Virginia

Four Inspiring Stories of Valor, Virtue, and Victory

Cathy Marie Hake

BARBOUR
PUBLISHING

Published by Barbour Publishing, Inc., P.O. Box 719, Uhrichsville, Ohio 44683, www.barbourbooks.com

Our mission is to publish and distribute inspirational products offering exceptional value and biblical encouragement to the masses.

eepa Member of the
Evangelical Christian
Publishers Association

Printed in the United States of America.
5 4 3 2 1

Dear Readers,

I've sometimes thought I was born in the wrong era. Seriously, now—have you seen the clothes women used to wear? Jewel-studded medieval brocade. Magnificent Elizabethan farthingale. Ultra-feminine hoopskirts. Elegant Victorian tea gowns. My best friend thinks I'm nuts. She reminds me those were the days when a woman owned only one or two dresses, had no running water, and there were weevils in the flour.

Okay, so I'll be thankful God didn't have me live back then. But history still fascinates me. Mom and Dad dragged me into antique stores all over the United States. They'd look at dumb stuff like furniture and weird kitchen items and horse things. Only it wasn't long before those things weren't dumb or weird—they were neat. History wasn't a dusty old book—to me, it became real. A loving mother sewed that quilt. A father used that gun and hunted for his family's meal. Over a hundred years ago, children loved wagons, too!

It captures my imagination to think of how our ancestors lived—the daily challenges they faced, the choices they made. When I write, though, I can't do so without having Christ as the center of the stories. He is my mainstay, and no romance is complete without Him.

The thing that strikes me is, no matter what year it might be, some things are universal: God is unchanging. Men and women work hard to make a living, but love is what makes that life sweet. Children are a blessing. What an awesome thought it is, to know the God who set the world spinning still holds our hands as we walk with Him. He is the Lord of might and power, yet He is also the Source of all tenderness and love. I met a young man in God's house when I was thirteen. Years later, we married. The month this book is released, Christopher and I will be celebrating our twenty-fifth anniversary. Facing the challenges of life has caused us to grow and change, but with God as our foundation, the years have been good.

Someday, someone may look at pictures or see the wedding and christening gowns from my cedar chest. They'll be heirlooms, then bits of history from long ago times. . .but most of all, I hope the faith I live is something that is passed on in word and deed because the real treasures are laid up in heaven.

For Christ, who saved my soul, and for Chris, who holds my heart—all my love,

Cathy

Precious Burdens

To my husband, Christopher—
for shouldering heavy burdens and loving me through it all.

Chapter 1

G od sends meat; the devil brings cookies." Emily O'Brien injected a light-hearted tone into her voice, even though she truly wished she could afford an occasional treat for her six-year-old brother. She turned away so he couldn't see her sadness, grabbed the nearly empty bottle, and poured a cup of watered-down milk for him.

"Emily," Duncan asked plaintively, "do you suppose it would be terrible bad if we invited the devil in just long enough to get a few cookies?"

"Ach! Now what kind of talk is that?" She turned back around in the cramped space between the food shelf and the table, set the tin mug down before him, and ruffled his red curls. "You're a good lad, Duncan. You'd never want to do business with that pitchfork-carryin' demon."

"Aye, right you are."

A tiny bleat of sound distracted Duncan's attention. He glanced over at the bed where their sister and her newborn lay, then lowered his voice to a bare whisper. "Our Em, what are you going to do?"

His innocent question nearly broke her heart. His childlike belief that she could handle this made her breath hitch. Emily forced a smile. "I'll go check on things today."

Emily pulled the thin curtains over the window, then smoothed the skirt of her mud brown serge dress and tugged her shawl tighter. "You know what to do, Duncan-mine. I'll be back quick as I can."

Emily left the one-room shack and waited until she heard the latch slide home before she started toward the docks. Hopefully, when she returned, she'd not be alone. They'd been faithful to pray for Anna's husband each and every day of his voyage. Mayhap the *Cormorant* had docked while Anna labored, and news just hadn't come yet. As the captain, Edward would be busy when he docked his fine vessel.

He has to be home. What am I to do if he's not? Duncan and Anna are starving, and the babe won't stay healthy if we've no coal. The midwife's still wanting her money, and rent is due. If he's not here yet, maybe I can at least get word on when the ship is due in.

Another blast of cold air swept by, causing Emily to cease her musing. Huddled beneath her shawl, she scurried to get out of the harsh wind. "Dear Lord in heaven," she prayed under her breath, "if You could see clear to helpin' Edward be home with enough jingling in his pocket to keep us from being so cold and hungry, I'd count it as a real blessing."

~ⁿ

"I'm looking for Edward Newcomb." Emily shivered as much from fear as cold while she stood at the bay side and made her inquiries. A more dangerous place didn't exist. Rough sailors passed by and treated her like a brazen hussy for asking about a man. No woman of decency came down here, but she had no choice. Desperation drove her. The men leered at her. One made comments saltier than the ocean air and grabbed for her. She hastily stepped backward, tripped, and fell over a coil of thick hemp ropes. A small cry curled in her throat as a haze of red engulfed her.

"Hey! Enough of that!" A tall, beautifully dressed gentleman strode up a narrow gangplank, along the sea-splashed dock, and crossed over toward her. The riffraff scuttled away like bilge rats in a storm. "Here now, miss. This isn't a safe place. You'd best get along home."

"Thank you," Emily said as he lifted her from the damp ground. The moment he set her back on her feet, she compressed her lips against the fiery pain that shot up from her left ankle.

He made no move to leave. Since he stood with his back to the sun, she couldn't see his shadowed face, but a kind tone urged, "You'd best go now, miss. This is no place for you."

For the first time since she'd set foot here, she felt safe. This man radiated authority and strength. Of all people, he could probably give her the best information. "Sir, I need help. I'm looking for someone."

He stared at her for a long moment, assessing her. Gulls cried, sails luffed, and the ropes mooring ships to the dock creaked. All around them, the bustle of dock life continued; but everything seemed motionless right here, and Emily fought not to squirm under this strange man's silent scrutiny. The fact that she couldn't clearly see his features made the whole situation feel even more awkward. She blurted out, "My sister's husband has been at sea for almost eight months, and I need news of his ship."

His voice softened with sympathy. "Well, then, let's get you some answers. Franklin!" The gentleman must have noticed her squinting into the rising sun. He stepped to the side so she could pivot. Finally she saw more of him than a mere silhouette. Dark brown, waving hair, heavy brows over deep-set, tea-colored eyes, and a strong, square chin. For a moment Emily almost gasped at how familiar he looked—but, no, that was merely a trick of the morning light. He was taller, broader, and far more handsome than Edward. She chided herself for being so fanciful when she needed to locate her sister's husband at once.

A portly man bustled up. "Aye, sir?"

"Franklin, this lady needs our assistance," the gentleman said. "Her brother-in-law's ship, the—" He turned and looked at her.

"The *Cormorant*," she supplied.

The men exchanged a telling look. Emily's heart skipped a beat. The gentleman discreetly leaned a little closer and lowered his voice confidentially. "Miss, the *Cormorant* came home and set voyage the last week in May." Pity stole over his face as he added, "And she just set sail again yesterday."

Emily felt the blood drain from her face. She stared at him and shook her head. "No." She swallowed hard and tried to mind her manners while grasping for one last hope. "Mayhap that was another *Cormorant*, sir. He wed my sister. Right and tight he did. Anna had the babe two nights ago. She's ailing bad."

The gentleman shifted his weight so the sun now struck features that carried a reassuring mixture of compassion and concern. "I'll see to it the sailor meets his obligations," he promised in a voice as reliable as iron. "What is his name?"

"His name is Edward, sir. Edward Newcomb."

The gentleman's eyes narrowed, and his face grew unrelenting and harsh as a blizzard. "Begone, wench. I'll not be taken in by such a tale."

" 'Tis the honest truth!"

"You wouldn't know the truth if it were served to you on a china supper plate." His voice went cold as sleet. "Edward Newcomb is my brother. I, of all people, would know if he were married. Now leave."

Emily stared at him in disbelief.

"Away with you. I'll not stand by and allow anyone to slander my brother's reputation or dishonor our family name with such an outrageous fabrication."

A wave of anger overtook her horror. "Fabrication? He's married, he is! He's a father now, too. You tell him Anna gave him a son." Pride aching, she straightened her shoulders. "You tell your brother that while he's been larking around, his wife's dinner plate was empty. That, Mr. Newcomb, is the truth—and you can just choke on your fancy china and lies!"

Back straight as a rod, Emily turned to walk off. She bit her lower lip against the throbbing in her ankle and hobbled faster. Each step hurt worse than the last. She wasn't going to show it, though. She managed to get clear past the docks and to the street before she couldn't bear to go farther. There she leaned against the trunk of a wind-twisted tree and closed her eyes in anguish.

What am I going to tell Anna?

⁓

John Newcomb watched the dignified woman limp off. Even dressed in what looked like a prim nanny's ragged castoffs, she'd stood regal as a queen. Now, straight-backed as could be, she walked away as if she were picking her way past rotted jetsam instead of a wealth of imports. He shook his head and heaved a deep sigh. "Where do they come from?"

"That was quite some yarn she spun," Franklin said.

"The woman's probably desperate to attempt such a ploy. Lame, thin, and wan as can be, she probably can't find either a job or a husband." John took a gold piece from his pocket and absently ran his thumb across the surface. 'Twas more money than she'd likely seen in several months, but he'd not even feel its loss. She didn't deserve anything for her scam, yet she must be in dire straits to have conjured up such a plan—unless there really was a hungry babe. Christ taught compassion instead of judgment. "Go give this to her."

∽

Later, when Franklin returned, he trundled over and shoved his hands in his pockets. "The woman gave me a message for you. She promises to pay back every last cent."

John scoffed. "That promise is about as honest as her woeful tale."

Franklin rubbed the furrows in his forehead. "I almost believed her. She clutched your coin tight in her fist and said, 'The O'Briens hold honor dear. They don't take charity.'"

John dismissed her words and set to work. Newcomb Shipping demanded his full attention. Fine Virginia cotton, wool, and hemp awaited loading into the hulls of the *Peregrine*. The *Allegiant*, now full of wheat, Indian corn, tobacco, and oats, required one last inspection ere she set sail. In a nearby berth, dockhands scurried to offload the coffee the *Gallant* had imported from Rio. The stench of tar and turpentine wafted past as the wind shifted—a reminder that he needed an update on the *Osprey's* repairs. John strode down the dock and set out his priorities for the day.

∽

The very next morning, Franklin handed John a note. "A lad brought this for you."

Intrigued, John unfolded the smudged paper and caught a penny as it slid out.

Dear Mr. Newcomb,
I'll be faithful to pay you back.
O'Briens don't take charity.

The brave little woman's words echoed in John's mind. She hadn't behaved as he'd expected her to. He'd thought she'd taken him for a soft touch, but she'd sent back this penny—a mere pittance. Was she hoping to reel him in for more?

As the day crawled on, her words kept haunting him. *Anna gave him a*

10

son. . .married. . .while he's been larking around, his wife's dinner plate was empty. . . . What if he'd misjudged the poor girl? Maybe she hadn't been trying to make fraudulent accusations in hopes of getting money. Was it possible one of the *Cormorant*'s crewmen actually misrepresented his identity and she believed her cause to be just? The sincerity in her tone and the look in her expressive green eyes certainly rang true.

The *Cormorant* had set sail on a prolonged voyage, so John couldn't even pose questions of Edward for several months. If the woman's plight was as dire as she'd implied, she couldn't wait for assistance. John determined to gather some facts. He sent for a discreet fellow he'd used to investigate sensitive matters in the past and engaged his services.

ᵔᔦ

Though he normally didn't personally oversee ships' departures, two days later John stood at the dock and watched the *Resolute* leave her moorings. He'd brought down a small case of heirloom jewelry. The bequest was to reach a young woman, and he'd not wanted any chance of its disappearing, so he'd specifically handed the treasures to the captain. The 4:00 a.m. turn of the tide made for an all-too-early awakening, but John shrugged it off. 'Twas part of his responsibility, and if ever he had a daughter, he'd want others to handle her cherished possessions with as much care.

Rather than going back home, he went into the shipping office. The register containing the contents of his warehouse lay open on his desk, but the figures of cotton bales, bushels of Indian corn, and bags of coffee beans could wait. Instead, John dragged his chair over by the stove. He'd barely started to nod off when the door opened.

"Sir, I found her—that woman you were looking for." The agent handed him a scrap of paper and slipped out the door as soon as John paid him.

Anna O'Brien, No. 6, Larkspur. Larkspur lay on the very outskirts of town, along the farthest edges of the docks—shantytown. John quickly drew on his warm greatcoat and set out. Instead of riding his horse, he took a wagon and ordered the driver to let him off about a half mile away from the address. This way he'd not have to worry his mount would be stolen. He hadn't been to shantytown since he was a callow youth. Back then it had looked dreary and sordid; time had only worsened its condition. A silvery half-moon illuminated the frost that sparkled on everything—reminding him of an iced deck. He'd rather be on such a deck than here—'twas less chancy than wandering this district.

"Wretched" described Larkspur perfectly. The dwellings were nothing more than shanties knocked together out of salvaged scraps of wood. Bitterly cold, tangy ocean air whistled between them; and ramshackle as they looked, John marveled, as he did every time he saw them, that they didn't blow over. One stood like a polished pebble amidst the rubble. Number Six. He stared at the gray, weathered

11

boards. Not a weed grew around them. In fact, a few flowers and tangled squash vines struggled to endure against the late autumn wind. He made a fist, then reconsidered. The wooden door was rough. No use getting splinters in his knuckles. Instead he used his boot to kick lightly on the widest plank.

Chapter 2

"J ust a minute," a sleepy voice bade.

Seconds passed while John impatiently flicked his gloves against his thigh. Each of his exhalations fogged on the cold, cold air. Even wrapped in the folds of his thick greatcoat, the air's icy bite penetrated to the skin. Across the way, the eyes of rats gleamed red like ingots fresh from Hades. Steps sounded, and a high-pitched voice asked, "Who is it?"

"John Newcomb."

" 'Tis John Newcomb, Anna. Do I let him in?"

Lamplight shone through small cracks in the house, so it came as no surprise that each word could be heard through the rattletrap boards. Thin wails of a babe wavered in the air. Anna must have nodded, because a latch slid free moments later, and a lanky boy with a sleep-tousled, red mop of hair peered out from behind a mere crack in the door.

"Thank you." John pushed his way in. As soon as he determined no danger existed inside the abode, he shut and secured the door. Slowly he looked about and took measure of the tiny, one-room shack. Shock rippled through him before he disciplined his features.

Such meager contents: a bed, two rickety chairs, a battered table, and a pathetic excuse for a stove. In the corner, behind a tattered bit of sailcloth that had been pushed back, a rumpled pallet lay directly on the sand-gritted flooring planks. He focused back on the bed and wondered how old the tiny woman in it might be. How could she, the lame woman, and this little lad—let alone a babe—possibly survive in circumstances this grave?

"John Newcomb," a faint voice said from the bed. "I didn't know Edward had a brother. How kind you are to come see your nephew!"

It took but three steps to reach the bedstead. The woman in it looked pitifully thin and weary, but even with those marks against her, John immediately recognized her similarity to the woman he'd met at the shipyard. Red hair and big green eyes attested that they were sisters, but her ashen skin warned that she'd been ill a long while. Just above the edge of a time-battered blanket, he spied a downy head.

The sickly woman smiled at John, then followed his gaze to look back down at her infant. "I've not named him yet. I hoped Edward would be here to help me decide on what his son is to be called." She painstakingly drew the covers

13

back a tad. Her fourth finger, John noticed, bore no wedding band.

Was she fighting modesty or just too weak to do the minuscule task? He leaned forward and looked intently at the tiny, swaddled bundle. In no way did the babe resemble Edward. In point of fact, the babe didn't take after anyone John knew. He looked like a wizened old man as he screwed up his face and let out a tiny bleat.

"Oh, now," Anna crooned softly.

John tried not to show his surprise when a shred of paper drifted out of the pillow slip. Knowing poverty existed was one thing, but seeing this timid little woman eke by with a paper-stuffed pillow defied belief. She reminded him of a tiny mouse, nesting in shreds of paper.

"Duncan, come be a dear and check his nappy for me. The puir, wee man-child is likely wet and hungry again."

For being on the young side, little Duncan handled the task with fair grace. The lad's arms were bony, and the baby's limbs looked like nothing more than matchsticks. From what he saw, John knew no one in this household had bene-fited from a decent meal in a long while.

Since they were occupied, John made no apologies for snooping about. A strip of salt-flecked, discarded sail gathered on a bit of string served as a curtain on the narrow window, but discarded newspapers covered the pane in a vain attempt to insulate the shack. Two shelves hung on one side of the window. A sparse collection of mismatched dishes perched on one. The other held nothing more than a pair of bruised apples, two pint jars filled with dried leaves, and a small glass bottle with barely an inch of milk. John's brows knit as he searched in vain for evidence of any other food.

His wife's dinner plate was empty. The words echoed again in his mind. They'd not been a melodramatic exaggeration. If anything, they'd been an under-statement. John's heart ached with pity, and he no longer wondered why the spir-ited woman had concocted her scheme to blame Edward for the paternity of the babe. She had come to his shipyard desperately needing to feed her family—but where could she be? And why had she paid back a penny when she should have bought food with it? What else had she done with the money?

He opened the stove and stirred the embers. The coal bucket next to the stove held one last small clump—certainly not enough to keep them warm for even half an hour more. He tossed it in, did his best to fasten the tiny grated door that hung askew, and asked in a deceptively casual tone, "Where is your sister?"

"She'll be home soon," Duncan answered. He tucked the baby in the bed. "There, then, our Anna. You were right about your wee little fellow wanting his supper. He's chewing on his fist. Put your arm about my shoulder. I'll help you turn a bit."

John watched the lad take his sister's frail, linen-covered arm and hook it about his own scrawny neck. Together they looked like a small heap of snowed-upon kindling. The lad didn't look half big enough to move her.

Propriety dictated John should turn his back. Anna O'Brien was a stranger, dressed in her nightgown, and lay in bed no less. A man of decency would never call upon a woman still in her childbed unless she were close family. Though circumstances rated as far less than fully proper, John couldn't stand by and allow this poor woman and her kid brother to struggle. "I'll help."

A smile brightened the lad's somber face. "Thank you, sir."

After Duncan stepped out of the way, John learned firsthand that Anna's profound weakness kept her from raising her own arms. Even after he stooped and gently lifted her arm, she could scarcely cup her hand about his neck. When he turned her, thin shoulder blades jutted out like bird wings beneath her gown. She shivered, not from his touch, but from the drafts coming through the walls. He gingerly tucked the babe close to the bodice of her gown and hastily situated the blanket around them. She rewarded his aid with a smile that glowed with gratitude. "Oh, you made that so easy for me. I thank you."

John tried not to show his horror at her thinness, but when the babe's wail echoed the wind whining between the walls, he asked quietly, "Do you have enough milk for the baby?"

"Not yet—but we're in the first days." A faint pink washed into her cheeks. "According to the midwife, three or four days usually pass before milk flows well."

John nodded. It wasn't that he truly agreed; he knew nothing about such matters. He did so because of the desperate hope and worry mingling in the new mother's voice. She needed privacy, so he excused himself. "The morning is cold, and your stove is near empty. I'll be back in a while with some coal."

"Oh! You'd do that for us? You're a generous man, John Newcomb."

He ordered Duncan to latch the door behind him and waited until he heard the slat slide into the warped bracket before he strode away. This neighborhood carried a hopeless mix of the poor, the drunken, and the unsavory. His hand went naturally to the reassuring knife he wore sheathed on his belt. Years on a ship had taught him how to wield it for any necessary task. Down here, protection was essential—yet Duncan and Anna lived helpless as lambs among this rabble.

The gold coin he'd given should have paid for warmth and food. Desperate as their needs were, why hadn't the other O'Brien woman used it sensibly? Her foolishness kept them hungry and cold. He shook his head in disbelief. What lunacy drove her?

John wisely came here without much jangling in his pocket. Providing such temptation would invite attack. Dawn hadn't yet broken, but the dingy thoroughfare lined with a smattering of shops sluggishly stirred to life. Lamps started to light windows and illuminate expansive boasts that the small businesses failed to fulfill. Even the bakery's fragrant aroma seemed to promise far more than simple loaves and buns.

First he purchased a basket and hooked it awkwardly over his left arm. By spending most of the paltry coins he'd brought, John determinedly filled it to overflowing. He'd done his share of bartering and marketing in dozens of ports and used that experience to make sure he got fair value for his coin. Badly as that lad and the new mother needed to eat, he'd not settle until he knew their bellies would be full.

"You there." He pointed at a stoop-backed man. "I need two full scuttles of coal taken to shanty number six, Larkspur Lane, right away."

"Aye, sir. I'll be right on yer heels!"

John arrived back at the shack and bumped the door once before young Duncan opened it. "Bless me, Anna—he came back!" He danced an excited jig as he said in astonished wonderment, "And he brought food!"

John set the basket on the table. He'd carefully set a handful of cookies atop everything else in hopes they wouldn't get broken. The lad spied them and did the inexplicable—he backed away. "Are y—you the d—d—devil?"

"Duncan!" his sister gasped.

Eyes big as saucers, Duncan whispered, "Em says, 'God sends meat; the devil brings cookies.' Anna, he brought cookies!"

John chuckled and pulled a small ham from the basket. "There, now. Meat. Does that put your mind at ease?"

Duncan still didn't look certain. He patted his sister's leg. "What are you thinking we ought to be doing?"

"All's well, boy-o." Anna gave John a winsome smile. "Please forgive him."

"There's nothing to forgive. Duncan is trying to protect his family." A knock sounded. John opened the door and accepted the coal.

Duncan spied the fuel. "Oh, sir! God bless you! Anna, this'll keep the baby warm all year!"

John chortled softly at the boy's innocence and enthusiasm. He didn't have the heart to deny the claim. Indeed, he'd arrange for coal to be delivered so Anna, her wee babe, and little Duncan would be warm for as long as they needed. He quickly added coal to the stove, wishing it wouldn't need time before the fire would catch and radiate more heat.

John pulled a slightly bent knife from the shelf. After the first cut, he traded it for his belt knife and sliced the loaf of bread and cheese. Ham had never been hacked into sorrier slabs, but he felt sure neither Anna nor Duncan would notice. He handed the lad some bread.

"Get water so I can put the eggs on to boil." While Duncan took a bucket and scampered outside to a communal pump, John carried the bread and cheese over to the bedside. As he gently lifted Anna's shoulders and head, he realized Duncan had taken his own blanket and spread it atop her.

Before Anna accepted a bite, she paused and dipped her head. Her pale lips moved silently in what he presumed to be a prayer. Though he knew she was half-starved, she took dainty bites from his hand. Her eyes shone with gratitude.

Duncan returned and filled a small pot, then set the eggs to boil. The remainder of the water went into a chipped porcelain pitcher. He gobbled up another slice of bread. "Soon as the eggs are done, I'll make you some tea. I'll cool the rest of the water a bit, and we can wash up the babe, too."

"You're a fine uncle, Duncan," Anna praised. She looked up at John and whispered, "As are you, John Newcomb. I've prayed for Edward to come home, but the Lord surely sent you in the meantime. You're an unexpected answer to my supplications."

John gave no reply. He'd made no claim to the babe and promised nothing, yet he felt guilty as a thief. After setting foot here, he could easily see why they sought a male connection. He never should have come. He wasn't a man to indulge in deception, yet his very presence hinted at a relationship that didn't exist.

He knew his brother well. Edward appreciated quality things, cultured women, and monied society far too much to consort with an impoverished, skinny Irish lass. Clearly, someone had hornswoggled this poor girl, but he knew it wasn't Edward's doing. Relief sifted through him that his brother wouldn't do such a contemptible thing. Despite his compassion and pity for the occupants of this shack, John refused to pretend any connection.

He finished feeding her slivers of ham, a small hunk of cheese, and the bread, then laid her back down. In his younger years, he'd seen a ship that had been caught in the Doldrums and the sailors had nearly starved. They gorged on food and became violently ill. As a result of that memory, he hesitated to offer her more. She'd barely eaten enough for a small child, yet she seemed quite satisfied.

"Oh, I thank you. That was wondrous good."

"There's more. You need to eat tiny meals several times a day to build up your strength."

"I've had gracious plenty. We'll save the rest for Emily."

Oh, so her name is Emily.

"There's lots for Em," Duncan said as he stood on tiptoe to peer into the kettle and check on the eggs. John clasped the boy's thin frame and lifted him away. He was far too short—couldn't they see he'd likely scald himself? *But what choice do they have? Where is Emily, and why isn't she here, tending these two?*

Duncan traipsed over to the bed. "Emily could eat all day and night. The whole basket is brimming. Mr. Newcomb brought us a feast, our Anna."

17

Anna's thin face lit with delight. "God be praised! We'll have a bit to eat on the morrow. Mr. Newcomb, you're too kind!"

"Rest," John bade gruffly. It pained him to see a woman so starved that she thought to ration such a modest offering. He'd filled the basket with whatever could be found, but this fare rated as exceedingly plain. The total of its contents was far less than the waste from his own table each day.

Cold seeped through the walls. He felt awkward covering Anna, but she'd weakly slumped onto her back again and needed warmth in the worst way. Her linen gown looked threadbare. He'd never given any thought to the bedding in his home, but one of his blankets measured thicker than both on her bed combined. As he tugged the blankets up higher and tucked them beneath her shoulders so they'd capture whatever meager heat she had, she shivered. From the appreciative, trusting look on her face, he knew it wasn't a shiver of apprehension but one of pure, cold misery. "More coal," he muttered to himself. "We need to warm up this place."

He strongly considered smashing a chair and adding it to the stove. The dry wood would catch and blaze quickly until the coal finally burned well. A single glance at the furniture in the place established the fact that not a single piece was worth salvaging. He'd use one of the chairs first. From the looks of them, one solid whack, and they'd shatter.

Before he could rise and carry out that plan, the door rattled. Having knelt to tend the coals, John needed to crane his neck to see past the table. The woman from the dock limped in. Worry creased her face, and he strongly suspected the redness of her nose and eyes wasn't just from the cold. She forced a smile that didn't begin to hide the worry in her big, green eyes. "What are my two loves doing up so very early?"

"Em! He came!"

She perked up and avidly scanned the tiny shanty. "Edward? Where?"

From the bed Anna said, " 'Tisn't my Edward, but it's the next best, Emily. My Edward has a brother! His name is John, and he came."

"He brought food and coal!"

Emily bristled. She stared at the basket, then said, "O'Briens don't take charity!"

John stood. "One could scarcely call it a charity, Miss O'Brien."

Her gaze bore right through him. "Oh, so you've decided we might be family now, have you?" She pulled a scarf from her head and shook out a fire fall of breathtakingly beautiful, thick, auburn hair.

Brazen, he thought. He stared straight back and felt a wave of disgust. What other work did a woman do at night but to be a harlot? His voice took on a sharp edge. "I've decided nothing."

A sharp gasp sounded from the bed off to his side. Anna's reaction accused him of hideous cruelty, for he'd just served her a terrible—if unintentional—insult. Too weak even to care for herself, the poor girl-woman now suffered from his temper, too. He'd just slurred her character in the worst way imaginable simply because he'd tried to take the starch out of her sister. Shame flooded him.

Emily opened the door. Her glower could set a bonfire. "Please leave."

He'd go, though first he owed Anna his apology. John looked over at her, but Duncan slipped between them. His little face puckered with confusion, but he took his sister's cue and tried to protect Anna.

"Emily," the little boy said, "I don't understand."

Anna began to weep.

"He started out by being so nice." Duncan's voice carried a plaintive tone. "He's Edward's brother, and he brought us food!"

Emily cast a glance at the basket on the table, then back at John. Weariness mingled with bitterness in her tone. "Duncan, he isn't here because he thinks we're family. He intended it as charity."

"Stop this nonsense and shut the door," John snapped. The woman had no more sense than a brick to be letting what little heat they had in the shack escape. Didn't she notice every breath any of them took condensed into a fog?

She adamantly shook her head. "Not until you're on the other side."

"Now see here!"

"No, you see here," Emily said in an unrelenting tone. "Edward Newcomb married Anna. I'll not let you insult my sister or besmirch her name."

"You have proof of this marriage?"

Contrary to her earlier assertion, Emily shut the door. The whole wall shook. "Aye, we do." She hastily tied her scarf back over her remarkable hair in a belated move of modesty, limped over to the far side of the bed, and produced a small fabric bag he'd spied earlier. From it she drew out a black book. Most of the gold from the lettering had long since rubbed off. For a second she reverently passed her chapped hand over the battered-looking leather cover, then laid the Bible on the bed and opened it. "We recorded Anna's nuptials here, and—"

"I'm not about to accept that as proof." John marveled at her gumption. Did she think him so gullible that he'd stupidly accept such a poorly executed sham? "Anyone can write whatever they jolly well please!"

"Not in the Holy Scriptures," Duncan protested, his voice full of shock.

"If that isn't good enough, then the license will speak for itself!" Emily took a folded sheet of paper out and smoothed it open. "Seeing as you're hostile, I'll thank you to step away from the fire ere I hand this over."

John made an impatient noise and reached her side. Stiff and straight as she stood, she barely cleared his shoulder. John resisted the urge to swipe the paper from her. Matters in this pitiable household were already strained enough without his acting like a brute—though he rather felt like one for having upset sickly little Anna. Try as he might, he couldn't block out the muffled sounds of her weeping. Nevertheless, he had to focus on the principal matter at hand. He stared at the page Emily laid on the bed and scowled. "This is nonsense!"

"Nay, 'tis Latin." Emily's tone carried a rich tang of sarcasm. Her hand shook as it hovered over the flower-embellished parchment. She pointed at several places but didn't actually touch the document. "Here. The vicar's signature. Here. Anna's. Mine. Edward's and our neighbor Leticia's. There were witnesses, so the marriage is legal as can be."

"My brother's middle name is Timothy, not Percival." He ignored the impatient flash in her eyes that accused him of concocting a falsehood and looked back at the signatures. The application of their tutor's ruler to the back of Edward's hand had taught him superb penmanship. John scowled. "Whoever signed this wasn't my brother. The scrawl on this is scarcely legible. Furthermore, if this is a marriage certificate, I'm a chamber pot. The Latin on here is a collection of words that mean nothing at all. 'Tis sheer gibberish."

The jut of Emily's chin made it clear she didn't believe him. Her hand dove back into the bag once again. Out it came. Between her calloused thumb and blistered forefinger, she held a ring. "And this? You cannot deny a family ring!"

John's breath caught. He took the ring from her. The thin band of gold held nothing more than a little ruby chip in the center. As jewelry went, the piece was cheap as could be, but John had given a similar ring to his governess when he was younger than Duncan. He recalled his mother taking him to a jeweler's, where there had been dozens of such rings with either rubies or sapphires. He'd thought the pinkish red stone fitting for a woman, so he'd chosen one of the ruby ones.

"Where did you get this?" He fought the ridiculously strong urge to curl his fingers and keep the sentimental little piece, even though there was no proof it was the one he'd once given. Undoubtedly hundreds of women owned such rings.

"It's Anna's wedding band, it is. Edward Newcomb himself put it on her finger. He said it had belonged in his family for generations. Anna grew afraid her pretty wedding band would slip off because she'd gotten so thin, so we kept it here for safety." Emily snatched it back. She meticulously put everything back into the bag.

"You've given me no real proof, Emily. Newcomb isn't an uncommon name. I could ride just one day's direction either way and find a good half dozen Newcombs. A man with a name similar to my brother's duped your sister. That is a pity, to be sure, but those facts and your so-called evidence aren't nearly enough to convince me a true and holy marriage exists between my brother, Edward Timothy Newcomb, and Anna."

Emily's jaw hardened. "Sir, take yourself out of here."

John tore his gaze from hers. He glanced over at the pillows. Beneath the covers, Anna's much-too-thin shoulders continued to jerk with every muffled sob she took. The babe began to cry.

"Now see what you've done?" Emily whispered hotly. "Begone!"

"And take this with you!" Duncan swept the basket from the table and shoved it at him. John's hands automatically closed around the handle. The little boy hadn't let go of the basket. He put all of his puny weight behind it to force John out. The effort didn't actually work, but John saw no point in tarrying where he wasn't wanted. He no more than stepped outside, and the door slammed shut.

Chapter 3

H e stood outside the shack and heard Emily's voice suddenly alter pitch. It went soft and wooing, carrying a gentle comfort only devoted love could produce. "There, now, our Anna. Never you mind that man. No, don't you mind him at all. We know the truth, and God does, too. That's what matters. Why, your sweet little son is all upset about his mama crying. Here, let me help the pair of you."

The baby wailed a minute more, then fell silent. A few moments later, the cries began again. John knew essentially nothing at all regarding babes, but even a fool knew they needed milk. Unless Anna suddenly had sufficient meals, she'd never have enough to suckle her child.

Duncan's guilty voice carried through the cracks. "Our Em, we didn't know. We didn't know he was bad. No, I never would have guessed it at all. You know, we got so excited that we even ate his food."

"Well, now, you needn't confess it so shamefully, boy-o. You didn't know. 'Twas an honest mistake you made. I'll still pray God blesses each and every morsel you swallowed. Go on ahead and take your full belly back to bed."

The boy's voice carried uncertainty. "I forgot about the eggs he gave us. I boiled them. Want me to pitch them out the door?"

"There's no use wasting good food." Emily sighed.

John quietly set the basket down by the door, but as he stepped away, he caught movement out of the corner of his eye. Rats. They'd take every last crumb. That didn't matter as much as the fact that he didn't want to lure the vermin to the shack, so he swept it back up and glowered at the closed door.

It wasn't his problem. He'd given her a gold coin and didn't expect repayment. He'd brought food and coal. That was enough. He owed them nothing.

John walked off.

He strode down past the other shanties to a busy street and hailed a passing carriage. Running his shipping business took all of his time and energy. If he didn't get moving, he'd not complete reviewing the manifests for the shipments due to go out on the next tide. Though his clerk could handle most matters and John trusted him well enough, a few transactions specifically demanded his presence or attention today.

～§

Two hours later, John slammed the *Freedom*'s log shut. He couldn't concentrate.

The basket of food in the corner nagged at him. Anna's soft weeping and Duncan's outrage haunted his conscience. Even if Emily sniped at him like a shrew, her brother and sister seemed nice enough.

He'd left in a temper, trying to convince himself they weren't his problem; but now that he'd cooled off, John felt differently. A Christian man owed the less fortunate his assistance. He'd never seen anyone more destitute than they. He decided to go back and offer little Duncan a job. Though no bigger than a minnow, the lad could carry messages and empty waste bins. That way they'd have a bit of money coming in, and the sacred O'Brien pride would be spared.

John didn't have time to go back to the shack, so he sent Franklin to fetch Miss Emily. "Bring her here and don't take no for an answer. She may fuss, but in the end she'll relent." He glanced at the basket and decided it would be best not to send it along as a reminder of the disastrous visit.

"I'll go at once, sir."

"Stop on your way to buy them more coal, a hearty meal, and a few quarts of milk. Leave the offering on their table. If they refuse it, point out that they cannot afford this misplaced pride. Regardless of whatever qualms Miss Emily holds, Miss Anna must eat to feed her baby son."

Franklin nodded somberly. John knew he could trust him to carry out his orders to the letter. Not only that, Franklin was a man of discretion. He'd not make this trip a matter of conjecture or gossip. Satisfied he'd fulfilled his Christian duties, John opened the ship's log and once again pored over the entries.

Franklin came back later—alone. Though normally rather impassive, he folded his arms across his chest and reported in a vexed tone, "I did some mighty fancy talking to make the small boy let me in. Miss Anna's lying abed with her newborn. I did not find Miss Emily at home, and when I inquired after her, the lad said she was at work; but before I could ask where, his sister shushed him. She seemed. . .ashamed."

"I'm not surprised," John muttered darkly.

"Neither the lad nor Miss Anna would say another word as to her whereabouts. The men at the docks probably gauged her correctly when they presumed her to be a doxy."

"She has no business gallivanting around. Her sister and that babe need her help."

Franklin grimaced. "Deplorable as the place is, I can see why she'd not be eager to spend her day there. At least they'll have enough coal to stay warm."

"What about the food?"

"The lad acted a bit stubborn, but I repeated your message. Bone thin, they are. I took gracious plenty and felt like I should have taken triple. The little mother looked down at her babe and told the boy they'd have to accept the food. Hungry though she must be, she instructed him to hold back some for their sister."

"After you left their abode, did you investigate the neighborhood and interview others to determine Emily's whereabouts?"

Franklin shrugged. "They're a closemouthed lot down there. I asked a few folk and might as well have been speaking a different language entirely. They pretended not to understand me or know a thing."

"You did as well as I could reasonably expect," John said. "Mayhap Emily will think to contact me when she sees fit to go home."

"I gave them the message that you want her to pay a visit here."

John nodded acknowledgment and turned back to his work. The day passed, but Emily never made an appearance. Thoroughly irked by her absence and probable occupation, John went out of his way to swing by Larkspur that evening. Duncan stood with his arms and legs spread in the doorway like a landlocked squid to bar his entrance. "Em said you're not allowed to talk to our Anna." He glowered. "You made my sister cry."

John couldn't very well argue with the truth—especially one as galling as that. He compressed his lips for a moment, then nodded. He looked at the lad. Duncan was a strange mix of belligerence, innocence, and protectiveness. John leaned closer and said in a low tone, "I'm here to offer you a job. Do I speak man-to-man with you?"

"Em won't have it." The lad cast a worried look over his shoulder. "Besides, I have to stay home because Anna and the babe need my help."

John glanced at the bed. Anna's face looked white as a sail in the moonlight. He whispered a quick prayer of thanks that she continued to sleep through his visit. The last thing he wanted was to upset her again.

"Duncan, I could pay you a bit in advance now for the labor you'd do later. I'd trust you to work it off."

The lad's scrawny fingers curled more tightly around the doorjamb. The unpainted wood had aged and dried until it looked gray as thunderclouds. "My sister wouldn't like me talking to you. No, she wouldn't. Last night you tricked me. I thought you were a good man, and I let you in our house. I won't let you fool me again. Go away." Behind him the babe let out a tiny squeal. Duncan slipped back inside and shut the door. A scraping sound let John know Duncan slid the small bar latch into the bracket to lock him out.

John walked to the end of Larkspur, then turned back to look at the shanty. The betrayal he'd read on Duncan's face ate at him. Somehow he'd make amends. Distasteful as it might be, the truth was, he'd have to deal with Emily. John hired a runner to keep watch on the house and fetch him when she finally returned.

Word didn't come until three thirty the next morning.

Short of sleep and shorter still of temper, John dressed quickly and set out to serve the older O'Brien sister a big slice of his mind. What business did she have leaving an ailing sister, a newborn babe, and a small lad alone all hours of the day and night? He'd wanted a few more hours of sleep himself, but if he didn't catch her now, who knew when she'd see clear to checking back in with her kin? He reached the dilapidated shack and didn't even bother to knock.

From being inside, he knew precisely where the bracket and stick were affixed to lock the door. John took the knife from his belt, slipped it between the door and its brittle frame, lifted the latch, and kneed the rough wooden panel.

Hopefully, Anna, Duncan, and the baby would be sleeping. He'd get Emily to come outside to discuss matters with him. It might well be her brother and sister didn't know how she spent her time, and he'd get more honest information from her away from their hearing.

The door creaked open. He slipped in and shut it behind him right away. Though a large man, he'd learned to move silently long ago. Now that ability stood him in good stead.

After allowing his eyes a moment to readjust to the dark, John noted Duncan slept in a tight huddle on his floor pallet. Though definitely warmer than it had been on his first visit, the shanty remained chilly. *Why didn't I think to have Franklin bring blankets for them, too?* John heaved a silent sigh. He should have ordered Franklin to tell them he'd continue to send coal. No doubt they'd rationed it to make it last, just as they had the food.

John's gaze fell upon the food shelf, and the contents of his warehouses scrolled through his mind. Flour, oats, corn, salt, coffee, molasses, syrup, and sweet potatoes he had aplenty. He'd convince Emily to send Duncan to work at the shipyard, and each payday John would contrive for a supply of those staples to be part of the lad's earnings. That arrangement ought to salvage the O'Brien pride.

John continued to scan the room. The small lump in the bed had to be Anna. Where was Emily? Had she gone out again?

Disgusted, John decided at least to add a bit of coal to the stove so the fire wouldn't burn out and force them to awaken to a cold home. He took care to move silently in order to keep from awakening Duncan or the baby. As for Anna—well, he seriously doubted she'd stir at all. After John rounded the table, he stopped dead in his tracks.

Emily sat on the floor with her back to the wall. Her head rested against the side of the bed, her magnificent hair billowing in loose, coppery waves to her hips. Thick auburn lashes lay in crescents on her cheeks, and her lips bowed upward in a charming half smile, making him wonder where her dreams carried her. A bitsy, half-made, white garment rested in her lap. The threaded needle still dangled from the minuscule sleeve, glinting in the dull light of the stove. She'd fallen asleep while trying to do something more for her tiny nephew. That loving task tugged at John's heart.

The dockhands and Franklin all thought she was a harlot, and her nighttime absence from the shanty confirmed that deduction. As much pride as Emily O'Brien displayed, it probably wounded her something fierce to sell herself; but her love for her siblings undoubtedly drove her to a woman's most unsavory profession. Faced with no other choice, she'd sacrificed herself for them. What else could she have done? Without a father or older brother to provide for them, Emily had to bring in money. No one would have hired her as a maid or laundress since she was lame and had the rest of her family to tag along.

In the still of the night, standing over her, John decided he'd lift the burden of providing for them from her shoulders so she could revert to a decent manner of living. He'd give her that chance. 'Twas a sound plan. Christ gave the woman at the well an opportunity to change her life. John would follow the Savior's example. If he approached this situation with mercy and compassion, she could listen to the gospel and turn her life back around.

Emily moaned ever so softly in her sleep, and as she shifted, the hem of her ugly brown dress caught on something. Her breath hitched, and she moved her limb a bit. A soggy cloth plopped from her ankle onto the floor.

John choked back a bellow. From the soft glow of the stove, he could see her foot and ankle were blackish violet and hideously swollen. Though he wasn't a man to gawk at a woman's limbs, her calf looked far too thin—even before he compared it to her bloated ankle. How could she bear to walk on that?

He leaned forward and looked more closely. 'Twas a very recent injury. His mouth went dry. She fell at the shipyard. He winced because he couldn't even recall asking if she'd harmed herself. *All this time, I assumed she'd been lame for years; but 'tis a new injury, one that requires pampering so it can heal.* How does she bear to walk on it at all?

Just as he began to kneel at her side, she startled awake. A terrified shriek erupted from her, and she tried to strike him.

Chapter 4

Emily! Stop. Stop!" He captured her wrists and gave her a moment to discover his identity and gather her wits; then he slowly released his hold. "I didn't mean to alarm you."

"Emily?" Anna whispered in a quavering tone.

"Want me to bop him?" Duncan stood just out of reach and gripped a pan in both hands.

"There's no need for that, lad," John said. For all of his intentions to sneak in and hold a whispered conversation, he'd managed to rouse everyone in the home—well, nearly everyone. Though he'd even startled Anna awake, the babe managed to sleep on.

John watched Emily struggle to quell the residual panic. Eyes huge, she stared at him and swallowed hard. Her narrow shoulders heaved with her rapid, deep breaths. Had he awakened with someone hovering over him, he knew he'd have swung to protect himself. Striving to inject a soothing tone into his voice, he reassured her, "Truly you've no need to be afraid."

Duncan scampered around to Emily's other side and clutched the pan to his scrawny chest. He didn't seem to be in any hurry to relax his guard. "My Em isn't ever scared. She's brave and strong, she is!"

Brave? Yes, he'd agree with that, but unafraid and strong—she was neither of those. Even so, John found Duncan's faith in his big sister endearing. Whatever her flaws might be, Emily had certainly earned the loyalty and love of her little brother.

Emily. John focused on her and fought the temptation to smooth back a springy wisp of hair that fell forward on her much-too-pale cheek. Instead he straightened up, clasped his hands behind his back, and kept his gaze on poor Emily. "All is well, Duncan. I just came to talk to your sister."

"No, I'll not let you speak to her—not now, not ever." Emily looked up at him and resolutely shook her head. "You already said more than enough the last time you came here."

"I wanted to speak to you," John clarified, "not Anna."

Anna looked up at him. Her eyes glistened with tears. "Emily is tired. Go away."

"I won't take much of her time."

"She has only three hours to sleep before she goes back to work," Anna whispered. "Leave her be. Leave us all alone."

John looked back at Emily. "Where do you work?"

"Wilkens's—"

"Silence, Duncan!" Emily ordered.

John's jaw dropped. "The asylum? You work with those raving lunatics?" Wilkens's Asylum sprawled across a fenced-in lot just down the street.

Emily's jaw jutted forward. " 'Tis no fault of their own that their minds snapped. You can think of them as wretched or miserable, but they are God's children just as much as you and I are."

"They're not safe!"

"So in your opinion they are undeserving of sound meals, a kind word, or a clean place to live? Christ said, 'Inasmuch as ye have done it unto one of the least of these my brethren, you have done it unto me.' "

He rocked back on his heels. She had a point, but he didn't cotton to the notion of such a young, vulnerable woman working in that kind of place. Those people could be violent! "What do you do there?"

"Honest work, 'tis, but hard," Anna whispered from the bed. "Cooking and cleaning. Soon as I get back on my feet, I'll go back and start cooking again. Em will watch the baby for me during the day; then she'll only have to work at night to do the cleaning."

John jolted at the underlying implication. "Emily, you can't mean to tell me you cook for all of those unfortunates and clean that whole place by yourself."

"Shush!" Emily cast a quick glance at the bed.

"With your limb like that?"

"Mr. Newcomb! Have you no decency?"

"Emily?" The paper-stuffed pillow rustled as Anna turned to her sister. "What does he mean?"

Emily picked up the baby gown, thrust the needle through the hem, and set it aside. Thoroughly irritated, she lifted the sodden cloth and glowered at him. He took her meaning and turned his back. He heard the small gasp she muffled and knew binding her ankle had to hurt—but she couldn't possibly walk on it without the support of the bandage. Next came a rhythmic, whispering *swish, swish, swish*. The cadence matched the tick of his pocket watch. Though he couldn't identify the sound, John figured he owed her a few moments of privacy.

The moment he heard her start to rise, he turned about and assisted her to her feet; but once she was upright, he surprised Emily by bracing her against his side.

"Mr. Newcomb!" She tried to pull away.

John tightened his hold, cinched her to himself, and murmured, "You need help balancing. Stop sounding so scandalized. I declare, you're half frozen!"

She gritted her teeth and said in an icy undertone, "Is there anything else you'd like to be saying to upset my youngers?"

The moment the words were out of his mouth, he regretted them. Obviously Emily hid whatever harsh realities she could from her siblings. Not that she could shield them from much. There were no more blankets in this poverty-stricken shack. Emily made sure her siblings stayed as warm as possible, even though it meant she suffered.

He looked at her, and she stared straight back at him. Vexation danced in her vivid green eyes. So did wounded pride. Those things registered, but so did something else: Emily O'Brien was nothing more than skin and bones. Her full skirt, billowing apron, and shawl might well hide the full extent of the truth; but as he held her close, she couldn't disguise the fact that she was—quite literally—starving.

"Duncan," he addressed the boy in a clipped, no-nonsense tone, "I'm taking your sister outside to the oak stump. We're going to have a private talk. You're to bring out Anna's shawl to help keep her warmer. After you do, I want you to add more coal to the stove and heat up some milk for Emily."

"The milk is for Anna and Duncan. They need it—I don't."

John scowled at Emily. He understood she didn't want her brother and sister to realize how dire matters were. They'd already thought to save food for her, but John seriously doubted they had any notion of how frail their stalwart sister was. He'd been fooled, and he possessed a sharp eye; love and Emily's acting ability, no doubt, blinded her siblings. He'd keep this secret for now, but he wanted Emily to know he wasn't going to back down. "We'll discuss this outside."

Weakly, Anna tried to prop herself up on one arm. "You don't have to go talk to him if you don't want to, Em."

"Yes, she does." He gave no chance for dissent. John kept hold and shepherded Emily toward the door. As long as she cooperated and hobbled alongside him, he'd let her walk; but if she dared balk, he'd sweep her into his arms. The temptation to do so was strong; yet he tamed it so she could keep her siblings in the dark awhile longer about her own sad condition. John guided her straight out of the hovel and over to a log. He set her carefully to the side, fully intending to take the place next to her.

Duncan trotted in his wake. John accepted the shawl, wrapped it about Emily, then jerked his head toward the shack in a silent order for him to leave. The little lad didn't cow easily. He braced his feet a bit farther apart and looked to his sister.

"I'm fine enough, Duncan. Go on now. Help Anna with the babe. The wee fellow ought to be waking soon." The moment Duncan shut the door, John sat to Emily's windward side and pulled her close once again. Hopefully, he'd give her a bit of shelter and some of his warmth.

She wiggled. "Turn loose of me. I've no business sitting by your side."

"Save your breath for something that matters." John kept his arm about her and reached across with his free hand to tug her sister's shawl up a little to protect her throat. He marveled at the blush the moon illuminated on her cheeks. For all of her boldness, she actually possessed a shy streak!

The swishing sound he'd heard when he turned his back suddenly made sense. A braid nearly as thick as his wrist now trailed over her shoulder, and a scarf covered her head. She'd taken that moment of privacy to tame her fiery hair properly and cover it. He'd spent the last two days thinking this modest little bit of goods was a doxy? The contrast between his wild imaginings and the mild truth forced him to realize he'd misjudged her badly.

Her stomach growled.

"When was the last time you ate?"

She didn't meet his eyes. "I couldn't say. I don't own a timepiece."

"Then how is it Anna knows you're to be back at work in three hours?"

"Mr. Shaunessey next door has a mantel clock. We can hear the chimes." She lifted her chin. "You'll find we don't lie, Mr. Newcomb, so you may as well leave off on trying to pounce on each matter as if you can capture us in something dishonest."

Her pluck won his grudging respect. This woman had mettle and fire. Still, he couldn't afford to smile and let her get away with this travesty. It was past time someone stopped her from trying to bilk blameless sailors, and it seemed circumstances had played out so he'd be the man who did precisely that. She wiggled ever so slightly, and the frailty of her build struck him anew. "You're so skinny you'd slip right through a fishing net."

"Waking me just to serve insults is hardly gentlemanly."

He muttered under his breath.

"Your opinion is not gentlemanly, either." She tried to push away.

John held her fast. "My apologies, Miss O'Brien. I came to settle some matters, but you have a penchant for disappearing. The ridiculous hours you keep make it impossible for me to connect with you at a decent time."

"Moaning about it doesn't change things, John Newcomb. Now that you've gotten my ear, could you please be hurrying with whatever it is you need to say?"

"I want to hire Duncan."

Shivers rattled her against his side. John wasn't sure whether fear or cold caused them. He wrapped his other arm about her, hoping to share his warmth with her. In bringing her out here, away from her brother and sister's hearing, he'd inadvertently opened her up to scrutiny if anyone happened to see them together. John regretfully ceased holding her in both arms and quickly dismissed the idea of opening his coat to share it with her. That would be just as ruinous. "Nay."

Emily's words jarred his attention back to the matters at hand. "Nay?"

"I pledged to pay you back. Duncan's not going to work off my debt."

"You're not indebted to me, Emily. The coin was—"

"Charity," she clipped off.

"A gift," he corrected in a coaxing tone. "And I'll be offended if you give back another cent. We both know you didn't spend it on yourself. Tell me why you didn't use that last penny to buy food."

"Your coin took care of our rent and the midwife's fee. As for food—we had enough to get by until I'm paid tomorrow."

"If Duncan works for me, you'll not have to suffer any hungry days."

She shook her head. "I won't put Duncan out to work. He's too young yet. Besides, Anna needs his help for herself and the babe while I'm gone. She cannot even get out of bed."

"How old is he?"

"Not quite seven years."

"As long as I'm being ungentlemanly, I'll ask: How old are you and your sister?"

"You're right." She stiffened. "That is ungentlemanly."

"You scarcely strike me as the coy type."

"No, according to your estimation, I'm more the scheming-and-lying type." She paused a second, then let out a beleaguered sigh. "You're wrong, but I won't waste my time arguing with you. Your curiosity is costing me my sleep, but 'tis plain to see I'll not get one wink more 'til you get your answers. So here you are: Anna just turned seventeen, and I'm coming up on nineteen."

"Babes, the whole lot of you." His hold on her altered. He cradled her more tenderly. He'd thought Anna might have been nineteen, but Emily—he'd imagined her a good eight years older. For all of her courage, she was far too young to shoulder the burdens she carried.

John recalled having lost his parents when he was about her age. He'd been fortunate enough to have Grandfather there still to give him both a solid home and teach him the business. He hadn't been forced to scramble for each meal or worry about providing for Edward.

Emily tried to hide her yawn from him. From the looks of her, she could stand to sleep the clock around one full time, if not twice. Feeling pity for her, he asked softly, "What are you doing, living on your own?"

"Master Reilly found it cheaper to send many of us off rather than keep us. Food being scarce and no more in sight, he made his choices and stuck us on a ship."

"He couldn't separate parents and children!"

"And why not? He needed the men to till his soil. We'd been sore hungry, and Da borrowed money for food. Master Reilly called in the debt and kept my parents instead of paying for their passage. Two years we've been here."

"Had you no family along?"

Her eyes closed in grief. "On the ship my sister Maureen died of the measles."

"Poor lass," he murmured. "I'm sorry for your loss."

"Thank you." She paused a moment, drew in a deep breath, then tilted her face up to his. " 'Twas soon after we arrived, and Mr. Wilkens was kind to give Anna and me our jobs. Say what you will, but that good turn kept us going."

"He took advantage of your situation, Emily. He knew you were desperate, so he's overworked you."

"It was better than my only other choice." She looked away. "No one else would help. I took the only way available to help my family."

"So, speaking of help, who gave you the ring?" he asked even more softly.

Emily turned toward him and glared. "Your brother put it on Anna's finger. I can see you don't believe me, and that's that." She pushed so hard, she tumbled from the log. Heated by her temper, she scrambled upright and slapped away the hand he offered to assist her. "It's a cruel man you are, John Newcomb. You find pleasure in insulting an ailing new mother, want to press a wee lad into labor, and drag a woman from her sleep just so you can dredge up her sadness until you can make her vulnerable. You've done your worst, but I'll take no more."

"Emily—"

"Back at the dock, you were willing to use your power to assure Anna's husband did right by her; but once you found out that man was your own brother, your resolve blew off like a scarf in a gale. You're a hypocrite, John Newcomb."

She held both shawls about her like a shield. "We may be poor and hungry, but we've never once stooped to dishonesty or hurt another soul. You look at us and see poverty—but you are the poorest man I ever met because your heart is empty. Don't come back here. You and your brother have done all the harm two men could e'er do."

She limped past him, and John stood aside. Her dignity and temper were a sight to behold. Two more hobbling steps, and she stumbled. He caught her arm and braced her before she hit the ground, but she didn't quite manage to stifle a whimper.

"Emily—"

With dignity worthy of a queen, she drew away and squared her shoulders. "Miss O'Brien to you." Pain drew her features taut, and tears glistened in her eyes; but she refused to let them fall. She took another step toward the house, then faltered.

He scooped her up and carried her back inside. "Until Edward returns, I'm assuming responsibility." He kicked the door shut and scowled at her. "God have mercy on your soul if I find this is all an elaborate contrivance."

Chapter 5

Emily couldn't find a speck of fault with how he treated Anna. After Emily and Duncan packed everything, John Newcomb placed the bundles in a shiny conveyance he'd summoned. He came back in and spoke softly to Anna, then went back outside and waited patiently for Emily to tend to any private care her sister might need. When she sent Duncan to fetch him, John returned, gave Anna a tender smile, and promised, "Soon you'll be warm and comfortable." With surprising gentleness, he gathered the bedding and wrapped it about Anna.

He's being so good to her, Emily mused. In all the times Edward had come here, for all his smooth ways, he had never seemed so genuinely caring and tender. *'Tis a crying shame 'twasn't John Newcomb who wed her. He'd make any woman a fine husband.*

John lifted Anna and carried her out to the carriage.

"Our Em, don't forget the jar," Anna whispered.

"Jar?"

Anna smiled up at him. "You're family. You can know. We've saved a wee bit to help bring Da and Mama over on the ship. Em keeps it in a jar under a floorboard."

Emily felt the accusation in his dark eyes. She turned away, and just as Duncan started to open his mouth, she pressed a finger to her lips. Duncan obeyed her silent command. She sighed with relief. She'd succeeded in silencing her brother before he told Anna the jar no longer held a single cent.

Even so, Emily couldn't face John. She murmured, "We've not left a thing behind," then crawled into the luxurious state carriage.

John simply gave the driver a few words of instruction and got into the conveyance. He did so with great care so neither Anna's head nor feet were bumped in the least. He slipped onto the wide, padded leather seat opposite Emily and Duncan and arranged Anna on his lap. Clearly she was too weak to sit up. He thrust a lush fur robe at Duncan. "Spread that across your laps." John then took another and gently tucked it about Anna. Her head lolled onto his shoulder, and she offered an embarrassed apology.

"Shh." The sibilant sound seemed strange coming from him. He didn't seem the type to give succor or compassion. Yet there he sat, plain as day, cradling Anna almost exactly like the stained glass window over at the church that showed Christ holding a child. Aye, and there was the reality—he might well have made a won-drous husband, but that wasn't the flavor of his actions in the least. He treated Anna with the gentle affection an uncle might bestow upon a favorite niece. Emily looked at him and hoped he'd see the gratitude in her eyes.

Their gazes caught and held. Suddenly feeling as if he were trying to see straight into her soul, she looked down at her tiny nephew and cradled him still closer to her bosom. Her hand shook a bit as she carefully tamed his fine, downy brown hair into a less wild arrangement. At her feet lay all she and her siblings owned. Against Mr. Newcomb's voluble protests, she'd taken their meager pos-sessions and knotted them in Anna's emptied pillow slip and Duncan's blanket.

Her brother sat beside her and clutched the precious bag holding the Bible and Anna's ring. Wide-eyed, he stared out the window at the sights passing by him so quickly and crowed his interest as the city came to life for the day.

John Newcomb chuckled at something Duncan said. Emily gave him a wob-bly smile, then cast a worried look out the window. "Soon as I get them settled, I'll need you to give me directions. I've gotten turned about a bit."

"Directions?"

"To the asylum."

"We'll discuss it later."

Dread snaked through her. Emily opened her mouth, then closed it as she sought the right words. After a moment's consideration, she said, "Those people are counting on me, and so is my family."

"Wilkens can find some other slave to do his bidding."

"Mr. Newcomb, the patients there need to eat!"

He made a sound of unadulterated disgust. "So did you. That miser earns a hefty sum each month to warehouse all of those unfortunates—the least he could do is hire sufficient staff and pay them decently."

"Oh, Em got a whole dollar a week!"

John's eyes narrowed at Duncan's disclosure. "Emily, you're not setting foot in that place again. I dispatched a message to him, and he knows you'll not be returning."

She moaned. "Oh, how could you do that?"

"I have four maids, and my home is a quarter of the size of that sprawling madhouse. The newest of my maids earns three times what you were paid to do that whole place on your own—and they have decent meals and warm quarters within the house."

Emily flinched at his words. She hadn't been properly trained to be a house-maid. When she'd come over on the boat, she hadn't even owned leather shoes. The pair she now wore were castoffs from a lunatic. Indeed, every last stitch she and her sister possessed had been left by patients who died or went elsewhere.

The carriage went over a bump, and the pots rattled. She screwed up her courage. "As for cooking—"

"I'll be sure food is sent to you."

"Mr. Newcomb—" Emily tried to modulate her voice. "We cannot rely on your kindness. I'm wanting to ask if your own kitchen might be needing—"

"No."

"Laundry—"

"No," he snapped.

"I see." *He doesn't want Irish beggars working for him.* "I do hope there's some way I can—"

"You can stop formulating a stratagem this very minute." He looked meaningfully at the way Anna lay limply in his arms, then locked gazes with Emily again. "Your sister needs you. Until such time as she and the babe are hale, you're not to leave her side."

"Sir, I can take care of my sister," Duncan declared.

"Aye, and so I can see you've done your very best." His features altered into a kindly visage, and his voice slid into a man-to-man, confiding tone. "But I have a whole pack of dogs that need caring for and a favorite mare that needs special currying. You'll be busy enough already."

"A horse?" Awe filled Duncan's voice.

"A fine bay. She's particular, so you'll need to handle her well."

A lump of emotion knotted in Emily's throat. If nothing else, this would finally allow Duncan to have time to roam and play a wee bit. At best he might actually prove his value and be taken on as a stable boy. It would give him a trade—an honorable one. Da would be pleased to hear his son had such an arrangement.

Emily's eyes felt grainy, and her head weighed too heavily on her neck. She fought against leaning into the corner of the carriage and dozing. It wouldn't be proper. Besides, she needed to keep an eye on John Newcomb. He'd stepped in and started making all sorts of decisions, but she wasn't sure if she approved of them yet. Things were changing so quickly, it made her dizzy. Just when she pulled herself back from the precipice of sleep for the third time, the carriage turned off the main road, between two massive hedges, and onto a long, tree-lined drive.

A small, vine-covered cottage rested off to the north corner of the property. Nestled in a neatly trimmed, chest-high box of hedges, the clapboard's two brick chimneys thrust skyward, as if to bear testimony to John Newcomb's promise of warmth. The carriage drew up to the east side of the wondrous home and stopped.

"You ladies stay here a moment. Duncan, come with me." John gently slipped Anna onto the seat, made sure the robe kept her snug, and stepped over

Emily's feet with catlike grace. He ordered the driver to hobble the horses and come back for the rig later; then he disappeared into the charming home with Duncan on his heels.

Though his caretaker's place was small, John suspected the simple cottage would seem like heaven compared to where they'd been living. It hadn't been inhabited for at least a year, and he couldn't vouch for what condition it might be in. Sheets covered the furniture, looking like ghost ships in the sea of dust.

Footprints disturbed the thick, gray coating on the floor and led to a closed door. They gave him pause to wonder who had been here. John frowned and made a mental note to instruct his staff to keep a weather eye on the place. Lovers could seek some other trysting place, for he'd not provide a place for immorality. This was to be a warm haven of rest for Emily's poor little family. The storms of life had battered them enough.

He followed the footsteps, paced to the door, and threw it wide open. No one occupied the chamber now, but it certainly had been used quite recently. Fresh, fluffy blankets covered the bed, and in contrast to the other room, no accumulated grime coated the surfaces of anything. Clearly the secret bower hadn't been just a spur-of-the-moment whim. That fact ired him even more.

"Dear me," Duncan whispered. He still stood by the front door. His rapture jarred John from his anger and caused him to see the cottage in a positive light again.

Because Anna was so infirm, the bedchamber's status rated as the most important consideration. John perused it. The bed was fair sized—certainly large enough for the sisters to share. Though the blankets on it looked fresh and heavy enough to provide sufficient warmth, he'd send over a few more so Duncan could sleep snugly, as well. John nodded his satisfaction.

Duncan peered around him, marveling. "Ohh, 'tis wondrous! Does the queen live here?"

"Nay, lad. Your sisters will."

He took Duncan's shoulder and led him a few paces toward the kitchen. A tiny alcove off to the side would serve nicely for him. "See this? You clean it up, and we'll put in a cot for you. It'll be your very own space."

The weak autumn sun barely made it past the murky windows. What little did shine through carried a host of silvery dust motes. A small shaft of light fell across Duncan's cheek as he looked up with absolute adoration. "Ooh, sir! Your brother told us he'd get us a fine home, but I never dreamed 'twould be so verra grand!"

"Anna and her babe deserve a nice place."

"Em, too," Duncan said all too quickly. "She works so hard for us."

"Yes, especially Emily," John promptly agreed. He couldn't fault the lad for his loyalty. Since Duncan mentioned his oldest sister, John snatched the opportunity and sought more information. "Speaking of Emily, she wouldn't let you say a word about the jar. You can tell me about it, now that Anna cannot hear."

The sparkle left little Duncan's eyes. His mouth curved downward, and his voice took on a melancholy flavor. "She kept money in a jar under a loose floorboard. She spent it all. Every last cent is gone now. She tried to be ever so careful, our Em did, to save a wee bit whenever she could. But when there wasn't any more food and every last treasure got pawned, Em used part of the money to buy us food."

"What did she do with the other part?"

"Mr. Rickers wanted money for our house again. Then the midwife wanted to be paid for helping our Anna birth the babe. We didn't have enough."

John shook his head in disbelief. "You managed to save money?" The thought baffled him. In the midst of their appalling poverty, they might have just as soon hoped to fly as to try conserving money for two transatlantic passages. The notion that Emily tried to set aside even a penny wrenched his heart every bit as much as it stretched his imagination. *Yet she sent a penny back to me.*

"Aye, and we had almost half the jar filled." Duncan blinked away threatening tears. "We'd been saving hard as we could to send for Da and Mama, but Em said we'll not be able to do that for a long while now."

John nodded somberly. At least he'd gotten the truth. Yet again Emily wanted to protect her sister from the realities of their plight. He squeezed the boy's shoulder. "I think Emily wanted to keep that a secret from Anna. Are you good at keeping secrets?"

Duncan's head bobbed up and down. "I keep lots of secrets for Em."

John tugged out a small wooden chair, lifted Duncan to stand on it, and looked eye to eye with the lad. He dropped his tone. "Duncan, we're friends. Friends don't keep secrets. I think you'd better tell me if there's anything important I should know."

Duncan wrinkled his nose, then pursed his lips. "You won't tell Anna?"

"Never."

Chapter 6

The boy leaned closer and whispered loudly, "Em pretends she's not cold, and she pretends she's full, too. It's a game, she said—but I'm not to tell Anna. I'm not supposed to tell Anna that Em cries sometimes, either. It might upset our Anna, and Em says since I'm the man in the family, it's important for me to make Anna feel happy and safe."

John nodded.

Duncan winced. "I should have asked Em first if I could tell you her secrets."

John cupped his hand around Duncan's thin shoulder. "Sharing that with me didn't break Emily's confidence in you, Duncan. She wanted to keep that a secret from Anna. I need to know things so I can help your sisters. You want that, don't you?"

The boy nodded somberly. "Em and Anna used to try to keep things from me, but that changed. Now Em and I keep things from Anna—'specially about the money. Em doesn't want Anna to know she spent it all—because now Da and Mama won't be coming for ever so long."

John schooled his features so they wouldn't betray the emotions churning through him. He looked at the lad and saw a longing in his eyes when he mentioned his mother and father. He injected a tone of cheer into his voice. "Well, Duncan-boy, 'tis true you don't have your parents with you right now; but you've been blessed to have two big sisters. And come to think of it, standing here all day won't accomplish a thing. We'd best get them out of the carriage."

Duncan perked up. "I'll go turn back the bed!"

"You do that." John smiled as the boy brightened up, hopped off the chair, and raced toward the bedchamber. "Fold back both sides of the bed, Duncan," he called. "Emily is tired, and I want her to sleep the day away, too."

"Aye, sir."

John reached the carriage and looked through the window. He felt a surge of anger at whomever the man was who had conned these women. Of course he expected Anna to be weary—she'd not yet recovered from her childbed, but the sight of Emily set his teeth on edge.

She'd fallen asleep, and the deep, dark circles beneath her eyes tattled at how profound her exhaustion had become. Either cooking or cleaning for that entire asylum rated as a herculean job, yet she'd done both—without decent nourishment

39

or sufficient sleep. Awakening her was beyond cruel. He'd simply carry her in, just as he planned to do with Anna. Even in her sleep, Emily managed to cradle the babe to herself with a fierce tenderness. It wrenched his heart to think of what she'd endured to care for her little family.

Compassion still wouldn't hold back the frustration he felt. How could he have imagined a single coin would make a difference? The fact that Emily had scrimped to save a pitifully insufficient jar of coins to pay passage underscored how deeply she longed for her father to come and resume the mantle of provider and protector—the very mantle she wore of necessity. No wonder Anna had wed some dashing sailor—this little family was desperate for security and provision.

The moment the well-oiled carriage door whispered open, Emily startled awake once again and banged the back of her head against the wall. "Oh, Mr. Newcomb!"

"You're exhausted. How could you possibly think you were going to work again today?"

"I'm strong."

"And I'm a mackerel," he snapped back. She started to rise, but he stopped her by lightly squeezing her bony elbow. "You dare not step down. The minute you put your weight on that mangled limb, you'll fall."

She clutched the babe to her bosom and stared at him with wide eyes. "Please take Anna first. She's fallen asleep again."

He glanced over at Anna, then turned his attention back to Emily. His eyes narrowed as he pinched the baby's blanket between his fingers and rubbed it. It had been doubled over and stitched, and he knew there were two more just like it. One draped Anna, and the other held that pathetic bundle on the floor. "Your own blanket—you cut it up for the baby."

She quickly tested the babe's skin. "Do you think he's warm enough?"

Did she ever think of herself first? John hastened to assure her that her sacrifice had been sufficient. "He's cozy as can be."

Just then the baby sneezed.

John frowned. "Let's get him inside, though. The fur will keep Anna snug for a few more minutes."

For the baby's sake, she relented. John tucked Anna's blanket and fur about her and assured himself she was far too weak to turn and fall; then he scooped Emily into his arms and drew her out. "Thank you, sir." She fidgeted as if she expected him to set her feet down on the ground.

"Mercy!" he said in an exasperated tone as he paced to the house. "Stop trying to conquer the world. You're lame, weary, and hungry. You're to do nothing more than rest and help your sister with the baby." He took her inside and paused for a moment to let her get her bearings.

Suddenly the festooning cobwebs, inch-thick dust, and shrouded furniture looked tawdry. He'd been a fool not to have a crew of maids come over to turn the place inside out, then gone back this evening to fetch the O'Briens. Wretched as their shanty had been, they'd kept it clean. This place would send most seasoned housekeepers into a fit of the vapors. Chagrin colored his voice as he muttered apologetically, "No one has been in residence here for a while."

"Ohh!" Emily drew out the exclamation in an expression of awe. She turned her head this way, then that, and peered over his shoulder. A deep sigh came out of her. "Mr. Newcomb, 'tis such a fine place!"

He looked at her, wondering if she was being facetious. It didn't seem so, but then he pondered whether she plastered on a smile to be polite. He couldn't mistake the truth. Emily's reaction was as guileless as it was gleeful. The way her eyes lit with undiluted pleasure delighted him to no end. He no longer regretted bringing her straight here. Had he left her, she would have gone off to work and undoubtedly swooned from a combination of exhaustion, hunger, and pain. Since the dreary appearance and accumulated grime didn't bother her, he could pretend to turn a blind eye to it. He'd let her sleep, then send help on the morrow.

As he held her, he remembered her spotlessly clean shanty. He had no doubt she'd probably scrubbed that sprawling madhouse until it gleamed, too. Her hair glimmered in the sunlight, and she smelled of fresh soap and water. Oddly enough, for all the expensive perfumes women wore, he far preferred the simplicity of a woman without those cloying scents.

What in the world am I thinking, finding anything favorable about this woman? Not only did the thought jolt him mentally, but he unintentionally jarred Emily.

"I'm sorry." A fetching pink suffused her cheeks. "I'm gawking around, and you need to go get our Anna."

John stepped into the bedchamber. "You'll share this room with Anna. That way you can help her at night." He took Emily to the bed and carefully lowered her, mindful not to bump her sore ankle.

She bit her lip.

"Did I hurt you?"

Her arms anchored the babe closer still, and she stared at him for a long moment. Finally she whispered tightly, "I didn't realize the place was more than that one room. I thought maybe the cottage was cut into halves or thirds and we were to share it with other families—after all, I spied two chimneys. This is all too much. Please understand, Mr. Newcomb—I cannot afford such fine lodgings. You were so good to want better for us, but I'm sorry. This is way above my pocket."

He scowled at her. "You're not paying for this."

Her cheeks went scarlet as she choked out, "Mr. Newcomb, I'm a good woman."

A good woman. Yes, once he'd learned of her working at the asylum, he'd accepted the truth. No evidence existed of her having earned money by plying a loose woman's trade, but plenty indicated she'd twisted herself in knots trying to care for her little family. He had assumed wrongly, and now he wondered how he could have believed such a wild notion. All of it boiled down to this awkward moment, and she felt it necessary to profess her moral standards.

Big, sincere eyes stared at him, and her face looked earnest enough. Then, too, her clothing rated as ragged, but proper and modest. She possessed nothing of value whatsoever. No two ways about it—he'd misjudged her. Now he hoped she hadn't discerned what he'd so foolishly presumed. The last thing she needed was to bear the injury of such a grievous and false accusation.

Emily started to scoot toward the far side of the bed. "I think you'd better take us back to our own house, sir."

"No." He hastily set a hand on her arm, then reached across and flipped the quilts to trap her on the bed. "I thought I'd been clear about the arrangements, Miss O'Brien. Until Edward returns, you, Anna, Duncan, and the babe are my guests. I'll hear no more of that. I'll go fetch Anna now."

"I thank you ever so much, Mr. Newcomb. Truly I do."

He turned to go, then hesitated. He stared at the far wall instead of facing her. "Before I fetch Anna, I must ask indelicate questions." He paused a moment to allow Emily to prepare herself for the shockingly personal things he needed to ask. No gentleman broached improper subjects with a woman, but he had no one to act as his intermediary. He whispered a quick prayer for tact. After clearing his throat, he forged ahead. "Anna's young and small, seemingly too small to birth a babe—though she obviously has. Duncan made mention of a midwife, but there are quacks aplenty who do far more damage than good. Did you summon competent help for her?"

"Aye. How could I not?"

"Good." He turned, looked down at Emily, and shrugged. "I'm not pleased with how weak she is."

"It's only been a few days, and she did have a hard time." She glanced up at him, her face etched with worry. "She's not gotten childbed fever. That's a good sign, to be sure."

He pushed ahead, although he knew the subject he broached—though necessary—was highly improper. So far Emily had been good enough not to fly into a dither over his prying. He ardently hoped she understood he asked these things only because he shared her concerns. "Has Anna's—well, is she capable—?" He drew a quick breath and blurted, "Does she have sufficient milk yet?"

"Today. It will come in today. I went to the vicar, and he got fenugreek seeds from the Benedictines for me. The tea will work."

Her face nearly glowed with embarrassment, but she actually continued to participate in this outlandish conversation. Clearly her love for her sister and nephew overshadowed her personal discomfort. That being the case, he was going to set out his expectations.

"I put little store in most curatives, but the Benedictine monks are reputed to be gifted healers. Still, I'll not have the babe fuss for wont of milk. I'll summon an apothecary or physician to come see Anna, and you are to follow his orders precisely. If she does not have milk by the morrow, we'll engage a wet nurse."

Having spoken his piece, John left. Once outside, he breathed a prayer of thanksgiving that they'd made it over that awkward hurdle. He tugged at his collar and smiled grimly at the memory of Emily turning a rather fetching pink. Hopefully, they'd not have to discuss such delicate matters again. He wasn't sure who had been more uncomfortable—but they'd made it through, and that was what counted.

John paused a moment. He looked over the lawn and past it up the drive. Set on a gentle swell of land, his mansion overlooked the ocean. It was far enough away to afford both households privacy, and he felt a spurt of relief that his home wasn't visible from this spot. The vast disparity between his wealth and the O'Briens' abject poverty couldn't be any greater.

The horse's whinny prompted him to go fetch Anna. In reality, only a few minutes had passed since he'd taken Emily from the carriage, but in that time they'd covered appreciable subjects. He'd never been around a woman who didn't simper and fawn over him. Emily's practicality made for a refreshing change.

John quietly leaned into the carriage, gently slipped away the fur so he could slide his arms under Anna, and lifted her. Even as he drew her from the dim recesses of the carriage into daylight, she didn't so much as stir.

Lord, have mercy on her. She's been through enough already. He strode toward the house and caught sight through the window of Emily moving about. *Father, while I'm praying, I'll ask You to touch her, too. She's bristly as a brush, but beneath it all, she has a heart of gold. If I can be Your servant to tend these little lambs of Your fold, use me.*

John carried Anna into the bedchamber and quickly noted how Emily hadn't only prepared for her sister to be settled in the bed, but also removed the smallest drawer from a bureau. In spite of the chill of the room, Emily had taken off her shawl and folded it to fit the bottom of the drawer. There, in that makeshift bassinet, she now placed the wee babe and smiled at him.

How little it took to make her happy. Before they'd left the shack that morning, John had insisted she finish eating the food Franklin had delivered. She'd relished each bite as if it were a delicacy from the king's own table. Then, too, she'd subtly seen to it that Duncan and Anna received larger shares. She wasn't a woman who put herself first, and that virtue shone through.

John released his small burden and watched as Emily tenderly straightened her sister's limp form, adjusted the blankets in which she was bundled, and added the rest from the bed.

He thought Anna looked ghastly. Had she truly fallen asleep, or was she in a deep swoon? Never had he seen anyone so weak. He no longer wondered why Emily had taken it upon herself to brave the shipyard in search of the man she thought was Edward. It no longer seemed a foolhardy venture—it had been a move of sheer desperation. John determined he'd send for Dr. Quisinby at once. Something was dreadfully wrong.

Lovingly, Emily smoothed back strands of her sister's hair. "Our dear Lord Jesus, please let this be the start of her coming back to health." Emily then turned to face John. A sweet smile lifted her lips. "She looks so warm and peaceful."

John felt like an intruder, watching that tender moment of hope and devotion. He had some thinking to do. *Emily prayed and cherished her Bible. Was it possible his brother had deceived these women? No.* John shook his head to dislodge that ridiculous, stray thought. He simply couldn't imagine it. As soon as the *Cormorant* docked, he'd bring Edward here. With Anna and Emily's description, Edward would undoubtedly be able to identify the sailor who bore responsibility.

Time would reveal the truth to these women. Even then, John decided he'd set them up as assistants to a haberdasher or seamstress and settle their little family into a cottage somewhere. He turned to be sure the babe was safe, then mentioned, "I noticed a few logs in the grate."

"Ah, then tonight we'll be snug as—"

"Not tonight—now. I'll see to it you have wood and coal aplenty. Food, too."

"Oh, Mr. Newcomb, you're too kind!" Emily went to the brick fireplace and got down on her knees. Her features pulled with each step, but she gave no complaint. She worked deftly to light the kindling beneath the trio of small logs and said over her shoulder, "I'll be glad to work—to be sure, I'll not be earning whatever it takes to live in such grand style, but I'd like to do my best. Duncan and I—we're just riding coattails, being here. Edward never promised us anything—just Anna."

He chafed at her words. Since he held out no expectation his brother was involved with Anna, he wanted to make sure Emily grasped how things stood. "Until Edward returns, we'll keep to this arrangement. In the meantime, none of you is to mention him."

She turned so quickly, she landed on her backside. Mouth agape, she stared for a moment. A look of utter betrayal altered her features. "Oh, Mr. Newcomb. You tricked me."

"I did nothing of the sort."

"Aye, you did. You brought us to a palace and promised every creaturely comfort. You won Duncan's allegiance by the promise of working with your animals, and my sister and her son will flourish instead of struggle. You said until Edward returned, you'd assume responsibility. I must have been a fool to think you changed your mind, but when you said that, I truly thought you'd reconsidered and were admitting Edward and Anna were wed."

"Now, Emily—"

"I was wrong to allow you to bring us here." Her voice shook, but he couldn't tell if it was with outrage or anguish. "Soon as Anna wakes, we'll go back—"

"No!" The word burst from him; then he cast a glance to be sure he'd not awakened Anna. He scowled back at Emily. "Look at her! You can't possibly last there another day. You're staying put."

She said in a sick hush, "You didn't tell us the cost of coming with you was Anna's dignity and our silence. You lured us here, but now you instruct us to live a lie."

"By staying silent, you're not living a lie, Emily. That marriage license is a fake."

To his horror, tears welled up in her green, green eyes, turning them into pools of infinite suffering. Until now she'd shouldered everything without weeping. He somehow had deluded himself into believing she was too strong to indulge in such feminine weakness. A solitary tear streaked down one pale, gaunt cheek.

Compassion tugged at him, but he needed to be careful. This was a temporary arrangement—until Edward made an appearance and things were resolved or the investigator turned up the real "Edward Newcomb" responsible for devastating these women. John reasoned softly, "You can live quietly here. Anna will recover nicely, and the babe will thrive. Surely you must admit that is more important than any other consideration. You're too tired to think this through. After you sleep a bit, it will all make perfect sense."

She shook her head sadly. "The only thing I know is I've taken cookies from the devil's own kitchen."

Chapter 7

Bone weary as she felt, Emily's turmoil kept her from resting. Once Mr. Newcomb left, she turned to her brother. "We've got work to do, boy-o." He sneezed, then laughed. "It's dusty in here."

"Aye, that it is. Scare up a broom. I'll knock down the cobwebs and sweep the walls and floor." She looked at the maize-colored drapery. "Do you think you could shove a chair over to the walls and scramble up it so as to take down the curtains?"

His wee chest puffed out 'til he looked like a proud little robin that just gobbled the longest worm in the park. "There's no doubt about it. I'll pull down every last one of them—just watch if I don't."

"I'm sure you can. Then we'll take them out and drape them on the hedges. You can beat them, and the wind will blow the rest of the dust out 'til they come clean enough. Now let's get to it." She made a shooing motion with her hands. "Find me a broom."

They got busy. No stranger to cleaning, Emily organized herself and efficiently rid the cottage of the depressing air of disuse. How could anyone neglect such a palace?

Her ankle hurt, but she'd learned to kneel on the seat of a chair to keep the weight off her ankle when the twinges got too bad. The chair could move about the room with her so she was able to keep working. She swept down everything once, then pulled the covers off the furniture. A collection of treasures lay hidden beneath those covers—a golden velvet settee, a rose-and-gold-striped wingbacked chair, two charming little nesting tables, an oak rocking chair, and a petit point footstool featuring a cabbage rose pattern.

Emily couldn't contain her delight over each piece as Duncan folded in the cloth to uncover it. "Oh, now, can't you just imagine our Anna, holding her babe in that rocker?"

Duncan rapped his knuckles on the smaller table. "Aye, and this is just the right size for me!"

The dust from the covers they removed made it necessary to sweep the floor yet again, but Duncan obliged. After that, they each took a wet rag and mopped the wooden floorboards until they gleamed.

Duncan found a crock of vinegar in the pantry and a bucket in the alcove. He sloshed water on the windows from the outside, and she used diluted vinegar on the inside of them so the sun could shine through.

Twice Emily stopped to help Anna with the babe. When she came back after the second episode, she sat down in a chair for just a second.

∾ঔ

"What in the world?" John squinted at the hedges. His brows knit. "Surely she didn't—"

Oh, but she had. The cottage's curtains flapped in the stiff noonday breeze like semaphores on a clipper. He dismounted from his prized bay and blazed right through the open door. Once inside, he stopped in his tracks. Duncan sat cross-legged on a spotless floor over by the window, crooning softly to the babe in his lap.

Sunlight flooded the cottage from the sparkling clean, curtainless windows, giving a cheerful air to the furnishings they'd uncovered. Hard work and devout prayer together shouldn't have accomplished half of the miracle he saw.

That hard work—and probably the prayer, too, he admitted to himself—*came from one very young woman.* Her temple rested against the wing of a rose-and-gold-striped chair. Dirt streaked her face and smudged her muslin apron. The cuffs of her dress remained turned up, as if she'd awaken any moment and resume what must have been a frantic pace of labor. Her bosom rose and fell in the slow rhythm of sleep. After she'd been slaving for Wilkens, John marveled she'd stayed awake long enough to do anything at all. He glanced about the cottage once more, then looked at her and decided on a course of action.

"Our Em is sore tired," Duncan whispered. "Anna says we must let her sleep."

"Not there. She looks horribly uncomfortable."

"I emptied our belongings from my blanket, sir. We can cover her."

John cast a look at the bedchamber, then thought better of carrying Emily to it. There was no telling what state Anna was in. He'd do better using the settee as a makeshift bed for this headstrong woman. Earlier he'd wondered what furniture lay beneath the dusty covers and suspected he might have to raid his warehouse to scare up replacement items if the mice had nested in anything. It came as a pleasant surprise to discover things were in good repair.

Emily was a short woman—the settee would accommodate her nicely enough for now. Anna had slept through his moving her. Certainly, as weary as Emily must be, she'd never know if he lifted her and popped her onto the settee. He drew closer and barely made contact, but Emily turned into a raging tigress.

Women, in his experience, were delicate and powerless. Ladylike, they'd never done more than swoon, rap a man's knuckles with a fan, or, even at their boldest, slap his cheek. Emily broke that rule. All four limbs went into action, taking a purposeful defense.

His arms tightened. "Calm yourself!"

From the first day in steerage on the ship, Emily had learned she had to protect herself. Working at the asylum had only reinforced that fact. The merest touch would send her into a defensive flurry. She kicked with her right foot. A strangled cry tore out of her throat as she arched in anguish. Fire shot through her, then ice. Emily fought to cling to the edges of reality as everything went cold and dark. Someone called her name, but she couldn't answer. For a moment she floated; then there was nothingness.

"Talk to her," she vaguely heard a man say. Someone patted her cheek lightly several times, then ceased that—only to start chafing her hand. "Emily. Come now, Emily. Wake up." The man's voice sounded quite concerned.

Emily stirred. A single slight shift, and the agony in her ankle mushroomed. Whimpers poured out of her. She bit her lip to silence that sign of weakness.

"Eh, our Emily," Duncan said from a long way off. "You're right fair. Aye, you are. All is well."

She struggled to open her grainy eyes and barely lifted her head. Waves of weariness and pain made her head droop back down. Where was she? It took a moment before she recalled John Newcomb bringing them to this wondrous cottage. . .but how had she come to lie on the settee? Her ankle hurt so badly, she barely managed to choke out, "Duncan?"

John Newcomb's face hovered into view. "Your brother is behind you, tending Anna's babe. Lie still."

"Anna?"

"Fine. She's just fine. In fact, she's probably in better shape than you are." Mr. Newcomb flipped a familiar-looking blanket over her. He seemed angry enough to spit anvils.

Now what have I done?

"The babe smiled at me, Em. I'm certain of it."

She kept her eyes trained on Mr. Newcomb while she whispered in a shaky voice, "Now isn't that sweet, Duncan! Anna's wee one is going to look up to you for love and protection."

"The way Anna and Duncan do to you?" John asked.

"Aye, and fitting it is. I'm. . .the eldest," she answered. Those few words seemed to drain her of most of her energy. She knew it was rude to ignore a guest, but everything wavered around her.

A warm hand curved around her jaw. Someone, somewhere, crooned in a deep, musical baritone to her. He bade her to rest, to sleep. Surely that couldn't be Mr. Newcomb. Her eyelids felt too heavy to lift, so she couldn't prove it; but as angry and mean as he'd been so far, Emily felt sure Lucifer would be wearing snowshoes before John Newcomb ever uttered a kind word to her.

"Things will be easier for you now. Be at peace."

~

"Emily. Miss O'Brien? Sorry to wake you when you barely got to sleep, but Dr. Quisinby is here."

Emily shook her head to dispel the lethargy grabbing at her. "Yes. Yes, thank you." She started to sit up, but large, strong hands touched her shoulders and pressed her back down into the luxurious, horsehair-stuffed velvet cushion. She blinked to clear away the haze of sleep and focused on none other than John Newcomb. Deep lines furrowed his brow. She murmured, "If you give me a moment, I'll make sure Anna is prepared for him."

"I've already examined your sister," a strange voice said. Emily looked past John Newcomb and spied an old, bewhiskered man dressed in a somber, charcoal gray jacket. Gold buttons on the garment hinted he conducted a very successful practice. Indeed, it didn't strain her mind in the least to believe him to be accomplished in his profession. Just his appearance inspired confidence in his ability. He studied her sternly but said nothing more.

His very silence alarmed her. "How is Anna? What about the baby?"

"We'll discuss that after the doctor examines you. Duncan and I will absent ourselves for a short while." John rose, and Emily belatedly realized he'd been kneeling at her side. He waggled his finger at her. "You cooperate. No more of your foolish stubbornness. Come, Duncan." He reached his hand around her brother's shoulder and led him out the door.

Emily started to sit up yet again, but Dr. Quisinby's stern look made her lie back down.

"Let's not put up any pretenses, miss. Anyone who could sleep through the wailing that babe was making must be suffering extreme exhaustion. Stay where you are, and I'll make this as simple as possible."

The front door closed, and Emily flashed what she hoped looked like a confident smile at the doctor. "Sir, I truly appreciate how you saw to my sister. I don't need—"

He held up a hand as if to silence her. His features altered into a scowl. "Mr. Newcomb was excessively clear in his directive."

Unable to refute that assertion, Emily resorted to the humiliating truth. "I understand his concern, Doctor"—she felt her face flame—"but I don't have a single coin in my pocket. It'll take me a long while to pay you back for seeing to my Anna."

He stepped closer and started to peel away the blanket. "You needn't fret over that. Mr. Newcomb already saw to my fee. He warned me you'd likely try to beg off. Furthermore, he garnered my pledge to persist. Now that that's settled, I may as well have a look—"

Emily endured the embarrassing questions and answered them as best she could while trying to preserve her dignity, but when he reached for her ankle, she tensed. No woman of decency—however rich or poor—permitted a man to view or touch such scandalous portions of her being.

"Miss O'Brien, it's obvious you've injured yourself. Mr. Newcomb is most concerned. He informed me you've hurt your limb quite badly and fell into a deep swoon today. You must be practical enough to allow me to assess the extent of the damage and treat you." The doctor's austere expression reinforced his opinion.

Planning to protest, Emily drew in a breath but exhaled without saying a word. Whatever argument she made would either sound foolish or be a falsehood.

"It would be an ill-considered move to refuse my assistance, since an injury of this nature could very likely cause you to collapse while you're carrying your nephew. Even if that didn't happen, you might well end up lame if this is broken. Then what help will you be to your sister?"

Emily grudgingly accepted the truth of his words. She compressed her lips and nodded. When the doctor took her calf into his hands, she nearly shot off the settee. As he started to unwind the cloth she'd used to bind her ankle, the swelling and discoloration became apparent. Emily had tried her best to keep Duncan and Anna from seeing the sad condition of her limb. When Mr. Newcomb accidentally saw it last night because he'd boldly let himself into their home, she'd nearly been embarrassed out of her skin.

"Yes, then, this looks quite sore," the doctor murmured in a sympathetic tone as he peered over his spectacles at her.

Emily feared she would be violently ill when he set aside the cloth and lightly ran his fingers over the beginning of the bruise above her ankle. She swallowed the bile, but he tightened his hold and began to turn the joint. The pain exploded.

❧

"Just leave the cloth over her brow." A deep murmur reached through the haze. "I'd rather not use hartshorn and revive her until I have this bound."

Emily forced her lids to flutter open. It took half of forever before she could remove the soggy handkerchief from her forehead or form any words, and even then they sounded faint. "Forgive me. . . . I'm not usually. . .this giddy."

"My estimation is that, you're normally a stalwart soul," the doctor said. He took a glass of water from Duncan and added a few drops of something to it. "Drink this."

She evaded the rim of the glass. "What is it?"

"Laudanum."

"Oh, Doctor, no. I don't think—"

"Don't quibble, Emily." She twisted a bit and realized John Newcomb was back. His dark countenance made her worry about what else had upset him. "Drink the stuff. You're not a brave little soldier; you're a hurting woman."

The doctor's whiskers spread apart as he grinned. "If you were a brave soldier, you'd be demanding a stiff whiskey."

Emily started to curl and set her elbow and hand on the settee to help push herself upright. Weak as she felt, she didn't mind John's silent assistance. He smoothly sat her up, then braced her as she fought a wave of dizziness. The men exchanged a few words, but Emily couldn't quite distinguish them. Everything sounded muffled and far away.

"Here." John Newcomb's voice registered. So did the sensation of something pressed against her lips.

Emily opened her eyes again. At least the dizziness had passed.

"Drink it. Come now, Emily. Every last drop."

She gave him a wry look but obeyed. For smelling so sweet, the contents of the cup tasted acrid. She suppressed a shudder. "How is Anna?"

"She's weak and malnourished," the doctor stated baldly. "Her milk is coming in, but she'll have to eat like a horse to build up a good supply."

"That won't be a problem," John stated crisply as he handed the cup to Duncan and pointed toward the kitchen drain board in a silent order to set it out of the way.

"She told me you've been brewing fenugreek tea for her," the doctor said. "That's precisely what I prescribe to increase milk, so you're to continue to give it to her thrice daily."

"Otherwise—" Emily cast an embarrassed look at John as he took a seat in the striped wingback chair she'd fallen asleep in a short while earlier. She then focused back on the doctor as she lowered her voice to a flustered whisper. "Is Anna going to fare well?"

"From the looks of things, she suffered through a difficult birthing."

"The midwife said as much."

Dr. Quisinby let out a small huff of air. His face and tone held a hint of sadness. "Judging from her condition and comparing it to my previous cases, I anticipate hers will be a lengthy recovery. In truth, you'd best prepare her gently for the fact that this son will be her only child."

Emily bit the inside of her cheek to hold back her reaction. Part of her wanted to scream at the injustice. The other part wondered if God had done this to save Anna from further humiliation since she was already a shunned wife.

"Her blood needs to be built back up," the doctor continued.

Emily nodded. Fretting over truth never changed the fact. Best she keep her mind set on the things that would make a difference and leave the rest to the

Almighty. God would get them through. "Just tell me what my sister needs. I'll do whatever you instruct."

"Plenty of sleep for both of you ladies. Generous portions of decent food to regain some strength."

"I'll have my cook see to them," John said. "What do you suggest?"

"Beef. Buttermilk. Egg custards and the like. Your cook is redoubtable—set the situation before her, and she'll see to matters." The doctor rummaged in a black leather satchel and produced a tall, square bottle. "This tonic should work nicely. Nasty tasting, of course, but the best ones tend to be that way. All three of you are to take a spoonful each morning."

Emily eyed the bottle. *If I don't take any, it'll last—*

John Newcomb leaned forward and rasped, "I don't like the calculating look in your eye, Emily O'Brien. You're not going to forgo your own doses so Duncan and Anna have more."

Emily felt her cheeks grow hot with guilt.

"Do I have your word?" John folded his arms across his chest and stared at her. Grudgingly, Emily nodded. "Aye, 'tis my word you have."

John gestured toward her ankle. "Is it broken?"

"Badly sprained," Dr. Quisinby said. "Very badly sprained. Pity of it is, sprains can take longer than a break to heal. She needs to keep off it. No gadding about."

John rose. He shook the doctor's hand. "I thank you for coming." He escorted the doctor out. Emily slumped into the corner of the settee. Minutes later, the echo of John Newcomb's fine knee boots on the wooden floor made her open her eyes.

"Here." A damp cloth draped from his fingertips.

"I'm thanking you," she whispered as she took the cloth and lifted it in both hands to bury her face in it. The spicy scent clinging to the cloth registered as both foreign and comforting. She inhaled deeply and proceeded to wash her face and hands. "Aye, I'm thanking you, John Newcomb, for seeing to my dear ones. Duncan and my Anna have suffered terribly. I'm ever so grate—"

"Hush." He whisked away the cloth and shoved a plate into her hands.

She whispered a prayer, then silently ate the slice of cold roasted beef, a dried fig, and a small chunk of bread, and drank a bit of pomegranate juice. "Oh, that was a fine feast."

"How is your, ah, foot feeling?"

Such a gentleman. Even if she was just a dirt-poor immigrant, he'd not mentioned her ankle. "It's much better, thank you." Emily manufactured a grateful smile as she looked at him. Both of him.

He took the plate from her hand and set it down on a nearby table. "You ought to sleep quite soundly now that the laudanum is starting to work."

"Anna—"

"Young though he is, Duncan is quite adept at assisting her." John fleetingly touched her cheek, and her heavy lids fluttered shut.

For the first time in years, she felt safe. Gratitude and relief flooded her.

"Emily, I'm going to carry you to your bed."

She forced herself to look at him again. "No, thank you." She patted the arm of the settee. "Sleep here. . .don't want"—she blinked—"bother Anna."

"As you wish."

The room started to melt sideways; then Emily realized it was because John had somehow moved her to the center of the settee. "Lie down, little one." He coaxed her to tilt back, then guided her shoulders onto the inviting seat cushions.

"That's the way of it," he praised in a croon as he lifted her limbs and tucked them onto the seat. Even muzzy as her mind felt, Emily knew he took great care not to bump her ankle.

"But the ba—"

"Stop fretting and sleep." He took the blankets he'd used earlier to cover her and draped them gently over her and tucked them about her shoulders. "Do you want a pillow?"

She sighed in pure bliss and shook her head. She'd been sitting by Anna's bed to sleep for so long that just lying down on something soft and having her own blanket felt like heaven on earth. Anna could keep the fine feather pillows. As the fingers of sleep reached for her, Emily remembered to mumble, "Thank you for everything."

❦

A few days later, the vicar paid a call. His arrival came as no surprise since Emily had asked John if he could send word to the vicar that they'd welcome a visit.

She'd been too worried to leave Anna and the babe alone for the few hours it would have taken to go to church. Indeed, she missed going to worship something fierce; but since she'd taken over both jobs at the asylum, she'd been unable to attend.

Emily consoled herself with the knowledge that this was only a temporary situation and that God had promised to be with her at all times. John Newcomb had entered their lives and displayed such generosity and kindness to Anna and Duncan—a fact that Emily counted as proof God still hovered close enough to hear and answer her constant prayers.

Duncan was off at the stables, and Anna lay napping soundly on the wondrously soft, big bed when the vicar arrived. For the first few moments, Emily fought with herself. Edward had brought along what might well have been a man simply posing as a parson. Could John Newcomb have taken a page out of that copybook and done the same thing? She knew she could put her trust in God; putting it in man was another issue entirely.

Emily invited the vicar to have a seat and tried to carry on polite small talk. Instead of plowing to the heart of the matter, he pleasantly carried the conversation, invited her to attend church, and spoke of how the choir would begin practice for the Advent services soon. His kindly concern and gentle spirit proved him to be a true man of the cloth. Swallowing her pride, Emily told him of their predicament.

"Well, now, why don't you show me the marriage certificate?"

She reverently took out the parchment and prayed ever so hard he'd tell her all was well. When Edward and the priest had brought the certificate with them, she and Anna had been thrilled with it. It wasn't simple paper—no, 'twas made of fine parchment, and the words were scripted on it in a fine hand. Roses crowned the top of a gold-embossed square that framed the whole affair, and she and Anna had been careful to sign their names on the lines with their very best penmanship. John's comment about Edward's signature rang true, though—'twas little more than a scribble.

The vicar accepted the page and carried it over to the window so he could read the script more easily. Clouds were rolling in so even that light seemed questionable.

"I'll fetch a lamp."

"No need, no need," he murmured.

Emily watched as his lips moved in silent reading. She couldn't determine any particular reaction. Finally he looked up. "Child, I'm sorry to tell you this is no marriage license. Someone went to a bit of trouble to create a beautiful imitation, but that's what this is: a counterfeit. It holds just enough liturgical words to fool someone who doesn't read Latin, but most of it is sheer babble."

Emily pressed her palm to her mouth to hold back a scream. Rage pulsed through her.

"Now, then, it's a crying pity."

"It's more than a pity—'tis a crime!" She wound her arms around her ribs. "I never suspected he was a scoundrel. He courted our Anna and charmed us all. When he brought the priest, I trusted that a man of God wouldn't do something amiss." She cast a horrified look at the bedchamber door, then looked back at him. Until now she'd hoped all of this was a case of John Newcomb's simply being wrong.

The full reality hit, and Emily knew she couldn't deny the awful truth any longer. "Poor Anna! Oh, my poor sister! What are we to do?"

"There's nothing to be done," the priest answered gently. "Some things in life you set behind you. Much as it pains me to speak the truth and even more pained as you'll be to hear it, this will have to be one of them you not only set behind you, but close the door on. As far as I can see, there's only one hope. John Newcomb is a righteous man. If the Edward Newcomb who signed this is John's brother, you can count on John to rectify the matter."

The fraudulent wedding parchment crackled as he set it aside. After a time of thick silence, he shook his head sadly. "The past is the past. We must now deal with the present. Why don't you bring the babe to me?"

Emily smiled at him gratefully. "Even if the marriage isn't real, you're willing to acknowledge him?"

"Every child deserves to be welcomed into the world. I'd be honored to pray for the boy. Perhaps, given the circumstances, it would be best if we simply tended my giving a blessing here." The kindly old man gave her a sad, aching smile. "With your sister ailing, I'm sure she'll find peace knowing we'll love and accept her son."

Indeed, that is precisely what they did. Emily served the priest tea until Duncan came home and Anna woke. Because Anna couldn't move without hurting, Emily went into the bedchamber and opened the curtains and windows so she wouldn't feel as if the visit were being conducted under cover of dark and shame. The damp smell of coming rain filled the room. She hastily combed and braided Anna's hair and tried very gently to let her sister know the vicar had confirmed John Newcomb's evaluation of the wedding parchment.

Anna's pretty eyes filled with tears, but she didn't say a word.

"Ach, now. You know Duncan and I love you. We know you didn't do a thing wrong, and the vicar said the selfsame thing. I'm supposing we could spend all of eternity being upset, but that won't change a thing. You have a babe—a sweet one at that. We love him dearly—all of us."

Anna cradled the little one closer to her bosom. She choked back her tears and agreed weakly, "Aye, we do."

"So let's forget entertaining regrets and make sure he grows up to be a young man who follows the Lord." Emily then gave the baby a quick swipe with a damp towel, popped him into a fresh nappy, and wrapped him in her own shawl.

"Are we ready?" Duncan asked from the doorway.

"Aye, I'm supposing we are," Anna answered in a hushed voice.

The vicar and Duncan came in. As they did, the clouds in the sky blocked out the weak sun. The vicar peeped at the babe, gave Anna a few kind words for herself, and exclaimed over what a fine child she'd borne, then took out a prayer book. Though she'd heard the words before, Emily listened even more closely this time. It was so very precious, having someone speak to the Lord about this beloved little child. The vicar paused briefly. "What name have you given him?"

A moment later, he repeated the name Anna tearfully decided upon. The skies opened up, and all heaven cried for the travesty.

Chapter 8

"Very good, Duncan!"

Duncan beamed and clutched the edges of the slate. He turned it so Anna could appreciate his work, too. "See? I knew that one, too!"

"Oh, now, aren't you a smart lad," Anna praised.

Emily had found a slate tucked beneath a stack of moldy books. Ever since Anna had started having trouble carrying the babe, they'd stopped giving Duncan his lessons. They'd gladly plunged back into them, and the slate made it all that much easier.

"Give me another one," Duncan begged.

"Hmm." Emily closed her Bible, then opened it. Her finger landed in the upper third of the page. She started to giggle.

"What's so funny?" Anna asked.

"Yes, please do tell me. What's so funny?" John asked. He leaned on the bedroom window and peeked inside. He grinned. "I don't mean to invade your privacy, but I don't believe I've ever heard Emily laugh before. I had to see if my ears were playing tricks on me."

"Oh, it's our Em, all right," Duncan said. He galloped over to the window and held up the slate. "We're playing a game. Em finds a verse in the Bible, and I'm to copy as many words out of it as I can spell correctly."

"There's a novel game." John looked at the slate, then reached in and rumpled Duncan's hair. "You did a fine job on that one. I still don't see why Emily laughed, though."

"Neither do we," Anna agreed. "What's so funny, Em?"

Emily looked back down at her Bible and spluttered into laughter again. "You'll never believe this," she warned. Her eyes shimmered with glee.

"I'm ready," Duncan declared as he poised the stylus over the slate. "Try me!"

" 'Jesus wept.' "

John watched through the window as Duncan's face twisted with confusion. Anna started to giggle, and Emily set aside the Bible and dissolved into hilarity. His own laughter boomed in, though it was more a result of the pure joy of seeing them all happy than at the fact that she'd happened to give her little brother such a simple verse.

Duncan set aside his slate, propped his chin on the windowsill, and asked in a bewildered tone, "Why are you all laughing when it says Jesus was crying?"

John grabbed him, dragged him through the wide-open window, and flipped him upside down. He playfully shook the lad until he laughed, then set him on his feet. "We laughed because Em wanted to stump a smart boy like you with a hard verse, and the best she could do was give you two little words."

"Em's a giggle box today."

"Oh, she is, is she?"

"Uh-huh." Duncan led him into the house and straight into the bedchamber, where Anna and Emily still battled to subdue their chuckles.

John watched Emily try to paste on a serene expression, but her lips twitched a bit. He wanted to start laughing all over again, too. He gave her arm a quick squeeze, then winked at Anna. Autumn sunlight filled the room, and the day seemed far more golden and warm than the calendar dictated. "So what set you into this jolly mood?"

"I'm afraid I started it. My pillow got a wee hole in it last night. I woke up wearing feathers in my hair," Emily began.

"And Anna said she looked like a loon," Duncan added.

"Then the baby got the hiccups," Emily said.

"And I got a funny brown mustache from drinking the hot chocolate," Anna confessed sheepishly.

"Duncan somehow accidentally got a nappy tucked into his waist and walked about like he had a tail for ever so long before he realized it," Emily said, her voice quivering with laughter. "And then he spelled 'beloved' as 'B-loved'!"

John belted out a laugh. "You're having quite a silly day!"

"So it's your turn. What have you done today?" Duncan asked.

John simply couldn't let the delight of the day fizzle just because he didn't have a confession to make. He theatrically tapped one finger on his chin, then shrugged. "I don't know. I'm having an ordinary day. I can't think of a single, solitary thing that's happened to me that warrants any laughter at all." Just as he finished speaking, he sat on the edge of a chair and let his elbow bump the side table so he'd have to bobble to catch the flower vase he'd upset. The laughter in the room was ample reward for his intentional clumsiness.

Soon the gaiety extended to their playing tic-tac-toe on the slate. Instead of using O and X marks, they drew pictures of animals. "Your cat looks more like a rat," Emily told John.

He gave her an exaggerated look of offense. "You had to tell me yours was a bear. I thought it was a monkey!"

"It didn't have a long tail," Emily retorted. She turned to Anna. "Tell him I drew a grand bear."

Anna's eyes grew wide with poorly feigned innocence. "Oh, that was a bear?

I thought 'twas a snowman with earmuffs."

"Fat lot you know," Emily teased back. "Your snake looked more like a worm than anything else."

The merriment continued. John deeply regretted having to leave for a meeting. He'd seen the O'Briens somber far too much. This slice of time came as a complete surprise—and a delightful one at that.

Adding to his relief, Duncan, Anna, and Emily had observed his one stricture: They didn't mention Edward's name in their discussions when others were present. Now that he thought of it, they didn't even mention his brother in his presence, either. Whether 'twas out of embarrassment or obedience, he didn't know. The simple fact that Edward's name remained unspoken and his honor and reputation were spared satisfied John.

When the situation warranted some form of reference, Anna simply said, "My husband." From that, everyone held the impression that she must be the wife of one of the shipping company's new captains—a false deduction John neither denied nor confirmed. As far as things went, the situation continued to unfold far more amiably than he'd expected.

"I'll have to look around the house," he said as he left. "I recall a cribbage board."

"Oh, that would be fine," Anna smiled.

"And Duncan could speed up on doing his sums by counting the hands," Emily chimed in.

"Do you play chess?"

Emily's brows knit. John had a wild urge to reach over and smooth the furrows with a gentle stroke of his finger. Instead he clasped his hands behind his back and listened as she said, "That's far too fancy a game for us simple folk, Mr. Newcomb."

He winked, then gave her a look of mock severity. "Miss O'Brien, no one can be terrible at everything in life. I've seen how you can draw. Surely your ability to play chess would have to be an improvement. Anything would be an improvement!"

"I think I've been insulted," Emily groused.

"Oh, no. Not in the least," Anna twittered. "Mr. Newcomb was trying to express his faith in your ability to learn the game of kings."

"Kings are boys," Duncan said. "If it's a boys' game, maybe Mr. Newcomb had better teach it to me instead."

"We'll make a date of it. I'll bring cookies and milk tonight after supper. I'll teach you all how to play chess," John promised.

Duncan started to chortle. "Oh, now you know what our Em will say about that!"

"No, I don't. What will Em say?" John's brows hiked as he looked to Emily. Emily shrugged.

"Remember what I told you once before? Em used to tell me that God brings meat; the devil brings cookies!"

"Duncan!" Emily gasped. Her cheeks went bright red—as red as the peppermint sticks John decided to bring that night.

∽

A few days later, Dr. Quisinby dropped in. After he examined Anna, he sat down to have some coffee with Emily. "Between that tonic and eating well, you and Duncan are looking far better."

Something in his tone made Emily stop cold. She set down her cup and stared at him in dread. "Anna—?"

"She's not recovering, Emily."

"What shall I do? Does she need other medicine? Should I—"

"Emily," he broke in. He shook his head sadly. "I had my suspicions when I saw her the first time. This visit merely confirmed them."

"You have to be wrong. She has a babe. A son needs his ma. Surely there's something—" When he shook his head again, Emily propped her elbows on the tabletop and buried her face in her hands. "I should have—"

"No," he interrupted. "She told me she was sick the last three months of carrying the baby."

"If she'd eaten more, stayed warm—"

He rose and came around the table and pulled her to face him. "Emily, none of that would have made the difference. I have rich, fat women who suffer this same malady. My medical text discusses it, but there is no cure. There is no blame to assume, no situation to second-guess."

"I don't want Anna to know. I don't want her to worry about her little one."

Dr. Quisinby nodded. "I concur. Let her last days be happy ones."

"Duncan—I don't want him told, either."

"As you wish. Perhaps 'twould be wise to let Mr. Newcomb know. Would you like me to inform him?"

Emily nodded. The doctor and room blurred as the reality sank in and tears started to flow.

∽

"Of all of the idiotic things in the world!" John roared. He lengthened his stride and hastened toward the small cottage as he served Emily his hottest glower. She stood in the doorway, her arms wrapped about her sister. The two of them looked ready to topple over any second.

John wedged himself between Anna and the doorframe, then swept her into his arms. Weak as she was, she melted against him like a candle accidentally left out in the sun. Appalled at the thought that they'd have both tumbled down the steps if he'd not happened along, he locked eyes with Emily. "Just what do you think you're doing, letting her get out of bed?"

"Anna was wanting some sunshine," Emily explained as she allowed him to hold the load she'd been struggling with. She tugged the hem of Anna's night-gown down to cover her limbs. "You cannot blame her—she's been inside for nigh unto three months."

"If she falls, she'll spend centuries in a pine box until the eternal trump sounds!" John was horrified by this whole turn of events. Emily's stricken look let him know he'd almost spilled the truth. Regret swamped him. He immediately softened his tone. "Forgive me. I'm complaining for no good reason. Here. Let me help."

In the recesses of his mind, he couldn't be sure whether he worried more about Emily or Anna, though. Neither of them was in any condition to endure the slightest exertion, let alone a tumble. Though rest and decent meals had perked up Emily, she had no business half carrying Anna when she still limped.

Dr. Quisinby had spoken circumspectly, but his message had come through clearly. Anna had little time left, and Emily—John gritted his teeth. The way she'd swooned the day he brought them to the cottage alarmed him. In those moments he'd finally seen beyond her fiercely brave façade to how truly weak, thin, and ragged she'd become. He'd held her in his arms and known for the first time a wave of inexplicable protectiveness. At that moment he'd determined to do whatever it took to shield and care for this woman.

Quisinby had confirmed his suspicions when he said Emily had undoubt-edly given her own portion of food to her sister and suffered hunger out of the selfless hope that Anna and the babe would fare better due to her sacrifice.

Even when she'd been sagging from exhaustion, Emily had clung to his ker-chief and tried with touching sincerity to thank him for all he'd done for her brother and sister's suffering—and never once confessed she'd been even more hungry and cold than they. And even as he'd tucked her in on that settee, her last thoughts had been of the baby and another vague whisper of thanks. He'd bent forward and taken up the kerchief again. The generous dose of laudanum the good doctor had given her had kept her placid as John dabbed one last smudge from her temple.

Now he wished he could wipe away the worried look in her eyes just as eas-ily. Keeping the secret from Anna had to be so very hard on her. To his aston-ishment, Emily hid this burden just as she'd hidden her hunger and thinness. To look at her quick smile and listen to her cheerful talk, anyone would guess she didn't have a trouble in the world.

Over the last week, John had thought to stay away from the small cottage.

It wasn't easy—in fact, it rated as impossible. Every day something essential gave him cause to stop by. While there, he sought signs that the sisters were resting and eating well. He'd ordered his cook over at the main house to send down hearty meals thrice a day. The place looked tidy as a spinster's parlor, and the tray of washed dishes bore mute testimony to the fact that the O'Briens were eating adequately.

At times John found himself wandering through the warehouse at the shipping yard to find things to deliver to them as an excuse to check in again each evening. For the first time since he'd taken command of Newcomb Shipping, he found his mind straying off business and onto the welfare of Emily's family. He'd never thought much of the fripperies that went out in the spare spaces of his vessels, but those caused him every bit as much happiness as they did for the O'Briens. Knowing how Emily felt about charity, he made it a point to have his cook leave the teapot and tea. He left the ball after tossing it with Duncan—stating they'd play with it again. Indeed they did—both for a good excuse for him to return and because playing with the lad was fun.

Then, too, there was something uniquely delightful about the O'Briens. In the midst of all their trials, Emily and Anna still found reasons to laugh. It seemed like the very sunshine of their love held back the cold season. Indeed, by sheer force of her will, Emily kept Anna blissfully comfortable and ignorant. Due to Emily's imaginative ideas, energy, and determination, John felt certain the caretaker's cottage had never contained so much love and laughter.

Until now.

He'd just groused at them and spoiled their joyful anticipation of this insignificant outing. He let out a sigh. "When the doctor wants her out of bed, at least be sure I'm here to help."

Anna barely pressed her hand on his shoulder. "Oh, please don't be cross with us. Dr. Quisinby paid a visitation here today, sir. When I asked, he said I could be in the sun if there was no breeze."

"Most likely he thought you'd have the sense to sit by a sunny window, not come parading outside."

"Oh." Anna's face drooped with dismay.

John felt ten times an ogre. He'd been in a sickbed a few times and recalled how he'd chafed to be up and about after only a day or two. Other than the carriage ride here, Anna hadn't been outside in ages. Indeed, she'd never again feel the kiss of a breeze or the glow of the sun unless they gave her that chance now. She may as well relish those simple pleasures one last time. He held her a bit more securely and grumbled, "Did your sister at least have the presence of mind to bring a chair out here and set it someplace secluded?"

Emily shot him an offended look. "Follow me, please."

Her stiff-backed posture would have amused him had she not seemed so very vulnerable. Emily O'Brien possessed a temper every bit as fiery as her hair, and it gave her a deceptive air of strength. He'd learned now to look beyond the façade she built so carefully and hid behind—but he wondered at times whether that was for her siblings' benefit or if she'd constructed it to mute the impact of life's unrelenting and unmerciful blows.

She was a woman of contradictions. The somber face she showed others and the simple joys she found with her family were like night and day. The joy of the Lord shone from her in her tender loving care and sweet laughter—but those moments stayed only within the walls of their home. How very sad she found it necessary to wear that cloak of wariness with others. It was as if she were hiding her light under a bushel—but because she feared the wind would blow it out.

As she crossed the well-manicured lawn, his eyes narrowed when he noticed her uneven gait. It bothered him, knowing she'd injured herself in his shipyard. Just because she endured without complaining didn't mean she still wasn't suffering. If he'd come to realize anything at all, it was that Emily O'Brien wouldn't ask for a scrap of attention or a bit of care for herself—even if she were in dire need. At first he thought pride kept her from it; but over the last days, he'd come to see she was a rare soul—one who simply loved others so deeply that she discounted her own needs as unimportant. He cleared his throat to garner her attention, but since she failed to take that cue, he called, "Emily?"

She paused and looked over her shoulder. "Aye?"

He strove to keep his voice mild. "You should still use the walking stick. Where is it?"

"I haven't the slightest notion." She started hobbling again. "I set it aside two days ago. It slows me down far too much."

John opened his mouth to command her to find and use it, but he quelled the impulse. He'd take up the matter out of Anna's hearing. Emily did her utmost to make sure her sister had nothing more to trouble her, and he agreed with that merciful decision. Emily's judgment on what her siblings needed had yet to be anything other than right on the mark.

"Duncan was playing with her walking stick last night," Anna said. "He pretended it was one of your beautiful horses. He kept himself busy riding back and forth across the bedchamber. I don't know where he set the cane when he grew tired."

"It doesn't matter," Emily replied blithely.

John paused for a moment when he rounded a hedge and reached the side of the house. Over at the edge of the yard, Emily had formed a little haven for her sister. The location was exceedingly clever. It caught the warm sun yet claimed the nestling shelter of being in the crook where the hedges formed a corner. A small box rested in front of the wicker chair—waiting to support Anna's feet. Off to the side, Emily had left what looked to be a picnic basket. In a crock she'd even gathered up a fistful of, well, flowery-leafy things. He'd never bothered to learn the names of plants, but the collection of color-changed leaves and dried-out stalks looked quite handsome.

John marveled at Emily's ability to turn what little she had into someplace so inviting. She'd done it here in the yard just as she'd scrubbed the cottage until it sparkled. Even that dreadful shanty had been neat as a pin, and she'd hidden the newspaper insulating its window with a colorful bit of cloth. There was something novel and admirable about a woman who found contentment so easily. Emily relished simple sunshine and a tiny, plain cottage.

Emily patted the chair. "Now here you are, our Anna-dear. Won't you have a grand time, turning your pretty face to the dear Lord's sun?"

"That I will."

After he settled Anna in her place, John straightened up and studied her for a moment. "Are you warm enough?"

She self-consciously gathered her shawl about her thin shoulders. "Aye. Thank you for asking. Would you care to join us? We're about to have nooning."

He didn't feel the least bit hungry, yet he nodded. "I'd be delighted to join you. Thank you for the invitation."

Emily murmured something unintelligible, then hastened back into the cottage and returned with the baby. John stood by Anna's side and took pains to be sure he didn't block the sun so she'd benefit from its meager warmth. He looked at the new mother and wondered aloud, "You know, I'm so used to hearing you call him the babe or man-child, I don't recall ever hearing the little one's proper name. So tell me, Anna, what are you calling your son?"

Anna's gaze dropped. In a heartbroken whisper, she answered, "Timothy Edward O'Brien."

Emily slipped her bundled nephew into Anna's arms. As she turned away, John saw how tears started to fill her eyes. He'd expected Anna to mention only a first name—not a full name. The ache in her voice made his guts clench, and he knew Emily heard it, as well. He cleared his throat. "Timothy is a fine name for a boy. Strong. A fine man in the Holy Bible, too."

Anna refused to look up. She protectively fussed with the blanket to be sure the babe's ears were covered. She avoided any eye contact as she said, "Mr. Newcomb, I thank you for your care. As soon as Em and I can arrange employment and housing, we'll be leaving."

Chapter 9

That's not necessary!" John stared at them in horror.

Emily drew close and set her hand on Anna's shoulder. She subtly shook her head to let him know she didn't agree with her sister. "We ought to stay awhile yet, Anna. Mr. Newcomb's been generous to help out, and I'm wanting you to be stronger before we go off on our own again."

Anna stubbornly asserted, "A change of arrangements will be for the best."

"Whose best?" John folded his arms akimbo and glowered. He'd just been congratulating himself on how happily things had turned out, and now he had to squelch this harebrained plot! At least Emily was being practical. Anna acted as if she didn't have the sense God gave a minnow. "You were starving. Freezing, too. You're both still weak as kittens. Think, Anna—who will care for Timothy while you work?"

"We'll work different hours." She mumbled the words to her lap and still didn't look at him. "I have no proof or papers. Your brother isn't home to confront, and I've decided I don't want to. 'Tis my son, so my voice is all that counts."

"Anna, if you don't want him to see you—"

"I don't want to see him ever again. What if he tries to take my baby?"

"Anna, I'm not concerned about Edward in the least. He's a rascal in some ways, but I cannot fathom he would ever stoop so low as to have done this to you. Truly I think 'tis one of his crew. I'm sure you and Timothy are safe."

Emily gave him a horrified look.

He cleared his throat. "On the obscure chance the babe is my brother's, I'll haul Edward to the altar. He'll wed you properly, Timothy will be legitimate, and I'll keep the *Cormorant* assigned to long voyages if that would make you happy. Instead of troubling ourselves about tomorrow, though, we need to concern ourselves with the present. You sweet women can't possibly make it on your own. Anna, your health is too poor. I can't allow this."

Anna looked up at her sister and whispered in a thready voice, "Emily, we can find work to do at home. Many other women do it. We can, too. Duncan will help. We're a family. We'll pull together."

John pressed. "I won't let anyone take Timmy from you. You cannot let foolish pride come before the welfare of your child."

Anna continued to look up at her sister. Tears streaked down her cheeks.

"Please take me back inside."

John swooped to snatch her out of the chair, but she quailed away. He regretted the fact that the truths he spoke went against her wishes. Still, he'd rather be the one to upset Anna than to have her feel Emily was betraying her. He strove to speak to her in his mildest tone. "Anna—"

"No," she whispered in a tearful tone. She stopped even looking up at her sister. Her head drooped as her shoulders shook with sobs. "No."

Emily knelt next to her sister and gathered her in her arms. Anna's weeping tugged at John's heart. He looked helplessly at Emily. She cupped Anna's head to her bosom and rocked her as if she were no more than a tiny lassie. He watched as Emily swallowed hard and blinked back her own tears. Yet, in the midst of the emotional tumult, she still managed to be sure the babe was in no danger of falling out of his mama's lap. How many problems can this one small woman juggle? How many burdens can she carry?

"We'll make it through, our Anna. Aye, we will," Emily promised in a voice thick with tears.

John stood over them and waited a moment. Surely, after the new mother had a few moments, she'd regain her composure. He'd heard women often did considerable crying in the weeks following a birth. He'd give Anna a chance to calm down. With Emily's tender ministrations, he felt certain she'd regain her composure. Minutes stretched. John realized he'd made a grave miscalculation.

Emily looked at him. Her eyes held fathomless sorrow. Deep inside, John felt something shift. At that moment he'd give all he owned to take away the ache in her heart.

In a soft, despairing tone, she said, "It would be best if you left us now, sir."

John paced away. For a moment he tried to tamp down his emotions. The practical side of him argued with his involvement in this whole mess. He'd done his best by them—providing shelter, warmth, food, and medical care. What more could he do?

Then he glanced back. Every logical excuse sank like an anchor. Anna, tiny little Anna—still thin as could be, so weak she couldn't even walk on her own. She was barely more than a child. She'd been swindled out of her innocence, robbed of the simple joys a young bride usually enjoyed. No matter who had fathered her babe, she didn't deserve to endure this.

Even more, he looked at Emily. Originally the woman had acted as prickly as a currycomb, but they'd worked past that. Day after day she'd welcomed him into the cottage, invited him to share their meals, and listened to his comments about work. He'd never before found a woman who was blind to his windblown hair, calloused hands, and rumpled, end-of-the-workday clothes. He'd given them a dwelling, but she'd turned it into a home—and warmly opened the door to him. He knew she was grateful, but her reception went beyond that. She didn't look at him and see wealth or power; she saw the sometimes lonely man who split his life between polished society and coarse seamen, and she accepted both aspects without reservation.

He watched as she used that same unconditional love with her sister. Finally Anna calmed down. Emily gave her a gentle squeeze.

Emily normally wore an odd, plain muslin apron that looked like a length of cloth with small ties at the sides and a hole in it for her head. She pulled it off and tied it to form a sash, then carefully tucked the babe in it. John sucked in a sharp breath. He'd never seen the condition of her gown. It was several sizes too big, and even careful stitching couldn't hide the fact that the bodice had been torn badly.

He watched her rise and oh-so-carefully lift Anna upright. One arm held the babe securely as the other wound about Anna's feeble form. Each step they took was an effort. Finally he could bear it no longer. The gravel of the path grated beneath his boots as he strode back to them.

He silently nodded to her, then presumed to stoop and gather Anna into his keeping. He said nothing but took her around the house, across the lawn, up the stairs, and back to her bedchamber. All of her weeping had left little Anna docile and limp. John felt an odd flash of gratitude that in such a state, she wouldn't realize how desperately she'd needed this basic assistance.

John stopped at the bedchamber door for a moment and stared at the bed. The blankets and sheets looked smooth, crisp—folded with military precision so one side lay open to give welcome to a weary woman. Practical, efficient little Emily must have done it when she came in for those few seconds to fetch the babe.

John paced to the bedside. His boots made a ringing noise on the plank floor. Emily followed on his heels. Her silent tread surprised him until he realized she was barefoot. At that realization he wanted to roar. Had he ever seen her wear shoes? He strained to remember, and he seemed to recall a battered pair of boots. Emily continued to wrap the babe in her cut-down blankets, too. He'd been a fool not to consider that they all desperately needed clothing.

Emily paused at the drawer for a moment and settled Timothy in it. She drew a blanket over him, then briskly tugged the hem of Anna's threadbare gown down before whisking the covers over her. John stepped to the side and watched as Emily's rough hand sweetly smoothed back Anna's hair. Softly she crooned, "Sleep now, our Anna."

Anna fell asleep with the speed only a child or an invalid might. Timothy started to fuss, so Emily took him from his makeshift bassinet and carried him into the kitchen. John watched in silence as she managed to warm some milk,

add molasses, and slowly spoon it into her nephew. She displayed no awkwardness with the task. Clearly she'd been doing this for days.

"I'll hire a wet nurse."

She looked at him and shook her head adamantly. "No. Anna still has some
milk. I'm able to fill in the rest by doing this. 'Twould break Anna's tender heart to
know another woman took over suckling her babe, and I cannot do that to her."

"Emily, blame me for not letting you leave. As for the *Cormorant*. . .she'll not
return for several months. Anna won't. . ." He cleared his throat.

Grief streaked across her face. She sighed deeply. "She won't have to face
him again."

"You will, though."

"That's a bridge I'll cross later. If I catch that rogue, I'm not sure what I'll do."

A wry smile twisted John's mouth. "You're too moral to commit mayhem or
murder. If you catch that scoundrel, you'll probably serve him a hefty slice of your
mind, then dash straight off to church to pray for his pitch-black soul."

She brushed a few errant curls away from her forehead with the back of her
wrist. "A blacker soul there never was."

John watched her shift the infant a bit. The prominent seams taken to repair
the rip in her clothing no longer lay hidden by the babe's blanketed form.
Though he dreaded hearing the answer, John still demanded, "How did your
gown get torn?"

" 'Twas torn when I got it."

"I'm not sure whether to be relieved or angry about that."

Emily shrugged. "It doesn't much matter. I'm handy with a needle. Do you
know any of the local dressmakers or milliners who might need a worker?"

"If you appear wearing that, they're not going to hire you. What else do
you own?"

A bright blush stained her cheeks.

His brows furrowed as he strained to recall the night he'd demanded they
pack and come away with him. "Duncan has a change of clothes. Anna's always
in her nightdress. I've seen her in two different—" He paused midsentence as
he realized Emily probably wasn't sleeping in a night rail. She'd given hers to
Anna!

Emily turned away and busily twitched an imaginary wrinkle from the corner of Timothy's blanket.

"How many day gowns does Anna own?" Just as surely as he knew his own
name, John knew Emily would have the same number or fewer than her sister.
He waited grimly for an answer.

"Two." Emily lifted her chin as she answered.

"I trust they're in better condition than the one you're wearing."

Emily's lips thinned into a straight line. She spooned another bit of milk into the babe and gave no reply.

"Answer me."

She continued to feed the babe. Her voice went brittle. "You asked no question."

John pulled out a chair and sat across from her. He leaned forward and rested his forearms on his thighs. Maybe she wouldn't feel so defensive if he didn't tower over her. Certainly, this matter needed to be discussed so he could determine their needs. He should have done so from the start. John waited a moment to let her get accustomed to his nearness, then softened his tone considerably. "Emily, I meant you no offense, and out there—I wasn't trying to be cruel to Anna."

"I know." She shot him a fleeting glance. "You spoke the truth, and as much as it shames me, I'm just as glad you did so I didn't have to." She said nothing more.

John let silence hover and hoped she'd hearken back to their conversation. She didn't. He finally pressed. "I didn't mean to upset you just now, either—asking about your clothing."

She continued to feed the child in silence, carefully drizzling milk from the spoon into little Timothy's tiny pink mouth. Precious little dribbles, patiently given, marked the passage of tense moments. Finally she spoke, but she didn't look at him. "If I'm embarrassed, it's my own fault. This whole mess is my fault."

"How could any of this possibly be your fault?"

"Because I was a fool to allow my sister to be beguiled by that monster. I hold myself to blame. Aye, I do. Edward Newcomb was a handsome man. Too handsome. Smooth, his charm was. Silver-tongued, too. I listened to him and fell for his lies as much as Anna did. Never did I suspect he would tell us a pack of lies."

She looked up at him. Her eyes glistened with unshed tears. "The Edward Newcomb who courted and ruined my Anna isn't so broad across the shoulders as you, and his dark hair defies discipline instead of obeying a comb as does yours, but he shares your strong chin. Then, too, his eyes are the same shade as yours—one I've not seen before or since. 'Tis like the color of tea left to steep fully."

John listened without interrupting. That description lined up too closely with Edward's character and appearance to leave him comfortable.

"He didn't wear clothes so fine as yours." She dipped her head and resumed feeding the babe. Her hand shook as she manipulated the spoon to coax the little one to take more nourishment. "He had quite a few garments, though. Once, when he tore a shirt, he cast it to the corner. We cut it down for Duncan and got a shirt and a few handkerchiefs from it."

John stayed silent. He sensed she wasn't finished speaking yet, but he couldn't understand where the conversation was going. He'd asked about her clothing, not about the rogue who ruined her sister. He bided his time and let Emily control the conversation. Her hands stayed busy, spooning in the milk, wiping the baby's chin.

"Edward made promises. He brought our Anna a ring and produced a man of God—one in vestments who carried a Bible and a missal. Anna's eyes were bright with love light, so I stood there and let her pledge her heart to that rascal. Only then we likened him to one of those princes in a fairy tale. We never suspected the truth.

"Looking back, I know I should have guarded my sister better. 'Twasn't a church wedding, but I overlooked that because we were both wedging the ceremony in the few minutes betwixt our shifts of work.

"Edward told us he had no family—none a'tall. His da perished at sea, and the rest of them died when their house caught fire. He said he'd missed being part of a family. He'd supposedly sold all he had in the whole world to buy the *Cormorant*, so he was living aboard the vessel in the captain's cabin. He said 'twas bad fortune to have a woman aboard a sailing vessel. Because of that, Anna stayed with Duncan and me.

"Edward brought fish for supper often enough. Proud she was of him, our Anna was. Her man could put food on the table. Each time he docked, he brought coal—but only enough to last for the nights when I went to work and Duncan got shoved over to our neighbor's. There never seemed to be sufficient money to buy us wood or coal, but Edward gave Anna a pretty little trinket every now and again.

"He had grand plans, he did. Promised Anna a fine home of her own—one with stairs and a maid and gowns aplenty—all of them beautiful enough for a princess."

Her voice shook as she added, "But he never so much as gave her a dress length of fabric or a bit of yarn so she could knit herself anything at all. He might have put a bit on our table, but he didn't keep a roof over our Anna's head for a single night or put a stitch of clothing on her back.

"He'd be gone for a voyage and return, and she'd be so happy to fall into his arms. We all prayed for each voyage to be successful, for him to be safe, and for the Lord to bless the business so he'd become a good provider for our Anna.

"Fish we'd eat—and he'd mourn that the voyage hadn't brought him enough profit to do more than pay back a little more of the hefty loan the bank held on the *Cormorant*. Even so, we kept faith in God and in Edward's best efforts."

John sat back in his chair and listened grimly.

Emily drew in a shaky breath. "That last time, I stuck my nose into their marriage. Getting sick most every sunrise, our Anna was, and we were sure of the reason. I got home early in the morning, and Edward sat there, staring at her like she'd told him his boat had run aground. She didn't even have to speak the words.

He'd guessed it right quick."

John dreaded what she'd say next, but he held his tongue and let Emily finish the heartbreaking tale. She needed to unburden her heart, if only for a moment.

"Edward didn't seem happy in the least about becoming a father, and Anna cried over his sour attitude. But he told her 'twas only because he'd hoped to have that splendid house for her before they started in on having babes.

"I nosed in then. I told him Anna didn't need a palace; she needed a warm cabin. He needed to stop dreaming up grand schemes for a day far into the future and care for his bride here and now. They could always change up to something better, but in the meantime he needed to start providing for her." Her voice dropped to a chagrined whisper as she confessed, "I told him he'd been having all the pleasures of a husband without assuming the responsibilities."

"You spoke nothing other than the truth, Emily. How long had this been going on?"

"The end of autumn and all of last winter."

"Four months!" John couldn't bear to sit through the tale any longer. He had to hear the rest, but he stood and paced over to the window. He shoved his hands in his pockets and clenched his jaw. He'd been to their shanty—in autumn, not winter—and the cold had been unbearable.

Emily fell silent. He stared at her faint reflection in the window. "You needn't fear me, Emily. I'm not judging you as a shrew at all. I don't know how you tolerated him that long. The circumstances were desperate, and you did what any sensible woman would."

"I'm not so sure of that," she confessed thickly. "Edward brought coal that night and set sail the next day. He'd told Anna earlier that he planned to be home for a whole week. I drove him away with my bitter words."

John wheeled back around. "No, Emily. I won't have you saying such a thing. Your words made no difference—this Edward was a blackguard. The minute a man of his ilk discovers his woman is with child, he decamps. If you'd have never said a thing, he'd still have abandoned her."

"We prayed for him and his ship every day. Aye, we did, and all of us worried the *Cormorant* might have gotten damaged or run aground—or worse. So many months passed without a word."

"And that's common enough, so you waited patiently," he filled in.

Emily nodded. "After he'd been gone a long while and things were getting bad, Anna acted so very brave when she parted with the wee gifts he'd given her. Every last one ended up at the pawnshop. She said 'twas like Edward had given her a way to take care of the babe she carried."

He groaned. Anna's love had let her hope and dream that her husband would come back. Emily's guilt made her assume she'd driven the man away. Neither of these innocents understood in all of those months that they'd been deceived, betrayed, and abandoned.

Emily swallowed hard. Her lips quivered as she said, "My sister had nothing left at all, John Newcomb—not a thing but a wedding ring and empty promises. I needed to make every last cent count. 'Twas more important to buy milk and coal than it was for me to have another gown. So you see, I deserve no more than I have."

I deserve no more than I have. Her words echoed in his head. John wanted in the worst way to quiet that aching confession. It kept repeating over and over, haunting him. She'd said she was coming up on nineteen. It sounded older and more responsible that way—but that meant she was eighteen. She'd been seventeen and Anna had been sixteen when a dashing sea captain took unpardonable advantage of their naïveté. Emily shouldn't punish herself for not knowing better.

Ah, but she would. She'd feel responsible; she'd hold herself accountable for anything that tainted the lives and hearts of those she loved. Under her crusty, brave front, she hid a heart too tender to believe. The sacrifices she'd made defied words.

John gently cupped her nape and thumbed delicate spiraling wisps of her beautiful, fiery hair. "Emily, you're worthy of a wardrobe full of fine gowns and a box full of jewels. You cannot punish yourself for what happened. The blackguard had a tainted soul and took sore advantage. Life brings tragedies, and this surely rates among them; but stop faulting yourself and chart a new course in life that will bring some happiness back into your heart."

She set aside the spoon, lifted wee Timothy to her shoulder, and patted his back. Without sparing an upward glance, she whispered, "You ask me to look past today. I cannot. The future holds too much heartache."

"Oh, Em," he said softly. He watched her shudder and gulp back a sob. He tilted her face up to his. "We'll make sure Anna is happy and comfortable."

She compressed her lips and nodded.

"Like you," he said in his quietest tone, lest Anna waken and hear him, "I know how very paltry that notion is. Day or night, you summon me at once if you need anything at all."

Chapter 10

John left the cottage and went to his stables. There he motioned to Duncan. The lad dashed to his side at once.

"Aye, sir?"

"I'd like a word with you." John clasped his hands behind his back and sauntered toward a fence. From the corner of his eye, he watched Duncan copy his posture and shadow his every step. The sight of his blatant imitation forced John to quell a momentary smile. The lad hadn't had a man in his life, so he'd begun to mimic John's moves whenever they spent even a few moments together. It was flattering in a sad but touching way. John silently vowed to be a good example. He stopped at a fence and stared at a frolicking yearling.

After a moment of silence, Duncan gave him a stricken look. "Did I do something wrong?"

"Nay, not a thing. It occurred to me I ought to know the stable boy I'm trusting with the care of my favorite mounts." John started out what he hoped sounded like a casual conversation. The lad was bright as a copper penny. He loved to chatter. All it took were a few seemingly casual questions, and Duncan gladly volunteered information. After getting him relaxed and assured, he was eager to please, and John managed to ask, "Did you ever see the courting gifts Edward gave your sister?"

"Oh, I did, sir! I truly did." Duncan cheerfully shared in great detail the treasures Captain Edward Newcomb had bestowed upon Anna months ago.

With each one the lad described, the gnawing in John's belly grew worse. The physical description Emily had given of Anna's so-called husband, the ring she'd shown, and the gifts Duncan mentioned—they all added up to a picture so appallingly clear that shame scalded him. John patted Duncan on the shoulder. "You're a good little fellow. I know Em and Anna tell you so, but I'm saying, man-to-man, you're a fine buck."

Duncan beamed with pride.

John excused himself, strode home, and looked at his calendar. It confirmed what he'd dreaded: He'd scheduled the *Cormorant* for monthly runs up and down the coast all through the previous autumn and winter. In fact, she'd been in and out at just the right time frame for a quick courtship and the four-month-long sham marriage.

Edward had always been resourceful and fun loving, but John never once believed he'd stoop to such a level—and he'd blindly defended his brother's honor at the O'Briens' expense.

Grandfather had left the entire shipping business to John, but Edward had always known that would be the case. He'd displayed virtually no jealousy five years ago when that plan became a reality. An adventurer by nature, he would never be happy tied down. Indeed, he'd seemed more than pleased when John made him captain of the *Cormorant*. He'd declared he got the better part of the bargain.

Occasional tales of Edward being indiscriminate with women and wine reached John's ears. Father died just as John was reaching his manhood, so Grandfather took it upon himself to discuss the importance of being morally responsible with women and temperate. John knew Grandfather had the same conversation with Edward, too. After Grandfather died and John suspected Edward hadn't taken that lesson to heart, he'd set aside time and reinforced the wisdom of living an upright life. That brotherly discussion and prayers obviously hadn't been effective.

Since Edward was at sea much of the time, it made no sense for him to keep a home of his own. Instead, John allowed his brother to inhabit the southern wing of the mansion. Rarely did John bother to enter those quarters, but he had every reason to do so today.

The maids cleaned in there on a weekly basis, but the wing was kept locked otherwise. It lay eerily silent now. John didn't know where his brother usually kept everything, but he remembered clearly that the porcelain figurine of a shepherdess customarily stood on the mantel next to a clock. That spot lay empty. The three little gold hearts that once dangled from the key to Edward's generously stocked liquor cabinet no longer hung from the braided scarlet cord. Though John had heard the truth, he needed to see it with his own eyes—and his eyes didn't deceive him as his heart had for the past days. The treasures Anna received from her so-called husband had come from Edward's quarters.

John sank onto a bench by the window. For a flash he dared hope mayhap it wasn't truly Edward. It couldn't be a deckhand, because none of them had entry to the house. Perhaps one of his employees had stolen his identity and masqueraded as him. Certainly a member of the household staff would have access to the trinkets—but the physical description haunted John. That last burst of hope faded. He knew the bitter, appalling truth.

He trudged out of the house, out to the stables. He quietly ordered a buggy to take him back to Emily's old neighborhood. The driver located the only pawnshop in the area by looking for the three balls hanging from the roof. John somberly ordered the driver to wait. He entered the dingy shop and looked about with a mixture of pity and disgust. Few were the items that carried any value at all. Those who lived in these blocks traded in goods too pathetic to be of value to anyone else. Aching poverty radiated from the sacrifice of a battered flute. Then, too, the better goods clearly hadn't come from this sector of town. The proprietor was savvy enough not to take things that could be traced easily, but some of these goods had come from either theft or burglary.

"Ah, sir!" The shopkeeper toddled up. His red, bulbous nose tattled about a fondness for drink. He quickly took in John's fine clothing, and an avaricious gleam lit his eyes. "Would you be looking for anything special?"

As if reciting loathed Latin declensions, John tonelessly rattled off the list of Anna's treasures Duncan had named.

"Ah, yes. I still have some of those things here. Nice, they are. Quality goods." He bobbed his head as if to punctuate those words. "Worth a pretty penny, too."

"Get them."

John could scarcely bear to stay in that pawnshop. The proprietor bustled about, then stooped to look in a cabinet. As he straightened up, his lower lip protruded. "My son must've sold the teak candlestick and the ivory fan." He assessed the things he'd managed to locate and named an outlandish price for them.

John looked at the counter and did his best not to snap at the pawnbroker. "Then I'll take those things." He slapped a coin onto the counter, grabbed the other three items Duncan had mentioned, and stalked out.

He'd paid too much, but he had to get out of there. The man was as dishonest as a praying snake, and he'd done his best to cheat John. How badly had he bilked valiant little Emily out of a few extra, much-needed pennies?

John looked at the cheap gifts in his lap. He didn't know whether to give them back to Anna or to keep them for when he confronted Edward. What he did know was that as soon as the *Cormorant* docked, Edward was going to have to do some fancy explaining. Even then words would count for naught. John had no idea how best to rectify this sordid mess, but he prayed for wisdom to handle it well.

As he rode back toward the better side of town, he stared at the little porcelain figurine in his hand. Years ago his mother had bought it to use as an example of a costume she wanted to commission for a masquerade ball. Though charming and sentimental, it carried virtually no monetary value. What had it gotten for Anna? An extra quart of milk? He fought the urge to fling it at the street and watch it shatter. The delicate bit of porcelain had been a tool to bribe an innocent. His fingers tightened about the swirling skirts until the edge cut into his hand.

The ground changed from mud to gravel to cobblestone. He'd left behind the ragged tide of poverty and had reached civilization. Sadly, civilization hadn't done anything to improve Edward's soul. He'd been the beast while the O'Briens, poor as field mice, displayed integrity and honor.

Suddenly something caught John's eye. He called out for the hack to stop, vaulted out, and hastened into a shop.

～✑

"Take it. Wear it!" John had waited until the next day to come by. He'd hoped Anna had calmed down and forgiven him. Obviously his hopes were in vain.

He gave Anna an exasperated look. He hadn't anticipated her reaction to his gift. He wanted to shower her with the pretty things that would lift her spirits and fill her last days with the simple joys most women took for granted. Not only that, but he knew Emily would take delight in her sister's excitement. But Anna wasn't excited. Why would the silly woman balk at having a simple, ordinary gown when she obviously needed one so desperately?

"Anna, yesterday you were planning to move away and find employment. If you are that serious about it, at least be sensible enough to admit you'll need suitable attire."

"Yes, Anna," Duncan agreed as he stood by the bedside. The lad tentatively ran his stubby fingers across the day gown's skirt, then pinched the fabric. "He's right, you know. You must wear it. The material is thick as can be! You'll be so warm in it!"

It bothered John that Duncan thought in terms of a garment for warmth.

"It doesn't even need to be mended," Duncan added.

John bit back a growl. When he'd been seven, he would have merely looked at a gown and thought it was a pretty color. The women in his life had never suffered cold, hadn't once borne the indignity of having to patch together the tattered remnants of someone else's cast-off clothing or been faced with relying on charity. They'd never once lifted their soft, lily-white hands to do any domestic chore or been forced to fend for anything more than a good seat at a soiree. Emily and Anna had endured far too much of the hard side of life, and Duncan had seen it all.

Duncan stuck out his thumb and poked it down the row of little pewter roses that marched one by one from collar to waist. "Look, our Anna! All the buttons are still on it!"

That did it. John swept the gown out of Duncan's reverent hands and tossed it across Anna's legs. He locked gazes with her, then gave her a boyish grin and wagged his finger emphatically. "I don't know what to do with you, Anna. You're supposed to help me here. If you won't put on your new gown, Emily won't, either. Don't you want her to wear hers?"

"Yes," Anna confessed with a sigh.

"Much better," he teased. He didn't want to bully her, so he hoped this change of tactics was in the right vein. "As soon as I leave, you can put it on. By three I expect Emily to be wearing hers, too. She ought to be home by then."

"Of course she will," Anna agreed.

John nodded. He knew she'd not jeopardize Anna's health by being gone long at all. She often found a quiet place to pray, so when he saw her Bible wasn't on the table and her shawl wasn't on its customary hook, he presumed she'd stolen away for devotions.

"What's happening at three?" Duncan asked.

"We're going for a ride in my buggy. Don't you think that would be a fun outing?"

"Oh yes, sir!"

"After the outing, we'll drop you off at the stables while your sisters and I have a talk. You'll get your new suit of clothes later because I've arranged for Mr. Peebles to give you a riding lesson." John left with the sounds of Duncan's excited whoops still ringing in his ears.

He arrived back at the caretaker's cottage at three o'clock sharp. He consulted his gold pocket watch to confirm the time, snapped it shut, and headed up the walk. He knew Anna would look nice in her new gown, but he especially wanted to see Emily. He'd chosen a fine, fawn-colored merino wool for her, one with a small vine pattern the exact same green as her pretty eyes. Instead of relying on an excess of lace and ribbons, the beauty of the dress lay in its simplicity—just as Emily's loveliness lay in her queenly posture and warm spirit. The moment he'd spied it, he'd known the gown would look stunning on her.

The carriage rolled up the drive as he mounted the steps. *Indeed,* he said to himself, *this will work out well enough. The women have had sufficient time to fuss and get ready.*

He planned to collect the O'Briens and take them on a simple outing. Anna couldn't stay out of bed for very long, but he'd spoiled her little picnic yesterday. He'd craftily planned this so he could entice Emily on a trip.

What could be better than a stop at the mercantile to let Emily and Anna choose some slippers and yardage? He'd be catching two fish with one worm that way. At least once in her short life, Anna would enjoy shopping for pretties and gewgaws, and Emily would get clothing she so desperately needed.

Women tended to prefer certain colors over others, so since he had no notion as to what they needed, he'd do well to let the O'Brien women look over the bolts and make their own selections. While they did that, he'd have a clerk help him fit Duncan with some breeches and shirts.

As for the baby, John couldn't begin to decide what Timothy required. Blankets, little gowns, and diapers he knew about—whatever else an infant required, he didn't know. Judging from the fact that Emily seemed to do a constant round from wash bucket to clothesline, he assumed she'd know best. But he'd bought twenty-five yards of white cotton on the advice of his laundress, Gracie. Aye, Emily was so clever that she'd make the tiny garments and cut out nappies.

John had arrived at some conclusions. After they returned to the little cottage, he'd sit Emily down and set her straight on matters. As for Anna, he'd gently let her know he was her ally and fully believed it was his brother who had dishonored her. He'd apologize both for his own stubbornness and for the pain Edward had caused her.

His brother was responsible for this mess. Not a shred of doubt remained in John's mind. He'd spent all last night anguishing over the fact that he'd been so busy with business, he hadn't been a good brother. He'd thought he knew his brother well, when in all actuality, he didn't. Family allegiance had blinded him, and even when proof mounted, John foolishly allowed himself to hope this was just a sad case of stolen or mistaken identity. In spite of his stubborn ignorance, the facts finally culminated in his accepting the galling truth. Honor demanded he start to right the wrongs as best he could. Several remedies existed—none of them seemed good, though.

At any rate, the O'Briens were ethically and morally—if not legally—family now. Determined to fulfill duty in his profligate brother's stead and salvage the family name to some degree, John forged ahead. He'd resolutely determined to put a fresh face on matters as of this noon.

The front door of the little cottage stood open, and Duncan stayed busy, sweeping the floor. John frowned. "Put down the broom and wash up a bit, lad. Where are your sisters? I was very specific that you were all to be ready to leave promptly at three."

Duncan propped the broom in the corner. "No, sir, they're not ready."

"I'm not in a mood to put up with two stubborn women digging in their heels and pitching a fit," he told the boy.

Duncan looked at him somberly. He reached for the broomstick and hugged it to his scrawny chest. "I don't think Anna's up to pitching much of anything, sir. Something's wrong with her."

"Emily?" John strode to the bedchamber door and knocked once. Emily didn't respond, and his concern mounted. "Emily!" He rapped harder, then gave up on proprieties and let himself in.

Emily didn't even turn to face him. She leaned over Anna and blotted her face with a wet cloth. In a strained voice, she said, "Oh, John—she just collapsed. Please fetch the doctor!"

Chapter 11

No one answered his knock, so John figured Emily likely had both hands full with the baby. He pushed aside the black crape ribbon, opened the latch, and stepped over the threshold. Though prepared to call out a muted greeting, the words died on his lips.

Emily sat on the settee. Duncan lay there, huddled into a sad little ball, resting his head in her lap. She held Anna's child to her shoulder and dully looked up at John. Grief rode her hard, robbed her eyes of their pretty sparkle, and left her cheeks gray.

"Emily," John said softly as he crossed the floor. He fought the urge to pull her into his arms. "Cook mentioned you sent for me."

"Oh." It took her a moment before she remembered why she'd wanted to see him. "I wanted to thank you."

He didn't reply. The funeral had been private. He and the vicar had agreed to bury Anna in consecrated ground. She'd been laid to rest in the warm woolen gown he'd bought her, and he'd added a small, gold cross about her throat. After Emily had gently caressed her sister's cheek and kissed her one last time, she turned away. John led her into the kitchen, clasped her to his chest, and held her as her sobs drowned out the sound of their closing the casket. The burial service had been simple, small, and quiet—just as Anna had been.

Now the babe fussed. Emily shifted him automatically. She looked down at her brother and back to John. "Would you still be willing to let Duncan have that job you offered?"

"Duncan does a fine job with my horse."

Her brows puckered slowly, as if something troubled and confused her; then she shook her head. "No, I meant the other one you mentioned when we were living at our own place. Duncan would work hard for you and could earn a wee bit. I trust you to be fair about his wages. I spoke with Madam Victorine, and she'll allow me to stitch for her at home so I can keep watch over little Timothy. If you—"

"Emily!" John stared at her in disbelief. "What are you thinking?"

She looked at him almost blankly. "We have to—" She paused and moistened her lips, then tried again. "It will work. I found a room—"

"No!" He wheeled about, stepped off three paces, then turned back again.

He couldn't let them go. The cottage usually lay vacant—it didn't inconvenience him to allow her to occupy it. Even if it did cause him a few logistical problems, he'd move heaven and earth to keep her here. At least then he'd know she was safe, warm, and fed. He locked gazes with her. "You're not going anywhere."

"I'll never forget your kindness to A–Anna."

"I did nothing for her!"

Emily stared at him. Her eyes held an ache he could barely stand to see. His voice sounded rough as he asserted, "You don't need to make any decisions right now. Stay here—at least for a few months."

Emily shook her head. "You've been more than generous. Even if Edward lied, you showed great personal honor to provide grandly for our Anna. He duped us, but that's all in the past now. Duncan and I never expected Anna's husband to take us on. I have to face the fact that a man who wouldn't even claim his own wife won't have anything to do with her relatives. He'll certainly never want a thing to do with a child he sired on the wrong side of the blanket."

"Don't you even think—"

"Oh, I've thought long and hard, Mr. Newcomb. My mind is set. I refuse to be a burden, weighing you down. We're not your responsibility."

"What if I want you to be my responsibility?"

"My brother and I will care for our own."

"You can't take care of yourselves, let alone a babe!" He scowled. "Besides, Timothy isn't just your nephew; he's my nephew, too!"

Emily's eyes shot fire. She gave her brother's arm a little squeeze. "Go check the nappies on the line to see if they're dry yet."

Duncan picked up on his sister's surge of emotions and hastened out the door. Emily watched him leave, then turned back to John. Her arms tightened around the babe. "You said the marriage wasn't valid. You never once recognized Anna"—her voice cracked as she said her sister's name—"never acknowledged her as Edward's wife. You have no reason or right to step in now and claim this babe."

"I was wrong."

"Well, you can just stay wrong! Don't you even think about calling Timmy your nephew!"

"We both know he is."

"You have no proof," she stated implacably, turning the tables on him.

John stared at her and tried to conquer his impatience.

Emily stared right back at him. Something in his eyes frightened her. All night she'd thought matters through. It was for the best that she move now. His reaction only proved it. She repeated herself. "No, you have no proof at all."

"Your Bible has the marriage listed!"

Emily cranked her head to the side and choked back a sob. How could he, of all people, bring that up now? "You yourself said anything could be written in a Bible."

John quietly closed the distance between them. He sat beside her on the settee. His closeness disturbed her, but she stayed still. Part of her wanted to leap up and dash away from him; a greater part of her wanted to lean into him and borrow his strength and consolation. She couldn't allow herself such weakness—especially now when he was suddenly changing his tune and making claims on Anna's wee babe.

John cradled her chin with a calloused hand and turned her face to his. "I know what I said, and I regret every word of it. You're old enough to understand that people sometimes say things they don't mean."

"Oh, yes. I've learned that." Her laugh sounded bitter, even to her own ears. She moved away from his touch. "Whoever he was, that scoundrel told lies aplenty and pledged a false marriage vow with his hand on that very Bible. I don't need you to tell me men say things they never intend to honor."

"You're ripe for the plucking, Emily, and there are many men out there who would take advantage of you. Stay here. Let me provide for—"

"Your offer is generous, but I'll not be a kept woman."

Impatience tinged his tone. "I had no scurrilous intentions! All I wanted was to make sure you could care well for my nephew."

Her heart clenched, and she bolted to her feet. "Anna went to her grave, shamed to the core of her soul. How could you even think to speak these words now? A week ago they would have helped. She admired you, and had you but even hinted you believed 'twas your own brother's child—" Words failed her. Emily took a few deep breaths to try to tamp down the violent storm of emotions raging in her breast.

His brows furrowed. "Emily—"

"It's too late now. It's much too late for you to change your mind." Unable to contain herself any longer, she darted to the bedchamber and shut the door behind her.

∽

John could hear her weeping. He paced back and forth a few times, unsure of what to say or do. Every single word out of her mouth had been true. Worse—she'd not flung them at him in spite. She'd said them out of the brokenness of her grief.

The whole while she'd clutched the babe as if he were ready to snatch him away. Didn't she understand he wouldn't cause her any further sorrow? Any fool who spent five minutes with her would plainly see her bottomless devotion to the babe. The way her face softened, the color of her eyes deepened, and her small body curled lovingly around little Timothy sang eloquently of how she cherished him. Clearly, to take the child from Emily's keeping would shatter her.

John's only motive was to make things easier for her, to ease her lot in life and make it possible for her to continue to mother her little nephew and Duncan without having to work herself into utter exhaustion. An inner voice whispered, *But how was she to know my reasons and plans?*

John looked about the tiny cottage. She'd considered it such a splendid home. She'd scrubbed and bustled and filled it with sunshine and laughter. For a few days, these plain walls hadn't been big enough to hold in all the love in Emily's world; now they weren't strong enough to contain the grief in her anguished heart.

Her crying continued. Every moment he fought the urge to go comfort her, but John feared he'd only make it worse.

Chapter 12

Shuffling footsteps made John turn around.

Duncan held a stack of nappies against his chest. "These are dry now." Once he heard his sister's weeping, his already lackluster face clouded over.

"Would you like me to take those to her?" John asked quietly.

Duncan's lower lip quivered. He stared straight ahead as he blinked. "I'm 'posed to be strong 'cause I'm the man of the family." His small shoulders lifted and dropped from a big sigh; then he turned a bit and gave John a defeated look.

John closed the distance between them, set aside the nappies, and pressed Duncan snug against his leg. "How about if I be the man, and you'll be my assistant? We'll make fine partners."

"We will?"

"Aye," he said, using his most definite tone. "We want good things for your sister, don't we?"

Duncan somberly nodded and blinked back tears.

"Emily is a special woman—a very special woman. She deserves the best we can do for her." He jostled Duncan gently and gave him a man-to-man look. "I need your help. I'll see to Emily, and you take care of Timmy. Can you do that?"

"Yes, sir."

The boy's bravery pulled at John's heart. He'd never spent time with children other than the occasional cabin boys aboard ship. They all counted a few more years to their short lives than this lad. Grief stricken as he was, he'd not misbehaved a bit. He'd followed Emily's example and tried to see to obligations far too heavy for him to shoulder.

John led Duncan to the doorway and let him open it. His heart lurched. She knelt beside the bed, her face buried in the blankets on what had been Anna's side. Her shoulders shuddered with her sobs, yet the baby lay securely in the bend of one of her arms up on the mattress. Her other hand clenched the blankets.

Just standing in the room brought back the sad memory from a few days ago when Emily had held Duncan tight to her side and whispered one last desperate prayer. Dr. Quisinby had looked over their bowed heads at John and subtly shook his head.

Sweet Emily had borne too much, and John knew he'd foolishly spoken the truth far too late and caused her more heartache. Quietly he knelt beside her and called her name. He picked up her hand and rubbed it. For an instant her fingers curled around his. He closed his hand around hers before she could reclaim it. Her hand fit in his perfectly—small enough to be fully protected, yet capable enough to partner him in whatever they eventually decided to do with the baby.

Slowly her head turned, and her lashes lifted just a bit. He couldn't be sure she'd even seen him through the tears.

Bless his little heart, John thought as Duncan went to her other side and cuddled close. "Are you praying, our Em?"

John stretched his other arm across and tucked them both into his embrace. "Prayer is always a good idea." He bowed his head and gave Emily's hand a light squeeze. "Heavenly Father, we've come to kneel at Your feet in the time of our greatest sorrow." As he continued to pray, Emily's crying tapered off, and she curled her fingers back around his hand.

When he finished praying, John patted Duncan's back. "Tuck the little fellow under your arm and carry him off to the main room. Most likely he needs one of those nappies you just brought in."

"Yes, sir. What are you going to do?"

John gently smoothed his hand over Emily's hair. "I'd like to talk to your sister."

Emily let out a choppy sigh and started to rise.

John sprang to his feet and helped her up. He kept hold of her elbow and led her back out to the settee.

Emily barely waited until he sat down. She wove her fingers together and whispered, "I flung words at you in anger, John Newcomb. I'm giving you my apology, but that doesn't mean I'm letting you get your hands on the babe."

"It was never my intent to take Timothy from you. You have my word—I'll never take him from you. That being said, I've earned your anger, Emily. So much of this is my fault. All this time I believed I knew Edward. I was so sure, but I was wrong. I grew so busy with work that I failed to take time as I should have to be my brother's keeper."

"No, John. I'll not have you blame yourself for the wrongs he did. They were his doing and his alone."

"But, Emily, even so—I should have known him well enough to suspect he was capable of this. Think of how close you are to Duncan. You'd know in an instant if he were up to mischief."

She gave him a sad smile. "But Edward fooled me just as much as he did you, John. You told me to stop punishing myself. I'm thinking you ought to pay heed to your own advice."

He reached over and gently twirled a few of her wispy curls around his finger. Delicate, yet strong. . .feminine, but fiery. He shook his head. "Dear little Em, what are we going to do?"

"You just prayed for God to lead us. I'm not overly good at waiting, but I'm supposing that's what's next."

He chuckled and drew her head to his shoulder. To his satisfaction, she rested her cheek there as if she belonged nowhere else in the world. For a spell he simply sat and cradled her in his arms. This moment of peace betwixt them felt right. Aye, it did, and that bore some reflection—but later. For now he'd simply relish these few minutes when she finally found respite from her sadness in his arms.

She stirred a bit, but he tenderly murmured, "Shh, sweetling. Rest."

A short while later, Duncan tiptoed up. "We did good, Mr. John. We are good partners! Look—you got Sis to sleep, and I have Timmy dry as a brick in an oven."

"Nicely done," John praised him under his breath. He wondered if Emily would stay calm if he carried her to bed. In the past she'd startled awake so violently. Then again, he just needed to shift her a bit and slip an arm behind her legs. "Em, everything's right as rain. You just keep dreaming," he murmured softly as he lifted her into his arms and rose. The reassurances worked. She didn't so much as wince.

After he tucked her in and shut the door, he went in search of Duncan. The lad was hunkered into a small heap on his cot near the kitchen. The babe lay bundled in Emily's old cut-down blankets in his lap. Duncan awkwardly tried to coax a spoonful of fluid into the infant. He looked up at John and wrinkled his nose. "Our Em is better at this than I am."

John sat down next to him and scowled at the way the babe let out a noisy howl. "I'll hire a wet nurse."

"Em won't like that. She loves babies and wants to care for him herself."

The baby let out another wail. John tentatively reached out and took him. He'd never held the babe. In fact, he realized as he fumbled to hold little Timothy, he'd never once in all his years held a single babe. Emily made it look so easy. He remembered how she carefully supported the head, so he curled his long fingers to cup the little fellow's skull. A shift here, an adjustment there—an awkward moment, then Timothy let out a bellow to make it clear he wasn't happy in the least.

"Eh, now. He's got his toes stuck in your watch fob," Duncan observed.

"Oh." John remedied that minor problem and murmured, "There. That ought to suit you, man-child."

Timothy wailed more.

John frowned. He cast a quick glance back toward Emily's door. Common sense said he needed her to come rescue him from his incompetence; pride made him want to master this minor debacle—both to prove to himself he was equal to the task and to allow Emily to nap.

Half an hour later, John sat on the cot in his shirtsleeves. He'd shed his suit coat quickly enough. Next, the slate blue silk vest had joined the coat on the table since the baby's little toes had kept getting tangled in the fob. He'd dropped the cloth Duncan used to mop Timothy's messy face, so he'd untied his crisp, white cravat and used it to dab at the streak of milk slipping from the babe's little mouth into his neck creases. That concoction of milk and goodness-only-knew-what-else smelled sweet enough, but Timothy had a knack for spitting out as much as he swallowed. The sleeve of John's shirt had an ever-increasing damp spot from all Timothy managed to eject. *No wonder Emily is so tired. She's waking up at night and going through this ordeal.*

Duncan watched in utter silence.

John glanced up at the lad, then nudged Timothy's lower lip with the spoon. "What are you thinking, Duncan?"

"It's a good thing you run a business better than you tend a babe; else you'd be a pauper, sir."

John chuckled at that assertion. "I can't deny a word you said."

"Em is good with Timothy. Tender and careful."

Something in the lad's tone made John study his somber little features carefully. "Duncan, have I ever said a word about taking Timothy away from you and Emily?"

"No, sir." The boy then blurted out, "You can't! He's ours. Em said Edward is a scoundrel. She's Timmy's aunt—almost his mother, you know—and I'm his uncle. She said we've got to go 'cause if Edward ever takes Baby Timothy, he'll turn our wee babe into a bad rascal. It's our place to rear him right and to teach him about God. I don't think Edward knows God, because he's a bad man."

John paused. Timothy let out an indignant squawk, so he quickly spooned in another dribble of milk. Duncan's explanation shed considerable light on why Emily wanted to move immediately. It nearly broke John's heart to see how she would willingly live in a dingy one-room habitation and suffer cold and hunger—all for the sake of her nephew's soul. He needed to do something—but what?

Timothy let out a pitiful sound.

"That does it." John stood.

Duncan scrambled to his feet. "What are you doing?"

"I'm going to get this babe fed."

Duncan scrambled along beside him. "Pardon me, sir, but you weren't doing such a fancy job of it."

John inexpertly held the babe over his shoulder. A second later, the babe rewarded that action with a sticky wet spot on his collar.

"You forgot the burp cloth." Duncan grabbed John's pant leg and tried to tug him to a stop by the front door. "Sir, I thought you were just going to walk him to calm him. You cannot take our baby away. Please don't do that. He's all we have."

"We're just going to get him fed and bring him back. You're coming along, so you can stop fretting."

John flipped a blanket over the babe, strode toward his home, and silently prayed that one of the women in the flock of cooks, maids, gardeners' wives—someone, anyone among the lot of them—was suckling a babe and had milk to spare.

๛

Late afternoon sun slanted through the windows. *Whatever am I doing, napping the day away?* Emily shoved off the blankets and got up. Someone tapped on the door. "Yes?"

"Supper's ready, Sis."

Emily smoothed her hair and clothes, then went out to the main room. John and Duncan both stood by the table. She felt her cheeks grow warm. "Pardon me for being a sluggard."

"The notion of you being a sluggard," John said, "is almost as ridiculous as me setting sail across the Atlantic in a washbasin."

Emily's smile faded abruptly when she saw the table. Three place settings awaited them. John came to dinner only when she invited him, and she hadn't done so now. The third place Duncan must have set out of habit—or his youthful hope that Anna would "come back." Her heart leapt to her throat.

"I have an evening appointment, so we'll need to talk while we dine."

As soon as John finished the prayer, Emily looked around. "Where is Timothy? He must be starving by now."

"Oh, you needn't worry, Em." Duncan smiled. "Mr. Newcomb made sure he got fed."

Feeding Timothy was no easy feat. Emily looked at their guest in amazement. In her wildest imaginings, she couldn't fathom how this huge man managed to hold a small feeding spoon in his great hands—let alone deliver it to a squirming, noisy infant. "You fed the baby?"

"I tried," he confessed.

"He's terrible at it," Duncan declared.

John took a sip of coffee. "I met with little success, so I asked my laundress to feed him. He's on a blanket behind the settee, if you want to be sure I brought him back."

Emily stared at John and shook her head. "I don't need to. You gave me your word you'd not take Timothy away from me. You're an honorable man, and you've never once lied to me."

The warmth of John's smile made her heart beat a bit faster. He tilted his head

86

toward her plate. "Eat. You're going to need your energy if you accept my plan."

"What plan?"

He blotted his mouth with a napkin, then smiled at her. "I'm sure you've noticed my cook is very accomplished."

She nodded.

He chose his words carefully in deference to the delicacy of the topic. "She is to be blessed with a child in the next month or so. My laundress already has a seven-month-old son. As I mentioned, she saw to young Timothy's hunger today."

Emily blinked at him, unable to comprehend why he would tell her these things.

"The laundress's mother, who's been watching the baby, is in poor health. My head gardener's youngest daughter, Mary, is twelve. I thought perhaps she could come stay with you during the daytime, and betwixt the two of you, you could tend Timothy and the other babies."

"Mr. Newcomb—"

"Oh, Em, you love babies so!" Duncan wiggled excitedly in his seat.

"And Gracie—the laundress—will wet-nurse Timothy each morning and evening when she drops off and picks up her little one. She can come at noon to feed him, too. Her own babe is eating some table food, so she has an abundance and doesn't mind sharing. When Cook has her babe, she'll come by, and she said she'll feed Timothy, as well."

Emily moistened her lips. "I'm to sit at home and rock Timothy whilst this young Mary tends Gracie's boy? We won't even have the cook's babe for another month. Mr. Newcomb, you're trying to dress charity in a comely costume, but 'tis charity, nonetheless."

He shook his head and flashed her a smile. "It's not charity at all. You'd be performing a valuable service for me. This way I can keep my staff." He looked at his plate meaningfully. "I don't want to think of losing my cook!"

Duncan and John carried on the conversation and quickly changed the topic. Emily felt they'd boxed her right into their tidy little scheme. The odd thing was, it didn't bother her. If anything, she felt relieved. She'd still be able to provide for Duncan and Timothy.

Lord, I give You my thanks. It's been so verra hard, but You've carried me through this far. I'm grateful. You've put John Newcomb in our lives—not just for the creaturely comforts he's given, but for how he's become a fine example to Duncan. Bless this man, Father, for how he's gone out of his way to help us. Amen.

"Emily!" Duncan tugged on her sleeve.

"Huh?" She suddenly realized their conversation had waned during the moments she had prayed and considered the new venture John proposed.

John gave her a strained look. He reached over and wiped a tear from her cheek.

She wrinkled her nose and gave him a watery laugh. "I'm being silly. I was thinking on how much easier 'twill be to care for three babes than all of the people at Wilkens's Asylum—and I'll have a helper!"

John shook his head. "A woman must be God's biggest mystery. She cries when she's pleased."

❦

"Crocuses!" Emily stared at the damp flowers in John's large hands.

He stamped slush off his boots, then came inside. "Aye. The promise of spring." He carefully handed them to her and looked her in the eye and said in a gentle murmur, "A reminder that there is new life through the Resurrection and God's hand tends everything, even through the darkest months."

"Oh, John, thank you. I needed to be reminded of that." Emily held the flowers and realized he'd brushed away the snow to cut them. That fact touched her heart even more. He'd been a godsend. On the days she grieved the deepest, John had a knack for saying something that brought comfort. Truly the Lord used him to remind her of His present and future solace.

John peeled out of his greatcoat and hung it on a brass hook by the door. "The new ship is to be delivered on the morrow."

"How big is it?" Duncan asked.

"A schooner. Three-masted. Same plans and size as the *Gallant*."

Duncan jigged from one foot to the other. "Can I see her?"

"Now, Duncan, Mr. John is a busy man." Emily gave her brother a stern look.

"We'll all go see her on Sunday after church," John declared. "I'm eager to show her off."

Emily poured water into her extra teapot and arranged the crocuses in it. She fussed as she set them on the table. No one had ever given her flowers. The gesture wasn't a romantic one, and she didn't mistake it as such, but the thoughtfulness of the act and the comforting words that accompanied it warmed her to the depths of her soul.

A knock sounded, and the door swung open without anyone answering it. Gracie and Cook both traipsed straight in. "Hello! How are the babies?"

"Fat and sassy," Emily said. "Gracie, that son of yours is starting to crawl."

Gracie and Cook bustled over to the table and set their baskets on it. By now they had the routine down. They delivered supper as they picked up their little ones. Often as not, John would instruct Cook to deliver his supper, too, so he could sup with them in the cottage instead of at his own table. Though it baffled Emily that he would do so, his presence always resulted in a lively discussion over the meal.

While Cook claimed Timothy and nursed him in the bedchamber, Emily and Gracie set the table. The laundress then took her wee one and left for home. "See you in the morning!"

With Cook still in the house and Duncan underfoot, Emily didn't fret about John's spending time there. No one could gossip about anything that innocent and open. She lifted little Violet from the cradle and carried her over to the table. The routine worked flawlessly. When Timothy finished nursing, Cook would come out, place him in the cradle, take Violet, and go back to John's big house. Since Cook was tending Timothy now, Emily sat down, and John asked a blessing on the meal.

"Family tradition is to wait to name a vessel until it is delivered," John said as he cut his roast. "I thought we could talk over some possibilities."

"What about the *Sea Tiger*?" Duncan suggested.

"That sounds exciting, but it won't work." John set down his knife. "My grandfather always named his vessels after birds—the *Cormorant*, the *Osprey*, and the *Peregrine*."

"Why did that stop?" Emily wondered.

"My father was a staunch abolitionist. He commissioned and got only one vessel before he died: the *Freedom*. When Grandfather started handing the reins of the business over to me, he told me to devise my own theme. I settled on using character traits."

"The *Resolute*, the *Gallant*, the *Allegiant*," Emily thought aloud. From their discussions, she knew much about John's business.

"Aye. So now I'm faced with trying to come up with something suitable."

"Loyalty. Honesty," Duncan suggested as he tore open a roll and slathered butter on it.

"Kindness sounds too. . .weak," Emily mused. She looked at John and knew kindness was an underrated force that had the power to change things. He embodied so many fine qualities. Surely another of his traits would make for a grand name for his new vessel. "Something stronger, perhaps. Stalwart. Courageous."

"Those have possibilities." John took a gulp of coffee. "Victorious. Persistence."

They continued to toss around names clear through dessert. By the time John took his leave, he'd narrowed his choices down to either the *Reliant* or the *Stalwart*.

Later, after she'd tucked both Timothy and Duncan in for the night, Emily fingered the crocuses and whispered, "Lord, thank You for this reminder of eternal life. Bless John Newcomb in a special way, Father, for his constancy and consolation. Between him at my table and You in my heart, I don't feel so alone."

༃

Three months later, John received a message from the captain of a frigate. Edward sent word that the *Cormorant* had limped into port in Georgia after a storm.

Many of the sails were shredded, and a portion of the starboard bulkhead had suffered appreciable damage when the mainmast snapped. Six other vessels also had sustained severe damage and required attention, so Edward estimated it would be another six weeks before all of the *Cormorant*'s repairs were effected and she'd be ready to return to Virginia.

Part of John itched for Edward to come home so he could settle the matters at hand. The other part of him got caught in an undertow of relief. He'd been praying for wisdom, but he didn't yet know how to handle this.

In the meantime, he stopped by to see how Emily was faring. No stranger to grief, she continued to accomplish whatever needed to be done. Even with the ache evident in her eyes, he saw her smile.

"Duncan carried heavy responsibilities and worries, but I'm thinking he needs a chance to be a carefree boy," she confided in John one afternoon. "I can sit and mope through each day, but then where does that put us? He's so very excited at how you've got him sitting up on a pony. Oh, and those books you brought? He's working hard at them. I'm hoping maybe I can talk to the teacher and find out what a boy his age ought to be learning."

"Emily, I've been meaning to talk to you about that. It was important for the two of you to comfort one another, so I didn't push to have him go, but I think it's time for Duncan to attend school."

"It's too far away, and it's much too late in the year."

John tilted her face up to his. "He can ride along with the other stable boys and the maid's little sister. They go each morning, and it'll be nice for him to get a taste for going to school."

"He'll be so excited. I've done my best to give him lessons, but it's nothing like having a real teacher. Just as he was getting old enough for book learning, Anna got sick and needed his help. We could only dream of him being lucky enough to go to school. You're making another of our dreams come true, John."

John chuckled. "That's really nothing on my part, Emily. The school welcomes all the local children."

The next day was a Saturday. John arrived with a slate, a fancy blue leather book strap, three schoolbooks, and a tin lunch bucket. "Come Monday morning, the wagon will stop right out on the drive for you, Duncan."

"Oh, Em! Can I go? Truly can I?"

Her laughter made the trip John had taken to the school and mercantile more than worth it. He loved her laughter. She didn't laugh nearly often enough—and he planned to change that fact.

"Well, now, the bucket isn't empty, Em!"

"It isn't?" She leaned forward to look inside.

Duncan clutched the bucket and giggled. "Cookies, Em! John brought cookies!"

Emily bit off the thread and threaded her needle. She'd stitched a shirt for Duncan, and from the scraps of cotton left, she'd cut out several handkerchiefs for John. With great care, she hemmed the squares, then chose dark brown thread—the exact color of his eyes—to monogram his initials on them. It wasn't much, but she wanted to do something to show her appreciation to him.

He'd often either have tea or a meal with her and Duncan. She came to look forward to his stories about his workdays and the events in town. He gave Duncan a small knife and was teaching him to whittle, and he'd been present for their celebration for Timothy's first tooth. He loaned Emily books, and they would discuss them. Their conversations about literature and the Bible gave her glimpses of his intellect, wit, humor, and character. The more she came to know him, the more intriguing he became.

Oh, John kept claiming she earned her keep, but she knew better. He had the gift of generosity. God had blessed him, and instead of hoarding his wealth, he turned around and showed kindness to everyone who worked for him. Aye, he was a man to admire—strong, kind, gentle. Emily told herself everyone felt that way about him, but in her heart she knew her feelings ran dangerously deep.

Chapter 13

John sat at the enormous oak desk in his office and stared out the window for the twentieth time that morning. After last night's summer squall, everything looked clean and slick. From his vantage point, he could see the entire dock.

He'd heard from a ship that just came in that the *Cormorant* was right behind it and should dock either today or tomorrow. John felt grateful for that news. It had been almost seven months since she'd been in port. Though he'd been praying about what to do, he still felt no sense of direction as to how he should handle Edward. Every time he considered how his brother had taken advantage of the O'Briens, his temper soared. The predicament was, if he unleashed his anger, he'd likely create more problems than he solved.

Late in the afternoon, John slammed a ledger book closed. He'd accomplished precious little today. If the *Cormorant* hadn't arrived by now, she wouldn't make it 'til tomorrow. No use waiting around here. He bade Franklin a good evening and left.

On his way home, John checked on the O'Briens. Judging from the line full of sun-dried nappies and snowy little gowns, Gracie must have been by earlier. She and Emily enjoyed doing the babies' laundry together. He felt glad Em had a woman friend to chat with.

He pulled a dozen of the cotton rectangles from the line and chuckled. A year ago he'd not known what shape of cloth a nappy was, let alone how to change one. Having Em, Duncan, and Timothy around domesticated him—and it was an improvement. Newcomb Shipping thrived, even with him there less. He'd started to look at the world around him instead of focusing solely on logs and ledgers.

The gravel crunched beneath his boots as he toted an armful of nappies to the door. He loved coming to the caretaker's cottage. Somehow, in the last month or so, it had come to feel like his own home. He regularly took his meals here, and Emily's presence at the humble table in this sunny kitchen was what made all the difference.

Duncan scampered down the five little porch steps just as John reached the door. The lad grinned and shoved the last bite of a bun in his already-full mouth and raced off to the stables. Emily didn't realize Duncan had left a caller at the door, so John stepped in, nudged the door shut, leaned against the sill, and took stock of her.

Over the past months, she'd eaten well and filled out so she glowed with good health. The green dress she'd made for herself brought out the color of her eyes. Late afternoon sun slanted through the window, giving her hair a burnished gleam. She radiated warmth and beauty.

She was reading her Bible and using her toes to tilt the runners on the cradle to keep Cook's daughter rocking contentedly. Gracie's babe lay on a blanket on the floor, an ivory teething ring he must have been gnawing on abandoned as he napped. Timothy lay beside him, his thumb in his mouth. So far, having Emily play nanny to the babes seemed to be working out beautifully.

At times Emily couldn't hide her grief. But right this instant she was the picture of serenity. He'd purchased the cloth for her dress, knowing full well society dictated she ought to be wearing crow black for mourning. Instead he'd chosen an unembellished cotton and hoped its plainness and her manners would keep her from fretting over the pretty, deep green color. In a move to acknowledge her mourning and quiet any qualms, John provided a black kerseymere shawl for her to drape over her shoulders. Emily deserved nice things in her life—she'd suffered long enough.

The day he'd arrived with that shawl, she'd had a small package wrapped in brown paper for him. How she managed to be so shy at times, then so fiery at others, never ceased to amuse him. She'd blushed and quietly handed him the package.

"Oh, look at this!" he'd exclaimed as he caught sight of the handkerchiefs. "Em, these are—"

"Little nothings," she'd demurred.

He'd lifted her face to his. "Emily, I don't ever recall anyone giving me a gift just because their heart told them to. I've been given birthday and Christmas gifts, but those were times when others traditionally make an effort. You—you did this, and I can't figure out how you made the time to do them." He'd folded one and tucked it into his pocket then and there. "But I'm thankful you did."

He always kept one of them in his pocket. She'd made enough for him to have one a day for a whole week. He stuffed his hand in his pocket now and wadded it up as he struggled again for the millionth time to decide what to do once his brother docked.

On his way home, John had decided to inform her of Edward's impending arrival. The caretaker's cottage sat next to the drive leading to the main house. It would be unfair to leave Emily unprepared for the sight of him. John had yet to discuss Edward with Emily and seek her opinion. Strong-willed as she was, he suspected she'd decided on a course of action.

"Oh!" Emily's pretty green eyes went huge when she glanced up and spied him. She closed the Bible and set it blindly on the small table beside her. "I didn't realize you were there!"

He chuckled softly. "When a woman is in the presence of the King and three cherubs, a man may as well be invisible."

A soft smile lit her face. "Now all of the wee ones are fat as cherubs, aren't they? 'Tis a welcome sight."

"Seeing you read the Word is every bit as wonderful." He tore his gaze from her before he embarrassed them both. He set the nappies on the table. "Where's Mary? I thought she was helping you."

"I let her go to the stables. Duncan said Blackie is whelping, and Mary wanted to see the puppies right away."

"I hope they hurried. Blackie's had three other litters, and she's quick about it. I suppose Mary and Duncan are claiming one apiece."

"Oh, no! Surely not!" Emily gave him a shocked look. "Duncan knows better than to expect such a thing!"

"Ahh, I understand." John nodded sagely. He paused for effect and fought a smile. "Duncan knows you get pick of the litter, Emily."

Emily spluttered, then started to giggle.

Mary dashed back to the door and announced breathlessly, "There's seven of 'em!"

John crossed the floor and picked up Gracie's babe. "Em, grab Timothy. Mary, you take Violet, and let's get going. I want to see the puppies, too!"

Emily gave him a scandalized look. "I'm thinking I ought not take the babes to such a place."

After making sure he had a firm hold on the baby, John pulled Emily from the chair. He couldn't hide the amusement in his voice. "Emily, our Lord Jesus was born in a stable!"

More giggles spilled out of her.

John felt sure he'd never heard anything half as delightful. He winked and urged, "Come on!"

Emily whisked the baby out of his arms. "Not yet." She fussed over the babes first. She changed their nappies, cooed to them, and wrapped them in a blanket apiece, regardless of the fact that the sun still shone. She handed Gracie's son back to him.

John chortled. "He looks like a stowaway, hiding in the spare, bundled sails."

They headed toward the stables at more than a genteel walk. In fact, had they each not been slowed down by holding a babe, John wondered if Emily might have actually let go of propriety and skipped a bit. He grinned at the thought, then worried Mary might hasten and be careless.

"Emily, let me carry Timothy, too. You take Violet from Mary, and she can run ahead."

Emily gawked at him, then shook her head. "Now, Mr. Newcomb, 'tis a fine man you are. Not a soul would deny you're capable as can be with clippers and men. Why don't you let me mind cradles and babes?"

He studied her face for a moment, then chuckled in disbelief. "Light as they are, you don't trust me to carry them both, do you?"

She took the babe from Mary, then pursed her lips and looked up at the scudding white clouds. A second later she trained her gaze on the baby he gently bounced against his shoulder. "Now you're not being fair. I've let you hold Timothy many a time. Much as I love him, you know what a show of trust that is."

"But you're not handing him to me now."

"Let's just say I think you've already plenty enough to handle, holding Gracie's strapping son."

John chortled again. He tilted the baby in his arms back a bit and talked to him. "Now how do you fancy that? You'd best keep that satisfied attitude. If you start crying, Emily won't let me touch the puppies!"

"I won't have to say a word." Emily cast an amused look at him. "Blackie will see to that."

A few minutes later, they sat on the floor of the stable. Duncan let out peals of laughter as the tiny puppies squeaked and wiggled around. He looked up at Emily with huge, shining eyes. "Blackie has seven babies, Em. Seven! Can you just imagine?"

"Aye, and a handsome lot they are," she said.

Duncan wrinkled his nose. "They're funny and wet. I suppose I shouldn't be too surprised you're thinking they're bonny. You said our Timothy was handsome as could be when he got born. I'm glad as ever he doesn't look like he did the first time I saw him!"

John let out a booming laugh at the look on Emily's face. He leaned to the side and scooped Violet from her arms. "Go ahead and set Timmy in the straw next to you. Blackie is uncommonly serene about folks touching her litter as long as they don't lift them away."

In fact, Blackie barely seemed to care that Emily gently stroked a single finger down the back of each puppy. Then again, Emily crooned to Blackie the whole while. "Ach! Now aren't you a fine mother? Seven in this pack. You'll be a tired girl, that's for sure. I'm thinking from the looks of them, they've all taken after you—their fur is almost all black as wrought iron."

"It's odd, but some whelps take after their sire while others take after the mother." John meaningfully glanced down at Timothy, then back at her. "That little fellow's got Anna's sweet temperament. I'm certain he's taken after her, clean down to the bone."

Duncan giggled. "Em was just saying last night that Timothy must take after me because he's always looking for more to eat!"

As Emily braided her hair that night, she remembered John's comment that he needed to discuss something with her. Somehow, in the excitement over looking at the puppies, they'd not had an opportunity to speak. She shrugged. He'd be by in a day or two if it was important.

How she'd come to look forward to the times he stopped by. He filled their cottage with—well, a lot of things. She didn't mean material things, though he was generous to a fault. No, he brought the important things with him—like safety and courage and companionship. Such a fine man.

He'd taken a shine to Duncan and even let him ride a pony every now and then—but only if he himself was walking alongside. Mr. Peebles, the stable master, had a grandson who was due to come for a visit soon. He and John had decided they'd give both lads riding lessons then.

Nearly half of Duncan's sentences started with "Mr. John says. . ." For Duncan's not having an older brother or a da to guide him, it did Emily's heart good to see how John Newcomb never made her brother feel like a pest.

Indeed, he never made her feel as if she depended on his charity, either. He allowed her to work so she could keep her pride and dignity. Others could see 'twas a simple business arrangement, so she never feared for her reputation. Clearly, he would never entertain any true affection for her. She accepted that fact, but in the moments before she fell asleep each night, Emily secretly mourned that she wasn't of his class so things might have worked out between them. Oh, 'twas nothing more than a silly fantasy, but she'd foolishly allowed her heart to weaken toward him. She saw his goodness, his strength, his kindness. She truly enjoyed his companionship. God shone through him, and that mattered most of all. No man would ever look toward her with courting in mind—with Duncan and Timothy in tow, she'd seem like a wallowing barge instead of a sleek clipper.

For all of his kindness, John Newcomb deserved a loving wife and a houseful of healthy sons. Emily wished all that for him, but she knew when that day came, she'd pack up and slip away, because she couldn't quite bear to witness a woman take the place she could never even dream to hold.

The fire had burned too hot late this evening, and her room felt stuffy. Instead of adding a log to last the night, Emily decided to let the end of the fire die out. The bright red sailors' sunset promised tomorrow would be a bonny day.

She fed Timothy one last time, changed his nappy, and tucked him in. After pulling the covers up to Duncan's neck, Emily returned to her bedchamber and knelt at the side of the bed. After a quiet prayer, she slipped into bed and fell asleep.

A bang startled her awake hours later. Emily bolted upright and wished she'd kept some of the fire so she could see better. She crept from the bed and hastily wrapped her shawl about her shoulders.

High-pitched giggles mingled with muffled footsteps. The bedroom door swung wide open, and a candle illuminated a man with a woman clinging to his arm.

"Edward!" Emily gasped.

Chapter 14

H urry, sir. Hurry! Em needs you!"
Duncan's shout echoed through the house as John dashed down the stairs. He'd barely thrown on his trousers and a shirt and run to see what led the lad to be so upset. Duncan stood in the doorway next to Goodhew, the butler.

Just then one of the stable hands ran up the steps and announced breathlessly, "Someone came to the little house!"

John had ordered Mr. Peebles to assign someone to keep an eye on the caretaker's cottage at all times. The fact that the dwelling had been used made him suspicious, and he'd worried most of all for Emily's safety if whoever had been trysting there should show up again.

Goodhew looked horrified. His nightshirt flapped about him, making him look like an albatross on takeoff as he spun about and pulled a gun from the drawer.

"Keep Duncan here." John grabbed the gun, ran down the steps, and vaulted onto the horse the stable hand had arrived on.

A three-quarter moon lit his way, and he rode down the drive, straight into Emily's small yard. He didn't bother to knock or announce himself; he burst in.

A woman sat on the settee, boohooing with great gusto. John barely paid her any heed because he heard foul curses coming from the other room. He followed the small yellow nimbus of light into Emily's bedchamber. "Emily!"

"Here!" she cried back.

Emily held a fireplace poker with both hands. Back against the wall, Edward held a candlestick in one hand and a wicked-looking knife in the other. He ignored John's arrival and continued to bellow at Emily.

"Emily!" John commanded. "Step out of the room."

"It's him. He's the one."

John wasn't sure whether fear or rage caused her voice to shake. He shoved his pistol into his waistband as he walked to her, then curled his hand around her shoulder. "I'll handle this."

"John! Get rid of that woman!" Edward made a show of setting the candle on the mantel and letting out a sigh of relief. "She's deranged—probably would have killed me if you hadn't gotten here."

"He's the one, John," Emily croaked. "That's Edward."

"I have no idea what this woman means," Edward protested. "I've never met her before."

Emily let out an outraged sound.

"Emily, step out of here. I'll take care of things." John gently pried the poker from her. "Trust me," he urged under his breath.

"He's got a knife."

"Yes, I can see that."

"Don't trust him."

Edward shoved the knife into a sheath at his waist. "Who is this spitfire, John? Your mistress?"

"You know I don't keep a mistress." Emily hadn't budged an inch. Asking her to leave again wouldn't accomplish a thing, so John set her to the side and stood between her and Edward. For a fleeting second, he thought to order her to check on Duncan, but upon finding his cot vacant, she'd undoubtedly come flying back in a panicked rage. Instead he addressed his words to Edward. "Leave here at once and don't come back."

Edward shoved away from the wall with another expletive.

John grabbed him by the collar and shoved him back again. "Keep a decent tongue in your head."

Edward made a choking sound.

"Report to me first thing in the morning at the shipping office." John flung him to the side and watched his brother scramble away and out of the bedchamber.

"Don't leave me!" the woman from the other room sobbed. The patter of her slippers could be heard following Edward's footfalls through the main room and out into the yard.

John turned to Emily. Her eyes glittered in the candlelight. She inched back and shook her head. "You let him go."

"Of course I did." John closed the distance between them and calmly drew her shawl together, then wrapped his arms about her trembling form. "I'll deal with him tomorrow, Emily. I had to get him out of here."

Her tears wet his shirt. "He's the one. He lied again. He said he didn't know me."

"Of course he lied." John did his utmost to keep his temper hidden. Emily needed calming in the worst way. He gently stroked her back. "Don't you understand? I wanted him out of here before the noise woke the baby. I didn't want him to know Timmy is here."

Emily's knees nearly buckled. "Oh, no!"

"Shh." John led her out to the parlor.

John lowered Emily to the settee, then stepped back into the bedchamber and brought out the candle and a blanket. He lit the lamp, then wrapped the blanket around Emily. She caught his sleeve. Both her hand and her voice shook. "I'm thanking you for all you've done for my kin, John Newcomb."

"Emily, hush. We need to plan what to do next."

She turned loose of him, dipped her head, and cleared her throat. "There's nothing left to do. I'll be gone by sunup."

"No!"

She shuddered at the word he roared. Still, she seemed more than firm on her decision. She turned toward the kitchen and raised her voice. "Duncan, come help me. We've packing to see to."

John cupped her chin and forced her to look up at him. The shocked worry in her eyes let him know she hadn't thought about the fact that Edward's shouting had to have awakened the lad. "Duncan is up at my house. He knew he could trust me—he ran to my place so I could come protect you. You can bet I'm going to do just that. You're not running away. You, Duncan, and Timmy belong here."

A sad, all-too-worldly-wise parody of a smile tugged at the corners of her mouth. "We don't belong in your world, John Newcomb, and well you know it. I'm taking my boys off before that dreadful man does something."

"What could he do? Think, Emily."

"Oh, I am. You were, too, when you thought of keeping Edward from finding the baby. Your brother's a rascal—" Her voice broke.

"Ahh, Em." John sat next to her and pulled her into the shelter of his arms. "I'll protect you and the boys."

"You can't," she said in a hopeless tone.

He slowly slid his hand down her hair. Soft little wisps curled about his finger and sprang loose, only to be replaced again and again. The wet warmth of her tears seeped through his shirt, but she didn't weep in torrents. Instead, her tears fell one by one in solitary anguish.

"I'm sorry for what he, uh, believed about"—she barely choked out the word—"mistress."

"You've nothing to be sorry for. Edward is responsible for his own thoughts—lurid and wrong as they may be. He's judging others for his own sin. Ofttimes guilty men do so."

"He h–had another woman—"

"Em, my Em, I'm so sorry." He felt her shudder and knew the impact of Edward's betrayal was hitting full force for the second time. The first time John had watched her limp away from the shipyard, and she'd had to handle the blow by herself. This time he'd not let her feel alone.

"I'm supposing I ought to be thankful the Lord didn't let him come barging in with another woman in front of Anna."

"That is something to be thankful for," he allowed, though he felt sick about the whole sordid mess.

"You'll tell Cook, Gracie, and Mary good-bye for me?"

John's arms tightened, crushing her to his chest. "You're staying right here."

She patted him and said in a tearful voice that managed to make pretenses toward soothing, "There, now, I'll be sure to sneak a message to you now and again to let you know how our Timmy's doing."

"You'll do no such thing! Emily, you can't leave. You and Duncan won't ever make it on your own, and who will watch the baby whilst you work? There are far too many problems. I'll not hear of this nonsense."

Emily pushed away and stared at him. The lamplight flickered in her glistening green eyes. "Best you listen and heed me, John Newcomb. I'll not stand by and let that man hurt my family e'er again."

Her spirit pleased him. John brushed a few of her tears away with his thumb. "He won't hurt you. I won't let him."

"You're not listening to me. I don't give a whit about myself. I'm worried about Timothy! What if he tries to take him away?"

"Em, Edward is too footloose to want to be tied down to a babe. Besides, there's no church record naming Edward as the father."

"Oh, sure and enough, he might not try to nab a babe; but give him a few years, and he could well change his tune. He's got the morals of an alley cat and the heart of a snake." She shook her head. "No. 'Tis a risk I won't take."

"Do you trust me?"

Emily drew the blanket around herself and stood. She paced away, then turned. Her mouth opened, then shut without her uttering a word.

John met her gaze unflinchingly. For all she'd been through, she had every reason not to trust another soul. Nonetheless, he wanted—no, he needed—her to trust him.

Emily turned away. "Forgive me, John. I'm not sure what to think right now. If ever a man has shown himself to be dependable and Christian, 'tis you. You're asking me to rely on your say-so, and my head tells me I can. But 'tisn't you I hold concerns about, and your brother already proved he leaves a heartload of grief and worry in his wake."

"I understand, Emily, but—"

"You have to admit you were blind to your brother's ways. You defended him." Her voice went hushed. "Even when Anna longed to be acknowledged as his wife, you never allowed her that. You'd never knowingly let him hurt us, but brotherly love veiled the truth back then. I can't help but worry that I'll rely on your word and it will happen again."

John sat there and let her speak. She'd not spoken out of bitterness. Her words came from the ache and worries he wanted to share, so he would listen as she spilled them.

"I don't trust Edward for a single minute. Anna's gone, and he's rich. He could pay a judge, just as he paid someone to pretend to be a parson. Even if he didn't want Timmy for himself, what if he tried to take him and give him to someone else?"

Silence filled the room. Emily gave John a look of resignation, yet she somehow managed to square her shoulders. "I'd best spend my night praying. You'll know when I've made up my mind."

John stood and nodded. He crossed the room and tugged the blanket even tighter around her. "I've no doubt they've tucked Duncan in up at my house. Let's take the baby on up there, too."

"Your brother will be up at the big house. I'm thinking my brother belongs back here with me."

"You're not thinking of slipping away in the middle of the night, are you?"

Emily stared at him. She chewed on her lip for a brief moment, then sighed. "I'd be telling a fearsome lie if I said the thought never crossed my mind."

"You've never once lied to me, Em. Give me your word you'll stay here—at least for tonight."

She shuddered. "I can't give you my word, John. If I do, what will I do if he comes back here tonight?"

"Em," he said softly as he tucked a strand of her soft hair behind her left ear, "why didn't you just tell me you were afraid he'd come back here tonight?"

She hitched one shoulder. "I suppose I'm not in the practice of whispering my worries to another."

He turned her, snatched up the lamp, and marched her back into the bedchamber. "Get dressed; then we'll talk."

"We've talked plenty. Sometimes it's best to stop talking and act."

Aware she had yet to give her promise that she wouldn't run off, John bent over, took Timothy from his cradle, and clasped him to his shoulder as he straightened. "I'm taking action, Em. Timmy-boy and I'll be in the other room."

A few moments later, the door opened, and Emily emerged from the bedchamber. Lamplight turned her hair to a molten gold and burnished copper combination. She'd gotten over enough of the shock that color now stained her cheeks.

John admired Emily for her character qualities. On several occasions he'd caught her at prayer or reading her Bible and appreciated the devotion she held for the Lord. Her wit and spunk amused him, too. Many times he'd even considered her hair to be lovely, and the day he'd bought her dress, he'd distinctly thought of what a lovely woman she was. . . . But at that moment, he looked at her in a completely different light. He couldn't hope to have a better ally in the troubled days ahead than this beautiful woman.

Emily crossed the floor and set the lamp on a small table. She knelt on the floor and silently reached up to take possession of the baby. Worried, even frightened as she was, her features softened with love as her fingertips grazed the blanket. She didn't say a word. Just the way she tilted her head a bit to the side and raised her brows silently invited John to relinquish Timothy.

Instead, John's arm curled a bit more tightly around the boy. He reached over with his other hand and slid it over hers, pressing it against the babe. "Em, we're in this together."

She focused on him. Even in the lamplight, he could see her eyes darken. A brave, sad smile fleetingly lifted the corners of her mouth. "If ever God made a fine man, surely 'tis you, John Newcomb." The smile disappeared, and she continued. "But 'tisn't right for me to depend on you or anyone else. This is my problem."

"Why is it any more your problem than it is mine?"

"Anna was my sister." Tears filled her voice and eyes.

"Aye, and she was a lovely, innocent young girl," John agreed softly. He curled his fingers to hold her hand more firmly. "But Edward is my brother. His dishonor caused this, so betwixt you and me, I'm more responsible for trying to right this as much as possible."

"I'll be disagreeing with you, John Newcomb. Most certainly I will. Anna gave Timmy into my keeping. He's mine. We both know full well that I'm far better able to handle this wee babe than you are to manage your brother. I can slip away, land a job, and make a new life. There's not a thing you could do if he comes here and takes Timmy."

"Enough of this." Her words burned his soul. John broke contact with her and stood. "Toss whatever you need for bedtime and some nappies into a pillow slip. You and Timothy are to be my guests tonight."

"Ach! We cannot do that!" She scrambled to her feet. "Have you not been listening? The scoundrel you call a brother is in that very house. I'll not stay under the same roof with him."

"I can be every bit as obstinate as you. Now you have a choice: You come with me, and we'll settle you in a room along with one of the maids so all proprieties will be observed; or I'll stay here the whole night long, and though we'll behave with the morals of pure saints, we'll scandalize the whole town, and your reputation will be in shreds. Take your pick, Emily O'Brien."

She glowered, then marched into the bedchamber. John stood in the doorway and watched as she grabbed a pillow and shook the feathered sack from it with notable temper. As she stuffed a nightdress and the shawl he'd given her into it, she muttered, "Every last angel and saint in heaven is likely blushing at your words, you rogue."

John chuckled. "I don't think they are, but you've turned a fetching shade of pink."

"I'm thinking you ought to make yourself useful, John Newcomb." She snapped a diaper in the air, then folded it. "Go fetch some breeches for Duncan."

⌒

She'd never been in such a grand home. Emily barely set foot in the foyer of John's place before she turned and bumped into him as she tried to exit.

"Did you forget something?" He tossed the pillow slip onto the beautiful marble floor.

"I forgot my wits," she muttered.

"You're never witless." John chuckled and tried to turn her around, but she didn't budge.

"I don't belong here. I'll wait outside whilst you send someone to fetch Duncan."

"Sir?" A tall man who managed to sound and look dignified in his nightshirt and robe stood by the open door.

"Goodhew, this is Miss Emily O'Brien. You've seen her nephew, Timothy, already. They're to be our guests tonight."

"Very well, sir. Eloise already prepared the blue suite, just in case." Goodhew shut the front door.

Emily wanted to moan at the loss of her exit.

"It's a pleasure to meet you, Miss Emily." The butler's tone carried a touch of warmth as he nodded polite acknowledgment of the introduction. He then turned back to John. "I took the liberty of setting a fire in the study so you could warm up, sir. Cook will bring in a light repast for you both as soon as you're settled."

Emily felt stuck. She searched for a way or excuse to leave, but her mind went blank.

John took her in hand and piloted her into the study as if she were a barge going through rough waters. Once there, she halted on a plush, ornate carpet. "I–I can't go in here," she whispered. "I didn't wipe my feet."

"Neither did I. Just step out of your slippers."

It wasn't until then Emily looked down. "Mr. John! You're—"

"Just leave the tray by the fire, Cook. Thank you for getting that ready." John's words cut Emily's observation short. He took the baby from her arms.

"Will you need anything special for the baby, Miss Emily?" Goodhew asked.

Emily tried not to gawk at him. She wasn't accustomed to being treated like a society lady. She stammered, "I give him milk and molasses."

"There's no need for that." Cook took Timothy from John and turned to Emily. "I'll take him on up to your room and feed him."

104

"Thank you, Cook." John tugged Emily over to a chair by the roaring fire and said under his breath, "Let her take him upstairs, Em. I don't expect Edward to come home tonight, but if he does, we'll want the baby hidden."

Goodhew slipped in from a side door and escorted Cook out. Emily stared at them, then turned to look at the ceiling-high bookcases that went around three of the walls.

John gently pushed Emily into a huge leather chair that nearly swallowed her.

Satisfied Timothy was in good hands, she then stared back down at John's bare feet. "If you point me to the kitchen, I'll get you a kettle of warm water. We'll wash your feet, and that'll warm them straight away."

"The fire will do." He eased into a chair and stuck his legs out straight. "I wouldn't complain if you served me some of that cake. It's one of Cook's specialties."

Calling upon the memories of the times she'd helped Mama serve guests at Master Reilly's house, Emily made a plate for him and also prepared his tea according to the preferences she'd already noted he held. *Odd, how I know such details about this man.*

After she served him, she perched on the edge of her chair.

"Emily, eat," John bade her quietly. "Put extra honey in the tea—it's good for your shock."

"I can't eat, so it's silly for me to fill a plate," she said simply. "It's not right for me to waste good food."

"You're here tonight. Refusing to eat or sleep won't help any. We need to be certain you are at your best to deal with things in the morning."

"I don't know what I'll do tomorrow—in fact, I don't even know what to do right now!"

"Let's have you rest." He held up his hand to keep her from interrupting him. "You and the boys are perfectly safe here. I can't even be sure if Edward will come home at all. If he does, he'll be in the other wing, so he won't have any notion at all that you're here."

"So you'd hide us in plain sight?"

He chuckled softly. "Cleverly put."

She watched him eat the cake in a few large bites. The fire crackled and popped, making the vast room seem cozy. Fearing he'd catch her staring at him, Emily looked at the portion of the room the fire illuminated. Master Reilly's home didn't begin to compare with the splendor of this place. At first glance everything was imposing, but another look changed her mind. Someone had taken care to add details that made this huge place a welcoming home. Every so often, on the bottom shelves, a child's toy sat next to the books. Portraits weren't strictly of stern-faced men and women—there were several of children with pets.

"See the framed picture to the right of the mantel?" John broke into her musings. "I did that when I was Duncan's age. I'd taken a mind to help myself to my father's inkwell and pen."

Emily gasped. The result hung there—plain as could be. A sheet of foolscap with a spill of ink and several fingerprints had been framed and displayed as if it were a Flemish master's work.

John chuckled. "Oh, the desk was a horrible mess, and my parents were justifiably angry. Grandfather came in just about then and roared with laughter. Without saying a word, he set aside the paper and peeled up the red felt on the blotter. There, on the leather beneath it, was a very old splotch of ink that had faded into a bluish tone. My father had done the selfsame thing when he was a lad, too."

Emily flashed him a smile. "So you were a rapscallion?"

"No more so than any other lad. Grandfather saved my 'picture' and hung it here. He told me it was a reminder that whatever trouble a man does, it leaves a blot on his soul. My father's blot was covered by red felt—and Grandfather chose red instead of green, because he thought it represented how the blood of Christ covers the blots of sin on our souls. It's a peculiarity in this home—you'll not see any green felt on the desks. It's all red."

"What a lovely lesson."

John nodded and rose. "You're weary. Let's get you settled in for what's left of the night." He padded over to the serving tray and cut a generous slice of cake. To Emily's surprise, he shoved the plate into her hands. "You just may want to nibble later. Now come with me."

Emily got halfway up the wide, sweeping staircase before she stopped cold. "Oh, no!"

"What's wrong?"

"My Bible!"

"You can borrow mine for the night."

She shook her head. " 'Tisn't just that. The marriage license and the matrimony page are in the Bible. If Edward goes back to the cottage. . ."

"I'll take care of it." John nudged her up the stairs and stopped outside an open door. "Wait here. I'll fetch you my Bible."

Emily did as he bade. Moments later, John handed her his Bible with the lovely gold leaf pages. "Will you be able to sleep?"

She shrugged. "I can't say. My body's weary, but my heart and soul are doing a jig."

John cupped her cheek and looked at her tenderly. "Then read Luke chapter twelve, verses six and seven."

Emily looked at him and nodded. With him touching her so kindly, she couldn't manage to speak.

"Sweet dreams." He walked back down the stairs, and Emily knew he'd left to go fetch her Bible.

His Bible rested heavily in her hands, almost as heavily as the burdens in her heart. She knew she needed to do something quickly to safeguard precious little Timmy. Duncan, too—because she didn't want him to see Edward Newcomb and know he was the wicked man who had tricked them all.

Lord, I don't know what to do. You know how scared I am. I love Timmy, and I'm sore afraid I won't be able to protect him from Edward. You'll have to give me a message. I'm not asking for anything grand—just a place I can take my boys and live peacefully. Reveal Your plan to me and calm my fretful heart.

Cook tucked Timmy into a cradle, then slipped out of the room. Emily sat on the edge of a beautiful four-poster bed and sighed. John hadn't once mentioned how she'd been shaking. Aye, and she had been—from the moment she heard the noise, clear up 'til now. It took every shred of her courage to make her voice sound stable, but her hands jittered like a blade of grass in a stiff wind. How kind of John to loan her his Bible.

Tired as she was, Emily knew she'd not be able to sleep a wink. Memories of Edward surfaced—of his wooing Anna, of how sour he'd been to discover he had a child on the way, of tonight when he'd pulled out that horrifying knife.

After all that, how can John expect me to sleep? The weight of the Bible in her hands commanded her attention. Since John had recommended a particular passage, she turned to it.

"Are not five sparrows sold for two farthings, and not one of them is forgotten before God? But even the very hairs of your head are all numbered. Fear not therefore: ye are of more value than many sparrows."

Emily stared at the verses and blinked. She'd just told God how scared she was. He'd known it even before she prayed and in His infinite wisdom and love used John to urge her to read these very words for comfort.

Her pulse slowed, and the weight on her shoulders lifted as she read the words once more. After she set the Bible on the bedside table, a maid came in.

"Miss Emily, I'm Clara. I'm to spend the night with you and the wee one. I just checked in on Duncan. He's next door, and he's sleepin' heavy as an anchor."

They spoke a few minutes; then Emily went behind the screen and changed into her bed gown. Once she came out, she peeped at Timmy, then crept into the huge bed. The feather pillow and comforters enveloped her. . .just like the little sparrows in God's hands.

Chapter 15

Emily woke the next morning to soft, musical crooning. She opened her eyes slowly and watched as John's laundress suckled the baby. During the night, Clara had slept in the room on a fainting couch. She'd insisted that Emily sleep, that she had plenty of experience with her younger brothers and sisters. She'd deftly mixed the milk and molasses, so Emily hesitantly agreed, with the caveat that if Timothy got stubborn, she was to be awakened.

Timmy and the maid must have gotten along famously. In fact, he seemed quite content now with Gracie, too. Emily yawned and blinked.

Gracie chortled softly. "I'll wager you've not slept more than a few hours at a time. It was that way right after I had my son."

"I didn't even hear you come in!"

"That's because you needed the sleep. Mr. John says you're to laze in bed awhile."

"Duncan—"

"Your little brother scampered down to the stable. Mary went with him. Blackie's puppies have us all charmed."

Emily sat up and stretched. In the morning light, this room looked like a little corner of heaven. The blue walls and the fluffy blue-and-white bedding made her feel as if she were floating on a cloud, and sunbeams coming through the far window made all of the golden accents glow. "Mercy! I was so weary last night that I didn't even take note of how beautiful this is. Mayhap I ought to see if I sprouted wings during the night, to be waking in such a place as this," she marveled.

Gracie laughed as she fastened her bodice. "It's pretty as can be. You rest on back. Soon as I get downstairs, I'll tell Teresa to send up your tray."

"Tray? Oh, no." Emily hopped out of bed. "I'm no highborn woman to be waited upon."

"Mr. John ordered it."

Emily grabbed her day gown and slipped behind a dressing screen. "Mr. John's a fine man, but he's got the wrong notion. I've never been waited on in my life."

Gracie chuckled softly. "Mr. John ordered us all to pamper you. You may as well give in graciously."

"We both know good and well I have plenty to do today. Sitting about is pure foolishness. Now where is your wee son?"

"Cook has him in the kitchen. He's gumming a biscuit she made for him. He'll be in a fine temper if you try to sweep him away before he eats half a dozen. Her own wee one is lying in a box on the table, cooing at her while she kneads bread."

Emily came out from behind the screen and started to brush her hair.

"Oh, Miss Emily! Your hair is pretty as can be!"

"Thank you." Emily rebraided it with the intent of putting it up into a coronet, but she suddenly stopped short. "Well, mercy. I didn't think to bring along any hairpins."

A tentative knock sounded on the door. Emily startled, then began to cross the room. Gracie called out merrily, "Come on in!"

Goodhew opened the door and stood at the threshold. "Miss Emily, you're awake. Mr. John ordered Cook to make you a breakfast tray. I'll have Teresa bring it right up. After you're finished, he'd like to meet with you in the study."

"There's no call to be fussing over me. I'll follow you to the kitchen, if you'd be so kind as to show me the way."

"Very well, miss."

⌘

John heard a baby cry and smiled. He'd arranged everything so Clara and Gracie would shift in and out of Emily's bedchamber and she could catch up on a bit of sleep. Clearly they'd slipped little Timothy out and brought him down here.

Upstairs his housekeeper and three of the maids were cleaning the nursery. He'd already inspected it and found it to be satisfactory, but Mrs. Thwaite clucked and tutted about its needing to be dusted and aired. Knowing her, she'd have it so royalty could eat off the windowsill.

As long as the *Cormorant* was docked and Edward was in town, John determined to keep Emily, Duncan, and Timothy here. He could come up with no better way to protect them. Emily could spend the days in the sunny nursery with Cook and Gracie's babes and Timothy. A safe place with a crib and toys, the children would fare well there, and Emily would feel securely tucked away. The moment she came downstairs, he'd fill her in on his plan. As for her future—well, he'd broach that subject later.

In the meantime, he needed to see to other matters. First and foremost, he needed to deal with Edward. For all of his prayers, he had yet to sense any direction to take or words of wisdom to apply. Simply put, all he felt was rage.

What should I do? Edward is my brother, my own flesh and blood. But so is Baby Timothy—and he's innocent. Edward made his own choices; Timothy doesn't deserve to live in poverty because of his father's sins. John rested his elbow on the desk and pinched the bridge of his nose, wishing he could be rid of this entire headache.

In that moment, when his eyes were closed, something rustled. Someone tugged on his sleeve. "Mr. John!"

John opened his eyes and turned. "Yes, Duncan?"

"I seen him. He's here. Down by the stable with Edward."

"Who?"

"The parson who came to my house and married Anna and Edward. He's here! You can ask him. He'll prove our Anna was really married!"

John stood, and Duncan tugged on his sleeve more urgently. "Please hurry."

They exited by the doors leading to the garden, and John lengthened his stride. Duncan galloped alongside him to keep pace.

"Are you sure he's the one?" he asked the boy.

"Aye, that I am. Only he's not wearing the same clothes this time. He looks like a fancy man instead of a churchy one. This way—they went 'round back, over by the extra water trough."

John stepped over a fence and lifted Duncan after him, then hastened on. What was Edward up to? Obviously it wasn't anything good, or he'd be doing it out in the open instead of behind the stables. John rounded the corner just in time to see a man mount a dappled gelding and ride off.

"Oh, no! He's going away," Duncan moaned.

Edward turned toward them. "Out for your morning constitutional, Brother?"

John glared at him. The man Duncan thought to be a priest was a notorious slave trader. "What are you doing, meeting with Phineas Selsior?"

"That's my business, not yours."

Duncan shouted, "He's the priest who married you to my Anna!"

Edward sneered. "Honestly, John. What are you doing, associating with these bilge rats?"

"You said you loved Anna!" Duncan cried. "You married her."

"Shh, Duncan." John drew the boy close, and the lad wrapped his arms about John's leg and held fast like a barnacle.

"We'll talk in the study, Edward." John could barely hold his temper. How dare his brother call Emily and her family bilge rats? And what business did he have with Phineas Selsior?

Edward shoved his hands into his pockets and shrugged. "There's nothing to discuss. You can stow that 'brother's keeper' nonsense. I'm a grown man, and I'll attend to my own business."

"You didn't mind your own business. You abandoned your wife."

"I have absolutely no idea what you're talking about." Edward leaned against a nearby tree trunk. He smirked. "I've never walked down the aisle."

'Twasn't a church wedding, but I overlooked that because we were both wedging the ceremony in the few minutes betwixt our shifts of work. Emily's words echoed in

John's mind. It sickened him to think of the lengths to which his brother had gone to delude them.

Suddenly the verse from Matthew flashed through his mind. "And if thine eye offend thee, pluck it out, and cast it from thee: it is better for thee to enter into life with one eye, rather than having two eyes to be cast into hell fire." He knew it then. He had to cast his brother aside.

"You're to leave and never come back. I'll have Goodhew pack your personal belongings."

Edward negligently lifted a shoulder as if it meant nothing to him.

"You'll no longer captain the *Cormorant*, either." John watched his brother's face go florid.

"You're wrong! She's mine!"

John shook his head. "You know full well she's mine." He looked off to the side where Selsior had ridden off, then looked back at Edward. "You've used her to bring in slaves, haven't you?"

"Not from the outside—just trading within our boundaries. All perfectly legal. Lucrative, too."

"Not with any of my vessels."

"Being self-righteous never filled your pockets." Edward pushed away from the tree and stalked closer to John. "Half of the shipping business, half of those ships, should belong to me. Grandfather changed his will because he found out I'd brought back a pair of slaves my first run out as Enoch's first mate. Bad enough I lived through the indignity of his leaving me to play lackey to old Enoch. I figured he'd punished me more than enough. The day the will was read and I learned how he'd cheated me of my birthright, I decided the Newcomb name meant nothing. I've used your ship to do as I jolly well pleased, and I've earned a tidy sum for it, too. Slaves bring good money—a hundred for a brat, four or five hundred for a breeding woman, and up to eight hundred for a strapping worker with some brains. Selsior gives me a full third of the cut."

John stared at him. "No more."

"Oh, that's where you're wrong. It didn't take much snooping. I saw the grave at the church. The headstone holds only one name—Anna's. There's no mention of an infant buried with her. Then I went back to the cottage. There's a cradle there."

John's blood ran cold.

"All I had to do was ask a few questions. Folks think Anna was married to a ship's captain—funny, no one knew who. You're going to deal with me. I get the *Cormorant*. In exchange, I keep my mouth shut, and no one will know that baby is a bast—"

"Enough!" John roared. He stared at his brother with absolute loathing.

"It's your choice. You know it is. He can grow up respectably, or I can make sure everyone knows he's—shall we say—'from the wrong side of the blanket'?"

"You're a wicked, wicked man!" Duncan cried.

"I always thought you were a clever lad." Edward sneered at the lad, then sauntered off.

Duncan couldn't hide his tears. "What are you going to do, Mr. John?"

John knelt and hugged the boy. "I'll have to pray about it."

"Em was wrong."

"What was she wrong about?"

Duncan sniffled and gave John a woebegone look. "She says the devil brings cookies. Edward is evil, but he never brought cookies."

∼∽

John calmed Duncan and left him in the care of the stable master. "Our littlest stable hand had a bad start to the day. Perhaps you could help him turn it around with a nice riding lesson."

"A fine idea!" Mr. Peebles rubbed his hands together.

Duncan looked up at John. "Are you going to go take care of Em and Timmy?"

"Aye, and you can be sure things will work out."

The lad stared at him somberly for a long count, then nodded once. "You never lied to us. Edward did, but you never have."

John lifted him to stand on a bale of hay. He stared him in the eye and pledged, "I'll always tell you the truth. Things are going to change. You don't have to worry. Before I go into the house, do you want to pray with me?"

"All right. Maybe I'd better pray now. You can save your prayer 'til you're with Sis."

Duncan dipped his head and folded his hands. John folded his big hands over Duncan's little ones. They bowed their heads until their foreheads touched.

"Dear God, I know I prayed hard and lots to have You bring Edward back, but I've changed my mind. Please make him go far away forever. Don't let him take our Timmy. Help Mr. John to be strong and brave. And, God, please bless Em and me so we don't have to go back to the way things used to be. Amen."

John squeezed Duncan's hands. For a moment he couldn't speak. Finally, his voice husky, he said, "That was a fine prayer."

As he walked back to the house, John let out a huge sigh. Aye, from the mouth of that little lad had come a prayer that said everything he'd been feeling, too. *Lord, give me wisdom. Guide me to do the right things.*

Inside his home, John followed Goodhew's tip and went to the nursery. Once he reached the doorway, he stopped. Emily had Timothy in one arm and Gracie's son in her other. Her back turned to the door, she was singing a little ditty he'd never heard before, and the lilt in her voice had both babes cooing. She moved with grace as she dipped from one side to the other in time with her song.

The nursery sparkled. So did she. It looked so right with babies in it; she looked so natural holding babies in her arms. Someday he wanted his own children in this nursery. *Our children.* The thought stunned him.

Suddenly he felt like a sailor who'd come home after a long voyage. How had he failed to see what was before him all these days? From his frustrations with her the first day, to his concerns, to his caring—why shouldn't it be a natural step to have come to love her?

Lord, thank You for her. Thank You for taking the blinders off so I could see Your plan for us.

"Emily?"

"Oh!" She startled and wheeled around. "Mr. John! I went down to your study, but you'd left."

"I had a bit of unexpected business. I need to speak with you. Will you walk with me?"

"But the babies—"

"I'm sure most of the staff will volunteer to mind them."

Emily smiled. "Ach, now there's a truth spoken too mildly. I went down to the kitchen, and every last lass there was willing to rob me of my wee ones."

John chuckled. "They're not the only ones. I fancy Goodhew embarrasses himself by neglecting his image in favor of spoiling the babies."

They quickly arranged for the babies to be minded; then John led Emily out of the house. She silently walked alongside him until they reached the crest of the hill. Once there, John looked out at the horizon and smiled. "Fair weather and a sound wind. My ships will make good distance today."

Emily pulled the edges of her shawl closer and huddled in its cover. She averted her gaze to the small stand of trees to their left.

"Are you cold?" John started to unbutton his jacket at once.

"No, no. I'm fine."

His fingers stopped, and he gave her a quizzical look. "What's wrong?"

She hitched her shoulder and remained mute.

He unfastened the last button, shrugged out of his coat, and stepped behind her. The heavy fabric enveloped her. It carried his warmth and scent. John folded his arms high across her shoulders and rested his chin on her head. The weight forced her to rest her chin on his arms. The hold felt strange—companionable, warm, and undemanding, but safe in a way she'd never imagined.

"Look out there," he coaxed in his velvety baritone. "Take a moment to appreciate the beauty. The ocean is one of God's richest masterpieces. It's always there, but never the same." He inhaled deeply, and his vast chest pressed against her back. "The salt tang is invigorating. Aye, 'tis. Just look at how the sunlight skips on the waves to turn them silver and gold. When you feel troubled, walk here, Emily. Gaze out at this, and let it give you peace."

She shuddered in his arms. He eased his hold and turned her around. Brows knit, he studied her. "What is it?"

"The sea gives you peace. For me, 'tisn't the case at all. When I look at it, all I see are countless miles of water, and every last one keeps me from my da and ma. You see the silver and gold because you make your living on the water. I smell the salt of all the tears I've cried in fear and sorrow."

She tried to give him a brave smile and shrug as if those feelings no longer bothered her. Suddenly the weight of his coat almost felt like the pressure of all the burdens she shouldered.

"Aw, Emily," he crooned. His expression softened with compassion. Gently he cradled her jaw in his big hand and studied her in silence.

She wanted to look away. Already he knew far too much about her. Life had denied her any privacy or dignity. The last thing she wanted was for him to sense how lost and alone she felt, but something about his eyes kept her staring up at him.

"I'm sorry, little one. I—"

She pulled away. "No. Oh, no, you needn't be sorry for me. I'm not to be pitied. Duncan and I have each other, and we're doing fine with little Timothy."

"Of course you've done well with Timothy."

"He's a grand man-child—growing bigger by the day."

"Be that as it may, Emily, you're entitled to want something for yourself."

"What with the other wee ones I care for, my days are full, and I want for neither bread nor shelter. Besides—"

"Hush!" He stepped closer and held her shoulders.

She wanted to squirm away from his hold, away from his piercing gaze and the way he made her long for the things she'd missed and could never have. He saw straight through the list of things she'd spouted. Yes, she truly meant she felt grateful for each and every one of them; but John seemed to hone in on the things she lacked, and she couldn't allow him to see the holes in her heart and soul. Most of all, she didn't want him to see the longing in her eyes. What woman wouldn't fall in love with a man like him? *Aye, but I'm ordinary, and he's extraordinary. I'm a fool even to think of this.*

"Emily, have you never longed for what other young women want?"

She tore her gaze from him and stared at his cravat. The laugh she forced sounded hollow, even to her own ears. The question made her ache something awful. Of all the men in the world, why did he have to ask? "What would that be? A child? I've two to rear. Boys, the both of them—and that is always what is most desired."

"What of a husband, a home, and beautiful clothes?"

114

She tilted her head to the side and gathered enough courage to meet his eyes once again. "Men rarely are worth much trouble, if you'll pardon my saying so. The landowner back home split apart all the families under his care without so much as flinching. Da couldn't keep his own children. Even here most of the men go off to sea and leave their wives behind to tend to the wearing realities of life. A good many of the seamen drink away their pay long afore they make it home."

"I can't contest the fact that you've seen more than your share of men who are rascals, Emily. Don't you know any who are decent, hardworking, God-fearing men?"

Only you, John Newcomb, she thought. Instead she tore her gaze from him and stared at the ground. "We both know there's not a man in five counties who'd ever look at me. I'm poor, uneducated, and have two lads he'd have to feed. I gave up dreaming years ago, John Newcomb. Dreams are for fools and children."

"Emily, you're wrong."

"Please don't feel obliged to give me any fancy words or promise I'll turn a corner and find true love. I decided long ago that it all came down to me relying on God to get me through each day. Whether due to intent or circumstance, others will end up letting me down. Edward was a scoundrel; Da couldn't keep us." She shrugged, then cleared her throat. "Aye, I know God will never fail me, so He's where I'm putting my trust."

"Joshua chapter one, verse nine: 'Have not I commanded thee? Be strong and of a good courage; be not afraid, neither be thou dismayed: for the Lord thy God is with thee whithersoever thou goest,' " John quoted softly.

Emily nodded. "Aye, now there you have it. 'Tis a verse I cherish, too. It's seen me through many a hard day, and God is always faithful to be there for me."

"Em, what if a man wanted to be in your life?"

Deep inside she winced at that question. Of all men, why did John Newcomb—the man she loved and could never have—ask her that? He unerringly hit her weak spots in this conversation. Unwilling to let him read any of her thoughts, she turned back to stare at the ocean. "A man who wants to start off his life with the likes of me and the boys? There is no such man, one willing to take on what he'd consider such burdens."

John stepped closer. She shivered ever so slightly beneath his coat. He gently tugged her shawl from beneath the jacket and draped it about her head and shoulders. Emily wasn't sure whether he'd chosen to stand between her and the ocean to arrest her view or block the wind. As his hands brought the edges of the shawl beneath her chin, he nudged her to look up at him.

"They're not burdens, Emily. Though the responsibilities have weighed heavily on you, you've never considered caring for your family a burden."

She smiled at him. "Love lightened the load."

"Emily." He slipped his rough hands up to cup her face, and his voice dropped to a deeper register. "God has given me that same love for you and your little family—I'll gladly take on such precious 'burdens.'"

"And I'm thanking you for having done so. You've been a true blessing."

"No, Em." He rubbed her cheek with his thumb and smiled. "I'm not talking about the little things I did to help you out. I'm talking about the future."

Why was he touching her like this? He'd been a comforting friend in the past, but this—it felt softer, more personal. . .like a caress. Her wits scattered in the wind. Emily stared at his cravat again. "Only God knows the future. The arrangement we have for now is wondrous, though. I do love minding the babes."

"Woman!" He said the word in an odd tone that hinted at both humor and exasperation.

Emily looked up at his face again.

His thumb slid over her lips. "I'm not trying to discuss a business arrangement. I'm asking you to be my wife!"

John watched as Emily's eyes glistened suspiciously. Her lips parted in shock, and the color drained from her face. She bowed her head, and he could see the tips of her russet lashes flutter as she blinked away tears.

"Emily?"

"John, you don't have to do this. Truly you don't."

"I know I don't. I'm asking you to be my wife because it's what I want." She still wouldn't look him in the eye. He sensed her emotional withdrawal and could not bear it. He'd not let go, and he could feel the pulse by her jaw thundering beneath his fingertips.

"You don't owe us a thing. You've been generous, but just because Edward—"

"Edward has nothing to do with this."

"You bear no responsibility, no fault. I'm so sad that you'd do this to try to mend some of his wrongs."

"I'm not."

"You're doing it to protect Timmy then, aren't you? What did your brother try to do?"

John tilted her face up to his. "Emily, this will shelter Timmy, but that's simply a bonus. As for my brother—I've ordered Goodhew to pack all of Edward's possessions. Edward won't be living here, and he's banned from any of my vessels."

"Oh, no! John, I lost my sister—must you lose your brother, too?"

"There is no other way," he said grimly. "No man is beyond the grace or redemption of God. I'll pray for Edward, but until he repents and seeks salvation, he's not welcome here."

"He put great store by the *Cormorant*. Surely he kicked up a mighty fuss over that." Pain streaked across her face. "Now you're proposing. What did he—"

He gave her a tender smile. "As if anything Edward might say matters at all."

"But—"

"Emily, from the first time I saw you, you caught my attention. Duncan charmed me, and I felt compassion for Anna—but you—you were different. Your spirit drew me. I finally came to realize why you've captivated me. I've not married because I never found a woman who I felt would be a suitable partner."

"I'm far from suitable! I'm poor—"

"Shh." He gently pressed his fingers to her lips. "Money can be made and spent, won and lost. Your wealth is superior, Emily. You have a wealth of love to share. Other women have looked at my business with a greedy eye—but they also knew my business forces me to deal with rough, rowdy men. In their presence I have to pretend that part of my life doesn't exist. When I marry, I want a woman who is my life partner—my helpmeet. One who isn't afraid of the rugged side I have."

Emily turned her head to free herself. "Oh, but, John, you're rich as King Midas himself! I'm telling you, that scares me silly. I wouldn't fit in as your wife here in your own house, let alone in society!"

"Love makes things work, and I have a heart full of love for you, Emily." He captured her hands and brought them up to his lips. He kissed the backs of her fingers. "Tell me you care for me. Agree to be my beloved bride."

"I do love you, John Newcomb. I love you straight down to the bottom of my heart. I just didn't imagine God would ever grant that desire because it's so impossible."

"Nothing is impossible with God." He drew her into his arms. "So I aim to make you my bride. I'll give you three days to get ready."

Her breath caught, but he silenced whatever she was about to say with a kiss.

❧

The next day Emily stood in the heavenly bedroom up in the big house. Down the hall she could hear a slight commotion. When she turned to go tend to it, the dressmaker stopped her. "Don't move!"

Cook laughingly instructed, "Clara, go make sure Lily and Mary are handling the babies. And you, Miss Emily, you'd best hold still as can be. Mr. John ordered me to be sure you had a wedding gown worthy of a fairy princess, and I aim to be sure you do."

Emily looked down at the silver-shot white satin skirts and murmured, "Oh, it looks more like an angel than anything. You must have stayed up all night sewing!"

The dressmaker chuckled softly. "I have two workers who helped. Mr. Newcomb is making it more than worth my while, so don't fret. The waist is fine, but the sleeves and hem look a tad long to me."

She marked them with pins, then said, "Let's slip it off you. I'll need to have you decide on what lace you like."

Emily carefully skimmed from the dress and looked down at the frilly petticoats and camisole the seamstress had brought. She sighed. "I've never worn anything so pretty. When you had me put these on, I never imagined the dress could be half as wondrous. Could I just trust you to choose as you see fit?"

The dressmaker beamed. "Of course."

Someone tapped on the door. Cook went to answer it, then turned around. "Miss Emily, you're wanted downstairs at once."

Emily hastily slipped into the fawn-colored dress John liked so much and stepped into her shoes. She pattered down the stairs with more speed than decorum, but John never rushed her, so she figured his summons must be important. Goodhew met her at the foot of the stairs.

"I'm to take you to the study, miss." He did just that, then flashed her a smile and patted her hand as he let go of her arm and opened the door. "I wish you every happiness."

Puzzled, Emily stepped into the study and into John's waiting arms. He embraced her and whispered in her ear, "I have an early wedding gift for you, sweetheart."

Before she could respond, a man said, "Now I've been waitin' far longer for a hug. Best you step aside, young man."

Emily let out a sharp gasp.

Both of her parents stepped out from behind a bookcase. John didn't let go. He swept her into his arms and laughed loudly as he closed the distance in a few hasty steps. "I'll share her."

༄

Emily stood at the back of the church in her beautiful, rustling wedding gown. Her father gave her a kiss and murmured, "He's a good man. He'll keep you happy."

She smiled at her father and nodded. Truer words had not been spoken. Since her parents' arrival, John had told her that the very day he'd learned her parents were still alive, he'd sent one of his own vessels clear across the ocean to fetch them. He'd never mentioned a word of it to her, fearing her parents might not be alive or located. That vessel carried food to be left behind, and John ordered it to be filled with those wishing to come to America. Several other families were celebrating reunions due to his kindness.

The organ began to play. It was time to forge a new family of her own. Emily whispered a quick prayer of thanks and let her father lead her to her beloved.

Chapter 16

Seven years later

"Hurry, Mama."

John swept his six-year-old daughter into his arms and chuckled. "Anna, Mama has her hands full. Be patient."

"The ship is waiting!"

"It's not going anywhere without my say-so," he reassured his daughter. He watched his wife with pride as she threaded her way toward him. They'd become separated in the throng, but that was nothing new. Emily often paused to speak to folks, and they adored her.

"Watch it!" Duncan yanked Timothy and Titus away from the rail. "You know what happens if you fall in!"

John smothered a smile at how both of the youngsters snapped to attention. Emily had planned this whole affair, and the boys knew if they misbehaved, she'd send them back to the house instead of letting them enjoy the picnic. The annual Newcomb Shipping picnic was far too much fun for them to risk banishment.

Emily had started the picnic the year they married, and each subsequent year, it turned into a bigger event. It looked as though half of Virginia had turned out for the ship's christening and picnic today. John watched his wife as she deftly handled the social demands as if they were nothing. God's goodness and love shone through her, and everyone responded. She'd been worried she'd not be able to handle high society, but she was their darling. Still, she'd not changed. The lowliest sailor's wife got the same reception as a debutante.

"Nonny, call Mama and tell her to hurry," Anna insisted. "She's your little girl. She has to 'bey you."

Emily's mother turned and fussed with Anna's hair for a moment. "Now, now, our Anna. Mama's letting folks make a fuss over Baby Phillip. They've not seen him before. Once she comes on up here, everyone's going to be paying attention to you, so he's getting his turn first."

"Papa, boat!" Lily said gleefully as she hung on to her grandfather's lapel.

"Aye, and a fine one she is."

"Who is fine?" Emily asked as John reached for her hand and helped her up the steps.

119

"You are, dear." He smiled at her. "You're magnificent. Ready?"

She nestled a bit closer and rearranged Phillip on her shoulder. "Yes. Everything is perfect."

They exchanged a loving look. They'd discussed names for the ship for months. Only yesterday had they agreed, so John had come down to the dock later that day and painted the name on the vessel himself.

Moments later, after John finished praying aloud and asking a blessing on the new ship, he put a bottle in Anna's little hands and helped her swing it. In a clear, high voice, she declared, "I christen thee the *Contentment*!"

Redeemed Hearts

*To my readers, who share with me in the faith, hopes, and
dreams of real life and still spend time to turn the pages of my books.
God bless you!*

Chapter 1

Virginia, October 1860

A ye, now, you're a beauty, to be sure." Duncan O'Brien reached out and caressed the sleek hull. Sawdust, pine tar, and salty air mingled to add to the sense of rightness. He'd just come back from a voyage and resolutely seen to the usual captain's duties before hastening here. Newcomb Shipping boasted a shipyard all its own. The vessel currently under construction would belong to him.

"We're making good progress," John Newcomb, his much older brother-in-law, commented as he slapped an open palm against a sturdy-looking bulwark.

Duncan moved about the dry dock with ease, sidestepping piles of lumber, ducking when wenched loads swung overhead, and striding up a plank to reach the deck. John followed right behind him.

Duncan looked about and grinned. "You were modest in saying you've made good progress. She's at least a month ahead of schedule!"

"It'll be a few months yet ere she's seaworthy. The framework is sound, and the men tell me the timber is cooperative. Old Kemper declares the last time he had a ship put itself together this easily was when he built it inside a bottle."

"Old Kemper? If he says so, that makes it even more remarkable." Duncan didn't bother to hide his smile. The master shipbuilder had cultivated a reputation for being surly. Indeed he had scowling down to a fine art. In the fifty years he'd been in charge of shipbuilding, Kemper had winnowed through many a carpenter to form the team that strove for perfection. As a result, Newcomb Shipping earned local fame for the vessels they turned out. Duncan reverently traced a joist. "This lady is a work of art."

"You'd be one to recognize that fact." John clapped a hand on Duncan's shoulder. "I doubt any other captain ever spent half as much time with the construction part of the trade."

"I paid my dues." Duncan nodded with mock solemnity. "It cost me half a licorice rope. The day I shared that rope, Old Kemper transformed into the best mentor a landlubber boy ever met."

John's eyes widened. "Is that what softened the crusty old man?"

"You tellin' tales again?" Old Kemper swaggered up. He shook his finger at Duncan. "How am I to command my men effectively if you reveal my weakness?"

123

"You earned their respect. That's all you need." Duncan slipped his hand in his pocket and pulled out a twist of paper. He palmed it to Kemper when they shook hands.

"You're a good man, Duncan O'Brien." Old Kemper made no attempt to conceal his gift. He tugged open an end of the paper, popped one of the dime-sized, chewy, black candy "coins" into his mouth, and twisted the paper shut once again. As he tucked the remainder of the licorice into his vest pocket without offering to share, he added, "And I'm not."

They toured the vessel and inspected every last inch. Afterward the three men headed toward the office. Once they finished reviewing the blueprints, Kemper hobbled off. John knocked his knuckles on the plans that lay across his desk. "You'll need to come up with a name for her soon."

"I seem to recall you didn't determine a name for the *Contentment* until the day before she was christened. I figure the right name will come to me in time."

"Well, well. I see you've truly outgrown your impulsiveness," John teased as he rolled up the plans and secured them in his desk.

"Probably not entirely. The responsibilities of captaining your grand vessels and crews have taught me the wisdom of paying consideration to actions and weighing decisions instead of trying to patch up mistakes. The ocean is apt to claim souls for any errors."

"Anticipating and solving problems in advance is a lesson a man learns more than once." John glanced at the clock in the corner. "Speaking of learning lessons—I know better than to disappoint my wife when she plans a special family supper. The last few evenings, I've had meetings. We'd best get going."

Duncan hefted his duffel bag and accompanied his brother-in-law out of the office. Duncan was a man who straddled two lives. One foot belonged aboard a deck; the other belonged on land where a loving family welcomed him with open arms. He counted himself blessed—a man couldn't hope for more than to be at ease with his family and his calling.

෴

Brigit Murphy heard a giggle. She glanced over her shoulder and gave Trudy a questioning look.

"I tied me pinafore a wee bit tighter." Trudy proceeded to dampen her finger-tips and smooth back a few stray wisps of her ginger-colored hair. "Miss Emily's brother just got home, and I'm wanting to look my best for him."

Brigit shook her head in disbelief. What would make a simple maid like Trudy think a man of distinction might give a fleeting thought to courting her? Such thinking led to pure folly.

Trudy had hired on only a month before her, but she was younger and of a more outgoing nature.

"Trudy, no maid ever keeps a position once her reputation comes under scrutiny," Brigit whispered, "even when 'tisn't her fault. Please—"

Trudy's lips pushed into a spoiled moue. "Oh, your mood's as black as your hair. You wouldn't be such a stick-in-the-mud if you knew Miss Emily was a cleaning woman afore she married Mr. John. What's wrong with a girl like me wishing for the same good luck? Besides, once you see this strapping man, you'll be trying to catch his attention, too. Why, Duncan O'Brien's the most dashing sea captain a lass ever saw!"

"I'm not about to chase after a man. Go on ahead and set your own cap for him."

Trudy waggled her brows. "Not that I'd mind catching the likes of Miss Emily's brother, but what cap?"

Laughter bubbled out of Brigit. The lady of the house didn't make her staff wear caps. In fact, Miss Emily didn't dress her maids in black, either. Shrugging at convention, Miss Emily ran her home in a unique manner. Cornflower blue dresses and rotating work assignments kept the maids a merry bunch. None of the maids held a permanent assignment—Brigit was just as likely to be asked to polish the silver or sweep out a grate as she was to be dusting the master's bed-chamber or minding the children. In fact, in the two weeks Brigit had been employed here, she'd seen Miss Emily don an apron and teach her oldest two daughters how to bake bread!

Taking care to tie her ruffled serving pinafore rather loosely, Brigit hummed appreciatively at the aroma filling the air as Cook opened the oven. Roast beef. Until she'd come to work here, Brigit hadn't tasted roast in at least four years. Another of the Newcombs' quirks was that the staff enjoyed the same entrées as the family. Miss Emily said it made for less work for the cook, but everyone knew better. The staff adored their mistress and took pleasure in telling Brigit from the very first day that Miss Emily had once held a job as a lowly servant and never assumed airs. Clearly she commanded her household by dint of affection, and it ran seamlessly.

Brigit knew the details of running a large mansion. As a landowner's daughter back in Ireland, she'd been reared with the expectation that she'd wed a well-to-do gentleman and manage his home. Mum saw to training her well. Then the famine hit. The blight on the crops rated as a horrible disaster, but Da always subscribed to the revelation of Joseph's dream in the Old Testament and saved for lean times. Year after year things worsened. Farmers left for the New World. Many of the house servants were wives, sisters, and daughters who went along. Brigit and Mum took over the chores.

Never once had they bemoaned the change in circumstances. Saint Paul's words from the fourth chapter of Philippians became the Murphy family's credo:

"For I have learned, in whatsoever state I am, therewith to be content. I know both how to be abased, and I know how to abound: every where and in all things I am instructed both to be full and to be hungry, both to abound and to suffer need. I can do all things through Christ which strengtheneth me." Even now, after they'd come to America and her parents lived in a tenement, Brigit willingly took on the role of a servant. She felt God's presence in her life and counted her blessings. Tonight one of those blessings would be roast beef.

Trudy nudged her. "Just you wait and see. Now that Duncan O'Brien is home, there'll be a parade of eligible girls coming through the door. He usually manages to talk Mr. John into sending him off on a voyage when the ladies start batting their lashes at him." She pinched her cheeks to bring up some color. "It'll be different this time."

Cook started carving the roast and missed Trudy's primping actions. "Aye, that it will," she said. "Trudy, dish up the carrots. Brigit, grab the pitcher of milk." As if she hadn't given the instructions, she continued, "I heard Miss Emily tell Mr. John it's high time she found her brother a wife."

Goodhew, the butler, wagged his finger. "Keep quiet about him for now. Mr. John wanted Duncan's arrival to be a surprise for Miss Emily."

Cook batted away Goodhew's finger and gave him a peck on the cheek. Anywhere else in the house, they conducted themselves according to their station; but in the kitchen, they switched back into a happily married couple. "It won't be much of a surprise. I had Fiona set a place at the table for Duncan."

Goodhew tugged on his coat sleeve. "Miss Emily will be so busy attending the children, she won't notice an extra plate. Mark my word, as long as no one says a thing, she'll be surprised."

Cook picked up her carving knife again. "Be that as it may, the real surprise will be on that young man. If he sets sail again without being pledged to marry, I'll polish every last piece of silver in this house myself."

Trudy and the other maid, Lee, exchanged looks. "Who do you think—"

Brigit took the milk and gladly escaped to the dining room. She didn't want to overhear the gossip. Then again, she did. In an odd way, everyone on the Newcomb estate was like a family. Oh, to be sure, she knew it wasn't anything close to the truth—but the kindhearted close-knit group of servants had made her feel welcome at once. Aye, and Miss Emily never once said a harsh word. More telling still—Miss Emily herself usually minded the children, but if she was busy, she directed Brigit to look after the lasses. The Lord's way of providing this position for her couldn't be clearer. A few tales wouldn't be harmful, but Brigit didn't want to risk stepping over the line and jeopardizing her job.

"Dinner is served," Brigit overheard Goodhew say. She quickly finished pouring a glass of milk, then scooted to the side and kept her back to the wall.

She'd learned the Newcomb tribe didn't waste time reaching the table. At eleven, Titus had the gangly legs of a pony. He galloped in ahead of six-year-old Phillip. Both had their mother's bright red hair. The five-year-old twins bumped into each other as they spilled through the doorway. June shrieked, and Julie giggled. They scrambled into their seats while Anna Kathleen and Lily tried to make more ladylike appearances. At thirteen and ten, they'd both just been warned to act less like hooligans, or their father threatened to cut off their lovely dark brown curls so they'd look like boys. Timothy came in, somber as a priest. At fourteen, he seemed far older than his years. Miss Emily smoothly swiped the book he carried and set it on the buffet before Goodhew seated her. Mr. John came in and gave her a kiss on the cheek, then took his own seat.

"I'm so glad you made it to supper tonight," Miss Emily said, smiling at her husband.

"Are you glad I made it to supper, too?" a deep voice asked from the doorway.

Miss Emily let out a cry of delight, popped up, and dashed over to the tall young man. His auburn curls picked up the lamplight and looked like polished copper. Laughter shone in his bright blue eyes. He lifted Emily and swung her around, then set her down and gave her a kiss on the cheek. "That makes it official. I'm home."

As he dragged another chair over to the table, Duncan started teasing the children. "I have things in my duffel bag, but only for kids who eat their vegetables."

Trudy brought in the carrots, Cook delivered the roast, and the other two maids followed in their wake with a basket of hot rolls and braised potatoes. Brigit filled the rest of the children's glasses and turned to leave, but the stranger halted her motion by resting his large, rough hand on her wrist. Startlingly blue eyes twinkled at her.

Duncan wore the smile of a rascal. "Don't I get any milk?"

Is he teasing me? She pasted on an uncertain smile. "If you're wanting some, sir."

"Aye. Some say 'tis a drink for the young, but it suits me just fine."

As she reached for his glass, Brigit wondered why he drank milk, of all things. It must not be an unusual thing after all, because when Fiona had set Duncan O'Brien's place at the table, she'd provided him with a glass as well as a coffee cup.

"Brigit," Miss Emily said merrily, "that's my little brother, Duncan, back from a voyage. He's a bit of a scamp and a tease at times, but he truly does like milk."

Duncan's brows lifted. "Little brother? Emily, you may be older, but you're the minnow in the family net."

While everyone at the table chattered, Brigit poured milk for the handsome sea captain and scurried back into the kitchen.

Trudy stood in the middle of the kitchen with her hands theatrically clasped over her heart. "Oh, just the sight of him makes me heart flutter. That man can sweep me off me feet any day."

Unaccustomed to the familiarity the staff displayed toward the family, Brigit busied herself with washing some pots and pans. Lee grabbed a dish towel and started drying. Cook came over and slipped another pan into the sink and let out a sigh. "You lasses keep an eye on Trudy. She wouldn't know proper conduct if she tripped on it, and she's liable to make a ninny of herself over Duncan."

"She wouldn't be the first woman ever to do that," Lee whispered.

"No, she wouldn't, but the others have stood a faint chance of actually qualifying as wife material. They all hailed from good families—not from the servants' quarters."

Brigit didn't marvel that women were attracted to Duncan's fine looks and rakish smile. Aye, and he'd be a good provider, too. He'd be a fine fellow for a lass to contemplate marrying, but any man who captained a vessel wouldn't be the type to sit back and let others do his matchmaking.

Miss Emily qualified as a force with which to be reckoned, and she had her mind set to play Cupid. If Duncan were half as adamant to remain single, things would be downright entertaining around the Newcomb estate.

Trudy primped in front of the tiny mirror over the washstand. "I mightn't be a ravishing beauty, but plenty a man's told me I'm fair pretty. Me mum always said, 'All's fair in love and war.' "

Lee snorted. "You'd best count on war, not love, Trudy."

Cook propped her hands on her ample hips and scowled. "You'll not be dallying with Duncan, do you hear me? It's not proper, and this is a proper home. Miss Emily's determined to marry her brother off to a nice young lady, and he deserves more than a servant who can't read her own name."

Brigit nodded her agreement. God was no respecter of persons, but man surely was. Common sense dictated a man of Duncan O'Brien's station wed a woman whose abilities allowed her to be his helpmeet. Servants were servants, even in America. Brigit Murphy expected no prince to sweep her anywhere. She grabbed the broom and set to work. The only thing getting swept around her was the floor.

Chapter 2

I 'll likely be here for three weeks, if you can stand me," Duncan answered his sister's query. "I need to see about several of the details on the ship."

"Which ship?" June asked.

"The ship he's building with Old Kemper," Titus scoffed. "Everyone knows the ship that's most important to a man is the one he calls his own."

Duncan shook his head. "Nae, lad. The most important ship to a man is the one he's captaining at any given moment. He's responsible for all souls on board, whether or not the papers say the vessel belongs to him."

John stared at Timothy, Titus, and Phillip. "You boys heed your uncle Duncan's words. That sense of responsibility and duty is why he's the youngest captain in my fleet."

"Dad, I want to go on a voyage," Timothy declared. "It's well past time."

"Me, too," Titus chimed in. "Uncle Duncan was going to sea by the time he was eleven."

Duncan gave the boys a long, hard look. " 'Twas a different time and different circumstances." He didn't enlarge on the particulars. The family took care not to make references to the period surrounding Timothy's birth. Duncan had been a wee lad, but he'd had to grow up fast. With Emily working all hours to provide for them, he'd tried to help his dying sister, Anna, with her baby son until John rescued them all.

A faint red crept from Timothy's neck up to his hairline. Though his nephew never said a word about it, Duncan knew he was sensitive about the fact that his mother's marriage to John's brother, Edward, had been a sham and that his own birth had eventually cost his mother her life.

Duncan cleared his throat and winked. "I've been talking to your father." He glanced at John. John was really Timothy's uncle, but for the sake of ease and love, he and Emily called themselves his parents. "I've tried to convince him to let the both of you go out with me on a voyage."

"Hurrah!" Tim and Titus both straightened up.

"Hold on for a moment," Emily cut in.

Duncan caught on that John hadn't spoken with Emily yet. "Oops. It seems I've let the cat out of the bag too soon. Now, our Em, surely you can see for yourself that these fine sons of yours are growing—"

"What I can see is that my brother and my husband are trying to pull the wool over my eyes." She gave him a stern look. "Not another word out of you, Duncan O'Brien, if you value your life."

"Em—"

"I said, not another word!"

He couldn't hide his grin as he gave a dramatic sigh, then muttered, "I was just going to ask for the salt."

John took up the cudgels. "How are you boys doing with your lessons?"

"I'm a full year ahead in my studies," Timothy declared. "And I've mastered every knot you and Duncan taught me."

"Me, too!" Titus wasn't about to be left out.

Duncan hid a smile behind the rim of his cup. Titus made up for his lack of size with an abundance of spunk. Emily would have a conniption if she knew he'd let both of the boys climb up the mast of the *Cormorant* the last time he was in dock; but his nephews had salt water flowing in their veins, and it did them good to use their muscles every bit as much as they used their brains.

"So you have me slated to go to the Boott Mills in Massachusetts this next trip?" Duncan gave John a conspiratorial look.

"Aye, that I do. Aunt Mildred lives up there."

"I'd like to visit her," Anna Kathleen declared.

Emily set her knife and fork on her plate. Her eyes glittered dangerously. "I'll not be badgered into any decision. Anna Kathleen, you're too young to travel alone; and, no, Lily, you going along would not make it any better. Tim and Titus, stop elbowing one another. You'll be black-and-blue by the time supper's over. I've a good three weeks to watch your behavior, and I'll take every last day of them before I make up my mind whether or not to let you go. Don't any of you dare try to bully me into anything. I'll not stand for it."

After supper was over, Emily dismissed the children from the table. Duncan and John remained behind with her to enjoy a cup of after-dinner coffee. Emily's eyes took on an appraising light, and Duncan felt the hair on the back of his neck prickle.

"So you'll be twenty-one in a few months."

"Aye, Em. We all know that."

"Yes, well, I'm assessing facts, as I said. I'm thinkin' it's well past time for you to find a pretty little wi—"

"Cast that thought aside!" Duncan's coffee cup thumped down on the table. "I've many a year left of bachelorhood."

"You'd do well with a woman to settle you."

"The only thing unsettling me is this crazy notion of yours. Em, don't try to play Cupid for me. When I'm good and ready, I'll find my own wife—and not a day before."

"There's no harm in my making introductions." Emily took a sip and gave him a pointed look over the brim of her cup. "You'll never find a sweetheart when you spend all your time at the docks or at sea, so I'm going to help out a bit."

Duncan rose and shook his head. "John, talk some sense into her."

To Duncan's dismay, John reached over and held his wife's hand. "Emily's always carried a full cargo of common sense."

"You'd best check the manifest and take inventory." Duncan tapped his head as he went out the door. "She's got a couple of empty crates in the upper cabin."

Brigit sat in the balcony of the church and kept her attention on the preacher. The yawn she hid behind her hand didn't reflect on his message—the blame ought to land directly on Trudy's shoulders. She'd been unable to sleep last night, so she'd come into Brigit's attic bedroom and mooned over the dashing young sea captain.

Brigit had spent more than half the night trying to talk some reason into her flighty friend. Her admonishments went in one ear and out the other. Trudy showed up for church this morning with an elaborate hairstyle she vowed would earn her Duncan's attention. Instead, Duncan sat with his family down below in the sanctuary, completely oblivious to the fact that he'd been the inspiration for such a creation. Then again, Trudy didn't suffer from his inattention. She'd fallen asleep.

The Newcomb household ran with flawless precision, thanks to Goodhew's discipline. Five minutes after the benediction, the servants took a carriage back to the mansion so they could put out changes of clothing for the children and have a meal ready to set on the table. Because she'd been assigned to travel with the children today, Brigit didn't go along with the rest of the staff.

She stood to the side of the children's carriage and minded June and Julie while Anna Kathleen and Lily took their places across from Titus and Phillip. Normally one of the maids and the younger children took one carriage while Mr. John and Miss Emily took Timothy and Anna Kathleen with them in the other. Today they'd been supplanted by Duncan—which might have been tolerable—but now Mr. John gallantly assisted a young woman into the carriage who settled into the space Timothy or Anna might have occupied. The young woman graced Mr. John with a thankful nod, then turned a dazzling smile on Duncan and patted the seat next to her.

Brigit ignored Timothy and Anna's mutinous expressions and let go of Julie's hand so the groom could lift the child into the wagon. June didn't wait—she scrambled up unassisted. A tangle of too many arms and legs filled the carriage, and Brigit had yet to take a seat. Just as she daintily lifted her hem, a deep voice from behind her said, "Hold now. This cannot be."

"Unca Duncan, ride with us!" Phillip's face lit up.

Duncan chortled. "This vessel appears to have plenty of bulk, but no ballast. I'm going to have to trim the load a bit. Phillip, dive over to me. Lily, be a good girl and come here. You can each ride with us in the other carriage."

"This isn't fair," Anna Kathleen protested.

Duncan gave Phillip and Lily a gentle push toward the other conveyance, then rested his forearms on the edge of the carriage. "No, 'tisn't. Many's the time you'll do what's required of you rather than what you want. Fair is nothing more than a child's justice or a weather prediction."

Brigit found his words quite true, and he spoke them with both certainty and a tinge of humor. She waited for him to move to the side. As he did, he took her hand and helped her into the carriage with all of the care and polish he would employ with a high-society lass. Aye, he was a gentleman through and through.

❦

Duncan strode back and took a seat beside Phillip. He gave brief consideration to holding his nephew on his lap since Miss Prudence Carston's extravagant hoops took up an inordinate amount of space. Miss Carston pasted on a smile and batted her lashes, but Duncan could tell she found no delight at a lad sitting between them. Manners forced her to feign amusement, but the young woman's lack of sincerity registered as plainly as a loudly luffing sail.

He'd told Emily not to try her hand at matchmaking, and this opening salvo had best also be the final one.

Phillip's nose twitched. "You smell like flowers."

Miss Carston preened. It might well take her half of eternity if she fluffed all the ruffles on her dress. "Roses. I always wear roses. I think they go well with my favorite color."

"I like pink, too," Lily said in an awestruck tone.

"Aren't you fortunate you inherited your papa's dark hair then? Redheaded women simply cannot wear pink." Miss Carston turned to Duncan. She artfully brushed a few tendrils by the brim of her hat. The hat looked remarkably like a pink iced cake, and her lace-gloved hand resembled a fussy tatted doily. The whole while, she studied his hair. "I hope you won't consider me too forward to say your jacket looks quite dashing with your auburn hair."

Forward? Aye, that she was. And insipid as could be. Men didn't take into account such trifling matters; furthermore, every last man in the congregation wore a black coat! This paragon of pink might well have Emily's approval, but she left Duncan as cold as a mackerel at midnight. As soon as they finished luncheon, he'd concoct a polite reason to slip away—if he survived that long.

John helped Emily into the carriage and took his place, then drove toward home. Emily tried to spark a conversation, and Miss Carston plunged in with notable enthusiasm. Duncan held his tongue. He didn't want to be a surly beast, but the last thing he needed was for social nicety to be mistaken for interest. He refused to lead a woman into hoping for church bells when the only chime he heard was freedom's ring.

Once home, Duncan assisted Emily's candidate out of the carriage. Little Phillip didn't appreciate the finer points of conduct and let out a whoop as he jumped onto Duncan's back. "Gimme a piggyback ride into the house, Unca Duncan!"

"Sure, little man." Duncan grinned at the young lady, who managed to quickly hide her look of shock. "We're an informal bunch at home, Miss Carston."

"How lovely. Far be it from me to spoil such leisurely comfort with formality. Please do call me Prudence."

While Emily and Brigit shepherded the children upstairs to change before lunch, Duncan suffered the necessary indignity of entertaining Emily's guest. She laced her hand into the crook of his arm and glided alongside him into the large parlor. Inspiration struck. He tilted his head toward the piano. "Do you play?"

"Modestly." The humble response might have come across more sincerely if she hadn't let loose of him and hastened to the bench. After limbering her fingers with a few scales, she folded her hands in her lap. "Oh. It's Sunday."

"Yes, it is."

"Papa allows only hymns on Sunday. He says on the Lord's Day we ought only play and sing unto the Almighty."

"I can respect that." Duncan wondered why that presented a problem. "Why don't you play a hymn?"

A faint blush filled her cheeks. "I don't see a hymnal. Everyone else is able to play from memory, but I can't seem to recall the particulars of any piece myself."

"Anna and Lily both take lessons. I'm sure there must be music in the bench." The minute he made that offer, Duncan knew he'd said the wrong thing. Prudence's face turned an unbecoming color, and her eyes flashed.

"I said I played modestly well. I'm not a novice." The words barely left her mouth, and she teared up. "Oh, I'm so sorry. How dreadfully rude of me. You didn't mean any insult, I'm sure."

Unmoved by her emotional show, Duncan continued to prop his elbow on the piano and gave her a bland look. Prudence managed to display a wide range of coy tricks. She tried charm, meekness, tolerance, friendliness, humility, temper, and tears. If he didn't miss his guess, ploys for sympathy and something to induce obligation or guilt weren't far behind. Tedious. The whole matter bored him to distraction. Instead of hastening to reassure her she'd not spoken amiss, he glanced down at the ivory keys.

"Anna's impetuous, but it puts fire behind her playing. As for Lily—she shows talent far beyond her age."

"How nice." Prudence dabbed at her cheeks with a lacy hanky, then looked up at him through her lashes. "Do you play?"

"Very badly."

"But you do so many other things well. Why, everyone knows you're the youngest captain around, and soon you'll even own your own boat!"

Boat. He inwardly winced. Calling his grand ship a boat would be like labeling Notre Dame a chapel.

⁓

"We'll walk downstairs like ladies," Brigit said to the Newcomb girls. Anna lifted her head and drew back her shoulders a shade; then Brigit nodded her approval. "Very nice. June and Julie, walk—don't bounce."

Lily clutched Brigit's hand. "It's not bad manners, is it—that I'm wearing pink, too?"

"Not at all. You look very pretty." All the girls were eager to get downstairs and be with Duncan and his guest, so it hadn't taken them long to change. Most children ate Sunday dinner in their church clothes, but Miss Emily wouldn't hear of it. She insisted best clothing ought to stay nice; and after watching the twins' predilection for spilling food, Brigit understood why. As soon as she installed the girls in the parlor, she'd go tie on an apron and help Cook serve the ham.

When they reached the entryway, Brigit could see over the girls' heads. Miss Prudence Carston looked as happy as a bee in honeysuckle; Duncan looked as if he'd just been stung. As soon as he heard the girls, he spun around and beckoned. "I just boasted to Miss Carston about your talent on the piano. Come play a tune for her."

Miss Carston stood and promptly sidled up to him. "Yes, darlings. Come play for us. We'd love to hear you."

Customarily, Julie and June would romp outside for a short while; but since Brigit could hear Mr. and Mrs. Newcomb approaching, and they had a luncheon guest, she knew the girls should remain inside. Brigit turned away and slipped into the kitchen. As she tied on her apron, she looked about to determine where her help was most needed.

"Have you ever seen a better ham?" Cook beamed at the platter she held.

"Virginia ham," Brigit said in an appreciative tone as she dodged Lee, who carried a pan of scalloped potatoes.

Trudy dumped green beans into a bowl and scowled. "Killing the fatted calf for Miss Pink-and-Pretty."

"It's pork, not beef," Cook snapped.

"Miss Carston comes from good family," Goodhew added. "I'll go summon them to the table."

Assigned to pour milk again, Brigit filled the children's cups as the family came into the room. She stood back by the buffet as Mr. John said the prayer; then she slipped quietly to Miss Carston's side. "Sweet tea or milk, miss?"

"Sweet tea, of course." She turned to Duncan. "I declare, just because I'm petite, people treat me as if I'm a child."

Brigit silently filled her glass and proceeded on to the next seat. Duncan smiled at her. "I'll have my usual, Brigit."

As she poured milk for him, Brigit heard Miss Carston's muffled gasp. That gasp then turned into a twitter of a laugh. "Oh, Duncan, aren't you a tease!"

Brigit admired Duncan for his tolerance. What man would appreciate his sister's blatant attempt at matchmaking? Miss Emily and Mr. John both cast appeasing looks at Duncan, but the young Miss Carston chattered on, and Brigit headed for the blessed escape of the kitchen. She strongly suspected Duncan would like to do the same thing.

◆

Three days later Duncan rushed into the library and shut the door behind him. He leaned his head against the door for a moment, then pushed away. He'd appeal to John to talk to Emily. Emily wasn't listening to a word Duncan said, and this simply could not continue. He'd been stuck with Pink Prudence after church on Sunday, then come home last night to supper with Adele-the-Able-Minded, who discussed the Lincoln-Douglas debates with far more passion than almost any man he'd heard. Now Emily had both of those girls and a few more in the parlor for tea.

He'd ducked in here, hoping to find his way to freedom. The seldom-used door to the garden promised a route of escape—except for the fact that the pretty new raven-haired maid stood over by that very wall, polishing the windows. She glanced at him, then concentrated on her work.

Good. She hadn't spoken. Knowing his luck, Duncan figured Emily might overhear Brigit and come to investigate. Duncan strode toward the exit with all of the resolve of a man swimming toward the only remaining hatch so he could escape a sinking vessel. As he approached, Brigit opened the windowed doors and concentrated on a small streak in one corner. He could see the amusement in her eyes.

The doorknob to the library rattled. He'd never make it through the door and out of sight. Quick as could be, Duncan shot between two bookcases. He gave Brigit a conspiratorial grin, then held a finger to his lips in a silent plea.

"Oh, that brother of mine." Emily sighed from across the room. "He was supposed to come home about now. I thought I heard him come in the front door, but he managed to give me the slip. Did he dash out to the garden?"

"No, Miss Emily."

"This would be so much easier if he'd just cooperate."

Brigit smiled, but Duncan appreciated how she said nothing. Now there was a fine woman. She knew when to hold her tongue, didn't lie, and understood a man needed to tend to his own business without interference.

"The windows are impeccable. You've done wonders in this room. Why don't you treat yourself to a book and read for a while?"

"Why, thank you, Miss Emily!"

Duncan felt a jolt of pleasure. She could read! A great portion of the Irish immigrants were illiterate. So many of the men on his vessels struggled over that very issue. Had he not been so very fortunate with the opportunities afforded him, he'd never have made it this far. Others who weren't so blessed would be stuck without choices if they couldn't read and write. Duncan offered a lesson each day on dock or at sea, and nearly half of his seamen participated.

The door clicked shut, and he waited a moment as he heard his sister cross back to the parlor. "Thank you," he said very softly.

The maid bit her lip, but her shoulders shook a few times, giving her away. Merriment shone in her eyes. "I'll not tell lies for ye."

"I'd not ask you to." He looked at the bookcases all around. The library held an extensive selection, one he considered the greatest material wealth of the home. "What book will you choose?"

She wiped her hands on her apron hem as she looked at the shelves. Anticipation lit her features, adding intriguing depth to her beauty. "I once read *The Last of the Mohicans* by James Fenimore Cooper. Have you any of his other works?"

"*The Prairie* is in here somewhere. I also liked *The Pioneers*." His eyes narrowed as he forced himself to turn and scan the spines. "The fact books are on the side closest to the fireplace. John keeps the fiction books shelved over here. Once upon a time things were alphabetical, but the kids tend to shove the books back in odd spots. I seem to recall that particular set by Cooper was bound in red leather."

Brigit smiled. "Now that'll cut my search down a wee bit, what with the blue, black, and brown covers all ruled out."

"And the green. Don't forget the green."

"Why couldn't it have been pink? That would have been so easy. There are but a handful of those—"

"Pink?" He shuddered. "Spare me. My current association with that hue is less than pleasant."

Brigit dipped her head and started to collect her rags and bucket. The haste with which she acted tickled him. "You've no right to be entertained at my expense, Miss Brigit," Duncan scolded playfully. "I deserve your compassion and pity. If my sister has her way, my single days are sinking as rapidly as a scuttled brigantine with too much ballast."

"So marriage is nothing more than a watery grave?"

He winced. "I'm not ready to get sucked into that whirlpool yet, and when I do, 'twill most assuredly be with the mermaid of my choice—not with Prudence-the-Pink."

"Prudence-the-Pink?" she echoed, her tone carrying an appealing lilt.

Oh, this new maid was a fun-hearted lass—smart as a whip and pretty as a china doll. Duncan chanced a glance toward the door when he heard footsteps and made sure no one was entering. He winked at Brigit and wiped his forehead in a gesture of relief. "Whew. Thought my days were numbered for the second time in a mere hour."

"You've had several more frightening escapades at sea, I'm sure."

"Not at all. There, I'm in charge and rely on God. Here, I'm at Emily's mercy—and I fear she has none at all. She's a single-minded woman. Once she sets a course, gale-force winds won't stop her."

"Aye, she's a woman of great will and heart."

Just then the faint sounds of a few piano chords sounded, and a screech-toned soprano started to butcher "Rejoice, Rejoice, Believers." Duncan rubbed his temple. "Talk about gales—there you have it! That's an ill wind that blows nobody good."

The lyrics served to underscore just how pathetic the situation had become: "The Bridegroom is arising." The soprano proved him right by hitting a combination of shrill notes that sounded just like the bo'sun's cat when a drunken sailor dunked him in the water barrel.

Brigit left the library with her rags and bucket. The sweet sound of laughter she diplomatically squelched before she exited was far more pleasing to his ear.

Chapter 3

"D uncan! You're whistling 'Rejoice, Rejoice, Believers.'" Miss Emily might
well have boiled tea in a pot with the heated look she gave Duncan as he
strode into the dining room.

"Why, yes, I am. It's a fine hymn."

Brigit slowly set a basket of rolls on the table and straightened the center-
piece. Truth be told, she didn't want to rush back into the kitchen. A bit of enter-
tainment was brewing, and she wasn't above wanting to watch it unfold. Duncan
O'Brien's inadvertent slip was landing him in deep trouble.

Brigit felt an odd kinship with him at that moment, though. All afternoon
the same tune had nearly driven her daft. Ever since Miss Emily's guest sang that
hymn in the parlor while Duncan was making his getaway, Brigit couldn't erase
the song from her mind. She'd hummed it, dusted to it, and tapped her fingers in
the cadence along the spines of the books in the library until she found the ones
Duncan had recommended. Now that selfsame song rushed back and netted him.

Emily crossed her arms and tapped her foot impatiently. "Well?"

*Miss Emily's shrewd to catch him on that, and he'll not be able to get himself out
of this hot water. Boiled Duncan O'Brien for supper.*

"All right." Duncan let out a longsuffering sigh. "I'm sorry, Em. It was wrong
of me."

"It most certainly was."

Duncan wore the lopsided smile of a charmer whose true repentance was more
for saying the apology than for committing the sin. "I shouldn't have done it."

"No, you shouldn't," Emily scolded, but her expression softened.

Duncan turned to Timothy, Titus, and Phillip. He gave them a sober look.
"Let that be a lesson to you." He paused for a split second, then added, "It is rude
to whistle in the house."

Miss Emily let out a squawk. "Duncan, don't you dare try to hoodwink me!
You'll tell me why you were whistling that tune here and now."

Brigit headed for the door to the kitchen before her merriment became
evident.

"Mama, Brigit was singing it all afternoon," Anna said. "Uncle Duncan must
have heard her when he got home."

"Oh, dear." As Brigit turned to the side so she could shoulder the swinging

138

door, she saw color suffuse Miss Emily's face. "Here I was, sure you must've come home and heard Antonia Whalen singing that very song. I'm so sorry, Duncan."

"Talk about sorry," Titus grumbled. "Miss Whalen massacred that song so bad I had to stick my fingers in my ears."

"Yeah. God will have to 'store our hearing after that terr'ble noise," Phillip chimed in.

"That's enough," Emily chided.

Brigit had to bite the inside of her cheek until the door shut and afforded her the safety of the kitchen. She'd heard Miss Whalen's singing, and it'd been more than enough!

Cook fussed over a tray on the table. "Miss Emily may well want to marry off that brother of hers, and I'd be happy as a clam at high tide to bake up a wondrous bridal cake; but will you look at this? Baked my poor fingers to the bone so Miss Emily'd have fine things for them young ladies when they was here this afternoon. We want to entice those young ladies to come visit more often. I put together nice things, and they didn't appreciate the fancy tea I set out one bit."

Lee popped a few crumbs from a piece of chocolate cake into her mouth. "I'd come calling if I'd be served such wondrous fare!"

Less than mollified, Cook grumbled, "Miss Prudence wouldn't eat a bite—and I know it's because she had that corset tied so tight. Miss Adele couldn't very well taste anything because she wouldn't stop yammering over why Mr. Douglas ought to be the next president of these United States."

"She's very well read," Brigit said.

"Reading is fine, but the woman is strident. The Newcomb family table has always been cheerful, and Miss Adele's grating ways would give everyone indigestion." Cook surveyed the kitchen with indignation. "I said I thought Miss Emily's plan to marry off Duncan had merit, but she'd best find better bridal candidates."

Trudy lifted her chin and tapped the center of her chest. "Miss Emily has the right bride here under her verra nose. Serving tea to those rich lasses today near turned me stomach. The Waverly sisters didn't think anyone would notice, but betwixt the pair of them they ate half a raspberry torte."

Cook wagged her head from side to side in a sorrowful manner. "If that wasn't enough, I had to mix up some warm lemonade for Miss Antonia after she strained her throat with that song. Lemons this time of year."

Lee wiped off the counter. "Good thing Mr. John provides well for his family. Couldn't've bought a lemon otherwise."

Antonia. Antonia the atonal. Brigit drew in a quick breath. *Lord, that wasn't kind of me at all. I'm sorry.*

"Stop fussing like an old hen. You've gracious plenty on that tray for everyone to have the dessert of their choice now," Goodhew chided in an affectionate tone. "*They'll* all appreciate your food."

Goodhew said no more. As a butler, he embodied self-control and tact. Then again, he'd mastered the ability to speak great truths with nothing more than a silent twitch of his brow. Though Brigit had been in service here for a slim month, she knew the wry allusion he'd just uttered was out of character. The insult to his wife's cooking exceeded his tolerance; and though he'd served the young ladies with civility, his approval didn't lie with any of them.

I hope Miss Emily has someone better up her sleeve. Brigit pumped water into the sink. *Then again, for Duncan's sake, perhaps I should hope she doesn't.*

꿍

"Taking some night air, Brigit?" Duncan smiled as he walked through the garden. With moonbeams catching wisps of her inky hair and making them go silver, it reminded him of a sprinkling of stars across a dark night sky. This woman made for a bonny sight.

"A fine night 'tis."

"Aye." He stopped by the bench she sat upon and lifted the book beside her. "Now what have we here?" He tilted it until the moon illuminated the spine, but the golden lettering didn't show up well enough for him to be sure of the title. A flick of his fingers opened the cover, and he read from the title page, "*The Pioneers.* So you found it."

"I did."

"I want to thank you for sparing my dignity this afternoon. No grown man wants to be caught escaping from his home because his sister is populating it with bridal prospects."

" 'Tisn't any of my affair." She daintily folded her hands in her lap and looked at them. "You needn't say anything more."

"*Saying* wasn't the problem in the dining room; *whistling* was." His humor must have struck a note with her. She glanced up and smiled.

"Now that you're wise to Miss Emily's plans, I'm sure you'll either find she has a suitable bride among the lot she's chosen, or you'll manage to keep free from the parson's trap until you can shove off to sea again."

"No doubt it's the latter. As I told you in the library, I'm not about to surrender to the war Emily is waging."

"Americans speak of war quite often."

"How long have you been here?"

She shrugged diffidently. "Long enough to know there's unrest in the nation, but there's serenity in the Newcomb home." A stricken expression crossed her face, and she popped to her feet. "Oh, I'm begging your pardon. I had no place, saying such a thing about your—"

"Think nothing of it." Duncan stayed where he stood, blocking her exit. "You complimented John and Emily. I happen to agree."

"Please excuse me." She took the book from him and scurried into the house.

Duncan watched her go. When he turned back, he spied her shawl. It had slipped off the bench and lay in a pool of—*cashmere*? He picked it up and fingered the fine fabric. What was a maid doing with such a pricey piece of goods?

"Duncan—I wondered where you went." Timothy strode toward him.

Duncan dropped the soft, pale yellow shawl on the bench. "Did you want me for something?"

"Yeah." A smirk tilted Tim's mouth. They fell in step and walked around a hedge, out of view from the house. Tim lowered his voice. "Mother is in rare form. She's bound and determined to stick you with a wife."

"So I noticed."

"Well, I thought you'd like to know she told Lily to gather flowers tomorrow morning so she and Anna could make arrangements for the parlor and dining room, and she asked Cook to make her Seafood Newburg."

Duncan stopped in his tracks. "Flowers are normal enough—but Seafood Newburg? Emily's escalating her schemes. Who's the next bridal prospect in her petticoat parade?"

"Opal Ferguson." Timothy toed a small rock. It skittered along and stopped at the edge of the path. "She seemed to have designs on Sean Kingsley, but he and Caroline eloped two weeks ago. Between Opal and her determined mama, you're going to be hard-pressed to slip out of the marriage noose."

Duncan groaned. "I thought we'd already scraped the bottom of the barrel. I've conversed with the abysmally misnamed Prudence. Adele actually drew a map in her mashed potatoes to demonstrate what portion of the States she estimates will revolt if Lincoln is elected. Antonia would break every glass in the house with that voice of hers. But Opal?" He grimaced. "I thought Emily loved me."

His nephew chortled. "She does. I overheard her telling Father a wife would settle you down."

"I'd sooner lash logs to a bathtub and row it across the Atlantic than be settled with Opal Ferguson."

"Opal generally gets whatever she wants." Tim shot him a pained look. "And she wants to be your wife."

"A spoiled henwit isn't to my liking. She cannot read or cipher any better than the twins. I'd never be able to go to sea and trust our home to her care."

His nephew poked him in the ribs. "You could take her to sea with you."

"I thought you felt a need to bite some salt air."

"Hey!" Tim gave him an outraged look. "Are you saying you won't take me if I don't help you evade the girls?"

"No, I'm saying nothing of the kind." Duncan wrapped his arm around his nephew and gave him a manly squeeze as he started to saunter along. "Though if I wed, according to family tradition, I'd be expected to take my bride on my next voyage—not my nephews. Any of Emily's prospects would cause me to jump overboard."

Timothy laughed.

"You, on the other hand—you'll be an asset. Aye, and I'm looking forward to having you help me teach some of the crew. The pity is, several of the immigrants who hire on can barely sign their names."

"I'd be glad to help, but I'm no schoolmaster or tutor, Duncan. I want to learn the ropes just as you did."

Duncan stopped and gave the teen a solid pair of pats on his shoulder, then broke contact. "Ignorance lives in us all, Tim. It's just that we all have areas where we shine. A man's dignity is important. You'll trade them your book learning for their seafaring wisdom."

"Are you saying I'm going out this next voyage?"

"Emily will have her final say, but I'm planning on it—unless she shackles me with a bride." He twisted his features into an expression of distaste. "Sure as the sun rises, it won't be Opal. Once I heard Sean married, I feared I'd be her next target."

"Why is that? Because Opal's mama is so scheming?"

"I refuse to delude myself, Tim." Duncan stared out at the horizon from the hilltop of the estate. Moonlight danced on the waves until the ocean blended with the night sky. "I'm of marginal class. I'm a full-blooded Irish immigrant, and every last one of these lasses—especially Opal—would turn up her nose if I didn't have a ship to my name."

He paused, then continued. "I'm accepted in society because of John's marriage to my sister, and it's known I'll provide well for my bride; but truth is, I'll not be tied to a woman who believes she lowered herself when she wed me. If 'tis my family connections and money that draw her, 'twill be a miserable marriage."

"And you think I'll be any better off?" Tim jammed his fists in his pockets and paced back and forth. "My real father didn't even marry my mother—"

Duncan listened to his nephew. Tim rarely said a word about his birth, so he needed to blow off some steam. Taking him to sea would be wise. He'd always been a somber child, and his feelings ran deep. As he stretched into his manhood, he would need self-confidence to counterbalance his true father's betrayal.

"It's proud of you, I am." Duncan stuck those words in before Tim could catch his breath and continue. Duncan had learned long ago that Tim rarely spoke his heart; and if he completely emptied it, he'd retreat in embarrassment. By listening to his nephew, then cutting the flow as it started to trickle down,

Duncan knew he would help the lad save face.

"Proud?" Tim gave him a stunned look.

"Aye. You're wise beyond your years. Many a man goes to his grave believing his worth is what others assigned to him. God gave His Son to ransom you—and that is your true value. Ne'er lose sight of that. Any man or woman who looks down on you isn't worthy of your love. John and Emily know that—and it's the secret of how they've made their marriage work."

"Then why is she trying to match you up with all these women? Can't she see how ridiculous it is?"

Duncan chuckled. "I wouldn't pretend to know the way my sister's mind works. The one thing I do know is I'm grateful for your warning about tomorrow night. I'll sorely miss having Cook's Seafood Newburg, but 'tis a loss I'll gladly suffer since it'll allow me to avoid Opal and her mama."

Tim let out a sigh. "You wouldn't happen to include me in your plans so I could miss out, too, would you?"

A slow smile tugged at Duncan's lips. "It seems to me I'll need some papers to show Old Kemper about the ship. Specifications. I'll leave them on the desk in my room. You might want to deliver them in the afternoon. Oh—and bring one more thing. It's very important."

"What?"

"Three licorice ropes."

Chapter 4

Brigit sat by the window up in her bedroom. She could see Duncan and Timothy out on the lawn. Guilt speared through her. Rattled at how she'd babbled to Duncan instead of remembering her changed station in life, she'd scurried off.

It was truly Duncan's fault. The rascal could charm a river into running backward. She'd been minding her own business, enjoying the peaceful evening, when he happened by. He didn't have to stop. In fact, he shouldn't have. *But I could have stayed silent or excused myself straightaway instead of sitting there, chattering like a magpie.*

She'd barely made it into the house when she realized she'd left her shawl on the bench. It couldn't stay out there—it was a special treasure. She'd gone back after it and overheard some of what Duncan said to Timothy.

Humility was a rare enough quality in men, but he'd taken it to an extreme. Why would a man like that feel he wasn't good enough for any woman in the town? With wonderful auburn curls and a ready smile, Duncan O'Brien looked as handsome as Adam must have on the day of creation; and from his conversations, anyone could determine he was as smart as a whip. Aye, and generosity and patience also counted in his favor—she'd heard about his concern to teach his men to read. Yet Duncan didn't give himself credit for those fine points; he dismissed them and assumed the lasses wanted him only for the jingle in his pockets.

Granted, a sound marriage needed to be based on more than financial considerations—no man or woman wanted to be viewed only for the depth of his or her pockets—but to Brigit's way of thinking, Duncan underestimated his appeal. When God had made him, surely He'd made a good man.

Some lass would be blessed to have him. She heard Trudy bumping about in the room next door. Brigit let out a moan. The poor lass still carried a torch for Duncan O'Brien. A sad thing, that. Trudy built up her hopes each day, only to get them dashed when Duncan stayed oblivious to her presence. Miss Emily must have noticed the longing in Trudy's eyes, because she'd been assigning her to tasks that kept her away from Duncan. For true, Duncan O'Brien deserved more than a mere servant as his bride.

᜔

"Blest be the tie that binds—" Duncan suddenly stopped singing.

Prudence, dressed in yet another pink frock, twisted around and sang the next line of the hymn while batting her lashes at him. "Our hearts in Christian love. . ."

Trapped in church. Wasn't there something about amnesty—no, sanctuary—that's what it was. Church was supposed to be a safe place, a house of worship and peace—not a matchmaker's hunting ground. The first hymn of the morning had been "How Shall the Young Secure Their Hearts?" which was followed immediately by "Love Divine, All Love Excelling." Now they were binding hearts in Christian love. *Lord, I'm sorry for the fact that I've ceased singing, but I'm sure You understand. I don't want to mislead anyone into thinking I'm planning a courtship. I'll just stay silent for this one hymn. . . .*

"How wonderful, knowing we are all bonded together in Christ's love." The parson beamed at the congregation. "Please turn in your hymnals to hymn number sixty-seven, 'O Happy Home, Where Thou Art Loved Most Dearly.' "

The pianist and organist both played the opening chords as Duncan glowered at Emily. A snicker sounded beside him, so he subtly stepped on Timothy's toes to hush him.

Lord, I'm a man of my word. I said I'd stand down for just that one hymn. Couldn't You have taken mercy and inspired the parson to choose a different hymn? Maybe "A Mighty Fortress" or "My Soul, Be on Thy Guard" or even "In the Hour of Trial"?

Duncan suppressed the sensation of being the center of attention and kept his gaze firmly on the cross at the front of the sanctuary. He took a deep breath and started to sing with the congregation. "O happy home, where Thou art loved most dearly. . ."

Chapter 5

P sst. Unca Duncan. C'mere."

Duncan spied his youngest nephew on the far side of the umbrella stand. It provided barely enough cover for the lad; Duncan wouldn't stand a chance of remaining unseen.

If Emily doesn't leave me alone, I'm going to start living aboard a landlocked ship or convince John to start sending me on the transatlantic voyages so I can get away from this never-ending petticoat parade.

Phillip pressed a forefinger to his lips and used the thumb on his other hand to point toward the dining room. In what Duncan supposed was intended to be a whisper, the boy announced, "Girls."

Duncan didn't need to be told. The cloying scents of several floral fragrances mingled and gave warning. He glanced toward the stairs, pointed upward, and reached out for Phillip's hand. Gleefully, Phillip launched from his hiding place. He snatched Duncan's hand, and they hastened for safety. They reached the first step, and Duncan let out a sigh of relief.

"Duncan!" Emily's cheerful voice stopped him dead in his tracks.

Phillip let out a loud groan. Duncan wished he could do the same. Instead he glanced over his shoulder. "Hello, Emily."

"I was rather hoping you'd be home for lunch. Please come join us. Phillip, did you wash your hands?"

"Yes, Mama." Phillip turned loose of Duncan's hand and wiggled his stubby fingers in the air. "See?"

"Good for you. Now go get your brothers." She gave him a Mama's-wise-to-you look. "I expect all three of my sons to be at the table immediately. Be sure to tell them Uncle Duncan is joining us."

"Yes, Mama." Phillip scrambled up the stairs.

Emily approached. Duncan couldn't decide whether to growl or smile at her. The words were on the tip of his tongue to tell his sister to stop this stream of marriageable material—he simply wasn't fishing. Then again, manners demanded he not embarrass her. The time would come for him to confront her when these young ladies were gone. In the meantime, at least he'd have his nephews with him so he could steer the conversation to include them and bore the women to tears.

"Several young ladies are here to visit Anna Kathleen and Lily."

146

"Is that so?" The ruse was so painfully thin that he felt a stab of disbelief. *Does Emily think I'm so stupid I wouldn't see past that lie?* Then another thought crossed his mind. If these scheming minxes were using his nieces as a means of getting to him, he'd put a stop to it here and now. He refused to allow his family to be used as tools.

Emily had threaded her arm through his and started toward the dining room. She must have felt his sudden tension, but she didn't stop. Lips barely moving, she said, "I need you to display your best manners. You're an example for my children, you know."

A stream of giggles filled the air.

Duncan groaned and shot his sister a heated look.

"You can make it through this. I'll help you." A charming smile lit her face.

How many times had Emily said that to him? She'd been true to her word each and every time. Long ago, when he'd been but six slim years, she'd taught him how to change Timothy's nappies. She'd held him close at their sister's graveside and made the same promise. Aye, and when they'd both needed to learn the finer points of gracious living after she wed John, she'd been his confidant and ally. They'd literally gone from rags to riches, but no matter what her circumstances, Emily was Emily. He loved his big sister for that.

"I'll do this for you." He gave her a tender smile.

"Thank you."

Duncan mentally battened down his hatches for the storm ahead. He would weather it. 'Twas but one insignificant meal. Aye, and with his nieces and nephews at the table, he'd most certainly find a way to enjoy the luncheon. A single step more, and he could see the staff had added every last spare leaf to the dining table, elongating it to accommodate twenty. Twenty!

"How long have you been planning this little event?"

"Since Sunday," Emily admitted in a gratingly cheerful tone. They walked into the dining room, and she singsonged, "Look who's joining us!"

Anna Kathleen twirled about. Her hoops swayed precariously, but rather than making her usual sound of exasperation, she beckoned. "Duncan! How wonderful! Do come meet my friends."

Duncan glanced about. A solid dozen or more young girls filled the room. Frilly party attire in nearly every pastel hue turned the room into a veritable feminine rainbow, and most of the girls were still young enough to wear their hair down. Relief coursed through his veins. He'd not been duped into a matchmaking scheme—these lasses still spent their days in the schoolroom.

Lunch passed with relative ease. Duncan found the youngsters refreshing. When Timothy shot him a stricken look, Duncan determined the brunette in the greenish dress seemed to be far more interested than his nephew wished.

Recalling the youngster on Tim's other side was named Bernice, Duncan smoothly went to the rescue. "Tim, have you told Miss Bernice about your plans for next month?"

The brunette clouded over, but Tim and Bernice both lit up. Tim shot Duncan a grateful look, then focused his attention on the red-haired girl. "I'm to help with the fittings on my uncle's new vessel, and I'll be going on the next voyage to Massachusetts."

Duncan congratulated himself. All went well enough. Since it was an unscheduled event in the middle of a busy day, he didn't mind the fact that he'd need to rearrange some of his plans. Family came first. Being the wonderful mother she was, Emily had concocted this little affair for her daughters and sons to enjoy their friends and learn the necessary social skills to help them through life. Duncan figured the least he could do was serve as an example.

Or so he thought until a flock of mamas and big sisters swept in to collect the girls.

Pink Prudence, Adele, and Antonia—whose name he'd not recall unless he associated her with a similar sounding name, A-tune-ia—all made appearances. Oh, and he'd been introduced to a few oh-so-available sisters who were home from finishing school as well as the gangly, bucktoothed granddaughter of their nearest neighbor. Decorum demanded he act with utter gentility. Under any other circumstances, he'd not mind a bit. This rated as different, though. Duncan felt like a sailor who fell overboard into a school of hungry sharks.

Tonight he would sit Emily down and make it plain. No more of this nonsense.

∽

Brigit sat in the nursery with the twins. She'd come up to mind them so Mr. and Mrs. Newcomb could have a quiet evening together. The little girls filled the last ten minutes with complaints, bemoaning the tragic fact that they hadn't been included in today's party. Leftover little treats from the luncheon party remained in the kitchen, so Brigit suggested, "June and Julie, why don't we have our verra own bedtime tea party?"

In no time at all, the three of them huddled at a small table. They weren't alone. Three tin soldiers stood at attention on the empty side of the table. "Now aren't you clever lasses?" Brigit nodded approvingly. "We've handsome companions for our party, and I doubt anyone ever saw such a scrumptious spread."

"I'd have to agree," a deep voice said from the doorway.

Startled, Brigit twisted in her chair to see if her ears had deceived her. No, they hadn't. Duncan O'Brien lounged against the door frame, his arms folded, his hair wind ruffled, and a twinkle in his eyes. He tilted his head to the side, and a rakish smile lifted the right side of his mouth.

"Do you want some tea, Uncle Duncan?"

Before Brigit could object, he pushed away from the door and started toward them. "Of course I do. I'm so thirsty I could drink the ocean dry!"

June went into peals of laughter; Julie giggled and managed to spill tea onto the saucer.

Duncan towered over the children's table, and Brigit wished he'd just bend down, gulp the tea, and depart. He didn't cooperate. No, he didn't. Instead he picked up each soldier, precisely set one to the left of each of them, then scanned the room. Who would have ever imagined what he did next? The big, handsome ship's captain swept a china doll from a bed. He pulled out the last little chair and folded his tall frame onto it. He sat the doll on his knee and surveyed the table.

"You've gathered a fine spread here. Shall I ask a blessing?"

The girls folded their hands and pretended not to peek. Brigit compressed her lips to keep from smiling at the fact that she and Duncan were doing the self-same thing. He said a short, sweet prayer, and they all chimed in, "Amen."

"Are you hungry?" June started pushing tiny plates at him.

"Ferociously hungry, and so is my little cousin, aren't you, Fortuna?" He toggled the doll and raised his voice into a falsetto. "Why, yes, I am."

"Fortuna?" Julie scrunched her face.

"Oh, haven't you ever met my cousin? How remiss of me. June, Julie, and Miss Brigit, allow me to present my cousin, Miss Hunter. Miss Fortuna Hunter."

Chapter 6

Brigit choked on her tea. She managed to murmur a greeting to the doll and watched Duncan waggle his brows. "I was sure you must have met her. All of her friends were here today to pick up their little sisters. She told me to be sure to have some cake."

"June, serve Mr. O'Brien—"

"Duncan," he interrupted.

Brigit nodded acknowledgment. "—Duncan some cake."

June leaned forward, then halted. "Do I have to use a fork?"

"If you use your fingers, I'll have to lick them clean."

Never had a tea party been so charming. Brigit delighted in watching how Duncan played with his little nieces. He unabashedly enjoyed them. Someday he'd make a wondrous father.

Miss Emily bustled into the room. Brigit suddenly sobered. *What am I doing?*

"I thought I heard merriment in here. Duncan, John wanted to speak with you about something."

"Mama, we're having a tea party!"

Emily petted her daughters' curls. "I can see, darlings."

"Tea and treats before bed," Duncan said as he rose. "I'm sure you'll have sweet dreams." He kissed June and Julie, then left the room.

Suddenly the whole room seemed far bigger and dreadfully empty. Brigit quickly picked up the mess and crumbs, placed everything on a tray, and dampened the end of a towel so she could wash up the twins.

"So you enjoyed your party?" Miss Emily asked as she helped her daughters into their flower-sprigged flannel nightgowns.

"Uh-huh." The twins answered in unison.

Brigit started to comb Julie's hair so she could plait it for the night. "They have very nice manners, Miss Emily."

"As do you." Miss Emily smiled easily. "You've said little about your family, but I'm guessing you're more accustomed to directing staff than being a member of one."

Her words made Brigit draw in a quick breath. "I'm sorry, ma'am. I—"

"No, no. You misunderstand me. We'll talk later."

Later. The taste of the much-too-sweet tea and treats suddenly came back and switched to bitter, and Brigit swallowed hard. *Lord, You know I need this job. Aye, You do. Whate'er I've done wrong, help me. My parents need the money I make, and if—*

"Ouchie!" Julie reached up and grabbed the base of her braid. "You're pulling too tight!"

"I'm sorry." Brigit loosened the weave a tad and deftly tied the tail of the plait with a bit of ribbon.

"She complains of that almost every night," Miss Emily said as she tied June's matching braid. "When you girls go to school next year, Julie's going to scream half the time when the boy behind her tugs on her pigtails or dips them in the inkwell."

"I won't let them do that to her." June's outraged words rang with certainty.

Emily laughed. "You might be too busy taking care of yourself to guard her."

June and Julie scrambled into the bed and snuggled together. Brigit picked up the tray as Miss Emily bent over to kiss her daughters. "Let's say our prayers."

"We already said prayers with Brigit and Uncle Duncan."

"You can't pray too much."

Brigit headed down the stairs, dread in her heart. In the slim month she'd been here, she'd seen Miss Emily shelter her children. The easy laughter in the nursery didn't mean all was well—it merely showed a mother's regard for her children's innocence. *Whatever she wants to talk to me about, it's surely not going to be a good thing.*

Miss Emily's words echoed in her mind. *You can't pray too much.*

ᵔᔆ

John wanted to give Duncan a receipt for a special order he had waiting in Massachusetts. The postal delivery brought the letter to the dock today, saying the ring for Emily was ready to be picked up. As brothers-in-law went, Duncan knew he'd been blessed with the best God ever made. Each year John made it a point to give Emily an anniversary surprise. For their upcoming fifteenth anniversary, he'd commissioned a diamond and sapphire ring.

If Emily caught wind of it, she'd cancel the order and spend the money on charity. John donated generously to any number of causes, but Emily always managed to ferret out some family in need. John had learned to dodge Emily's openhandedness by sneaking around and evading her questions. When he managed to give her the gifts, she was always so touched that she cherished whatever it was. . .and John would simply assure her she could name whichever needy situation she knew and he'd give twice as much to it.

Diamond and sapphire. Duncan saw a sketch of it. Emily was still a simple woman at heart, and she'd not want anything ostentatious. John and the jeweler traded letters until the design reflected the perfect style. Duncan hid the slip of paper in his Bible, knowing full well he'd be sure to take it with him on his next voyage.

He came out of his bedchamber as Brigit carried a tray down the stairs. Now there was a fine lass. Her startling eyes matched the blue dress she wore, and it seemed a smile never left her lips. He'd stood in the doorway of the nursery, watching how she sat at that little tea table with his nieces. Not a one of the young women in Emily's Bridal Brigade would have ever set up such an enchanting party for two little children and join in as she did. The few minutes he'd watched her, he'd been impressed by the way she gently took the opportunity to reinforce basic decorum and yet encouraged the girls to use their imaginations and pretend.

How had she known June and Julie had felt left out today? Duncan remembered being that young. His sisters were so much older, and once Emily was to wed John, Duncan felt that he didn't exactly belong in their world. He wouldn't admit it to a soul—it would have sounded babyish—yet John understood. Just before the wedding, John took Duncan aside and gave him a shiny, new Seated Liberty quarter. He'd told Duncan he was a worthy part of the family—a full quarter of it. John, Emily, Duncan, and Timothy—there were four of them, all starting a new life together. If ever he felt he didn't belong or wasn't wanted, John ordered Duncan to pull that special quarter from his pocket and rub it. He'd not needed to. The quarter itself served as such a potent reminder that Duncan counted it as his greatest earthly treasure. He watched Brigit disappear behind the kitchen door and jingled the coins in his pocket. She'd understand. Aye, a woman like that who bothered to make children happy would. And it made her a treasure in her own right.

෭

Later. Later turned out to be a mere half hour after they tucked the twins into bed. Miss Emily passed by Brigit and murmured, "Come to the kitchen."

Too nervous to do much of anything, Brigit sat at the kitchen table and kept her hands knotted in her lap. Miss Emily set the creamer on the kitchen table next to the simple earthenware teapot and started to stir her cup. "The day I hired you, your speech and mannerisms told me you'd not grown up in a humble village cottage. Plain as could be, you'd known what it was to have a fine education and social exposure. Oddly, though, your hands weren't the soft, smooth ones of a person of leisure."

Since the lady of the house posed no direct question, Brigit held her silence.

"Each time I've an opening, I ask the dear Lord to bring the right lass to that position. He gave me that sense of rightness about you, Brigit Murphy. I hired you on, but I didn't pry one bit. No, I didn't—but I am now." Miss Emily took a sip of her tea, then softly urged, "Tell me how you came to be here."

" 'Tis the same story I'm sure you've heard many times over by now. The blight struck, and the famine grew worse."

"But your family owned the land; they didn't till it."

Brigit nodded.

Miss Emily reached across the table and pushed Brigit's cup and saucer closer. "If a sip of tea cannot soothe you, you're surely not Irish. Drink up, lass."

The sip of tea did give comfort. Brigit smiled.

"I live in a fancy home, Brigit, but 'twasn't always the case—and sure as the sun rises, you've heard that fact. Fortunes can change just as fast as a tide. 'Tisn't the surroundings that define who we are; 'tis our hearts."

Which is why she's so comfortable sharing tea with me in a humble kitchen instead of her fancy parlor.

"So let the tea loosen your tongue," Miss Emily said, "and share your heart with me."

Brigit traced the edge of the saucer with her fingertip to delay answering the personal invitation. "Mum always said there wasn't such a thing as too much tea, but I doubt she'd shared a children's tea party ere she made that pronouncement over her next cup."

"Where's your family now?"

"Mum and Da live in town." She lifted her cup and half-whispered, "On Willow Glenn." Naming the street that teemed with tenements left a sour taste in her mouth, so she took a hasty sip.

A beauteous smile brightened Miss Emily's face. "So you're not here alone. Have you any brothers or sisters?"

"Nay—just the three of us there are." Though Miss Emily treated her with great warmth and Christian kindness, Brigit tried not to pour out all her private business. This woman wasn't her friend; she was her employer. "God be praised, we all stayed together."

"Do your parents have enough to eat?"

The tea nearly sloshed over the brim in Brigit's cup. "That they do, ma'am, and I thank you kindly for asking."

"Before I met my husband, about all I could buy was milk; and even then I had to water it down. We near starved."

"So that's why Duncan likes milk now."

Miss Emily gave her a slow smile. "Aye, and it's sweet you are to understand that fact."

Miss Emily asked several leading questions, then finally poured herself a second cup of tea and let out a satisfied sigh. "I can see my faith in the dear Lord wasn't misplaced. Truly, you're an answer to prayer." Miss Emily asked Brigit to take on the duty of working with Anna Kathleen and Lily on social skills—conversational abilities, personal grooming, and the curbing of their hoydenish tendencies.

"Anyone could see you possess the refinement to handle those matters, Brigit, and the responsibility also carries with it an increase in wages." The grandfather clock chimed from deep within the house. "Now then, since we've settled things, I'm supposing we ought to turn in for the night."

Brigit rinsed out the cups and pot, then barely slept that night because she lay in bed praising the Lord for His generosity and goodness.

~❦~

"Bad pennies always turn up."

"I beg your pardon?" Brigit stopped dusting the dainty porcelain statue of a shepherdess on the hallway table. With no one else around, she thought Duncan had addressed his words to her.

He cleared his throat. "I—um—I was trying to recall the old saying 'Bad pennies always turn up.' What of the good pennies?"

She shrugged. "Mayhap some kind soul spent those in a charitable way."

"Could be." He walked off, muttering to himself.

Pennies. Brigit smiled to herself. She'd been waiting for Duncan to leave so she could go clean his chamber. Last night, Miss Emily had assigned her the responsibility of regularly tidying his chamber. Nothing specific was said, but Brigit gathered Miss Emily had caught wind of Trudy's infatuation and wisely chose to place distance between Duncan and the giddy maid.

The sheets smelled like fresh air. The scent filled the room as Brigit snapped the sheet to unfold it across Duncan's bared mattress. She smoothed it, tucked in the corners, and swiftly added the top sheet and covers. Crisp cases slipped on the pillows, curtains drawn open, and water exchanged from his washbowl, and she'd gotten a fine start on her chores for the day.

Arms full of sheets, she headed into the hallway and ran smack into Duncan. "Oh, I beg your pardon, sir."

He braced her elbows and frowned. "Aren't you working awfully hard?"

Brigit wrinkled her nose. "Not at all. Sprucing up a home is a constant thing, but Miss Emily is diligent to keep matters well in hand. Besides, Mum always said hard work ne'er hurt a body."

"Hmpf."

"If you'll excuse me, sir—"

He turned loose of her and peered over her shoulder into his room. "Are you done now?"

"Not quite. I'm to salt-sweep the carpeting; but if you'd rather, I can come back after I've done a few other chores."

Duncan pushed past her and scowled at the beautiful green-and-gold Turkish carpeting in his room. "It looks perfectly fine. There's no need for you to tend the flooring."

What man worried over the details of housekeeping? Baffled and also torn by allegiance to Miss Emily, Brigit moistened her lips and murmured, "I'll check with the mistress."

"I'll talk with Emily. If you wait a moment, I'll give you something to place in Timothy's room. He asked to study star navigation, and I have a few charts. . . ."

Mindful of propriety, Brigit stayed outside the chamber as Duncan went in. She watched Duncan cross the room with his self-assured stride. He stopped at his desk and reached for the key in the lock, then froze.

Duncan turned around. "There were tiny golden hearts dangling from this key."

"Perhaps they fell off."

He stepped back so he could survey the carpeting. His scowl evaporated. He stooped and grabbed what looked to be short, thin red cords with a trio of hearts. "Here we are."

"Now aren't those pretty wee things!"

"Aye, and I'm glad they're not lost. Many a year ago they belonged to my sister Anna—God rest her soul. Em and I plan to give them to her namesake someday. In the meantime, I'm to keep them out of sight. Last night I decided since little Anna Kathleen wouldn't be in my chamber, I could put them on my keys and enjoy them myself for a time."

"I'm sorry you lost your sister."

"Did I hear my name?" Miss Emily came down the hall.

"Aye." Duncan grinned at his sister. "Anna's three golden hearts fell off the key, but they're found."

"Good!" Miss Emily beamed. "Timothy said you'd promised him navigational star charts. I thought to take them to the library instead of his room. Titus is curious, but he'll crumple the edges. Best we think to unfurl them on a table downstairs."

"Fine." Duncan lifted his chin in an unconsciously imperious move. "Brigit, I'll take the charts below. You may leave."

∽૭

Duncan waited until the maid was out of earshot, then gave Emily a thunderous look. "Do you need more funds to run the household?"

"Why, no. John is quite generous. What makes you ask such a thing?"

"You're working Brigit too hard."

Emily gave him a withering look. "Now, our Duncan—"

"Don't you 'Now' me. That lass is underfoot no matter where I go. She said you'd ordered her to salt-sweep my carpeting."

"I did."

"It doesn't need it!"

Emily smiled at him in her I'll-be-patient-with-you way. "I won't let things get filthy ere I see to them. Maintaining a smooth home means doing things on a routine. 'Tis time for your carpeting to be either beaten or swept. The salt will brighten the colors, but if you'd rather have all the furniture moved so Brigit can beat—"

"No. Absolutely not."

Emily hitched her shoulder. "Then 'twill be salt-swept."

"Then don't have her change linens and dust, too." To escape Emily's calculating look, Duncan turned to rummage through his desk. "I may have been but a scrap of a lad, but I remember all too well how exhausted you were from cleaning before John brought us here. I thought you'd kept sensitive to not overworking anyone else as you'd been."

"Has Brigit said anything to you? Complained—"

"Not a word," he interrupted. "It's just that everywhere I go, she's right under my nose. I don't see you working any of the other maids that much."

"Brigit is well educated. The children love her, and I have her work with them more as a result."

"That might account for a portion—but not enough."

Emily let out a choppy sigh. "Very well. I'm keeping Trudy and Lee working together. Trudy's developed an infatuation for you, so I took pity on you and—"

Duncan lifted his hand. "Enough said. After she leapt into my arms from the stairs, I've taken to avoiding her like the plague. And since we're on the subject, Em, I insist you cease playing Cupid. I won't stand for it."

"We've always been a social family. I'm not about to stop having people over because you're marriage shy."

"You're not just having 'people' over; you're bringing in eligible women. I'm not fooled for a minute."

"The women's circle sews together every other Tuesday."

He snorted. "What about that gaggle you had in last week?"

Emily gave him an exasperated look. "If you had any manners, you wouldn't refer to that. MayEllen Reece is in confinement, and we all wanted to celebrate the coming little blessing."

"I might grant you that one, but every other day you have a lass here for a meal. Em, don't prevaricate. It's as if you toss out birdseed and every last goose and henwit in the county takes a turn pecking at our table."

She muffled a sound he couldn't quite interpret. To be sure, she looked displeased. "I have the perfect name for your vessel. Based on the way you're acting, it should be called the *Recalcitrant*."

"I'm not recalcitrant; I'm independent. When I determine I'm ready to wed, I'll do my own choosing. I'll court a woman with common sense and a kind heart. Until then, Em, cut it out."

"There's nothing in the world wrong with my letting you have a look at who's out there."

"You're wasting your energy. By the time I'm ready to wed, every last one of these lasses will be married and have a babe or two." He gave his sister a hug, then decided he'd made his point and it wouldn't hurt to praise her a little. "I know your motive is good. I'm thankful you have a happy marriage, and it's endearing to know you want the same for me. When I'm ready, I promise you'll be the first to meet my girl."

Emily beamed up at him. She stood on tiptoe and patted his cheek. Duncan felt a spurt of relief. He'd finally gotten through to her. He smiled.

"Duncan, boy-o. You're in the right of it. I will be the first to meet your girl. That's why I'll have to introduce the two of you!" Emily twisted from his hold and hummed as she walked away.

It wasn't until she started down the stairs that Duncan identified the tune: "The Time I've Lost in Wooing."

Late that night, when Duncan climbed into bed, he caught himself ironing his hand over the crisp sheet. He pulled his hand back and growled under his breath. That pretty Irish maid with the beguiling blue eyes had changed this linen and smoothed it in place so nary a wrinkle marred the surface. She'd plumped his pillow, too. He took it, turned it over, and thumped it for no reason whatsoever.

No matter where he turned, there were women. He'd grown accustomed to living at sea, being surrounded by men. Even in the close quarters of a ship, men understood how their crewmates needed solitude and space. Here on land where room abounded, women clumped together and clucked over every little thing. It could drive a man daft.

The last thing Duncan wanted was to come into his chamber and have thoughts of that maid, Brigit, haunt him. Her quick wit, bright eyes, and attention to detail left her all too perceptive—not that he had anything to hide; but she'd been here, fussing at Emily's insistence. She'd straightened his things, dusted his bookshelves, and even left the faintest hint of citrus behind. Was it lemon and beeswax polish, or did she wear lemon verbena?

That did it. He was an orderly man. He kept his cabin on his vessel clean, and he could jolly well make his bed at home. He'd tell Emily not to have Brigit in here again.

Chapter 7

So that's how it's to be for now."

Brigit bit her lip and nodded.

"There now," Miss Emily crooned. "Duncan's in a foul mood, and 'tisn't your doing. 'Tis mine, truth be told. Aye, that it is. I've crowded a few too many lasses about him, and he's needing his chamber to be a refuge."

"Yes, ma'am."

"Your position is safe here, Brigit. I'm delighted with you. So let's discuss your duties for today."

Brigit listened and diligently carried out each assigned task. The Newcombs ran an odd home—the help worked only a half day on Sundays, and they each had another day off during the week. In addition, each of them also had one evening off on a weekly basis. Tonight she'd go visit Da and Mum. That thought warmed her as she collected the laundry and delivered it to the laundress.

When she entered through the kitchen, Cook flashed her a smile. "I just took inventory of the pantry, and I'm needing to rearrange things. A handful of girls are due in tomorrow to help me with canning. Have the other maids told you about this?"

"No. I'm willing to help. I'm not precisely sure what to do with those orange things, though."

"Pumpkins." Cook smiled at her. "They make a wondrous custard or pie." She flapped her hand back and forth. "But that's neither here nor there at this moment. I'm going to have Trudy and Lee wash out jars for me. Goodhew put crates in the pantry, and you'll go help me sort through the jars."

"What are the crates for?"

"Why, Miss Emily sends a crate of jars to the staff's families along with flour, sugar, and such so they'll have the essentials for holiday baking. It's a household tradition. She does it once a season—autumn, Christmas, Easter, and summer."

Brigit stared at Cook in astonishment.

Cook tugged her into the spacious pantry and whispered, "Miss Emily was practically starved to death when Mr. John found her. She'd given her portion of food to Duncan and their sister, Anna. Anna—bless her soul—made it through birthing Timothy, but she was just too weak. The very first thing Miss Emily did as mistress of Newcomb House was to come into this pantry and make boxes for the maids' families. Now where shall we begin?"

Brigit looked around at the countless tins, sacks, barrels, and jars. Shelves, cupboards, and bins filled the large, square room. Canned apricots sat at eye level on the nearest shelf. "Oh, Mum loves apricots," she blurted out.

Cook laughed. "Then help yourself. While you're at it, put a pair of jars in the next crate for my sister."

"Glory be," Brigit said slowly. "The dear Lord's in heaven, and He's reaching down to provide for us."

～

He had no one to blame but himself. He'd taken Emily to task for overworking Brigit, so now Emily had the maid taking the girls to Newcomb Shipping's warehouse for an afternoon of hunting through the bolts of fabric. They were to select flannels for the women's sewing circle to make blankets and nightgowns for the local orphanage.

The girls would be underfoot at the house with the autumn canning, so the excursion made perfect sense. All in all, the plan should work out beautifully—except for the fact that John had an appointment, so Em decided Duncan could drop them off on his way to the dock and pick them up later.

So here he had June standing between his legs as he drove the carriage, and Brigit sat beside him with Julie on her lap. Anna Kathleen and Lily took up the other seat, much to his relief. Until they were seated and others were out of range, his nieces practically killed anyone who ventured close with their parasols. He'd have to talk to Em about teaching the girls to handle those dumb things better; else they'd blind someone.

As the carriage rolled down the main tree-lined street in town, another carriage stopped alongside his. Opal and her mother were riding along with Prudence and another woman. He couldn't very well ignore them, so he tipped his hat.

June asked loudly, "Uncle Duncan, which one of them is Fortune Hunter?"

The outraged expressions and sounds coming from that conveyance made it clear all of the women heard June's question.

"June, the name is Fortuna, darling." Brigit's words rang out. "Fortuna was an imaginary name for the dolly. It means to be blessed or lucky. We all need to look for the blessings in our lives."

Grateful for Brigit's quick thinking and diplomatic solution to the sticky situation, Duncan nodded, then smiled at June. "And you want to be a blessing to others."

"Is that why we're getting 'terial for the orphan babies?"

"Yes," he answered.

" 'Tuna Hunter didn't get a blessing," Julie pouted. "She got lost. I can't find her."

Anna Kathleen called over, "You all are welcome to join us if you'd like!"

Duncan bit back a groan. If the ladies accepted Anna's invitation, there was no way he could leave society ladies in the warehouse. He'd be obliged to go along and endure them all afternoon. Brigit had enough common sense to mind the girls and keep them together with her. She'd capably select practical fabrics with a minimum of fuss or bother. Compassion had filled her eyes when she'd been told of the purpose of this outing, and Duncan knew beyond a shadow of a doubt that the only material she'd want would be for the motherless children. He'd be able to assign a man to push along a cart for Brigit and assure their safety, then leave and tend to his own business.

On the other hand, visions of Prudence pulling out yards of pink satin or Opal heading toward the brocades made Duncan's hair stand on end.

He strove to school his expression. "Someday we'll have to plan some other kind of outing, Anna. The ladies are wearing such fetching dresses, they'd never want to get them soiled in a musty old warehouse."

"Yes, well, we will be coming to the ladies' sewing circle next Tuesday," Opal singsonged as she ran her fingertips along a ribbon on her day gown. "You girls go on ahead. Be sure to pick out some lovely little pieces so we can brighten the days of those unfortunate waifs."

Prudence leaned forward. "I'd be happy to help today."

Opal's mother cut in. "Pru, dear, your mama would swoon if I took you home with cobwebs and dust all over that rose taffeta."

"Another time. Good day, ladies." Duncan drove off and didn't even try to smother his smile. Pink had some use after all.

Chapter 8

D etails. They're just minor details," one of the carpenters grumbled as he tromped off with a toolbox.

Duncan held his tongue. It wouldn't serve any purpose to bark at the men. The frustrations he faced were myriad; yet none of them would be lessened by snapping at someone. His ship still needed appreciable fittings before it would be seaworthy and capable of handling a fully laden hull. After listening to the discussions around him, Duncan felt more pressured to hasten the maiden voyage.

Hotheaded men already scrapped with one another about politics, and everyone had an opinion about the Lincoln-Douglas debates. Whichever leaning they held, those men weren't above trying to convince others to see matters in the "right" way. He had his hands full keeping the workmen on task and off the political bandwagons. More often than not, Duncan found it necessary to stop a scuffle between his workers because some staunchly advocated secession, while others firmly believed in preserving the Union. All he needed was for someone to get upset and sabotage the vessel. Once it was launched, he would have far better control over who came near it.

Newcomb Shipping boasted fine crews of seamen, and there'd never been anything but cooperation at sea. Discipline was both rare and fair. Some of these hotheaded men could tear apart the crew's harmony. Duncan made mental notes of the few who were rabble-rousers and also of those who were peacemakers.

Duncan wasn't a man to vote by party recommendation—he studied the candidates, prayed, and finally came to the decision he felt was best. The word "secession" came up often, and folks were hot under the collar. He wished the Lord's peace would be poured out on the nation.

"Duncan, I'm needing more timber," Old Kemper called from several yards away.

"Fine. I'll have a draft ready for you at the office. When do you want it?"

Kemper sorrowfully shook his head from side to side and swaggered up. "Nay, that's not the issue. 'Tis that the mill's behind on deliveries."

"Then we'll send wagons for whatever you need. Probably ought to lay by some extra if they're running late on our orders."

"I was hopin' you'd say that. Can't take my men, though. I need every last man jack. You'll have to pull some deckhands. Sooner you do it, the better off we

161

are." Kemper brushed some sawdust off the front of his shirt. "I'm already look-ing at a delay because of this."

After arranging for a team of sailors, Duncan sent them off with Old Kemper to get the lumber. He went to examine the sails on another vessel and dickered with a supplier over the rising cost of tar.

Every last contact contained some reference to the election. Duncan didn't want to engage in political conversations. He tried to sidestep them as best he could. Folks lost all reason when they found someone didn't share their leanings. Duncan planned to cast his vote in the privacy of the ballot box and prayed what-ever the outcome, his loved ones would be spared any of the discord's ravages.

John met his gaze and subtly tilted his head toward the shipping office. He rarely sought a meeting in private. Most of their discussions took place out in the shipyard or on the docks. The fact that John indicated he'd rather handle a mat-ter out of sight let Duncan know it must be important.

Duncan cupped his hands to his mouth to create a bullhorn. "John—I need to get some papers signed. Can you meet me in the office?"

His brother-in-law nodded.

Duncan hadn't lied. He did need John's signature on a few things. Those matters were resolved in minutes. Unfortunately, folks kept coming in and out. John grimaced. "Let's have a quiet supper tonight. I'll instruct Emily that she and the children can eat early. Hey—have you seen my fountain pen?"

"No. Why?"

John shook his head as he rummaged on the top of his desk. "I can't find it at home and wondered if I accidentally carried it here or if you'd borrowed it by chance."

"Sorry. Haven't seen it."

John heaved a sigh. "It'll turn up. As to the other matter—we'll dine in the library at seven, if you're free."

"Done." Duncan figured John had plenty on his mind. They'd both been busier than a one-armed man in a rowboat. 'Twas time to compare notes.

⌇

"I'm needing butter." Brigit surveyed the cart and determined what else would complete the meal.

"Here you go." Lee plunked down a small dish.

"I'll be happy to wheel that on in." Trudy bustled over and curled her hands around the handle of the ornately inlaid wooden cart.

"I imagine you would, but you're not going to." Cook used her ample hip to bump Trudy away. " 'Tis dishes for you tonight. Get with it now."

Trudy let out a gust of a sigh and pouted. "I don't know why I can't take the tray in to the gentlemen. I've been here longer than Brigit."

Brigit didn't want to be party to this conversation. She popped the domed covers over the plates to hold in the heat and filled the creamer.

Cook didn't mince words. "You're not assigned that task, and for good cause. You make a pest of yourself every time you get in the same room as Duncan."

"I do not!"

"And just who dropped beets on his arm yesterday?"

Trudy looked completely affronted. "That was an accident."

"I've never seen anyone so accident-prone," Lee added in a wry tone. "The way you tripped on the stairs and he had to catch you—"

"Oh, stop! Mishaps occur to everyone." Trudy pressed her hand to her bosom. "No one can begin to imagine how mortified I was to tumble down the stairs in front of him."

Lee snapped a dish towel at her. "For it being such an embarrassing calamity, Goodhew said you sure did manage to cling to Duncan for a long while."

"I could have broken my neck. He rescued me, and I was suffering a reaction."

Cook folded her arms across her chest and narrowed her eyes. "Tripping down one measly step wouldn't break your neck. It's a crying pity you didn't thump your noggin and knock some sense into yourself. Any other lady of the home would dismiss you for the way you're literally throwing yourself at a family member. 'Tis unseemly. Stop whining and do your job, and be glad you've kept it thus far."

Brigit turned the cart around and bumped the swinging door with her hip to open it. She backed out of the kitchen and drew the cart after her until the door shut. Once out, she seesawed the cart back and forth at an angle until she had it turned around. The library lay just a few doors down the hall.

Goodhew waited until she brought the cart to the door, then opened it and announced, "Dinner, sirs."

"Yes. Good." Mr. John's voice drifted out of the room along with the pleasant scent of the fire Brigit had lit in the room an hour before.

She pulled in the cart, and the door shut behind her. Mr. John sat behind his desk, and Duncan stood by the fireplace. Brigit got no cue as to their desire, so she asked, "Will you gentlemen be dining off the cart, or would you prefer to use the desk or one of the tables?"

"That table there will do just fine." Mr. John gestured toward a table flanked by a pair of deep green leather wingback chairs. He then turned his attention back on Duncan. "It's not a matter of greed. Emily suffered from such poverty. I'll never have her in a position where she needs to worry again."

"And you have my undying gratitude for that." Duncan grabbed an andiron and poked at a log. The logs let off a cheery popping sound, and sparks flew.

Brigit quietly spread a small, plain white linen cloth across the table, then set the plates down and laid silverware beside them. She took pains to make as little noise as possible. The somber tone of voice the men shared brought forth memories of when Da and Mum were discussing the grave matters of sending the farmers to America so they wouldn't starve. Tears misted her eyes.

She poured coffee for Mr. John and placed the glass of milk for Duncan next to the other plate. Once everything was in place, she pushed the cart off to the corner, came back, and removed the warming domes. "Supper is served."

The men took seats, and Duncan asked a blessing. Brigit waited until he finished before she set the domes on the cart. It would have been disrespectful to make that racket while he was addressing the Almighty.

"We need to set up priorities at once," Mr. John said. "Plan. I'll hire some men to do patrols on the grounds."

"Thank you for the milk, Brigit." Duncan took his glass.

Mr. John continued. "I expect our vessels to be conscripted right away. Supplies are of the utmost—"

Duncan lifted his chin at a self-assured angle and spoke in an uncustomarily sharp tone, "We'll have Goodhew summon you if we need anything, Brigit."

"Very well."

She gladly left the library. Whatever the two men were discussing, it should be between only them. The very fact that they were holding this private meeting underscored the importance of discretion, and Brigit felt horribly intrusive standing there. Servants were supposed to be invisible and silent—but she'd been out of place when the men so obviously wished to hash out this business.

"Back so soon?" Trudy simpered once Brigit reached the kitchen. "Don't you know to stay and clear away? Men don't take long to eat."

Jealousy dripped off each word, and Brigit decided to put Trudy's fear to rest. "That may be, but Duncan dismissed me. I'll just have to go back later."

Later. Hopefully much later—after the men had finished and left the library. Brigit felt completely unsettled. Memories flooded back of so many evenings of similar conversations filled with concerns and burdens her parents had held. *Lord, whatever is weighing on the hearts of those men, please help them carry the load.*

༜

"It's heating up and will hit boiling point all too soon." Duncan set down his fork. "I'm striving to stay impartial in public."

John nodded. "There comes a point when a man has to stand up and be counted. When the time arrives, we'll not be silent. Until then, we have to set priorities and keep as neutral as possible."

"I'm thinking of protection."

"As am I." John took a gulp of coffee and grimaced. "Cook must've measured the coffee wrong. This stuff is so weak, it needs crutches. Why did you have that maid leave?"

Because she looked worried and pale. Brigit's normally been bright as a copper penny, but she wasn't tonight. Pushing that cart in here, she was the cheerful-hearted lass I've become accustomed to seeing; but within seconds she changed. She's perceptive, and she sensed the ugliness of what we're discussing. She gave us a trapped look, and tears filled her eyes—I wanted to spare the lass. It all sounded so melodramatic. Duncan hitched a shoulder. "We have no reason to think she's untrustworthy. I prefer to have no one privy to our conversation, though." He paused, then tacked on, "Women ought not be burdened with such dark matters anyway."

"True enough. So as for protection—I want to purchase guns. Several of them."

"And you don't think that will raise suspicions?"

John grinned. "It's customary to give gifts at the boat's christening. We can order a goodly number of navy Colts and present them to Old Kemper and several of the other men. No one is going to keep a precise count, so we'll be able to keep a reasonable stash here."

"What about Timothy and Titus learning some marksmanship?" Duncan chuckled at the memory of the horrendous fuss his sister had kicked up the first time she learned John had taken him out to do some target practice. "Do you think Em will allow it?"

"While you were away on your last voyage, I went down to the caretaker's cottage to talk to your father. He and I have been working on Emily a bit at a time—dropping hints so she could grow accustomed to the notion. At first she pitched a fit, but she's had a chance to let the idea sink in."

"I could tell her a Colt is more manageable and accurate for the boys. Safer by far, too." A distinct memory of that first time he'd fired John's rifle flitted through Duncan's mind, and he winced at it. "The kick from a rifle would knock them over."

"Your father sneaked Tim off a few weeks ago and let him discover that fact firsthand." John unconsciously rubbed his right collarbone. "I smuggled Tim some liniment that night to lessen the bruise, but he sported an impressive one."

"Gunpowder and bullets—what is your plan about those?"

The men talked long into the night—making plans and setting priorities. If war didn't occur, they'd easily use all the supplies in the course of time. If matters continued down the road of doom Duncan predicted, they'd need every last bit.

Aye, that was the sickening part of it all. The United States looked as if they weren't long to remain united. In a war, the North and the South would surely inflict wounds that would be slow to heal. With Virginia counting itself as the South and participating in the Southern economy, it would be doubly difficult since the capital was right there. This region would be in the middle of the skirmishes.

In the event of a war, Newcomb Shipping would be an immediate target for the factions. Each side would want to lay claim to the vessels. The very thought that the vessels they used only for peace would be conscripted for war left both men cold. By loading half the ships and setting up long-term voyages and trade agreements, John planned to keep a good part of the fleet out of the fray. His strategy ought to work well enough to keep them from being party to a good portion of the predicted violence.

John drummed his fingers on the table. "How do you stand, if it comes to fighting?"

Chapter 9

Duncan stared him directly in the eye. "I'm not eager to take a life; but if it comes to the point that we go to war, I'd represent our family. I want you to stay out of the fray. Em and the children need you too much." Duncan didn't want John to give him any grief over that assertion, so he smoothly changed the direction of the conversation. "Have you thought about what you want to do with the family? Will you keep them here since we were discussing firearms earlier?"

John shook his head. "It's one of the reasons I'm sending the boys with you to Massachusetts on this next voyage. It'll give you a good reason to drop in on my aunt. Discuss the matter with her. If she's amenable, I'll have Emily and the children stay with her for a season or two until the danger passes."

"You think Em will go for that?"

"She'll battle me." John wiped his mouth. "But Em loves the children, and in the end that will tip the balance in my favor. She'd do whatever is necessary to keep them safe."

Duncan absently swirled his glass until the milk turned into a whirlpool. "No matter whether you have a Northern or a Southern sympathizer, everyone is sure that if it comes to a battle, the whole matter will be over in a few months."

"We can only pray if it comes to that point, they're right. Now let's determine what supplies to stock up on and how to go about it."

Plans. They made their plans in seclusion over a fine meal and by a warm fire. Detail after detail needed consideration. The very next morning both men started to carry them out. Within days Duncan was glad they'd buckled down right away. Events around him made it abundantly clear they had assessed the political situation all too accurately. The nation was teetering on the precipice of civil unrest.

"Hey—did you read the article in *The Spectator* about Yancey's speech?" the sailmaker asked as Duncan inspected the cloth he proposed to use. "It says here, 'As a declaimer and specious reasoner, he has few superiors. As an ingenious debater, seeking to place fairly and frankly before the country a faithful record of facts and an incontrovertible accumulation of unimpeachable testimony, he was, in his effort of Wednesday, totally and painfully deficient.' "

"Hmm." Duncan tested the thickness of the fabric and frowned.

"Are you unhappy with the editor's opinion or with my goods?"

"I was considering having you make an extra set of sails to keep on hand. The last storm cost us dearly, and 'twould be wise for me to place an order." Duncan rapped his knuckles against the cutting table. "You can deliver them as you make them."

"Yes, I believe I could work in your order."

"Fine. Draw up the order and have the papers delivered. John or I will sign them and send a deposit. John may wish to order additional single sails or cloth. Be sure to include pricing."

The sailmaker couldn't hide his greedy smile. "Of course. Of course. I'll be right on that."

"Excellent." Duncan made a speedy exit and silently congratulated himself. He'd managed to tend to yet another of the priorities he and John agreed upon. If, indeed, war came, Newcomb Shipping needed to be wholly independent. Even if it meant sending some of the ships off on extended voyages to safeguard their fleet, they'd be able to do so if he and John continued to split these meetings and make acquisitions without raising any suspicions.

If anything, the fact that his own vessel was in the works made it that much easier. Each time he placed an order, merchants presumed he was fussing over his "baby." He could, in all honesty, confess that to be true. He did attend to each and every last detail. 'Twas no lie, and he held no shame for that fact. A ship carried souls across the unforgiving ocean; and the least little mishap, miscalculation, or mistake could be disastrous. He freely said as much, too. Everyone promptly agreed—some out of wisdom, others out of greed. Nonetheless, it allowed him to place an order for half again as much lumber because he'd nearly run out, for twice as much hemp rope, and for a full ton of iron for his blacksmith to make fittings.

ᴇᴈ

The next day Duncan came down to breakfast and was asked to drop Emily and the children off at the shore. John and Emily decided since the weather was turning and today looked to be fair, the children would do well to have a nice outing. Though John said nothing, Duncan fully understood his motive. If things settled down after the election, the children's trip to the shore would still be a fun time; if politics got ugly and the Newcombs decided to take the children away, they'd have a fond memory.

Emily left the breakfast table claiming she wasn't feeling well. Before she left, Emily asked Brigit to fill in and supervise the outing. According to plan, Duncan would leave her and the children at the shore, where they'd hunt for shells and enjoy a picnic. He'd simply pick them up a few hours later, after he conferred about his new vessel and booked cargo for the upcoming voyage.

Seven children, a dog, a blanket, art supplies, and a picnic basket took up the entire back of the wagon. Brigit turned three shades of pink when Duncan said she'd have to ride up on the bench seat with him. That very fact charmed him—it also made him decide he'd not allow her to trade places with Anna Kathleen, as she started to suggest. She might well be in charge of the children, but he was in charge of the outing.

"You're a quiet one," he said after they'd traveled down the road a ways and she'd not said a single word.

She shot him a nervous smile. "It's kind of you to drive us to the beach."

He tilted back his head and chortled. "Brigit, you might think I'm the worst kind of cad by the time I come to reclaim you. I'm stranding you with a wild tribe."

"But the day is lovely. We've sun to keep us warm, plenty of room to romp, and enough food to feed the town."

Once he selected a spot and stopped the wagon, Duncan hopped down, then reached up to assist Brigit. His hands spanned her tiny waist quite easily. Once more he appreciated how gracefully she moved. She thanked him prettily, and yet again he noticed her speech and conduct seemed far too refined for a simple housemaid. If Emily wouldn't make rash assumptions, he'd ask her about Brigit's family and background. As it was, he didn't dare. Satisfying that idle flash of curiosity would tilt Emily back into her matchmaking mode.

"Titus, you carry the blanket," Brigit said as she took visual inventory of the supplies. "Timothy, you're the strongest. I'll ask ye to carry the picnic hamper. Lily, be a dear and carry the wee crate with our paints and such. Yes, there you have it. Phillip, I'm trusting you to keep hold of Barkie's leash. Anna Kathleen—the twins will be yours and mine. I fear 'twill take the both of us to keep them in line."

Duncan stood back and watched. Brigit organized the children in short order. Instead of running off willy-nilly, they listened and obeyed. He helped settle them, then promised to return later.

Timothy and Titus swam like fish. So did Barkie. Duncan barely reached the shipyard ere he realized he'd not ascertained whether Brigit could. Not a one of the girls could swim a stroke, and Phillip wasn't any more accomplished than they. He should have given stern warning to the children that they weren't to get wet. What if one of them got overeager, went out, and—

John slapped him on the shoulder, jarring him from his concerns. "Wait until you see your cabin. The fittings are in."

"Yes. Um, John—can Brigit swim?"

John nodded. "Em asked her."

"Good. Good." But what use was the skill when Brigit's skirt used a full five yards and she undoubtedly wore the customary three layers of petticoats beneath that? Sodden skirts like that would work like an anchor.

"Franklin arranged for an entire load of cotton for Massachusetts, and the *Cormorant* is ready to set sail, but Josiah's taken ill."

Duncan glanced over at the vessel and nodded. "I can make the run."

"I hoped you'd volunteer. The delivery's set for the Boott Mills in Lowell." John batted away a pesky gnat. "I've talked Em into letting you take Timothy and Titus along on the next voyage—but this trip is unscheduled. If you'd rather pass or handle just one of the boys, I'll certainly understand."

"It's good news all around. My cabin's together, Franklin closed a deal and saved us time, and the boys are to get their feet wet." Duncan shook back a stubborn, curly lock of hair that the wind kept flinging down his forehead. "It's no trouble for me to take both. Tim might have wanted to be alone for his first voyage, but I'm thinking Titus will keep him good company."

John squinted at the rigging of a nearby vessel. "Aye, there's that."

Duncan dropped his tone. "And they need to meet relatives up North. If your plan becomes necessary, they'll do better if they're familiar with the new surroundings."

"Go on—see your vessel, and pick up the children afterward." Worry lined John's face. "Wind's taking on a bite to it, and I don't want them catching whatever Emily's come down with."

⁓

"Brigit, I need to pack the boys' bags for their voyage."

Brigit stood up so quickly that she banged her shoulder on the banister she'd been polishing. "When?"

"Now. Duncan just told me the captain of the *Cormorant* is sick, so he's taking the helm. The boys will be going with him. Have Trudy and Fiona finish polishing the wood, and you come help me."

"Yes, ma'am." Brigit washed her hands and passed on Miss Emily's instructions to the other maids, then went upstairs to join her. She found Miss Emily standing by the wardrobe in the boys' room. She had one hand braced against it for support. Brigit hurried to her side. "Miss Emily, you're white as a cloud. We'd best tuck you in bed straightaway."

"I'll lie on one of the beds and supervise; you can put everything in their valises. The laundry's fresh and ready so you can pack it now, and the boys can wear what they have on today when they board in the morning."

"Sure as can be, God must be smiling down on this plan for all to be ready like that."

Miss Emily settled onto the mattress and gave her a weak smile. "I like the way you think, lassie."

"Why don't I borrow a blanket off this other bed—"

"Stop fussing. We have work enough to do." Miss Emily closed her eyes and started to list the items they would need. "Two good shirts for when they're in Massachusetts. Two of the old ones to wear at sea. . ."

As Brigit carefully folded each garment and layered them into the boys' bags, she decided not to trouble Miss Emily with the details. A quick look through drawers and the wardrobe provided most of what they needed, and the rest of their necessities lay on the washstand.

Emily wiggled on the bed and let out a resigned little sound. "Poor John and Duncan. Most men are tense, what with worrying about the future of our nation. Feelings run high about such matters. John says he hopes once the election is over, things will settle down."

"That would be a pure blessing indeed."

"Brigit, I hope for miracles from God, not from man. John and Duncan are up to too much at the shipyard and spending too much time talking to each other in low tones."

"Is that what's wrong? Have you been worrying yourself sick?"

"What turns my stomach is that Newcomb ships have always been used for peaceful commerce. Even when others transported slaves, the Newcombs refused to make money in such a dreadful manner. John and Duncan fear that if war comes, the ships will be conscripted and fitted with cannons."

Brigit shook her head as she latched the valises. "There's a sorrowful thought."

"Duncan's been cantankerous as a shark with a toothache, but it's my fault for making this trip home so miserable for him. He's normally quite charming, and I hoped to help him settle down. You might have noticed I invited a few young ladies over."

Brigit compressed her lips to keep from laughing at that understatement.

"It seems I didn't spark a match; I sparked his temper."

"I'm sure it's not just that one thing." Brigit tried to watch her words. "Your brother must know you love him very much."

Emily sat up and grasped the covers on either side of her hips. "Ohh."

Brigit reached out and steadied her. "Perhaps you ought to lie back down."

Rubbing her fingertips across her much-too-pale forehead, Miss Emily said in a faint tone, "I planned to handle preparing Duncan's things myself. I don't think I'd better. Please, will you do me the favor of packing for him?"

"Of course I will." Brigit took Miss Emily's arm. Miss Emily steered them into Duncan's chamber and promptly melted onto his bed.

"Be sure to include that new shirt I had you sew." Miss Emily yawned. "He'll need everything you put in for the boys, and he'll also need his lucky coin."

❦

How in the world is a man to keep his sanity? Duncan headed down the companionway to his cabin. Two days at sea. It felt like an eternity, and he could hold the weather only partially to blame. It used to be he couldn't wait to set sail again. He'd no more than dock, and he'd be itching to cast off again. He liked the jig and reel world of his rowdy crew and the brotherhood of the sea. So why did he want to be on land?

Emily's matchmaking schemes would have made a lesser man break out in hives. I ought to be glad I escaped. Aye, I should—but I'm not. And it's all that blue-eyed maid's fault. The realization made his mood grow even more foul than the weather had been.

Duncan shut the door to his cabin and trudged toward his bunk. Salt chafed his skin, and wherever salt didn't, damp clothing did. As far as voyages went, this one rated as downright miserable thus far. They'd set sail and started out with fair weather and good hopes. By midafternoon a squall had blown in and battered the *Cormorant.*

Timothy had been horrendously seasick. Even now, he lay on Duncan's bed and looked downright puny. The lad's face still carried a sickly tinge of green. Titus, on the other hand, sat in the center of a hammock they'd suspended across the cabin. He rocked it like a swing and whispered, "He's still sleeping."

"You ought to be, too. I have plans for you in the morning, so you'd best rest up." Duncan waited until his nephew plopped down and was nearly swallowed up in the hammock. He let out a sigh of relief as he shed his clothes, sponged down, and put on a dry outfit. His stomach rumbled.

"I'm hungry, too." Titus popped back up. "I know how to get to the galley."

"I'll bet you do; but aboard a vessel, men don't pilfer the way you sometimes did when you wandered into the pantry and kitchen at home. That kind of undisciplined access to the provender could leave us all stranded and starving."

"Oh." Titus waited a beat. "You're the captain. You can do whatever you want."

Duncan hung his wet clothing up on pegs and slipped a thin strip of twine across them so they'd not sway free and plop on the deck. He scowled at a pile of fabric in the corner. "What is that mess?"

"Huh? Oh. My clothes."

Duncan crossed the cabin in a few long strides and unceremoniously dumped his nephew out of the hammock and onto the deck. "Aboard a vessel nothing is left out. It shifts and slides, and a man can trip as a result. There's no maid here to baby you. You'll be a man and clean up after yourself."

"Yes, sir."

Duncan left the cabin. When he returned, Titus's clothes occupied pegs and were secured with twine. "Well done. Come share a bite with me. Afterward I'll dump you into the bunk with Tim and take the hammock. I'm warning you now, I'm going to snore enough wind to send us clear to Massachusetts by morn."

Titus muffled his chuckle and scrambled to the captain's desk. They shared a hunk of cheese, some soda bread, and a pair of apples. "Uncle Duncan, do you think Mama misses us?"

"Emily is bound to miss you. Me? She's used to me coming and going." Brigit's image flashed through his mind. He suppressed it at once and cast a look over at Tim. "Has he kept anything down at all?"

"Lemon drops." Titus pulled out a small tin and rattled it. "Brigit gave them to us. She said they would settle a tipsy stomach, and they did."

The mention of that maid he'd just thought of only served to sour Duncan's mood. Women. God created them for His purposes, and Duncan acknowledged that. He even granted they made the world a far better place—but only from a distance. Marriage? That lay several years in the future. *Then what am I doing, thinking of Brigit and marriage at the same time?*

Duncan cleared his throat. He didn't want to grouse at his nephew any more than he already had. "Enough. You go climb in with Tim. I'm manning the hammock."

Weary as could be, Duncan barely managed to finish thanking the Lord for pulling his vessel through bad weather and watching over his family before he mumbled amen and fell asleep. He didn't dream one bit; but when he opened his eyes, he had a strange sense of having traveled back in time. Years ago he'd awakened in a hammock in this selfsame cabin when he accompanied John on voyages. The memory was a fine way to start the day.

Duncan spotted the valise he'd secured on a peg next to the wardrobe when he'd boarded back home. It would take a few minutes to unpack, so he started in.

Emily always insisted on packing for him. The way she didn't fuss yet showed her love in countless ways warmed his heart. When he married, he wanted a good woman like Em—one whose capabilities and caring would make for a happy home.

Each article of freshly starched and pressed clothing fit in his compact wardrobe. A new shirt appeared—a fine one at that—not a fancy one for Sunday best, but one that featured full-cut shoulders and plenty of sleeve to allow ease of motion while on board.

He'd felt oddly bereft the past few days, realizing he'd left something important ashore. Duncan knew he couldn't very well order the ship back to port to allow him to run home and get his special quarter, but its absence had left him uneasy. . .until he felt something in the fabric of the new shirt—his quarter! *God bless Em for seeing to that detail.*

He treasured that assurance and always kept the coin with him on his voyages—a touchstone that reminded him he had a home and loved ones awaiting his return. He curled his hand around it and glanced at Tim and Titus. *I'll bring them back to you, Em. You can count on it.*

Chapter 10

The *Cormorant* docked in Lowell, Massachusetts. Duncan made sure all was well and gave orders for the Southern cotton to be delivered to the Boott Mills. He traced his finger down the register. "See here, Tim? The agreement is for the entire cargo. Every last bale, each of them approximately one hundred pounds. The mills run by water power, but the water level there is low, so the bales will travel by barge."

"Do you have to arrange for the barges?"

"Your father or Franklin already tended to that matter. Because we do this run so regularly, Newcomb Shipping is able to book for the services."

"Uncle Duncan, can't you take something home that's better than dumb old material?" Titus wrinkled his sunburnt nose. "We already have millions and millions of bolts in the warehouse."

Duncan shook his head and ignored the exaggeration. "A deal was struck. A man sticks to his word. We've lined up buyers for the fabric. Already most of it is earmarked for Europe. It'll go out the week after Christmas."

"On your new ship?"

"Aye," Duncan said, stretching the single syllable into a long, satisfied sound. " 'Tis to be my new home at sea. For now, though, we need to pay our respects to your aunt."

After his nephews were settled in with Aunt Mildred, Duncan went back to the docks. The lads needed to stretch their legs, and their aunt had plans to keep them busy. Especially if they would have to come live here, they'd need to forge a comfortable relationship, and Duncan didn't want to run interference. Business wasn't just a necessary obligation; it also supplied a reasonable excuse for him to take his leave.

The next three days, bales of cotton left the holds of the *Cormorant* and rode the barges to the mills. The space vacated filled with bolts upon bolts of cloth. Brightly printed calicos, practical shirting, and sheeting accounted for the greatest portion of the order. Duncan spot-checked the loads to assure the quality didn't waver. He also made a trip to the warehouse and selected a variety of the finest fabrics Lowell had to offer. Those bolts were muslin wrapped and stored with additional care.

The bustle and rhythm of commerce appealed to Duncan. He thought to take Tim and Titus with him for a day as he tended to business, but he dismissed that plan immediately. Almost to the man, each contact slid into some political discourse.

Duncan had hoped the rhetoric wouldn't be so strident since they were so far north. Though he privately agreed Lincoln would be a godsend as the president and didn't support disunion, he also understood some of the economic issues driving the unrest in the South. He personally believed all men were created equal—that his Irish roots didn't make him any less God's child; so why would African roots make a man less worthy of respect or God's grace? The hopes he'd held that Lincoln might heal the rifts evaporated as rapidly as the steam that powered the looms in the mills.

After the ship's hold was filled with the goods and they were set to sail with the tide the next evening, Duncan sat down to supper with Aunt Mildred and the boys. He rather hoped if he broached a certain subject, Aunt Mildred would volunteer to assist him. "Emily wanted me to buy some prints for the staff."

"Prints?" Aunt Mildred's eyes widened. "Now that's different."

"Mama doesn't like to do things the usual way," Titus said. He took a gulp of potatoes.

"She's a very uncommon woman," Aunt Mildred agreed. Her voice held no censure. Indeed, Duncan recalled she'd been infinitely kind to Em when John had wed her and she'd needed to learn the ways of society. "I confess, I like the blue she's used for your household staff. Black is so dreary."

Duncan leaned forward. "Come along and help me make appropriate selections. You'd have a better notion of what Em would like."

"I have every confidence you'll do fine. I already promised Tim and Titus I'd take them to the museum."

Duncan nodded. He couldn't begrudge the boys a nice outing.

Timothy started to chuckle. Duncan shot him a questioning look, and the chuckle turned into a full-throated chortle. "Buy pink. Nothing but pink. I'll bet Prudence Carston suddenly stops wearing it if you do, because she'd never want anyone to think she's an ordinary woman instead of one of society's darlings."

Pink. The next day after he picked up the ring John had ordered, Duncan stood in the warehouse and stared at the fabrics. He glanced at the pinks and winced. *How did I let Em saddle me with such a ridiculous errand? As often as she goes to the shipping office and rides by the warehouses, she could have gone in and chosen whatever suited her fancy.* Duncan gave fleeting thought to pleading that he was simply too busy, and it would have been the utter truth; but the special quarter in his pocket reminded him of how family cared for one another. He'd do this for Emily.

Em wanted prints. She'd also specified they were to be pretty and of good quality. He'd handled cloth aplenty, and judging quality presented no problem. The real problem lay with selecting something reasonable. Pretty prints abounded—many made with the newest aniline dyes so they had eye-catching color. He wanted to make this a quick grab-and-dash type of task; but to his consternation, he couldn't.

"As you can see, they're arranged on the shelves by color." The warehouse-man waved his arm in a wide arc to encompass a veritable rainbow. "The blacks and browns are practical. Keep the dirt and wear from showing."

Duncan headed toward the grays.

"Those are especially suitable for second-year mourning attire."

Disenchanted by that bit of information, Duncan turned toward the blues. *Blue. The color of Brigit's extraordinary eyes.* No, he refused to be beguiled by her. Besides, Em was tired of blue.

"Greens are favored this year." The warehouseman leaned against the cart he'd pushed along.

Greens looked fresh. *Appealing. They'd set off Brigit's hair and*—Duncan cut off that line of thought. *Yellows would show every last smudge. As often as she—no, all the maids,* he corrected himself—*dusted, the gown would look filthy.*

Ah. Respite. White. Duncan felt a wee bit of the tension drain away. He'd been wanting to buy some white for himself. Aye, he did. When he got home, he'd get Emily to tell him who had sewed that new shirt. She'd placed the order, so she'd be able to direct him. He'd never had a better fit—the generous cut across the shoulders didn't bind, and the extra length made sure it stayed tucked in. He'd supply more cotton and place an order for her to make him a good half dozen more. He'd make sure, though, that he'd simply handle the transaction in writing. Knowing Emily, she'd hired some comely seamstress in hopes that he'd fall in love. He'd rather swim to England than deal with his sister's ridiculous romantic machinations.

A single bolt—that was all he'd need. Straight off the loom, a bolt held sixty yards. The printed cloth was processed and cut into half that length. Duncan squinted and noticed the bolts of white had also been halved. He shrugged. Thirty yards would keep him in shirts—what about John and the boys? Titus and Tim both washed their shirts aboard the ship and nearly tore them to shreds. They were growing fast. Duncan chose two bolts of white. White. Aprons. Emily always had the staff wear them. Brigit had a charming habit of slipping her hand into her apron pocket and tilting her head to starboard just a bit—a telling cue that she was thinking something through. He chucked a third bolt onto the cart.

"I thought you said you were wanting colored prints."

The voice behind Duncan pulled him from his thoughts. He stared at the cart and couldn't believe what he'd done. *Ninety yards. I just grabbed ninety yards of white.*

"Don't mistake me. You chose the finest white that we carry. Mayhap I misunderstood—"

"No, not at all. I also want prints." Duncan strode ahead to the next set of shelves. *Pink?* He shuddered. *The shade of Prudence.*

Only women of ill repute wore red.

He turned the corner and gave up on trying to reason through what choices to make. Duncan impatiently grabbed several bolts and heaved them onto the cart. Even then Duncan kept picturing how Brigit would look dressed in almost every swath of cloth he touched. *Brigit. Aye, she is quite the lass. Pure of heart, quick of mind, and kind in spirit. A rare woman indeed.*

Duncan halted dead in his tracks and marveled under his breath, "Well, blow me down. I was so set on swimming free of Em's marriage net that I jumped right out of the water and into the boat."

"What was that?"

"Show me your bridal material."

Chapter 11

Home. While at sea, Duncan felt the ocean was his home; but when he landed and rode up the drive to the Newcomb estate, his heart filled with an unmistakable warmth that told him he belonged here. He cast a glance over at Tim and Titus. Clearly they felt that same tug. They unconsciously kneed their mounts, and all three of them galloped the last mile.

"Why are there so many carriages and ribbons?" asked Titus.

"Can't you remember anything?" Timothy gave his brother a scathing look. "It's Phillip's birthday. I'll bet that's why Duncan got so pushy about us setting sail."

"I wasn't pushy. I was emphatic. A captain sets his timetable, and the crew needs to adhere to it. Discipline and control are essential on any vessel."

"Yeah, well, those are all right, I suppose." Titus wrinkled his nose. "I just didn't like some of the other rules."

Duncan gave him a long look. "No more shedding your clothes like a snake. That voyage trained you to be a man. Now act like one."

"I'll make you proud." Titus stared back at him. "You have my word of honor."

His word of honor. Duncan nodded. Honor. Integrity mattered to him above all but God and family. The one thing he couldn't abide was dishonesty or deception. He couldn't very well come home and pretend indifference to the woman he loved.

What would he do about Brigit, now that he'd returned? In the time he'd been gone, he'd reconsidered the whole situation and come to the same conclusion over and over again: He loved her. She'd been in his thoughts nearly every waking minute, and he'd dreamed of her, too. She read well and enjoyed the same books he did, could carry on an intelligent conversation, and showed devotion to his family. Aye, she was a sweet woman.

Marriage to her wouldn't be a trap; it would be a joy. He'd need to court her a bit. Women put store in such customs. If he had his way, he'd just stand up in church Sunday and let the parson help them speak their vows. The first step would be making sure the feelings were mutual; then he'd do the right thing— go to her parents as well as settle her in with his own folks down at the caretaker's cottage. That way he'd see her every day while the women took care of the social details of arranging the wedding. It shouldn't take long. After all, he'd already seen to getting the fabric for her bridal gown.

Brigit. There she was, standing on the veranda, holding hands with June and Julie. The cashmere shawl about her shoulders drew Duncan's attention. He wanted to use it to tug her into his arms for a welcome-home hug and kiss, but he'd not do such a thing.

"We're home!" Titus shouted.

"We've been waiting!" Julie and June shouted back. Both tried to tug forward, but Brigit held them back. A wise move, that. If they were to shriek or move rapidly, they might startle one of the boys' horses.

Brigit didn't meet Duncan's gaze. Instead she smiled at Timothy and Titus. "We're looking forward to hearing all about your grand adventure as sailors."

"Tim got seasick the first day," Titus blabbed.

"Titus was homesick the whole time," Tim shot back.

The girls both giggled at their brothers' rivalry, but Brigit squeezed the twins' hands. "Now will you be taking a chance to fill your eyes with the sight before you? Your brothers left as lads, but I'm sure as can be they've come back men now. Taller and smarter, too."

"What about Uncle Duncan?" Julie asked.

"Your uncle." Brigit stretched out the words to allow herself time to respond. Duncan wondered how she'd get herself out of this. He didn't have to wait a second more. "Your uncle was already tall and smart before he left."

"Let me tell you how smart," Tim chimed in. "Wait until you hear about when we were at the—"

"We can all wait," Duncan cut in. Brigit rated as one of the most clever women he'd ever met. She weighed her words carefully around the children, and that discretion rated as a fine quality indeed.

"It won't take me long to tell the story—" Tim protested.

" 'Tis Phillip's birthday." Duncan put the slightest bit of pressure on his horse's side to keep him from dancing and bumping hindquarters with Tim's mount. "We need to go stable these mounts so we can celebrate Phillip's special accomplishment, too."

"What 'complishment?" June asked.

"He got older." Duncan nodded his head to give weight to his ridiculous comment. "It won't be many years ere he's taking to sea, too."

⌇

Brigit wanted to go hide in the kitchen and help Cook. One look at Duncan let her know she hadn't been exaggerating how handsome he was when she thought of him. He looked so manly with his brown, caped greatcoat flying behind him as he'd ridden up, and his roguish smile and deep voice gave her the shivers. She might very well make a fool of herself if she didn't mind her actions. The last thing she wanted was to lose her job because she flirted with a member of the family she was supposed to be serving. *I thought Trudy acted like a lovesick puppy, and here I am, twice as bad.*

She and the twins were supposed to greet the birthday party guests, so she'd been out on the veranda, planning to welcome a dozen or more rowdy little boys. Brigit had seen a trio on horses in the distance and expected they were more guests. She'd felt her heart lurch when she recognized who the handsome young man was, riding between the two youngsters. Duncan had come back.

Brigit promised herself she'd keep her distance from Duncan. What with all the guests, that ought to be an easy thing to do. She figured the last of the guests must have arrived, so she went back inside with the twins.

Miss Emily believed in simple, honest fun. Instead of setting up several parlor games, she'd specified that Phillip's guests were to come in warm playclothes. With everyone assembled, she turned them loose in the back. Soon they were chasing a ball and rolling down the hill.

The maids and the stablemen stayed out on the lawn, overseeing the children's safety. Brigit soon gathered up some of the children and lined them up to join her in a game of tug-o-war. Duncan didn't stay in the house with the adults; he'd come outside, too. Phillip shouted with glee, and Duncan eyed the rope and the boys.

"I want to be on your team," Phillip said.

Duncan strode over and had his nephew flex his biceps. He tested the little arms and nodded. "You're stronger. I think you and your friends should pull against me." He looked at Brigit and added, "And her. Just the two of us against all of you mighty little men. What say you?"

"Aye!" Phillip didn't answer alone. His friends all chimed in with him.

As they prepared to tug, Brigit stood in front of Duncan and warned, "You made a bad decision. You won't be getting much from a weakling like me."

"You'll put your heart into it. That'll make us winners."

He turned out to be right on the first match. On the second, Brigit couldn't dig her heels into the earth well enough. Her boots slid, and her back knocked Duncan down, and she fell over him—or had he let go and caught her so she wouldn't fall? She couldn't tell. The very thought that he'd be so chivalrous made her heart patter. She scrambled to her feet.

Duncan rose. "Are you all right?"

"Fine."

Many of the little boys gravitated toward the strapping man, much to Brigit's relief. It let her scoot farther away. In no time at all, "Captain Duncan" had the "crew" of youngsters making forts from hay bales and ice blocks. It made for a glorious mess.

"Brigit!"

She turned when he called her name. White exploded all around her. Duncan stuck his hands in his coat pockets, looked up at the sky, and started to whistle as if he were innocent as a babe.

"Unca Duncan got you!" Phillip shouted from inside the makeshift fort. "He made a snowball by chipping an ice block."

"That was a sneaky thing to do," Brigit protested.

"You know what else is sneaky?" Phillip grinned at her. "He made me one for my birthday!" Phillip threw that snowball at her, but it fell short.

"I'm needing soldiers and warriors," Brigit called out. "Duncan O'Brien just declared war, and Phillip is in his camp. Who's going to stand by me?"

"We can play Capture the Flag!" someone shouted.

In no time at all, an epic "battle" ensued. In the midst of it, Duncan charged across the yard, vaulted over Brigit's melting fort, and tossed her over his brawny shoulder. He plowed through the broken-down bales of hay and headed back to his side. "I've got the princess! I captured her. We win!"

The children went wild, and the adults cheered.

Breathless—more from his contact than from being carried over his shoulder—Brigit couldn't say a word. He stopped and set her down next to his team's fort. Standing like Colossus with his hands on his hips, he asked loudly, "So what say you now, my raven-haired maiden?"

Oh! I'd have been just as happy for him to carry me away. If I stand here, I'm going to make a fool of myself. I can't let him know I have tender feelings for him. "I'm not a flag!"

"But you're holding your team's," he pointed out. "And I got you."

Brigit grabbed the scrap of red cloth someone had draped over Duncan's fort. "But you let go, and I have your flag now! You counted your chickens a minute too soon."

He looked at her and nodded slowly. "We both did."

"We did?" She sucked in a sharp breath and squealed as a chunk of ice slithered across the back of her neck.

Duncan swept both flags from her hands and chortled. "Well done, Phillip."

Several of the children cheered and clung to Duncan, and his laughter rang out. The man loved children. Aye, and they adored him back.

Even after the party ended and the house quieted down, Duncan sat on the floor and voiced his admiration for the gifts Phillip had received. Brigit gladly finished picking up the last of the mess and hastened out of Duncan's presence. He'd kept slanting her glances she couldn't interpret. *Lord, I don't understand why he's giving me those looks. Has he guessed that I hold feelings for him? What am I to do?*

Chapter 12

The first rays of sun shimmered on the dewy lawn. Brigit looked out her window and touched the ice-cold pane. Another day. "Lord, be with me today. Keep me strong and give me wisdom to behave as Your daughter."

After washing up, Brigit donned one of her blue wool gowns and brushed her hair until it crackled. Her fingers fumbled with the hairpins as she recalled what Duncan had called her yesterday. *My raven-haired maiden.*

The man was a rascal. That he was. He'd acted like an overgrown boy. She refused to give him another thought. All it did was rob her of her peace and sanity. Brigit savagely stabbed one last pin in place. On days like this, she reconsidered her opinion of Miss Emily's no-cap policy. Wearing a cap might well have merit. In fact, Brigit thought she'd vote for a complete night-styled mobcap if given the chance. Wouldn't that be just perfect? Then Duncan couldn't say a thing about her hair. He'd never see it.

She dropped her buttonhook and had to get down on her hands and knees to fish it out from beneath her bed. After she used it to fasten her ankle boots, Brigit frowned at the bed. She'd mussed up the counterpane. That wouldn't do. No matter that another soul wouldn't know. She'd know, and that was reason enough to flick it back into order. Miss Emily provided individual rooms for the maids, and the appointments in them far exceeded what a girl in service might ever dream.

Aye, and I'll be in service until I'm no longer a raven-haired girl, but a gray-haired old woman, she thought as she closed the door and headed down the stairs. *Those silly feelings I thought I had for Duncan? Well, they were just a momentary weakness—nothing more. I'll keep away from him until I regain my balance. Now there's a bonny plan—full of good sense.* She sighed. *If it is such a great plan, why does it make me miserable?*

Duncan stood at the foot of the stairs. Brigit wanted to spin around and run back up in the pretense of having forgotten something—but that wouldn't be the truth. She squared her shoulders and continued down.

He gave her an appreciative smile. "You're a comely lass, Brigit Murphy."

"Thank you." She tried to brush past him.

"Brigit." He captured her hand and stopped her. "Stop avoiding me."

"I've work to do."

"Yes, you do, don't you?" His deep voice flowed over her. "Emily tells me you made that fine new shirt I like so well. I told her I want a dozen more—all made by you."

She snatched that as an excuse. "With all that stitching to do, I'd best get right on it."

He squeezed her hand, then turned it loose. "I'll let you go for now—but we'll talk later."

Brigit shook her head. "We've nothing to discuss."

He dared to reach over and touch a tendril at her temple. "I disagree."

"I'm needed in the kitchen," she stammered. With a total lack of grace and decorum, she dashed for safety.

∽

John glanced up from the newspaper. "*Pennsylvania Telegraph* didn't mince words today. Listen to this: 'We have no notion or idea that Abraham Lincoln will be defeated as a candidate before the American people for the presidency of the United States; but if such a calamity should occur, it would be the worst blow that ever was inflicted on the laboring men and mechanics of this country. It would arrest our progress in every improvement, by opening all the paths of industry to the competition of foreign and domestic slavery.'"

Duncan nodded and set down the ship's log he wanted to review. "Strongly put."

John folded the paper and slapped it down on the desk. "I've never prayed as hard for our nation as I did when I cast my ballot today."

"I need to go vote." Duncan looked about. "Things are far calmer than I expected. How did you manage to make the men keep their opinions on the vote to themselves?"

"Franklin passed the word: Anyone stirring up dissension or stumping for votes is fired. The men need their jobs too much."

Duncan rested his hands on his hips. "I'm supposin' Gerard O'Leary protested you were curbing his right to free speech."

"Yeah, but Old Kemper nipped that in the bud. Told O'Leary his speech wouldn't be free if he was drawing wages when he said his piece."

"Commonsense men like Kemper would straighten out the political mess in no time." Duncan arched his back to stretch out a few kinks. Em often rubbed John's shoulders to banish the tautness. *Soon Brigit will be my wife, and I'll relish that kind of closeness myself.* He thought for a moment to inform John of his decision to wed, then squelched the notion. He'd given Em his word that she'd be the first to know.

∽

"Miss Emily," Brigit asked that afternoon, "I'm wondering where that lovely little figurine went—the one of the lass in the pretty gown and a lamb at her side. 'Tisn't on the hall table anymore."

Emily looked startled. "That's where it always is. I chose that spot because it's farthest away from the children's rooms and won't get bumped. I hope one of the girls didn't borrow it. It belonged to my sister, Anna, God rest her sweet soul. I'd be heartbroken if something happened to it."

No one confessed to knowing where the pretty porcelain piece went. For a brief instant, Brigit wondered if the man she occasionally saw from her attic window might have taken it, but she dismissed that thought. He'd never even come close to the house. In fact, the times she'd spied him, he'd always been by a shrub or next to a tree. Hadn't she overheard Mr. John say he hired men to patrol the grounds? Whoever the guard was, he'd be competent—John Newcomb would engage a bulldog of a man for the sake of his family.

Brigit forgot about the missing statue because she was due for her evening off, and she planned to go visit her parents. Bless Cook's heart—she remembered Mum loved apricots and wrapped a jar of them along with a small crock of whipped cream for Brigit to take home.

Surrounded by her warm cashmere shawl and holding the sweet bundle to give to her parents, Brigit felt blessed. She loved to be able to give even the smallest thing to help them. As she hurried home, she whispered, "Lord Almighty, I'm thankin' You from the bottom of my heart for the ways You provide for my family."

"Hey, there, Brigit Murphy! What are you doin' here?" a lass asked as Brigit turned a corner and headed down the side street toward her parents' building.

Brigit stopped and smiled at the young girl she'd met on the boat as they'd voyaged here. "I'm paying a visitation." She cradled the apricots and cream in her arms and tilted her head toward them. "I've something small that'll be sure to please my mum."

⌘

Duncan stood in the shadows around the side of the tenement building as he heard Brigit speak. When he left the polling place, he'd spotted her bright blue dress and contrasting yellow shawl in the distance and recalled Emily mentioning it was to be Brigit's evening off. Duncan had quickly followed Brigit to the edge of town until they reached here and counted his blessings that the Lord had presented him with this unexpected opportunity. He needed to know where her father lived so he could obtain permission to court her and seek her hand in marriage. Duncan smiled to himself. He'd rather the courtship part of the arrangement be quite brief and hoped Brigit would feel the same way.

He'd thought 'twas fitting that the woman he intended as his bride would catch his attention. And why wouldn't she? A comely lass she was and quick minded. But in the last few days, she'd avoided him. In fact, she'd ghosted away whenever he entered the room. Once she'd been underfoot all the time. No matter where he turned in that house, she'd been there. He smiled. He'd been attracted from the start, and the fact that he'd been so aware of her was ample proof. He suspected the reason she'd begun hiding from him, and he'd help her get over that shyness. He'd likely scared her with that playful romp at Phillip's party. As soon as he made it clear he had honorable intentions and would safeguard her reputation, the woman would light up his world with her smile once again.

He'd overheard her say something about having a little something to please her mother. Duncan lounged against a tree and folded his arms across his chest. His bride was a dutiful woman. Devoted, too. The mental list he'd started of her fine character qualities kept growing.

He'd have to do something at once about her parents' housing. They'd be his family now, too, and he didn't want them living in this dangerous, squalid place. Duncan didn't even want her in there right now. He thought to ask which room her parents rented, but a trollop approached him and offered her services.

Duncan shook his head. "I'd like information is all."

"It'll cost ye." The tart gave him a coy smile.

"Brigit Murphy—do you know what room or floor her family is on?" He placed a coin in the woman's hand.

"I couldn't say. There are Murphys aplenty, so I don't bother to keep them straight. Brigit doesn't live here. She's hired out in service to a fancy family." The trollop gave him an assessing look. "You'll have to tell me. Has old Mr. Murphy done something wrong? Is there a reward for him?"

"No. Not at all."

She heaved a sigh. "I didn't think so. They're one of the goody-good families. Her da walks her back to the grand place where she's a maid; my da turned me out to make money."

Duncan looked past the rouge and gaudy clothes. "If you were offered a decent job, would you give up this way of life?"

She shook her head. "Sinnin' suits me fine. Money's not bad, either."

Her attitude left him feeling soiled. Duncan straightened up and walked off. He'd found out what he needed to know. Brigit's father would return her safely this evening, and Duncan planned to wait for him.

He went home with a sense that his life was about to change—and for the good. Aye, 'twas a grand feeling. He'd have a wondrous wife and a fine ship, and if the election went as he'd voted, the country would have a wise man at the helm.

The minute Duncan entered the house, Goodhew took his coat and told him in a grave tone, "Mr. John and Miss Emily wish to speak with you at once. They're in the upstairs parlor."

Well and good. I'll tell them of my plan to wed Brigit. "Thank you, Goodhew."

The minute he entered the small upstairs room, Duncan knew something was wrong. Em's eyes were puffy and red. John stood by the window, tension singing from every last inch of his frame. Duncan shut the door. "What is it?"

"We have a thief in the house."

Chapter 13

A thief!" Duncan echoed the words in disbelief.

The fire in John's eyes made it clear he'd determined the truth.

"Who is it?" Duncan demanded.

"I haven't pinned that down yet," John grated. "But as soon as I do—"

"I'm really not sure anything's been stolen," Emily confessed. "I could have misplaced my cameo, and I recall allowing Anna Kathleen to borrow my fan. She mightn't have returned it."

Duncan let out a relieved gust of air. "Is that all?"

"No." John cleared his throat. "I've left money out on purpose—and, I confess, not a single cent of it has been taken."

"I'd think money would be the first thing to be taken. If it's left alone, then perhaps Em's right and those other things are simply misplaced."

John sat next to his wife and took her hand in his. Duncan could see how hard he was trying to contain his anger so Emily wouldn't suffer any more upset than necessary. He waited. John wasn't a man to jump to conclusions. He was probably doling out the bad news a bit at a time to soften the impact on Emily.

"A book I'd been reading seems to have grown legs and walked off, and you know about my grandfather's fountain pen. Anna Kathleen told Emily today that her locket is missing, too. None of those things alone amounted to much of anything. In fact, most of them could have simply been misplaced. Emily and I decided to keep watch, but we said nothing since we've never had cause to mistrust the household staff."

Emily whispered, "We were hoping things would turn up again." She gave Duncan a look that melted his heart. "But now our Anna's pretty little statue is gone."

He jolted. "The shepherdess?"

Emily tearfully confirmed, "Anna cherished it so."

John thumped his fist on his thigh. "Julie's china doll is gone. The truth is clear enough: The stolen goods are ones a woman would want. Whoever's taking them has to have free access to the house. That means—"

"The thief is on staff," Duncan finished. He shook his head in disbelief. "Let's try to put together the pieces of the puzzle."

"Goodhew and Cook have been with me forever." John stared at the door.

"My grandmother hired them, and they've served faithfully for decades."

Duncan agreed. "No suspicion could be cast in that direction."

"That leaves the maids," John said grimly. "Em and I were trying to apply some deductive reasoning before you came in. Trudy and Fiona can scarcely read, so it makes no sense that they'd take a book or a fountain pen."

"But since you might have just misplaced those, we can't rely on that." Emily tugged on his hand. "You've been so busy that you're a wee bit absentminded, you know."

"Fiona is patient as can be with the girls, so she'd have ample opportunity to take a doll; but she's awkward as a pelican," Duncan thought aloud. "I can't imagine her tiptoeing around—she'd crash into something first."

"Trudy's made a pest of herself mooning over Duncan," Emily told John. "I've been keeping my eye on her or assigning her to tasks along with another maid so she'd be supervised. I'm doubting she could have managed to pilfer anything."

"That leaves Lee and Brigit." John's face tightened. "They can both read."

"We have to trust them." Emily looked from John to Duncan and back again as she asserted, "I do, I'm telling you."

Duncan shoved his hands in his pockets. It had to be Lee then. His sweet little Brigit wouldn't ever—

John forged ahead. "I've been trying to put the facts together. Lee was gone on her days off when the locket and cameo were taken. That leaves Brigit."

Sick anger washed over Duncan. *I trusted the lass. I was ready to make her my wife. How could I have been such an idiot? She's been playing me for a fool all this time.* She'd been clever and quick about helping him over a rough spot or two with Emily's matchmaking—but now he realized she might well be a woman well accustomed to keeping secrets. 'Twas also a way she turned him into an ally so he'd drop his guard and not be suspicious. Oh—and that habit she had of slipping her hand into her apron pocket that he'd thought was so endearing—was it a sinister thing? Had she been swiping things from under his very nose?

Recalling the bundle she'd carried into the tenement tonight only fanned the flames of Duncan's mistrust. Hearing her boast that she had something sure to please her mother—well, that about cinched it.

Brigit—she'd duped him as easily as John's brother, Edward, had gulled Anna. *At least I discovered the truth before the marriage. Thank the Lord for that small miracle. This is already debacle enough as is.*

Duncan felt as if he'd swallowed a fistful of barnacles as he agreed, "It's Brigit."

"No, it can't be," Emily insisted. "I trust her. You must, too."

"Trust? You expect me to trust her? Em, I saw her carry a bundle into a building tonight. Before she disappeared, she boasted about how she had something to please her mother. It's plain as can be what's happening."

John stood. "I'll dismiss her this minute."

Emily tugged him back down. "You're jumping to conclusions—that's what's happening. Why, Brigit is the one who pointed out the figurine and the doll are both missing."

"It sure seems like more than a simple coincidence that Brigit 'discovers' the items are gone. It's nothing more than a smokescreen. It's her way of looking innocent while she's probably pocketing the goods and pawning them."

"It doesn't make a lick of sense. We've countless things a thief could take that would bring a far better price than what's come up missing."

"Let's talk about what's missing." Duncan struggled to get Emily to face the facts. He felt as if he'd been gut-punched and understood her shock, but pain was best dealt with right away so they could get rid of the problem. . .get rid of Brigit. "Think about it: Nothing ever got taken until she came to work here."

"Brigit has a pure heart. She'd not take a thing, I'm telling you." Emily folded her arms across her bosom and glared at him. "I know my staff."

"She has you bamboozled."

"Do I come down to your vessels and pass judgment on the men you hire for your crews?"

"Em," John said in an I'm-trying-to-be-patient tone, "that's an entirely different matter."

"Indeed it is." She agreed all too quickly. "Here at home if I employ a bad staff member, the worst that can happen is some little trinket is taken; if you sign on a man who does something wrong out at sea, it can cost lives."

Duncan refused to try to reason further with her. Until his sister came to her senses, he'd have to protect the family from Brigit's pilfering. "I'm going to shadow her and see what she's up to. What we need to do is keep this quiet. The best way to catch a thief is to let her think she's safe. If she doesn't suspect we're wise to the problem because she's taking only paltry items, she'll keep at it." *I'll catch her red-handed.*

"Josiah is hale again." John nodded. "You can stay home, and he'll take the *Contentment* out since you just did his run with the *Cormorant.*"

"It won't be necessary. I'll do this next run with my crew. Mark my words—it won't take long to get proof on"—he saw the look on Emily's face and hastily changed the end of his sentence—"the thief."

Emily heard his plan and let out a humorless laugh. "You've far better things to do with your time. I'll make no bones about it: You've lost your mind. If you're searching for anything at all, your wits ought to be at the top of the list."

Duncan stood and left the room. As he shut the door, he thought, *If only it was just my wits. I've lost my heart.*

Chapter 14

D a walked her back to the Newcomb estate and gave her a kiss on the cheek. Brigit hugged him tightly and whispered in his ear, "I love you, Da. Take care of Mum."

"I worry about you." He looked up at the mansion and shook his head.

Brigit's heart beat heavily with the sadness she felt. Not so long ago, Da had been the owner of such a fine home. Aye, he had. Now he couldn't even land a steady job. She gave his hand a squeeze and tried to lighten her tone. "Worry? Now there's a fine waste of your time. You're supposed to lay me at the Lord's feet and not fret a bit."

She went upstairs to her attic room and waved out the window until Da was out of sight. A hasty splash at her basin, a quick change into her warm flannel nightgown, and she had a bit of time to read her Bible. After she closed it, she blew out her lamp, walked to the window, and stared out at the ocean as she prayed.

The Lord's world was vast. Aye, and He could reach out His mighty hand and do anything. *Tonight, heavenly Father, I'm asking You for just a small thing. Insignificant really. Well, it is important to me. Please, will You help Da to come into his own here in America?*

After she finished praying, Brigit continued to look outside. A sudden movement caught her eye. There he was again—the man who sometimes crept to the very edge of the trees and shrubs before the clearing around the house. He stood there in the dark of night. Once she'd seen him there at the break of dawn.

Who is he? Is he the man Mr. John said would be patrolling the property? Can it be in connection with the private meetings Mr. John and Duncan held about the possible war? She'd seen the crate filled with fine wooden boxes down in the corner of the library. Titus had gotten snoopy and opened one while she was dusting. Because of that incident, Brigit knew the boxes each contained a fancy-looking firearm. It all probably linked together.

Brigit balanced on one foot and rubbed the back of that calf with the toes of her other foot. War. Politics. She wrinkled her nose. Such matters were for men. She needed to mind her own business.

In the few seconds she'd not paid attention, the stranger disappeared. Someone was walking straight toward the house. She pressed her face closer to the window-pane and squinted. Oh. It was Mr. John. Clearly whomever he'd met wasn't of any danger to the household. Since Mr. John saw fit to slip out of the house and hold his meetings in the dark, Brigit decided 'twas best she ignore them. Aye, that was what she'd do. She'd forget she ever saw a thing. Maids were supposed to ignore, disregard, and overlook any matter that wasn't set squarely in front of them. She'd do just that—especially because she liked the Newcombs and wanted to be the best maid they'd ever employed.

⁓§

"Oh, let me guess: Emily's gearing up for her holiday entertaining." Duncan sauntered into the dining room and smiled at Goodhew and Brigit.

"She does this every year. It wasn't much of a guess," Goodhew said to Brigit.

"I heard that!" Duncan drew closer to where Brigit sat on the floor in front of a massive oak and marble buffet. He gave her a playful smile. "Maybe you can explain it to me. Why do women think they have to put the food and drinks in these fancy dishes? Men just want a plateful. In fact, if the plate is full, we can't very well tell if it's a fancy one or a plain one."

"Ladies don't fill their plates." The twinkle in her eyes let him know he'd managed the right approach.

"But who cares about the plate as long as the food on it tastes decent?"

"The ladies do," Goodhew said with a sigh. "Which is why I'm doing inventory. It's just as well. I'll need to replace a few things."

"Is something missing?" Duncan forced himself to sound only passingly interested.

"Just a cup here or a plate there—the ones the children managed to chip or break. That lovely, rose-shaped silver tray is gone, but it's because Mrs. Waverly declared it was hers after a church tea and carried it away. Miss Emily was too much of a lady to squabble over it."

Duncan took the lid off a crystal candy dish and popped a gumdrop into his mouth. He offered the dish to Brigit and Goodhew; both declined, so he set it back down and helped himself to another before replacing the lid. "Do we have enough trays then?"

"Eight," Brigit reported. "Eight silver trays. Miss Emily has as many china ones—lovely, hand-painted ones. The two glass ones bring the total up to an even dozen and a half. We haven't even looked at the large trays yet. I'm thinking she has trays aplenty."

Duncan slowly chewed the gumdrop. "Enough that she won't miss one or two?"

Brigit smiled at Goodhew. "She'd probably not miss them, but Goodhew certainly would!"

Goodhew nodded urbanely at that praise. "Thank you, Brigit. Now how about the chafing dishes?"

Brigit dipped her head and walked her fingers on the rims of some silver pieces. "There are four chafing dishes and four—no, five—pairs of candlesticks."

Duncan watched as Goodhew scribbled the figures on a pad of paper and nodded.

Brigit leaned into the piece of furniture and took a closer look. "I'm thinking the candlesticks are wanting a good polishing. They're showing tarnish about the bases."

"You're right. That simply won't do. We'll see to that later, after the inventory. The Newcombs always host a New Year's Eve ball. All the families from the shipping company are invited. We'll need the punch bowl. Do you see it?"

Brigit scooted a bit closer to the other edge of the cabinet. "Which one? There are two in here. One's all silver; the other's silver and crystal."

"Emily prefers to serve the punch in crystal and wassail in the silver." Duncan went back for more gumdrops.

"I'm thinking that would look quite festive." Brigit reached into the center of the nested punch bowls. "There's something in here." She carefully unwound a length of red velvet.

Cook came in the room. "Ah, look! You found the dinner bell." She bustled over and grabbed it. She rang it a few times and smiled at the clear, high tinkling tone. "Isn't that the prettiest little thing you ever saw? Years ago, when 'twas just old Master Newcomb and John living here, I'd use that to summon them for meals. I don't remember why we stopped."

Goodhew took the bell from her and handed it back to Brigit. He gestured for her to wrap up the bell and put it away. "The children make a fair bit of noise. Especially with the lasses playing the piano, the bell simply wasn't practical."

"They both play well." Brigit put away the bell and shut the cabinet. "Miss Emily said the twins will begin lessons soon."

"I need to speak to Miss Emily," Cook said. "We've just finished counting the linens."

Duncan watched Brigit tense. He'd done the same thing.

The butler looked at his wife. "Is there a problem?"

"Not exactly. They're all there. It's just that a few of the table linens are showing wear, and the one from supper is hopelessly stained. It'll have to become a picnic blanket. Miss Emily will want to replace them."

"I'm a fair hand at stitching." Brigit stood, closed the buffet doors, and discreetly dusted off the back of her skirts. "If those pieces need only a bit of mending, I could see to them."

"I can attest to that from the shirt Emily had you make for me."

Brigit flickered a quick smile of thanks.

"No use wasting your time on old tablecloths, lass." Duncan glanced down at the shirt covering his chest, then back up at her. "Your efforts would be much better spent by sewing more of those fine shirts for me, and I brought home material for just that purpose."

Cook snorted. "You're a scoundrel, Duncan O'Brien. This very morning I told Miss Emily the staff is needing new aprons. Don't you be thinking to steal away Brigit and her needle."

Sticking to the truth always worked best, especially when spinning a web. Duncan let out an exasperated sigh and looked at Brigit. He waggled his brows playfully. "She's right. I am a scoundrel, and you'd best be warned."

He left the room, pleased as could be. Brigit had just gotten an eyeful of things that any thief would happily snatch, and she seemed quite relaxed. It shouldn't take long at all now.

~⚬

Brigit dusted the downstairs and hummed under her breath. She looked at the gumdrops and scrunched her nose. Duncan was an odd fellow. He'd picked out the black ones. Aye, that was the only color he'd eaten. She should have accepted one—she could have put it in her pocket and given it to Mum. Too late now. She wasn't about to invite herself into the Newcombs' candy dish.

The library was the last place she'd need to dust. She saved it for last because the scent of the place always brought her such an intense longing for home. The mingling of smoke from the fireplace, the leather from the countless volumes on the shelves, lemon and beeswax furniture polish—'twas her idea of what heaven might smell like.

Top to bottom, one side to the other. Dusting didn't take any concentration—'twas a grand chore for that very reason. Brigit enjoyed having a chance to be alone with her thoughts. In fact, she liked having a chance to be alone.

Especially after having been around Duncan awhile earlier, she needed to remind herself of a few choice facts. Duncan had been pleasant and polite to her in the dining room, but he was that way with everyone on the staff. When Trudy ended up falling from the stairs into his arms, hadn't he made sure she wasn't hurt before he set her down? When Fiona asked him to read a letter from home to her, hadn't he stopped what he was doing and read it twice so Fiona could relish all the news? Aye, Duncan O'Brien might have a devilish smile, but he had the heart of a choirboy.

Brigit rolled the ladder toward the left side of the far wall and climbed up. As she dusted, she tried to rub out any personal thoughts of Duncan. She needed her job, and the fastest way to lose it would be to be moon-eyed over him.

The door opened as she climbed down at the right end of the row. Duncan and Timothy entered. Timothy held a book and exclaimed, "I thought the punishment was cruel."

"Why is that?"

"Because she bore it alone, and she couldn't have gotten with child unless—"

"Why, Brigit!" Duncan interrupted his nephew. "So you're dusting in here, too?"

"I have the downstairs today. Would you gentlemen prefer for me to come back later so you can have some privacy?"

Duncan gave her a keen look. "You've done a fair bit of reading. Have you read Nathaniel Hawthorne's *The Scarlet Letter?*"

She could feel the heat rush to her cheeks. "It was given to me as a gift. I ceased reading it when I came to realize the nature of the subject."

"Sidestepping the indelicacy, do you agree with Tim that the punishment was cruel?"

"From what I recall, it seemed unnecessary." Brigit chose her words carefully. "The child's existence made the issue clear."

"Exactly," agreed Timothy.

"What of other crimes and punishment?" Duncan leaned against the desk. "Say. . .theft. What would be reasonable?"

"I've read that in some places in the world," Tim said with relish, "they cut off the thief's hand."

Brigit shuddered in horror. She turned back to continue dusting. The whole time she worked in the library, Duncan and Timothy carried on a lively conversation about various forms of punishing criminals. Duncan managed to use examples of discipline problems aboard a sailing vessel. He capitalized on the opportunity to mentor Timothy and give him advice on how to maintain control. His theory of discipline versus punishment held merit. Brigit found herself thinking Captain Duncan O'Brien undoubtedly earned his men's allegiance fairly.

༄

Duncan felt restless. Surely something would happen soon. He'd made certain Brigit viewed things she could easily steal and pawn. For a while he'd almost forgotten himself. He'd managed to track Brigit into the parlor and immediately snagged the twins as an excuse to go in and monitor the maid. Brigit ended up teaching the girls a simple tune on the piano. When they'd each learned it, she set them a few octaves apart and let them play it as a duet. They made up several silly lyrics to go along with the music, and Duncan had to admit Brigit was quick to find a rhyme and had a sense of whimsy.

She'd also not forgotten to do her tasks; once she had Julie and June set up on the piano bench, Brigit flipped the cushions, plumped the pillows, and rolled up a rug. Not long thereafter, Duncan saw her fling that very rug over a line and beat it. Cold as it was outside, she'd come back in with rosy cheeks.

He refused to be beguiled by her pretty face. Sooner or later she'd slip up, and he'd know it. Duncan sensed that time was at hand. He'd retired to his bed-chamber, but rest eluded him. Duncan finally took off his shirt and shoes yet restlessly prowled until he got rid of some of his energy. At long last, he looked out in the hall, yawned, and left his door ajar. He didn't bother to fold back his bedding—he lay atop the counterpane and dozed.

The slightest rustle and click woke him.

Chapter 15

Brigit woke to a shout. She yanked on a robe and hastened into the hallway. Lee, Trudy, and Fiona stumbled from their rooms, too.

"Did someone die?" Lee quavered.

Trudy ran for the stairs. As she struggled to yank open the oftentimes stubborn door, she wailed, "If somethin's awrong, I'm finding Duncan. He's strong enough to protect me!"

Fiona tromped down the stairs, fluttering her hand under her nose and muttering, "That perfume she's wearin' is strong enough to revive Goliath and make him keel over dead a second time."

By the time Lee and Brigit reached the second floor, the family was up and standing in a knot by the master suite. The children were in nightshirts, and Miss Emily's flannel nightgown peeped out from beneath her roomy shawl. Mr. John had his arms around Miss Emily, who was weeping.

Duncan wore a pair of black britches and a blacker scowl. He folded his arms akimbo and spoke through gritted teeth. "We've been patient far too long. Enough. Enough, I say. Whoever's the thief, confess now."

"Thief?" Trudy's gasp conveniently bumped her right up against Duncan.

Duncan righted her and took an aggressive step forward. He shoved the children behind his back. "The ring. I want it now."

"What ring, Unca Duncan?" Phillip asked as he scratched the cowlick at the back of his head.

"Anna's wedding ring." His voice rivaled a thunderclap.

"Anna's got a wedding ring?" Fiona yawned. "That makes no sense at all. The lass isn't even betrothed yet."

"Timothy's mother was named Anna," John said somberly. He continued to shelter his wife in his arms and rub his hands up and down her back. "Emily kept the little gold band in a special place. It was to go to Timothy's wife someday."

"No further explanations," Duncan rasped. "Everyone is to go to his or her room. One at a time, you're to visit the necessary. Open the laundry chute, then close it. Whoever took the ring is to slide it down the chute. We'll not be able to determine who took the ring, so you can keep your wicked little secret."

Emily wiped her eyes and quavered, "Whoever took it, I just want it back. If you're in dire straits and needed money, you could have come to me. I'd have willingly helped you. I still will. Please—just give back Anna's ring!"

Brigit blinked to keep from crying along. She swallowed hard and held her hands tightly together at her waist. She'd once had a ring—a pretty little emerald Mum had given her for her thirteenth birthday. What a treasure it had been—a symbol of her becoming a young lady. When they'd arrived in America, Da barely had any money left. Brigit had sneaked away the second afternoon and pawned her ring. They'd eaten three meals before Mum noticed Brigit's ringless finger. The memory still tore at Brigit—not because of the sacrificed ring, but because of the anguish on Mum's face. Miss Emily looked as bereft as Mum had.

"Back to your rooms now." Duncan looked fearsome as could be, and Mr. John had his hands full trying to calm Miss Emily.

June stared up at her uncle with saucer-sized eyes and tugged on the leg of his trousers. "I'm not big enough to open the laundry door."

Julie added, "Me neither."

Duncan's craggy face softened for a moment as he bent down and rumbled, "Now there's a fact, but I'll not fret over it. Neither of you is tall enough to have reached the ring in the first place."

Titus poked Phillip in the side. "That leaves you out, too, shrimp. You're too short."

"Am not!"

"Are too!"

"Boys!"

Phillip got up on his toes and stood shoulders to ribs with Titus. "I opened it before and threw Julie's do—" He cut off the word and flushed brightly.

"Phillip, you'll keep those feet on deck here." Duncan set his hand on the lad's shoulder to make his point. "I'll deal with you about the doll."

Emily pulled away from John. "Phillip, did you take the ring?"

"Why would I want some stupid, old girl's ring?"

"The rest of you go to your rooms," Duncan ordered. "In ten minutes you're to start making your trips to the laundry chute."

❧

"No ring." Duncan paced in the library. He wheeled around and frowned. "How did you and Em both sleep through someone sneaking into your room?"

"We weren't in the room." John cleared his throat. "Em—well, I'd carried her to the necessary. She's not feeling her best in the early mornings. It looks as if you're going to be an uncle again."

The news stopped Duncan in his tracks. He looked from his brother-in-law to his sister and back. "Well, I'll be switched." For a moment he grinned. *Babies. Em loves babies. But at her age? I'm almost twenty-one. That makes Em. . .thirty-five.*

A surge of anger swelled. "That does it. You can't have this kind of upset in your delicate condition!"

"Delicate?" Emily let out a watery laugh. "Family, yes; delicate, no. I'm healthy as a draft horse. I'm just so s–sad that s–someone is embarassed to c–come—" She dissolved into tears again.

"Whoever it is isn't embarrassed; she's wicked. And we already know who it is, so let's stop beating around the bush."

John jerked to attention. "You saw who took it?"

"No, but I told you and Em—"

"He made a wild accusation when he said 'tis Brigit." She sobbed into John's chest as she clung to his shirt. "I know he's wrong. I just know it."

Duncan heaved a sigh. The last thing his sister needed was for him to add to her agitation. He gave John a look, and John nodded. They'd take care of it later. Duncan then said as softly as he could, "Our Emily, don't be in a dither. I won't do anything rash. You have my word on it."

She lifted a tear-stained face to Duncan. "Stop sounding as if I made you gargle vinegar, Duncan O'Brien. This whole thing is a tragedy, and I'll not have you add to it by accusing an innocent. No, I won't."

He had no trouble giving her his promise. "I won't harm an innocent." *I'll catch Brigit red-handed.*

༕

The uneasiness in the house was palpable—between the election results and the theft, everyone was on edge. Miss Emily had Goodhew call the staff together while John was at work and the children were at school. Brigit watched her as she pasted on a tremulous smile.

"I've lived through lean times, and I know what a strain it can be. Each of you is a valuable part of this household. I've decided since it's too hard on someone's pride to ask for help, the best thing to do is intervene. Instead of having distrust and tension, I'm simply increasing everyone's salary."

Goodhew sniffed. "I'll not take a cent more. I won't be painted with that extortionist's brush."

Everyone else started to chime in, but Miss Emily held up a hand to silence them. "No one is to speak of it again. Not a word. I've made a decision, and it's a condition of your employment."

Brigit shook her head. She'd never seen such a sad set of circumstances—or so she thought until later that afternoon when she was clearing away the luncheon dishes. Poor Miss Emily had no more than risen from the table when she collapsed into a dead faint.

Trudy let out a screech.

"Stop that noise and go fetch Goodhew," Brigit commanded as she raced to

Miss Emily's side. She immediately loosened the throat of Miss Emily's gown and chafed her hands.

A shadow fell over them, and Duncan boomed, "What did you do?"

Brigit glanced up at him. "She swooned. I don't know why."

He scooped Miss Emily off the floor and headed for the stairs. "Fetch Cook to help me and have Goodhew send for the doctor."

Trudy, Cook, and Goodhew arrived at the same moment. Cook must have spilled something in her haste. The front of her dress and apron was drenched. "I'll see to her," Brigit volunteered and hurried up the stairs right behind Duncan.

As soon as he settled his sister on the bed, Duncan turned his back. He rasped, "Loosen her. . .dress improver. She oughtn't be wearing one in her condition."

Brigit gave fleeting thought to ordering him out of the chamber. It wasn't proper for him to be there. It wasn't even proper for him to allude to such an intimate issue. Squabbling with him wouldn't tend to Miss Emily, though. Brigit quickly unfastened Miss Emily's gown, unlaced her corset, and covered her with a blanket. She then dipped a cloth in the pitcher and draped it over Miss Emily's forehead.

Duncan wheeled back around. "Leave."

For the next three days the young captain who once sparkled with humor and intelligence prowled around the house like a hungry panther, ready to pounce. Brigit counted the days until he set sail again. The man was wound like nine days on a seven-day clock.

Brigit's heart went out to Miss Emily. The poor woman was distraught, and she didn't do well at hiding that fact. Oh, to be sure, she tried; but 'twas clear as an icicle that her feelings knotted her something fierce. Brigit tried to do tiny things to ease Miss Emily's sadness. She made an effort to open drapes to let in the weak wintry sunshine. She hummed lilting tunes. Cups of tea, an unasked-for footstool—anything Brigit could think of, she did for Miss Emily.

Phillip, the wee scoundrel, had taken Julie's doll and dumped her down the laundry chute. He'd confessed that rotten deed, yet the pretty little china doll never ended up in the laundry bin in the basement. Duncan brought in a small grappling hook. He cleverly dropped a rope down the chute, tied the hook to the end, and slowly pulled it upward. By doing so, he recovered Fortuna Hunter.

Later that day Brigit saw Duncan tinkering with sliding more things up and down the chute. She figured he'd come to the same hope she had: Mayhap the ring had been sent down the chute and got lodged as the doll had. Her hopes soared, then crashed as Duncan finally slammed the chute and stalked away.

❧

The world was turned upside down. Folks seemed to want to pick on one another. To hear half the folk talk, President Lincoln was the devil incarnate; the other half would drag a chair up to Christ's right side for him. Slave and free, rich and poor, North and South—strife and contention fulminated just beyond the property line. Until now it had stayed there—but the peace of the Newcomb home and life was no longer assured.

Duncan watched for an opportunity to restore that peace. He'd not managed to nab absolute proof that Brigit was the thief, but every last fact pointed toward her. He'd heard the rustle and click before he discovered Anna's ring had gone missing. The door to the servants' quarters in the attic clicked. He'd checked, and it sounded like the noise he'd heard. Then, too, the very last maid down to see what the ruckus was about just so happened to have been Brigit. She must have taken a few moments to hide the ring.

Duncan gave consideration to tearing the attic apart to locate the ring, but it was such a wee band, it could be in countless places—many he'd not even consider. As soon as he proved her guilt, he'd force Brigit to reveal where the ruby ring had gone.

Aye, 'twas she. Logic gave firm reason to rule out every other member of the household staff.

Emily pointed out that Phillip had swiped Julie's doll, and they'd all presumed it had been stolen. Most of the other items were minor and could easily have been misplaced. But she couldn't explain away the figurine or the ring.

John vacillated between trusting Emily's judgment and wanting to fire all the maids. Because it would upset Em too much, he didn't want to tilt her precarious peace of mind based purely on conjecture.

Waiting. Of all things, Duncan counted patience among his weakest traits. A man of action, he hated to stand by and let time pass without doing something. Clearly something needed doing.

Chapter 16

Brigit cleaned the windows in the library. *I should have traded with Trudy. I could be scrubbing the tub instead of this. Then I wouldn't have to be here, remembering how Duncan O'Brien hid in here, trying to escape from Miss Emily's marriage candidates.*

Deeply troubled by the shadow hanging over the household, Brigit tried to banish any worries or suspicious thoughts. She'd done nothing to earn anyone's distrust or animosity. Duncan alternated between being his suave, clever self and rumbling with all of the fearsomeness of thunder. 'Twas a crying shame he'd lost his peace.

Oh, he'd not outright say so. A man had his pride and didn't want others to know when things bothered him. It was just that Duncan never seemed much of a mystery to her. From the day she'd been a coconspirator by keeping his presence in the library a secret, she'd thought they'd gotten along well enough. Reading his thoughts came as easily as scanning a newspaper. The only problem was, Brigit kept getting the wild notion he was watching her.

Miss Emily kept telling her to go the extra mile, to be sympathetic about the pressure Duncan was under. What with the political matters at a near boiling point and the frustrations of dealing with supplies that weren't arriving on time for the shipbuilding, Duncan simply wasn't himself—at least, that's what Miss Emily said.

On top of all of that, they were having foul weather. Men pontificated about how the *Farmer's Almanac* had rightly predicted this relentless stream of storms, and Brigit had felt the icy sting of the sleet on several occasions. For the past few days, the temperature had dropped even farther, and they'd experienced snow, of all things! Surely, for the men to be working out of doors gave adequate cause for Duncan to come home in a black mood.

Since he'd announced a thief was in the house and spilled his ugly thoughts, Brigit had become increasingly self-conscious. Thoughts about finding a new position filled her mind, but with the uncertainties in the political climate and the facts that she had no funds upon which to fall back and her parents relied on her, she had to stay. Brigit decided to keep vigilant. She loved Miss Emily and wanted to help put an end to this travesty. She'd do it because it was the right thing to do, but also because Miss Emily had been so kind to Mum and Da.

Mum and Da had looked so pleased when she'd brought what Cook called "the autumn baking crate." Why, with just a bit of meat and eggs, they'd have most of what they needed to eat for quite some time. Aye, and that extra jar of apricots Cook had given—Brigit had nearly cried with delight over how good the Lord was to add that extra bit of sweetness to her parents' life.

She'd been giving almost all of her pay to them when she visited on her day off. Da picked up a day job here and there, but mostly bosses wanted to hire stronger, younger men. The voyage over had left Mum frail of health. She'd not last a month if she took on any labor. Each day Brigit woke with a sense of gratitude that God provided this job.

Beautiful things filled the Newcomb estate. Aye, the home boasted grand rooms with fine appointments. Upkeep on such a place was a never-ending proposition. Miss Emily kept the staff busy. In the past two days, she'd taken to giving orders here and there that should have been customary; but what with the suspicion that a thief might be in their midst, the chores took on a different flavor. The tensions stretched tight.

Brigit swiped at a tiny streak along the edge of a pane. For all she'd endured until now, she'd always found contentment in her circumstances. She suspected Duncan O'Brien felt that same way. Whoever was behind the robbery had stolen Duncan's serenity as certainly as he'd taken all the goods.

Worn out from yet another busy day, the entire household retired early. Brigit stood at her attic bedroom window and fidgeted. When Duncan had come home, he'd been in a good mood—as if the sea winds had blown away the worries he'd carried when first he set sail. Now he hovered. Every time she turned around, he seemed to be there. His smile didn't reach his eyes, either. Like a lightning bolt, the realization struck her as she mopped the floor tonight. *He's hunting for the robber, and he thinks I'm guilty!*

Holy Savior, what am I to do? I can declare my innocence, but what would that accomplish? She rested her forehead against the icy pane and blinked back tears of frustration. A pair of verses from the twenty-fifth chapter of Proverbs ran through her mind. *"If thine enemy be hungry, give him bread to eat; and if he be thirsty, give him water to drink: for thou shalt heap coals of fire upon his head, and the Lord shall reward thee."*

Feed Duncan. Fill his glass. Be kind. *Such seemingly simple things to do—but with the suspicious way he's behaving toward me, Father, those acts will take every last shred of my will and a boatload of Christ's love to accomplish. I don't want to obey Your Holy Word only to keep my job. If I did that, 'twould be living by law and not by grace. I'm praying now for wisdom and a forgiving heart. Help me, Lord. Help me minute by minute. I cannot do this on my own.*

Sleepless, she continued to stand at the window. A slight movement caught her attention. She spied the stranger she'd seen on those other occasions in the yard. She couldn't tell much by the weak moonlight, but maybe he was involved somehow. *I simply cannot stay silent about seeing him any longer. If he is a guard, he's had to have seen something; if I've been wrong about presuming he's a guard, then I need to get one of the men to capture him.*

Brigit's heart pattered as fast as a toe dancer's feet as she slipped into a wrapper and ran to the servants' staircase. She grabbed the knob and twisted, but the door refused to open. The stubborn thing wouldn't budge.

"Oh, no!" She tried twice more, each second pounding with her heartbeat. *He'll get away. I'm fiddling with this stupid door, and that man is getting away!*

Frustrated and unwilling to let the matter alone, she dashed back to her room. Ignoring the icy weather, she opened her bedroom window and crawled out onto the roof. Slick it was, and so cold that it felt burning hot beneath her hands and knees. Normally Brigit rather enjoyed looking out her window, but looking down from this vantage point didn't give her any pleasure—it nearly scared the wits straight out of her.

She tried to recall the house's floor plan. Could she go right and drop down onto one of the children's balconies? No, wait. Right would be Duncan's—well, she did need to get him. She stood and wobbled. Clumps of snow slid away and made soft, distant *plops* as they hit the ground. She started to pray aloud, "Dear Lord Almighty, don't let me turn into one of those plopping sounds myself!"

Cold. Oh, cold, cold, cold. Each step she took made her shiver worse. Brigit strove to keep her footing as she crossed the roof, then groaned as she drew close to a chimney. In her effort to keep from slipping right over the edge, she'd gone too far. Both arms stuck out to help her balance, she looked behind her. No. She couldn't possibly turn and go back. She'd barely kept alive going straight ahead. Turning all the way around would be pure folly. "Lord, You know I'm not here to kill myself. Aye, You do. I'd take it kindly if You'd grant me deliverance."

The trellis—the very tips of a trellis stuck up beyond the edge of the roof. She whispered her thanks to the Lord, then swallowed hard. He'd given her a way down, but it wasn't going to be easy. Then again, how many times had Da said most of the good things in life didn't come easy?

Sure she'd skid right over the edge if she took another step, Brigit took a deep breath to steel herself. As it was, she slipped as she laid down on her belly with her feet toward the drop-off. Her fingers scrabbled for any hold, but it was a vain effort. She skidded over the edge and barely muffled her shriek as she caught the trellis and held on for dear life.

For a second she closed her eyes. "God, don't stop now. I need Your help, and I'm needing it badly." She opened her eyes and saw violets. Violets? Oh! Her gown and robe were hooked on the trellis—as if God had snagged her there for safety's sake! She had to hold on with one hand while she freed her slushy garments with the other. The clammy fabric slapped at her legs, and she shuddered. When she got hold of Duncan and he apprehended the stranger because of her tremendous effort, that man was going to owe her at least a dozen apologies.

It being winter, the vines on the trellis were dried-out, rough things. Nary a leaf remained—something Brigit counted as a blessing, because she'd end up slipping on them or wearing them if they were present. The whole trellis wobbled, and she didn't waste time. It might snap.

She also hurried because she needed Duncan to nab that stranger. The longer it took her to alert Duncan, the greater the chance was that the intruder would slip away.

"Fine thing for a young lady to do in the dead of winter, in the middle of the night," she muttered as she climbed down. " 'Tis nothing short of a miracle I haven't broken my neck."

A big, rough hand clamped around her ankle. "That could still be arranged."

Chapter 17

One quick yank, and Duncan pulled Brigit off the trellis. He caught her—a chivalrous thing to do, all things considered. The mud puddle there would have been a just reward for her perfidy.

"Duncan!"

"Surprised?" He clamped a hand over her mouth and hauled her toward the kitchen. He didn't want her crying alarm and warning her partner. Hopefully, John would catch him. It took every last shred of decency for Duncan not to shake her senseless. What had she taken this time, and to whom was she going to pass it?

Just tonight, after everyone else went to bed, he and John had a quick exchange. The two of them concocted a solid plan to capture the thief once and for all. Duncan no more than set foot into his bedchamber and went to shut a crack in the curtains when he saw a bit of snow slide over the edge. It wouldn't have been anything to catch his attention, but then several more followed. Realizing someone was on the roof—of all things!—he ran outside.

He could scarcely believe his eyes. Brigit. Regardless of what logic told him and the way he'd been behaving over the last two weeks, deep in his heart, Duncan secretly still fostered a thread of hope that she was innocent. The thread snapped, and the full weight of her betrayal hit him. He'd trusted her with his family and almost with his heart—he'd been ready to propose! Anger mixed with incredulity. He nearly bellowed her name, but cold reason washed over him. If he startled her, she'd likely slip and break her neck; he wanted the satisfaction of doing that deed with his own hands—not that he would, but the thought satisfied a savage need inside of him. Besides, if he made a noise, he'd scare off her accomplice.

For having been as skilled as she'd been with her other episodes of theft, she wasn't smooth this time at all. The daft woman had let out a shriek loud enough to wake Methuselah, then muttered to herself the whole time she scrambled down the trellis. No doubt about it, the woman had a death wish.

Now Brigit didn't act innocent. No, she surely didn't. She squirmed and struggled—even tried to bite his hand. He got her in through the kitchen door, kicked it shut, and bumped into the counter ere he reached the table. The whole while, Brigit gave him more grief than a tiger in a burlap sack.

He dumped her onto the table where Cook usually kneaded bread. Keeping his hand firmly over her mouth, he anchored Brigit in place by clenching the belt to her robe. "Don't you make a sound."

She reached up and closed both hands around his wrist. Though she tried, she couldn't yank his hand away. Before Duncan could imagine the depth of her desperate insanity, she turned loose and threw herself backward. A tug and loud rip ensued. Within a second, she ended up in a heap on the floor; he stood with a soggy belt to a flowery robe in his hand. He tossed it aside and dove after her. She smacked at him and yelped, "You're letting him get away!"

Duncan pinned her to the floor. "Let me guess: He won't even bother to come after you. Regardless of the cliché, I've found there is no honor among thieves. You're going to have to shoulder the blame yourself."

ᵕᢟ

Brigit stared at Duncan in disbelief. Here she was, trying to unravel the mystery and catch whomever it was who had been robbing this good family of their treasures. What happened? Duncan considered this as proof that she was the guilty party.

She glowered at him. "While you're wasting time with that ridiculous notion, the thief is making his escape!"

"I'll settle for one of the pair." He reached across her and grabbed the torn belt. Quick as could be, he grabbed both of her wrists in one of his massive hands.

"If you—" She tugged against him, but to no avail. He had her well and truly bound, knotted faster than a schooner in a gale.

"Be silent, or I'll use the other length to gag you."

Duncan stood and lifted Brigit to her feet. He pulled out a chair and nudged her into it.

Nothing he did made sense. He'd actually been quite gentle when he'd lifted her; and the minute he had her seated, he hastily jerked the flaps of her robe shut. How could a man have the mind of a jackal and the manners of a saint?

She started to shiver. Her soggy garments, her bare feet, and the unheated kitchen combined to make her miserable. Brigit swished her head from side to side, trying to get a swath of hair that had worked free from her braid to cease drooping over her left eye. All she succeeded in doing was to whip herself with the wet plait.

"Fighting won't get you anything." Duncan scowled. "Now tell me who your partner is and where I can find him."

Utterly frustrated, she glowered back. "I don't have a partner because I'm not a thief. I was coming to get you because I saw a man in the yard!"

"So you nearly broke your neck, crossing the roof in order to reach me."

"The door is jammed. I had no choice."

Duncan shook his head, skepticism painting every last feature.

"That's right. Go on ahead and scoff. You've been pointing your finger at me, and I was working to prove my innocence. I had to do something—as long as that villain is free, you'll keep blaming me."

"Obviously for good cause," he said in a voice rich with vindication. "An innocent person wouldn't be sneaking around at night, and I caught you dead to rights. I won't let anyone steal from my family."

"Neither will I. You're falsely accusing me, and if I do nothing, it'll cost me my job. You'll be stealing the very bread out of my parents' mouths!"

Chapter 18

Hush!" He barked the order in a hoarse tone. Memories of his young years—of his family being cold, hungry, and sick—flooded Duncan's mind. He'd not yet reached his seventh birthday, but he'd known things were dire. Even so, Emily had never once stooped to thievery. Duncan held no sympathy for this maid.

"But—"

"I'll not listen to another of your lies. You've betrayed the trust and kindness of this family. Don't try to justify it by trying to earn my pity or sympathy with sad tales about your family's woes. The truth stands—"

"Aye, it does!" Brigit stared him straight in the face.

Tears glossed her eyes, but fire burned in her cheeks. She'd been caught, and 'twas nothing more than embarrassment and anger that caused this reaction. Duncan refused to be moved by her words.

He yanked out a chair, slammed it down next to her, but failed to take it. "Not another word out of you. John will be here soon, and I'll have him waken Emily."

Brigit's gasp only fired his temper more.

"Oh, yes. Emily will be told. You couldn't believe we'd leave her ignorant of your role in this. The children will have to be warned, too—so don't think you can weasel your way back into anyone's good graces—not after what you've done."

"I'm telling you, I didn't do anything!"

Duncan scoffed. "If you were innocent, you'd still be sleeping in your bed—not climbing down a trellis at this hour. John will have to determine whether to turn you out or turn you over to the authorities."

As if on cue, John came into the kitchen. He lit a lamp and stared at Brigit. "There are tracks out in the mud. Most have a dusting inside them, so I know they're left over from the party. There is one set that's fresh. I saw a man, but he ran before I could get close."

Duncan noticed that Brigit's fiery denial of guilt didn't settle any better with John than it did with him. She pled that she would never steal—not as an upright Christian woman and because she needed to keep her job so she could provide for her parents.

John's jaw hardened as he stared at her. "You're giving yourself plenty of motive."

Brigit lifted her chin in a dignified manner that was at direct odds with the lock of hair hanging down her face and her spongy garments. "Supposing you men are right. Try explaining why I'd be risking my neck to walk across a snowy roof when I don't have a single treasure on me!"

Duncan gritted his teeth. She had a point. He'd not caught her red-handed.

A rustling in the doorway made Duncan and John whirl around. Emily entered the kitchen with a shocked look on her face. Brigit couldn't help herself. "I didn't do anything wrong, Miss Emily. Honest, I didn't!"

John hastened to his wife's side. Tears streaked down her cheeks, and she clutched him. "Come on, sweetheart. I'll take care of this."

Emily shook her head. "Something's wrong."

"I know, dear. Duncan and I are handling this. You go on back to bed."

"But everything's back." Emily gave her husband a bewildered look. "Up in the hallway. There's a towel, and everything that's been stolen is on it—the statue and the cameo and our little Anna Kathleen's locket and your book—it's all there except my sister Anna's ring."

Duncan couldn't bear to see Em cry. She rarely wept—except during the months when she was carrying a babe. Then she cried enough to float an armada. He would process the information about the returned articles in a few moments. For now he intended to block Emily's access to Brigit. Tenderhearted as Emily was, she would—

"What is that odd sound?" Emily's tears were tapering down to the hiccup stage, and she pulled away from John.

Duncan and John took a quick look at one another, then both focused on the same thing at the same time.

"Look at the poor girl!" Emily ran to Brigit's side and quickly flipped back the silly lock of hair to expose the maid's pale face.

At first, Duncan thought her lips were quivering in a theatrical attempt to earn pity, but then the truth dawned. Her teeth were chattering. Even then the noise wasn't from that. It was because her chair rattled on the floor from her shivers.

"You've scared the lass." Emily looked down and let out a breathless shriek. She fumbled with the binding. "You've tied her! Undo this at once."

Duncan yanked a knife from the butcher block and sliced clean through with a single swipe. He kept a hand on Brigit's shoulder. Originally it was to keep her from trying to bolt, but now it was to keep her from falling out of the chair. He frowned at her. The woman felt cold as sleet.

As he was in just shirtsleeves, Duncan didn't have a coat to offer. He swept Brigit into his arms and growled, "Em, you come along and see to it she changes." He headed up the stairs with his sister pattering directly behind him. When they got to the stairway to the attic, Em managed to open the door without the least bit of effort. Duncan shot a yet-another-lie look at Brigit. It was wasted effort. The lass huddled into a ball in his arms. Aye, she did—but at least she exercised enough intelligence not to cling to him.

Emily went ahead of them and opened the third attic bedroom door. A blast of cold met them. Brigit had left the small window open, and the room felt like the inside of an icehouse. While Duncan lowered Brigit onto a bed she obviously hadn't slept in, he rasped, "Emily, don't shut the window. The floor may be slippery over there, and I don't want you to fall and hurt yourself."

"Nonsense." The window slammed shut. "We need to warm her up at once."

He straightened, turned, and wagged his forefinger at Emily. "No arguments. Make sure she dresses warmly and pack the remainder of her belongings. You have five minutes."

Temper had him wanting to bellow the words, but discretion demanded he not. The last thing he needed to do was wake the whole household. Emily needed a chance to accept the betrayal before everyone else was told. He went back to the stairs.

The door stuck.

❦

Brigit wrapped her shawl more closely about her shoulders. *Lord, I'm in such a mess. What am I to do?*

Duncan carried her valise and kept one hand clamped around her elbow as he led her down the road. Brigit refused to say a word. She didn't dare. The minute she opened her mouth, she'd humiliate herself by weeping. Her boot hit a rut, and she started to tumble, but Duncan jerked her upright.

"Are you all right?"

She couldn't bear to look him in the eye. Right about now she'd vow the boots he wore hid cloven hooves. How could she once have believed him to be charming and kind? If anyone was guilty of deceit, Duncan O'Brien topped the list.

He stopped. "I asked if you were all right."

She nodded. He let go of her elbow and tilted her face up to his. He stared at her but said nothing. Brigit turned away from his touch and started to walk again.

"No." He took hold of her arm and drew her the wrong direction. "Come this way."

So that's the way of it. Mr. John wanted me thrown out of the house at once. He couldn't even wait until sunrise to get rid of me. They were just pacifying Miss Emily with the tale of Duncan giving me a ride into town. He's really going to take me to the edge of the estate and send me on my way. Brigit swallowed, but the big lump in her throat didn't move. The sooner she put some distance between herself and this place, the better. She walked alongside Duncan in absolute silence.

"You're still shivering. That shawl isn't warm enough." He started to remove his thick, brown greatcoat.

Brigit bit back a cry. The last thing she wanted was to be wrapped in this hateful man's garment. "Leave me alone." She sped up until she was nearly running.

Duncan caught her in a few strides. "Slow down before you slip again." He gained a better hold of her, and his voice took on a rough edge. "You'll stay with my parents at the caretaker's cottage. They've just returned home from a long trip. I'll arrange for the rest of the staff to think you're here to help my folks air out the place and spruce it up."

Brigit shuddered. Her reputation was in tatters, and she'd never get another job without references. What would happen to Mum and Da?

Duncan opened the unlocked door to the caretaker's cottage and nudged her inside. She could barely see the embers glowing on the hearth. He led her over to a settee and whispered, "Lie down here. I'll stir up the fire."

Woodenly, she seated herself in the corner of the settee. She watched Duncan's broad back as he squatted at the hearth, added kindling and a pair of logs, and brought the fire back to life. Even when the room radiated with its warmth, Brigit couldn't stop shaking.

Duncan walked behind the settee. He spoke in low tones to someone, but Brigit was too stiff to turn and couldn't understand what was said. A few moments later, Duncan stood before her and unfolded a thick quilt. He draped it around her shoulders and managed somehow to raise and twist her so she was bundled in it. By the time he finished, he'd laid her down and robbed her of her shoes.

༚

Duncan decided to spend the night in the wingback chair. He could keep watch over the fire and Brigit. He'd been so sure of her guilt. John seemed convinced, too. But Em—Em vouched for Brigit's goodness.

And that attic door stuck.

Then that moment out on the road changed everything. The ache in Brigit's eyes nearly knocked him to his knees. In that split second, everything settled in his mind. He knew for certain this woman—the woman he still loved—was innocent.

From the time he'd started dealing with business, Duncan discovered he'd been given a gift of discernment. He could sense the character of a man and determine whether or not to hire him or contract his services. Even weasels like the sailmaker knew better than to try anything shady with him. From the first time he'd seen Brigit, he'd seen the goodness in her. Aye, he had. She'd filled his glass with milk that time, then gone on to fill his heart with sunshine.

But he'd been a fool. In his rush to avoid marriage, he'd not trusted the gift the Lord had given him. It took a voyage away from Brigit to make him come to his senses, but once he'd returned, he'd let the octopus of doubt nearly strangle him. Looking into Brigit's eyes, he'd seen the truth. Oh, he had. She was innocent; he was guilty. His heart had been right from the very start, and he'd been a fool to allow circumstances to cloud his judgment and test his love. He'd hurt her because of it.

He had a lot to make up for.

Duncan hadn't followed John's edict to get rid of Brigit at once. He'd made up his mind, and John could bluster all he wanted. Until Duncan could prove Brigit was blameless, he was going to shelter her reputation and feelings by having her live with his own parents. He'd vouched for her innocence just now when he told his parents who she was and why he'd brought her here.

It had taken a long while for her to fall asleep. Silent tears streamed down her face until she did. Though Duncan knelt by the settee and tried to reassure her, she was too far gone to hear a word he said. Between cold and shock, she just lay there and trembled. Mama offered to brew tea, but Duncan doubted Brigit would be able to swallow it. Papa cleared his throat, beetled his brows as he looked at Brigit, and hesitantly suggested, "Medicinal brandy or whiskey might do the trick."

So on top of all of my mistakes, I'd give Brigit the humiliation of thinking I'd made a sot of her.

He shook his head. "Rest. What she needs is her rest."

Dad nodded. "I'll have Mama make up the bed in the spare room."

John had added a fair-sized bedroom and a workshop onto the other side of the kitchen years ago, but Duncan shook his head again. "Mama needs her rest, and the fire here's what the lass needs more than anything."

Both of those statements were true, but they were only an excuse. He couldn't bear to leave Brigit alone in this calamity. Even after she fell asleep, he couldn't stand to be more than just a few feet away.

Still alarmed at how cold she'd become, Duncan tiptoed over to make sure she'd warmed up. Even though Brigit lay exactly where he'd put her, she'd managed to curl into the quilt tighter than the coil in a seahorse's tail.

At least the shivering had stopped. He counted that as a good sign. He'd have to settle for that one sign, because nothing else looked very promising. Dried tears pasted wild strands of her ebony hair to her face. Just days ago, playing with the children in snow had caused those same strands to form springy tendrils around her hairline. He tenderly fingered the strands. *Lord, help me make this up to her. Help me make things right.*

Duncan went back and took his station in the wingback chair. Thoughts swirled in his mind. He had no right to claim his love for her until he earned her trust. He'd nearly shattered her with his accusations, and a sensitive woman like

Brigit would need time to get over such ugliness. The best thing he could do was show his support for her and prove her innocence. Once he did, God willing, she'd become his bride.

Sweat rolled off his forehead, but Duncan popped another log onto the fire. Purgatory probably felt cooler than this parlor, but he refused to risk Brigit's catching a chill. Finally he settled back into the chair and decided he could afford to doze. On the slim chance she woke up, Brigit wouldn't be able to get away. He had her shoes beneath his chair. Even more, he had her in his heart.

Chapter 19

Y ou did what?" The force of John's bellow could have filled every last sail on a clipper.

Duncan didn't mind the bluster. He'd expected it. Locking eyes with John, he said very clearly, "I took Brigit to my parents' cottage. She's staying with them until this matter is cleared up."

"It's already solved, and I won't have her on my property."

"She's not on our property, dear," Emily whispered. "You gave the cottage to my parents. It was very generous of you. You did it right after you added on that nice, big second room."

"This isn't a game." John glowered at them.

"No, 'tisn't," Duncan agreed. "I'm saying here and now, Brigit is the woman I love. The devil can have a holiday in a suspicious mind, and I was fool enough to let him—but no more. We have no proof against her. None. What I do have is my faith in her and in the Almighty."

Emily yanked on John's hand. "John—"

"Don't be taken in by love, Duncan." John gave him a world-weary look. "Remember Anna."

"If I would have minded that advice, I'd have never wed you," Emily said quietly.

Duncan nodded. "I'll prove Brigit's innocence; and once I do, I want her welcomed back with open arms. She's going to be my wife."

❦

"Christmas is just around the corner." Nonny O'Brien's cheerful announcement didn't much lift Brigit's spirits. Not wanting to cast a pall over Duncan and Emily's mama's happy mood, Brigit plastered on a smile and nodded.

"We want to celebrate the holiday in the Old World way. I ken 'tis an imposition, but I was thinkin' to ask for your help." Soon Nonny had Brigit firmly entrenched in her plans. They sewed doll clothes for the twins, painted a whole fleet of ships for Phillip, and polished up little jewelry boxes Papa O'Brien had made for the older girls.

Being involved in those holiday customs helped Brigit regain a few shreds of her serenity. She always loved the holidays, and she could see how much Nonny and Papa loved their family by the affection in their eyes and voices and how they lavished thought and time into making a special gift for each grandchild. Brigit knew the children would be delighted.

Truth be told, Brigit had a second reason for looking forward to Christmas. Duncan's new vessel would be finished any day. As soon as Christmas was over, he was due to take the ship on her maiden voyage. From what she'd overheard, she gathered it would be an extended voyage. She needed to have time away from him.

Duncan came by each day and promised to prove her innocence. To his credit—or was it Emily's?—the rest of the Newcomb staff had been told Nonny O'Brien needed Brigit's help with several Christmas projects. It was the truth, but Brigit felt it was only a half-truth, and such things made her squirm. What else could she do, though? At least she'd not been subjected to public scrutiny or shame, and every bit of her salary still came so she could take care of her parents.

Mum would take one look at her and know something was dreadfully wrong, so Brigit didn't want to go home. Bless his heart, Papa O'Brien delivered the money to her parents and came back with a handful of cheerful stories and the assurance that all was well with them.

Someone pounded on the door. Brigit ran to answer it. The minute she saw who stood there, she wanted to slam it shut. Duncan's arms were full of fabric.

"Emily's asked if you'll make new gowns for the staff."

Brigit stared at the two huge bolts of material and blinked to be sure it wasn't her overactive imagination. Indeed it wasn't. Miss Emily hadn't sent solid cornflower blue serge or wool. No, she hadn't. She'd had her brother deliver a dainty green-and-white ivy print and a stunningly feminine, very stylish pink cabbage rose.

Duncan stood in the doorway and gave her an amused look. "You needn't decide betwixt the pieces, if that's why you're hesitating. Emily wants you to make a gown from both fabrics for each of you."

"My. Oh, dear me. Yes, well. . ." She backed away from the door and gestured for him to come in. *I've been a bogbrain, leaving him out in the cold.*

Duncan conscientiously wiped off his boots before he stepped over the threshold. He carried the bolts over to a small table on the far side of the parlor and propped them up against it. After making sure they wouldn't slide and fall, he set down a small wooden case. "There you are."

When he turned back around, Brigit forced herself to keep her hands folded at her waist. "Miss Emily chose bonny cloth, to be sure."

"So you like it?"

Brigit nodded. She didn't want to prolong the conversation. In fact, she wished Nonny would come out of the kitchen and ease this dreadfully awkward encounter.

Duncan took a seat and made himself at home. Brigit wanted to shove him straight back out the door; but it wasn't her home, and she had no right. He'd dropped by at least once a day since she'd come here. Now 'twas a good thing for a son to be dutiful and loving. Clearly he displayed both of those laudable qualities toward his parents—but he'd been checking up on her. He and she both knew part of his intent was to hover like a hungry hawk, and she was the field mouse he'd nab if the merest opportunity presented itself. Oh, he'd said he intended to prove she was innocent, but Brigit's trust in him was too badly shaken to allow her to believe him.

"Em sent you the whatnots in that case." He leaned forward and rested his elbows on his knees. The man looked comfortable enough to stay a good long while. "She wanted to be sure you had everything you needed."

At your request, so I wouldn't steal? Brigit held her tongue. Regardless of how upset she felt, antagonizing him wasn't right. "Please let Miss Emily know I'll get to sewing at once."

"My sister is a bit distracted these days. If you find you require anything else, just let me know."

Brigit nodded.

Duncan must have figured out she didn't care to pursue a conversation, because after silence stretched between them, he stood. He walked toward the door and stopped directly in front of Brigit. "You didn't catch a chill from the other night?"

He sounded almost concerned. Brigit could scarcely credit it would matter to him at all. Likely Miss Emily wanted to know. Staring at his shoulder, she said, "I'll save the scraps for the girls' sewing baskets."

Duncan made an impatient sound and tilted her face to his. Before he could speak his mind, Nonny's laughter sounded from the other side of the room. "Nonsense. You'll keep those scraps yourself. Duncan-mine, I'm wanting a wee bit of satin. The palest blue, if you have it—just scrap is all. About a yard or so will do nicely." She came over and patted his chest. "Drop it off whenever's convenient."

"I'll see to it." After giving his mother a quick and sure hug and kiss, he left. Brigit went to the fabric and touched it.

"I'll have ye know, our Duncan chose those prints," Nonny said in a gay lilt. "Our Em had him get them in Lowell. You'll be a pretty sight in that green, come Christmas."

"I'll be sure to make up that print for the girls first."

Nonny shook her head. "Dinna be thinkin' you sneaked that by me with your sweet vow. You're to make one for yourself, too."

Brigit busied herself with some housekeeping, then ventured toward the small wooden box. Inside were needles, thread, scissors, a tape measure, a slip of paper with everyone's measurements, and a thimble. Another bit of paper had been folded and wedged into the lid.

"Blessed are ye, when men shall revile you, and persecute you,
and shall say all manner of evil against you falsely, for my sake.
Rejoice, and be exceeding glad: for great is your reward in heaven:
for so persecuted they the prophets which were before you."
MATTHEW 5:11–12

Brigit folded the verse and tucked it in her pocket. *God, please bless Miss Emily and Nonny for their kindness. To be sure, I'm in the fiery furnace; but You gave them to me just like You allowed Shadrach to have Meshach and Abednego with him during his trials.*

During the next week, she took out the slip of paper and read the verse over and over again. Oh, she knew that verse. Back when she was but a small lass, she'd committed it to memory. That was all well and good, but now it served two purposes: It prompted her to keep her eyes on the Lord in her troubles, and it reminded her someone still had faith in her honesty.

Duncan continued to drop by. Sometimes he had a good excuse—like with the blue satin. He'd brought by no less than five different shades of blue so his mother could make a choice that suited her fancy. There was no mistaking it—Duncan O'Brien cherished his family.

Most times he just came by. He didn't seem to have any reason at all, but Brigit knew the truth—he was there to intimidate her and spy on her. She tried to make herself scarce during his visitations, but that wasn't very easy in the small cottage. She felt clumsy as a cow with him around. Awkward and fumble-fingered as a twelve-year-old lass, and all because he made her so self-conscious. Every last thing she did fell under Duncan O'Brien's scrutiny. Each time he left, she'd breathe a sigh of relief.

Working helped keep her mind off her troubles. Brigit stayed industrious from the minute she woke until Nonny O'Brien chided her into blowing out the lamp at night. She already had Cook's and Lee's dresses nearly finished, and she'd cut out Fiona's and Trudy's today. As both of them were identical in size, it made more sense to tackle them at the same time.

After having cut out all of those gowns, Brigit still had cloth left. . .cloth originally earmarked for her. She wouldn't make it up. No, she wouldn't.

That night she waited until Nonny and Papa went to bed; then Brigit sat by the hearth and carefully embroidered. When her eyes grew too weary, she tucked away her stitching and turned in for the night. After she blew out her lamp, she climbed into bed and curled into a ball of misery.

Da always said God had a purpose for everything. Aye, and he also said anything worthwhile was hard won. *Lord, I don't understand what I'm supposed to be learning from all of this.*

A faint scraping sound interrupted her prayer.

Brigit slid out of bed and threw on her robe. Her bare feet made no noise on the floor as she crossed into the doorway. A man had nearly folded himself in half to fit through the window; but when he turned, a shaft of moonlight illuminated his face.

He was the man she'd seen out in the yard all those nights!

Brigit didn't even pause to consider her actions. She ran across the room and used the seat of the chair as a stepping stool in order to leap onto the man's back. She wrapped her arms around his neck and her legs around his waist as she screamed, "Help!"

Papa O'Brien ran out and managed to belt the intruder in the middle.

The door crashed open, and Duncan thundered in with a bellow. Brigit continued to cling to the stranger as he wheeled around. Papa was in midswing and couldn't stop. He accidentally knocked her off. She hit the wall as she saw Duncan lunge and heard him hiss, "You!"

Chapter 20

The tide had come in late that night, and Duncan had needed to be there to meet a vessel. He'd ordered special gifts for John and Emily, and he didn't want them to find out. As he rode by his parents' cottage, he heard Brigit's screams. He vaulted off his mount and tore through the front door.

Seeing her hit the floor made his heart stand still. Seeing Edward made his blood run cold.

The uppercut he served Edward hit true, as did the blow to his middle. Edward crumpled over; but the odd part of it was, he'd never put up the slightest defense. "Fetch some rope," Duncan barked.

"I know where there's some," his father said, panting. "Just a minute."

"Brigit? Are you all right?" Duncan knelt by her and bit back a roar as she dazedly lifted her hand to her head. "Come here, sweet." He scooped her up and carried her to the settee. He didn't want to turn her loose or put her in the other room. He refused to let her out of his sight, but Edward's moan let Duncan know he couldn't turn his back for a single second.

"I've got her, son." His mother patted his arm.

"Rope." His father came back into the room, holding aloft a fair length. "Good sturdy rope 'tis. We'll bind him to a chair."

Duncan thrust Edward into the chair and set to work. He yanked the rope tight and knotted it once more for good measure. That task done, he wheeled around and strode to the settee. His mother was clucking over Brigit, whose wide eyes and pale face made his heart lurch. A quick glance at the spot on Brigit's temple told him she'd have a headache and a good-sized lump for a day or so. Even so, he couldn't resist cupping her cheek. "Are you all right?"

"I'm fine."

"No, you're not," he rasped angrily. "Stop sitting here. Lie down. Da, I'm asking you to go fetch the doctor."

"I don't need a doctor."

"Nonsense." Duncan lifted her and cradled her for an instant to assure himself she'd not really been hurt any other way. "There's a knot on your head, so you're not thinking clearly. I want you lying down until the doctor says you can get up."

"Then lay her down," his mother urged.

"I'm deciding where to put her. She's cold. Look at how she's shivering."

His father crossed the room. "You left the door open and let in the winter night air. I'm thinking that's as good a reason as any for the lass to be shivering." He slammed the door shut.

Brigit jumped and winced at the noise.

"I'll go into town and get the doctor," his father said, "but I'm yanking on my boots first."

Duncan studied Brigit's features. "Are you seeing double or feelin' like you might lose your supper?"

"The only double I'm seeing is that man," she whispered. "He looks like John Newcomb."

Duncan murmured some nonsense to calm her, then settled her back on the settee. He shed his greatcoat and covered her in the depths of its thick, brown folds.

"You turned into a fine young man, Duncan," Edward said softly. "You treat a lady well."

"At an early age, I saw you do the opposite." Duncan shot Edward a venomous look. "I learned my lesson from that."

Unable to tolerate the sight of the man who had betrayed his loved ones, Duncan strove to contain his temper. He strode to the window and stared sightlessly out into the yard. Since the day he'd learned Edward had duped his sister Anna into a sham marriage and abandoned them, Duncan had longed for justice. In a flash of characteristic honesty, he admitted to himself he wanted more than justice—he wanted revenge.

"You killed Anna. Aye, you did." He didn't turn to make the accusation. "Granted, you never actually plunged a knife into Anna or shot her—but you did worse when you deceived and betrayed her. You left her, knowing she carried your child. Aye, you left her to freeze and starve.

"Here, in this very cottage, Anna passed on. She passed on shamed to the depths of her soul, her heart broken because she finally learned of your betrayal."

The cottage stayed chillingly silent. Finally Edward confessed, "Everything you say is true. I cannot begin to—"

Duncan's father slammed his fist into something. "Then say nothing."

Duncan clenched his jaw at the wave of sorrow that washed over him. His arms shook with the effort it took to keep his fists at his sides.

"What more did you plan to take from my family?" he demanded in a low roar of fury. "Haven't you already done more than enough?"

"I have." Edward's voice carried no challenge. "And I—"

Duncan wheeled around. "Why? Why did you come back here? And spare me your lies. I've had a belly full of them already."

"I've told more than my share of lies. I came here tonight to try to make right a small portion of my wrongs."

"Impossible."

"There's an envelope in my pocket. Read the letter. You've nothing to lose by reading it."

Duncan's father jerked the envelope from Edward's pocket. He strode to the fireplace and almost threw it in, but Edward shouted, "No! Anna's ring is in there!"

"Anna's ring! What were you doing with that? You had no right." Duncan grabbed the envelope and opened it with a savage rip. He cradled the thin golden band with the tiny ruby chip in his palm. He hadn't seen it since he was a lad, and the broken promises it represented washed over him. "You put this on her hand with deceit in your heart. You're not worthy to touch it."

"You're right. I'm not worthy." Edward bowed his head. "I'm a sinner of the worst sort. I have no excuse for the evil I did, and any apology wouldn't erase the wounds I inflicted."

Duncan's mother stopped dabbing at the bump on Brigit's temple. "Then why did you come back?"

"Because God sought this lost sheep. I'm in the fold of Christ now—bought by His precious blood. Only now can I look back and admit the wrongs I've done." He shook his head and sighed. "Anna loved me with all her heart."

"Aye, and you broke that sweet heart of hers," Duncan bellowed.

"I did. I'm ashamed of that. Though the Lord has forgiven me, I don't ask it of you. I have no right. I've come to realize what a treasure I had and gave up in Anna."

Father moaned. Mama sniffled.

Duncan glowered. "Some new leaf you turned over. You found another lass, teamed up, and stole. So tell me now who you had in the house as your accomplice."

"I have no accomplice." Edward shook his head. "I sneaked into the house. There are passageways built in the walls where I've hidden. I discovered them when I was a boy. I took the things I'd given Anna—not so I could keep them, but because I've had replicas made of them. I wanted to have reminders of her."

"You don't deserve—"

"I don't. But it wasn't a matter of justice. I wanted to ensure Timothy would get the ring; and while I was looking for it, I happened across some of Anna's other things. I found I longed for a touchstone—memories of the few times in my life when I'd been happy. She did make me happy, Duncan. I gave back everything I took."

"You're a liar. You took more than just Anna's things, and you kept back this ring." He held out his hand to display the unmistakable evidence.

Edward cleared his throat. "I took the other things so you wouldn't notice a pattern. I gave them all back, except the ring. The letter is written to Timothy. I wanted him to have the ring, hoping someday he'd be able to give it to his sweetheart. The joy on Anna's face when I put that ring on her finger—I want my son to see that same joy on a girl's face someday."

"Tim's an honorable man. When he weds, it will be a true marriage, and he'll provide and protect as a husband should."

"That knowledge pleases me. I pray my son turns out better than I did."

Duncan sucked in a deep breath. Edward wasn't saying a word in his own defense. He clamped his teeth against the vile things that wanted to spill out, then unfolded the letter.

My son Timothy,

It's a sad day when a father's first words to his son are an apology and come only after the boy has already grown into his manhood. You deserved better.

I'm only now writing this, not contacting you in person because I gave up any right to you when I abandoned your mother. I was a sinner of the worst sort. Anna was an innocent, and her very goodness drew me to her. She gave me her heart, and she pledged her love. It shames me to say I took all she so freely gave, then left her.

God took Anna home, and I knew about you. Though I acted hard-hearted, I felt such deep shame that I wanted you spared my influence. Emily and John had fallen in love, and I knew they'd rear you far better than I could. All these years you thought I'd spurned you; the truth is, leaving you was the one sacrificial act of my life. Seeing the young man you've become gives me peace about that decision.

My conscience has haunted me all these years. The Holy Spirit wouldn't allow me ease. God, our Good Shepherd, sought me. He untangled me from the brambles of bad living and redeemed me by the blood of the Lamb.

Two years have passed, and my walk with the Lord has deepened. I came to a point where I knew that though I'd been forgiven, I still had to make restitution for my wrongs.

When I left, John told me I'd be welcomed back if I got right with God. I came back fully intending to be a prodigal brother. That night, though, I heard you in the garden, pouring your heart out to Duncan. I realized then that I couldn't return home because the cost of my reunion would be far too great, and you would be the one to bear it.

I deserve nothing. Still, over the years, I've come to realize the days I shared with your mother were the sweetest of my life. Looking back, I now know I loved her—as much as a selfish, evil man could. The one thing I wanted for you is the legacy of love Anna carried in her heart. The day I put this ring on her finger, she glowed. By all rights it should be yours to give to your sweetheart someday. Let it always remind you of the constancy of unconditional love.

I wronged you and am worthy of your resentment and hatred. There are no words to say how sorry I am. Forgiveness is a sacred thing, something only God or His children can grant. I was unworthy of His mercy; yet He granted absolution. My sins were cast into the depths of the sea. Timothy, you will sail those seas. It is my hope that you will not let my sorrows and sins burden you and cause your spirits to sink.

Anna is with the Lord; and by the Savior's mercy, I'll see her in heaven someday. It is my prayer you will serve God and live a rich, full life, so I can finally see you face-to-face in paradise.

Edward Timothy Newcomb

Duncan finished reading the letter aloud.

"I want nothing from you," Edward said softly. "I just wanted to leave the letter and ring here. I've made a life for myself—one that is full, save the fact that it is lonely. Wealth, I've discovered, is empty when love is absent. I've set up an account for Timothy, and he's named as my sole heir."

"Your money willna mean a thing to the lad," Duncan's mother whispered tearfully.

"I don't expect it will. It's all I have to leave him, though."

Brigit was trying to muffle her sobs. Duncan strode over to her. The poor lass looked woozy and overwhelmed. He shouldn't have allowed her to stay in the room and witness this private business, but it was too late now.

"Ah, Brigit." He pulled a kerchief from his pocket and dabbed at her cheeks. "Your poor head. It must be aching something fierce."

" 'Tisn't that at all. It's none of my business, but it's all so verra tragic."

"You've such a tender heart. I'm sorry—"

"I'm sorry, too." She clutched his hand. "I've read the newspapers and heard people talking about a coming war where brother would fight against brother. The war already came to this family. 'Tis more than enough to break my heart."

Duncan let out a deep sigh. "There's already been enough hurt, hasn't there?"

Brigit nodded. The action made her draw in a sharp breath and close her eyes. Her grip tightened as more tears seeped from beneath her lashes. The sight of it made Duncan want to roar, but she whispered, "He's not defending his reprehensible actions. He called himself a sinner and confessed."

"Stop fretting over that now. You're hurting."

Her eyes opened, and a touch of a smile tugged at her lips. "It would take far more than a mere bump to bother a hardheaded lass like me, Duncan O'Brien. Go pay attention to the important things."

"I am."

Her brows puckered. "What are you planning to do about him?"

Arguing with her wouldn't accomplish anything, and he did need to make some hefty decisions. "This has knocked the wind out of my sails. I need some time alone to pray." He turned loose of her hand and tunneled his arms beneath her. "Let me carry you into the other room. My mother will stay with you. Da will go fetch the doctor."

Once he was alone in the room again with Edward, Duncan didn't feel ready to talk. He knelt by the fire and whispered, "Father, he's done such awful things."

They're all forgiven.

"He killed my Anna. Tim's been without a father."

Anna is with Me. I'm Tim's eternal Father, and I gave him John so he'd have a godly man as his example. You are there for Tim, too. Will you teach him bitterness and vengeance, or mercy and grace?

"How can I forgive Edward? I've carried hate in my heart for him all these years. I didn't think I had, but I have. Seeing him here brought back everything."

Forgive him as I forgive you, My son.

Time passed; and for every thought and protest Duncan had, God met him at the point of his hurt.

Slowly Duncan stood to his feet. He went to Edward. "Knots aren't just things in ropes. They're in hearts and souls and memories." He took a knife from the table. "I don't want to be bound by them any longer." He sawed through the rope. "God's grace and mercy go with you, Edward."

Chapter 21

*A*bsence doesn't just make the heart grow fonder—it makes me a bit crazy. Duncan stood in the entryway and scanned the stairs and open doorways, hoping for the impossible: to catch Brigit. The doctor had ordered that she stay in bed for a few days due to the bump on her head; and once those days were up, she had come back to the big house. John had insisted on making a personal apology and escorting her back himself. Duncan felt more than a little surly about that second fact. He'd looked forward to having at least a few minutes to walk with Brigit and speak to her privately.

It's been nigh unto a week, and I've seen only that woman's back as she scurries off. I saw more of her when I had her living with Da and Mama.

Oh—evidence of her presence surrounded him. The scent of her perfume lingered in rooms. Swags of pine and holly she'd made festooned the house both inside and out. Ribbons and wreaths had always been a tradition, but this year they abounded. The twins spent hours on end at the piano, plinking out the simple melodies to two Christmas carols Brigit had taught them. Duncan wanted to enjoy the holidays before he set sail. It was difficult to, though. Each time he tried to get near Brigit, she slipped away. It used to be that he couldn't avoid her. Then he'd needed to make a bit of effort to stop by his folks' each day to check on her and enjoy her company. Now that she was back in the main house, he could barely find her.

Emily didn't help one speck, either. Just about the time Duncan would locate Brigit and approach her, Emily would call her away or send someone to summon her with a ridiculous matter that was "urgent."

"Emily." He closed the parlor door, shutting his sister in. "We need to talk."

"Very well." She handed him a tiny key and pointed toward the window seat. "Open that. I have something I need to hide in there."

He removed the pink-and-cream-striped cushion and unlocked the hinged lid. "What is this all about?"

Emily laughed. "Since the first year I married John, I've used this as my hiding place for Christmas gifts. It's the one place nobody ever bothers. John bought Timothy a sextant, and I need to tuck this in before someone finds it. We thought that was a fitting gift for him this year. Don't you agree?"

Duncan didn't bother to open the handsomely carved wooden box to admire the piece. He'd let Tim have the honors, then speak his praises on Christmas. "You always make fine choices." After he took care of that matter, Duncan sat Emily down and held her hands in his. "Em, I want you to stop interfering."

"Inter—"

"Don't you dare try to play innocent. I know you far too well."

She huffed. "You're impossible to please. You told me you weren't ready to settle into marriage and insisted I cease what you called the 'petticoat parade.' Well, I have, and now you're not satisfied."

"You look entirely too pleased with yourself," he muttered. "I am consistent. I've told you not to interfere, that I'd choose my own wife."

"Wife?" Emily gave him an innocent look.

Duncan squeezed her hands and let go. "You'd try the patience of a saint, Em. I've made up my mind, and I'm going to win Brigit's heart. I can't very well do it if you keep hindering me. Stop helping her get away from me."

Patting her slippered foot on the floor, Emily gave him an impish smile. "It took you long enough. How many unsuitable lasses did I have to march past you before you finally figured out the perfect woman was under our verra roof?"

"You were trying to match me with Brigit all along?"

"Isn't it just the funniest thing in the world?" Emily smoothed her skirts. "You're so very much like my John—you live in a gentleman's world, but you work with a rowdy crew. Brigit comes from a fine family. They eventually lost everything due to the famine, and she's been supporting her parents by working here."

Duncan moaned.

"Aye, Duncan-boy-o. She's well educated and cultured, but she never once minded putting her hand to any task—however small or dirty it might be. She'd been here only two days ere I wondered if she'd be the one for you. The night you and she shared that tea party with the twins, I knew your future was assured. I even took Brigit aside that night for a pot of tea and found out more about her. While you were busy denying the truth, I was getting to know my future sister-in-law."

"If you were so certain, why did you keep shoving those other women at me?"

"Contrast. It was simple contrast." Emily gave him a mysterious smile. "It's taken you far too long to see the jewel that was right under your nose."

"Then stop delaying it further. I have a plan. You can help me."

☙

Brigit knew Duncan's new vessel was finished. Emily planned a christening the day after Christmas, and the ship would then go on her maiden voyage. That day couldn't come fast enough.

He'd thought her guilty. Aye, he had. Once she'd gotten a chance to think back, Brigit came to the galling realization that Duncan had been doing everything he could to set her up and capture her—he'd been trying to charm her, make her feel safe. He'd shared in her tea party and piano lesson with the twins. He'd discussed books—oh. Her heart twisted at the memory of how he'd toyed with her. He'd asked her about what punishment was appropriate for a thief!

And to think she'd actually fancied him a bit. That stung even worse. She'd given him her trust, and he'd barged right into every activity he could to find her weaknesses. The man was a scoundrel.

At least I didn't make my feelings known. I don't have to be humiliated that way. Sure and certain as can be, I'll never think of him favorably again. It may well be my job to serve the whole family, and I'll do it to the best of my ability, but I don't have to waste my breath talking to him.

༷

Duncan thought it quite telling that he had such cooperation with his scheme. Aye, the children thoroughly approved. He didn't have to give them the name of the lass whose heart he wanted to net. They all guessed, and he didn't bother to deny a word.

It hadn't taken much at all to enlist their help. Duncan simply went out and came home with an armful of mistletoe. He'd no more than walked in the door, and Lily peered down at him from the second floor. Her face lit with glee. "I'll fetch Anna Kathleen. We'll help!"

In almost no time at all, she and Anna tied the mistletoe into dainty little balls and sprigs. Timothy and Titus came over to investigate what they were doing and offered to help Duncan tack up the mistletoe in every doorway. It was gratifying, knowing they supported his plan.

Timothy stood back and stared at their handiwork. He smirked and elbowed Titus. "Our Duncan's a man on a mission."

"I'm thinking it's a dangerous one," Anna chimed in as she looked up at the doorway where they'd just hung the last sprig. Her brows puckered; then she stood on tiptoe to straighten out a twisted ribbon. While Duncan wondered how she'd managed to turn into a fastidious young woman under his very nose, Anna gave him a pitying look. "Brigit's good and mad. I don't blame her one bit."

"I can't see why." Titus propped his hands on his slim hips.

"He's too young to understand." Lily tilted her nose at a superior angle.

"Hey. I'm older than you are!"

Lily gave her brother a hopeless look and shook her head so emphatically, her dark curls bounced. "What woman would want a man who didn't court her?"

"He's got mistletoe all over the house. She can't possibly miss it."

"Worse," Anna said softly, "what woman would want a man who didn't believe in her?"

"What kids wouldn't want some of Cook's gingerbread?" Duncan pointed toward the kitchen. "I'll bet you could talk her into letting you have some. Can't you smell it?"

They went off to the kitchen, but Duncan stayed behind and scowled at a small, fuzzy mistletoe leaf on the floor. Anna's words troubled Duncan. *Does Brigit think I don't believe in her?*

Never a man to stand by and do nothing once a problem was identified, Duncan sought Brigit at once. *At least this time Emily won't call her away.* That thought did him no good. Duncan methodically searched the house from attic to basement and couldn't find the woman. Out of frustration he finally pulled Emily away from the piano teacher who was discussing music selections for the girls as if the decisions were of the gravest importance.

"I wasn't done yet," Emily protested.

"You can go back in a second. Just tell me where Brigit is."

"Oh, Mama needed her." Emily patted his arm reassuringly. "Da came by this morning and asked if Brigit couldn't help out. According to him, Mama and Brigit had some last-minute details to do on a Christmas gift."

Duncan yanked on his coat and headed for the door. Goodhew nodded and opened the door as he murmured, "Happy hunting, sir."

"Practically broke my knuckles dragging her back to the main house, so where does she go? Back to the cottage," Duncan muttered to himself. "The woman's a thief after all. She's robbed me of my sanity."

"She's robbed you of your heart, if I might say so."

Duncan gave Goodhew an exasperated grin. "You may not say so—even if you are twice my age and a valued person to my family."

"Close to thrice your age." Goodhew's mouth and cheeks looked as impassive as his voice sounded, but his eyes sparkled with merriment.

"I'm going to go talk some sense into my woman."

"You're a better man than I am, sir. I've been married thirty-five years and have yet to accomplish that feat, but it is good to hear you call Miss Brigit your woman, sir."

Duncan left without another word. He marched down the road to the caretaker's cottage and noticed John had already managed to get the door replaced. Worried about Brigit when he'd kicked it in, Duncan hadn't given a thought to the damage, so the whole thing lasted only one slim day after the scuffle ere it turned into kindling. The new one looked sturdy, but he didn't bother to knock.

"Well, what a lovely surprise!" His mother smiled up at him.

Duncan glanced about and folded his arms akimbo. "Enough of you women conspiring against me. Where did you put her?"

"I haven't put anyone anywhere. Would you like a cup of tea?"

"I want Brigit. Em said she's here, and I'm tired of this game. Where is she?"

"Oh, Brigit was here this morning. She's such a lovely girl—talented, too. Did you see the wondrous tablecloth she embroidered for the twins? A tea party tablecloth, she called it. Said they—"

"Mama, you can sing praises about Brigit's talents another day. Tell me where she's gone."

Da wandered in. "Why, didn't you know? Em's good about making sure her maids have days off, she is. Thoughtful. Little Brigit is thoughtful, too. Did your mama tell you—"

"Where is Brigit?" Duncan didn't want to be rude, but he'd lost what little patience he had.

"The lass said this is her afternoon off."

Duncan headed out the door. Barely containing his frustration, he managed to shut instead of slam it—but only because he respected his parents so much. *Tim wasn't wrong one bit—I'm a man on a mission.* He momentarily wished he'd ridden a horse and knew he could easily go to the stable to fetch one, but a walk would settle him down. In his present frame of mind, he'd likely scare the wits right out of Brigit. *I've been operating under a grave misconception, and all it accomplished was to muddy the waters. Now that I've figured out the problem, I'm going to solve it—just as soon as I catch up with that woman.*

ᏺᏚ

"Brigit."

Brigit froze when she heard her name. She'd been holding Da's arm, listening to him as they walked out of the ramshackle tenement building. Everything in her rebelled. She refused to turn.

"Why, now who's that handsome lad callin' out your name?" Da stepped forward a bit and took a good gander at Duncan.

Oh, she'd stuck to her guns and not taken the slightest peep at who had spoken—but she'd know Duncan's voice anywhere. "It's cold out, Da. Let's get going."

To her consternation, her father didn't budge. Duncan did. He came on over and shook her father's hand. "Duncan O'Brien, sir. I'll be wanting to speak with you about your daughter just as soon as I talk with her a bit."

Her father tapped the toe of his boot on the ground. "Oh, so that's the way of it, is it?"

Brigit finally looked up at Duncan. She glowered at him; he winked. "He's a rascal, Da. Don't waste your breath."

"Of course he's a rascal. What with a fine Irish name like O'Brien, I'd have to expect as much. He can't be all bad if he's taken a liking to you."

"Da!"

"I came to walk her home, sir."

"Now there's a fine man. Manners. Protective." Da nodded approvingly. His eyes narrowed. "Just whose home?"

"The Newcombs. Emily Newcomb is my sister."

Da's chuckle made Brigit's stomach churn. He gave her a bit of a squeeze. "This Duncan's something, all right. Everyone knows John Newcomb owns the shipyard, and your young man's standing here—"

"He's not my young man!"

Her father tilted her face up to his and said softly, "I know you too well, daughter. Your strong reaction tells me you hold some feelings for the man, and his presence here tells me plenty."

A scalding wave of embarrassment washed over her. "Da!"

"From what I see, the pair of you need to settle a wee bit of a tiff."

"We'll get things worked out, Mr. Murphy." Duncan took hold of her other hand.

She snatched it back.

Da gave her a kiss. "Off with you now. Be happy."

Brigit watched in shock as her father walked back inside, effectively abandoning her.

Chapter 22

I t's cold out. Let's get going."

Brigit jolted. "Don't you dare repeat my words and use them against me."

"Do you want me to hire a ride for us, or would you rather walk?"

"Both." She flashed him a heated look. "We'll each do one of those."

"We'll walk. The chilly air might cool your temper." He said the words so blandly that he managed to get a fair hold of her arm and start leading her off before she even realized what he'd done.

Brigit dug in her heels and hissed, "I need my job. You're going to spoil it all."

"If you'd cooperate even the least little bit, that wouldn't be a problem."

She let out a long-suffering sigh. "You're making a scene, and the only way I'll make it through is simply to go along. It doesn't mean I have to talk to you at all."

"That's fine." They started to walk again, and he added, "I'll be happy to do all the talking."

Brigit quickened her pace. "You're impossible. The next thing I know, you'll be blaming all of this on me because I helped you escape that day. I can't regret it, though. No, I don't. I spared those lasses being married off to the likes of you. You would have broken their tender hearts."

"I'm thinkin' you're the one with the tender heart, Brigit."

"Can't you just leave me alone?"

He curled his hand around her. "No."

Brigit could feel tears burning behind her eyes. She refused to cry. "Let go of me. I declare, if I weren't such a lady, I'd smack you."

"I can see I'm perfectly safe then. It's clear as a cloudless sky that you're a lady."

"Don't you try to be charming, Captain O'Brien. I won't fall for it. No, I most certainly won't. I already know the truth."

"What truth is that?"

"Shakespeare said it quite well in *Hamlet*: 'A man can smile and smile and still be a villain.'" Brigit moaned and braced her forehead with one hand as she stared at the slushy ground. *I can't believe I said that to him. Oh, dear Lord above, I'm digging myself a grave here. If I say another word, I'll likely lose my job.*

"So I'm a villain."

Brigit didn't reply. She concentrated on the toes of her shoes. The hem of

231

her blue dress was getting a wee bit damp. Rain had fallen very briefly today and promptly iced the edge of the path. Not that it should matter. She really didn't care a whit about her appearance. It wasn't as if she wanted to impress anyone—especially Duncan.

They walked in silence for a ways. Duncan shot her a bold look and mused aloud again, "So I'm a villain. What is my crime?"

"You've stolen my peace of mind," Brigit snapped. She lifted her arms in the air in an impatient, flinging gesture and started to walk faster still. "I can't believe you just prodded me into admitting that. Don't you dare act as if it just happened, because you planned it. You're a man who plots his course carefully, so I know you meant to hound me. Didn't anyone ever teach you it's rude to provoke a woman?" She groaned. She'd told him she wasn't going to speak to him, and here she was, babbling. "If I speak to you any longer, someone is going to certify me a lunatic."

"I could lock you in the attic. The door sometimes sticks. No, wait. I can't do that. You'd end up breaking your neck, climbing out on the roof."

"Your humor is—"

"To mask how I've lost my own peace."

Brigit cast a glance at him and burst into tears. "You dreadful man. Don't you even begin thinking I feel the smallest scrap of pity for you."

"I don't want your pity; I want your forgiveness."

When she started crying, she lost track of where she was going. Brigit plowed into a bush, and Duncan yanked her back and turned her around. He opened his greatcoat, pulled her to his chest, and wrapped her in his arms and warmth. He held her while she soaked his shirt with tears.

Brigit sucked in a choppy breath and managed to hiccup in the most unladylike way as she let it out. She muttered against Duncan's chest, " 'Tis said God watches out for children and fools. He surely must be watching me now. Honest and true, I've made a fool of myself sobbing like a baby."

"God is nigh, my sweet. I have no doubt of that. I've been calling upon Him to help straighten out this mess, and it's time we talk. I've hurt you badly, and I'm sorry to the marrow of my bones for that."

Brigit wiggled out of his arms. Duncan promptly shed his coat and draped it around her shoulders. He held it there by wrapping his arm about her and nudging her to walk.

"I've plenty to say and am trying to decide where to begin. I was so busy fighting Emily's matchmaking plans that I closed my eyes to any woman. When I took the lads on that voyage with me, I was miserable. Oh—'twasn't on account of them. 'Twas because from the first time I set foot on a Newcomb ship, I've loved to go to sea. That whole trip I didn't find a moment's pleasure with sailing. All I did was think of you."

Brigit trudged on in silence.

"By the time I came back, I'd determined you were all I could ever hope for in a bride—a solid Christian woman, you lit up the room when you came in, and you lit up my heart. I nearly kissed you during the games on Phillip's birthday, but I came to my senses in time. I didn't want to give anyone call to cast aspersions on our character."

He stepped over a fallen branch and lifted her over. Before he set her back down, Duncan waited until Brigit looked into his eyes. Sincerity shone in the depths of his eyes. "I'm ashamed of what I'll be saying next, but I cannot ask forgiveness if I don't confess."

Brigit bit her lip and nodded.

Duncan tucked her close to his side, and they continued toward home. "John and Emily told me we had a thief. They'd narrowed down the possibilities until 'twas one of the maids. We talked long into the night. The Bible says perfect love casts out fear. My love for you was far from perfect; and as John and I started to piece together the facts, they all pointed at you."

"I never did anything!"

"I know." He sighed. "A book and a fountain pen were taken. Trudy and Fiona can't read or write. Since Trudy started acting moon-eyed, Em always assigned her to work with someone else, so we knew she couldn't have taken the fan or cameo. Fiona is too clumsy to sneak into any room unnoticed, though we agreed she spends a fair amount of time with the twins and might have taken the doll."

"Phillip admitted he took the doll."

"Sure and enough, Brigit, he did. The problem was, we didn't know that at the time. Nothing had ever been stolen until you started working for John and Emily. That alone weighed heavily against you. Worst of all, you'd discovered the little shepherdess statue was missing, but then I saw you with a bundle. You stopped outside your parents' building and boasted about having things to please your mother."

"Cook gave me apricots for M—" She stopped herself, then shrieked, "You followed me?"

"Shh. I'd gone to vote and saw you walking down the street. At the time I needed to figure out where your father was so I could ask him for your hand— so, yes, I did follow you. At the last minute I recalled a promise I'd made to Em. I told her when I found the right woman, she'd be the first to know. I couldn't very well break my word, so I came home. I went to her, but that's when she and John told me about the missing things."

"So instead you condemned me for being a thief and wanted to chop off my hand." Every last word made her tight throat ache.

"All of the evidence was there, Brigit. Wrong as it turned out to be, it stacked up against you. By now you know how Edward hornswoggled my sister Anna into a sham marriage. I hadn't recovered from that. My pride had me believing you'd been hurting my family right under my nose. The betrayal I felt cut deep. When I saw you on the roof, the last flicker of hope I held got snuffed out."

"So now you think to woo me? No, Duncan. I don't want a man who cannot hold more faith in me than that."

"That's where you're wrong."

Brigit closed her eyes in horror. She'd just presumed far too much and humiliated herself. Duncan wouldn't let her pull away, though.

"I looked into your eyes that night and knew deep in my heart that you couldn't have stolen a thing. I went against John's orders and took you to my parents. I wanted you to be sheltered until I could solve the mystery. All along I tried to prove to you that I stood by your side. I came by each day. I made sure you still got your salary, and the household staff figured you were special because I'd chosen you to go help my mama. I even put that Bible verse in the sewing box for you."

"You did that? The verse came from you?"

"Aye, Brigit. I wanted to encourage you. Until I cleared your name, I had no right to speak my heart. I was trying my hardest to brace you up, but I've come to see you didn't understand."

"How could I? You'd been trying to trap me all along. I thought you were hovering just to scare me because you thought I'd betray your parents."

Duncan groaned. "I'm accustomed to working on a ship with a crew of men. As it turns out, I'm none too good at figuring out how a woman thinks."

They'd finally arrived at the back of the estate. Duncan turned her to face out over the ocean. Ships bobbed along the dock. "God's given me a love for you, Brigit Murphy. It's big as the ocean. Our ship went through a mighty storm and got stuck on treacherous shoals. Tide's coming in, and I want our ship to float free. With your forgiveness and God's blessing, we could sail through life together." He turned loose of her and walked around so he stood directly in front of her. Taking her hand in his, he knelt right in a thin layer of ice. "I'm not just asking your forgiveness, Brigit. I'm asking for your hand and your heart. I love you, lass. Marry me."

The door flew open, and Titus dashed out. "Don't you hear the bells? Come on!"

"Bells?" Duncan and Brigit repeated the word in unison.

"Hurry. Dad and Tim are saddling horses." Titus slapped Duncan on the arm. "The church is on fire!"

᪻

Brigit clutched Emily's hand and bowed her head. "Heavenly Father, please watch over our men. Keep them safe. Oh, please keep them safe. A pretty church can be rebuilt, but a fine man—I can't replace Duncan. I'm asking You not to take him away from me just when You've brought our hearts together. Be with Mr. John and Timothy and Titus and all the other men, too. . . ."

After praying, Brigit sat in the kitchen with Emily, sharing a pot of tea. She spent considerably more time stirring her cup than drinking from it. The grandfather clock chimed the quarter hour, and she remarked on the obvious. "They're still not back."

Emily said nothing.

"I'm worried," Brigit confessed. "Duncan is there—he could get hurt. I'm supposing I ought to have faith; but the truth is, faith isn't a shield against bad things happening."

A melancholy smile chased across Emily's face. "That's true. Believers still have problems. Sickness and death visit their homes."

Brigit took a gulp of tea and stared at the rim of the cup. The tea had grown tepid, and she couldn't even warm her hands around the cup. "I can't imagine living with the worry and not having God to lean on. I'm scared, but I know He's with Duncan right now—and with Mr. John and your sons."

"And the Lord is with us, too." Emily stood and added more hot water to the teapot. "Love puts your heart at risk. There's always the danger of the one you love hurting you or being hurt. The thing that gets us through is knowing that grace redeems us. Whether it's God's grace and forgiveness through Christ or the forgiveness we grant one another, it's what gives us another chance."

"The way Duncan gave me another chance, even when I looked guilty."

"And the way you've forgiven his doubts."

The cup clinked softly as Brigit put it on her saucer. "My father is fond of telling me nothing good comes easy. If he's right, I'm supposing my marriage to Duncan ought to be the finest ever."

Emily cried out delightedly, "He asked? I thought maybe he hadn't had a chance to propose yet."

Brigit started to giggle. "Aye, he asked. But I didn't have a chance to answer him before he ran off. Should I be wondering if he'll keep running in the opposite direction now that he'll have a chance to reconsider his offer?"

"Not at all. If anything, that'll bring him back. You've given him every reason to come home."

They went through another pot of tea. The clock chimed again. And again.

"Even with the rough start you've had, you and Duncan are a good match." Emily smiled. "You've both lived through being rich and poor, you both love the Lord and want to serve Him, and the very height of emotions that sparks between you proves much is possible—if only you give it a chance."

"I do want to. Just as we were saying: God set the example; forgiveness grants the gift of redemption.'"

"That's right." Emily sweetened her next cup of tea. "John and I stayed up late into the night talking about that very thing. He tracked down Edward today."

"Well, praise be!"

"Duncan sent a wee gift along—he and I decided Edward ought to have the little golden hearts on the red cord that he'd given to our Anna. John told me Edward was speechless."

Cook walked into the kitchen. "The gentlemen are back and stabling their mounts. I presume they'll be hungry."

The front door opened. "Brigit!" Duncan yelled.

"Oh, dear. Now what did I do?" She stood up.

Emily rose and pushed her toward the entryway. "From the way that brother of mine is bellowing, the whole world is about to find out."

Soot-covered and disheveled, Duncan was halfway up the stairs. "Where is she?"

"I'm down here," Brigit called.

He jumped over the banister and strode up to her. "Before I raced off, I asked you a question, lass. I haven't heard an answer."

"The church burned down," Timothy advised. "If you always wanted a church wedding, you'd best tell him no. He's too impatient to wait for them to rebuild."

"He ran into the church and carried out the altar." John chuckled. "That ought to count for something."

"They're pests, but I love them." Duncan took her by the hands and started to pull her toward the parlor so they could have some privacy. "Putting up with me might be hard, but do you think you can stand them?"

"I love you, Duncan O'Brien. I'll gladly wed you and take them in the bargain."

"He got her under the mistletoe!"

"Fitting it is, too," Emily said. "She'll be a Christmas bride."

Brigit didn't hear another thing, because Duncan took her in his arms and kissed her senseless.

Epilogue

Mr. Duncan asked that his bride be given this." Goodhew stood in the doorway and handed Emily an envelope. He stood on tiptoe, looked over Emily's head, and smiled. "And might I say, Miss Brigit, you look radiant."

"Thank you."

"Everything is ready downstairs. Mrs. Murphy, the cloth you stitched for the altar is exquisite. It covered the burned edge so no one can see the singe marks at all."

Brigit's mother beamed. " 'Tis kind of you to be saying so."

Nonny and Emily both fussed with one last bow on Brigit's gown. They'd been stitching it in secret since Duncan had brought back the satin from his trip to Lowell.

Brigit waited until Goodhew escorted Nonny, Emily, and Mum out; then she opened the note.

Beloved Brigit,

The day John married Emily, he gave me a shiny new quarter to signify that I was one-fourth of their family. Through the years, it's been a reminder to me that I was wanted. I've enclosed a brand-new gold Indian Princess dollar. I'm trading up. You are my whole world, my princess, and our future is golden. Let it serve as the first of many reminders that you are loved, my bride.

—D

Late that evening Duncan carried his bride across the gangplank and onto the *Redeemed.* Just yesterday the bride had christened the vessel. Tonight the captain's cabin would be their honeymoon suite. In two days the *Redeemed* would go on her maiden voyage, carrying cotton to Ireland. In accordance with the family tradition, the bride would sail with her groom.

Anna Kathleen had caught the bridal bouquet, and she'd tossed it back into the carriage as Duncan and Brigit departed. Brigit put the bouquet down on the table in the cabin, and it made an odd sound.

"What was that sound?" Duncan looked around.

"It's a wedding wish."

"Oh?" He wrapped his arms around her waist and nuzzled her temple.

Brigit urged, "Look at the ribbon on my flowers."

"I'd rather look at you."

" 'Tis the coin you sent me. I tied it to my flowers for our wedding."

"And God tied our hearts together at the altar. I'm going to love you forever, Brigit-mine."

Ramshackle Rose.

To my dear friends,
Sulynn Means and Cathy Laws—
I've known you for ages.
You give of yourselves unstintingly,
and with nothing less than your whole hearts.

Chapter 1

Rose Masterson knelt by her picket fence and carefully culled a few more withering leaves. She stopped her tuneless humming as she got to her feet. For a moment, she wrinkled her nose at the way the white paint cracked and peeled on the slats of the fence that leaned inward toward her house. It would be lovely to paint the wood and brace it so it would stand upright like everyone else's did. . .but then, that would uproot the morning glory, and she couldn't bear to do that.

Turning her back on the fence, Rose started to hum again. She lifted a wicker basket and headed toward her cottage. Along the way, she picked some foxglove to give to Doc Rexfeld. He said it helped three of his patients who had heart palpitations, so Rose made sure she always kept some on hand. While she was at it, she cut some daisies and decided to drop them by Old Hannah's place.

Just before going inside, Rose lifted the hem of her cream-and-olive-striped wash-day dress and scraped the mud off her high-top, Vici kid, lace-up shoes. She ought to polish the durable, soft-as-glove leather, but that could wait until Saturday night so they'd look good for church.

"Miss Rose! Miss Rose!"

Rose turned and smiled at the freckle-faced towhead who stumbled up her brick path and stopped mere inches from her. "Bless my soul! If it isn't Prentice, I'm not sure whom I'm looking at."

He giggled and opened his grubby hand. "Lookit! I lost two teeth!"

"Gracious! You're halfway to being a man already. I'll have to talk to your daddy about putting a brick on your head to keep you from growing up so fast."

Prentice jigged from one foot to the other. "Iff'n you tell him I'm that growed up, p'rhaps he'll get me a pocketknife."

Rose set her basket aside and crouched down. It wasn't exactly a ladylike position, but it let her get close enough for Prentice to see her face a bit better. Walleyed and nearsighted to boot, the six-year-old missed much of what went on around him. Rose knew he'd settle down if only she'd take a moment with him. She cupped her hand around his shoulder and carefully considered what she should say next.

"I really want a pocketknife," Prentice told her breathlessly. He stopped wiggling and gave her a toothless grin. "Lotsa boys got 'em."

"I suppose that's true."

"They can do stuff—whittle, carve—do all kinds of nifty stuff."

The image of Prentice clumsily slicing his fingers with a sharp blade made Rose shudder. Inspiration struck. "You're right about the other boys having knives, though I think most of the ones who do are a far sight older than you. Seems to me that's fine for them, but you. . ." She squeezed his shoulder. "You, Prentice, are an exceptional young man. It seems to me, you ought to think more along the lines of something a bit more extraordinary."

"What's 'strod'nairy?"

"Extraordinary means something different and wonderful."

He scratched his side and heaved a sigh. "I'm already different 'nuff. I wanna be like all of the guys at school."

"Prentice, God wants you to be the person He made. If you're busy trying to be like everyone else, who's going to do the job the Lord has in store for you?"

"D'ya really think Jesus has something for me to do? I'm. . .different."

"Seems to me, God needs special people to do special jobs. Why don't you think about that for a while?"

"I reckon I could." He tilted his head to the side and turned a bit so he could focus on her more easily. "Just seems a fellow could use a pocketknife to do 'strod-'nairy things."

"I've seen men do extraordinary things with paintbrushes. In the right hands, any tool can be made to do beautiful things. The trick is, each person has to discover what the tool is that God has in mind for him."

He scratched his side and heaved a sigh. "Can't think of nothing like that. I figured a pocketknife does lotsa stuff, so maybe I'd get good at doing something."

"Hmm."

"You stitched up my pocket. I wouldn't lose a knife."

Rose gave him a quick hug. "Oh, Prentice, I'd rather stitch your pocket shut than to have you put a knife in it just yet. There are other things a fine boy like you ought to keep in his pocket."

"You got something in mind, don'tcha?"

"As a matter of fact, I do."

His little head wagged a bit from side to side as he tried to get a closer look at her. In his excitement, he could scarcely stay still. "You gonna tell me what?"

"Better than that." Rose playfully tapped the tip of his nose. "Come in and look at my catalog with me. I'll show you!"

Prentice scrunched his freckled nose. "You mean, we'd send away, mail order?"

"Certainly. It makes it so much more fun. Each day, you get to wonder if it will come. Anticipation means waiting with excitement for something to happen. You'll get to anticipate your. . ." She paused for a moment, then said with hushed, drawn-out relish, "Harmonica."

"Harmonica? A harmonica!" Prentice tugged on her full leg-of-mutton sleeve and confessed, "I don't know how to play one."

Rose nodded. "I know. That's what makes it even better. You'll come to my house every day, and you can learn in secret. It shouldn't take much time; then you'll be walking down the street, astonishing everyone with your grand talent."

"I'd leave it here?" His features fell for just a moment. "But I can come every day?"

"There might be a day every now and then when I'm not at home, but you know you are always welcome, Prentice. Why, you could come right after school."

"Hurrah! Will you have cookies sometimes?"

Rose laughed as she stood. "Of course I will."

"Won't it take forever for the harmonica to come?"

"Just about the time you decide it's never going to arrive, it comes. Besides, you'll need a tiny bit of time to start letting those new, grown-up teeth come in."

"Stinky Callahan tole me they're going to come in all bucktoothed."

"No one can foretell the future."

Prentice kicked a pebble and sent it skittering away. "He said my teeth would be as crooked and ugly as your fence."

Rose sat on the stoop, and Prentice flopped down next to her. She slid her arm around his thin body, and he wiggled closer. From the way he dipped his head, she knew he was trying to hide the tears that threatened to fall. Rose threaded her fingers through his corn-silk hair.

"I could change my fence if I wanted to, Prentice. I could, but I won't. Weak and wobbly as it is, it does a very special job right now. When I think on that, it gives me joy. It makes my fence beautiful to me." She bowed her head and kissed his hair. "I don't care if your teeth come in straight as a row of soldiers or crooked as can be. As long as you smile at me, you'll be handsome."

His little arms wrapped around her knees. "You make me wanna smile, Miss Rose."

❦

Garret Diamond dusted the last shelf of canned goods and nodded to himself. His emporium already looked better. Then again, that wasn't saying much. When he'd bought it two weeks ago, the emporium qualified as the most pitiful business he'd ever seen. As Buttonhole's only mercantile, this place should have been a thriving concern; but between the lack of customers and the abysmal figures in the books, the place simply wasn't turning anything close to a profit.

Ever ready to tackle a challenge and wanting to put his mark on the world,

Garret took ownership and promptly locked the doors upon the completion of the transaction three days ago. Since then, he'd scrubbed, dusted, swept, sorted, and ruthlessly cut his losses. A list of things to order that ran at least two sheets long sat on the counter each evening. A heap of things sat near the back door—items that were of inferior quality, badly outdated, spoiled, or even chewed on by mice. Tomorrow he'd haul it all out to the dump. Come Friday, the wagons would arrive bearing his new merchandise.

The post office occupied a back corner of the mercantile. In fact, the small rent the post office paid and the fact that its customers would have to wander through the store influenced Garret's decision to buy this particular store. He and the gnarled old postmaster, Mr. Deeter, got along well.

Garret hefted a box of canning jars and hauled them to the back door. Carefully, he set it down next to a crate of sun-faded fabric. The lids on the jars bulged, warning him if he jostled them and the glass broke, he'd end up with a stinky, explosive mess. As he straightened, someone rapped smartly on the glass window of the storefront.

Wiping his hands and face clean with a damp cloth, Garret headed toward the waiting customer. He knew the Pinaud's Brilliantine in his hair must have attracted an appreciable layer of dust, but that simply couldn't be remedied. Hastily readjusting his leather work apron to disguise the streak of dirt over his heart, Garret decided this was all he could do for the moment. It wasn't the best first impression, but. . .

He opened the door and couldn't think of a word to say to the woman standing there.

She wore a worn-out, striped dress that might have been pulled from a missionary barrel. What could have passed as a becoming hairstyle that morning now featured a wheat-colored topknot that slid precariously off to the left and a good dozen wisps and coils corkscrewing around her face and neck. Midafternoon sun illuminated her from behind, making her hair glow like a golden halo. Her eyes were more green than gray—definitely her best feature. She held a little towheaded boy in front of herself.

"I'm sorry, ma'am, but we're closed still. The mercantile will open for business again on Saturday."

"We've come just to visit the post office. Surely, we can purchase a few stamps and mail a letter."

"Mr. Deeter is out to lunch." He couldn't very well send them away or leave them standing out in the sun, so Garret opened the door wide and gestured for them to enter. "You're welcome to wait a few moments if you'd like. Please watch your step. I'm rearranging things and trying to establish some order. Allow me to introduce myself. I'm Garret Diamond."

"It's a pleasure to meet you, sir. I'm Rose Masterson. This is Prentice—"

"Man, oh man!" The little boy gawked about. "It's all different in here!"

The woman kept her hands on the boy and looked up at Garret. "Indeed, it is, but the post office is still in the corner. Imagine how hard it would have been to move all of the metal mailboxes and counter!"

The little boy giggled. "And the bars on the window. Daddy let me pull on the bars on his window at the bank. No one could ever move a window made of bars."

"I'm sure you're right." Garret glanced about the store, then grinned apologetically back at the mother and son. "Mr. Deeter has the post office shipshape. Wish I could say the same thing about the rest of the place."

"Prentice, there are boxes on the floor in this aisle. Let's go around to the far wall. We can play a game of draughts while we wait."

Garret took a closer look and noticed the boy had a problem with his eyes. The woman managed to guide him around the dangers. "I could hold the letter for you and give it to Mr. Deeter when he returns."

She smiled. "Why, thank you. I'd appreciate that." She handed him the letter and reached into the pocket of her apron to find her money.

Garret frowned. Her letter was addressed to Sears, Roebuck and Co. in a flowing, elegant script.

"You mightn't need to order things, ma'am. I have fresh stock arriving tomorrow. Saturday will be the grand opening."

"Thank you, but Prentice and I read all of the descriptions in the catalog and decided on one particular item."

Not one to dissemble, Garret still felt it reasonable to state his case. "I realize the emporium has fallen into disrepair and may not have met your needs. Those times are past. I've bought the place and plan to make it a going concern and serve Buttonhole's every need. If the article you wish is of a personal nature, I guarantee I'm a man of discretion."

"I appreciate your assurances, Mr. Diamond. Prentice and I have made our choice."

He inclined his head. "As you will."

The little boy tugged on her skirts. "I'm not going to get to lick the stamp now, am I?"

"I suppose not."

Garret smiled at the boy's wide, toothless mouth. "Looks like you would have done a fine job. Not many teeth in the way of your tongue." He snapped his fingers. "You know, I think I remember having a stamp. Let me check."

A few minutes later, he found his stamp book. "Aha! Just as I recalled. I have one last first-class stamp."

"Thank you for checking." The woman handed him two battered pennies.

"I lost my teeth today." Prentice diligently licked the stamp and stuck it in the corner of the envelope. His mother had stooped to hold it for him, and Garret noted how she made subtle allowances for her boy's vision problems, yet honored his independence. Prentice had her light hair, but he otherwise must have taken after his father. His mother's features were too finely chiseled, her form far slighter in build.

"I've been busy, so I haven't had an opportunity to meet anyone in town yet. Where do you folks live, and what does your husband do?"

Prentice giggled. "Miss Rose doesn't have no husband."

"My apologies," Miss Masterson interjected in a laughter-filled voice as she straightened up. "I should have thought to be more forthright. I moved to Buttonhole two years ago and went through the same confusion, so I understand precisely what lies ahead for you. I'm a spinster and live down the street and around the corner."

"The house with the tip-tilty fence," Prentice added.

"Prentice and his father live across the street from me. His father is Hugo Lassiter, the bank teller."

Garret nodded. Miss Masterson had done him the kindness of subtly letting it be known that Prentice had no mother. No doubt, she minded the boy. *Lucky kid. She has a ready smile and a gentle heart. Odd that she seems so blithe about being a spinster. Any other woman would be embarrassed or coy, but she seems content as can be.*

"We ought to leave and allow Mr. Diamond to get back to his tasks." Miss Masterson set the envelope by the postal window. She took hold of Prentice's hand.

"You promised I could see Tom."

"Yes, I did." She looked up at Garret and explained, "You have a mouser named Tom who likes to sleep under the back porch steps. Would you mind if we exited from the storeroom?"

"I'll need to assist you." Garret lifted Prentice onto his shoulders. "I have discards piled by the back door." He offered his arm to Miss Masterson and led her through his store.

She halted and gasped when they got past the curtain that led to the storeroom. "Mr. Diamond, surely you cannot mean to waste all of these things!"

"I'm not disposing of all of it. Much of it is out of season, so I'm hauling it up to the attic." He frowned at several bolts of fabric. "Between the sun and the mice, those yard goods are ruined. The lids are bulging on those jars, and I won't sell anything that I think is spoiled or might make a customer sick."

Miss Masterson squeezed by him, opened the back door, and tugged Prentice free. She set him down and ordered, "Go see Tom Cat." After the boy left, she turned back. "Mr. Diamond, Cordelia Orrick is a widow with three lit-tle girls. She lives in the green cottage at the far east end of Main Street. If you cut the first few yards off of those bolts, the fading problem is gone, and Cordelia is resourceful enough to work around the other parts. I'm sure she'd find the flan-nel particularly useful. As for the jars—if you empty them, I'll wash them. They can be filled with soup for shut-ins."

Garret leaned against a shelf and looked at the piles of junk. "A widow shouldn't have to mess with mouse nibbles."

"Ruth and Naomi gleaned." She smiled. "I have no doubt they ran into a few field mice."

Garret frowned. "Sharing the field with mice is to be expected; sharing flan-nel isn't."

Miss Masterson let her gaze wander about the storeroom. "Cordelia is a hard worker. You said you have stock arriving on the morrow. I'm not one to tell you how to run your business, but I'm willing to mind her daughters for the day if it would help." Before he could reply, she sashayed out of his store and collected Prentice.

Garret watched Rose Masterson wander down the street. He had the odd feel-ing she was completely unaware she'd left home without a hat. She'd worn dainty lace gloves, but she had a smear across her apron that looked suspiciously like jam. It matched the level of Prentice's mouth, a fact that Garret found charming. If the rest of the town were half as delightful, he'd settle in quite happily.

Chapter 2

Your emporium looks wonderful, Mr. Diamond."

"Thank you, Miss Masterson." The store owner tucked a pencil behind his ear. "You deserve part of the credit for its condition. You recommended Mrs. Orrick and watched her daughters after school yesterday. She was a tremendous help. I doubt I'd have gotten everything ready in time without her assistance."

"I did nothing; Cordelia is industrious as a bee. Bee—oh, that reminds me. I need honey."

"I'll be happy to get some for you."

"Piffle. I'm going to enjoy wandering about. I'll discover where you're keeping it." Rose turned away and sauntered through the mercantile. She hadn't voiced empty praise. The place shone. In the two years she'd lived here, Buttonhole's only dry goods store had been pathetically understocked and dingy. The change was startling.

Rose finished scanning all of the shelves and displays, then set her wicker basket on the counter. She'd purposefully waited until the end of the day. From the steady stream of folks who'd gone by her street all day, she'd surmised the mercantile's opening had, indeed, been a grand one. Plenty of small tasks had kept her busy, and she'd been just as glad to tend to them and avoid the crowds. "Since the store's been closed a few days, I guess most of the townsfolk were happy to come by."

"It's been a pleasure to meet my new neighbors." Garret Diamond looked down at the meager contents of the basket she'd brought, then back at her. "Were there other things you required? I'm happy to deliver the order to your home so you don't have to carry it."

"You're so very kind to make the offer, but I have what I need."

He looked at the box of shredded and spindled wheat breakfast biscuits. "I'm carrying a new product. It's a ready-made breakfast cereal with a far more pleasant flavor and texture. C. W. Post calls it Grape-Nuts, but it's actually a wheat cereal, too."

"I already have Cream of Wheat at home, thank you."

He nodded. "I had some of that for my own breakfast this morning. I confess, I have a decided weakness for adding raisins to it."

Rose smiled and lifted the single banana out of her basket. "Brown sugar is my usual, but when they're available, I prefer sliced bananas in mine."

"Ah, and the very last one, I'm afraid. I'll be sure to keep them in stock. They've become quite the thing, haven't they?"

She set it down and remembered softly, "I had my very first one at the Philadelphia Centennial."

"I didn't have the pleasure of going to the centennial, but I went to the Chicago World's Fair. I count it one of the great adventures of my life."

"Oh, my! Did you ride on the Ferris wheel?"

He nodded. "Fifty cents to rotate on it twice. A shameful extravagance, but I don't regret it at all." He patted the counter next to her banana. "But I didn't have one of these there. Did you see the oranges I have in the crate over by the apples? They're fresh from California. Train brought them straight through."

"I'm sure they're pure extravagances, too, Mr. Diamond, but my own trees are laden with a variety of other fruits, and I'm already going to be busy trying to preserve their bounty."

He propped both elbows on the counter and leaned toward her. "Perhaps I could tempt you to buy some sugar, paraffin, or canning jars?"

Rose burst out laughing. "I suppose I could use a loaf of sugar."

"Ah, but I don't just carry loaf or cone sugar, Miss Masterson. I have granulated sugar by the bag—so much more convenient, don't you think?"

"Buttonhole is going to be spoiled by the fancy goods you're importing."

He winked. "I certainly hope so. The sacks it comes in are double thickness, so you'll end up with a useful swatch of fabric."

Lula Mae Evert had toddled over to hear about the sugar. She reached up to primp her mousy brown marcel waves into place, then patted Rose on the arm. "Useful. Now there's a clever salesman. He already figured out the perfect word to hook you into making a purchase." She turned her attention to the storekeeper. "Rose, you'll soon discover, is the most practical woman the dear Lord ever created."

"Now that is high praise, indeed."

Rose felt a flush of warmth over those words, because that closely matched her prayer. Each morning, she asked the Lord, "Make me a blessing to someone in Your name today." It wasn't pride—it was her calling. God had been faithful in opening her eyes to places where she could be His servant.

"Five pounds or ten of that sugar, Miss Masterson?"

The man had an almost playful air about him that could charm even the grumpiest old crone. Rose drummed her fingers on the counter. "Why, Mr. Diamond, I'm shocked. You don't have it in twenty-five-pound sacks?"

"I do, but I'm afraid if I tried to sell it to you, picnic ants might carry you off."

She smiled at the outrageous picture his words painted. "Very well. I'll take ten pounds since I'm starting to can fruits. If you have any more of the bags with the tulips on them like you sold to Mrs. Sowell, I'd like that print, please."

It didn't take Mr. Diamond long to tally up her order. The man was quick with ciphering but accurate. He settled each item back into her wicker basket with care to keep it balanced—something most men wouldn't have thought to do. Rose tucked that fact away in the back of her mind. Mr. Diamond was not only clever and conscientious; he was also thoughtful.

As if he could tell what she was thinking, he turned the basket toward her and pushed the sugar off to the side. "I'll bring that sugar by after closing. It's too heavy for a lovely lady to carry."

Lula Mae Evert giggled. "Rose is strong as an ox, Mr. Diamond."

Rose gave him exact change and lifted her basket, then hefted the ten-pound bag of sugar—in the tulip print, as requested. "I'm quite capable. I thank you for your offer. I do hope many of your customers have thought to extend an invitation to church tomorrow."

"A few have."

Lula Mae lit up like a Fourth of July sparkler. "Well, of course you'll come, Mr. Diamond. Afterward, you just march right on over to my house. We're having pot roast, and I insist you share it."

"I'm afraid I'll have to turn down your kind invitation, Mrs. Evert. I'm going to Sunday supper at the reverend's."

Rose headed out the door and dipped her head just a shade so no one could see the smile tugging at the corners of her mouth. Gossip swept through Buttonhole at hurricane speed. The moment someone learned that the new owner of the emporium was a bachelor, every last mama with a marriageable daughter revised the Sunday supper menu, thus providing a dandy excuse to visit the store today. Lula Mae would mope all week for having missed this opportunity to snap up a fine young man for her daughter, Patience. By showing up so late in the day, she'd given all of the other mamas and daughters a head start at trying to attain the attentions of the charming—and probably richest—eligible man who'd just moved to town.

Oh, and if things went as Rose suspected, the matchmaking was going to turn into quite a show. Handsome Mr. Diamond would be in church tomorrow, but if any of a dozen young ladies had her way, he'd be at the altar for an entirely different reason within the season. Poor Mr. Diamond.

⌒§

Mrs. Evert watched Rose Masterson leave, then murmured, "Bless her heart."

Garret knew full well those three fateful words were a Southern belle's stock phrase for jumping in and dishing out gossip. He wasn't one to tolerate talebearing, even if it came wrapped up in pretty words or under the guise of news.

"She's just as sweet as that sugar you sold her."

"What a kind thing to say." Garret felt a twinge for having misjudged the woman.

She fussed with the large jet button at her throat. "Well, I'm only speaking the gospel truth. Rose Masterson is a dear, dear woman. She's different, you understand." The woman's voice dropped. "We all make allowances for her. Somewhere along the way, her parents failed her miserably."

"I thought Miss Masterson said she'd only been living in Buttonhole a short time." Garret had the feeling if anyone needed allowances to be made, it was more likely Mrs. Evert. She wasn't making sense. "You knew her parents?"

"Of course I didn't know her parents. They're dead, young man. She's an orphan."

"Such a shame. It's a good thing they reared her to be so capable and independent, though."

Mrs. Evert ignored every word he said and babbled on. "They went on to the hereafter due to the same tragedy, so she lost them both at once. Terrible as it is that she was left alone to fend for herself—they left her virtually penniless, too. She ekes by in that little house of hers and declares she'll never marry. Have you ever heard of such nonsense? Well, at first, we all assumed she was heartbroken from her loss, but she's never snapped out of her strange notion. She wouldn't do a body harm—so you needn't ever fret yourself over that. The woman's a glowing example of Christian charity. It's just that she's. . .well, dotty."

The minute Mrs. Evert paused to draw in a breath, Garret cut in so she'd cease the talebearing. "It's always a pleasure to learn a sister in the Lord is gifted with such charity. Was there anything else you'd like to buy, ma'am?"

The remainder of the day flew by. Garret finally swept up, locked the front door, and counted out the till. Business had boomed today, but that could be attributed to curiosity and the fact that he'd kept the store shut for almost a week. Of course, the volume of customers was astronomical. Sales showed it, too. He'd turned a tidy profit. Good thing he'd filled the storeroom and had another shipment of goods due in on Monday.

It didn't take long to fill out his account book, but Garret had always found working with numbers quite easy. Organization was the key. He kept the financial ledger, then a record book for stock on hand and what he'd ordered. In a matter of a few months, he'd have a fair notion of the volume sold on average of each item so he could keep his store stocked appropriately.

Garret knelt behind the counter, removed the secret panel he'd installed, and opened the lock on the Gruberman and Sons wall safe. He'd need to make a bank deposit on Monday. For now, he'd keep his funds secured here. He set them inside but kept out his tithe and offering for tomorrow. Once the secret panel clicked back in place, Garret stood and stretched. It had been a long day.

For the next hour, he restocked his shelves. Funny, how he'd learned so much about his neighbors by what they bought. Lumbago salve, Belgian lace, paregoric, and a Bailey teething disk—Garret had a glimpse of the town and its individual inhabitants.

And Rose Masterson—what did her purchases tell him? He turned a jar of honey so the label faced the front. She'd bought only necessities. Staples. No frills—nothing but the basics. Even if he'd had several bananas, would she have bought more than just that one? For all of the customers he'd had throughout the day, he could still recall each of the items that barely filled the bottom of Miss Masterson's basket: honey, a single banana, cereal, yeast, one can of Borden's condensed milk, and half a pound of lentils. Oh—and the bag of sugar. Mrs. Evert's comments led Garret to believe Rose didn't have any leeway in her budget. He hoped he hadn't embarrassed the young lady by suggesting purchases she couldn't afford.

If Miss Masterson suffered a pinching purse, why had she recommended he ask Cordelia Orrick to assist him with the store? As it was, he'd already arranged with Mrs. Orrick to come dust and mind the store for a few hours a week. Depending on how the store did, Garret figured he could probably also hire Rose Masterson. The Lord instructed His sons to mind the widows and orphans, didn't He?

The lamplighter passed by, singing as he lit the fixtures along the way. The man had a pleasant baritone. Who was it who said she was his sister-in-law? The sparrowlike woman with the two hip-high sons who nearly danced a jig when Garret offered them each a sour ball—Mrs. S—it started with an *S*. Sowell—that was it. Garret smiled to himself. He wanted to put names and faces together as rapidly as he could. Miss Masterson was right about the confusion of meeting so many new people at once.

Rose. The name suited her. Oh, she wasn't a hothouse rose. If anything, she was a wild rose—a hearty yellow one with a fair share of thorns and a heady fragrance. Between watching the Widow Orrick's daughters and Prentice, she seemed to collect children about her. This Rose, no doubt, would have a handful of crickets and ladybugs about her. Garret shook his head. Normally not given to fanciful thoughts, he chalked up that whole vision as one triggered by overwork and exhaustion.

He turned off the light and headed up the stairs to his living quarters. He'd no more than made it up a few of the risers when a knock sounded on the store's door.

Chapter 3

Rose shoved an errant curl back from her forehead and tried her best to ignore the mosquito bite on her right shin. The more she tried to forget that silly irritation, the more it itched. She'd dabbed camphor on it earlier today and gotten some relief, but her petticoats must have rubbed off the cure. Then again, the benefit of wearing long skirts was that she could balance on her right foot and use her left heel to—

Fingertips resting on the building, Rose nearly tumbled into the emporium when Mr. Diamond abruptly opened the door. "Mercy me!" she exclaimed.

His strong hand caught her arm and righted her. "Miss Masterson, are you all right?"

"Yes." She could feel the warmth clear through the wool of her cape and the serge of her gray dress. She couldn't very well explain what she had been up to. No lady confessed to scratching as if she were a mangy pup, and she certainly didn't refer to her limbs in the presence of a man. "Thank you. I lost my balance."

"It's my fault. I need to sand the step. It's a tad rough, and I can't have any of my customers tripping. Are you sure you're not hurt?"

"I'm fine. Just fine. You've had a busy day. I thought you might be tired. Here." She stooped and lifted a basket, then shoved it into his hands.

"What is this?"

"Just a warm supper. I doubted you'd feel much like cooking anything after working so long and hard." She flashed him a smile. "The jar ought to look familiar enough. It's one of your own."

He lifted the blue gingham cloth and smiled. Rose was glad she'd decided to bring by the simple meal, after all. It didn't take any longer to make a big pot of chicken stew and a large pan of corn bread than it did to make small ones for herself.

Mr. Diamond closed his eyes for a second and inhaled. "This smells great. I'm hungry enough to eat the basket, too."

"I slipped a pair of peach tarts under the corn bread, thinking you could have one for dessert and the other for breakfast. If you're that hungry, you could eat them both tonight. I hope you enjoy your meal." She stooped and lifted her other basket.

"I will. But wait—what is that?"

"Oh—this is for Mrs. Kiersty. Bless her heart, she's down with a terrible case of quinsy. Soup and tea are about all she can tolerate."

"I'm sorry to hear that."

"Doc Rexfeld started her on slippery elm lozenges, and that honey I bought from you today ought to be quite soothing, too, don't you think?"

Garret looked into her eyes and nodded. "I'm sure the honey will be helpful. I recall using honey and lemon for coughs and sore throats. Permit me to send along a lemon."

Her lips parted in surprise but quickly lifted into a smile. "Oh, that would be so kind. I'm sure she'd appreciate your generosity."

He left the store's door wide open and set his supper basket on the counter. "It'll only take me a second." The fruit display to the left of the register held a full complement of choices. Rose watched the storekeeper ripple his long fingers over the fruit to select the lemon. He returned to the door. "Here you go."

"Thank you, Mr. Diamond." She accepted the fragrant lemon, slipped it under the cloth and into the basket, and turned to leave.

"Wait. You shouldn't be wandering alone in the dark. Let me escort you to her place and back home."

Rose gave him a startled look. "The lamps are lit, and Buttonhole is safe as a sanctuary. You're kind, but your worry is needless. God bless you, Mr. Diamond."

"God bless you, too, Miss Masterson."

She made it all of three steps down the walk before he had hold of her arm. "Where does Mrs. Kersey live?"

"Kiersty. She's at the boardinghouse."

"Why doesn't the cook at the boardinghouse make her soup?"

"Mrs. Kiersty is the cook. I'm afraid the owner, Mr. Hepplewhite, is able to scramble eggs and sear meat, but that's about the full extent of his culinary skills."

Garret chuckled. "Add to those two skills the fact that I can make hot cereal and slap together a sandwich, and you have the full extent of my kitchen expertise."

"Ah, but you can always open up a jar or can of something."

"Eating into my profits, eh?" He swiped the basket from her. "I confess, I've had the Hormel canned meat. Smoked oysters and tinned sardines aren't too bad. To-night I strongly considered celebrating by sitting down with a box of Cracker Jack."

Rose stopped beneath the lamppost and gawked at him. "Mr. Diamond, you cannot be serious!"

"Truth is the truth. You're right. After such a busy day, I was far too tired to bother cooking." He hefted the basket. Jars clinked against one another. "This basket is far too heavy for you to carry. How much soup did you put in this?"

"Two jars. I also included some applesauce."

"I smell bread, though."

"Yes, well, Mr. Hepplewhite and the others need bread. There are a few loaves for them."

Garret stared at her for a long moment, then quietly stated, "I'll bring flour, yeast, and eggs to you tomorrow."

"There's no need—"

"I agree," he interrupted smoothly. "There's absolutely no need for you to do the labor and supply the ingredients. I'm new here, but I aim to be part of the community. You wouldn't want to make me feel unwanted or unnecessary, would you?"

"Mr. Diamond, you've most assuredly chosen the profession best suited to your skills. I declare, I've never met a man who could find a bit of down fluff on a sleeve and sell the person a Christmas goose—at least, I never had until I met you."

His scowl looked anything but genuine. The glint in his hazel eyes and the lilt in his voice proved so. "Miss Masterson, I'm affronted by such an accusation. I'd never sell a customer a Christmas goose at this time of the year. Pillows would be far more suitable as replacements during spring-cleaning."

"Joel Creek's farm isn't far out of town. His wife tends to bring eggs, butter, and milk in once or twice a week, and she made a few superb pillows last year."

He held her arm as they stepped off the boardwalk and crossed the street. "You are a treasure trove of information, Miss Masterson. I can see I'll need your assistance in getting to know everyone."

Rose didn't mind being friendly or making introductions, but if all Mr. Diamond wanted was to coax information out of her so he could sell things, he was barking up the wrong tree. But no—he'd just offered her staples so she could bake for their neighbors, and he'd wanted Mrs. Kiersty to have an expensive lemon to help her throat. Surely that proved him to be compassionate and concerned.

"I chose to open my store in Buttonhole because the town seems to have a gentle charm and caring about it."

She remembered aloud, "I came for the same reason. I visited several places before I decided to live here."

The jars clinked softly in cadence with his steps. "Meeting so many folk today confirmed my impression of how friendly everyone is. It heartens me to see how you're an integral member of the community after living here just a few years."

"Seeing the changes you've made and how you want to conduct a quality emporium, I can promise you, everyone is going to embrace your presence here. I daresay it took me almost a year to be regarded with the ease with which you've been welcomed."

"Why would that be?"

"I'm afraid they didn't quite know what to think of me. They eventually despaired of fitting me into a normal mold and decided I'm a bit dusty in the attic."

"Dusty in the attic?" He echoed her words with a measure of amusement equal to that which she'd instilled in them. "Just what is so dusty about your attic?"

"When I moved here, most of the gentlemen in Buttonhole felt I needed a man to tend my personal business, but I neither depend on nor answer to any-one except the Lord. Their wives and marriageable daughters felt I posed competition for the eligible young swains. It took them some time to realize none of that was true. Now they accept me with genteel amusement. The fact is, I'm happy to be a spinster. The apostle Paul wrote about the ability of a single person to serve unhampered by marriage, and I find delight in doing just that. I confess, it's not the usual choice a woman makes, so they've decided I'm gently daft."

He pursed his lips and whistled a few notes. "Miss Masterson, as long as we're making confessions, I'm afraid I have one of my own to make."

"You do?" She stopped and looked at him.

The left side of his mouth kicked up in a rakish grin. "I'm just as dusty in the attic. At least, I plan to keep a very dusty attic for a few years."

Rose held her silence. She knew full well the mamas in the town were about to turn the table on this salesman. All day long he'd charmed and convinced them to visit his store and tempted them to snap up what he offered. *Have you seen my wonderful. . . ? Wouldn't you like. . . ? It's perfectly suited to you. . . .* Tomorrow he'd be in church, where those selfsame women would have their daughters gussied up. *Have you seen my wonderful daughter? Wouldn't you like to sit with us? The church is lovely, isn't it? Perfectly suited for a beautiful wedding.*

"For shame, Miss Masterson."

Rose snapped out of her thoughts and gave him a startled look. "I beg your pardon?"

Mr. Diamond chuckled. "I hoped you'd be a kindred spirit and accept me as a man who needs to establish his business before he could devote himself to one of the local ladies and start a family. I can see you've already cast me to the vagaries of the matchmakers and consider my cause lost."

"I know the matchmakers."

"Ah, but you don't know me." He took her arm again and steered her toward the boardinghouse. "Suffice it to say, I'm about to confound Buttonhole's citizens by failing to fall madly in love with one of the fair maidens."

"Do you read much, sir?"

"It's among my favorite pastimes."

"Perhaps it's best if I just quote from Robert Burns. 'The best-laid plans of mice and men oft go astray.' "

He opened the door, and his breath washed over her as he dipped his head and added in a tone only she could hear, "Don't stop there. 'And leave us naught but grief and pain for promised joy.' I'm not about to be ensnared by the plans and promises of others. I've plenty of plans for myself."

༄

Punctuality, for being a virtue, should carry with it some level of protection. The wry thought made Garret smile as he wiped the last dab of shaving lather from his chin. He'd determined to show up on the church steps just two slim minutes before the service began. After worship, he'd gladly greet his new neighbors, then make his excuses and go to the parsonage to dine with the minister and his wife.

Garret had concentrated his attention on setting up the store, and he'd been so busy with the grand opening, he'd failed to see the obvious. Rose Masterson did him a great favor by letting him know he was considered eminently eligible. Or was that imminently?

He'd awakened this morning with a plan in place—he'd keep a friendly distance and let the good parson and his wife spread the message that Garret Diamond couldn't commit himself to a bride until he'd established himself.

Oh, he'd certainly not mind meeting the young ladies who were prospective bridal candidates. It would be wise to get to know them, learn of their temperaments, personalities, and quirks. Rushing recklessly into marriage simply wouldn't do. If he kept a slight distance at the start, it would permit him to meet the full selection instead of misleading one particular young lady into thinking he'd been smitten by love at first sight. It wasn't right to dally with a girl's heart, and since he had to wait to marry until his business flourished, it was essential to make his decided lack of romantic intentions quite clear from the start.

When the time came, he wanted a woman who would be his helpmeet in the fullest sense of the word—to help with the store, to be a loving wife and a good mother. Hardworking. Sweet spirited. Caring. Virtuous.

Caring and virtuous. . . He thought of Miss Masterson. She hadn't bought the honey for herself. It wasn't expensive in the least, but if Miss Masterson's finances were half as strained as Mrs. Evert claimed, her small sacrifice of giving that jar to Mrs. Kiersty was akin to the widow in the parable who tithed her last mite. When he delivered the flour, butter, yeast, and eggs he'd promised, Garret would slip in a jar of honey for her to keep for herself.

With that decision made, Garret smiled at himself in the small mirror over the sink. He purposefully avoided splashing on his customary bay rum, snapped his elastic suspenders in place over a spanking new French percale shirt, and secured a turn-downed collar he'd saved for today. He felt a momentary twinge of homesickness. Great-Aunt Brigit knew just the right amount of starch to use.

The school bell pealed. Parson Jeffrey had mentioned the church didn't have a bell yet, so they used the school's bell as a call to worship. Half an hour ago, it rang twice. Now it rang thrice. Ten minutes until the service. Garret donned a subtle charcoal-and-black vest, grabbed his suit coat and hat, and went downstairs. He allowed himself a few minutes to eat a shiny red apple before he stepped out his door. . .and into a sea of pastels and foamy lace.

Chapter 4

ood morning!" a chorus of sopranos sang out.

"No better way to start the day than with worship." He shut the door to the mercantile and removed his hat. A gentleman didn't keep his hat on in the presence of ladies. It also gave him something to do with his hands. "I'm sure the preacher has a good message for us today."

"You won't hear a word of it if these gals won't stop flocking and clucking like hens." A spry old man hobbled through the bustled dresses and batted away a few feathers arcing from Sunday-best hats. He extended his hand. "I'm Zeb Hepplewhite, owner of the boardinghouse, and I'm invitin' you to come sit by me on the bachelor bench."

Garret had no idea what the bachelor bench was, but from a few crestfallen sounds the girls around him made, he surmised he'd just been tossed a rope. He shook Zeb's hand as if it were a lifeline. "Pleasure to meet you, Hepplewhite. I'd be honored to join you."

Once seated in church, Zeb rumbled, "This back bench is bachelor territory. Back bench t'other side's for the mamas with crybabies. Front pew on the left is for the parson's family, and front pew on the right is courtin' row. A buck sits there with a gal, and the good folks of Buttonhole take it to be a declaration of intentions."

Garret nodded his understanding as he looked at the rows of oak pews that lined the boxy white church. "Thanks," he said in a low tone. "I might have blundered badly."

Zeb opened his hymnal and covered his chuckle with a rusty cough. "Wouldn't be the first person to. Miss Rose sat here on the bachelor bench the very first Sunday after she moved to town. As it turns out, 'twas a fitting choice. Oliver Sneedly told her she was in the wrong place, so she scooted across the aisle. Was a few months afore the folks hereabouts stopped squawking and let her be. She has a knack of taking a fussy babe and hushing it."

As the congregation stood to sing the first hymn, Rose Masterson slipped into the crybaby pew. Garret had seen her three times by now, but this was the first time he caught sight of Miss Rose when she'd bothered to tend to her appearance. She made for quite an eyeful. Tamed coils of golden hair framed her face and peeped out beneath a sensible black straw hat trimmed with a minimum of folderol. The midnight blue silk military loop and hooks on her snowy bodice might have looked mannish on someone else, but the way they graduated in size from her tiny, cinched waist up the front served to prove just how feminine she could be. Her deep blue skirt draped over a very modest bustle, giving her a silhouette any man would find admirable. Then her head turned.

She had a smudge of white on her right cheek.

Rose didn't have a vain bone in her body. If he were a gambling man, Garret would bet his bottom dollar it wasn't powder on her cheek. It had to be flour. He reached up and brushed his own cheekbone in a silent message.

She didn't understand.

"Flour," he mouthed silently.

Any other woman in the world would have been mortified. Rose's eyes lit with appreciation, and she swiftly rubbed away the white with her gloved hand as she sang every verse and the chorus of "Come, Thou Fount of Every Blessing" by memory. She looked back at him, her brows raised in silent query.

Garret nodded and grinned. She'd erased the evidence of her baking, at least from her face. As she lowered her gloved hand, the flour made a faint swipe on the side of her dark skirt.

By the time Parson Jeffrey finished an excellent sermon on living by faith and the congregation stood to sing the benediction, Rose held a sleeping baby in each arm. Instead of her full sleeves ballooning out as fashion dictated, they both caved in. The knot in the uppermost military cord loop was soggy from having become a teething chew. A suspicious damp spot marred her skirt, yet she wore a look of utter contentment.

The scripture of the day from the third chapter of 1 John ran through his mind again. *My little children, let us not love in word, neither in tongue; but in deed and in truth. And hereby we know that we are of the truth, and shall assure our hearts before him.*

Yes, he'd come to the right place. Good people—people like Rose Masterson—lived here.

༄

"King me!" Leigh Anne clapped her hands delightedly.

"Now weren't you clever." Rose slipped a draught atop one of Leigh Anne's red ones. They sat by the cracker barrel in Diamond Emporium and chattered as they played the game. Rose knew Leigh Anne's grandma timed her shopping to coordinate with the end of the school day, but she'd been a bit late today. It was too hard for Leigh Anne to walk about the store due to the heavy steel and-leather leg braces she wore, so Rose challenged Leigh Anne to a game of draughts.

"I get a lot of practice at board games." Leigh Anne tried to be subtle as she scratched below her knee.

Rose knew the brace often rubbed, so she leaned across the board and whispered, "Do you need some salve?"

"I ran out," Leigh Anne admitted.

Garret sauntered over. He looked quite dashing in a casual sort of way. Instead of wearing a suit coat as he worked, he always wore a vest and gartered his shirtsleeves.

From the way the young girl blushed, Rose decided to say something so Garret wouldn't know what the conversation was about. Leigh Anne loathed her braces and would probably rather be shaved bald than to have them become a topic of conversation. Rose teased, "Seems to me you've said the same thing about root beer barrels in the past—that you've run out."

"Root beer barrels?" He squatted down beside Leigh Anne and studied the checkered board. "Looks like you have Miss Masterson on the run. Why don't you hand me one of those draughts you captured?"

Leigh Anne happily handed over one of the black wooden pieces.

Garret hefted it in his hand a few times, then stood. He grabbed a few root beer barrel candies and soon was juggling the draught amid a flurry of candies. When he stopped with a flourish, he dumped the candies into Leigh Anne's lap. "Miss Masterson trounced me in a game a few days ago. From now on, any time you beat her, I'll pay you a piece of candy. We've got to stick together, you and I."

"I'll share with you, Miss Rose."

Rose shook her head. "No, Leigh Anne. You earned those candies."

"Grandma says a girl should only accept gifts and candy from a man if he's her beau. I can't have a beau."

"You are a bit young," Garret agreed.

Leigh Anne shook her head so vehemently that her dark brown curls swirled. "I'm almost fourteen. Gladys is twelve, and her initials are already carved in the sweetheart tree. No one will have me."

"Leigh Anne, you don't know that," her grandmother refuted, having just arrived. "God might have someone special just for you."

Hands knotted around the candies in her lap, Leigh Anne whispered, "I'm crippled."

Garret hooked his thumbs in his suspenders and scowled. "Miss Leigh Anne, your limbs might be on the weak side, but your mind's sharp as a tack, and your heart is sweet as honey. It occurs to me, one of these days, some smart fellow is going to count himself mighty lucky to have an excuse to sweep you into his arms and carry you about."

"You're so romantic, Mr. Diamond." Leigh Anne drew in a quick breath and blurted out, "Why aren't you married?"

"Leigh Anne!" Her grandmother pressed her hand to her bosom and nearly had apoplexy.

The door to the emporium opened, and as a couple of ladies entered, Garret nodded his greeting, then blithely turned back to Leigh Anne. "You're asking what everyone else is wondering. The truth is, a man has no right to call on a woman when he doesn't have the time to attend her. I need to build my business so I'll be able to provide well for a family. When the time comes, I want my emporium to be stable so I can dedicate myself to being a good husband, just as Christ cared for His bride, the church."

"Why, now isn't that sensible of you?" Lula Mae Evert cooed as she came closer. "As busy as you've been, it should not take long at all for you to realize great success with your store."

"It's thriving. Everyone says so," Mrs. Busby agreed.

A little boy at her side tilted his head far back so he could look up at Garret. "Papa says you'll be ready to marry up by Christmas."

"Is that so?" Garret nearly choked on the root beer candy he'd popped into his mouth.

Rose stood and started smacking him between the shoulder blades.

"Yeah, to my cousin, Missy Pat—"

His mother's hand clapped over the boy's mouth. "We really must hurry. I just stopped in to buy. . ." Her voice died out, and her already-pink cheeks went positively scarlet.

"Some?" Garret recovered enough from his choking that he rasped out the prompt.

"Matches," Mrs. Busby said in a strangled tone.

Rose had to credit Garret. He resumed his professional demeanor and ignored what amounted to an embarrassing pun. He acted as if the simple request couldn't be interpreted in any other manner and nodded sagely. "Matches. Parlor, small box, or vest matches?"

"Mr. Busby doesn't smoke. I believe I'll take some for both kitchen and parlor."

Garret walked toward a nearby shelf, tapped the edge, then turned around. "Mrs. Busby, I know my predecessor sold lucifers, and I have the remaining stock on the shelf. Keeping them there goes against my grain. I'd far rather give you a flint striker than sell you these old-fashioned phosphorus lucifers. I don't think they're safe. I have Red Top matches due in later this week."

"Oh, la!" Mrs. Busby waved her hand dismissively. "I learned to cook and keep house with lucifers, and I've never once had a single spark go astray."

Mrs. Blanchard bobbed her head in agreement. "They're ever so much more convenient. Why, I simply keep a quart jar of water close by to douse the match when I'm done."

"I've seen too many sparks from those for my own comfort. I took to mail-ordering Red Tops a year ago," Rose said.

"As do I." Leigh Anne's grandmother put a can of Wedding Breakfast coffee on the counter. "Leigh Anne, are you and Rose about finished with your game?"

"About six more moves, Grandma."

"I'll be sure she gets home," Garret promised as he headed to the counter. Rose noted he'd not taken matches along with him for Mrs. Busby. Instead, he'd stubbornly taken along a striker. "I'll be sure to keep sulfur tops for you ladies. There's no reason for you to need to order such necessities by mail."

He tallied up everyone's purchases and sent them on their way, and Leigh Anne finished the last move of her victorious game. As Rose stood and shook the wrinkles out of her gown, the shop bell rang.

"Mr. Diamond, I'm going to have to throw myself at your mercy." Trevor Kendricks shuffled by the door. "Ma's under the weather and wants some embroidery stuff—pink." His face matched the color he requested.

"Embroidery floss. . ." Garret folded his arms across his chest. "I have it by the skeins, but I'm hopeless as can be when it comes to choosing a matching hue."

"Did she tell you a name or number?" Leigh Anne asked softly. "Corticelli numbers the spools."

"Can't rightly recollect. I get the numbers all squirreled up in my brainbox. I have a strand here in my pocket."

"While you youngsters match that up, I'm going to go ahead and buy a postage stamp." Rose went to the counter and slipped two cents to Mr. Deeter.

"Here you are, Rose." He slid the stamp to her and jerked his thumb back toward some brown-paper-wrapped packages on the counter. "You had more parcels come today, but they were too late, so Tommy will be delivering them tomorrow. If you needed either of these immediately, I thought you might want to know they're here."

Rose smiled. "Oh, I'll carry the smaller one home with me. I've been waiting for it."

Garret called over, "I'll be happy to carry the other box to your house after I close tonight."

"How very kind of you."

Mr. Deeter bobbed his head. "He's a good'un. Garret, you'd best come claim it now. I'm liable to lock up the post office while you're busy with customers, and I don't want Miss Rose to think we forgot about her parcel."

Garret strode over as Rose licked the stamp and applied it to the corner of the envelope.

Garret's features went taut, and Rose knew he'd read the address: Sears, Roebuck and Co.

Chapter 5

Rose swept up the smaller package. "Isn't this convenient? The post office and the mercantile working hand in hand. I declare, Mr. Diamond, you've made your emporium such a cheery place; it's a pleasure to stop in."

"Thank you." From the hectic blush on her cheeks and the way she suddenly plunged into chatter, he could tell she was embarrassed. She undoubtedly didn't want to hurt his feelings, but she'd grown accustomed to mail-order shopping. It might take a short time for her to change her ways. He could be understanding and bide his time. Garret decided to wait until he could speak with her privately. Though she expressed the firm wish to remain single, Miss Masterson's business was worth courting.

"We found it!" Leigh Anne called out.

"Wonderful." Garret hefted the larger box and carried it over to his work counter.

"And Leigh Anne shared her candy with me," Trevor said. He sounded like he had a marble in his mouth.

Garret turned so the youngsters couldn't see him and gave Rose an exaggerated wink. He went over to them, then praised, "That does look like a dandy match. Miss Leigh Anne, are you about ready to go home now?"

"Yes, sir."

"I'm still trying to figure out where everyone lives."

"Oh, we're neighbors. Leigh Anne's two doors down from me on Elm." Trevor handed the spool of embroidery floss to Garret and dug into his pocket. The penny he pulled out bore a fair coating of lint, which he rubbed at. "Sorry."

"Not a problem." Garret flipped the penny onto the counter and lifted Leigh Anne into his arms. "Miss Masterson, would you please mind the store for me for a few moments while I escort this pretty young lady home?"

"Now wait a minute." Trevor handed the floss to Leigh Anne. Her hand closed around it as her mouth formed a perfect O. The strapping teen grabbed the dainty girl from Garret.

"I'm happy to mind the store." Rose pulled an apron from a hook on the wall.

"Seems to me Mr. Diamond ought to mind his own store." Trevor's arms tightened. "Leigh's my neighbor. No use in him wandering around when I can take care of her far better."

"Miss Leigh Anne." Garret reached for her. "I promised your grandmother I'd be sure you got home."

"You're keeping your word. You can be sure I'll carry her home safe as can be. Leigh, hook your arm 'round my neck. We need to get going. Ma's wanting her floss, and you don't want your grandma fretting herself about you."

Rose tugged Leigh Anne's skirts down to keep her ankles covered. "Mr. Diamond, I can personally vouch for Trevor's character. He's dependable as the day is long and strong, as you can plainly see."

"Miss Leigh Anne." Garret beetled his brows and gave her a stern look. "If you aren't comfortable with this arrangement—"

Her arm wound around the lad's neck. "Miss Rose says it's acceptable. I think we're just fine. Thank you for asking, though."

Garret held the door, then shut it after they left. As he turned around, Rose didn't bother to hide her smile. She shook her finger at him. "For shame, Mr. Diamond. You don't want anyone playing matchmaker on your behalf, and here you are, nocking an arrow on Cupid's bow for those two."

"Am I supposed to understand what you're talking about?" The deep creases bracketing the corners of his upturned mouth made it clear he knew precisely what he'd been doing, and his sudden ploy at innocence was just another game.

She took off the apron she'd donned and draped it over his shoulder. "I'll take that package with me now."

"Speaking of packages, Miss Masterson, you've gotten a total of three in the week since I've been here."

Rose's step faltered. *Please, Lord, don't let him ask me about it.*

つ

"I'm sorry the mercantile didn't meet your needs in the past and certainly hope you'll allow me the chance to carry the goods you need now that I've taken over."

Color stained her cheeks.

Garret felt like a cad. "I understand there are times when a lady might wish to purchase items of a personal nature through a mail-order catalog. Please don't think me indelicate. My intent is to run a business where you are able to find any of your other needs."

"I've been here twice in the past week to purchase things. If you'll excuse me, I must go."

She swept out of the mercantile with equal amounts of speed and grace. Garret watched her go, then set about reworking the display of homeopathic curatives and medicaments. They were no more than a jumble of tins, bottles, and jars in a case he'd not yet reached. As he started to empty the case and examine the contents, he groaned. Most of the bottles contained spirits and unnamed ingredients. Two were so old, sludge had formed in the bottom. A jar of Vaseline, a tin of bag balm, and Red Clove liniment were all he salvaged. The rest, Garret dumped into a bucket. He'd ask Doc if any of them were worth keeping.

As he set the bucket in the storage room, Garret couldn't help thinking the woman on the jar of Magnificent Mane looked quite similar to Rose Masterson. She had the same delicate features, and he imagined when Rose unpinned her hair, it would be every bit as luxurious.

He shook his head. *I've seen several lovely girls today—all tidy as can be, who would do credit to any man they wed. Missy Patterson, Hattie Percopie, Anna Sneedly, Constance Blanchard. . . Each of them from fine family backgrounds, soft-spoken—and utterly boring. Rose—mussy little Rose who forgets her hat half the time, whose topknot skids around, whose sash is more likely to be mangled than tied in a pretty bow—she's the one I think of. What's come over me?*

He tilted his head and rubbed the back of his neck. The memory of her flowing script on that envelope addressed to the catalog flashed through his mind.

Then and there, he determined he'd win her business—all of her business. He'd come to Buttonhole full of dreams of making his mark in the world. He didn't imagine himself as building a business empire. More than anything, he wanted to be a man who served the Lord and his fellowman. To his way of thinking, if every man loved his family and bettered his community, the world would be a far better place. Once he stabilized his emporium, Garret figured the Lord would send a wife his way. One step at a time—one foot in front of the other in a sure and steady walk.

He had no way of knowing what Miss Masterson ordered. Simply put, it stretched his imagination that she'd needed four different shipments of things of such a private nature that she'd needed to mail-order them in such a short span of time.

On occasion, he'd even ordered from a catalog or two himself. The catalogs always promised their prices were lower than those of local merchants—a fact that Garret felt was not borne out. Nonetheless, if Miss Masterson was barely eking by, she might well have been convinced by the catalog that she'd be saving money by dealing with them. Garret decided he'd show her the truth by looking through the pages of the mail-order book and demonstrating that his prices were quite comparable. The convenience of having the purchases on hand rather than waiting for them and paying postage ought to tip the scales in her mind. After all, she did seem like a reasonable woman.

Indeed, she was a reasonable woman, and he was a rational man. With that level of practicality betwixt them, she'd come to see the light.

Garret wouldn't begrudge her a final item. In fact, he'd promised to personally deliver the two other boxes that had come for her. It would give him an excuse—no, he corrected himself—a reason to go speak to her this evening.

The store was a bit slow. Garret didn't want to pay a call in the rumpled shirt he'd worn all day, so he stuck an iron on the store's potbellied stove. Great-Aunt Brigit always made ironing look so simple. Garret realized the chore was far more complex than he'd imagined. He couldn't decide whether to start on the collar or the sleeves. He scowled at the shirt. *Or do I start in on the main part?*

He slung a shirt over the board and decided to proceed from one side to the other. As soon as the flatiron heated up, he attacked. With more zeal than skill, he mowed over the buttons. Just then, he felt something underfoot. A quick downward glance revealed that one sleeve dragged on the floor. He flipped it up, then sniffed. Something smelled— "Oh no!" He jerked the flatiron off the shirt and scowled at the arch-shaped, yellow brown scorch marring the garment.

An hour later, the rest of the shirt looked passable. Garret covered up the damage with a vest and coat. He applied fresh pomade to his hair and decided to take along something to sweeten up the lady. The row of clear glass candy jars caught his attention.

Mints? No. She might think he was telling her she had bad breath. Sour balls? Garret shook his head. He didn't want her to misconstrue them into an odd symbol of him thinking she was tart-tongued. No man took chocolates to a woman unless he intended to court her, so he ruled those out at once. She hadn't wanted any of Leigh Anne's root beer barrels. Tootsie Rolls! Yes, that would be the ideal candy. It would be a subtle reminder to her that Diamond Emporium carried the finest, the latest, the best. They would also take a little while to eat, so that would stretch out the visit long enough to permit him sufficient time to state his case.

༈

"Just a few more; then I'll help you." Rose switched the cold flatiron for the hot one, then slid it over Hugo's worn blue chambray shirt. She'd mended it as best she could, but the garment wouldn't last much longer. Mary Ellen had sewed these very buttons on it the first time she and Rose had shared a cup of tea. Now that shirt was Hugo's favorite—a reminder of his dearly departed wife's devotion.

"D'ya really think I can do it?" Prentice's glasses bobbed upward as he scrunched his nose. "Lotsa folks say I'm clumsy."

"If you always bother to listen to bad opinions, you won't have time to live your life. I hold with the notion that it's far better to try and not quite get it perfect than to sit still and never see or do anything."

"That's why you're so fun."

"Why, thank you, Prentice. I take that as quite a compliment."

Heavy footsteps sounded on the porch, and a few solid, thumping knocks announced the arrival of a man.

"C'mon in, Hugo!" Rose called as she brushed more water from the noodles she'd boiled a few hours earlier onto the placard of the shirt to starch it. Pressing the iron to the cloth, she detected the faint aroma of noodles rising in the steam. It sharpened her appetite.

"Dad's bringing wood." Prentice galloped over to the door when it didn't swing open. He jerked it open, then stammered, "Miss Rose, it's not my daddy."

Chapter 6

R ose put the flatiron back onto the stove and glanced over her shoulder. "Mr. Diamond! Do come in."

"I have those other packages for you."

She scanned the room. "Oh yes. Could I trouble you to place them over by the hall tree?"

"I'd be glad to."

"We already got our surprises in the mail today." Prentice eagerly followed behind the storekeeper.

Rose held up her forefinger. "But we both know it won't be a surprise if you tell anybody what it is."

Prentice jerked his hand out of his pocket.

"You may sneak past Mr. Diamond and go put your special thing beside mine in the drawer of the parlor desk."

"Yes'm, Miss Rose."

Garret straightened and watched the boy leave the room, then gave her ironing board an assessing look. He cleared his throat. "There you are. I'll be going now."

Slipping the shirt onto a hanger, Rose laughed. "If you don't mind me finishing Hugo's shirts, you're welcome to join us all for supper."

"I, uh. . .thanks, but—"

"Prentice and his father live across the street. We exchange favors. I do their laundry, and Hugo hauls wood for me and refills my stove and lamp gas. Since I need starch on laundry days, I usually make a noodle casserole. It's silly for me to make one just for myself, so they always join me on washday for supper."

"That's quite an arrangement. Practical."

"It's sensible. The evening's still warm, and there isn't much of a breeze. Please feel free to remove your coat. Hugo always dines in his shirtsleeves."

Mr. Diamond's face went ruddy. He curled his fingers around his lapels and closed the distance between them. He looked down at her and lowered his voice. "Perhaps you could give me a bit of advice regarding laundry."

Rose felt a bit dizzy from his nearness. She busied herself arranging the last shirt on the ironing board and tried to sound casual. "Do you have a stubborn spot that won't wash out?"

"I haven't tried to wash it yet."

"That's probably a point in your favor. The wrong solution or temperature can set a stain. What is it?"

He let out a sigh and peeled out of his jacket. With a hooked thumb, he dragged the right side of his vest's neckline farther to the side of his chest.

"Oh, my. That's a nasty scorch." She looked up at him. "I take it you're unaccustomed to doing your own laundry?"

"Correct. I don't have the talent you're demonstrating at this moment. I looked away from the ironing board and failed to keep the iron in motion. Have I ruined the shirt?"

"Did it burn all of the way through, or is what I'm seeing the worst of the damage?"

"The very tip is darker."

"Daddy!"

Prentice's shout rescued Rose from gawking at Mr. Diamond. He'd continued to stand close enough that her skirt brushed his leg, and the line of the scorch arched right up toward his shoulder, accentuating the breadth of his shoulders. She'd almost reached up to touch the mark—just to check the severity of it, she hastened to tell herself. She cleared her throat and called out, "Hello, Hugo. Supper and your laundry are about ready."

Hugo dumped an armload of logs by the hearth, dusted off his hands, and mussed Prentice's hair. "Sounds great. Were you a good boy today?"

"Pretty good. I can't stand on my head yet. Miss Rose is going to help me learn how."

Suddenly it all sounded wrong. Rose could only imagine what these men must be thinking—that she'd demonstrate for Prentice by upending herself in a completely undignified display of petticoats and limbs. She'd just told Prentice what others thought didn't matter, but she started reconsidering that statement. Hugo would surely understand, but how could she sit across the supper table from Mr. Diamond if he believed she'd—

"Miss Rose taught you how to ride a bicycle and walk on stilts," Hugo said smoothly. "It makes sense she'd be the one to show you that, too."

"I'm sure all it will take is for someone to stabilize Prentice," Rose murmured. "Hugo Lassiter, have you met Mr. Diamond, the new mercantile owner?"

Hugo walked over and shook Garret's hand. "So are you—oh, I did the same thing—scorched a shirt. Mine looked much worse. I came to Rose for help with that disaster. Though I'm sorry your shirt met the same fate, it's reassuring to learn I'm not the only man in town who botched up his shirt."

Garret's mouth twisted into a wry smile. "The only domestic skills I possess are sweeping and eating."

"So he's joining us for supper." Rose switched flatirons again and shoved a few curls away from her forehead with the back of her wrist. "Hugo, do you mind if he borrows one of your shirts so I can apply some peroxide to that scorch?"

"Not a bit."

Rose made sure she didn't offer the blue chambray. It didn't take but a few moments to pop an extra place setting on the table, and soon they all bowed their heads for grace.

"You'll never imagine what came on the train," Hugo said once they started eating. He didn't wait for anyone to actually guess. "A washing machine for Cordelia Orrick! Nice, big, modern one."

"You don't say!" Rose set down her glass.

"It's another one of those mystery gifts." Hugo mixed honey with his peas and used his knife to lift them to his mouth.

"Mystery gifts?"

"Yes, Mr. Diamond. It seems folks in Buttonhole look out for one another. Every so often, something someone needs just. . ." Rose spread her hands, palms upward. "Appears."

"Miss Masterson, are you telling me someone secretly bought the Widow Orrick a washing machine?"

"My daddy told you; she didn't." Prentice slurped some milk. "Ever'body else calls her Miss Rose. How come are you calling her Miss Masterson?"

"We've only recently met. It's mannerly to address one another that way. Miss Masterson deserves my respect."

Rose smiled at him and nodded her head. "That's most kind of you, but in truth, I'm of the opinion that respect is better shown than spoken of. We're all brothers and sisters in the family of God. I'd take no offense to you addressing me by my given name."

"Likewise."

Prentice squinted through his thick glasses. "Your name is Likewise?"

"It's Garret."

Rose watched how Garret made an effort to lean down a bit closer each time he spoke to Prentice. He didn't slow his speech as if he were talking to a baby, and his tone carried warmth. More than anything, that convinced her of his character. A man who showed kindness to a gawky little boy had to have a good heart.

"Mr. Garret, wanna know 'bout other mystery gifts?"

"Sure!"

"Mrs. Percopie got a fancy icebox for the diner. Mr. Creek got a great big plow for his farm when the old one broke to smithereens. Hattie's pa got a rifle."

"A Marlin repeating rifle—a fourteen shot," Hugo added. "He's kept that family in meat for the past two winters with the hunting he's done."

"He's quite a hunter," Rose agreed. "Bless his heart, he's been kind enough to give me some delicious roasts."

"Even though I've been here but a short time, Miss Rose," Garret said as he chased a noodle to the edge of his plate and speared it with his fork, "I'd guess you shared every last one of those roasts with someone."

"Roasts are meant to be shared." She smiled. "The Secret Giver sent me a bicycle."

"Do you have any idea who it is?"

Hugo propped his elbows on the table and nodded. "My boss at the bank is wealthy enough. The gifts are all on the expensive side."

"I think it's Mr. Hepplewhite," Prentice said. "He always finds pennies and nickels behind kids' ears. Maybe he finds money other places, too."

"And what about you, Miss Rose? Do you have a suspicion?"

"Almost everyone in Buttonhole wonders." Rose gave a dainty shrug. "Conjecture is normal enough. My thoughts have taken a different path, though. It occurs to me that more than one individual is capable of showing kindness anonymously."

"She acts all calm now." Hugo chuckled. "You should have seen her the day her bicycle arrived. Our Rose was absolutely giddy."

"I've had hours of enjoyment riding about. Is everyone ready for dessert? I made peach cobbler."

Over a large piece of cobbler, Garret Diamond turned into a sleuth. He and Hugo discussed how the first mystery gift, an organ for the church, arrived the Easter before Rose had moved to Buttonhole. They decided it had to be a husband and wife or a brother and sister. Only a woman would have thought to order a baby's layette with express delivery for Mrs. Andrews when she adopted a foundling. Then, too, they reasoned that only a man would have known the particulars involved in selecting the right plow and would think to include a supply of the proper-sized cartridges with the gift of a quality rifle.

Rose dumped the dishes into the sink to soak while she continued to remedy the scorch in Garret's shirt. Dabbing peroxide on the large mark bleached away much of the discoloration, but she couldn't help inhaling the fragrance of bay rum that drifted up from the fabric. Normally the homey scent of noodle starch steamed up from her ironing board; Garret's bay rum smelled heady and masculine.

The sheriff dropped by, accepted a chunk of cobbler, and mentioned, "Sneedly's brood is croupy again, and Doc's out on a call. You got anything that'll help out, Rose?"

"Let me see." She excused herself and went into the spare bedroom. Instead of bothering to turn on the gaslight for just the few minutes she'd be there, she brought a candle she lit from the stove. The bottom drawer of the five-drawer chest over by the window held her supply of medicaments, and she quickly walked her fingers along the bottles, tins, and jars until she pulled out two items. Holding one container in her hand, the other in the crook of her arm, she managed to grab the candle and return to the gentlemen.

"Sheriff, I do have a couple of things that ought to help a bit." She blew out the candle and set it on the buffet.

"Oh, good." The sheriff pushed away from the table and started to leave. "I hoped you'd scare up a cure. Those kids are barkin' up a storm."

Rose took the bottle from the crook of her arm, jostled it, then held it up to the light. "I'm afraid I'm about out of the Jayne's Expectorant." She looked down at the chunky blue green container in her other hand. "This is a new tin of camphorated salve, though. I'll go over and help make mustard or onion plasters."

"Jayne's?" Garret's brows rose. "Is that stuff any good?"

"Doc recommends it. I think it works fairly well, especially if the children breathe in steam vapor." Rose reached for her cape.

Garret swiped it away and draped it over her shoulders, smoothly enveloping the ample volume of her leg-of-mutton sleeves. "I have a bucketful of curatives I took out of the store and put in the back until Doc could take a gander at them. A fair number of those bottles strike me as nothing more than false hope. I'm sure I saw a few bottles of Jayne's."

Rose perked up at that bit of news. "With Red Riding Hood on the glass?"

"Oh, is that who it was?" Garret chuckled. "I'll have to take a closer look at the bottle now. We'll drop by the store, and you can check to see if anything else there might help the children."

"Do you mind if I finish your shirt later and return it tomorrow?" She searched for her apron pockets beneath the cape and slipped the bottle and tin into them.

"Not at all. I appreciate your help. It's looking a world better already." He held out his hand. "Why don't you let me carry those?"

"I'd rather ask you to bring the rest of the cobbler if you don't mind. I doubt Mrs. Sneedly had a chance to cook a decent meal if the children are ill." Rose handed him the still-warm metal pan and swiftly tucked a fresh loaf of bread, a bag of split peas, a hunk of paper-wrapped bacon, and almost a dozen fresh peaches into a flour sack.

"I'll fill your stove while you're gone," Hugo called as she headed toward the door.

"Take your laundry. It's ready to go." She swept out the door. Garret's stride carried him alongside her, and she halted abruptly. "You forgot your suit coat."

"I'll get it tomorrow. Those poor kids are waiting for help."

"More likely their parents are. The Sneedlys have six children. They've lost half again as many. I've never seen folks suffer so with the hay fever and croup."

"I have a whole bin of onions at the store. Remind me to grab a couple for the poultices."

Rose smiled at him. "Thank you. You know, you could have rubbed a bit of raw onion on the scorch—"

"And made my shirt reek for eternity." They turned the corner, and he led her diagonally across the street so they'd reach his store a few steps faster. "I'd rather lose my shirt to stupidity than to stink."

"Now that Cordelia Orrick has a washing machine, you might hire her to do your laundry."

"Miss Rose, don't you dare try to get me to trade a ring around my collar for a ring through my nose."

Chapter 7

I t's nothing short of a modern-day miracle," Cordelia Orrick said for the third time since she'd come into the shop. "A Number Three Western Star washer. A Number Three, mind you! Why, I won't know what to do with all of my spare time now that I won't be using my washboard much."

Zeb Hepplewhite rubbed his nose with the ball of his thumb. "When I got word you'd gotten that newfangled washer, I was hopin' you'd feel thataway. What, with Mrs. Kiersty getting up there in age and battling her quinsy, the laundry's not caught up at my boardinghouse. When it comes to doing the wash, I'm as useless as hip pockets on a hog. Perhaps I could hire you to be the laundress."

Garret smiled to himself and put several new dime novels out onto the shelf. *I'll bet whoever the Secret Giver is, that's what he had planned all along when he ordered that big new washer.* Whoever the mysterious benefactor was, he seemed to have a knack for selecting practical items—at least most of the time. An icebox for the diner, a plow for a farmer, a hunting rifle for a family man, the washing machine for a mother. . .but a bicycle for Miss Rose seemed like an odd choice.

Why a bicycle? Then again, everyone in Buttonhole seemed to think she was, as Mrs. Evert said, "dotty," or as Rose confessed, "dusty in the attic." It stood to reason that the Secret Giver chose something a bit less ordinary for that reason. Besides, hadn't Rose pedaled down Main Street this morning with a basketful of her fresh peaches to share with some townsfolk? He still remembered the supper she'd made. He'd never tasted finer. The woman surely had call to boast about her culinary skills.

He heard the train pull out of the station. About a quarter hour later, the mailbag was brought to the post office—along with a box bearing a label from Sears, Roebuck and Co. for none other than Miss Rose.

Garret argued with himself over the whole matter. Miss Rose was only one person, a maidenly woman of very modest means. How she spent her money was none of his affair. Then again, where she spent her money—well, that was his business, or more to the point, it *wasn't* his business. The rest of Buttonhole seemed quite pleased with Diamond Emporium. Folks were voluble in their praise, and sales stayed steady if not downright brisk compared to what he'd expected from the size of the town and the financial books the previous owner had shown him before he bought the place.

So what if Miss Rose buys things from her catalog? She comes in here to get her staples and perishables.

It didn't matter. Not really. But it irritated him. Garret took it as a personal challenge. He was going to prove to that woman his store would give her top-notch service, fair prices, and far more convenience than the well-thumbed book she kept on her parlor table. Surely she could see for herself that he carried superior items.

The bell rang over the door. Garret glanced up and gave a neighborly nod. "Hello, hello," Lula Mae Evert singsonged. The pink splotches in her cheeks were every bit as bright as the ones painting her daughters' cheekbones. The daughter on the right practically towed her mother along; the taller daughter on Lula Mae's left had to be dragged forward. "Charity and Patience both talked me into letting them have new dresses."

"Mama says you have exquisite yardage." The younger one flashed him a guileless smile.

"How kind of her to say so." He secretly wondered which one was which, but he didn't dare ask. Judging from the way Lula Mae had waxed poetic on Patience's domestic talents, he presumed she was the elder one with the sulky expression.

Lula Mae gushed, "I'm sure my daughters have never seen such lovely trims, either. Why, you have a positively wondrous selection of lace, ribbons, and buttons."

"I'm glad you think so, Mrs. Evert. Take your time, ladies." He gestured toward the area he'd created for the fabrics, patterns, and sewing notions. "I'm sure you'll find something to your liking."

The taller daughter let out a beleaguered sigh. "Sewing is ever so dreary, Mama. Can't you hire a seamstress like Julia's mother?"

Garret couldn't hear what Lula Mae whispered back, but from the set of her jaw, he could tell she wasn't about to put up with her daughter's plan.

A buxom woman who longingly ran her fingers over the Singer treadle sewing machine Garret had on display offered, "I'd be willing to sew for you. I'm planning to turn my parlor into a seamstress shop."

"Thank you, Lacey," Lula Mae said as she cast her daughter a quelling look, "but my daughters are quite adept at sewing."

The older daughter scowled; the shorter daughter continued to smile. She was cute in how she didn't mind that her front teeth overlapped just a bit. Garret didn't doubt that in another year, her mama would instill a self-consciousness about that sweet flaw and drill her until she habitually spoke and laughed behind a gloved hand. For now, though, she reminded him of a little bunny. She scooted into the corner and started to look through the patterns while her sister huffed her dissatisfaction at each bolt of fabric her mother pulled out.

Garret made a mental note about Patience. If the attitude she displayed now was her usual, she wasn't the sort of woman he'd want to share a box supper with, let alone marry. Every pattern required too much work, and each length of fabric elicited a disdainful rejection.

Finally the younger Miss Evert turned and huffed at her. "Honestly, Patience, if you don't care, I'll pick out something I like. All your dresses get passed down to me, so one of us may as well be happy."

Oh, so I was right. The younger one is Charity. Garret smothered a smile as Patience developed a sudden interest in a length of blue she termed "robin's egg."

"Don't you think this will be ravishing on Patience, Mr. Diamond?" Lula Mae draped a yard around Patience, who glowered at him.

"Pretty as a peacock."

"Same color as one, too," Zeb said from over by the nail barrel.

Patience shoved away the fabric. "I don't care if he's rich, Mama. I'm not—"

"Shh!" Lula Mae fumbled with the bolt and dropped it. Squeezing her daughter's arm to silence her was obviously more important than fine taffeta.

Snorting with glee, Zeb dumped the nails back into the barrel and folded his arms across his chest. Two ladies standing by the canned goods whispered to one another behind their hands, and Garret hadn't ever been more thankful for the chime on the door. It gave him an excuse to turn away. *Saved by the bell.*

"Isn't it the most gorgeous day?" Rose struggled to fit a pair of baskets into the door. She couldn't seem to look up from them long enough to do more than laugh. Oh, and she laughed so freely. Even with her hands empty, she wouldn't lift one to cover her mouth.

Garret started toward her, but she finally wiggled through. A breeze shut the door behind her, and she tried to take a step, only to have giggles spill out of her.

"Rose, whatever is so entertaining?" Mrs. Kiersty tipped back her head so she could see beneath the brim of her flower-and-ribbon-bedecked straw hat, then looked over the edge of her spectacles.

"I seem to be stuck." Rose shoved one basket into Mrs. Kiersty's hands and the other into Garret's. She twisted to the side, opened the door, and yanked in the portion of her brown paisley skirt that had gotten trapped. Yards of the fabric swept in. What was once probably a pretty gown now qualified as hopelessly bedraggled. It was clean as could be, but the triple row of golden ribbons encircling the hem had puckered, and the hem itself was frayed. Rose didn't seem aware of those flaws. She smoothed the skirt and announced, "There's quite a breeze kicking up."

"Peaches and apricots," Mrs. Kiersty whispered in an oddly rough tone. Garret figured her voice still sounded faint and gravelly from her bout with quinsy. She intently inspected what lay under the basket's blue-and-purple-checkered cloth.

"Fresh from your trees, I presume," Cordelia said as she came over.

"Oh yes. I just picked them. You'll never imagine what I found while I was picking them!"

Garret felt the basket in his hands move at the same time he heard a small sound. He glanced down and didn't need to imagine. He could see the answer for himself. "Kittens."

"Yes!" Rose lifted a calico bit of fluff and held it high for him to inspect. "Have you ever seen anything so adorable?"

"Rose, dear, you don't bring wild little animals inside. Certainly, you don't take them into the mercantile." Mrs. Kiersty set aside the basket of fruit and snatched the kitten from her hands by the scruff of the neck. She dumped the mewling baby back into the basket and clucked her tongue. "It's just not done."

Garret agreed—in principle. He just didn't like the way the old biddy plowed in and took charge without regard to Rose's feelings. "He is cute, Rose, but perhaps—"

"Gotta be a she-cat." Zeb sauntered over. "Calico cats are always females."

"Everyone's saying the mice are particularly bad this year." Cordelia Orrick picked up a bottle of bluing. Garret presumed she'd also need to buy all of the ingredients for making more laundry soap for her new laundry venture. She set it back down and came over to look at the kittens. He made a mental note to help her gather up all of the necessary chemicals—ammonia, salts of tartar, potash. . *.just as soon as I coax Rose to take her furry little creatures back outside where they belong.*

It made perfect sense for a mercantile to have a mature cat that would prowl the premises at night to keep vermin away. A mouser was a valuable asset; a playful kitten that could tangle yarn, fall into storage bins, or streak out of nowhere and make customers stumble would be a disaster.

Unfortunately, Rose seemed blissfully unaware that Mrs. Kiersty was right and the basket of kittens ought to go. Instead, she petted each kitten with just her forefinger as she told him, "Garret, I heard Tom Cat passed on, and I was sure you'd want one for your back porch to protect your merchandise. You get pick of the litter!"

"You heard about old Tom Cat?"

"Prentice told me. He was terribly upset."

Garret nodded. Just about every afternoon, he'd find Prentice sitting out on the back porch of the mercantile. The boy would have the tattered old tabby on his lap or lazing beside him. The visit never lasted more than ten minutes, but the day old Tom died and Garret saw Prentice's face, he knew the cat had meant more to the boy than he'd realized. He'd knelt down to comfort Prentice, but the little guy had sobbed a name and ran away. He knew the little boy had gone to Rose for comfort.

"Why don't I let Prentice choose and keep my cat?" *There. Nice solution.*

Diplomatic. Everyone ought to be satisfied.

"Cats make Hugo sneeze and itch." Rose smiled at him. "They can't have one, but it's kind of you to offer."

Garret couldn't resist. He reached down and petted the calico. "He could keep one at your house."

Rose continued to smile. "I kept the runt."

"Isn't that just like you?" Patience Evert simpered.

Garret looked at the young woman and could see by her patently insincere smile that she'd not meant it in a complimentary way, but her mother gushed, "It is. Rose has a soft spot in her heart for anything or anyone that's. . .different."

"Why, thank you, Lula Mae." Rose smiled at her.

"Mama, isn't the tabby cute?" Charity wiggled through the knot of people and scooped one of the pale orange ones out of the basket. She lifted it and giggled as he started to climb up her sleeve.

"You're ruining your dress," Patience snapped.

"Don't let it near your collar." Lula Mae flapped her hands fretfully. "His claws will shred the lace."

"And that's Belgian lace," Mrs. Kiersty whispered as she adjusted her spectacles and repinned her hat farther back on her head. She leaned in so she could see it better. "I remember that piece from when you made it for Patience. Pretty as a snowflake."

"And it was stylish back then," Patience tacked on.

Rose reached over and covered Charity's hand with her own so they both stroked the kitten together. "Style may be fleeting, but beauty and grace are eternal."

"That's what I taught my daughters, too." Mrs. Kiersty bobbed her head so emphatically that Garret marveled her hat didn't flip off and roll away. Surely that one hatpin wasn't designed to withstand such a challenge. She glared pointedly at the basket, which held only one kitten now since Cordelia cupped the other tabby to herself and Zeb was tickling it with its own white-tipped tail. "But I taught them that animals belong outside."

Garret fished out the calico Rose had originally held out to him and set aside the empty basket. "These are fine little beasts." *I don't want a cat.*

"Aren't they?" Rose beamed at him.

"Mama, could I keep this one?" Charity gave her mother a pleading look. "I'll give up having a new dress."

Whoops. This little basket of trouble is cutting into my business. I need to get it out of here.

"You don't need a cat." Her mother took the kitten from her. "You need a dress."

Whew.

The tabby rubbed his head back and forth against Lula Mae. The woman melted faster than a chip of ice in the sun. "Aww. He is a precious little thing."

"Mr. Diamond, you were to choose first." Cordelia Orrick looked like she'd burst into tears if he took the tabby she held.

"I don't need a cat. Why don't you take that one? He certainly looks at home in your arms."

Cordelia perked up. "Oh, and since Rose found him in a peach tree and he's this color, I'll name him Mr. Peaches!"

"And ours can be called Apricot—Cottie for short," Charity decided.

"Two down, one to go." Zeb looked pointedly at the one in Garret's hands.

"I just said I didn't want a cat. Why don't you take him, Zeb?"

Zeb held his hands out, palms upward. "Nuh-unh."

Garret raised his brows. "How about you, Mrs. Kiersty? Wouldn't you enjoy this little ball of fur when you're out in that handsome garden you've planted?"

For a moment, her face lit up.

Hurrah! Did it. That was easy enough.

"I said no, and she lives and works at my boardinghouse." Zeb's words cut short Garret's premature self-congratulations.

"He'd dig up my garden anyway," Mrs. Kiersty said with a sigh. "I used fish in the mulch." Zeb took her arm and pulled her toward the door. They scurried out as if Garret would chase her down and slip the cat under her hat if she didn't get away fast enough. The other two ladies who had been twittering behind their hands and the one by the sewing machine followed in their tracks.

The little calico kitten started to purr loudly. The vibrations beneath Garret's fingertips enticed him to continue stroking her.

"I need to check in on Mrs. Kendricks, Garret. Remember when her son, Trevor, stopped in to buy embroidery floss for her? She's still unwell. Even if you don't want to give that kitten a home, could you keep her for an hour or so?"

He cleared his throat and nodded.

"Thank you." Rose picked up the fruit basket, and Cordelia grabbed hold of her arm.

"I'll walk with you. You can stop in for a moment to see my new washer. It's a Number Three Western Star!"

They left, and Lula Mae clasped the tabby to her bodice. "Since Patience can't decide on material, we'll just take this baby home and settle him in."

The door closed, and Garret looked around the store. Empty. Completely empty. He'd had seven—no, eight—customers in here just moments ago. He lifted the calico kitten so they were nose to nose. It let out a tiny meow and continued to purr loudly.

"Stop sounding so content. Everyone just left, and not a one of them bought a single thing."

Chapter 8

Garret, I'm afraid I owe you an apology," Rose said as she hurried up to the mercantile.

Garret stopped sweeping the boardwalk and turned to face her. His brows knit. "I beg your pardon?"

Rose laughed. "You have that backward. I was begging your pardon. I got busy with Mrs. Kendricks and lost track of the time. You've been stuck playing nanny for a kitten you don't want."

He folded both hands on the end of the broom and extended his arms fully. The sleeve fabric pulled until the green-and-black-striped garters no longer left even the slightest ripple in the length. Other than the barber, who always looked awkward and silly as he swept, Rose couldn't think of any other man she'd seen with a broom in his hands. Garret managed to make the broom look every bit as masculine a tool as a rifle or ax.

Rose batted away a ribbon from her hat that fluttered against her cheek. "I came to collect the kitten and hope you'll accept an invitation to supper as restitution."

"That depends."

"On what?"

"Yes, on what—what we're having for supper. And if you're making one of your scrumptious cobblers for dessert. Minding kittens isn't without its dangers."

"Oh no!" Terrible images of what havoc the kitten must have wreaked in the store flashed before her eyes. "What did the kitty do?"

"Nothing too terrible. Just kept me on my toes. She seems to like tight places."

"Tight places?" Rose echoed back the words and had a sick feeling inside.

Garret shrugged and took a few last swipes with the broom. "She tried to hide behind the shovels and such. While I picked them up, she crept behind the brooms."

Rose groaned. She could picture it all vividly—shovels, hoes, and rakes tumbling down. "I'm ever so sorry, Garret."

"Her adventures tired her out. She took a nice nap."

Rose let out a small sigh of relief.

"On the blankets. Scared Mrs. Blanchard out of a year's growth, I'm afraid."

Dread laced her words. "Where is she now?"

"Mrs. Blanchard or the kitten?"

"Both." That one word stuck in her throat and came out like she was being strangled.

Garret opened the door and motioned her inside. She'd just begun to cross the threshold when he said, "Mrs. Blanchard is at home with a new bottle of smelling salts."

"Smelling salts?"

"I'll have to order more. They were quite effective." He set the broom in the corner and wiped his hands on a damp dishcloth he had hanging from a wooden ring by the counter.

Rose's nose twitched. The mercantile used to smell mostly of dust. At the grand opening, she'd noticed a wonderful mingling of lemon and beeswax, pickles, new leather, and fresh apples and oranges. This morning, it had carried that same delicious mix of aromas. Now all she could smell was dill.

Garret leaned his hips against the counter and rested his hands on either side of him. He looked utterly relaxed as he casually stated, "Pickle is upstairs in my bedroom."

"Pickle?" Rose's head swiveled to the side. The three-gallon glass jar that usually rested on the far side of the counter was gone. The dill smell permeating the mercantile suddenly made sense. She covered her face with both hands and burst out laughing.

Ten minutes later, Garret handed her a dipper of water. She'd laughed herself right into a fit of hiccups. "I'm sorry. *Hic.* Truly I am, Garret. You know I'll—*hic*—gladly reimburse you for the pick—*hic*—kle jar and the smelling s—*hic*—salts. I'll stay and scrub your—*hic*—counter with soda. That ought to take a—*hic*—way some of the dill."

"Stop apologizing and tell me: If we bathe the kitten in soda, will it take the smell off her?"

Rose choked on the water and barely kept from spewing it everywhere. "She didn't just—*hic*—knock over the jar?"

"I'm afraid not. She must've thought the pickle was a fish. When the jar fell, the brine washed right over the kitty. The only thing I could think of was that tomato juice is supposed to take care of skunk odor. I'd resigned myself to smashing a few dozen tomatoes in one of the galvanized tubs and dunking Pickle in it."

"Pickle and catsup?" Rose hiccuped and started laughing anew.

Garret chuckled. "I wasn't brave enough to do it on my own. I can just see that little scamp wiggling away and leaving a red streak all over the store."

Rose drew in a deep breath and spoke as rapidly as she could in hopes that she'd manage to say everything before she hiccuped again. "I'll take her home and get her cleaned up. After you—*hic*—close the store, come over for supper.

I'll give you a choice: roast—*hic*—chicken or panfried pork chops."

He motioned her to take another sip of water. "What about my apple cobbler?"

The water seemed to banish her affliction. She handed back the dipper. "I'll bake two cobblers, and you can bring the second one back to have all to yourself. It's the least I can do after what the kitten did."

Garret didn't leave to fetch the cat. He set aside the dipper, folded his arms across his chest, and rocked from heel to toe and back again. "You can't bathe the cat without me. I get to watch."

Rose bent to pick up the basket in which she'd brought the kitten. As she straightened, she caught the ornery twinkle in Garret's eyes.

"So the old saying is true," he mused aloud. The corner of his mouth tugged into a rakish smile.

"What saying?"

He looked pointedly at the basket, then scanned the mercantile as he drawled, "Criminals return to the scene of the crime."

"How am I to know that you didn't teach that poor, innocent kitty all of those bad habits? She never knocked things over, scared the wits out of a woman, or broke anything at my house."

"It's a woman thing. I'm sure of it. She was trying to rearrange my store, was being catty about Mrs. Blanchard's bilious-colored dress, and gave in to a temper fit. I'll bet you found the kittens because she was causing a ruckus and threw peaches at you."

"Garret Diamond, you missed your calling in life." She picked up one of the dime novels and waved it like a fan in front of herself. "With the tales you make up, you should have become an author."

❦

"Rose Masterson, you missed your calling in life," Garret said half an hour later as they stood on opposite sides of a table she'd set up. "This arrangement you have here could turn into quite an enterprise."

An old maple table sat in the middle of her yard. Two buckets and a pair of washtubs sat on it—all full of warm water. In the middle of the table were a scrub brush and a box of baking soda, and two more full buckets waited on the grass under the table. A stack of towels sat on a chair behind her. He nodded approvingly. "Everything necessary to bathe a cat."

"Don't go making any grandiose proclamations yet. The second I get that cat wet, we're going to be wet. I gave the runt a bath this morning, which is why I have twice as much water and three towels."

Garret unbuttoned his sleeves and rolled them up. For good measure, he used the garters to hike his sleeves up past the muscles of his forearms. "I'm not about to let a cat get the better of me."

Five minutes later, Garret shot Rose a quick look, then grabbed Pickle by the scruff of the neck and struggled to wiggle her so she'd let go of the edge of the tub. He'd barely managed to dunk her the first time, and she'd shot out of the tub with a hair-raising yowl. Rose managed to dump half of the box of soda into the water, and she tried to use the scrub brush to help work more into the kitten's fur.

"Watcha doin'?" Prentice asked from the other side of the sagging fence.

"Washing a kitty." Rose sucked in a quick breath as Pickle scratched her wrist. "Oh, dear."

In a matter of minutes, several of Buttonhole's children and a few of the adults were witnesses to the remainder of the kitten's bath. Afterward, as Prentice sat and held a towel-wrapped Pickle, Rose served peach cobbler to everyone. Garret sighed and told her to cut into the second pan—his pan. Rose giggled. "I imagine since you've never seen my backyard, you're hoping the peach tree is large."

"Guilty as charged, Miss Rose."

"It's rather small." She paused strategically. "But the other two peach trees toward the back of the yard are huge."

"I'll make it a point to come peach picking, Miss Rose." He took up a few plates and helped her serve the rest of that second cobbler, and Rose licked the last of the sweet peachy syrup from her silver server. Having a scamp like Garret over to pick peaches suited her just fine.

"Know what?" Prentice announced in a loud voice to everyone while conscientiously keeping hold of the cat. "Mr. Diamond is Miss Rose's beau. She called him 'dear.'"

"Balderdash." Garret turned to her, then immediately added, "I mean you no disrespect, Miss Rose."

She laughed. "I took none. Prentice, I said, 'Oh, dear,' just as your mama used to say, 'Oh, my,' or Mrs. Busby says, 'Mercy me.'"

"I've never heard such piffle. Rose isn't the marrying type at all," Lula Mae singsonged. "Rose, you simply must give me your recipe for this cobbler. It melts in my mouth."

"I'll write it down for you and bring you peaches tomorrow."

Garret frowned at Rose. "You oughtn't be picking peaches—not with those scratches."

"I have peroxide."

"Yes." Hugo chuckled. "Remember? She used it on your scorched shirt."

Cordelia frowned. "I can bandage those scratches while I'm here. Where do you keep your peroxide?"

"The bottom drawer in the spare bedroom."

"You stay out here and mind your daughters. I'll fetch it," Mrs. Blanchard said. Garret suspected her motive was less to help than it was to get away from the cat. Chances were good the only reason Mrs. Blanchard had stopped by in the first place was because this impromptu gathering featured a sweet and a chance to chat. For being as skinny as she was, the woman had a terrible sweet tooth. She stopped into the store each day to get a full penny's worth of candy, and Rose's cobbler rated as far more desirable.

Neighbors drifted off, and Mrs. Blanchard reappeared with the peroxide, a dishcloth, and some salve. She clucked her tongue as she set them down on the water-splashed table beside the tubs and buckets Garret had emptied and stacked. "Silly woman. She's playing with kittens when there's dust at least half an inch thick in her spare room and parlor." She spiraled her finger in the air right beside her temple and whispered, "I tell you, she's touched."

Garret lifted the dishcloth Mrs. Blanchard had brought out and studied it. Made from an old white flour sack, it still bore the faintest outline of Minnesota Pink Label. On the opposite side and end, Rose had embroidered "Sunday" and a cheery-looking sunshine in the corner. He continued to look at that silly decoration and said softly, "I, for one, am glad she used her time to bake those cobblers instead of dusting. Aren't you, Mrs. Blanchard?"

"There's no law that says she couldn't do both." The woman stuck her nose in the air and stomped off.

Hugo steered Prentice past the table and across the street. They were the last to go. Rose stood by the porch holding Pickles while the runt she'd mentioned slept on the windowsill behind her. Garret called over, "Rosie, put down the cat, and let's take care of your scratches."

Angry weals lined the full length of all the thin, long scratches. Garret frowned as he inspected her wrists. "I know you already washed these, but I think you'd best suds them again. Cat scratches are known for causing infections and fevers."

"Oh, a splash of peroxide will do me just fine."

Garret wouldn't let her pull her hands from his. "Soap first. I'll apply peroxide, then some salve. What about bandaging them for the night?"

"Stuff and nonsense!"

He gave her a stern look. "If this were anyone else, you'd insist on that treatment."

Rose let out an irked sound, but she didn't deny the truth. "Would it satisfy you if I promised to apply salve and to wear gloves tonight?"

"It'll spoil your gloves—make them greasy." As he spoke, he dipped her hands into a fresh pail of water and gently washed the scratches. Such wonderful hands she had. Her nails were short, her fingers slim and long. Instead of being milky white, her hands and wrists carried the slightest bit of coloring—no doubt from the hours she spent gardening and picking fruit. The backs of her hands were soft as could be, but the palms bore small calluses that tattled on how she wasn't afraid of pitching in and doing work. They reminded him of his great-aunts, Brigit and Emily. They'd spent a lifetime of doing good deeds, and he'd considered their hands beautiful.

Rose slipped her hands from his and cupped them, palms upward. She pursed her lips and blew, sending bubbles floating into the wind. Her laughter floated along with them as she dunked her fingers to rinse off the remainder of the soap. As she dried her palms on the Sunday dishcloth, she asked, "Did I tell you that 'Pickle' is a marvelous name for the kitten? You'll have to help me think of a name for the runt."

Garret carefully applied the peroxide, watched it bubble, then applied the ointment. "I see his coloring is like the other two."

"Yes, there was only one calico. The runt is a girl, though. Any ideas for her name?"

He slowly stroked the salve along the next scratch. Most of the time, women wore gloves. This contact with Rose seemed so warm, so personal. He was in no mood to rush through it. "Mr. Peaches, Apricot, and Pickle. The others are named for food. I'm trying to think of something that's orangey tan. Crackers? Caramel? Cobbler?"

Rose shook her head. "Cobbler would be too confusing. I like Caramel. That's cute." Her nose wrinkled.

"Did I hurt you?" He paused and continued to gently hold her hand.

"Oh no. Not at all. I was just thinking that Pickle and Caramel make for an odd couple of names." To his acute disappointment, she pulled away and left him feeling oddly incomplete as a result.

"If anything. . ." She paused to laugh again. "When I call them, it's probably going to give everyone fodder to think I'm slipping further into my nonsensical morass."

"Rose, I'm about convinced your attic isn't dusty—it's drafty as can be if you think I'm letting you keep my cat." He dumped out the bucket, scooped up Pickle, and walked off. He was halfway back to the store before he realized something. Pickle didn't smell of dill brine any longer. The faint but unmistakable fragrance of tea rose wafted from her fur.

He threw back his head and laughed. Rose had anointed his cat with her perfume!

Chapter 9

L et's try it again." Rose cupped her hands around the harmonica and
watched as Prentice bobbed his head and drew in a deep breath. He lifted
his own nickel-plated Hohner harmonica, and they started to play a duet.

"I think Susannah would say, 'Oh!' all right if she heard us play that,"
Prentice moaned after they finished. "Miss Rose, we sound terr'ble."

"I've heard better," she admitted. "I know we wanted to keep this a secret, but
perhaps it's time for us to seek out help. Who do we know who plays a harmonica?"

Prentice stuck out his tongue through the empty spot where his teeth once
were and played with the gap. "I dunno."

"Hello."

Rose jumped a bit and swiveled around. "Garret!" She motioned him over
enthusiastically. "What a wonderful surprise. What brings you here?"

He opened the gate and sauntered into her backyard with long, lazy strides
that still managed to close the distance between them quite quickly. "Cordelia
Orrick is minding the store. I came to pick peaches."

Prentice elbowed her and whispered loudly, "Ask him!"

"Ask me what?"

Rose lifted her harmonica. "Can you make this silly thing work?"

"I've been known to puff a tune or two." Garret accepted it and polished the
nickel on his sleeve. He took a seat on the step next to Rose. "The first trick is, you
have to shine it up and make sure it's warm. A cold one makes your mouth stick
so the mouth organ won't slide easily."

"Wow. He's gonna be great!" Prentice hopped up, raced over, and plopped
back down on Garret's other side.

There wasn't enough room, so Garret scooted closer. Rose gathered her
skirts and started to inch away, but he curled his arm around her shoulders and
halted her movement. "You needn't run away, Miss Rose. I promise not to deafen
you with too many sour notes."

She smiled. "I'm just scooting over a tad."

"Better not. You'll fall in that—what is that thing?" He leaned forward and
squinted.

"A strawberry barrel. By cutting holes all over in the barrel, I can harvest a
fine crop of berries in a small space."

Garret's arm tightened, and he yanked her closer. Rose muffled a surprised squeal. "That settles it! I hold a definite liking for both you and strawberries, so I refuse to let you fall."

Rose couldn't remember the last time someone had hugged her. The feeling of being sheltered washed over her. Garret's easygoing nature and scampish smile made her settle in close beside him with a contented sigh. Life couldn't be richer or sweeter than to have good friends and a sunny day and to be surrounded by the blessing of God's bounty.

Rose watched as Garret cradled the harmonica like she would hold a tiny chick. An odd thought streamed through her mind. *I like the way he moves—his confident, steady gait, the effortless manner in which he hefts heavy things, the supple gestures he uses, and now—the way he wraps those long-fingered, strong hands around the little instrument.*

"Here's how you do it." He patiently showed Prentice how to hold the harmonica, how to sense and hear the right notes, and how to play as he both inhaled and exhaled. Soon Prentice was playing recognizable snippets from songs.

"You taught him more in fifteen minutes than I have in three weeks," Rose praised.

"You practice more, little man. Rose is going to hold a basket for me while I pick fruit." Garret held up a finger to silence her before she could protest. "You are not going to pick anything until those scratches are completely healed."

"They're already much better." She held them up and wiggled her fingers.

"Miss Rose," Garret said in a low tone as his brows knit, "you'd best be thankful your yard doesn't have a hickory tree in it."

"Hickory?" She glanced around, then gave him a baffled look. "Why?"

"Where I come from, folks got a whuppin' with a hickory switch for stretching the truth beyond all recognition."

Rose tilted her nose in the air. "I'm not telling a falsehood. They've not festered as cat scratches can, and I kept salve on them all night."

"You ought to soak them."

"I did." When he gave her a stern look, she sheepishly added, "In a manner of speaking. They were in warm water whilst I washed the dishes."

"You've misbehaved enough for the day, if not for the week." Garret handed her an empty basket. "You just stand there. I'll fill it." He reached up and plucked two peaches from a branch and placed them in the basket.

"This is ridiculous. I want to be useful."

"You can be useful by deciding where all of these. . ." He picked two more and held them up before tucking them in the basket with the others. ". . .are going to end up."

"They're all coming ripe at the same time. I'll can as many as possible." She tipped her head back and looked up at the heavily laden branches. "I have enough to feed an army."

"I have empty crates at the emporium." His movements were so fluid that it didn't seem as if he was working at all, yet the basket she held was filling up fast. He paused a moment and looked at her. "We could send peaches to the orphanage in Roanoke. Don't you think those children would enjoy them?"

"What a wonderful idea! The train comes through tomorrow morning. We could do that, couldn't we?"

"I have a feeling we could do just about anything we put our minds to."

"As long as the Lord blessed the task," she tacked on.

"Look at all of this. It would be a sin to waste it. After you decide how much you want to keep for your own use, I'd be happy to carry some to the boarding-house." He took the full basket from her, set it on the steps next to Prentice, who continued to puff into his harmonica with more zeal than talent, then came back with another basket.

Rose had already picked three peaches. She lay them in the basket, and Garret groused at her, "You need to learn to follow directions, woman. No more picking. You just hold this."

"You're downright bossy, Garret Diamond."

"If my skin were as thin as the skin on these peaches, I'd be mortally wounded by your harsh words."

"Doc Rexfeld is talented." She laughed. "I'm sure he could pull you through."

"He was just in the store yesterday. Struck me as a competent, likable fellow." He rapidly filled that basket. "Hey, speaking of the emporium, I wouldn't mind putting some of your fruit out. You could make a bit of money on all of these extra peaches and apricots, you know."

"Oh, I couldn't! I'd much rather give them away." She lifted the basket higher. As it filled, it grew increasingly heavy.

Garret hitched his right shoulder. "If that's what you want. I'd be willing to give you some jars or sugar if you want to can or preserve more. Knowing you, you'll be giving most of it away."

His generosity and enthusiasm for giving to others touched her deeply. "I really have enough jars. Could I talk you into giving the jars to Cordelia? Her girls love peaches, but she's sensitive about taking charity. Perhaps if you worked it out as part of her pay. . ."

"I still have some of those I emptied when I took over the emporium. I'll just stick them in a wagon and have Prentice wheel them over to her house. If you take the peaches over tomorrow, she's bound to—"

Prentice came over. "Listen to this!" He played "Three Blind Mice" with just enough accuracy to allow them to guess the tune.

Garret gently rubbed a freshly picked peach on his sleeve and handed it to the little boy. "That deserves a prize. Here you are." As they finished filling the bucket, he brushed a leaf off Rose's shoulder and puffed out her sleeve.

Rose laughed. "I'm a wreck, and you did all the work."

"All the work? We're not stopping already. I haven't even gotten to climb a tree yet."

She looked from the tree to him, then back at the branches. "I don't even let Prentice climb the peach, apricot, or plum trees. The limbs aren't strong enough to bear weight."

"Killjoy."

She couldn't believe her ears. "Did you just call me a name?"

He grabbed the bucket from her and leaned close enough that the sparkle in his eyes warned her he might say something outrageous. "Well, I guess I'll take solace in the fact that Prentice's harmonica playing didn't harm your hearing." He added, raising his voice, "Even if you are a spoilsport."

"Oh. Are they spoiled, Miss Rose?" Prentice pouted. "You were going to make jam."

Garret took that as an invitation to harvest several more bushels. They picked peaches and apricots aplenty. He carried a few of the baskets into the kitchen and set them on the table.

Rose scampered alongside and tried to reach the table first, but she didn't quite manage. The Sears catalog lay open to the pages featuring sewing machines, and Garret leaned forward to study the selection. "What are you getting?"

Rose slammed the book shut and stammered, "The, uh, moquette rug," she barely choked out.

"I see." He folded his arms across his chest and drummed his fingers on the opposite upper arms. "I have moquette rugs. Just got in a nice selection. What color were you thinking of?"

"Medium. It's floral." Rose reached up and loosened the suddenly too-tight collar band on her shirt. "I just want a yard of it to put by the sink."

"Medium isn't much of a color. That's one of the drawbacks of dealing with catalog purchases. You're buying things sight unseen. You can choose exactly the hue that suits your fancy at my mercantile."

"I like being surprised."

"I see. Well, I need to be getting back to the store."

He picked up the envelope next to the catalog and offered, "Would you like me to post this since I'm going back to the store?"

"I'd appreciate it." *Though I'd have been far happier if you'd never seen it.* She smiled. "Thank you, Garret."

Without another word, he walked out of her house.

Rose sank onto a chair and crumpled her apron and skirt in her fists. *Oh, no. Oh, I never wanted this to happen.*

Prentice came in. The door banged behind him. "Miss Rose, can I take my ha'mon'ca home now? It's not a secret anymore."

"Huh? Oh. Yes." She blinked at him and forced a smile. "Sure, honey. Go right on ahead. I want you to enjoy it."

"You gonna give away all this stuff, or are you baking with it?" Prentice wore a toothless smile as he tucked the harmonica in his shirt pocket. He helped himself to an apricot, twisted it in half, and ate the half without the pit. Juice slid down the edge of his hand.

"There's gracious plenty. I'll probably share some, can some for the winter, and do a bit of baking. How does that sound?"

"Could you dry some of these 'cots again like you did last year? Daddy and me really liked them."

"Sure. Why don't you help me when you come home from school tomorrow?"

" 'Kay." He licked the juice, then popped the other half of the apricot into his mouth and went to the dustbin, where he proceeded to spit out the pit. The sound it made when it hit the metal never ceased to make him smile.

Rose grinned along with him. She'd taught him that perfectly horrid trick not long after Mary Ellen died. Prentice had been crying for days and had no appetite, so in an attempt to get him to calm down and try to eat, Rose demonstrated that vile stunt. He'd been entranced. She counted it a true miracle that the boy didn't end up with a miserable bellyache that night, because he'd eaten a full dozen apricots.

Rose looked at the bushels and didn't feel her usual sense of contentment. Instead of representing God's providence and a way to bless others, those bushels served as a reminder that Garret had picked each piece of fruit and shared a perfectly enjoyable afternoon with her. Then that catalog had spoiled it all.

Garret had made marvelous changes at the mercantile and took the time to assure her he'd gladly order or carry any item she desired. He'd even looked at her catalog one afternoon and proven that with the shipping costs added on, the items she'd mail-ordered weren't any better a bargain than what he kept conveniently on hand right there in Buttonhole.

But she'd ordered that dumb rug from her catalog, and he'd found out. The rug was like almost everything else she ordered—just an excuse to send an envelope to Sears. Everyone in Buttonhole thought she was a woman of very modest means, and the poor condition of the mercantile in the past few years had given her ample reason to choose to do business by mail order.

But now—Garret is sharp as can be, and I was careless. How could I have left the catalog open like that? To the sewing machines, of all things! I didn't lie. I really did order a yard of that stupid carpeting—but the envelope is heavy and has two stamps on it, and the carpet will only be a dollar. Why didn't I think of something else? I hope he's too busy to notice the envelope is too thick for just one dollar, or he's likely to figure out that I'm the Secret Giver.

Chapter 10

"G ood day," Garret said, returning Mr. Sowell's greeting. At least part of that statement was true. He'd felt quite free, taking his very first afternoon off since he'd come to town. The young Widow Orrick proved to be quite able to help out at the store, so he'd gone off to spend his time with Rose.

They'd had a wonderful time in the yard, picking fruit. Prentice had scared away the birds with his awful harmonica playing, but Rose's laughter had more than made up for the shrill notes. The envelope rested in his coat pocket, the slight weight of it taunting him. Everything had been fine until he'd seen that atrocious catalog—but Garret refused to let that darken his mood.

He'd assessed Rose Masterson from the start and known she'd be a tough customer. He'd never met a more independent woman—she knew what she wanted, and nothing else would satisfy her. He could normally entice a customer to try something new or buy a little something different. It would really test his salesmanship to get the hardest customer to switch her allegiance from Sears to his emporium, and that person was Rose.

Nonetheless, he liked the challenge.

He nodded emphatically as he told himself that with time and patience he was going to prove his mercantile worthy of all of her patronage.

"Well, as I live and breathe! It's you, Mr. Diamond—out for a constitutional in the middle of a workday?"

Garret turned toward Mrs. Patterson's voice. She held a watering can, and the potted plants along her porch rail dripped down the railing, leaving a muddy streak. Finicky as Mrs. Patterson was, she'd undoubtedly wash the streak away. "Hello, Mrs. Patterson! Are you enjoying that new rocking chair?"

"Absolutely." She beamed and beckoned. "Come see how lovely it looks in our parlor." As he walked up to the porch, he quelled a smile. She'd leaned over the railing and used the last little bit of water to rinse off the unsightly streak so her house would be picture-perfect.

After he agreed the rocker she'd purchased looked far better in her home than in his store, Garret got a sinking feeling as Mrs. Patterson gave him a calculated smile. "It's quite hot today. You must join Missy and me on the veranda for a glass of sweet tea."

He drank enough sweet tea to float the Spanish Armada. While Mrs. Patterson filled his glass yet again, Missy dutifully mouthed another oh-so-appropriate platitude about the weather. "Don't you simply adore this breeze?"

He nodded. "Very refreshing."

"The blossoms are setting nicely." She smoothed her skirts needlessly. "Mama says we'll have a bumper crop of tomatoes. Daddy says *The Farmer's Almanac* predicted that, too."

"I suppose you'll be busy canning them."

"Oh, Missy loves working in the kitchen, don't you, dear?" Mrs. Patterson prompted.

Missy nodded obediently and blotted the corner of her mouth with a spotless linen napkin.

She is just what I should be looking for. Pretty. Gentle and poised, too. But Garret couldn't help comparing her polished ways to Rose's engaging exuberance. He hoped he wasn't too abrupt when he took his leave.

He saw Mrs. Sneedly on the street and asked about the children. "Hale as can be now, thanks to Rose. Thanks be to God, too!"

"I'm glad to hear they've improved."

"So am I." Mrs. Sneedly bobbed her head. "And since they're so much better, Anna is able to fiddle around in the kitchen again. Why, she's famous hereabouts for her carrot cake."

"Is that so?"

"Absolutely. You mustn't think I'm exaggerating just because she's my daughter. Why, the parson's wife herself suggested that Anna enter her carrot cake in the county fair."

"That's quite a compliment."

"You'll have to come by and sample it for yourself."

Garret managed to bring the conversation to a close and wandered off. Any man would love a woman who could cook like Anna, and she was tame and biddable as could be. Her apron was always spotless, and he'd never seen her go out without a hat. She didn't have Rose's fire and zest for the simple things like using a blade of grass for a whistle. Life would be very predictable with Anna.

I always thought I wanted an easygoing woman who'd be like her—she'd be proper and excellent at keeping the store neat as a pin. What's the matter with me that there are a half-dozen suitable women in town, and the only one who appeals to me is stubborn, wild little Rose?

He thought about going back to the store, but as he drew closer, he could see Cordelia through the window. Cordelia had a pair of stockings draped over her shoulder and was holding up one of the expensive, lace-edged Madame Mystique corset covers for a customer's approval.

That in itself was enough to make him hesitate about entering, but then he saw Lula Mae in there with Mrs. Blanchard. Not a day went by that those two women didn't come into his store on some flimsy pretext or another. Lula Mae sang her daughter Patience's praises, and Mrs. Blanchard made her daughter Constance sound like a paragon of every virtue known to man.

The two mothers had practically used him as a tug-of-war rope after church last week, each asserting he ought to come to her home for Sunday supper. Bless her heart, Rose had breezed over and tucked her hand in the crook of his arm. "Hugo and Prentice look like they're wilting with hunger, and I made that peach cobbler you all like so much. Are we ready to go now?"

"I sure am, Miss Rose."

If he went in the mercantile now, those two mamas would start in on their matrimonial machinations again, and he refused to put himself in the middle of such nonsense. He'd like to choose his own wife, thank you very much. Quite frankly, at this moment, he'd had enough. He didn't think he could endure one more conversation. He had some thinking to do. He cut to the back alley and headed down Elm Street to escape that encounter.

Garret tried to think of a place he'd like to go. If he went to the diner, Mrs. Percopie would be sure to have her daughter serve him; then she'd give Hattie a break so she could sit a spell.

Absently, Garret reached up and smoothed his hair. He could use a haircut, and the barbershop had to be safe. It was the town's male bastion—a place where he could escape mothers and the countless tales of their daughters' accomplishments. It would feel good to get a trim and a shave—to relax and not have to listen to the fluttering of Cupid's wings.

Garret walked into an empty shop. Mr. Busby gestured toward the chair. "Have a seat."

Garret eased onto the red leather seat, leaned back, and closed his eyes. Peace. Safety. He let out a sigh of unmitigated relief.

Mr. Busby pulled the comb through Garret's hair. "Same cut as the first time you came in?"

"Yep."

Mr. Busby whistled a few notes through his teeth. Garret couldn't help thinking he sounded a lot like Prentice on the harmonica. *Snip. Snip.* Comb. *Snip.*

"So how are you liking Buttonhole?"

"Great town. Glad I came."

The barber grunted his agreement. *Snip. Snip.* "Great place to settle down."

"I can see that."

"Next thing you know, you'll be wanting to marry up." Mr. Busby shifted and started snipping at a different place. "Got a handful of pretty gals, but none better than my niece. I'm sure you've met her—Missy. Missy Patterson."

"I saw her at church." Garret didn't want to say much. He could end up bald or butchered. He kept silent as Busby dropped endless, anvil-like "hints" that Missy would make a fine wife.

"Ready for a shave, too?" Busby already had the razor in hand and had smacked it across the strop.

Garret pulled off the towel and shook his head. "Not today. Thanks." He paid for the haircut and walked out as fast as decorum permitted.

Garret walked until he hit the edge of town. He didn't want to talk to anyone now. His thoughts shifted to Rose Masterson, and suddenly there she was—a streak of dust on her cheek, a dirty cloth hanging out of her pocket, and Dutch-clean windows sparkling behind her as she pushed Old Hannah's wheeled invalid chair into a shady spot.

He ought to keep walking, but he couldn't force himself to. Garret couldn't take his eyes off Rose. Why would a woman with her warm, sensitive spirit purposefully conduct her business with a mail-order company located outside her own community instead of with someone she'd invited to dine at her very own table? Things didn't add up.

Why was the catalog open to sewing machines if she was buying carpeting? Rose didn't sew much, or her clothes would be newer or in better condition. Lacey Norse positively coveted the sewing machine at the mercantile; Rose hadn't paid more than fleeting attention to it. She'd just swish by it and head to Mr. Deeter's post office window and mail a letter.

Rose had no family. She'd once mentioned in conversation that she rarely corresponded with her old friends—they'd married and grown busy with children. Yet she mailed off something each week or so. The envelope he'd promised to mail for her was heavy—too heavy to contain a single dollar. Garret stared at her as realization dawned.

Within minutes, Rose's arms were full of lavender and pink sweet peas, and she set them on the frail old woman's lap. Garret watched as Rose picked up a tendril of the pink flowers and pinned them around the lady's sparse little bun. "Hannah, you look like an angel with a halo!"

Garret cleared his throat. Both women looked up at him. He shook his head. "Ma'am, I beg to differ. You look like a queen." He focused his attention on Rose. She'd frozen in place, her fingers still hovering over Old Hannah's hair. She met his gaze, stepped away from the old woman, and wiped her hands on the sides of her dress.

"You need to stop by the mercantile on your way home, Rose."

Rose wished that bell over the mercantile door didn't clang so loudly. The town didn't have a bell for the church, but this one was noisy enough that they ought to wrestle it from Garret Diamond and stick it in the steeple! Her gaze darted about the emporium. No one was there. Mr. Deeter had already closed the post office.

What am I doing here? I'm a modern woman. I don't need a man to dictate my actions. I tend to my own matters. I have the right to order goods from anywhere I want, anytime I want. What business does Garret have, ordering me to make an appearance? I can't believe I actually listened to him and came in here! I don't owe him an explanation for what I buy from Sears and Roebuck.

She made an impatient noise at her foolishness for obeying such a high-handed order and wheeled about to march out the door.

"You're not running away, are you?"

She closed her eyes and muffled a moan.

Garret climbed down from the ladder and dusted his hands as she slowly turned back around.

Rose didn't want to look him in the eye after she'd complied with his command, so she glanced up and saw the new banner he'd hung that advertised Calder's Saponaceous Dentine. She said the first thing that came to mind. "Are you trying to sell that stuff or give small children nightmares? The teeth in that picture are enough to terrify them."

He folded his arms across his chest and stared at her steadily. "Your diversionary tactic isn't going to work, Rose. You know exactly why you're here."

His shoes made a solid sound on the beautifully polished floorboards as he closed the distance between them. He tilted her chin upward and said in a low tone, "I know who you are, Rose Masterson."

"Of course, I'm Rose Masterson."

He pulled an envelope from the pocket of his leather apron and tapped it in his palm. "This is heavy—far too heavy to hold one thin dollar for that moquette rug."

"I ordered other things, too. My personal expenditures are hardly your concern."

He pinched the thickness of the envelope and stared straight into her eyes. "That rug provided a very clever excuse for you to send an order off to Sears, but the time has come for you to admit that those other things you ordered aren't for you. I strongly suspect this envelope's order contains instructions for—"

"I'm not going to stand here and listen to your cockeyed suppositions, Garret Diamond. When you gave me your word you'd mail that letter, I never dreamed you'd withhold it."

He ignored what she said and traced the two stamps with the blunt edge of his forefinger as he mused aloud, "I've been here long enough to see an interesting pattern. You mail off an order and get something from Sears. Just about the same time, something mysteriously arrives from the Secret Giver for someone in town."

Maddening man! Why doesn't he tend to his own matters and leave me alone? She lifted her chin. "As often as I order things, you can scarcely consider that a pattern."

When Garret leaned forward, she could smell his bay rum. She'd already felt unbalanced—that heady scent only added to the way her senses whirled.

"You, Rose Masterson, were in the mercantile when Cordelia mentioned her washboard needed to be tacked together again; then she received that washing machine."

"Several other people were in the store at that time, and I know for a fact that Hugo repaired the washboard very cleverly for her."

He gave a maddening shrug, then started tapping the envelope in his open palm yet again in a nerve-racking beat that matched the much-too-rapid beat of her heart. His voice dropped in volume and tone. "I wonder if Lacey Norse is going to get that new sewing machine she needs to start up her seamstress shop."

Rose's eyes grew wide, and she felt a wave of heat wash over her, but she said nothing.

The corner of his mouth tilted in a smirk, and he gave her a slow, sly wink. She could see the golden shards in his hazel eyes glint with intelligence. "I'm on to your secret."

Flustered, she grabbed the envelope from him and held it behind her back as if that would make this all go away. "Mind your own business."

"I do mind my own business. The good people of Buttonhole seem to think I do a fair job with the mercantile. You, on the other hand, seem to be minding everyone else's business."

"Are you implying I'm a busybody, Mr. Diamond?"

That slow smile widened into a full grin. *Calder's should have used his teeth for their illustration—they're far better looking than the ones on that dreadful poster. Mercy, how could I let my mind wander at a time like this?* Struggling to regain her wits, she inched back from him.

"Yep. I'm saying you've been busy, Miss Masterson. Busy in ways no one but me seems to have detected."

Rose stared at him and tried to think of a way to end the conversation. The problem was, she didn't want to lie. So far, she'd managed to speak the truth each time the subject of the Secret Giver came up. Folks might well have misinterpreted her meaning, but she'd never told a falsehood.

"You may think you figured everything out, Mr. Diamond, but my business is just that—*mine.*"

"You minded Mrs. Percopie's business when you bought that fancy icebox for the diner. You minded Joel Creek's business when you bought the plow." Garret didn't give an inch of space or argument. He drew closer again and continued on in a relentless litany. "Mothering might be considered family business, and you sent Mrs. Andrews that layette for the baby she adopted. You set Cordelia up in a laundering business with that high-volume washing machine."

Rose lifted her chin and countered, "I wasn't even living here when the church got the organ."

"I admit, that threw me. Then I recalled you saying you'd visited Buttonhole before you moved here."

She forced a laugh. "Plenty of people pass through town. It could have been any of them."

"It could have been, but it wasn't—" He gave her a stern look. "Was it, Rose? You saw a need, and you took care of it."

"The Secret Giver sent me something, too."

"That was downright clever of you. Diverting attention like that. . ." He shook his head in amazement. "Bet that fooled a few folks, too. You managed to do things like that, and ordering a rifle was a jim-dandy idea. You cooked up mighty interesting ways to keep the curious off your tracks."

Rose fell silent. She'd run out of words, and the exasperating man had her backed into a corner. He'd discovered her precious secret and confronted her. The envelope crackled as she clutched it in her fist. *Now what do I do?*

Garret stepped closer still. "Give me the envelope, Rose. It's time to mail it." He slipped his arm around her and closed his hand around hers.

Clang! The bell sounded as the shop door opened.

Chapter 11

A loud gasp sounded.

Garret kept Rose from bolting by wrapping his other arm around her shoulder and pulling her close. "Mrs. Blanchard. Mrs. Jeffrey," he greeted in an urbane tone that didn't match the thundering heartbeat Rose heard beneath her ear.

"Land o' Goshen!" Mrs. Blanchard blurted out.

"Oh. It's just Rose." Mrs. Jeffrey's tone carried pure relief. "Nothing untoward is happening, Bessie."

"Then what is he doing?"

Garret didn't move hastily. Rose desperately wanted to pull away, but her knees felt too weak, and she realized the wisdom of his actions. Jerking apart would only reinforce something indecent was under way. Instead, Garret kept hold of her.

Good thing, too. The thundering sound filling her ear couldn't possibly be his heart, after all. Rose fought the dizziness that threatened to swamp her.

"I'm afraid I gave Miss Rose a shock, ladies."

"She is pale," Mrs. Jeffrey said. "Look how pale she is."

"Are you okay, Rose? Has something dreadful happened?"

Garret confessed, "I gave her a fright."

"Why, you could scare a body witless, coming down off that ladder. You need to be more careful, young man."

He managed to rob Rose's nerveless fingers of the envelope and scoop her into his arms. Rose tried to make a sound of protest, but he shushed her.

Mrs. Blanchard fumbled in her handbag. "I have those smelling salts in here."

Garret carried Rose to the press-backed oak chair over by the men's boots display. She felt safely anchored in his arms, and when he let go, the mercantile rippled around her once again. "Here you are, Miss Masterson. Sit down and take a few slow, deep breaths to steady yourself."

Mrs. Jeffrey shoved him to the side and muttered, "Give us a moment with her." A few seconds later, Rose felt something yank at her sides and back. Jerking motions. . . *What?*

"I've loosened her stays," Mrs. Jeffrey whispered. "Can't you find those smelling salts?"

The acrid scent of ammonia and Rose's violent cough answered that question. Rose jerked away from Mrs. Blanchard's vial and gasped.

Garret stood over by the water barrel, struggling not to laugh at Rose's predicament. With his back to them, he called out, "Shall I bring over a cool cloth or a dipper of water?"

"Yes. Yes, that would be just the thing," Mrs. Jeffrey said as she smoothed hair back from Rose's face and pinned the loose strands into the bun she now anchored firmly in the correct location.

"Here you are." Garret subtly winked as he handed the cloth to Rose. With quiet intensity he said, "Rose, you don't look like yourself right now. I'll remain with you here while the ladies find what they need; then I'll close the store and escort you home to be sure you make it there safely."

"That's unnecessary." Rose tried to stand.

Mrs. Blanchard pressed her back down. "For once, stop acting hale as a horse, Rose. It's only your pride speaking. Why, I nearly fainted recently, and Mr. Diamond escorted me home, too. It's the gentlemanly thing to do."

Mrs. Jeffrey patted Rose's cheek. "Your color is returning. This is what comes from eating those ridiculous cold cereals for breakfast, dear. I know you're alone, but you simply must stop shaking that nonsense out of a box and fix yourself an egg and toast."

"And prunes," Mrs. Blanchard added. "You need to start off your day with wholesome foods. Clearly your health is slipping."

⁓

Ten minutes later, with her corset strings and shirtwaist all tucked back into her skirt—thanks to Mrs. Jeffrey's kind assistance—Rose found herself being escorted by Garret toward her house. He'd flatly refused to let her go home alone, and the way he kept hold of her, she would have needed dynamite to blast him from her side.

Completely unsettled, Rose struggled to figure out what to do. Garret had just knocked her whole world off its axis. She wasn't the sort to swoon—was this how women normally felt when they grew faint? Was it because she wasn't accustomed to a man standing so close, or was it this man—who'd just discovered her quiet activities and posed a threat to her secret joy?

"Rosie, we're almost home," he soothed. "Are you feeling any better now?"

Embarrassed and desperately wanting to escape him, she muttered, "I'm perfectly fine, and you're wasting those prunes." She referred to the small box he carried—placed in his hands by Mrs. Blanchard with explicit instructions that Rose needed to have no less than three a day. The thought of eating that sickeningly sweet fruit each day was more than enough cause to make her swoon all over again. She shuddered. "I loathe prunes."

"You're not the only one. They're one of the few fruits I can't stand." He shook the box. "You can give them to Old Hannah the next time you go clean her house." He led her past her ramshackle fence and up toward the house. "Here we are."

She stopped at the threshold and took a stance that would make a suffragette proud. "I'd be lying if I thanked you for bringing me home."

Garret ignored her bravado, opened the door, and nudged her inside. Before she could gather steam, he ordered, "You go put on some tea. We're going to talk."

"Unthinkable." She gave him a wry look. "The good citizens of Buttonhole think I'm dotty, and they're most likely right; but I'm not about to do anything as foolish as inviting you in and risking my reputation and yours."

"You're right. We'll have to be circumspect about our partnership."

"Partnership?" She gawked at him as her stomach somersaulted. Was there no end to the ways this man could find to disturb her? Rose shook her head. "We have no partnership, Mr. Diamond."

He looked into her eyes. "I wouldn't be too sure about that." When he got intense, the gold in his hazel eyes overtook the brown. She'd have to remember that.

"I'll go off to the diner and eat so folks will know I've left you here. I'll sneak back after dark. We'll meet in the backyard by your strawberry barrel."

"You can wait until the crack of doom before I do such a thing."

"You still must not be feeling well. You're not your usual, cooperative self. Go rest. I'll see you later." He turned and whistled loudly as he left her standing at the door.

Rose fought the urge to slam her door, but she refused to give him the satisfaction of seeing her reaction. *I have to remain calm if I'm going to convince him to— Who am I trying to fool? Garret Diamond is just as stubborn as I am.* She closed her eyes, rested her forehead against the door, and let out a loud, unladylike groan.

༒

Sitting still and dallying over a cup of after-dinner coffee tried Garret's patience. He'd made a point of going to Percopie's Diner immediately after leaving Rose. The incident in the mercantile could have been a catastrophe, and with the way news spread through Buttonhole, folks would be quick to comment if he'd have spent more than just a few moments at Rose's.

"More coffee, Mr. Diamond?"

He glanced up at Hattie, then picked up his cup and tilted it. "I still have half a cup. That'll do. Thanks for asking. You brew a fine pot here."

Hattie scanned the diner. It was early yet—too soon for much of a supper crowd, so she slipped into the chair directly across from him. "Mr. Diamond, I wondered if—well. . ." She sighed and glanced over her shoulder. Her face flushed as she whispered, "I need to ask a favor."

He wondered why she was whispering. "What is it?"

"There's been some talk around town of earning money for a church bell. That always means an auctioned box social." She sighed again. "Please don't be offended, but I—well, I don't want you to bid." Her gaze skittered toward the door, to the kitchen again, then down toward her lap. "Some of the nicest young men in town aren't as well off as you."

Garret took a gulp of coffee. "Anybody I know?"

"Lester Artemis." Her eyes took on a sparkle. "He works at the *Gazette*. He just loves my fried chicken."

"He's a lucky man. I wish you both well."

Hattie popped up from the chair and whispered, "Thank you! Oh—will you please tell Mr. Hepplewhite, too?"

Garret nodded and left the diner, sure he'd wasted sufficient time there. The fact that Hattie had spent those few minutes sitting with him certainly helped keep folks from speculating that he'd set his cap for Rose.

He stopped midstride. *Rose. I'm setting my cap for Rose. When did that—how did that happen? The woman has worked her way into my heart, and I'm going to have a real fight trying to turn her affections toward me when I can't even get her to buy stuff from my store!*

As soon as it grew dark and the lamplighter finished his rounds, Garret slipped out of the back door of his place and headed toward Rose's back door. He had to protect her reputation, so he didn't take a direct route. Finally he reached her house, sneaked around, and tapped lightly on the back door. When she didn't respond, he got irritated. She was trying to ignore him, and he wouldn't put up with it. He rapped more firmly.

Rose finally flung open the door and glowered at him. From the light of the lamp she held, he could see she still wore the same dress she'd had on at his store. Judging from the color in her face, she either had a high fever or a raging temper. "What is all of that racket?"

His own temper flared to life. Vexed that she'd taken her sweet time to answer, he scowled right back. "The crack of doom. Now get out here."

Chapter 12

Her eyes widened at his audacity. "Garret Diamond, I don't know what's come over you, but you're bossy as a war general. I have little patience for anyone who decides to try to run my life."

"Come outside."

"What if I said I'd get too cold out there?" She gave him an exultant smile.

He'd never cross her threshold at night, alone, and she clearly realized it. He wasn't about to let that irritating fact stop him. "It's a balmy night. If you said you'd be cold, you'd be lying. . .and you don't lie. Which is why you didn't deny what I said back at the store." His patience was slipping faster than a skinny man's sleeve garter. "You, Rose Masterson, are the Secret Giver."

Her eyes nearly shot fire at him. "You, Garret Diamond, are a pain in the neck."

He leaned back against the post and chuckled. "Now that we've established our identities, let's negotiate."

She crossed her arms and glowered at him. "Are you trying to blackmail me?"

"Not in the least. What I'm going to do is join you. From here on out, I'm a coconspirator."

"This isn't funny."

He heard how her voice quavered and realized fear had triggered her temper. "I agree, Rose. This isn't funny; it's important work. It's a ministry."

Some of the fire seemed to leave her eyes. "I still don't think you ought to stick your nose into my business. The sixth chapter of Matthew, verse three says, 'But when thou doest alms, let not thy left hand know what thy right hand doeth.' That being the case, you really do need to stop prying."

He looked through the screen and lowered his tone. "Was it prying when you told me Cordelia Orrick needed that fabric?"

"Of course not."

"So what is the difference if we work together to make life better for our Christian brothers and sisters?"

She rubbed her temples as if he'd given her a terrible headache. "I don't want anyone to know."

"I agree. There isn't any reason for others to know. It'll be a pact between us. I think you've been wise to keep your identity a secret, and you've chosen to give things that equipped others to work and earn for themselves."

Her shoulders drooped as she let out a long, slow sigh of capitulation.

Garret opened the screen door. "Now hand me that lamp, and bring along your precious catalog. We have work to do."

"It's silly to order from the catalog anymore. The only reason I did it was to stay anonymous. The things can come from your store now." Her eyes grew glossy, but she blinked away the moisture. "I felt terrible, hurting your feelings by not making some of those purchases from the mercantile."

He reached in, took her hand, and gently tugged her outside. The screen door banged shut. "You were doing it for the right reason."

Rose handed him the lamp and gathered her skirts about herself as she sat on the uppermost step of the porch. "I was going to get the four-drawer New Queen sewing machine, but I really like the Singer you have at the mercantile much better."

"Then why didn't you plan to order one of those?" He sat beside her and fought the urge to wrap his arm about her shoulders.

"It's not in the catalog. Oh, don't glower at me. I'm telling the truth." She fished the crumpled envelope from her pocket and smoothed it out on her lap. After taking a deep breath, she tore it open and shook out a small stack of money and her order sheet. "You have plenty of fabric at the mercantile, but I thought it might be nice for her to have some supplies on hand. Often folks take the material to the seamstress but don't think of all of the notions that go into making a garment."

Garret moved the lamp so he could scan the order sheet more easily. She'd ordered a case of thread, hooks and eyes, Selisia waist lining, buttonhole twist, stays, and lace. Garret set aside the form and took her hand in his. He trailed his fingers across the edge of her cuff. A small, frayed section made him frown.

"Rose, how can you buy all of this for Lacey when you need new gowns yourself?"

She turned her hand so she could inspect the spot he'd touched. Relentlessly, he skipped his fingers along the stained apron pocket, the tattered ribbon trim of her skirt, then up to her collar where he traced the washed-and-worn-until-limp fabric. Very quietly, he stated the fact again. "You need new clothes."

Her nose wrinkled as she took stock of her garments. "Oh, my. I haven't paid much attention. I really have let myself go. These are shabby, aren't they?"

Soft laughter bubbled out of him. "Rose Masterson, you are so content helping others that you're blind to your own needs. You're the only woman I know who lacks even the smallest scrap of vanity."

"I am content, Garret. Very content. I don't want you to ruin my secret."

He winked at Rose and covered her hand with his. "I'm not going to ruin it;

I want to share it. In fact, I'm going to steal a page out of your copybook. We're going to throw everyone off our tracks. Do you have some paste?"

"Yes." She gave him a wary look.

"Good. Get it, a pair of scissors, and this week's *Gazette*."

"What for?"

"You'll see."

In no time at all, they sat side by side with a pair of Rose's serving trays across their laps. Rose leaned over and laughingly added the "orse" she'd cut from the word "horse" after an "N" Garret pasted at an odd tilt. "Good. Now where did the sewing machine go?"

"Here." Rose handed him the little snippet of paper. She'd found it on the back page of the newspaper as they searched for the necessary words.

"Thanks. You know, I ate at the diner, and supper hasn't agreed with me. The chicken was a mite bit greasy." He winced and rubbed his stomach. "Could I trouble you for some bicarbonate?" While Garret continued to paste the rest of the message, Rose went in search of a cure.

By the time she came back outside, he'd started to fold the letter. Garret set it aside and accepted the glass she held out to him. "Thanks, Rose."

She held a plate with bread on it—the bread sparkled in the lamplight. Carefully, she stepped around the trays of paper scraps and scissors and sat beside him. "Bread can help, and so does a little peppermint. My nanny used to make this for me. Try it."

Garret accepted the thick slice of buttered bread that wore a mantle of crushed candy. It smelled yeasty and minty. Just before he took a bite, he raised his brow. "Nanny?"

Rose watched as he chewed. "Nanny." She moistened her lips. "Garret, I've not corrected the folks' assumption in Buttonhole that I'm hard-pressed financially."

"So you have a little nest egg that allows you to do as you will?"

Rose nodded. "So you finished the letter? I want to see it all put together."

He thought about putting her off, but she'd find out soon enough. Garret handed it to her. She leaned to the side a bit to catch more light on the cut-and-paste letter, and her gasp told him she'd read the last line.

"Rose, you just admitted your clothes have grown shabby."

"I can buy or make my own clothes."

He swallowed the last bite of bread. "That's not the point. Other people have noticed the sad condition of what you wear, even if you haven't. To their way of thinking, the Secret Giver would want you to have some new clothes. Hiring the seamstress to do a good deed while buying the sewing machine for her is exactly what everyone would expect, and it'll keep them looking elsewhere for the benefactor."

She gave him a disgruntled look. "You may be right, but I was right, too. You, Garret Diamond, are a pain in the neck."

༽

The next afternoon, Rose wanted to serve a healthy slice of her mind to her pain-in-the-neck partner. He'd slipped half of the money in her sugar bowl when she wasn't looking, and now he was hustling her into the mercantile. "Garret, I'm busy! You're entirely too commandeering. Can't you see how I need to—?"

He opened the door to the mercantile and announced loudly, "Here she is—show her the note!"

No less than nine chattering women and girls surrounded Rose; all started talking at once, trying to give her the news. Lacey Norse clutched the pasted-together gift letter and wept for joy. Rose didn't have to feign any emotion. It was a touching moment. She glanced over at Garret. He smiled and headed toward the storeroom.

It was turning into quite a pleasant little party. Rose had to smile. All of her lovely friends were celebrating the Secret Giver's wonderful plan to provide Lacey with the much-needed sewing machine while providing Rose with new clothing. They wanted to help choose the fabric and patterns and crowded into the sewing corner of the store.

Mr. Deeter watched from the window of the post office and called out, "Don't you all go fancifying Rose until she's nothing but flounces and froufrou."

Rose laughed. "Simple is best. I have to be able to ride my bicycle."

"This. Just look at this," Leigh Anne's grandma said as she lifted a bolt. "A plaid wool is sensible and stylish for her."

"Grandma, it's summer. Wool is going to be too hot and itchy for her."

Patience Evert sneered at Leigh Anne. "A lady wouldn't speak of such things."

Rose smiled at Leigh Anne. "I was about to say exactly what you did, dearheart. The summer heat can be so oppressive."

"And she got swoony just yesterday," Mrs. Blanchard said.

"I'm perfectly fine," Rose huffed. "It was nothing, I assure you."

"Twaddle." Mrs. Blanchard produced a dark blue muslin. "The only reason you're feeling better is because you ate your prunes this morning. This is practical and will wear well."

"It's a nice shade." Rose reached out to touch it.

"Nonsense. This is a time to cast practicality to the wind and be whimsical." Cordelia lifted a green, water-stained taffeta. "You need a new Sunday-best dress, and this green will do wonders for your eyes."

"Yes, it would," Lacey agreed. "I can just imagine you in it. Mrs. Busby, the ivy print dimity beside you is ideal for a shirtwaist for her."

"And this would make a perfect match for the skirt!" Charity added.

"It would," Rose agreed. "Oh, it's all so very pretty. It's been awhile since I even paid attention to fashion, and these fabrics are marvelous."

"What do you think, Mr. Diamond?" Missy Patterson asked in an adoring tone. "Won't our plain Rose look lovely in it?"

He picked up Pickle and put her in Leigh Anne's lap. Rose secretly wished Garret would like this green. She truly favored it; and since these clothes were his idea, it would be nice if he was pleased with the choices, too.

He cocked his head to one side, then pressed his lips together in a thoughtful line. "Miss Rose will look fine in those. Green suits her—pulls out the green in her gray green eyes. I confess, though, I'm partial to something. . . ." His voice trailed off as he spiraled his hand in the air in a hopeless gesture.

"More feminine," Mrs. Jeffrey filled in. "What about this cotton print?"

Rose was about to admit it was pretty, but Garret jumped right in. "Now that's a good one." He jutted his chin and added, "The flowery one just to the side of it is easy on the eyes, too."

The bell over the shop door clanged. "Shiver me timbers, what's goin' on in here?" Zeb Hepplewhite hobbled into the middle of the store and gawked at everyone.

"The Secret Giver struck again," Garret said.

"He slipped a note under the mercantile door," Lacey said as she pointed to the six-drawer Singer that now held a conspicuous spot in the middle of the store. "I'm getting that wondrous sewing machine!"

"Well, how'd ya like that?" Zeb scrunched the side of his face and waved his hand in Rose's direction. "What does that have to do with you all hanging enough bunting off of Rose to make her the grandstand for a picnic?"

"That's the funniest thing I've heard all morning." Rose laughed as she disentangled herself from clinging ivy dimity, sprays of cabbage roses, and clinging mossy green. She paused and fingered the floral that Garret said brought out the green in her eyes. It was one of the prettiest things she'd seen in a long time. "I'm especially fond of this one."

"The Secret Giver wrote that I'm to make Rose three new outfits and. . ."

While Lacey filled Mr. Hepplewhite's ears with the goings-on, Mrs. Blanchard tugged on Rose's sleeve and hissed, "Don't be mush-mouthed, young woman. You're going to ruin Zebulon's fun if you don't say that a bit louder and let him know just how much you like this piece. Haven't you figured out yet that he's the Secret Giver?"

"Well. . . ," she stammered.

Mrs. Percopie cut in, "No, he's not. It's the banker."

Mrs. Jeffrey shook her head. "No, no. The reverend and I finally figured it out. It's Mr. Deeter."

"The postmaster?" the other two women asked in hushed unison.

Mrs. Jeffrey's head bobbed emphatically. "He was appointed to the position because he comes from good family—one that actually managed to maintain its wealth after the War Between the States. He's been paid a steady salary all of these years from the United States Post Office Department. Besides, from sorting the mail, he knows everybody's business."

Rose glanced over and caught Garret looking at her. A wave of warmth washed over her. She'd never had a man pay attention to her or notice the color of her eyes. Oh, a handful of years ago, there had been a few swains who'd known she'd inherit Daddy's fortune. Mere boys, they'd acted like lovesick puppies, and she'd not felt anything but disappointment that they'd seen only the green of dollar bills instead of the green of her eyes. Garret hadn't known about her wealth; he'd simply cared about her.

He winked very slowly, then turned and headed toward a display.

"Isn't that so, Rose?"

"Huh? Oh, I suppose, if you say so." She had no idea what she'd agreed with, but it certainly put a smile on Constance Blanchard's face.

Mrs. Busby muffled a twitter behind her hand. "I declare, Rose, it's a blessing you decided not to marry. If you hadn't noticed that man was better looking than chocolate cake until Constance said so, you simply were intended to be alone."

Chapter 13

"Mmm-mmm-mmm." Garret stood at the front door and hummed his appreciation loudly. "Peaches. I don't rightly recall the Good Book saying what heaven smells like, but I declare, this is the scent." He muttered under his breath, "Too bad they don't taste anywhere as good as they smell."

"Let yourself in," Rose called. "I'm busy."

Garret opened the door, and Caramel slinked out and rubbed against his leg. For being the runt of the litter, she'd still managed to thrive under Rose's loving care—but that came as no surprise. Everything and everyone Rose touched flourished.

Garret stepped in, set down the twenty-five-pound bag of granulated sugar, and peeled out of his coat. After hanging the coat on one of the hall tree's hooks, he carried the sugar into the kitchen. "Looks like I'm just in time with this."

Rose didn't turn around. "Please pardon me, but I don't want these to scorch."

"Not to worry. The view's as pleasant as the fragrance." He smiled at the sight of her standing by the stove in her old brown paisley skirt. Damp tendrils curled all around her face and the nape of her neck, and her cheek bore a hectic flush from the heat of the stove. Her apron was askew, and her hips and bustle jostled in cadence with the vigorous way she stirred the pot.

A good four dozen jars of peaches sat in higgledy-piggledy rows on the table, and several smaller jars sat in steaming rows. "Just say the word. I'll move the pot for you. In fact, I can hold it and pour the jam directly into the jars if you direct me."

Rose cast a surprised look at him.

He shrugged. "My great-aunts loved to cook, but they were both getting frail enough that they couldn't lift a heavy pot. On more than one occasion, I rolled up my sleeves and helped out."

Minutes later, he curled his hand around sunny yellow crocheted pot holders, hefted the pot, and took it to the waiting jars. In a matter of minutes, he and Rose managed to fill all of them. She hastily wiped the jar mouths clean, popped on the lids, screwed the collars in place, and set them in a water bath to seal them.

"Whew!" She lifted the water dipper for him to take a sip, but he shook his head. After taking a long, cool drink, Rose set it down and smiled. "Thank you for your help. That went much faster and easier."

Garret swiped his forefinger through a blob of jam on the edge of the table and wiped it off on a damp dishcloth. "I'll help with the next batch if you'll give me a jar. I'll send it to my great-aunt Brigit. She'll love it."

"Bite your tongue, Garret. I'm done with peaches for the day. You just feel free to take one of these jars and let me rest."

"From the looks of it, you're done canning for the year. What did you do? Go strip every last peach from the trees?"

"No." She laughed. "This is only a portion of them. I'm going to deliver peaches to Cordelia tonight. Mrs. Kiersty already took a bushel, and she's sending Mr. Hepplewhite for more tomorrow."

He looked at the empty tulip-decorated sugar sack she'd set aside. "Want to refill your canister before I put this sugar in the pantry?"

"It was generous of you, Garret, but I think you'd better take it back to the store."

"Balderdash." He opened the door to her pantry and stared at the room in shock. "Woman, what—"

"Now, now. You have to understand Sears ships things by weight. I often had them use bags of sugar or flour to bring the weight up to one hundred pounds so the price of freight dropped."

Her so-called pantry was actually a third bedroom. He'd never seen such a collection of things. Speaking aloud, Garret took stock. "Thirty. Forty. Fifty pounds of sugar. Fifty pounds of flour. Beans. My word, you have enough beans in here to feed all of Buttonhole for a month!" He continued to scan the room.

"Maybe Cordelia could use that sugar you brought to me."

He turned and scowled at her. "Maybe Cordelia could come grocery shop here at your house!"

Rose's smile faded. "Cordelia doesn't know about what I keep in there. She's been very careful not to take liberties with my home."

"Why? She's not starchy like some of the other women."

"This was her childhood home."

"You don't say." He felt his unreasoning anger fade. Rose had stocked this room and used most of the contents to make meals for Old Hannah, soups and teas for Mrs. Kiersty and the boardinghouse folks, countless lunches and suppers for Hugo and Prentice. . . .

Rose turned back toward the kitchen. She cut a fresh loaf of bread, took the slice, and sopped it in the bottom of the jam pot. When she held that treat out to him, Garret covered her fingers and gently pushed it back toward her mouth. "You have it. I'll take the heel."

"No." She grinned. "I feed the heels to the birds."

"Woman, you never cease to amaze me. You can find something nice to do for anyone or anything."

"I've had nice all my life. There's nothing wrong with me making sure others have a turn at it, too." She cut a slice and handed it to him.

As he slowly pretended to dredge his own slice, yet soaked up no more than a speck of the still-warm jam that lined the pot, he asked, "What's our next Secret Giver project going to be?"

"Shirts, I think. Mary Ellen used to sew all of Hugo's shirts. He's nearly worn them out, and he's not gotten a new shirt since she passed on."

Jealousy stabbed at Garret for a moment. Rose did Hugo's laundry every week. Indeed, Garret had seen Hugo stringing up a new clothesline for her just last Sunday. Hugo relied on Rose for meals, laundry, and babysitting. With all of those essentials met, Hugo did nothing more than fill Rose's stove and lamps and made sure she had firewood. Hugo didn't seem like the type to take advantage of a woman's sweet and generous heart, so that meant he must be biding his time before he convinced Rose that Prentice shouldn't be a motherless boy. That argument would hold a lot of sway.

Garret barely tasted the dot of jam on the bread that he shoved in his mouth. Two chews, and he swallowed as he scowled.

"It occurs to me that you wash, mend, and iron Hugo's shirts. The least he could do is mend your fence."

"I wouldn't want him to."

"That's beside the point." He took a quick glance out at the fence. Caramel leapt up on it at that moment, and even the kitten's slight weight made the rickety fence wobble. Garret looked back at Rose and demanded, "Has he ever offered?"

"No." She gave a small shrug and nibbled on her bread.

He wiped his hands off on a damp towel. "Well, I'm going to see to it that your fence is repaired. It's an eyesore."

"No!" Rose shook her head adamantly. "Leave my fence alone."

"Tell me why, Rose." He folded his arms across his chest and waited.

Rose stared straight back at him, her gray green eyes sparkling with defiance. Her hairpins must have come loose as she shook her head. A few pinged onto the floor, and her not-quite-on-the-top topknot started to uncoil. Hectic color filled her cheeks, and she reached up to keep her hair from coming down. Realizing she still held the jam-covered heel of bread, she halted the movement.

Garret froze, too. He'd love to see her hair flowing over her shoulders. Her blush made him do the gallant thing. "Allow me to help." He hastily collected the pins he could find and stood behind her. She shifted uneasily. "Being antsy and fidgeting is making it come down. Hold still, Rosie."

Garret tucked the pins between his lips and gazed at the ever-loosening honey blond mane. The tiny tendrils at her nape weren't damp anymore, he noticed.

Soft. Her hair felt incredibly soft. He knew he ought to simply try to crank it back into a tighter twist and jam in those pins. As soon as he did, she could wash her hands, excuse herself, and go make herself presentable again.

Instead, he held the bulk of it in his left hand. Tresses spilled from his grasp in a warm, satiny fall that went past her hips. Rose shivered and let her bread drop into the sink as she curled her hands around the edge of the counter.

Garret took a steadying breath and finger combed the portions by her temples and forehead back into his hand with the rest. At first, he started to twist the abundant mass counterclockwise, then changed his mind and went the opposite direction.

Rose inched to the side a bit, her movement nervous. She turned as much as she could and looked at him from the corner of her eye, over her shoulder. He could see vulnerability in her expression that he'd not seen before. She usually looked so self-assured and carefree. This was a different side of her—unguarded, unsure. "You needn't fuss, Garret," she whispered unsteadily. "Just—"

"Seems to me," he said around the pins in his most soothing tone, "you're the one who's fussing, Rose. Your hair is glorious."

He'd never dressed a woman's hair. Never wanted to—until now. At least twenty different shades of honey, wheat, and gold shimmered in his hands. From having been twisted so tightly together, the strands still hung in a long, loose spiral. As he twisted them and coiled the length back onto her crown, Garret knew he wasn't arranging it as she would have. Rose always crammed it tightly into a knot that would fit in a stingy teacup; he'd eased it into a. . .a delicious cinnamon roll–like coil that took his entire hand span to keep in place as he anchored it with the pins.

Lazily putting the pins in and resituating them so they'd hold, he asked, "Why wouldn't you want me to fix your fence, Rose? You're always willing to help others; I'd love to help you."

"It isn't that," she said quietly.

"Then what's the problem?"

"Cordelia needs it the way it is."

He had only two hairpins left. He paused before choosing where to put them. "What does Cordelia have to do with it?"

Rose started to turn around. He wouldn't let her.

She sighed. "I told you this was her home. Not long after I moved in, I went out to cut down the morning glory, take down the fence, and replace it. Admittedly, it's in terrible condition. Cordelia was taking a constitutional, and she stopped to chat. One morning, her beau came by and took her for a walk. He picked a morning glory from the vine, and she started to apologize for it being there. It's a weed, you know."

"Yes, but a pretty one."

"Jonathan told her it was called bindweed. He professed his love and proposed to her there by the fence. He said she'd twined her way into his heart, and he wanted her bound there forever."

Garret placed the last hairpin, took Rose by the shoulders, and turned her around. Tears turned the gray shards of her eyes silver. She blinked away the dampness.

"How could I be so selfish as to destroy something that gives a lonely widow such comfort?"

Garret studied her quietly, then murmured, "Of course you couldn't, Rose."

Tempted to pull her into his arms, Garret cleared his throat. "I need to get going. I just wanted to drop off that sugar."

"I'll bring you some peaches and jam tomorrow. You'd burn yourself on the jars right now."

"Fine." As he headed toward the door, she turned toward the other portion of the house. Garret shut the door and shook his head. He'd been so caught up in paying attention to Rose, he'd forgotten the sugar. Oh well. It didn't much matter. She'd undoubtedly use it somehow.

He turned and saw Hugo standing by the sagging, peeling fence and nodded. "Lassiter."

"Diamond." Hugo still wore the brown suit he'd worn to work at the bank, but now the coat was unbuttoned. He glanced at his pocket watch meaningfully, then closed it and tucked it back in his vest pocket.

The action rated as utterly ridiculous. Businesses were closed for the evening, but with it being late spring, the sun hadn't even set. *Rose always says Hugo is just a friend and neighbor, but she's sure that's all I am, too. This isn't the first time I've suspected he's sweet on her. Well, too bad. She's mine.*

Garret strode toward him.

"Rose isn't exactly mindful of appearances," Hugo started in.

"She doesn't need to be. She's beautiful just the way she is." Garret didn't hesitate for a moment to speak his mind. Hugo had been looking at his watch—well, he might as well learn what time it was. Time for him to turn around, go home, and mind his own affairs. "Anybody who thinks otherwise is both blind and heartless."

Hugo chuckled and raised both hands in a gesture of surrender. "You don't need to convince me. I wasn't referring to her looks, though. I'm pointing out that it's not proper for a man and woman to be—"

Garret bristled. "Are you intimating that Miss Masterson and I have conducted ourselves—?"

"No. Absolutely not." An all-too-entertained smile lit Hugo's face. "Miss

Rose is so dead set on staying single, she'd be oblivious if a gentleman came calling with candy and flowers."

"And you'd know that because you've tried?" Garret rasped.

"Nope. Rose is like a sister—any affection I hold for her is purely fraternal. You, on the other hand, seem to be getting a mite possessive."

Relieved at Hugo's words and more than ready to stake his claim, Garret stared him straight in the eye. "Yep. I am."

"So that's the way of it." Hugo's smile grew wider still. "Truth be told, I have my eye on Cordelia Orrick. Hired her to start doing my laundry. It made for a good excuse to go on over to her place."

"She's a fine woman." Garret didn't bother to hide his grin. Things were turning out even better than he'd dared to hope.

"Nice little daughters, too. They get along with Prentice just fine. I don't think it'll take long before I can pop the question." Hugo gave him an amused look. "Convincing Rose is going to take some doing on your part."

"I'm equal to the task."

Hugo seemed to think about it for a minute, then nodded slowly. "I can believe it." He extended his hand. "I'm not above scheming if it'll result in her being happy. Let me know if I can help you out."

Garret shook hands with him. "Thanks."

Chapter 14

The next day, Rose sauntered toward the mercantile with two jars of peaches and another two of peach jam. The afternoon sun felt wonderful on her cheeks. Of course, that meant she'd forgotten to wear her hat again, but feeling heaven's warm kiss was worth more than bowing to silly rules about fashion.

She could hear Garret and Prentice before she opened the door. Unwilling to spoil the moment with the clang of the bell, she walked around to the back of the mercantile and sneaked in. Pickle scampered past as she tiptoed across the storeroom floor, but Rose tried to determine where they were. The curtains were open just a crack, and she shifted to peek through.

Prentice sat cross-legged on the counter, and Garret perched alongside him, his long legs dangling. His right foot tapped in the air to keep beat as they played a duet of "Shoo Fly" on their harmonicas. As soon as they finished, Prentice begged, "Again!"

"That was four times in a row, Buster. I'm going to run out of breath."

Unwilling to be an eavesdropper, Rose set down the jars and clapped as she walked through the curtains, into the store. "*I'm* breathless. That was a wonderful performance."

Prentice shoved his glasses higher on his nose. "You don't sound all squeaky and barky like the Sneedly kids do when they can't breathe."

Garret chuckled. "Rose, Doc tells me those kids are doing better."

"Praise the Lord, they are."

"Miss Rose makes ever'body feel better." Prentice blew a few notes on his harmonica, then added, "Doc says the herbs she gives him from her yard keep Mr. Ramsey's heart going, and Daddy says she's the onliest one around who can make Mr. Van der Horn smile."

"Now that's really saying a mouthful." Garret tucked his harmonica into his shirt pocket and reached for the jar of licorice. "I reckon I'd best get back to work now. Why don't each of you have a treat?"

"Wow!"

"Prentice, mind your manners," Rose chided softly.

"Thanks, Mr. Diamond!" Prentice took the licorice stick and scrambled down from the counter.

Rose caught the ball of string Garret used to tie up packages as it went flying. As she got ready to put it back on the counter, it felt odd. She glanced down and groaned at the bedraggled shape it was in. "Pickle?"

"Yep." Garret shrugged. "It's a definite improvement over the pickle jar. At least string doesn't leave her smelling funny for days on end. Did you come for any particular reason?"

From the way he glanced at Prentice, Rose couldn't be sure whether Garret was asking whether she'd come to fetch the boy or whether he was reminding her they had an audience so she shouldn't say anything about the Secret Giver.

"I need some cheesecloth and wire-mesh screen. Do you have any?"

"What will you be using them for?"

She walked past him, around the counter, and into the mercantile. "I fear I've used my Peerless food dehydrator so much, the screens on it are giving out in protest."

"And we're gonna make dried 'cots," Prentice informed Garret. "Miss Rose washes them, and I twist 'em in half. Only I don't spit out the pits."

"I'd hope not." Garret went to the hardware section and located the proper mesh. "A gentleman should never spit in the presence of a lady."

"Lotsa men chaw and spit." Prentice wiggled and bumped into the door. "It's yucky."

"Prentice, please prop open the door. It would be nice to have a breeze come through." Garret redirected his attention to Rose. "This mesh is thirty inches wide. How much do you need?"

"Five yards of each, please."

Garret leaned back and gawked. "Five yards?"

"Yes, please."

"Oh, now isn't that simply splendid!" Mrs. Kiersty stood in the open door and beamed. "Rose, I wondered if the day would ever come."

"What day?" Rose and Garret asked in unison.

"What's happening?" Mr. Appleby slipped past Mrs. Kiersty and entered the mercantile.

"Rose is buying five yards of fabric—and not one kind, but two! Two, mind you. She's decided it's time to—"

"Excuse me, Mrs. Kiersty, but I'm not buying fabric. I'm buying mesh so I can make dried fruit and fruit leathers."

"Oh." Mrs. Kiersty looked entirely too dejected by that revelation.

Mr. Sibony, on the other hand, perked up. "You do have a way with those. I remember the strawberries you dried last year. The missus and I sure relished them when you left them behind that day you came to help her with the darning."

"Darning?" Garret's brow wrinkled, then softened as he smiled. He stooped, lifted Pickle, and absently petted him.

"Mrs. Sibony broke her arm last winter." Rose smiled at Mr. Sibony. "It healed up, good as new. She showed me that quilt she's piecing. The colors in it are beautiful."

"Well since we're talking about material. . ." Mrs. Kiersty tugged on the cuff of her glove. "I still think Rose ought to buy some and make a dress for herself."

"Nonsense." Rose walked over and took the mesh from Garret. "Everyone knows the Secret Giver provided a very generous new wardrobe for me."

"Then why aren't you wearing one of those new skirts?" Mrs. Kiersty scowled at Rose's old cream-and-green-striped dress.

"I'm spending the day in my kitchen, preserving fruit. It would be impractical for me to wear nice clothing, and I'd be mortified to offend someone by ruining those pretty new dresses with sticky sap and juice."

"I've decided who that someone is." Mr. Sibony's voice dropped. "Mr. Milner—he's the Secret Giver. I'm sure of it."

"How did you reason that out?" Garret took the mesh back from Rose. He winked at her as he did so. "Five yards?"

"Yes, please."

Mr. Sibony and Mrs. Kiersty accompanied them over to the cutting table. Mr. Sibony said, "Hank Milner got that inheritance—remember?"

Mrs. Kiersty's head bobbed.

"It was just before you moved to Buttonhole, Rose." Mr. Sibony nodded his head emphatically. "The timing is just right. He's the one."

Garret cut the mesh and began to roll it up. "I'm still meeting folks in town. Other than shaking Mr. Milner's hand at church, I haven't spoken with him. Mrs. Milner seems like a kindhearted woman, though."

"Oh, she is." Rose had to restrain herself from grabbing the mesh and running out the door. These situations were dreadfully uncomfortable. She refused to lie, but this time she hadn't needed to even hedge because of how cleverly Garret managed to turn the conversation. "I've heard she's organizing the bazaar so the church can raise money for a steeple bell."

"That'll be a lot of work." Garret snipped a length of string off the battered ball and tied the mesh into a tidy scroll. "But it's for an excellent cause. If there's a committee, I could volunteer to help out. One of the blessings of being single is that I'm free to use my spare time however I wish."

"Rose says the same thing." Mrs. Kiersty sighed. "Well, I can't spend all day jawing. I have hungry boarders to feed, and I'm clean out of baking soda and running low on lard and salt. If I don't have biscuits, pie, or cookies, we're likely to have a riot over there at supper."

"Seems to me, Zeb wouldn't allow anyone to bother you." Garret drummed his fingers on the tabletop. "He's a quick-thinking man."

"Quick thinking, but not quick moving," Mrs. Kiersty called over her shoulder as she headed toward the shelf with the baking ingredients on it. "His gout's making him miserable again. Actually, his misery is making me miserable. The man sits there all day, grumping and groaning about his feet, of all things. Feet! That kind of talk in a kitchen is enough to turn a body's stomach."

"Speaking of feet—I came in for about fifteen feet of chicken wire." Mr. Sibony shoved his hands in his pockets. "The missus says she thinks we have 'bout enough store credit from her eggs to cover it."

"Eggs are twenty-two cents a dozen, and you folks have fine laying hens. I wouldn't be surprised at all if you had gracious plenty. Let me check."

Garret nodded, then reached for the credit ledger. Suddenly he turned, stooped, and rose with the jars in his hands. A slow smile lit his face. "Rose, I can't believe you brought all of this. Why don't you take some of this jam over to Old Hannah while I see to Mr. Sibony and Mrs. Kiersty?"

"I already took her some." Rose figured he was trying to get rid of her so he could discuss the Sibonys' financial situation in private. "I did hear Wilbur Grim's ailing."

Mrs. Kiersty gasped. "Rose Masterson, you have no business paying that man a visit!"

"He's the town drunk," Mr. Sibony whispered to Garret in a confidential tone.

Rose felt Garret's gaze. She stared straight back at him. "He lost a limb in the War Between the States, and he's bitter. But he has never once been hostile to me, and he has a twelve-year-old son, Aaron. Aaron and Trevor were here last Monday, playing draughts with Leigh Anne."

"Oh. I somehow got the notion he was Trevor's brother."

"Coulda been." Mr. Sibony chuckled. "The Kendricks have a sizable brood—I can't keep 'em all straight, and I grew up in Buttonhole."

"This can't be right." Mr. Deeter's exclamation startled them all. He stood up behind the barred window in the post office and shook his finger at Garret. "You gave me your word that if you ordered anything heavy through the post office, you'd give me fair warning."

"I did agree, and I've kept my word." Garret gave him a baffled look.

"I just got a note that says you've got a huge crate, heavy 'nuff to take a full team to pull, waiting at the train."

Garret shook his head. "I have a shipment due in on Friday, but I plan to pick it up. It'll be several boxes—but nothing heavy or large. There must be some mistake."

Mr. Sibony scratched his arm. "I've got me my wagon and team hitched outside."

Garret tugged at the garter on his sleeve. "You might end up with credit enough for that chicken wire and more. Mrs. Kiersty, I'll just put the baking soda and lard on the boardinghouse's tab."

"I can scrape together enough to get by until tomorrow. Let's go see what came!"

"I'll need to sign for the delivery." Mr. Deeter came around and locked the door to the post office, and they all traipsed out of the mercantile. Garret flipped over a CLOSED sign and locked the door while Mr. Sibony unhobbled his lead horse.

Garret curled his hands around Rose's waist so he could lift her up into the wagon bed. He drew her a bit closer, squeezed, and murmured under his breath, "What have you done this time, Rose?"

She just laughed.

Chapter 15

This thing weighs half a ton." Garret grunted as he and the other men shoved the crate into a space he'd cleared in the mercantile. Half of Buttonhole's citizens had gotten involved. They all stared at the crate with great anticipation.

"Let's open 'er up," Mr. Deeter said.

Garret grabbed a crowbar and carefully pried off the crate's lid. Everyone leaned forward, only to sigh in dismay. "Lots of packing straw," he said aloud. "I'll have to open the front."

"You're testing my patience, young man." Mrs. Kiersty took off her glasses and waggled them at him until her hat bounced from the emphatic action. "You're purposefully trying to string this out, and my old heart can't take it."

"Are you expecting something, Mrs. Kiersty?" Rose asked softly.

"Nothing but heart failure if he doesn't hurry up," the woman confessed in a sheepish mutter. "I feel like a guest at a birthday party. The gift is his, but I'm excited as can be for him!"

Nails screeched as Garret pried the crate open. He loosened one side, then the other. He looked at Mr. Sibony. "How about if you yank on that side, and I'll get this one?"

"Thought you'd never ask."

The huge front panel made a loud crash as it hit the floor. Bits of straw fluttered in the air like confetti. Garret brushed off more of the packing and uncovered bright blue cloth.

"Well, what is it?" Mr. Deeter impatiently reached in and dusted off more on one end. "Material? Material can't be this heavy."

Garret spied an envelope. He snatched it and pivoted around. "Rose, why don't you open this and read it for us?"

"If you insist." She waved him back toward the contents. "You go on ahead and unload."

If he didn't know for a fact that she was behind this, Garret would never suspect that Rose had anything at all to do with it. She waved at him again. "Hurry. I want to see!"

As the men pulled the heavy fabric from the box, she read aloud, "Instructions for installing your awning. Well, what do you think of that? Your emporium is

320

going to have the prettiest blue awning the people of Buttonhole have ever seen."

"We all expected great things from you when you came to town, Diamond." Mr. Deeter slapped him on the back.

Removing the fabric caused more of the packing straw to sift and fall, revealing not just the necessary metal ribs and posts to support the awning, but also wrought iron. "This is too much."

"It is wonderful," Mrs. Kiersty gushed. "Don't you think so, Rose?"

"I think those benches will look perfect out front." Rose shoved the instructions back into Garret's hands. "Let's all work together and put them there right away."

The men crowded around, grabbed hold of the heavy pieces, and carried them back outside. Mrs. Kiersty, in her bossiest tone, made sure the men centered each bench beneath the windows on either side of the door. Garret stared at the custom benches in awestruck silence.

The glossy black metal didn't carry the usual curlicues or floral designs. A low arc crowned the back with a circle in the center containing a diamond shape. Two thick solid bands with diamond shapes were at the top and bottom of the back, with DIAMOND'S EMPORIUM metal lettering filling in the middle section. The diamond-in-a-circle motif formed the seat, arms, and legs of both of the seven-foot-long benches.

"Son," Zeb Hepplewhite said as he hobbled over, "you're not gonna be able to move those things again. To my way of thinking, you're stuck in Buttonhole for life."

"He's not just stuck here; he's volunteered to help out." Mr. Sibony turned to Mrs. Milner. "He said he'll help you with the church bazaar so we can finally get that steeple bell."

Garret nodded. He was listening, but most of his thoughts centered on something other than the bell. Stinging from the fact that Rose considered him in need of such an act of charity, he decided he'd have to sit her down and explain a few facts—the first of which was, he was in stable financial condition. He had become her partner so they could have a ministry of giving. Receiving was out of the question—well, he corrected himself, she needed those clothes Lacey Norse made, and wearing them was an act of kindness because Rose made for a beautiful advertisement.

He kept looking at Rose. She'd made sure Leigh Anne got to sit on the bench first, and when Mrs. Jeffrey stopped her to say something, Rose gave her a quick hug and nodded. She and the town had a rare affinity for one another. Sweet, wild Rose. She'd cultivated a family for herself here, and her roots went down deep.

Rose sat down on the other bench, and Prentice hopped up and wiggled until he was plastered to her side. She curled her arm around his shoulders and laughed as Mrs. Altwell and her children joined them.

"Mr. Diamond!" Rose called merrily. She leaned forward to glance over at the other bench, which held a full load of citizens. "Look at this. Just look! I think the Secret Giver might be allowing your fine mercantile a bit of advertising here, but I'm sure he must have intended these benches as a gift for everyone in town. Why, the only thing that's going to improve this is that awning. Surely, this is a fine day for Buttonhole!"

Garret felt the knot inside of him untie at her sweet words. Dear Rosie— she'd just turned the tables on him. He'd been thinking of the selfsame excuse of advertising as a way to give her clothing. Everyone on the benches chattered happily, but Rose—well, she positively glowed with joy. He couldn't very well spoil her happiness by fostering foolish pride.

"The woman's right, you know," the banker agreed. "Buttonhole's folks do need a place to rest now and then."

"I'd have to say there's no better town than Buttonhole." Garret nodded, then turned to Mrs. Milner. "I have a few ideas for the bazaar. Have you set a date?"

"Hugo Lassiter said he could meet tonight. Cordelia Orrick can watch his little boy for him."

"Fine." He saw Rose directing Trevor and Aaron as they carried the wooden panels from the crate out of the store. "Hey! Wait a minute. We're going to need those for a booth for the bazaar."

"Why, yes. Waste not, want not," Mrs. Milner said.

Garret dropped his tone. "It's for a kissing booth."

Mrs. Milner squealed.

"Ma'am?" He wondered if he'd offended her with that plan.

Clapping her gloved hands, Mrs. Milner called out, "Everyone listen! We're having something different this year for the church bazaar—something perfectly scandalous." Her eyes sparkled with glee. "Mr. Diamond is going to build a kissing booth!"

"Diamond, you're going to kiss the women?" Joel Creek teased.

Garret tapped his foot on the hard-packed street. "Nope. All of Buttonhole's pretty maids are going to pucker up."

"I don't know if I want my daughters doing such a thing," Lula Mae spluttered.

"It's harmless fun." Rose patted her arm. "And just think—you'll want the steeple to have a bell to peal on their wedding days."

"Did you all hear that? Miss Masterson has given her approval." Garret grinned. "We'll all make sure she sets a good example and spends some time in the booth."

Chapter 16

Rose paused at her hall tree before she left the house. The beveled mirror reflected her new floral dress. Lacey had done a lovely job sewing it. Rose glanced up and caught sight of her hair. "I look a fright," she said to herself as she tried in vain to reposition some of her pins to make the bun look fashionably soft and secure.

"Oh!" she finally said in exasperation. She snatched her straw hat off a hook and slapped it on her head. *That ought to do.* It even made her presentable—not that such a thing ought to matter. She simply needed to go buy a few yards of ribbon and lace so she could pretty up the jars she'd canned for the bazaar. Well, at least that was her excuse. She needed to ask Garret a few things, but their partnership required that she concoct reasons to visit the mercantile.

They'd been stealing a moment here and there to pray together, seeking wisdom and guidance for how the Lord would have them meet the needs in their community. God had been faithful. Just last week, Garret showed her a trunkful of merchandise he'd found in the store's attic that included a sturdy toolbox with a beginner's assortment of tools. She'd come up with the thought that Aaron Grim could be paid if he helped construct booths for the bazaar.

On an afternoon when Cordelia managed the store, Garret went through the merchandise and decided what he ought to sell and what the Secret Giver should send to someone. Garret told Rose to come with a list of needs; he'd made a list of goods. Truly, God's hand was on them. The lists were a perfect match.

Rose smiled at the benches on her way into the store. They'd turned out even better than she'd dared hope. Garret had been fit to be tied with her at first, opening that big crate. At that moment, it had dawned on her that she might have stepped amiss and hurt his feelings.

The warmhearted smile he'd given her when he finally calmed down and agreed that the benches were really for the townspeople meant the world to her. He understood the gift wasn't for him alone. Yes, he'd been able to see the truth and accept it with grace. With the shade from the awning covering the benches, folks could rest and visit before or after they spent time in his wonderful emporium.

The door opened, and Mrs. Blanchard smiled. "Rose! Are you ready for tomorrow?"

"Not yet. I have to get a bit of lace and ribbon to put around my jars of peaches."

Mrs. Blanchard backed into the store and drew Rose in along with her. "Dear, you need to use a bit of lace and ribbon on yourself. We'll fix you up for the kissing booth!"

Rose laughed. "Garret was just teasing me. I'm not going to actually spend time at the booth. We want to make money for the bell. Missy, Hattie, Patience—"

"Piffle!" Mrs. Blanchard towed her toward the colorful array of ribbons. "Dear, many a man would be happy to part with a few cents to get a peck from you. Isn't that right, Mr. Diamond?"

Rose turned and smiled at him. He must have just gotten back from the barbershop. His hair looked a bit shorter and was freshly treated with Brilliantine, and she caught a whiff of bay rum—the heady, masculine scent she'd come to associate with him.

He studied her from hat to hem, and Rose suddenly felt her amusement change to. . .anxiety.

"Don't answer her, Garret. I'm far too old to play such games."

"Rose, Rose, Rose." He shook his head. "I'm not about to let you demure. We've all heard of 'putting your money where your mouth is.' You'll be lending your mouth, Rose, and the men of Buttonhole will be donating their money."

"I'm going to be busy enough already. I'm helping at the cakewalk, and I promised Old Hannah I'd wheel her over so she could look at the quilt and crochet booth."

"I'll take your shift at the cakewalk." Cordelia smiled, and her cheeks filled with color as she averted her gaze. "I was going to ask you if you'd mind. I'd count it a favor."

Mrs. Blanchard whispered, "Mr. Lassiter is working the cakewalk, isn't he?"

Rose felt disoriented. *How could I have missed that? Hugo's started taking his laundry to Cordelia, and she watched Prentice when he went to the planning meetings for the bazaar. Why, they're sweet on each other!*

Garret grinned smugly. "There you have it! Cordelia will do the cakewalk, and you can do the kissing booth. I'm certainly planning on getting my two cents' worth!"

The next day, Rose watched as Missy Patterson left the kissing booth with a jar full of coins to take to the counting table. Hattie Percopie, dressed in a fetching lavender organdy dress, stepped into the booth. Folks laughed as Lester Artemis hopped right up to be first in line. As soon as he paid his two cents and got a kiss, he went straight to the back of the line to get another.

Young love. That's what it is. Rose smiled at the sight, then headed toward the edge of the park so she could go get Old Hannah. She stopped by the counting table where the mayor and pastor sat side by side, drinking Hires root beer that the bank had donated. Leigh Anne sat under a big, candy-striped lawn umbrella. A sign in the grass next to her featured an outline of a bell. Thin horizontal lines had been penciled in, and when that sum of money had been raised, she'd color in the corresponding segment.

Rose arrived at Old Hannah's home, only to find Mrs. Jeffrey and Mrs. Busby there already. They all fussed over Buttonhole's oldest citizen, then turned on Rose.

"I'm so glad to see you wore that dress. It's so very feminine," Mrs. Busby gushed. "The green positively matches your eyes, and the sash—well, almost every woman I know would nearly perish to have such a tiny waist to show off like that."

"I brought my rose petal paper," Mrs. Jeffrey chimed in as she pulled it from her pocket. "A tiny bit of this will put a little more color in your cheeks." She nudged Rose into a chair and applied the tint.

"Bite your lips so they'll redden up a tad, too," Mrs. Busby insisted. "See? You look fresh as a flower. Wonderful! Just wonderful."

"Blushing and bloody—now there's a face that will scare away any male from knee pants on up." Rose tried to inject a touch of humor into her voice. Secretly, she still hoped to avoid the kissing booth.

She'd endorsed Garret's vaguely scandalous plan for the booth because she knew the men in Buttonhole were gentlemen and wouldn't behave in an unseemly way toward the young ladies who took a turn. Still, she hadn't imagined Garret would rope her into serving a spell in the booth! Why, she was five and twenty—no longer young and dewy, but a spinster. The men would want to spend their two cents for a kiss from a pretty young woman at the first blush of her womanhood. Rose was well past her prime, and it would be humiliating to have only one or two gallant men pity her and pay for kisses they did not want. She'd rather spare them—and herself—the embarrassment.

From the looks of how the young ladies were doing when she left the bazaar to come here, Garret's idea was garnering a healthy addition to the funds. Combined with foods, toys, quilts, and several other moneymaking venues and ventures, Buttonhole stood a fair chance of amassing enough to fund the much-longed-for bell. Rose figured if she merely lagged and dallied, Buttonhole would reach the goal. Leigh Anne would color in the last line on the bell, making it unnecessary for Rose to take a turn in the kissing booth.

Hannah's son showed up and whistled at his mother. "I'm going to have to beat back the old gents all day. You're glowing like a young girl."

"And how about Rose?" Mrs. Jeffrey prompted.

"I'll help him beat back the old gents," Rose volunteered.

"You'll be busy at the kissing booth," he countered. "In fact, I mentioned to Mrs. Milner that I was coming back to get Mother, and she said Patience Evert is balking."

"Bless her heart, Lula Mae has her hands full with that one." Mrs. Busby shook her head.

"Well, Rose is to run on ahead and take her turn in the booth. Mother, I'll take you, and Rose can show you the quilts and such later."

Rose couldn't quite figure out how they managed it. Mrs. Jeffrey and Mrs. Busby each took her by an arm and hustled her toward the park. She didn't have a chance to protest. Hattie Percopie stood in the kissing booth, her penny jar half full, and Lester Artemis was turning his pockets out to scrounge up another two cents.

"Lester, why don't you escort Hattie over to the counting table?" Mrs. Jeffrey didn't bother to hide her smile behind her gloved hand. "It looks to me that the reverend and the mayor will have plenty to add to the bell fund, Hattie."

Mrs. Milner and Garret walked up. Garret wore his Sunday-best suit and a natty new straw hat, which he gallantly swept off. "Ladies."

"Good, you're here, Rose." The strain around Mrs. Milner's eyes eased. "We can't have the kissing booth go empty—it's the biggest success I've ever seen!"

"I'll ruin that record." Rose eyed the booth with trepidation. Garret and Aaron had built it, using the wood from the benches and awning. "It's a grand booth, though."

"Charity and Mrs. Kiersty made the bunting." Garret reached over and tugged her away from the safety of standing between the other women. "Now it's your turn to do your part."

"Garret, I really don't think—"

"You're not here to think, Rosie. You're here to pucker." He took a jar from a shelf he'd cleverly built inside the booth and thumped it down in plain view on the ledge, then sauntered off.

Plink, plink. Pennies fell into the jar. Rose turned in surprise to see who would waste two cents to kiss a spinster.

Chapter 17

Hi, Miss Rose!"

"Prentice." She let out a sigh of relief. She'd never been kissed before—well, other than by a child or her parents. This would be simple enough.

Hugo held Prentice a bit higher, but Prentice wouldn't stop wiggling until he knelt on the ledge and grabbed hold of her shoulders. "I earned my pennies by playing my ha'mon'ca for Daddy."

"I'm honored."

She accepted Prentice's kiss and gave him a hug. Hugo helped him down, then dropped a dime along with his two cents into the jar. Rose opened her mouth to tell him, but he shook his head. "Rose, there's two cents there for me; then the rest is for my son, Cordelia, and her daughters. We're all thankful to you for your kindness and friendship." He brushed a kiss on her cheek.

"Hey, now, what is that?" Zeb reached up and did his sleight-of-hand trick. He pulled a quarter from behind her ear, gave it a surprised look, then dropped it in the jar. "Rose, my girl, never had me a daughter, but I like to imagine if I did, she'd a' been like you." He puckered up and gave her a fatherly kiss.

Rose could scarcely imagine the sweet things those men had told her. They warmed her heart and made her glad Garret had forced her into this booth, after all. She looked out and gasped. A line of Buttonhole's males trailed around the edge of the park. Young and old, married and single, rich and poor—the men were all lined up to kiss her!

"Took us a minute to recognize you, Miss Masterson," Mr. Deeter called out. "Take off that-there hat so we can see the sun shine on your hair and know it's really our Rose."

All of the old fears eased: *Don't fidget, Rose. A proper lady. . . The mannerly thing. . . People of our social station. . . Be sure to. . . Never. . . Always. . . Mind your posture, dear. . .* The stuffy rules of society, the pretentious code of behavior, the impossible strictures swirled in her mind. Mama and Papa had been gentle, but persistent, in her guidance. When her parents had passed on, though, the rules had nearly stifled Rose. Unwilling to spend her lifetime steeped in artifice, she'd sought out a place where others wouldn't inconvenience her if she stepped awry while, as Thoreau would say, she kept pace with a different drummer. She'd chosen Buttonhole and found happiness. Here, she could be herself—she could love others and be loved just for herself instead of her bank account or social status.

Jesus, thank You for this. My heart is so full!

Overcome with joy, she took off her hat and flung it into the air. It sailed over the park, landed in a tree, and sent several birds into flight. She clapped in delight as the men cheered.

Aaron Grim paid two cents—hard-earned money he couldn't afford—to give her a kiss. "You always treat me like I'm somebody instead of a drunk's boy. I'm gonna be somebody someday, Miss Rose. I'll make you proud."

"You're already somebody special, Aaron. I'm already proud to know you."

Trevor Kendricks spent his two cents and winked. "You and Mr. Diamond did me right, playing matchmaker for me and Leigh Anne. Won't be long before that bell's gonna chime at our wedding."

"You know I'll be delighted to help with the plans and reception. Leigh Anne will make a beautiful bride."

By the time Mr. Sibony stood before her, he eyed the jar. "Reckon I couldn't get two cents in that thing if I had to. Got another jar on hand?"

Rose gawked at the jar. She'd been so busy talking and blinking away emotional tears, she hadn't paid attention to the money jar. It was brimming!

"I'll take this jar over to the counters." Garret stepped up, switched jars, and gave her a lopsided grin. "Your sash is coming loose."

Rose reached around behind herself and fumbled with the wide bow Lacey insisted looked so chic over a bustle. "I'll be with you in a moment, Mr. Sneedly."

"Don't tie it too tight. You're always coming over to help when my kids get to wheezing and gasping from their croup. Last thing I want is you being breathless."

Mrs. Blanchard stopped by to say, "The quilt raffle brought in almost six dollars, and Cordelia says the cakewalk is coming up to nearly a dollar and a half now."

"How much more do we need for the bell? I can't see Leigh Anne's sign from here."

"I'll check on it."

Mr. Oates hefted his five-year-old twins and set them on the ledge. "Polly says she wants a kiss just as much as Peter does. Since I didn't see a sign that said otherwise, I figured you'd be one to bend a bit and take a peck from a girl."

Garret came by with a glass of lemonade for her. He raised it and announced to the men still in line, "I'm making sure Rose keeps enough pucker power for all of you fellows."

She laughingly accepted the glass and took a quick sip. "Garret, I'm supposed to take Old Hannah to see the quilts. Who is supposed to take the booth now?"

"You're staying put. Mrs. Altwell showed her around, and now she's under the umbrella with Leigh Anne."

"Rose, are you playing mother hen again?" Reverend Jeffrey asked.

Rose gave him a startled look. She'd never imagined she'd have anyone line up to kiss her, but the pastor?

"I'm cutting in line. I need to get back over there so the mayor can come, too." He dropped a nickel into the jar and kissed her hand.

The banker chortled. "Now how am I supposed to follow a fine show like that?" He pulled a whole dollar from his pocket and put it in the jar.

Rose stared at it in utter astonishment.

He grabbed her glass, took a gulp, and carried it off without taking a kiss at all. He whistled a tune as he went, but Rose couldn't tell what it was because of the men's throaty laughter.

As the laughter died down, Leigh Anne let out a squeal. "We did it!"

The mayor stood by her and clapped his hands to get everyone's attention. "Ladies and gentlemen, I'm pleased to announce that the bazaar has been such a success, we've earned the money for the bell."

The banker turned around and stared at the nearly empty glass of lemonade. "What about the money in Rose's kissing jar?"

"I plan to add to it," Joel Creek called out as he stayed in line. "Schoolmarm's been saying she needs maps, and Mayor's been jawing about Buttonhole needing a library. I figure we'll find a good way to use it."

The bazaar continued. Folks started talking about what the extra money ought to buy. The line of men at the kissing booth shortened only because each man attending had bought a kiss—not a one had walked away. Garret came at the end.

He dropped two shiny new pennies in the jar and smiled. "Looks like I'm the last one."

She glanced around and lowered her voice to a mere whisper. "Looks like we won't have to plant that envelope, promising the Secret Giver will make up a shortfall."

"When you concocted that plan, you underestimated your appeal, Rose." Garret cupped her face in his hands. He studied her features slowly, one at a time. His gaze settled on her lips. "A man—especially this man—knows a beautiful woman when he sees her." He dipped his head.

Though flustered, Rose tilted her face up for the little peck. She expected the same friendly smooch she'd gotten from all of the other men. She puckered up a bit, but the minute their lips touched, there wasn't that little popping sound and Garret didn't pull away. Her head felt too heavy, her lids fluttered closed, and his lips stayed tenderly against hers. Everything inside of her melted.

Garret stood stock-still. He rested his forehead against hers and continued to hold her face in the chalice of his hands. "Rose, you are the sweetest woman God ever created."

She slowly opened her eyes and looked straight into his. This was her partner, her friend. He might not feel that overwhelming warmth and jumble of feelings, but she sure did. At the ripe age of twenty-five, she'd just had her first real kiss. She'd never imagined how it would make her knees tremble and her heart thunder. Suddenly common sense washed over her. She and Garret had a pact. *Everything will be ruined if I let my heart fill up with utter nonsense.*

Panicked, she croaked, "Excuse me." She wheeled around and ran home.

Chapter 18

Garret drummed his fingers on the counter. He'd about lost patience. It was high time for Rose to stop acting silly. He'd seen the alarm in her eyes. The kiss he'd intended to be just a little touch of tenderness had given him away. She'd learned of his intentions sooner than he planned. Then she'd run off like a scared rabbit.

For the past week, she'd been hiding, too. It irritated him, the way she avoided him. Instead of coming to the store to pray with him to seek God's guidance for the next Secret Giver project, she'd simply sent a note saying she'd support whatever he felt led to do.

Far too cunning for her own good, she'd come to shop for her eggs, butter, and milk when he had his afternoon off and Cordelia was minding the store.

To celebrate the successful bazaar, Mr. and Mrs. Milner invited him to supper. Mr. Milner happened to clear his throat, waggle his brows, and mention that the missus might have invited Rose. Garret intentionally waited ten minutes after he saw Rose pass by his window before he left. By the time he gained entry to the Milners', Rose already had knotted on an apron and was helping in the kitchen.

Garret didn't feel in the least bit sorry about the arrangement. She couldn't make a scene, take off her apron, and stomp home. He tried to make eye contact, but the silly woman refused to look at him. He consoled himself with the fact that when the evening wound down, he'd offer to escort her home, and simple manners would cause her to accept.

Biding his time never took so long.

The mantel clock chimed eight. Garret rose from the parlor chair and nodded to Mrs. Milner. "It's turning late. I thank you for a lovely meal." He shook Mr. Milner's hand. "Pleasant evening. Very pleasant. I'll be happy to escort Miss Masterson home."

Rose stood stiff as a tin soldier as he slipped her summer shawl about her shoulders. "Thank you." The words came out of her as if someone were squeezing her so tightly that she could barely whisper a syllable.

They stepped outside, and he tucked her hand into the bend of his arm. *Finally. Finally I can talk some sense into this silly, lovable goose.*

"Rose?"

She turned toward the fence. "Yes, Sheriff?" Garret bit back a groan.

"Doc's tied up with a couple of dimwits who got into a brawl over at the saloon." The sheriff rested his hand on the chest-high green picket fence and buffed his badge with the other shirt cuff. "Sneedly's gone to Macon, and the missus is alone with her brood. She sent the oldest to see if you could help out. The kids are all croupy from the hay fever again."

↜

Rose twisted and wrestled to fasten the last button on her dress. That one between her shoulder blades had never seemed to be so difficult before—*before Garret made sure I had all of those new dresses, skirts, and shirtwaists.* The completion of the thought made her ache. From the first day they'd met, her life had never been the same. It hadn't taken long for a comfortable friendship to develop between them. How could she have lost her senses and let one kiss turn her world upside down?

A glance in the mirror proved that the heat she felt showed in the form of a virulent blush. Even her drab, old, brown paisley day gown didn't tame the effect of the color. Until she could regain and maintain her composure, she'd have to avoid Garret.

In the meantime, she'd been keeping busy. By filling every hour of her day with a chore, task, or deed, she actually managed to suppress the memory of that kiss—sometimes. Rose grabbed her hairbrush and started to untangle the snarls she'd gotten during another restless night. Somehow, the braid she normally wore to bed had come unraveled. Stroke after stroke, she tried to talk sense into herself. When she started to twist her hair, she knew forgetting Garret was an impossible task. Even this simple action brought back the time he'd pinned up her hair. She shivered at the memory.

Think of something—anything—to do today. I could bake. Pea—no, nothing peach. Definitely not a cobbler. I don't want him thinking I was trying to pander to his whims if he should stop by. He'd better not stop by. Why hasn't he stopped by? She shook her head. *I can't let that man drive me daft. Something else. I have to think of something else. . . . Apple. Yes, apple. Not a cobbler, either. A pie. There. That's a good idea. I could take it to share with Cordelia and her girls.*

Rose stuck in one last hairpin, then left her bedroom and headed straight for the kitchen. Tying on her apron, she frowned at the bowl in the center of her table. Three apples nestled in the center of it—shiny red apples. They were the wrong kind for baking, and there weren't enough of them even if she could have used them. She'd dehydrated apples aplenty, but the thought of making a dried apple pie in a season when fresh fruit abounded seemed ludicrous.

Bread. She could use a loaf, and the Sneedlys went through three loaves a day. With the children still sniffling and coughing, Lorna didn't have the time to bake. Rose grabbed her largest bowls and set to work.

A little less than two hours later, the yeasty smell of bread filled the kitchen. With the summer heat, the batches of dough rose far more quickly than usual. The first loaves were still in the oven, and the second batch would follow as soon as she took those out to cool. Rose had scoured the flour from her cutting board, mopped the floor, and washed the measuring cups, spoons, and bowls. She looked about for something to do.

Even in the few moments when she was between tasks, her mind whirled. *Why did Garret do that? Kiss me like that? We were supposed to be friends. How are we ever going to be friends again? He's a man of the world—how could he have risked our partnership, all for one meaningless kiss?*

She'd had dozens and dozens of kisses that day. Not a one of them had made her feel anything more than neighborly warmth. Then Garret's kiss had sparked something deep inside she'd never known existed. *He hasn't even tried to see me. The kiss meant nothing to him at all. For him, it was a two-cent donation. For me, it was everything. I have to stop thinking about it. I have to forget.*

The Sears catalog caught her eye. Desperate for diversion, she pulled it from the shelf and set it on the table. Aaron Grim was in critical need of new clothes. Rose turned to the index, found the proper pages, and flipped to them. What size would Aaron wear? She winced at the requirement of height, weight, and measurements.

If Garret were here, he'd know the right size.

"Nonsense," she said aloud. "I did just fine before he ever came. I'll do just fine on my own."

But we're partners. We've been praying, and God has been gracious to guide us.

"God blessed me long before I had a so-called partner," she muttered as she thumbed through the pages, waiting for something to catch her eye.

The women's clothing captured her attention. Cordelia hadn't had new clothes in ages. She was always busy sewing something for the girls since they were growing so fast. If Hugo was serious about courting her, Cordelia needed to have some pretty things to wear.

Why, I don't need to order anything from the catalog. I can go to Lacey. She'd do such a nice job, and Cordelia could choose what she likes. We all had so much fun when we decided on the fabric and patterns for my clothes. I know! I can order some drawers and vests for her and the girls from the catalog, and I can make one of those cut-and-paste letters and direct Lacey to make clothes for Cordelia.

Rose started to fill out an order form for the items. She could never provide for such needs with Garret present. This was all for the best. Oops. She'd written "best" instead of "vest."

She started the form over again, only to smell something burning. She jumped up from the table.

The edge of one of the loaves was singed—not badly. She could keep that one herself. Consoled by that thought, Rose stuck the second batch into the oven and went back to her catalog.

She filled out all of the necessary information for fine, pure Swiss-ribbed, summer-weight silk vests and merrily ordered one in each color: black, salmon, apricot, white, and light blue. Vests for the girls were easy enough—all she needed to record were the girls' ages and the type of vests desired. Drawers for Cordelia; pantalets for the girls.

No, no, no. Rose crumpled the order form and tossed it into the stove. Cordelia was sure Zeb Hepplewhite was the Secret Giver. She'd be mortified if she thought for a second that a man had dared to buy lingerie for her and the girls.

That left clothes. Rose grabbed a *Gazette* and a blank sheet of paper. She had to hunt high and low before she recalled sticking her scissors in with her strips of bandaging after she'd had to patch up Prentice's knee the last time. Since she was out of paste, she made some with a dab of flour, a dash of salt, and a bit of water.

This was so much more fun by lantern light on the back porch with Garret.

The thought stopped her midsnip. Caramel meowed and jumped up into her lap. She started to purr loudly. Rose set down the shears and cradled the kitten in her arms. "Oh, Caramel, there's nothing worse than a lonely spinster pining for a love that was never meant to be."

❧

"I'd like to speak with you about something." Garret waited until Cordelia placed the last tin of Parlor Pride stove polish on the shelf and turned around.

The corners of her eyes crinkled. "It's about Rose, isn't it?"

He nodded. It occurred to him that he'd propped the doors wide open to allow a pleasant breeze to blow through, but he didn't want this conversation to become community gossip. No one was sitting on the benches, but he didn't want to take a chance, so he walked toward her. "I stopped over at her place again today, but she wasn't there. Talking sense into a woman might not be easy, but I don't have a fighting chance if I can't track her down!"

"I confess, I saw you kiss her."

Cordelia hadn't spoken loudly, but she'd not taken the hint to mute her tone, either. Mr. Deeter must have overheard her, because he called out from behind the window, "Half of Buttonhole saw him kiss her. Whoo-oo-ie!"

Cordelia had the grace to look chagrined that she hadn't been more mindful of the delicate nature of the conversation. She leaned a bit closer and murmured, "I have an inkling what kind of sense you aim to impart."

Garret didn't reply. He wasn't ashamed of his love, but he figured Rose ought to be the first woman he told.

Mr. Deeter called over, " 'Bout time you went and bought a ring 'stead of selling 'em, if you ask me."

As he chuckled at his clever opinion, Cordelia coughed to muffle her laugh. Garret drummed his fingers on the closest shelf. "That's what I need to talk to you about. Could you give me an estimate of Rose's ring size?"

Cordelia perked up and bustled over to the locked jewelry case. "She's a five. I'm positive she's a five. She loaned me some of her gloves last Easter. Glove and ring size are the same, you know."

Garret sauntered over to the case. "See anything in there you think is pretty?"

"She was looking through her catalog just a few weeks before the bazaar and asked me the very same question. That one on the far left with the little swirls is similar to the ring we both decided was the prettiest."

"Hmm. Would you mind trying it on?"

A minute later, Garret slid the ring on Cordelia's finger. "Oh, Garret, it's beautiful."

Mr. Deeter cleared his throat, but it didn't cover the gasp.

Garret glanced over and saw Mrs. Jeffrey and Rose in the doorway to the store. Mrs. Jeffrey grabbed Rose by the arm and yanked her off the stoop. Garret raced for the door. "Rose!"

The women were across the street, and two wagons traveled the normally quiet road in opposite directions. By the time they passed, Rose was gone.

Chapter 19

You should stay here for the night." Mrs. Jeffrey patted Rose's arm. "After such a disquieting event, it's not right for a body to be alone. The bed in the spare room is all made up, and you can borrow a nightgown."

Rose set her knife and fork across her plate. She'd forced herself to eat two bites of each dish her hostess had served. Every last one of them got stuck halfway down, and now the food sat like a cannonball in her stomach.

Reverend Jeffrey muttered something about a deacons' meeting and excused himself. As he passed by Rose's chair, he patted her shoulder. "Romans 8:28 says, 'And we know that all things work together for good to them that love God, to them who are the called according to his purpose.' This trial has already been through the heavenly throne room. We'll keep you in prayer and have faith that this will turn out according to God's will."

She nodded. He was right, but it still hurt. After she helped do the supper dishes, Rose wanted to be alone. "Thank you for the solace of your company today. I truly appreciate it, but I need to go home now. Caramel—my kitten—needs to be fed."

Bless her heart, Mrs. Jeffrey didn't argue. "Okay, dear. After you feed her, if you decide you'd like to come back here, the door is open, and you're more than welcome."

"Thank you." Rose slipped out the back door and went home. Once there, she started heating water for a bath and sat down to read her Bible. The faded, plum-colored ribbon marked where she'd left off yesterday in the fourth chapter of 1 Peter. Verses 12 and 13 leapt off the page at her: *"Beloved, think it not strange concerning the fiery trial which is to try you, as though some strange thing happened unto you: But rejoice, inasmuch as ye are partakers of Christ's sufferings; that, when his glory shall be revealed, ye may be glad also with exceeding joy."* Suddenly common sense washed over her.

She stared at the words. "Lord, it is strange. I don't understand why this is happening. I thought Hugo and Cordelia were falling in love, and I was so happy for them. It was bad enough when I thought Garret didn't return my feelings, but for him to be betrothed to Cordelia—it just makes my heart ache. It's so selfish of me. I should be thrilled for them, but all I feel is so lonely and empty. Was this part of Christ's suffering? To be single and watch others find the contentment of love and marriage? Until now, there's never been anyone who stirred my heart. Now my heart is breaking. I don't know what glory there is for You in this. I don't see any joy in it. Help me to understand, Father."

❧

Garret gave Cordelia some of the new Bayer headache powder from Germany. She'd managed to weep herself into a migraine, and Mr. Deeter kindly walked her home after leaving the post office in the hands of Percy Watkins, the postman, who had finished his deliveries for the day.

Garret didn't care about keeping the store open; he wanted to track down Rose and explain matters. In just those few seconds he'd seen her, her beautiful green eyes had gone huge with shock, and her face—her pretty face—had turned white as the wicker basket she usually carried.

He hadn't had a chance to get to Rose. Mrs. Blanchard had plowed in like a yacht under full sail. She'd not come alone, either. Mrs. Busby and Leigh Anne's grandmother were in her wake. Mrs. Blanchard stabbed him in the chest with her forefinger to accentuate her words. "How dare you upset our Rose!"

"I didn't—"

"You most certainly did, young man. I heard it from an eyewitness. Bad enough you did it at all, but in front of that poor child!"

"What? Now wait a minute."

"Don't you deny it. Poor little Prentice saw and heard it all. You've been an utter cad, and we will not stand for it, will we, girls?"

"No. Never," Mrs. Busby hastened to agree.

Leigh Anne's grandmother edged around and squinted at him. "I expected better of you. You're no green-behind-the-ears boy; you're a grown man. There's no excuse for dallying with a woman's affections—especially someone as sensitive as Rose Masterson."

"I agree." His quiet, confident words didn't register. The women had come to speak their minds, and he figured he might as well let them. It would take less time than trying to defend himself. Mrs. Kiersty came in, caught the drift of the conversation, and gave him a heated look that could have boiled an egg.

"Hugo and Cordelia belong together. They both have children. I've been coaxing them into each other's arms ever since Christmas, and if you've ruined it for them and those darling little children, I'll never buy so much as a grain of salt in this store again," Mrs. Kiersty announced.

"You'd be bored to distraction with any of the demure younger girls." Mrs. Blanchard gave up poking him in the chest—she jabbed at his arm instead. "Oh, I admit, I wanted you to sweep my Constance off her feet. It didn't take long for me to realize the two of you simply wouldn't suit. You need a woman of Rose's spunk."

"Amen." He nodded.

"It's not fair to judge her by her ramshackle appearance," Mrs. Busby quavered tearfully. "Her apron might be smudged, but it's because she's always cooking for someone or minding a child to help out."

"She has a gentle touch," he said softly.

"God looks on the heart, young man," Mrs. Lula Mae Evert declared.

"I'm glad He does, and Rose has the purest heart of anyone I've ever met; but I'm a man, and I'm more than pleased to look at her outward appearance. She's a charming woman."

"Well, then, if that's not your problem, then let me say: Time was, I felt scandalized at her willy-nilly, disorganized ways." Mrs. Sowell tapped him on the chest with the handle of her parasol. "But Rose's house would look neat as a pin if she wasn't always off helping someone else."

"Because she dusts for Mrs. Sneedly and washes Old Hannah's windows?" Garret held his ground. "Or because she spends all sorts of time minding her herb garden so Doc has curatives for folks?"

The women fell silent and exchanged baffled looks. Garret folded his arms akimbo. "You ladies don't need to champion Rose Masterson. I already have my heart set on her, but I had hoped to tell her so before the rest of the community knew."

"Then why did you give Cordelia a ring?"

"Cordelia was just trying on a ring so I could get the right size for Rose."

"Boy, do you all look like a flock of gossiping hens." Percy Watkins smirked from the post office.

"You all love Rose and were protecting her," Garret said diplomatically. "You've been her family, and I appreciate how you rushed to defend her. It does my heart good to see you all care for her so much, and as soon as I can declare my love to her instead of telling it to half of Buttonhole, we'll all celebrate. Now if you'll excuse me, I need some quiet time to pray and decide how to unravel this mess."

"I could go to her," Mrs. Kiersty offered.

"I'll handle this myself." His tone brooked no argument.

Garret fasted from his evening meal and prayed instead. Shortly thereafter, he headed toward Rose's house. A single light shone in the kitchen, but that proved she was home and awake, so he knocked on her door.

Rose barely opened the door a crack. Her nose was red, and her eyes held an ache that made his heart twist. She said nothing at all.

"Rose, we need to talk."

She shook her head.

Garret pushed the door open a bit farther. "Rosie—"

"I'm having my devotions."

"Come out on the veranda, and we'll share them. We haven't prayed together for a week and a half."

"No. Good-bye, Mr. Diamond."

"Garret. My name is Garret."

She tried to shut the door, but he wouldn't let her. Instead of struggling, she walked away. He could see her pick up her Bible and carry the lamp to the back part of the house.

Garret intentionally left the door open. He crossed the street, spoke with Hugo, then came back with a big washtub and a shovel. The moonlight and street gaslight fixture illuminated Rose's yard quite adequately. He went to the fence and started to work. The shovel bit into the ground.

"Garret Diamond, you stop that this very minute!"

Chapter 20

Rose stood in her doorway and stared at him in horror. It had taken every shred of her resolve and faith not to fall apart when he came to the door. Tears burned behind her eyes, and her nose tingled with suppressed emotion, but she'd managed to be civil and told him to leave. Barely. She'd wanted to run away from him; she'd wanted to throw herself into his arms. Honor and dignity forced her to turn and walk away. The sound of digging in her yard brought her back, though.

"Quit that!"

He ignored her. A hefty swoop, and the shovel bit the earth. He stomped on it a few times, then wiggled and removed the shovel, only to repeat the action in the dirt just inches to the right.

Rose ran out and grabbed his arm. Anger gave her strength. "Stop this. You can't do it. You can't. I won't let you."

"You already gave me permission."

Affronted by his galling lie, she shot back, "I most certainly did not!"

"I have the note you sent me. You gave me permission to do whatever I felt was appropriate for the Secret Giver. You even said you'd be a full partner. Well, Partner, you're donating these plants, and I'm giving my strength."

"You're not giving; you're taking away. You know how much these mean to Cordelia. Destroying them won't erase her memories of Jonathan. Don't do this. It'll hurt her."

Garret forced the shovel into the earth yet again, but he let go of the handle and wiped his hands on the sides of his trousers. "Cordelia is like a sister to me, Rose."

She wanted to believe him, but he'd given her every reason not to. She'd seen him place that ring on Cordelia's finger. Rose looked at him in silence. Meeting his eyes was almost impossible.

His hands cupped her face—just the way they had when he'd kissed her. A cry tore from her chest as she tried to jerk away, but he didn't let go.

"Rose, it's you I love. Didn't my kiss tell you that back at the bazaar?"

"That kiss," she whispered brokenly, "was nothing more than a moment of madness."

"Then I'm headed for a lifetime of insanity, because I'm counting on marrying you."

"You can't mean that. I saw you put that ring on Cordelia's finger, and she was thrilled. She said it was beautiful."

"I had two ulterior motives. Hugo asked me to see if there was a special ring she liked. Yes, he aims to propose."

Rose could barely understand what he said. Everything was so mixed up. A confused mind and an aching heart were a deadly combination.

"That's why I'm digging up the bindweed, Rosie. We're going to transplant it over to Hugo's yard. It's his way of letting Cordelia keep a bit of her past while making new memories with him."

"Oh, Garret—that is so precious!" *How wonderful it is for Cordelia to have a man love her like that.* With her next breath, Rose couldn't stop the purely selfish thought, *But why can't Garret love me with that same kind of burning devotion?*

"Hugo and Cordelia's courtship isn't the most important thing happening. Listen to me, Rose. The main reason I had Cordelia try on a ring was so I knew what size to get for you." He slipped his hand into a pocket and withdrew an ornate band with a sparkling diamond. "Rose Masterson, I'm head over heels in love with you. Marry me. I need you in my life—you're already in my heart. Be my helpmeet, my wife."

Her breath caught. She wanted to say yes so badly. Oh, how she wanted to. Instead, she forced herself to whisper, "You know nothing about me."

"I know all I need to know. You have a heart as big as heaven."

"I–I'm different. I can't keep my gloves or apron spotless, and my hair's always a fright. I'm not supposed to know it, but they call me and my house ramshackle. Did you know that?"

With his thumb, Garret brushed away the single tear she hadn't managed to blink away. He slowly, tenderly twirled his forefinger so some of her escaped wisps of hair curled into a ringlet by her left temple. The action made her weak in the knees.

"You're perfect the way you are, Rose. Your beauty is in how you don't fuss with the details and how you radiate with joy over everything. Your gloves are smudged because you hug grubby little boys who don't have a mother. Your apron is smeared because you cook and bake and cut flowers for others. Those aren't flaws, sweetheart. They're badges of love."

"You're just trying to be honorable. Of course you want a woman who is young and pretty and—"

Garret shook his head. He gazed at her steadily. "There are young women in town, and they're pretty in their own ways; but to me, they're all pretty boring, too. I want a woman with spirit and depth. I've fallen in love with a woman who is every bit as beautiful on the inside as she is on the out. I want you, Rose."

"But you don't know." The anguish she felt rang in her words.

He rested his forehead against hers as he invited, "Then tell me. Whatever it is, we'll work through it. I don't for a second believe God would give me this love for you if He wouldn't also give us strength to overcome any obstacle in our path."

"Could we sit down?"

"Sure, sweetheart." He walked her to the veranda and sat beside her on the small oak bench.

Rose steeled herself for what was to come. The lawyer hadn't spared her feelings when he'd explained her financial status. *There are two kinds of men—those who will want to marry you because of your money and those who won't want anything to do with you because you'll unman them when they discover you could buy and sell them a thousand times over.*

Garret crooked a finger under her chin and turned her face up toward his. "Folks here assumed you're an orphan and were never married. Is that right?"

"I've never been married. For that matter, my daddy never approved of anyone who came calling, so I've never been courted." She felt heat scorch her cheeks. "Until the bazaar, I'd never been kissed."

"There's only one man who's ever going to kiss you again, Rose. I'm that man."

Raw possession rang in his tone. Instead of making her feel afraid, it actually calmed her and gave her the courage to tell him a little more.

"Daddy's business necessitated a move to Georgia, so when he and Mama passed on, I was essentially on my own." When Garret didn't respond and continued to wait for her to say more, Rose tried to ease into the topic as carefully as she could. "I do have an aunt up in Boston. Other than that, Buttonhole is my family."

"Before the war," Garret responded, "my family was in the shipping business—the Newcombs. I have a few distant cousins in Boston. What's your aunt's last name?"

She couldn't hold his gaze. Her focus shifted downward.

"Rose," he asked very slowly, "is your last name really Masterson?"

After a prolonged silence, she grudgingly admitted, "It's Masterson-Cardiff. I chose to shorten it when I moved here." She glanced up to see how he was reacting to that news.

Garret stared at her for a long moment, then shook his head in disbelief. "You're the heiress of the Cardiff railroad fortune? Rose, you could travel the world and live in luxury, yet you choose to live in Buttonhole, Virginia?"

She pulled away from his touch. "It's where I'm happy." She braced herself for his reaction. He was too generous and honorable to be a greedy fortune hunter. That meant he was going to decide they were unsuitable matches after all.

Garret stretched his long legs out, cupped his hands behind his neck, and leaned his head back. The whole bench shook with his deep, throaty chuckle.

That was the last reaction she'd expected from him. Rose twisted on the bench and demanded, "Just what is so hilarious?"

"I was just thinking how much fun we're going to have. Sweetheart, the emporium is booming. I've made more of a profit in three months than the previous owner made in a year and a half. We can live very comfortably on what I make, and we can use the rest to play Secret Giver from now until the cows come home."

Rose stared at him in astonishment. He didn't care. He honestly didn't care that she had money or that tidiness eluded her. Then something in his expression shifted. Her heart skipped a beat.

"As long as we're trading secrets, there's something you ought to know."

She gulped, then lifted her chin. He'd had faith and love enough to stand by her. Well, she had faith and love enough to do the same for him. "You said with God's help, we'd make it through whatever obstacles lay in our path."

He let out a big sigh. "Rose, I'm just going to say it straight out."

She mentally braced herself for whatever dreadful information he needed to share.

"I hate peaches."

She blinked at him in utter amazement. "You hate peaches? Is that all?"

He shrugged. "Well, I've tried every trick in the book to be with you, and I've managed to avoid eating your peach stuff most of the time. I just can't imagine you spending all of that time and energy to make me peach cobbler when I'd rather have something else."

"What else would you like?"

His large, warm hand cupped the back of her neck as he leaned closer. "Your kisses are all the dessert I ever want or need." His breath washed over her, and Rose shivered at the delicious thrill of knowing he loved her. "Tell me you'll marry me," he said.

She scooted closer. "I love you, Garret. I'd be honored to be your wife."

"Then I'm ready for some dessert." He kissed her until her toes curled in her shoes, then slipped the ring on her finger.

❦

Four weeks later, Rose wore her mother's wedding gown. Cordelia was the matron of honor, and Hugo served as best man. Proud as could be, Zeb Hepplewhite walked Rose down the aisle to Wagner's "Wedding March"—played on the harmonica by Prentice.

No one mentioned that the bride's gloves had a smudge or that the groom's cuff links didn't match. Somehow it just seemed right. Mrs. Jeffrey and Cordelia had spent half the morning and an entire card of hairpins to anchor Rose's hair and veil into place. Zeb decided he needed a peck on the cheek before he gave her away, and the veil tilted a bit to the back while her hair shifted to the right.

"Would you like my wife to help fix you?" Reverend Jeffrey whispered.

Garret shook his head and took Rose's hand. "This is my girl. She doesn't need to be fixed because she's just right the way she is."

"Hair looks like Miss Rose now," Prentice said as he shoved his harmonica in the pocket of his new pants. "But are you sure that's who's under all of that?"

Garret raised his brows. Reverend Jeffrey shrugged, and Rose laughingly nodded. Garret lifted the veil and told her, "I have a feeling we're not going to always follow convention, but we'll always follow Christ and live in love."

They said their vows and sealed them with a kiss. The church's new bell pealed for the first time to celebrate the marriage, and the newlyweds went off to honeymoon in an undisclosed location.

Two months later, Mr. and Mrs. Garret Diamond returned from their honeymoon. Rose gasped as they drew up to the house. Gone was her old, tilted, peeling fence. In its place was a beautiful white picket fence. Someone had planted yellow climbing roses along it.

A fresh coat of paint covered the house, the gardens were all weeded, and the inside of the house was spick-and-span. No one admitted to having any part in these projects. Mr. Deeter shoved his hands in his pockets and said, "God's the source of everything. Folks 'round here know it."

Lula Mae nodded. "I guess maybe we all have a bit of the Secret Giver in us if we follow that Bible verse about giving without one hand knowing what the other's doing."

Garret nestled Rose close to his side. She smiled up at him. After they'd visited Niagara Falls and the Statue of Liberty, he'd surprised her with a trip to Chicago. They'd spent two days wandering through the huge Sears, Roebuck and Co. warehouse that was crammed with possibilities.

Now as they stood with their friends, Garret wondered what Rose would think when all of the books he'd ordered for a town library arrived. And as she gazed at the young rosebushes, Rose wondered what Garret would do this evening when she told him about the baby.

Restoration

For those who gave an unseen part of themselves away in service to our country and the women who love them through it all.
May the day come when wounds heal by the grace of God.

Chapter 1

Virginia, 1918

Tonight, when they're asleep, I'll burn it. Russell Diamond stared at his uniform in the drawer. He hadn't intended to find it, but now that he'd stumbled across it, Russell was certain of the action he had to take. No one would have to know—at least, not for a long while. By then, maybe he'd have the words to smooth over the whole situation.

The olive drabs looked so innocuous, all pressed and clean—just as they had the day he'd first put them on. By the time he got home, the uniform still held blood, mud, and sweat, as well as sea salt from the quick "laundering" it was given aboard the passenger liner the army used to transport the wounded back from Le Havre. Russell loved his country, but he hated war. He wanted no reminder of what he'd seen and done. For now, he took care to glide the bottom drawer of the walnut wardrobe shut and headed for the backyard.

Not many folks had an orchard for a backyard. Big, old, beautiful peach and apricot trees near the house gave way to younger apple trees farther away. Dad had planted a dozen of the apples the year he and Mom married—mostly because he didn't care for the taste of peaches.

Mom and Dad sat on the porch swing, sipping lemonade and enjoying the sunset. Russell didn't feel like talking, so he bobbed a curt nod and plowed on past them. His leg ached as he limped at his best speed. He knew he should have been warmer to his parents, but it wasn't in him. Instead of ruining their pleasant evening, he'd go off on his own. Snagging a pair of buckets and slipping out of sight, he hoped they'd assume he was off to weed a bit.

Among the trees, with peach, apricot, and nectarine blossoms drifting down on him in a gentle Virginia breeze, Russell sat on the ground and jerked weeds until the first pail overflowed. He set it aside and collected more to fill the second. The pain in his leg intensified, but he kept working. Coming across a withered apple core, Russell pitched it into the bucket with the bitter knowledge that he'd missed harvest this past year.

It's too late—or far too early, he thought wryly, *for even gathering any windfall.* Mom always took the bird-pecked or bruised fruit and turned it into sweet cider, cinnamon applesauce, peach jam. . .something. She could find the good in even the worst of situations. *But she was never in war.*

Russell continued to scan for weeds. Anything—anything to keep him busy so he wouldn't have to think.

He finally sat and leaned against a tree his father had planted the Sunday after Russell's birth. At twenty, it was vibrant and straight—a contrast to the dried up, gnarled way Russell felt inside. Home was just the same as always— Dad working at Diamond Emporium, Mom busy with charitable tasks and cooking far too much food. Sis had married one of Buttonhole's fine young men, and they'd be blessed with a baby in a few months. Folks visited over picket fences with their neighbors, bachelors still had a special pew at the back of the sanctuary, and old Mrs. Blanchard still missed about every fifth or sixth note as she played the piano in her parlor.

But I've changed. I'm different. I'll never be the same.

Pain rolled over him again. Russell closed his eyes and let his head fall back against the rough bark. Minutes passed; memories swelled. Everything suddenly shifted when a soft footstep sounded. Russell jolted and grabbed for a rifle that wasn't there.

"Son."

"Dad." He rasped that single word and tried to act casual as he pulled his arm back into his lap, but his heart still thundered.

Dad's step faltered; then he sauntered the last fifteen yards or so, weaving past trees. *He can't stride through his own orchard because of me—I've taken away the pleasure he always took in his evening strolls.*

In days gone by, Dad would have reached out to give a fatherly squeeze to Russell's shoulder, but he'd learned sudden moves and sounds set Russell on edge, so he didn't venture any form of touch. Russell ached for the missing contact.

"Your mother and I would like to talk with you."

"Yes, sir." *The time's come.* Russell got to his feet and walked in silence beside Dad until they reached the back porch. *Dad's slowing his pace to compensate for my limp.* Russell resented the need for it.

Mom, her hair in its usual mussed bun and her apron slightly askew, patted the seat of the porch swing next to her. He sat there, and she handed him a glass of lemonade.

"Thanks, Mom."

Russell could feel her studying him in the waning light. Dad set to lighting a lamp. Unable to look them in the eyes, Russell watched his father's hands as he performed the simple task. Once done, Dad sat on an old wooden chair.

"You're hurting, Son—and I'm not talking about your leg."

Russell shifted his gaze and stared at a droplet of water meandering down the side of his glass. His father's quiet words were so typical of him—direct, open, and unadorned. The very stark quality of them made the truth all that much more painful. The distraction of watching such a mundane thing allowed Russell to consider a response. Finally he opted for honesty. "Yes."

"We knew going away would. . .be hard on you." Mom practiced no artifice, and her candor and sincerity had been qualities he'd come to admire very early on. It tore at him that she felt the need to measure her words so carefully.

Until this evening, he hadn't known she'd also been watching her actions just as cautiously. Mom hadn't washed and hung his uniform back in his wardrobe; she'd laundered it and quietly slipped it away in the bottom of the wardrobe in Sis's old room. If he hadn't been looking for the battered old valise they kept in the drawer, he wouldn't have seen the painstakingly folded olive drab pants and shirt just awhile ago.

Russell chugged down the lemonade, mostly because it bought him a few more moments. He set aside the glass, then looked from one parent to the other. "I mean no disrespect. This is hard." He drew in a deep breath. "I can't stay here anymore."

Mom wrapped both of her arms around his right arm and leaned her head on his shoulder. She was holding on tight, just as she had the evening before he took the train to leave as a soldier. "You haven't finished healing yet. The cast just came off. Wait. Stay just a little while until you're more stable."

He'd known she'd resist his plan, but Russell still knew what he had to do. Dad searched his eyes, and Russell couldn't take the scrutiny. He looked away and subtly shook his head. Waiting was out of the question.

"Have you prayed about it?" His father's face looked drawn.

Russell couldn't lie, even though he knew the truth would burden them. He'd not taken the matter to God—in fact, he and the Almighty were on very shaky terms. "No."

Mom gasped, and Russell knew he'd let her down. Her voice showed it when she finally said in a strained tone, "Aw, honey."

Mom's faith was deep and dear to her; he'd strayed from the path of righteousness. It was one of the biggest reasons he couldn't live here.

"You should still stay, Russell." She rubbed her cheek on his shoulder. "It takes time when a man's been hurt for his body and soul to settle with all he's gone through. We understand. It doesn't change how we feel about you."

Russell gently separated from her and stood. He and his father exchanged a momentary look—one that silently agreed to shield Mom from as much of the pain as they could. Russell dipped his head and pressed a kiss on her hair. "I love you, too." The scent of peaches and cloves that always clung to her gave him a scrap of comfort.

Dad took a deep breath and let it out slowly. "We have something else to discuss."

Though he wanted to escape to the solitude of his bedroom, Russell forced himself to sit back down on the swing. One last night, he'd sit here. He'd discipline himself to pretend things weren't so bad. It was the least he could do.

"A letter came today," Dad said. "My great-uncle Timothy passed on. The family house belonged to him. He boarded up the place, and no one's lived in it for several years. The day we learned you were coming home, he wrote his will and left the house and all of his wealth to you, Russell."

"Money won't cure what ails me."

"No, it won't." Dad sighed. "And I'm glad you have the wisdom to see that, but you said you need to leave. You'll always have a place to come back to here, but in the meantime, you have a home and funds to take care of yourself."

Russell nodded. Words seemed futile, and Mom seemed far too fragile.

Mom tilted her head and looked up at him. She tried her best to give him a brave smile even though tears glossed her eyes. "Think on this more. Sleep on it. Your dad and I will pray." Pain radiated from her as she added, "If you still feel you have to go, we'll be supportive."

They all sat together as night engulfed the yard. Crickets chirped and cicadas whirred. The wind soughed through the branches. He'd left as a boy and come back a man—but for this one evening, Russell relished the one thing that he'd not been stripped of: the unvarnished, uncomplicated, unconditional love of his family.

If he stayed here, the ache in his soul would ruin that. He knew he had to go.

❧

Crack! Lorelei Goetz looked down at the two pieces of glass in her hand and grimaced. They hadn't broken along the line she'd scored. Setting down the smaller segment, she focused her attention on the larger. If she tapped it a bit more with the ball end of her scoring tool, she might still get the cut.

Minuscule glass slivers caught the sunlight pouring in through her workroom window, turning the edge of her table into a kaleidoscope of red, gold, and blue. She paused for a second to appreciate the prisms the clear shards added to the mix. Papa had called them the beams of joy. He'd taught her the art of stained glass, and at times like this, it was bittersweet to see the beauty but not have him here to share it.

"You start early today, *Ja?*"

Lorelei looked over her shoulder and smiled. "Ja, Mama. I'd like to finish this window a few days early if I can. Mr. Grun said he'd be going to Portsmouth next week, and he'd be willing to deliver it for me."

He mother smiled and nodded. "*Wunderbar!* He will be very careful. Herr Grun is a kind man."

Lorelei turned back to the glass. "Yes, Mama, he is." She paused a moment, then added in a firm tone, "It doesn't mean I'm going to pack up and go marry his cousin in South Dakota. This is our home—yours and mine. We're staying here."

Mama clucked her tongue. "You are a pretty girl, my Lori. There is no reason for you to spend your days breaking glass and putting it back together when you could be married and having babies. Your papa would want you to."

"Yes," Lorelei agreed pensively. "Papa would have been a wonderful grandpa."

Taking advantage of the opening, her mother rushed to add, "I was married and had you by the time I was your age."

"Twenty isn't old, Mama, and Papa also wanted me to find a man who would love me the way he loved you. He told me not to settle on anything less than a perfect fit—not in a window, not in my marriage."

"If only he were here. He would talk sense into you. There is a difference between wishes and wisdom, Lori."

She turned around. "Mama, what's wrong?"

Her mother came into the workroom and perched on a wooden stool. She looked like a chickadee—a plump, compact woman with brown and gray hair; she wore a faded gray apron over a brown and black dress. Instead of folding her arms as she'd normally do, she shoved them into the apron pocket—a sure sign she was worried. Instead of speaking, she shrugged.

Lorelei set down the glass, blew on her hands to remove any glass slivers, then went to her mother. "Mama, we have each other."

"But we have little else!" Her mother blurted out the words, then bit her lip.

"You're worried about money?"

"Yes, but more—I'm worried about you. So many still look at us as the enemy."

The injustice of that hurt. Papa had gone to fight for America, yet because they had German ancestors, still spoke German at home, and had a German last name, folks reviled them. It wasn't until after Papa died and the government sent a soldier in a fancy uniform to give them shiny medals in Papa's honor that many of the townspeople finally shifted from hostility to wariness.

"There are hard feelings—ones that won't fade for a long time. Too many of the young men refuse to be seen with a German girl even just for a date. They won't want you for a wife." Mama pasted on a smile. "If you go to South Dakota, you will have a husband and children."

"Arranged marriages ended in the Dark Ages. I'm happy here with you. We'll pray that if God has a husband in mind for me, He'll bring him to our doorstep."

Mama shook her head. "What am I to do with you? Men are not like bottles of milk that get delivered to your porch."

Lorelei laughed and gave her mother a peck on the cheek. "Last Sunday, the pastor told us to seek God's will and to pray specifically, in faith."

Mama finally pulled her hands out of her apron pocket and rubbed her legs. "Child, I'm going to end up with flat knees from all of the hours I spend kneeling in prayer for you."

Chapter 2

S on." His father's voice carried grim determination. "I want a promise from you."

Russell stood near the backyard porch steps, by the barrel Mom grew strawberries in. He plucked a dried leaf from one of the plants. Mom was inside, putting together some food for him to take. From how red and puffy her eyes had looked at breakfast, he knew she'd been up half the night weeping. He'd come out here because. . .well, because.

"You write your mom. Let her know how you're doing."

Swallowing hard, Russell lifted his chin and stared at Dad. He gave a curt nod. "You have my word."

"And you have my word that if you need me, I'll be there. If it would help, I'm ready to come along right now—just me. I have a sense that you're fighting mightily to shield Mom from things."

Knocking the heel of his hand against the barrel, Russell cleared his throat. Dad had built the emporium from a failing, little, backwater shop into a thriving concern. For him to be willing to leave it all at the drop of a hat underscored the love he felt. "Dad, I appreciate the offer, but you were right last night. I have to be alone."

"Son, you're not alone; God is with you."

"I told you last night—I'm not talking to God anymore."

"I heard you." His dad came down the steps and plucked a strawberry. He dusted it off gently and popped it into his mouth.

He chose the fresh, sweet berry; I'm standing here clutching the dead leaf. Russell let out a bitter laugh.

Dad shoved his hands in his pockets and didn't take offense at Russell's mirthless reaction. "It's not your leg that's troubling you; it's the ugliness you endured. It's a soldier's burden, one I hoped you'd be spared. My great-uncle Tim was battle scarred and struggled mightily with his feelings and his faith."

"I don't remember much of him—just that he didn't get married until he was real old."

"He took what little was left of the family shipping business after the war and threw himself into rebuilding it. Business and the sea were his lifeblood, but his escape—his refuge—was the old family house."

"He left it."

"Originally, he went back home after the war. With time, he finally found peace there. When his wife developed consumption, the doctor recommended they move. It wasn't until then he left. You'll find peace there, Son. I have faith."

"I heard old Mr. Sibony has a matched pair of geldings he wants to sell." Russell hoped his father would go along with the change of subject. "I figure I'll just ride to the coast."

Shortly thereafter, with a blanket tied to the rear of his saddle and packs tied to the second gelding, Russell left Buttonhole. Following the directions he'd been given, he rode for two days until he passed through a seaside town and arrived at the outskirts where the road branched off. To the right, he spotted a charming little cottage with two chimneys, a budding garden, and sheets on the clothesline, snapping in the stiff breeze. That breeze also carried a woman's voice.

He didn't want to deal with others, so instead of following the curving dirt road, he cut across a spread that once must have been a well-kept lawn. He could see stables in the distance off another fork in the road, but ahead loomed the old Newcomb house.

Russell halted the horses near a clump of overgrown shrubs and studied the house. He listened intently for any sounds of inhabitants and heard none. Not a single track or footprint marred the earth. Satisfied the place hadn't been approached from this direction, he tethered the geldings and reconnoitered on foot.

He continued to scan the ground for signs of footprints and the windows for faces or moving curtains. Several of the windows were cracked. A few panes were missing entirely. What glass remained intact looked murky with age-old, undisturbed dust. *Good. No one's been here.*

Water would be his most basic need, so he strode down a weed-encrusted cobblestone path to a well. Someone had wisely fitted a cover over the well for safety's sake. Russell nodded approvingly. He dragged it to the side, looked about for a rope and bucket, and realized neither was present. Inhaling deeply, he could smell the sweet, damp aroma of fresh water. He flipped a small stone in and heard a satisfying splash.

Russell made his way to the front of the house and allowed himself to look up and assess the architecture. It must have once been a graceful place—a large antebellum mansion meant for rearing a big family. It would accommodate sizable crowds, and from family stories he'd heard, the Newcombs had done considerable entertaining.

The roof lacked a plethora of shingles, warning Russell the inside undoubtedly suffered water damage. Some of the upper story's windows were cracked; a few were even missing. The ground-floor windows had been boarded up, and sections of clapboard on the seaward side of the house looked thoroughly rotten.

The veranda sagged here and there.

It looks like I feel.

Dad had told him his great-uncle had found refuge here after the ravages of the War Between the States. *It can be my hideaway now, too. There's plenty of work to be done, and it doesn't matter how long it takes.*

Russell trod carefully—not just because of his leg, but because the steps and veranda sported broken or missing planks. He curled his hands around a gray, weathered board and yanked. Nails squealed, and the piece pulled free. After that, he pried two more slashes of wood free and revealed a leaded-glass window. Russell rubbed dirt from the panes and peered inside.

Cloth lay over a lump he presumed to be a piece of furniture, looking like a gray-shrouded ghost. This had to be the foyer. *How did I imagine I'd find refuge in this desolate old place?*

Russell plotted a course across the veranda and yanked several boards down from across the front door. Whoever had driven the nails in had meant them to stay. It took considerable effort to clear the door. When revealed, the entrance boasted a matching pair of panels that bore elegant carvings of dogwood blossoms. The doors showed no evidence of a lock, but Russell still expected significant resistance when he simultaneously twisted and pushed both door handles. To his great surprise, though, the doors groaned loudly, then swung open with ease.

Russell forced himself not to press against the doorway, to pan across the foyer with his rifle. The fact that he didn't have his rifle had a lot to do with why he refrained from the action. The habits he'd developed to survive had become ingrained. Russell wondered if he'd ever get over feeling the need to exercise such extreme vigilance. He entered the house, then closed the doors behind himself.

And promptly sneezed.

The sound echoed up the great wooden staircase, into all of the rooms, then died out. Dust, inches thick, covered every surface in sight. Not a footprint marred the floors; no handprints disturbed the stair rails or doorsills. Enveloped in nothing but dust and silence, Russell closed his eyes and let his shoulders slump. At least he'd found the solitude he craved.

∽

"It's beautiful," Mama said in a hushed voice as she looked at the nearly finished window on Lorelei's worktable.

Lorelei painstakingly rubbed one of the hand-painted segments with a soft cotton rag. She'd spent hours on that one piece because the angel's wings needed to convey the shelter of God's provision of protection. "I'm happy with the way it turned out."

"Your papa would be so proud."

Lorelei ached as she heard the tears in her mother's voice. The pain of losing him was still fresh. "It makes me feel close to him, working on these windows. I sent him a sketch of this one in my last letter."

Mama hugged her. They huddled close in the workshop, surrounded by a pair of sturdy tables, frames, lead cames, pieces of glass, and assorted tools of the trade. Papa had loved working on church windows, and they both felt surrounded by echoes of his love whenever they were in the workshop.

When Papa had gone to war, they couldn't afford to stay in town. Rent was too high. Then, too, having a German last name and accent didn't exactly make them welcome. A friend of Lorelei's had told them about this cottage. Lorelei had walked out to it that very day, looked over the little cottage, and decided it would suit their needs admirably. As far as she was concerned, the workshop cinched the deal.

She'd found the attorney who handled the property, and he'd gotten special permission from the old man who owned the place to rent it. The rent was ridiculously low, and Lorelei suspected it was a move of compassionate pity; but since the budget looked grim and orders for windows were slow, she'd thanked God and signed the papers for a long-term lease.

She'd worried she'd lose that special feeling of being close to Papa when they moved, but her fears were unfounded. Even Mama, after they'd settled the last soldering rod into place, remarked that it all felt "right."

"Did you know," Mama whispered in a tight voice, "after we lost Johann Junior, your papa painted his face for an angel in the church window?"

Lorelei gave her mother a playful squeeze. "Not until he and I went to Richmond to install another window at that church. I saw it and asked Papa why he'd painted my pesky brother as an angel."

Mama pushed away and clucked her tongue in her special way that she used to try to induce shame.

"You're not fooling me, Mama. You only make that sound when you know you'll end up laughing if you talk!"

"Oh, my Lori." Mama reached up and patted Lorelei's cheek. "You are God's gift to me. When the shadows of life fall across my heart, you cast them away with your sunny laugh."

"Let's hope my laugh lasts long enough for us to run out and get the sheets off the line. It looks like we're about to get a spring shower!"

They scampered outside. Lorelei ran ahead while her mother grabbed the wicker laundry basket. By the time Mama met her by the clothesline, she'd gathered the slips and underwear they'd made from carefully bleached flour sacks and pillowcases. Lorelei dumped them into the basket, then started whipping the clothespins off one end of the sheet while Mama dislodged them from the other. Ocean winds were unreliable and often grew brisk enough to sweep any unsecured items right off the line, so they'd learned to secure everything—just in case.

She and Mama had the simple chore down to a quick routine. She matched the two bottom corners while Mama matched the two top ones. They'd snap the sheet, fold it in half lengthwise again, then meet in the middle. Today, as the first sprinkles hit, they dumped that sheet into the basket instead of finishing the folds.

Lorelei laughed as she skidded around the clothesline and yanked the next sheet. Her action sent clothespins pinging into the air like crickets.

"Your Sunday dress! Get it first," Mama called as she pulled her own Sunday-best black skirt free from the pins.

The skies opened up with a flash shower. They threw the last few items into the basket, each grabbed a handle, and they ran to the house. Mama stared at the basket, then scowled at Lori. "In South Dakota, they would not have storms from the ocean."

"In South Dakota, they don't have sunrises over the ocean, either."

"Hmpf."

Lorelei pretended Mama's reaction was to the top layer of laundry that had gotten soggy. "I'll help you hang up whatever is still damp. I have some twine in the workshop."

"You will do more on that window. I will hang the clothes." Mama wrinkled her nose. "I'll let you do the ironing later while I read the Bible."

"I ought to have time to do that later this afternoon since God is watering the garden for us." Lorelei took a few steps closer to the window and tilted her head as if doing so would help her see around a clump of trees. "I thought I saw a man walking a horse."

"Sweetheart, no one would be out in this rain, walking a horse—riding one, maybe." Mama raised her hands, palms upward in a who-knows gesture. "But not walking it. If the horse were lame, the man would have stopped back at the Rimmons' instead of coming up this old road."

Lorelei didn't see anything more. German Americans suffered all sorts of persecution, and the newspaper habitually carried articles denouncing the "Huns." Since they'd moved out here, no one had bothered them, but Lorelei still felt wary.

"Usually, I am the one who worries," Mama teased. "I tell you, no one is out there."

"I suppose you're right." Still, Lorelei folded her arms and tried to rub away the shivery feeling that wasn't from the rain.

Chapter 3

Pure, sweet, clean rain. Russell had just finished walking through the entire house, including the attic, when the spring storm hit. He'd moved from room to room, shutting doors in hopes that the stiff breeze wouldn't find too many cracks and blow the dust around that had him sneezing repeatedly. He'd have to tackle the chambers one at a time, collecting the worst of the grime before he tried to air out the house. He'd grown up doing a lot of dusting and cleaning for Dad at the emporium; he knew the routine well.

Russell headed for the kitchen, having decided that he could open the large windows and push open the door. The draft ought to race through and blast out a fair bit of the mess. An ancient straw broom in a small closet by the pantry came in handy. He used it to dislodge a pair of massive cobwebs that swagged like fishing nets from the ceiling to the stove and worktable. He'd need somewhere to set his gear, so he whisked off the tabletop and cast aside the broom.

Unsteady due to his healing leg, he loped outside toward the shrubs to fetch the geldings. "Hey, boys." The large workhorses lifted their heads and snuffled. "You've kept busy, haven't you?" Russell stroked the closest one's damp withers.

The horses didn't mind the rain in the least. From the looks of the uneven grasses, they'd satisfied themselves by foraging. "Come on. I have a place in mind for you." He'd not checked out the stable yet, and Russell refused to keep his mounts there until it was cleared out and held fresh water. The horses obediently walked along as Russell led them to an ivy-covered overhang off the small wing near the kitchen. Half a dozen old, large urns lay there, tipped on their sides. Russell dumped out what little dirt remained in them, then set them upright to collect the downpour from the roof. He swiftly unburdened the first horse of the saddle and the second one of the bundles, then went back inside.

The pump in the kitchen needed to be primed, but he rather doubted it would work even then. The gaskets and cups inside must have rotted out long ago. Determined to work through the fiery pain in his leg, Russell dragged a tottering wooden chair toward the cabinets. He dropped heavily onto it, then jerked open each drawer and cupboard within reach.

A single plate. A chipped mug. A coffee can filled with mismatched knives and forks. . .battered pieces. *Like me.* He gathered them into a pile and left them when he happened along a set of large mixing bowls. Russell swiped the bowls under the water cascading from the roof, then started collecting drinking water in them.

That task accomplished, he recalled other receptacles he'd spotted during his tour. Soon his odd collection of pans, wash pitchers, two slop jars, a metal milk pail, and a battered steel washtub sat in strategic spots throughout the house, catching leaks. It made for an odd symphony of pings, drips, and drumming sounds, but something about it took the edge off his restlessness.

Aware he couldn't clean the whole place in a single day, Russell decided to focus on the largest bedchamber upstairs. The dust nearly choked him, so he tied a kerchief over his nose and mouth, then yanked the fancy draperies from the rods. He dragged them across the floor to help get rid of a goodly portion of the grit, then dropped them over the banister into a heap on the floor of the foyer. Just that small amount of handling had the fabric disintegrating.

"What am I doing?" His words echoed in the house as he looked down at the billowing dust he'd sent into the air. "I'm not going to find peace here."

Thunder boomed over the roof.

I have nowhere else to go. May as well make this place habitable. Russell figured he'd do better to shake out a blanket or sheet and hang it over the window. He thought of the sheets he'd seen on the neighbor's clothesline and felt a pang of envy for how fresh and clean they'd be. He'd be sleeping wrapped in a blanket tonight—much as he had in the trenches.

Russell shook off that awful analogy, surveyed the room, and quickly settled on priorities. He retrieved the broom and used it to sweep down the walls. Cobwebs and dirt banished, the walls looked the same shade as the sky when it went from blue to that first tint of twilight lavender. The floor was, to his relief, sound as could be. It creaked here and there, but that didn't much matter. He could fill the spots with talcum to solve that paltry irritation.

Russell limped about, using the water collected from the leaks to sluice off the bedroom floor. He quickly swept out the tiled upstairs washroom and bathtub, then used the next round of water to do a cursory wash down of that room, too.

Clothes damp from rainwater and sweat, Russell sat on the old tub's edge. *At least no one is here to witness how weak I am.* The notion of being out of shape stuck in his craw. Tall, broad-shouldered, and well-muscled, he'd never been limited. *I refuse to give in now.* He shoved away from the tub and left the room, his uneven gait ringing like a never-ending taunt on the tiled floor.

He braced himself in the door to the hallway. *This is my haven? This? Supposedly Uncle Timothy found contentment here, but I can't see how. Maybe he was just better at fooling folks into thinking he was at peace. He left it behind as empty and forgotten as a snake leaves its old skin.*

Russell's leg ached abominably, but he refused to acknowledge it. He headed for the kitchen, opened the door, and saw the horses contentedly drinking out of the rain. He stuck his hands out into the rain, scrubbed his face, and turned back toward the house. Mom had slipped in some of those little tablets she considered to be cure-alls. He shook two of the Bayer aspirin into his palm, shuddered at the bitter taste, and washed them down with rainwater.

Hungry, Russell unwrapped the last two slices of bread Mom had sent along. He had canned provisions, as well, but for now, he didn't much care what he ate. No matter what he put in his mouth, it all tasted like sawdust. Even Mom's famous peach jam failed to give him any pleasure.

Russell looked about the kitchen and let out a deep sigh. This old place was a filthy hulk. His survey of the structure showed the roof and veranda needed immediate and extensive attention, but the rest of the house was fairly sound.

He didn't dare try to start a fire in one of the fireplaces or the stove. Even if there weren't nests in the flues or stovepipe, he didn't have much in the way of usable fuel. Then, too, the wooden structure was dry as could be. One spark, and the whole place would become a torch. He'd need to varnish, paint, and polish the place from top to bottom to protect it.

Time. It would take time—not just days or weeks, but months. That was okay with him. He had the time. He needed the time. *Even after I restore every last inch of this old house, I'm not sure I'll find this place to be a refuge.*

The drumming and pinging in the pots called him back to action. Using the broom as a cane of sorts, he grabbed his baggage and limped back upstairs. The water went into the tub; then he set the pans back in place to catch more.

Russell ventured back into one of the smaller bedrooms. Gritting his teeth against a wave of pain, he leaned against the doorframe and rested a moment. He bent forward, kneaded his thigh to break a cramp, and grunted as he straightened up.

After knocking his way through gargantuan cobwebs, Russell pulled out a dismantled metal bed frame and dragged the parts to his bedchamber where he put the pieces back together. A bedroom door lay across the springs. He sat on it. "Rock hard," he groused. "You'd think they'd have left at least one decent mattress behind."

He'd worn himself out. Russell unrolled both thick wool blankets, used them to form a mattress, then pulled a jacket over himself for a cover. He stared out the window at the rain and realized it was only midafternoon.

Unaccustomed to being unwell, he'd pushed himself all morning in an effort to tamp down any memories or thoughts. Now he'd pay for it. The rest of the day and night stretched ahead, and he had nothing to occupy his hands. Against his will, his mind started heading down the tormenting paths he'd worked so hard to avoid.

✎

"Mama, I'm sure someone is up at the big house."

"You said that yesterday, and then the Rimmons' boy came by, looking for their cow."

Lorelei shrugged. "I know."

"So why are you so jumpy? Do you feel we are not safe out here, away from the town?"

"I wouldn't have rented the cottage if I thought we weren't going to be safe, Mama."

Mama bobbed her head in agreement. She sliced cabbage into thin ribbons—some to be coleslaw, the rest to become sauerkraut. She snorted. "Besides, no one would come here to make trouble. That old house is a wreck, and we're too poor to rob."

"The way you're wielding that knife, no one would dare bother us."

"I'd offer them some of my coleslaw and make the enemy my friend, just as the Bible tells me to."

Lorelei shredded carrots. "Where does the Bible talk about coleslaw?"

Mama tried not to smile, but her eyes twinkled. She set down the knife and drummed her fingers on the cutting board. "You shouldn't concern yourself with that. Concentrate on where the Bible talks about children respecting their parents and girls getting married."

Dumping the carrots into the bowl with the cabbage, Lorelei teased, "Mama, don't tell me the Bible mentions South Dakota along with your coleslaw."

Mama pursed her lips and pretended to think on it for a minute. "Remember in Proverbs where it says a meal of herbs in harmony is better than a fatted calf with a contentious wife?"

"I thought we were praying for God to deliver a man to our porch."

"Oh, so that is why you keep thinking you see a man."

Mama's sly look made Lorelei shiver. "Mama, you'd better not be doing anything more than praying. If I find out you've been trying to help God by playing matchmaker, I'm going to be perturbed."

"When have I had a chance to be a matchmaker?" Mama tossed mayonnaise and only a skimpy bit of sugar into the bowl, then started to stir. "Once a week, we go to church. The iceman and the milkman come to make deliveries, but they are both married. I'm going to go to my grave without ever becoming a grandmother."

Lorelei dipped a fork into the bowl, swiped a sample of the coleslaw, and ate it. "Since you're hinting that we have only a matter of hours or days left before God calls us home, I'd go to my grave happy, having tasted your cooking. It's heavenly."

"Heaven should be filled with the sound of children laughing, not the taste of a humble salad."

Though they carried on the conversation as if it were a lark, Lorelei knew her mother was serious. She'd been talking about the future and marriage nonstop ever since Monday's storm. Once Mama got a notion in her mind, it was there to stay. Unwilling to continue the conversation, Lorelei took off her apron and hung it on the hook behind the kitchen door. "It'll be another thirty minutes before the casserole is done cooking. I'll go work on that window a bit more."

"You do that. Be sure to keep your eyes open for that strange man."

"So you do think someone's here!"

Mama shook her head. "No, Lori, I don't." She turned away and added in a pained voice, "It would be nice to have a man at our table again."

In the months since Papa had left, then after they learned he'd died, Lorelei discovered that Mama would turn to her if she wanted consolation. When Mama spun around the other way, she wanted to be left alone. Respecting her mother's desire for privacy, Lorelei slipped outside.

Lord, this hurts so badly. I miss Papa terribly, and Mama pretends she is okay when I know her heart is broken. Please help us.

Chapter 4

"Mabel, get on out here." While the storekeeper shouted those words, he kept staring at Russell.

A rawboned woman muttered something under her breath as she came out of the back room. A two-inch brooch secured a red, white, and blue ribbon to her bodice. Russell didn't have to see the picture on the brooch to know it was their son. He braced himself for what he knew would come next.

"We got us a soldier!" The storekeeper came around the counter, headed for Russell, and rubbed his hands in delight. "I can tell by the set of your shoulders— that military bearing is unmistakable."

Russell's stomach started to churn. He hadn't thought to eat before he came, and the emptiness in his belly underscored how little he cared about even the most basic things now. *I just want to buy some stuff and leave.*

The woman shocked Russell when she threw herself at him and hugged him like a long-lost son. "You dear boy! Where were you? Did you meet my Herbert?"

"Herbert Molstead. He's with the First Division." The storekeeper's voice rang with pride. "Eighteenth Infantry Regiment."

Russell awkwardly patted the woman even though he wanted nothing more than to get out of there. "Sorry. I was with the Twenty-eighth."

"Oh." Disappointment creased her face, but she still clung to him.

"Twenty-eighth? That's under Bullard! We got us a whiz-bang hero, Mabel. They beat the socks off the Krauts at Cantigny." The man stood a bit straighter and stuck out his hand. "A pleasure to be in your company, young man."

Still patting the woman with his left hand, Russell reached out and shook hands. "Sir."

"Mabel, turn loose of him and let him tell us all about it."

The last thing Russell wanted to do was talk about the war. These people wanted to hear stories about glory and victory; his memories were gory and vicious. He gently pulled free and indicated the brooch. "What do you hear from Herbert?"

"That boy." Mabel Molstead tsked. "He said he's up to his ankles in mud all of the time."

"Trenches," her husband added knowingly. "Mama's sure he'll catch a cold. She sent him socks."

"I'm sure he'll appreciate them." Russell wanted out of there. He quickly revised his plans. Not wanting to let anyone know he'd taken up residence, he'd ridden to a town just north in order to buy supplies.

On the way there, he'd decided to buy a buckboard so he could haul a mattress back to the estate. Knowing the buckboard would enable him to transport supplies made it a good investment, and the thought of having a comfortable, soft mattress lightened his mood.

Now those things didn't matter. What he needed most was to get away.

"Oh! Oh, mercy me. You would still be over there unless. . ." Mrs. Molstead's voice died out.

Mr. Molstead cleared his throat. "Yes, well, then. We've been nattering on, and I didn't even ask what you came in to buy."

"Just a few basics." Russell spied a folding cot and reached for it. "Do you have bread, or is there a local bakery?"

Ten minutes—an eternity—later, he secured packs to one horse and mounted up on the other.

"Here, son. The missus wanted you to have this." Mr. Molstead held up a pair of home-knit socks.

"Much obliged." Russell forced a smile, nodded, and rode off. He'd barely accomplished a thing coming here. No mattress, scant repair materials, and the groceries would last only a few days—especially since he didn't have an icebox. At least he'd gotten parts to repair his pump.

Since his last name was Diamond, the Molsteads wouldn't connect him with the Newcomb family or house. He'd still have his refuge. That and the thought of sleeping on the cot gave Russell grim satisfaction.

❦

"I can see what you mean, Miss Goetz." The sheriff frowned at the big old house. "Someone's definitely torn down most of the boards. Footprints are fresh, too. I'll go in and take a look-see."

Lorelei nodded. As soon as the sheriff crossed the veranda and stepped foot into the mansion, she scampered up behind him.

"Miss, you'd best not come in here. No telling what I'll find."

"You've taken the county championship for pistol marksmanship for the past three years, Mr. Clem."

His chest puffed out a bit. "Could be whoever's squatting here is outside. Stay close so I know where you are."

"All right." Chills chased down her spine. Lorelei glanced about the entryway.

"Only one fella," the sheriff whispered. "See? One set of boot prints. Dust in here is thick. He's got a bum leg—see how the stride's uneven?"

"Looks like he's gone upstairs a few times." Dust still coated the stairs, but in a very thin layer that bore fresh scuffle marks.

"We'll check downstairs first." Sheriff took his pistol from the holster. "You stay right behind me. Even if he's not here right now, no telling if the floorboards are rotten."

Lorelei felt a spurt of relief that he'd thought of that potential problem. She'd been gawking around from the moment she'd entered and now paid more attention to the floor. She tapped her toe, sending puffs of dust swirling about her worn shoes. "This is marble."

Sheriff started toward the left. "Typical enough of these old houses. Rest of the place ought to be fancy wood floors. No linoleum in the olden days, you know."

"I'd not thought of such a thing." She carefully followed his footsteps through a parlor, then into what must have been a ballroom. The long room at the back of the house where the windows overlooked the ocean held an enormous buffet and a few chairs. "They must have had splendid suppers here."

"Kitchen's likely through these doors." Sheriff Clem cast her a warning look. "The evidence from the outside and the footprints show he's been in there a fair bit. You stay back." A minute later, he called, "It's okay in here."

So far, the rest of the downstairs hadn't been disturbed in ages. Gray tan dust clung to every surface, giving a dismal air to what once must have been exceptional beauty. She couldn't tell what furniture formed the lumpy shapes under canvas sheets. The sheriff didn't bother to search beneath them because none of the footsteps that stood out in shocking relief on the floors ever approached the abandoned pieces.

Lorelei couldn't believe the difference as she sidled into the kitchen. Clean. The walls, counter, and floor gleamed from a fresh scrubbing. The iron cookstove off to the side was big enough to prepare food for an army. A small hodgepodge of dishes peeked through the glass-fronted doors on one cabinet, and stacks of canned food, neat as a row of soldiers, sat in another.

"Whoever this is, is planning to stay a good long while." The sheriff nosed into the pantry and tilted his head toward another door. "Best be getting on with the search."

An entrance to the other wing hadn't been traversed, so they bypassed it and peeked through the rest of the downstairs, including what had to be one of the most dismal sights Lorelei had ever seen: book-filled shelves in a library, a treasure trove left ignored in the passage of time.

Once upstairs, they discovered the squatter had trundled up and down the hall a few times, but the most noteworthy thing was that he'd scoured the master bedchamber and made it into his own place. A bureau, a table-sized Turkish rug, and a cot showed the mysterious occupant had made an effort to create a tidy, functional place for himself.

"See that cot? Made up right and tight—the military way. We got us a soldier boy here, Miss Goetz. Gotta be careful. Some men go to war and come back teched in the head. Could be a dangerous situation. I'll see if I can't catch this fella, but until I do, you and your mama might be wise to stay in town."

Lorelei stood in the room and closed her eyes. Sadness swamped her. She opened them and blinked away the tears that threatened. "Whoever this is, he has been here awhile and never bothered us."

"Never know." Sheriff Clem shook his head ponderously and escorted her out of the room. "I reckon you and your mother can ask around to see who'll take you in for a few days until I can come back and lie in wait for this soldier boy. I've got me some important things to do for the rest of the week. 'Bout middle of next week, I could see my way clear to coming to set a trap for this trespasser."

Her step faltered at the top of the stairs. She stopped and pled, "Must we do anything? Maybe he just needs to rest awhile before he's on his way."

"Trespassing is a crime—and before you let that tender heart of yours come up with excuses, no one had to post signs. The boards on the doors and windows gave the message loud and clear."

They descended the gritty stairs and went back outside. Sheriff kicked one of the boards that must've once blocked the front door. "Suppose I'd be ten kinds a fool to bother tacking that back up. If he's just resting up, he'd best be gone by next week." His brows beetled, and he gave her a meaningful look.

"I'll talk to Mama and see what she thinks."

He nodded. "You do that, Miss Goetz. It shouldn't take you long to pack a few necessities and walk to town."

The sheriff mounted up and tipped his hat. He rode off down the lawn and across past the shrubs and took the shortcut to town through the wooded area. For all of his warnings and concerns, he'd not offered to give Lorelei a ride back to her cottage.

She hadn't expected him to. He had two sons in the American Expeditionary Force "over there." Like so many townsfolk, he couldn't quite ignore her last name, accent, or Nordic coloring. He'd done his duty by coming out here to investigate, but the delay in any attempt to apprehend the trespasser because he had "important" things to do made it clear he'd rather wash his hands of the affair.

৵

Russell winced as he exited the narrow passageway. Once he closed the secret door, he limped to the window and braced himself as he watched the man ride off and leave the girl behind.

He'd heard them coming and slipped into the hideaway. Dad had told the story of how the black sheep of the family had experienced spiritual revival and used that passage to get into the house and borrow some keepsakes so he could reproduce them. The missing items had caused Great-Uncle Duncan to suspect one of the maids was a thief. Once matters had been ironed out, Duncan had ended up marrying the maid. Aunt Brigit had been one of Dad's favorites. As soon as he'd prepared a decent place to sleep, Russell had remembered that family lore and located the secret passageway.

Prying busybodies. They had no call to bother him. He'd kept entirely to himself.

Russell watched as the girl walked the weed-encrusted gravel road that arched around toward the main thoroughfare. She moved gracefully, with a fluid step that made her hem sway. Cutting across the grass would have saved her time and distance. Why would she stay on the path, and why hadn't the sheriff given her a ride back to the cottage? For all of his brave talk about safety, the sheriff had done nothing. He'd left the girl behind, alone.

Pretty thing, too. Tall and willowy. Had sunbeam yellow hair. She halted for a moment, stooped, and rose. Even from her profile, he could see her smile. She held up something and pursed her lips. *Wishing on a dandelion?* "Honey, don't you know wishes and prayers are for children?"

He startled himself by speaking those words aloud. He'd heard everything the sheriff had said while they'd been in the house, but her voice had been too soft for Russell to hear most of what she'd said. The lawman had called her Miss Gets.

Before enlisting, Russell had worked at his father's emporium. He recognized the material of Miss Gets's dress—one of the economy prints that sold for a paltry three cents per yard three years ago. Money must be tight.

But the sheriff was right—she and her mother shouldn't be living out here alone. Russell knew the caretaker's cottage they inhabited was part of his property. He'd write a letter to his attorney and tell him the place wasn't for rent any longer.

Chapter 5

There's definitely someone living up at the big house, Mama." Lorelei tugged the baby blue table oilcloth straight, then put a small vase of pansies in the center.

"It is not our concern. We have no responsibility for that old place."

"I didn't want to worry you, so I went to town and asked the sheriff to meet me there. We went inside."

Mama whirled around so quickly from rinsing radishes, she showered water in an arc around the kitchen. "Lori!"

"It was perfectly safe. You know Sheriff Clem. He even wore his pistol. He walked ahead of me every step of the way."

Mama turned away, banged her hands on the sink to supposedly shake off the water, then came toward the table. The effort she put into wiping her hands off on the dish towel told Lorelei she was trying to control her temper. "What did you think you were doing, to walk into danger like that? Do not tell me Mr. Clem would protect you. He is one who believed your father went to fight with the Germans. Even after the army delivered those medals saying Johann was a brave American soldier who died for this country, Mr. Clem did not apologize for his ugly lies."

"His wife always talks to us at church."

Mama sighed. "What am I to do with you, child? You want to believe good of everyone. The world is not like that. It is why Jesus came—because man is sinful. You cannot give away your trust so easily."

"I need to talk with you about that very thing." The chair scraped the battered linoleum floor as Lorelei pulled it out. She sat down and patted the table in an invitation for Mama to join her.

Mama sat down and folded her hands on the table. Just as quickly as she folded them, she unfolded them and reached out to hold Lorelei's hand. "What is it?"

"Until Sheriff Clem can meet the man who's living at the big house, he thinks we should move back to town. He said it's not safe here for us."

Mama didn't say anything, but her hold tightened.

"I promised him I'd speak with you about it." Lorelei leaned forward. "Mama, I don't want to go back to town. I wouldn't have the workshop, and it's important for me to honor my promises to complete the windows on time."

"Your safety is more important than a thousand windows."

"I feel that way about you, too, Mama." She shrugged. "I don't feel scared at all out here. Even when I was in the mansion, I didn't worry."

"Tell me then why the sheriff thinks we are unsafe here."

"From what we saw, only one man is there. Mama, he's probably a soldier. Sheriff Clem judged the footprints to be made by a lame man. More than that. . ." She paused and tapped her temple. "The sheriff thinks he could be dangerous because war can change men."

"This is true. It can." Mama ran her forefinger down Lorelei's arm. "You have been thinking. I can see it in your eyes."

"I have." Lorelei leaned forward. "Mama, if Papa had come home from war with an injury, we wouldn't love him any less."

"Of course not."

"I was thinking, if the injury wasn't a physical one—if his mind or spirit was hurt—we would still love him."

"So you are thinking this soldier man hiding in that old house might bear an unseen wound. Though the sheriff's warning seems prudent, your heart tells you otherwise."

Lorelei smiled. "Oh, Mama, I was hoping you'd understand."

"This isn't something you decide without prayer. While you make sandwiches, I'll read the Bible. We can pray and talk about it during lunch."

Papa had always read the Bible and said family prayers at the close of supper. When he'd shipped overseas, Mama had reasoned that France was six hours ahead of Virginia, so if they had their devotions at lunch, it would be at the same time Papa was. That way, they'd all read the same chapters and worship together as a family. Mama started reading from the second chapter of Nehemiah:

Wherefore the king said unto me, Why is thy countenance sad, seeing thou art not sick? this is nothing else but sorrow of heart. Then I was very sore afraid, and said unto the king, Let the king live for ever: why should not my countenance be sad, when the city, the place of my fathers' sepulchres, lieth waste, and the gates thereof are consumed with fire? Then the king said unto me, For what dost thou make request? So I prayed to the God of heaven. And I said unto the king, If it please the king, and if thy servant have found favour in thy sight, that thou wouldest send me unto Judah, unto the city of my fathers' sepulchres, that I may build it.

Lorelei drew in a deep breath and let it out slowly. "Mama, those verses—they never really meant anything to me before. This time, they jump out. If this man has a sorrow of the heart, I want to help."

Resting her hand on the thin pages of the open Bible, Mama fell silent.

Lorelei wanted to plead her case. The verses spoke so clearly to her of a man who had suffered and needed to find a safe home again. Still, the decision wasn't hers to make—at least, not alone. Whatever they did, Mama needed to feel at peace, too. Mind racing, Lorelei thought of things she could say that might convince her mother to agree to befriend the stranger. Failing that, she thought of people in town Mama might stay with if she felt scared.

The knife cut through the bread at a slant, creating uneven slices that told of her impatience. Mayonnaise. Lettuce and tomatoes fresh from the garden. Some salami. It took only seconds to make lunch, but in that time, Lorelei prepared an argument worthy of being heard by the Supreme Court. She turned back to her mother.

"Don't," Mama said softly. "I know what you want, Lori, but this is not about what we want; it is about what God would have us do."

Lorelei let out a guilty laugh. "You're right. Still, Mama, there can't be anything wrong with leaving a little food for him."

"How do you know he's hungry?"

"There hasn't been any smoke from the chimney or stovepipe."

"So you are imagining this soldier is going without his daily bread?" Mama shook her head. "Lorelei, if you feed him, you encourage him to stay."

"He's not a stray cat!" Lorelei set the plates on the table and let out a short laugh. "It's too bad he's not. Have you seen how many field mice we've had around here?"

"Deer, rabbits, gophers. . ." Mama gazed out the window. "They're going to eat up half of my garden."

"He's living up there and hasn't stolen a single thing from the garden, Mama. Did you notice? It would have been so easy for him to help himself—especially at night."

"If you weren't so talented at making such beautiful windows, I would say your time is wasted here and you should stay in town and sell things. You could make a poor man buy a wallet!"

Lorelei laughed guiltily. "Okay. So let's pray and eat."

They stretched their hands across the table to meet in the middle. Mama's hands felt cool, slightly rough, and reassuring. Even so, Lorelei missed Papa's big strong hands turning their grasp into a triangle.

"Heiliger Vater in Himmel," Mama began. She always prayed in German.

Holy Father in heaven. The rest of the prayer poured forth, but Lorelei clung to the very first words. War had robbed her of her beloved earthly father, but he'd taught her to rely on her heavenly Father—and that brought solace in times like this.

ᴖᴧ

Russell froze as he heard footsteps on the veranda. They were tentative. *Because someone is sneaking up on me? No. The weight is too slight, the shoes heeled. If the woman is scared, why would she bother to come here?*

He heard her next few steps, and realization dawned. She tested each step she took before putting her full weight on it—wisely checking to see if the rotting boards were safe. The footsteps finally stopped, only to be replaced with three uncertain knocks on the door.

He'd hoped the sheriff's warning would be sufficient. Clearly, someone had ignored it and decided to get snoopy. Folks were like that, but Russell didn't want to be around anyone. He refused to go answer the door. He stood stock-still and waited until he heard the woman leave the veranda. A wry smile twisted his mouth. She made faster time on her retreat. More likely, she was scared of him rather than it simply being a matter of her retracing her steps so she'd use the boards she knew to be safe.

He quietly crossed the parlor and drew back the very edge of the heavy draperies. From that vantage point, he could see the lissome blond sauntering back down the road. Her flour sack dress swayed with each step, swishing gently from side to side in a uniquely feminine way. Odd, how many little things he'd forgotten while living in the muddy trenches with men.

About twenty feet from the house, she turned around and gave a fleeting look at the porch. A smile chased across her face; then she looked up at the upstairs windows. Her smile faltered, but Russell felt a stab of relief that she didn't sense where he stood. He didn't want any connection to anyone.

"Go home, Buttercup," he whispered. "You don't belong here."

As if she heard him, she whirled around and walked out of sight.

He'd been going from room to room, trying to decide which projects needed immediate attention and what could wait. He'd been up on the roof. The whole thing needed to be stripped down to the base and completely reboarded and reshingled. Russell couldn't haul the wood up and do the work alone, and he didn't want to have to deal with others, which led him to the dismaying conclusion that he'd need to hire others to come do the task.

While in town, he'd go ahead and purchase supplies for several other repairs. In fact, he'd buy a buckboard. By loading it high, Russell reckoned he'd be able to stock up on enough that he'd be able to avoid making several trips.

Last night, as he fell asleep, he'd already made a mental list of half a dozen items he needed. Upon awakening and walking around, he'd added to that list until he needed to actually write down everything. Tomorrow or the next day, he'd grit his teeth and ride in.

For now, he'd leave the parlor and library as they stood. Due to the way the wind blew off the ocean and their intact windows, those two rooms had the least amount of grime in them. Russell took a quick peek under the heavy sailcloth at an ornate set of nesting tables. Once the rest of the room was restored, these would make a nice addition to the furniture.

Then again, so little furniture remained that he'd have to be satisfied with what was on hand unless he went to town to shop for more or made it himself.

Russell chewed on the tip of the pencil, then scrawled on the paper, "boards for porch." He couldn't risk someone falling through the disintegrating planks. Maybe he hadn't wanted to do that as a first project, but given the curiosity factor of his neighbor and the sheriff, he didn't have much choice.

In the meantime, he'd go ahead and shore up the existing porch for safety's sake. A fistful of nails, his hammer, and the boards he'd ripped from the windows would do the trick. Russell opened the front door and stopped cold.

A small basket sat there, a rust-colored gingham cloth covering its contents.

Russell wanted to ignore it. If he accepted a neighbor's gift, he'd end up having to interact and be sociable. The thought curdled his stomach. He stepped over the basket and avoided looking at it again as he assessed the planks. As he scanned the boards and visually measured their lengths and condition, the basket kept coming back in view.

Seeing it was bad enough; smelling it was worse. The aroma of fresh-baked bread sneaked past the cloth covering and tempted him to eat his fill. Russell swallowed and turned away. One nail. Two. Three. He banged each in place and lied to himself with each of them. *I don't want bread. I don't. Not a bite.*

He sat back on his heels and studied the porch a bit more. *The first week I was in Buttonhole, your mama stopped by with a big old basket of corn bread, chicken stew, jam, and applesauce.* His father told that story often enough. Mama was famous for her baskets. Russell had grown up watching her cook far too much, then slip extra loaves of bread, jars of soup and jam, vegetables, and cookies into her baskets and set out to deliver them to whomever she fancied might need them.

"I'm not a charity case." He punctuated his rough words with a few bangs of the hammer. The basket jumped.

Try as he might, he couldn't ignore the aroma. Russell argued with himself, hated his weakness, but still leaned back, snatched the wicker handle, and yanked the basket onto his thighs. He swept off the checkered napkin and inhaled. Several slices of bread, a pint jar of jam, an earthenware crock of baked beans, another of coleslaw, and a savory, two-inch-round length of bratwurst filled the basket to overflowing.

His lap was full, but his heart and stomach ached with emptiness. Russell stared at the offering. When he saw the neatly printed label on the jar of jam, he lost the battle. Peach jam. How many hundreds of jars of peach jam had Mama cooked and delivered? She'd done so in her special way—with that gentleness of wanting to be kind to another. The young woman—Buttercup—had done the self-same thing. That fact slipped past his defenses.

Russell scooted backward until his spine rested against the house, unscrewed the lid, and dipped his finger into the jam.

✧

Russell waited until night fell. He'd kept busy all day, then washed up. Round about midnight, he slipped out of the mansion and approached the small cottage on the edge of the property. At least two hours had passed since the lamps in the cottage had gone out, so he felt certain the women were fast asleep.

He knew two women lived there. The laundry on the line broadcast that fact. He'd also been spying from his attic window. Buttercup lived there—probably with her mother, from the looks of things. A pathetically small woodpile slumped along the back fence, one of the two chimneys lacked a few bricks at the top, and the place needed basic repairs.

Carefully, quietly, Russell walked from his home to the cottage with his arms full. He stacked several logs onto their woodpile and carried a few more to their back porch. He wouldn't need all that much for himself, and he'd have all summer and autumn to chop more. It was the least he could do as repayment for the food they'd given.

By returning the basket and dishes and leaving wood, he turned their charity into a barter. Satisfied with that arrangement, he turned to go home.

A small whimper stopped him in his tracks.

Chapter 6

P oor girl," he said as he approached the small form. Fifteen minutes later, Russell carefully peeled his shirt from around the mutt and gently petted her between the ears. Glad he'd cleaned out the stovepipes the day before, Russell started a fire in the stove to provide some radiant heat for the dog and to boil water to cleanse her wounds.

The poor beast looked like she'd been struck by a motorcar. One hind leg and her tail were injured—just how seriously, Russell couldn't tell. The dog seemed to sense Russell meant to help her. She weakly licked his hand as he finished bathing away the dirt and blood. After dipping a white cotton dishcloth into the boiling water several times, Russell tore it into strips and used them as bandages. It wasn't until he finished that he let out a rueful laugh.

"You're going to have a limp just like me. Same leg, even. We're a sad pair."

The dog yawned and rested her muzzle on his thigh. Russell stroked her ears. "I guess I'm stuck with you."

⁓

Sunday morning, Lorelei left a basket on the porch of the big house and scurried back down the road. She and Mama needed to hurry so they wouldn't be late for church. This was the third basket she'd left for the strange soldier.

Both times she'd left baskets, he'd returned them along with doing a chore as payment. They now had plenty of firewood and the well sported a new rope and bucket. Lorelei didn't want him to think he had to barter for the food they gave, but it was nice to have someone see to the details that slipped her notice or strained her abilities.

Mama came out of the cottage and tucked a hanky into her purse. "Hurry. We don't want to be late for church."

"We'll be on time."

Mama wrinkled her nose. "I want to be there a little bit early. It's past time for Sheriff Clem to tell us what he's found out about the man up at the house."

"He hasn't bothered to do anything more, Mama."

"Unless he benefits, the sheriff lets matters slide." Mama fell into step with her. "He claims to be busy, but most afternoons, he either sits at the counter at Phoebe's drinking free coffee, or he goes off to play poker at David McGee's."

Lorelei laughed. "I suppose we ought to be glad he's coming to church.

Perhaps his heart will be touched."

"Maybe we can ask Mr. Rawlin about the house." Mama walked around one side of a mud puddle while Lorelei went around the other. "He's in charge of the property. When we wanted to rent the cottage, we had to work with him."

Lorelei nodded. Mr. Rawlin had taken care of the matter—even though she'd suspected he didn't want to lease to them. "Maybe he could rent the place to the soldier. It would be a fair trade if he could stay there for all of the cleaning and repairs he's doing."

Mama stopped. A stricken look chased across her face. "We ought to have invited him to come to worship with us."

"I did, Mama. I slipped a note in with the basket on Friday."

"I'll be back soon." Russell petted the dog as he spoke. She'd lapped up half of the can of beef broth. "They've gone off to church, so I'll slip down to the cottage. I'll be back before you know it."

The unbandaged tip of her tail wagged weakly on the kitchen floor. Russell didn't know exactly what to do for her, but he'd applied the first aid he'd been taught and hoped it would be enough to let the dog heal.

Russell had wanted the women to leave for church, and he'd hoped it would be late enough in the morning that the ground would have dried from any dew. Ever since he'd returned home, Russell couldn't stomach the smell of morning-damp earth. Rain didn't bother him: It carried a sweetness to it that helped. But he'd spent too many frigid predawn hours in the trenches with the loamy smell of dirt overpowering him.

He stepped outside and breathed through his mouth to minimize his sense of smell. *Okay. It's okay.* He let out a sigh of relief, then hefted a few scrap lengths of planking over his shoulder and grabbed a small crate containing nails, a hammer, folding measuring stick, pencil, and saw. On the way to the cottage, he managed to stumble twice due to his weak leg. Anger welled up. Though no one had witnessed his awkwardness, Russell still hated it and all it brought back. He went to the front of the cottage and dumped the boards with a satisfying clatter.

Then he saw it: the flag in the front window. The background was white, just like the draperies, which is why he hadn't seen it from far off. In the center was a star—but not the blue one that proclaimed the family had a son, brother, or father at war. This one featured a gold star carefully stitched over that blue one—a heartbreaking testament that their man wouldn't be coming home.

Russell stood and stared at the flag. Fury welled up. He took another look at the small porch and went into a frenzy, completely shattering the warped boards and dismantling the entire structure. As soon as he pried the last board free, he stared at the mess he'd created. What was supposed to have been the simple replacement of a few boards had resulted in this galling destruction. He'd been enraged at the loss these women had suffered, but his actions had only caused more problems. He let out a long, deep sigh.

He couldn't very well go into town on Sunday and buy boards, but tomorrow he'd be able to get the lumber to do the job. Then again, he didn't dare leave the porch as it was. He searched about for wood.

A stack of storm windows lay on the leeward side of a fair-sized workshop. Russell selected those with the sturdiest wood and carried them to the front door. By setting them in place, he created a temporary walkway. Anxious to leave before they returned from church, he left a note under the front door.

~§

"Miss Goetz, I need to speak with you for a moment." Mr. Rawlin looked at her steadily as his wife bustled away to claim their youngsters from Sunday school.

"Oh, good." She slipped out of the pew, into the aisle. Mr. Rawlin invariably discussed matters out of earshot. She figured as an attorney, he had to guard his tongue and weigh his words more carefully. That being the case, she waited to mention anything about the stranger staying at the house until they got outside.

"The sheriff mentioned someone's living up at the big house," Mr. Rawlin said.

"Yes. He's fixing things up and cleaning."

The attorney nodded sagely. "Makes perfect sense. He's undoubtedly the new owner. The old one died, and I contacted his heir—a great-great-nephew." He smoothed his tie. "He's a good man—a war hero. I'm sure you and your mother will be safe."

"Thank you. He hasn't troubled us at all."

~§

He hasn't troubled us at all. Lorelei's words echoed back in her shocked mind as she stared in horror at the porch when she and Mama got home. *I spoke too soon.*

"Mercy, mercy!" Mama blotted her forehead with her hanky. "Will you look at that!"

"I am." The two words caught in her throat and came out in a strangled croak. "That just proves it."

Lorelei bowed her head in defeat. She and Mama would have to find somewhere else to live—but where?

"God provides our every need." Mama smiled. "That old porch—you are slender, and it doesn't mind you, but it's started to creak and groan under my feet. I was nervous to use the front door anymore." Nimble as a mountain goat, she climbed the three makeshift steps, crossed the storm window "porch," and opened the front door.

"Mama, be careful."

Mama turned around. Her eyes twinkled—a rare event these days. "You're too late to say that, Lori. Come now. Oh, look! We have a message here."

Lorelei joined her mother in a flash. On the back of a long list of tools and supplies, in a bold scrawl done in pencil, he'd written, "Wood was rotting and dangerous. Be careful. Will finish soon."

"Isn't that nice of him?"

"Yes, it is, Mama."

"What a pity that he didn't come to church, though."

❧

It was too late by the time he spotted her. Busy thinking about what more he could do for Mutt, Russell hadn't paid attention. Monday morning, he went out the front door and nearly knocked over the girl. "Whoa!" He instinctively grabbed her arms to keep her from tumbling backward.

She let out a gasp, then got her footing. Color flooded her cheeks even though he released her. "Excuse me. I brought you this." She nudged the basket into his arms and stepped back. "Your list. . .tools and wood and things. . ." She nervously moistened her lips. "I thought you might want it back."

He nodded curtly.

"I–I heard a woofing sound when I came the other day. There is a bone for your dog."

His chin came up. *She's been spying on me.*

"Thank you for the firewood and the porch." She'd inched back toward the steps, and the morning sun glinted on her pale hair and necklace—a very plain, rather small, silver cross. "It is very kind of you to help us, sir." He gave no reply, so she whispered, "Good-bye."

As she walked off, Russell stared at her back and felt a bolt of hatred nearly consume him. *She's German.*

Chapter 7

As he rode down the path toward town, Russell cast a quick look at the cottage. He'd given his word that he'd repair the porch, and he'd honor it. Then again, he owned the property. He didn't want anyone living there—especially not the enemy. He sought out the lawyer's shingle as he rode down Main Street.

"Mr. Diamond." The attorney reached out to shake hands.

Russell automatically scanned to be sure Mr. Rawlin didn't have a knife or pistol in his other hand. The notion was ludicrous, but life in the trenches taught a man to be cautious. Satisfied no danger existed, Russell shook hands and refused the proffered seat.

"What can I help you with?"

"I don't want anyone on my property. Get rid of the renters."

Mr. Rawlin slowly eased back to lean against his big mahogany desk. "I'm afraid that's not possible. Your great-great-uncle signed a ten-year lease with the Goetz women."

"Ten years!"

Drumming his fingers on the desktop on either side of his hips, the attorney nodded. "It was old Timothy Newcomb's idea. I confess, I tried to talk him out of it. Stubborn old man wouldn't be swayed. He wanted to be sure the women would have a safe haven. I suppose by now you've determined they are of German heritage."

Russell folded his arms across his chest.

Mr. Rawlin heaved a sigh. "I confess, at the start, I wasn't any happier about it than you are."

"Then find a way to break the deal."

The attorney shook his head. "Johann Goetz gave his life for this country. Last year, when the War Board started gearing up for us to enter the Great War, they knew they'd need reliable men who spoke German. Being close to D.C. as we are, they had a few scouts come out and nose around. Johann was a shade older than they wanted—thirty-nine—but they needed him, and he went."

Russell didn't move an inch or say a word.

"Gossips whispered plenty. Your great-uncle always had the *Gazette* mailed to him. It's featured several articles about the vandalism against Germans in this area. Just north of here, a German was lynched, and the jury found the men who did it innocent. In that same edition, a letter to the editor hinted that Mr. Goetz went off to fight with the Jerries." He paused. When Russell said nothing, the lawyer continued, "Just about that time, Lorelei came to me and asked to rent the cottage. I didn't want to, but as a professional I had to set aside my own feelings and serve my client. I contacted him, and he gave me instructions."

"A decade was extreme." Russell scowled at him.

"I thought so, too, but that's what your uncle specified. He was worried someone might take a mind to smash up her place like they have others."

"From the looks of things, no one bothers them at all."

"Perhaps because they moved out of town. Problems happen—especially here along the coast where folks have lost their sons at sea even before we got sucked into the war."

Russell had heard of such events. He thought of the star flag in the cottage window. *But anyone could put that up. It doesn't actually prove their man was fighting with the Americans.*

"Most of the gossip stopped when posthumous awards arrived for Mr. Goetz," Rawlin continued. "Your uncle figured it's been hard on those women and that they deserved better."

The star stitched on the flag in the window was gold. Russell couldn't argue with what he'd been told. If anything, he owed that widow and her daughter some help—it was a soldier's duty to see to a fallen comrade's family.

"The bank is expecting you to come by and put your signature on file." Clearly, the attorney chose not to press the issue of his renters any further. "The inheritance is in your name, and you can draw on it as you see fit." He glanced down at the papers in front of himself and read the latest bank balance.

Russell stared at the papers in shock. *Dad told me I'd have enough to live on. He didn't tell me I'd be rich. Ten men couldn't squander that much money in their lifetimes.*

"I took the liberty of opening an account for you at Sanders' Mercantile so you can get supplies. Did you require anything else?"

"No." Russell started to walk out. He stopped at the door and turned. "The house needs to be reroofed immediately. Do you recommend anyone?"

"Want it done cheap, or want it done right?"

"Right." Even if he hadn't inherited a fortune, he would have given that answer, but the fact that the lawyer even bothered to ask the question seemed bizarre.

Rawlin jerked his thumb toward the north. "Pinkus Bayley. Gray house with the red shutters. Don't let his age fool you. He used to be a shipwright. He can gather the best men in short order. Let him buy the supplies—he'll get a better deal."

"Thanks."

378

The livery had hitches for his team and a sound-looking buckboard. The man in charge sat on a stool, showing a couple of strapping teens how to splice rope. "Don't suppose you got any work out there at your place, do you?" one of the youngsters asked.

"My boys are hard workers," the livery owner added.

Russell didn't want people all over his place. Then again, he'd have the crew doing the roofing. *I might as well get it all over at once and be done with it.* "My stable's a wreck. Needs a thorough cleaning."

The younger lad's voice cracked and went up several notes. "We're used to mucking out stables. You came to the right place to hire yourself some workers."

"Show up tomorrow—two hours after daybreak. I'll pay you two bucks a day apiece." Russell watched how their eyes lit up. "For that kind of money, I expect you to be men—not boys who need directions."

"We can do it!"

"Fine. I've got things to see to here in town. My horses could stand for some decent feed—corn and oats. I'll be about two hours, so take care of them now, then have them hitched and ready to go."

At the feed store, Russell arranged for corn, oats, and hay to be delivered at the end of the week. By then, the stable would be ready to hold the supplies.

Next, Russell stopped by the post office and mailed a letter to his mother. He'd taken pains to write more than the fact that he'd arrived at the mansion. After two paragraphs, he'd included as much as he could concoct, then signed, "Love, Russell." It wouldn't win a prize, but it fulfilled his promise. He hoped it would settle Mama's fears.

By the time he reached the diner, Russell's leg ached abominably. He slid into a seat and ignored the assessing looks of others by staring sightlessly at the menu. It would be like every other menu nowadays—featuring so-called patriotic dishes like victory burgers and liberty cabbage, and a reminder about meatless Mondays and wheatless Wednesdays.

"Have you decided what you want?"

"I'll have the blue plate special," he ordered without glancing up. In an attempt to keep from having to strike up a conversation, he pulled the list from his pocket and reviewed it. When the waitress slid a plate of liver and onions in front of him, he winced.

A brawny, middle-aged man swaggered up, grabbed the plate, and shoved it back at the waitress. "That's not fit for eatin'. Give him meat and 'taters. Bring me a steak while you're at it." He slid into the seat opposite Russell and leaned back with more show than a rodeo pony. "Chester Gimley. Figured you'd be lookin' to have someone do the work out at that old place. I can do anything you want. Cheap."

"And I reckon," the waitress said as she thumped the plate back down in front of Russell, "Mr. Diamond can eat anything he orders. In case you didn't notice, he's concentrating on his work."

"Mind your own business, Myrtle."

"Gimley?" Russell looked at him, and the stranger's eyes brightened with greed. "I don't hold with a man treating a woman with disrespect."

Gimley went ruddy and blustered, but he didn't apologize.

Russell deliberately picked up his knife and fork and cut into the revolting slab of liver. He took a big bite, promptly washed it down with his coffee, and realized it didn't taste any better or worse than anything else he'd had in weeks. He ate because he needed to, but everything got stuck halfway down and had to be washed past the ever-present ball in his throat.

Gimley snorted derisively, shoved away from the table, and stomped off.

Half an hour later, Russell left the diner with his stomach churning. He stopped at the gray house with the red shutters, struck a deal with old Pinkus Bayley to replace the roof, and gladly accepted a glass of bicarbonate before he left.

The mercantile made him suffer a momentary pang of homesickness. Dad's emporium carried the same wondrous mixture of aromas—briny pickles, sweet, fresh fruit, the tang of new leather goods, and the honest scent of soap. Drawing the list from his pocket, Russell started searching for the items. In a matter of minutes, Mr. Sanders and his daughter, Olivia, were both helping him. It didn't take long before his order filled the entire counter and formed an appreciable heap on the floor.

Staples, eggs, produce, three one-pound cans of coffee, and a crate overflowing with cans and jars of food sat next to a frying pan, cast iron pots, and a kettle.

"Looks like you're feeding an army," Mr. Sanders teased.

Russell ignored the comment and added molasses to the supplies. The beans Buttercup had brought in the first basket had been sweetened a tad with molasses, and he'd had a hankering for more. *I can make them for myself. I don't want her cooking for me.*

"I have just the thing for you: Kirby's Ezee 'Grasshopper' vacuum cleaner." Olivia demonstrated it and added, "It requires no electricity."

Russell hastily propped it against the icebox. Doing so knocked the Johnson's Prepared Wax for the floor from atop the stack and created quite a ruckus.

Russell startled at the sound and broke out in a cold sweat. For a few horrible moments, he was in the trenches again, hearing the clatter of equipment. His heart raced, and he kept clutching his fists as he reminded himself that he didn't need to grab his rifle or knife. Everything within him screamed to retreat, yet Miss Olivia stood there giggling behind her hand while her father unrolled a mattress for his inspection.

The mattress. I need the mattress. I have to get this stuff so I can stay home and not come back for a long time. Russell snatched the dipper from the water bucket and gulped several mouthfuls, then croaked, "The mattress is fine. I'll take it."

Folks in the store chattered just like they did back in Dad's place. Russell knew it was all just neighborly talk—snoopy, helpful, good-natured. Nonetheless, he was on edge. He'd turned down at least half a dozen housekeeping offers and didn't care what they thought his total bill would come to.

". . .sheets, a pillow, and blankets?"

Russell realized Mr. Sanders had asked him a question. He nodded and rasped, "Add it all up and put it on my account. I'll go fetch my buckboard." He got out of there as fast as he could limp.

♦

Lorelei hoed the garden and watched the road. He'd taken both horses and headed toward town. She wanted to ask her neighbor a favor, and it had taken her hours to build up her courage after he'd scared her this morning. She heard the trundling sound of a wagon and the jingle of harnesses before he came into view.

As she wiped her hands on a rag, Lorelei went to stand in the middle of the road. Mr. Diamond looked about as cheerful as a thundercloud when he pulled the team to a stop.

"Mr. Diamond, I have a favor I'd like to ask of you." When he made no reply, Lorelei wrapped her arms about her waist and forged on. *Nothing ventured, nothing gained.* "Mama and I garden. We've planted a Victory Garden—like they have in England—and many folks in town buy our produce. I wanted to ask you to let me sharecrop a tiny section of your land."

"I'll think about it."

His reply surprised her. She'd braced herself for a flat refusal and dared to hope for agreement. Never once had she thought he might delay making a decision. Lorelei blinked at him for a moment, then tucked a wind-whipped strand of hair behind her ear. "Thank you."

He stared off to the side. His eyes carried a haunted look, and the set of his jaw didn't invite further conversation. In fact, the raspy quality to his voice made it sound as if he rarely spoke.

Lorelei sidled off the path and watched as he nickered and the handsome pair of geldings set the buckboard in motion. She'd wanted to intercept him without Mama overhearing the request. Worried as she was about money, Mama would get her hopes up or be in a dither that the neighbor would deduce their finances were strained. This way, Mama wouldn't know a thing if he refused them.

Lorelei went back to the garden and picked up the hoe. She carried it to a small shed, then washed up at the pump and went back to the workshop.

Mama was sweeping the workroom floor. Lorelei stooped, held the dustpan, and smiled at the tinkling sound as all of the tiny bits hit the thin steel. "In my fanciful moments, I imagine that's what the angels' laughter sounds like."

Mama smoothed her hair. "Ah, my Lori. It takes so little to make you happy."

"You're the one who taught me to count my blessings." She rose and dumped the sweepings into the wastebasket as she began to sing:

> *Count your blessings, name them one by one;*
> *Count your blessings, see what God hath done;*
> *Count your blessings, name them one by one;*
> *Count your many blessings, see what God hath done.*

Mama had joined in on the last two lines. Afterward, she brushed away a tear. *"Du bist mein Segen, Lorelei."*

"You're my blessing, too, Mama."

"It would be nice to have the blessing of more orders." Mama fiddled with the last remaining order slip on the board.

"Papa always said, 'God will provide.' He'd want us to have faith."

"Yes, he would." Mama tugged a hanky out of her sleeve and wiped her cheeks. "I will take some lettuce and cabbage into town tomorrow. It will buy more flour for us."

"See? God provides."

༖

Sleep didn't come easily or well for Russell. Even on his new mattress, he'd jerk awake and reach for his rifle. He'd rolled out of bed before dawn and made a pot of coffee. As he finished the last sip, wagons rolled up.

I told them not to come until two hours after daybreak. Irritated, Russell thumped down his empty mug and went outside.

"She's a beauty," Pinkus Bayley said as he admired the old house. "We'll have her looking grand as can be in no time at all."

"Warn your men that the veranda is rotting in places and they'll need to test their footing. I don't want anyone breaking a leg."

"Hear that, men?" Pinkus clapped his hands and rubbed them together. Russell estimated it was more out of eagerness to begin than from a need to warm them. "Even from here, I can see you're right. We'll take it clear down to the joists and put up all new slats, felt, tar paper, and shingles."

"I'll set a water bucket and dipper here for the men."

"Jim-dandy idea." Pinkus turned back to his men. "Daniel, go check out the chimneys to be sure they're sound. Jake and Ed, I want you to scythe the grass over yonder. We'll dump the old shingles and rotten wood there. We'll have us a bonfire when the job's finished."

The liveryman's sons rode up together on a swaybacked mare. *Can't anyone in this town follow directions or tell time?* Russell took them over to the stable and pulled open one of the creaky, weathered doors.

"We'll oil the hinges, Mr. Diamond," the elder boy said as he put his weight behind the companion door and got it to budge. "Pa said we need to be sure to wash down everything after we clean it out. No putting your team in here until then, else they're like to take sick."

Russell frowned at the boys' worn shoes. "Might be snakes in here. I'm sure every last spider in Virginia is. Go on back to town and tell Mr. Sanders to put you in boots."

The boys exchanged a worried look.

"A man pays for the tools and equipment for jobs on his place. Boots—sturdy boots—are a necessity. He's to put them on my account."

"Pa don't cotton to folks takin' charity."

Russell gave the boys a steely-eyed look. "I don't cotton to someone else giving orders to my hired help. While you're here, you'll do as I say."

"Yessir."

Russell headed back toward the house. The work there literally started with a crash bang. Shingles and boards slid off the roof and smashed onto the earth. Pinkus jerked his chin toward Russell.

"Yeah?"

"Most of the chimneys are in fair condition. The mortar needs some patching, but that's not much. The one to the parlor needs to be torn down at least to the bottom floor and rebuilt. It's about to topple. I'll need to be getting sand and gravel to make cement and a load of bricks. Daniel's best as they come on chimneys. After we're done, he'll clean 'em all. Until then, don't set any fires."

"Okay." Russell squinted toward the cottage. *It's my property, and I'm responsible for it.* "Have Daniel repair and clean the chimney over at the caretaker's cottage while he's out here."

"Aye. Fine notion. My men brought lunch buckets today, but most often, folks feed them when they work. Mrs. Goetz is a dandy cook. Think you can talk her into setting up our dinners?"

"We'll see." Russell looked back at the top of his house. The smallest effort made shingles come loose and skid. Much to his relief, all of the men were wearing safety ropes.

Pinkus cupped his gnarled hands and shouted, "Ed! Wind and rain pattern would hit the southeast corner hardest. I expect the boards there are weak. Don't go over there. You've eaten too many of your wife's noodles!"

The men chuckled, and Russell knew he'd gotten the right man for the job. Pinkus slanted him a sly look. "I know what you're thinking. I'm older than dirt. Seventy-one. Fought in the War Between the States."

Russell didn't reply to that revelation, though it surprised him.

"When I got home, I didn't want to talk to a soul." Pinkus squinted at the roof and rubbed his chin. "I reckon folks are makin' pests of themselves. I told my men they're to concentrate on this job, not on whatever's happening 'over there.'"

Russell froze. The old man's insight stunned him.

"I'm glad you're takin' care of the Goetz women. Things are tight for them 'specially since they lost Johann. Admirable Christians, staunch Americans. You gonna have little Lorelei replace your broken windows?"

"Windows?"

"She took on her father's trade. Good at it, too. A dab hand at glazing windows and puts together some mighty fine stained-glass church windows. From the looks of it, you have plenty of cracked and broken panes."

"One thing at a time." Russell didn't want to have anyone here at all—let alone a woman. A pretty woman.

One who was German.

They parted, and Pinkus went to holler orders to his men as Russell trudged toward the caretaker's cottage. He started toward the front door, then recalled he'd torn the porch to shreds. As he knocked on the back door, he secretly hoped no one would be home.

Chapter 8

Pale blue, striped curtains with cherries dotting them parted. Buttercup—*Lorelei*, he corrected himself since he'd learned her name from Pinkus—peeked out. She smiled and opened the door.

"Why, hello."

"Is your mother here?"

"No, she went to town today. Can I help you?"

Russell shifted his weight from both feet onto just the left. His right leg ached. "I need to speak with her."

"She should be home later." She bit her lip for a second. "Is something wrong?"

"No." He hated to have to ask for help. Waiting only meant he'd have to come back. "I'm going to need dinner for the workmen each day. 'Round about noon—something good and filling. Counting the boys cleaning out the stable, there are ten of us. Do you think your mother could cook?"

"Yes. Yes! Mama loves to cook. We have a wagon. I can help her pull the food up to the house."

"You can't very well walk into town and drag back the rest of what you'll need in a kids' wagon. Can you drive a buckboard?"

Her eyes sparkled as she nodded.

"Do you have an icebox?"

"Yes. Ice is delivered every Thursday."

"We won't need food today. Starting tomorrow at noon, I want solid meals. No skimping. I'll give your mother a note for the butcher and the mercantile so she can get whatever she needs." At that moment, Russell realized the mercantile wouldn't be a problem, but the butcher might well be ugly about selling meat to a German. He added, "I'll make it clear she's my cook and feeding my workmen, so there shouldn't be a problem with her buying the necessary bulk."

Lorelei smiled. "It will be a lot of food. How many days will they be working?"

"Two weeks." Her question took him by surprise. He'd expected her to ask how much he'd pay. "New York housemaids earn eighteen dollars a week." He'd decided twenty would be fair, but Pinkus's words echoed in his mind. *Things are tight. Lost Johann. . .* A closer look showed Lorelei's dress and shoes were both nearly worn out.

"Eighteen dollars!" Her eyes grew huge. "But that is New York."

"I'm sure cooks make far more, and I'm asking your mother to feed several hungry men, even if it's only one meal a day. Tell her I'll pay thirty a week on top of whatever the food costs."

He spun around and made it down the steps before she stammered, "Do you have dishes and tableware enough for ten men at your house?"

Dishes and tableware enough, he repeated to himself. *It's not just her voice that sounds German. She puts the words together wrong.*

"We have dishes if you don't." She spoke the words softly, tentatively.

Russell thought of the mismatched left-behinds he'd gathered. He didn't own enough to have one guest at his table, let alone nearly a dozen. The notion of doing any formal entertaining left him cold, but he refused to depend on someone else for anything as basic as table service. "Get dishes. None of those painted steel things—real ones."

"Fancy china?"

Having worked at Diamond Emporium and ordered stock through catalogs, he knew far more than most men ever would concerning domestic goods. He could handle this. Relieved to be dealing with something straightforward and unemotional, Russell turned.

"Haviland. They have an everyday pattern called Ranson that will do. If that's not available, get Spode's Tower."

"Ranson," she repeated in a tone that matched her astonished expression. She leaned into the doorsill. "What about glasses and such?"

"A case of whatever pressed glass they have on hand. I'll probably use most of the glasses to mix paint or clean brushes. When the house was locked up, they left a mishmash of cutlery that ought to work, so don't bother getting any silverware."

"Very well."

That settled, he turned to leave. The women would feed the workers, and he could make himself scarce by continuing to work on the interior of the house. He said over his shoulder, "I'll also have the boys plow a garden for you once they're done cleaning the stable."

"Thank you!"

"I'll have the buckboard here in ten minutes."

"Make it twenty minutes, Mr. Diamond. I have cinnamon rolls in the oven."

༷

Lorelei laughed at how the pots rattled and the toy wagon wheel squeaked as she pulled it up the road. The combination made for a comical symphony, and she delighted in the music because it reminded her of how God had provided this opportunity for them to make money. This wasn't a tiny sum, either—it was enough to provide for a little while.

Mama would be coming in ten minutes, after the tarts came out of the oven.

The men could start in on the main part of the meal first.

Mr. Diamond left his buckboard parked in the yard to serve as a buffet table of sorts. She reached it, spread a cheery scarlet tablecloth over the bed, and started arranging the dishes.

"Chow time!" one of the men hollered to the others.

It wasn't necessary for him to shout. Two of the men had seen her coming and whistled. Part of her wanted to smile at how silly it was for them to do that, but the other part felt embarrassed. It didn't feel any better to have them all crowding around as she put a big roasting pan on the buckboard table.

"What did you fix us?"

"Today," she said as she picked up a kettle and a big saucepan by their handles and plunked them on either side of the roaster, "is pot roast, braised potatoes and baked carrots, peas, salad, and rolls."

"Got any gravy?"

"In the speckled pot that's still in my wagon." She didn't bother to get it. No less than three men dove to grab the gravy. They were all hardworking men, but when it came to food, they acted like starving little boys.

Old Mr. Bayley cast a woebegone look at the now-empty wagon. "No dessert?"

Lorelei smiled. He was such a nice man. "Mama knows you like berry tarts. She's taking them out of the oven in a few minutes."

The men heaped food on their plates and sat in the dirt to eat. Mr. Diamond wasn't anywhere to be seen, and Lorelei feared the men would dive in for seconds before he had a chance to get anything. She took a plate, placed generous portions of everything on it, and went around the back of the house toward what she'd learned was the kitchen.

A chair propped the back door open. "Mr. Diamond! I'm leaving food here for you." She stayed on the doorstep and peeked inside. The kitchen was homey, and the scarred cutting board made Lorelei think many happy hours had been spent in this room. The sensibly arranged room held a huge, ancient stove. Beside it lay a bedraggled-looking, heavily bandaged dog.

"Oh, you poor baby!" She remained outside, set the plate on the chair, and tugged a little piece of the roast free. "Here, puppy. Are you hungry?"

The dog barely paused to sniff, then gobbled it. The very tip of her tail, free of a bandage, swished to and fro in a sign of pleasure.

"What are you doing in here?"

Lorelei jumped at the harsh sound of Mr. Diamond's voice and whirled to face him. "You were not there. I saved food for you."

"You don't belong here."

He cast a disparaging look at the food and made an impatient sound. "Not just here in the house. You don't belong up here at all. You had to hear the men whistling at you."

Embarrassment washed from her bosom to her scalp in a scorching wave.

"It's foolhardy for you to deliver dinner alone. I hired your mother, not you. From now on, she's to bring the food. You can come only if she's with you."

"You are here, as is Mr. Bayley. I am safe enough."

"No one is ever safe." His voice rang with pain and bitterness.

"God is with me."

His face hardened, and his eyes narrowed as he shot back, "Where was God when your father died?"

⁓

Russell helped Mrs. Goetz put the empty dishes from yet another fine meal into the wagon. Today's corned beef and cabbage, soda bread, and carrot cake tasted wonderful. Truth be told, she'd managed to bring something different every day so far, each meal far surpassing what he'd expected when they struck their bargain.

Rationing and food "rules" restricted what women cooked. Mrs. Goetz studiously adhered to the government's recommendations, but it never seemed as if her meals lacked anything at all. Fish and fowl dominated the menu instead of beef—just as the pamphlets advised. On "Meatless Mondays," she made hearty soup from Lorelei's vegetable garden or filling casseroles. On "Wheatless Wednesdays," she'd serve chicken with potatoes or rice and make puddings or baked apples for dessert. With sugar and butter being limited so more could be sent overseas, she still managed to use honey, molasses, currants and raisins, and cooking oil so creatively that the men actually asked for the recipes for their wives to use.

She deserved praise for her hard work, but Russell wasn't in much of a mood to talk.

"I'm leaving this here for your dog." Mrs. Goetz set a small earthenware bowl on the buckboard. "Lorelei scraped from yesterday's chicken bones the marrow and made a special gruel. It helps the puppy grow healthy again."

"Thanks."

"Lori and I—we are grateful to you for plowing the garden for us."

"She was planting stuff yesterday."

"No. She was mixing in ash and horse droppings to enrich the soil." Mrs. Goetz curled her fingers through the handle of the toy wagon and crammed her other fist into her apron pocket. "She will have to come with me here tomorrow to get the buckboard. I must go to town for more food, and I do not drive."

It was the first time anything had been said about Lorelei not coming up to the house anymore. For a whole week, she'd stayed down at the cottage. Clearly, Lorelei helped cook the enormous meals, but never once had she ventured anywhere near the mansion.

Russell fought with himself over whether to go talk to her. He'd spoken in anger, and in doing so, he'd caused her grief to deepen. The memories of how she'd flinched at his words and the tears that filled her eyes haunted him. Her hand had trembled as she lifted it to touch the small silver cross hanging on a fragile chain about her neck. *Almost as if she were trying to shield her faith from my cruel onslaught.*

"How many more days do you need me to make the lunches? It looks good—this roof of yours. The men are working hard and fast. They will be done soon."

"Another week." He cleared his throat. "They'll also be repairing your roof and chimney, but I'll do the porch myself."

Mrs. Goetz shook her head. "No."

"I understand you're worried about whether it's safe to have the men there. Perhaps you could make a few meals ahead and go into town with your daughter so she's not around them."

"This is not the problem." Aching pride showed in her careworn face and squared shoulders. "We do not want anything from you."

"What's that supposed to mean? It's my property. I'll do whatever I deem fit."

Tears silvered her eyes, making him remember how Lorelei's had glistened. "Patching a porch does not fix hurt feelings."

He inwardly winced at that observation and didn't pretend to misunderstand what she was saying. "I made your daughter cry. It won't happen again."

"My Lori has a big heart. She cares easily for others."

He shook his head. "Not after how I spoke to her. She's been glad to keep her distance."

"That is where you are wrong, Russell. Lorelei wants to bear your burden as a Christian should, but you have made it clear you want nothing to do with her or with God."

"She's not responsible for me or my soul."

"You are responsible for your soul," the older woman said in a matter-of-fact tone. "But as Christ's followers, we believe we are our brothers' keepers. You were trying to be mindful of her safety when you told her not to come alone." She hitched her shoulder. "That time, you were being your sister's keeper."

Her comment didn't amuse him. "I upset her. You can tell her I'm sorry. Warn her I'm going to work on the porch so she can avoid me."

"Lorelei needs no warning. Perfect love—the kind God gives us in His name that we are to show one another—this special caring knows no fear."

Mrs. Goetz left, pulling the wagon behind her. Russell watched her leave. What would it be like to live without fear?

❧

"Here, girl. Come to me. Yes. Good girl." Lorelei crooned softly to the dog and knelt to capture her. No longer bandaged, the brown and white mutt still looked. . . well, like a mutt. One ear cocked up while the other flopped to the side. One haunch bore partially healed scrapes and was missing most of the fur. "What are you doing out alone?"

Lorelei gathered her in the basket of her arms, rose, and realized she'd never be able to carry the dog back to Mr. Diamond's house. He cared for this dog, and once he discovered she was missing, he'd be worried. Lorelei's gaze fell on the wagon. She managed to lay the dog in it, then worried she might hop out once the wheel started squeaking. Once she finished tying down the dog, she grabbed the handle, steeled herself with a deep breath, and headed toward the forbidden mansion.

Soon she started to sing:

Are you ever burdened with a load of care?
Does the cross seem heavy you are called to bear?
Count your many blessings, every doubt will fly,
And you will be singing as the days go by.

"What are you. . ." Mr. Diamond's voice died out as he strode down the drive. His gait seemed steadier, his limp far less noticeable. His forehead creased, then he let out a disbelieving bark of a laugh. "My dog is wearing your apron?"

390

Chapter 9

It was the only way I could be sure she wouldn't bound out. She is healing well, but I didn't think her strong enough to walk back here." Lorelei started to untie the apron strings she'd wound around the wagon to keep the dog inside.

Mr. Diamond knelt on the other side of the wagon and loosened a stubborn knot. "How did you get out, girl?"

The dog woofed and licked his hand.

"She probably smelled your cooking. I can't blame her for following her nose. Old Pinkus Bayley told me the men are taking their time to do a good job, but they might be working a tad slower than usual because of the food you're making."

"Mr. Bayley is a kindhearted man."

"And I'm not."

His words jolted Lorelei. She didn't know what to say. *Jesus, please give me the right words. I need Your wisdom and kindness.*

Mr. Diamond looked at her and said gruffly, "I'm not proud of how things went last week. I had no call to say what I did. Whatever gentility I once had is long gone. Stay away from me. I had the good sense to leave home so I wouldn't hurt those I love; this is my refuge. Once I have this place fixed, I won't have to bother with anyone else."

"It is no sin to hurt inside or to question God, Mr. Diamond." Her apron wadded in her hands as she quietly confessed, "God has heard more than a few of my questions and knows my grief. I would be wrong to judge you, let alone find you guilty of what I have done myself."

"I saw your tears." Each word grated out of him. "You walked out of my kitchen weeping—because of me."

She closed her eyes for a moment, then opened them. "It was because of you. In this, you are right; but you are also wrong. I didn't cry for myself. I cried because I cannot imagine the pain you try to bear alone. In Psalms, it says the Good Shepherd is with us when we walk through the valley of the shadow of death. Many days and nights—even in the midst of my sorrow and questions— that has been my only comfort. I have been angry, and I have asked, 'Why?' but I have always leaned on the assurance that God is beside me. My heart aches to think you are without that comfort."

"You can't expect me to find peace when I've lived though war."

"Peace is not a place; it is a serenity that comes when we trust God that He will make all things right in His time."

He shook his head sadly. "Buttercup, I meant it. Keep your distance."

Buttercup—I like that he called me such a beautiful name. Deep inside, this man longs for good things. She reached out to pet his dog. "When you doctored her and bandaged her, did she try to bite you?"

Lightning fast, he reacted. "I'm not a stray dog for you to heal."

"No, you are not, but just as you understood she didn't mean to hurt you, I also accept that you reacted out of pain. Now that I see what is in your heart, I'm not afraid."

Pinkus sauntered up. "Good, good. The two of you are talking. Lorelei, knock some sense into this stubborn man's head. Tell him to hire me to paint the place after you put in the new windows."

Lorelei felt her face grow warm. "I cannot do this, Mr. Bayley." She'd secretly hoped Mr. Diamond would give her the commission to replace his broken windows. The job would bring in enough money for her to slip some into the savings sock. Now, though, since Mr. Diamond had made it clear he wanted nothing to do with her, she couldn't very well make a bid for the work.

"Why not?" The old man's face crinkled into a hundred wrinkles as he turned to Russell. "You unhappy with the job my men have been doing?"

"I'm pleased. The roof and chimneys look good."

"Then what's the holdup? While we do the roof and chimney over at the cottage, Lorelei can get to work on your windows up here."

"I didn't order the paint yet," Mr. Diamond said.

Something about the set of his jaw made Lorelei take a second look. He put down the dog, and as the dog gingerly tested standing again, realization dawned. *He's offended because his leg is weak. Climbing the ladder will be too hard, but he doesn't want anyone to treat him like a cripple.*

Lorelei sat in the wagon and folded her hands in her lap. "What colors did you decide on, Mr. Diamond? When you paint the inside of your house, will you do different colors for the rooms?"

"He can paint them whatever color he fancies. Don't make no nevermind to me," Mr. Bayley snorted. "And the outside—well, to my way of thinking, it would be a crying shame to paint this grand old woman anything other than white." He directed his attention back toward Mr. Diamond. "Russ, reason it through. By the time you buy ladders and scaffolding, you pert near hired my crew to do the outside of this place. They could really use the work, and you have plenty that needs doing on the inside to keep you busy."

Clearly, the old man's reasoning went a long way toward salvaging Mr.

Diamond's pride. Mr. Diamond hooked his thumbs through belt loops and drawled, "Slate. I want slate for some of the detail work."

"Slate blue or slate gray?" Lorelei ruffled the fur between the dog's ears.

"Isn't it the same?" both men asked in unison.

She shook her head. "What colors do you want inside?"

"Back to that, eh?" Bayley chuckled.

"Well, if he wants to use silver, pink, and black inside, then he should use slate gray." She tilted her head toward Mr. Diamond. "If you want to use blues, lavender, and gold, you should use blue slate."

"Sounds to me like the lass knows what she's talking about. She going to do the windows before we set to painting?"

"I need to go back home." Lorelei wondered why she'd bothered to try to look so casual. She stood and reached for the wagon handle, the whole time feeling embarrassed that her neighbor didn't want her around and hadn't offered her the job. "Good-bye."

"What's awrong with her?" Mr. Bayley muttered as she dragged the wagon down the gravel.

Mr. Diamond mumbled something, but Lorelei couldn't tell precisely what he said. Then again, maybe that was best. *Perhaps he has been too polite to say it, but the real reason he doesn't want me around is the same reason others have shunned us. Yes, he asked Mama to cook, but he was desperate. The truth is, he doesn't think I'm American; he thinks I am the enemy.*

⁓

"Miss Goetz?" Russell stood in the doorway of what looked to be her workshop. Lorelei was welding something on a table, and he'd waited until she put the soldering iron down so she wouldn't burn herself. In those moments, he'd promised himself that he would mind his words so he didn't hurt her again.

"Yes?" She glanced over her shoulder at him.

"I'd like to speak with you."

"Come around toward the window." She swept her hand in a fluid gesture. "I have not swept and do not want you to get glass in your shoes."

He walked around the perimeter of the room and hated how his uneven gait sounded on the cement floor. If Lorelei noticed it, she managed to hide her reaction. She sat on a tall stool, had a pencil shoved haphazardly into her hair, and wore a supple leather apron that nearly covered her everyday dress.

As far as he knew, she owned three dresses—a "Sunday-best" gray and black one and two "everyday" dresses. He strongly suspected the sunshine yellow dress had been her Sunday best until she'd needed to make the gray-and-black-striped one for mourning.

"What are you making?"

She fussed with the edge of the window. "A piece for the Mariners' Chapel."

"Can we hold it up so I can see the design?"

"I need to weld a few more places before it can be moved."

"Okay. I'll wait." He watched as she exchanged the soldering iron for another that she had waiting on a potbelly-type affair. Even with all the windows and both doors open, the heat made the workroom feel sticky and hot. *But that thing isn't enough to keep this big drafty room warm in the winter. I'll have to put in a larger one. Maybe she'd rather have a second one in the opposite corner.*

"There's another stool. You are welcome to have a seat." She bent over her task and concentrated on each action with precision that made her features take on an intensity that caused her eyes to glow. The heat from soldering and her passion for what she did made her cheeks rosy.

"You love what you do."

"It was a gift from my papa. He taught me."

He didn't want to talk about her father. He'd seen too much death in his short time in the trenches to want to think of it now. Instead, Russell tried to keep the conversation focused on her work. "What is this one called?"

"Fishers of Men."

"Do you design them yourself, or do you have a book of samples?"

"Each window is a new opportunity. I talk to the person who commissions it and see what they have in mind; then I make sketches and have them select what pleases them." She handled the flux, soldering wire, and iron with a deftness that bespoke many hours of practice.

"The racks there for storing your glass are clever."

She laughed. "You are teasing me."

"I'm serious." He looked at the wooden fixtures that held a veritable rainbow of glass panes in an orderly vertical array. *The attorney said my uncle feared her place might be vandalized. No wonder he worried. All this glass. . .*

"Every business has to organize the material," she said in a practical tone.

Her words pulled him away from imagining what danger she and her mother might have been in, in town. He didn't want to think of that, and conversing about how she had things set up seemed easy enough. "You can see everything, and it doesn't take much storage space."

She glanced up from her work. Her eyes danced with unrestrained humor. "Some were broken when we moved here, so I use noodle-drying racks on the end to hold the smaller pieces."

"Noodle-drying racks?" He took a closer look. "No wonder you thought I was teasing you."

Setting aside the soldering iron, she offered, "We can lift this now so you can see it if you are still interested."

"Let me help."

"Just a minute, please." She rotated a crank, and a length of sturdy rope snaked down from a pulley hanging from a ceiling beam. The rope forked into two equal lengths. Each held substantial hooks. "This will make it easy." She stood on one of the rungs of her stool and stretched forward as far as she could.

"I'm closer." He took the hooks and threaded them through rings she'd affixed to the top of the window. "There."

Slowly, carefully, she operated the crank until the window hung suspended in space. "Come to this side so you can see the sun coming through the panes."

Russell didn't need to be asked twice. He'd already gotten the general flavor of the piece and wanted to see its full splendor. He reached her side and looked at the work in awe. Boats floated on rippled glass that looked just like water. The fishes' scales were iridescent, and the faces on Christ and the men He'd called to become His disciples had been painted with undeniable artistry. "Incredible."

"You like it?" She watched him eagerly, clearly wanting to see his reaction.

"That belongs in a museum."

"There is a second one." The implicit offer came out in a shy admission.

"Show me!"

She left his side, went to another crank, and raised another piece off a nearby sturdy table. In the foreground, a young sailor gripped a ship's wheel. Jesus stood behind him, one hand on the sailor's shoulder, the other extended, pointing the way. The thin black paint stroked on the glass gave grain to the "wood," folds to the "cloth," and strands to "hair."

"You're such a wonderful artist. What will you do for my house?"

Lorelei gave him a wary look.

"You don't just do religious windows, do you? What about something old-fashioned?"

"You would have to show me which window." She still looked less than eager.

"Lorelei—I'd like to call you by your given name, if you don't mind." She nodded her permission. "I couldn't put you in a dangerous situation. I worried you might get hurt, climbing a ladder and trying to glaze the windows."

"That is not the only reason." She turned away. Her shoulders were hiked clear up to her ears with the tension that sang through her. "I would not have a lie between us. It is better to be honest, even when it hurts."

He sighed. "All right. I'm sure you guessed it anyway. Your mom and I had a discussion. You've got a tender heart, Lorelei. I decided to keep my distance because I don't want my bitterness to poison you."

"Then why are you here now?"

"Because Pinkus showed me how I can remove the window frames and bring them to you. You'll be working from home, and I won't show up if I'm in a bad mood."

She looked doubtful, so he pressed, "Next week, while the men are working on your roof and chimney, you and your mom can come to my place. You can number all of the windows and measure them. We can decide on some of the places to hang some of these masterpieces, then we'll all go to town and buy whatever glass and supplies you'll need."

"Tell me, Mr. Diamond—"

"Russell. Call me Russell."

"Tell me, Russell." She paused as if to bolster her nerve, then blurted out, "Do you really want us at your home? Many do not, because they think we are German."

"I'm English and Irish; you're German. We're both American."

His answer came too quickly—as if he'd rehearsed it. Lorelei paused. *Do I want to pursue this or let it go?*

He shifted his weight and looked uncomfortable. Her silence must have prodded him because he began to speak again. "I admit, the first time you spoke and I heard your accent, it surprised me."

"It was not a happy surprise."

He exhaled slowly. "No, it wasn't. I won't bother lying. Heines. Huns. Krauts. I've heard it all, and I've even said it myself. Living like a rat in trenches, soldiers are crude and desperate. They have to build up hatred so they can kill the enemy. It isn't easy to come home and hear echoes of your enemy in your neighbor's voice."

Chapter 10

I am not your enemy."

"Of course you aren't. I've come to know that full well." Russell's features tautened. "I've seen the gold star in your window. I know you've paid the ultimate price for our country."

Lorelei bowed her head. Her eyes and nose stung with tears. "Papa wanted to go. He loved America and wanted to help."

Russell cleared his throat. "Then there's no problem with me hiring you to replace my windows or commission stained glass—unless you're already backlogged."

"Fishers of Men was the last piece I had on order." She pasted a brave smile on her face and hoped he wouldn't ask why she didn't have stacks of orders waiting. Before the war, they'd always been backlogged with commissions; now, no one wanted to do business with German Americans.

Russell nodded. "It's selfish, but I'm glad. I need you to work for me."

"I am able to start on your house right away."

"I have to go get paint in a few days. We can pick up some windowpanes while we're at it. How do you keep the glass from breaking when you transport it?"

"It's not easy. Sometimes one of the neighbors who has a motorcar drives for me. When we moved here, I layered straw in the bed of a wagon, then laid the glass between our blankets." She cast a glance at the noodle-drying racks. "The pieces that broke, I kept. I can use them still."

"Are you able to match glass?"

"Sometimes. Why do you ask?"

"There's a leaded-glass window in the parlor that has a few bars of color here and there. I like the effect, but about half of the window is broken. Temporarily, I'll have you replace the whole thing with plain glass, but eventually I'd like to have you restore it."

"If you show me, I can see what kind of glass it is. Even if there is none in town, we could put in a special order. I should warn you, red glass is most expensive. Gold is used to make the red glass, thought it would not seem so to look at it."

He gave her a look she couldn't interpret, and Lorelei felt gauche for having to broach the subject. "You have much work to do, and the cost must be a great burden. I wanted to let you know so I can keep my windows for you affordable."

"I see."

"I could replace the regular windows for you first, because those will be cheapest. When the new garden plot begins to yield a harvest, Mama and I can sell your share or can it for you, and you will end up with a little bit more money."

He scanned her workshop and pointed at a dowel. "What are those metal, snakelike things?"

"Lead cames. They are the channels the glass fits into and come in different widths and shapes. The U shape is for the edges, and the H shape is for the middle." She smiled. "Like when you put together a puzzle—the inside pieces must have nooks and crannies to hold on to one another, but the border must be smooth."

"When I got here, you were using solder and flux."

"Yes." *Such an intelligent man, gathering information so he can calculate the costs of materials.* "When I do more delicate work, I sometimes use copper foil. If you have any lamps which are in need of repair, that would probably be the technique I would employ."

"Where do you buy all of this stuff?"

"The store is starting to order it for me again." As soon as the words were out of her mouth, Lorelei regretted them.

Russell's eyes narrowed. "Starting to? What does that mean?"

"It is of no consequence now."

He tilted her face up to his. "They persecuted you for being German, didn't they?"

"No longer. And during the time I needed things, Mr. Bayley was most helpful. He very kindly used his connections with stores in other towns to obtain whatever I lacked."

"So the old codger is really a guardian angel in disguise, huh?"

Russell's tone was warm and rich with approval, so the words didn't seem disrespectful in the least. Lorelei smiled and nodded.

"We'll go to town day after tomorrow." She detected a slight edge to his voice as he added, "Make a list. Don't worry about which stores we'll go to."

"I need to ask Mama. She might need my help with the cooking or something."

"Lorelei, it would have been dishonorable for me to come speak with you if I hadn't already gotten her approval."

"Oh." She looked into his unfathomable eyes. "I did not mean to insult your integrity."

"No offense taken."

"Well?" Mama stood in the doorway. "What do you—oh, Lori! The window ist wunderbar!"

"You like it?" Lorelei vacillated between being delighted that her mother loved the work and being worried that Russell would get upset at hearing a few German words.

"Ja!" Mama waggled her finger at Russell. "I told you my girl, she makes beautiful windows."

"She does. I'll be here day after tomorrow to take her to get supplies. Perhaps you could come with us to the house now so she can get a feel for what she's going to need."

"I cannot go. I have food almost ready for the stove—potato soup, green beans fresh from the garden, and bread, of course. It is just humble food, but perhaps you should eat supper here."

Lorelei watched indecision flit across his handsome features. "Put it in the wagon. You can use my stove. I need to fire up the oven, anyway. Mutt is sleeping next to it at night."

"This is good, yes. We can come together this way." Mama bobbed her head approvingly. She spun about and headed back to their cottage.

Russell sat on a stool out of the way as Lorelei took care of the small oven so the fire would go out, then let down the stained-glass windows and put things away. "Where's your broom, Lorelei?"

She shook her head. "I am odd. I prefer to sweep in the morning, before I start to work. The little slivers of glass welcome me, and I like the way the morning sun turns them all into sparkles. It makes me happy to start to work again each day."

"Are we ready?" Mama stood in the doorway again.

"Not yet." Russell slid off the stool. "I'm virtually living in the dark. I have one lamp. It would probably be wise for us to take one of your lamps or a candle along so I can get you back here safely."

Lorelei slanted him a funny look. "This, coming from a man who leaves logs in our woodpile at night?"

༜

Russell woke, rolled out of bed, and grimaced as his leg cramped. He'd overdone it yesterday, and he'd pay for it dearly today; but since he'd spoken with Lorelei and they'd cleared the air, he felt better.

He'd wondered yesterday if she'd just been in a good mood after finishing that incredible window, so he'd gone down to the garden and tried to act casual as he watched her garden. "Russell! Hello!" Lorelei's warm smile had drawn him closer.

"I'll hold that." He'd taken the bucket off her arm and watched as she deftly started filling it with beans. To his surprise, the smell of soil hadn't bothered him. He'd absently picked some of the string beans and added them to the harvest. After that, they'd each filled a whole basket with tomatoes. He'd spoken very little; she had chattered sunnily and hummed under her breath. Contentment had radiated from her, and he'd basked in it.

Unwilling to lose the ease he found in her company, he'd urged her to come measure more windows last evening before they'd make the trip to buy supplies. Mrs. Goetz had invited herself along and again made supper for all of them, then puttered around the downstairs as if she belonged there. Only after she'd left had he discovered Mrs. Goetz had worked wonders in the parlor.

Rubbing the morning stubble on his face and staring down at the fresh scars on his leg, he willed away the pain—but the pain didn't obey. The doctors had removed whatever shrapnel they could, and they'd set his leg—but his leg had healed an inch shorter, and some of the shrapnel remained in place.

I have my leg. I'll take the pain. Russell shuddered at the memory of them discussing amputation. He'd shouted himself raw, telling them not to do it. In the end, they'd been worried about infection and damaging nerves, so they'd left shrapnel behind—a permanent reminder of war. *As if my memories and limp aren't enough.*

In a sour mood, he glared at daybreak's first ribbons of light streaming through the window. The blanket that normally hung there was missing, and he jolted. *The windows!* Today he and Lorelei would go into the village and get the supplies to do more work on his house.

Dressed but with his shirt hanging open, Russell hobbled into his kitchen. The aroma of coffee sped his uneven gait. Mutt's head lifted, and her ears perked up. Slowly, she struggled to her feet and headed for the door. Russell let her out and grinned at the stove.

Just before she'd left last night, Lorelei had put a pot of coffee on the back of the stove. "It has far too much water. During the night, the banked embers in the stove will cause the extra water to steam away. You will start your day with a good cup of coffee."

Mmm. He reached for a cup and could hardly wait to get a mouthful. It was a fine trick—one he'd remember, just as he'd keep a big kettle of water on the stove each night so he'd have warm water with which to wash and shave in the mornings.

By the time he hitched the horses and drove the buckboard to the cottage, Russell came to a stunning realization: For the first time since he'd come home, he didn't mind being with other people.

Well, not exactly. He didn't want to cope with everyone in town, but he found an odd comfort in Lorelei's company and an undemanding nurturing in her mother's presence. Odd, but he felt a kinship with them: They didn't want to have to interact with some of the people in town any more than he did. *If Lorelei can face those people, I can, too.*

❧

Lorelei laughed the minute Russell drove up. "So you brought your friend?"

He twisted and urged the dog to sit in the back of the buckboard. "Silly dog is starting to follow me everywhere. She jumped aboard as I was leaving."

"You have doctored her well, that she can jump." She hefted a bushel of vegetables and swung it into the buckboard. "Mama said you told her we could take the produce to town to sell."

Russell got down and wrested the next bushel from her. "Give me that."

Mama came out of the cottage, crossed the brand-new, brick-edged cement veranda he'd made, and started for the buckboard. Russell made an irritated sound, went to her, and grabbed the box of quart-sized canning jars from her. "What do you think you're doing?"

"Taking the produce to town, as you told me I could." She toddled along beside him. "You brought the dog. Do you think whoever the owner is will claim her?"

He stiffened for an instant, then shrugged. "We'll see."

Once they reached town, it didn't take long to unload the produce at the mercantile. The money went toward their store account, so Lorelei turned toward the paint. Russell stopped her. "Did you need anything?"

"Not today, thank you."

He stared at her, then asked in an undertone, "I should have asked before we got here. What do you need?"

"Just two days ago, Mama and I came with your buckboard to buy the food to feed your workers. Our kitchen is quite full. If you have the paint, we can go on to get the glass."

"Okay."

Russell barely finished loading the paint into the buckboard when an energetic group of boys raced up and encircled him. "Is it true? Were you in the war? Did you kill a bunch of Krauts?"

Lorelei saw sweat bead on his forehead and upper lip as the boys continued to pepper him with questions. The haunted look about his eyes intensified, yet he remained completely silent.

"We want to hear all about it!"

"Not from me." Russell pushed past them and helped Mama into the buckboard.

"Heroes do not boast, boys," Lorelei said softly as she slipped past the boys. As they drove off, she leaned forward and whispered to Russell, "We can get the glass another day."

"No." His voice was low and harsh. "Whatever needs doing is getting done on this trip."

Chapter 11

Lorelei rolled the putty into a long, smooth, snakelike cord, then carefully positioned it along the edge of the glass. Once she laid it there, she used her putty knife to press the doughy substance into place and smoothed it so the seal would be sound and the glass secure.

Windowpane after windowpane, she'd done this. A simple skill, glazing a window didn't take a lot of thought, but each one gave her a sense of satisfaction. This particular window sash held four panes; two were originals, and she'd replaced the other pair. The original ones had a faint undertone of lavender to them, and she'd searched among all of the panes of available glass to match it. Old glass often had ripples, bubbles, or a tint to it, and on the day they'd gone to buy glass, Russell had said he wanted to restore the house to be comfortably livable but have it maintain its old flair. He'd been genuinely pleased at the notion of trying to approximate color matches instead of doing wholesale replacement of all of the windows.

Russell. Ever since that day when the boys wanted him to talk about the war, he's become more reserved.

"Ready for lunch?" Mama asked from behind her.

"In just a minute."

Mama's footsteps died out, and Lorelei carefully replaced the lid on the putty can before going to the cottage. Once there, she washed up.

"You stopped singing today," Mama said as she fished corn on the cob from the kettle with a pair of tongs. "Usually you sing as you work. What worries you?"

"Russell."

"Ahh." Mama's voice held a wealth of understanding.

"For a while, I thought maybe he just needed to meet people. He started being more sociable for a little while, but then he got grumpy again. He's all by himself up at that house, day in and day out. It's not good, Mama."

"He's hurting. Not his leg—his heart. Men who go to fight can do this. Some call it 'shell shocked,' but he is not crazy in the head or dangerous. He has curled away from the world because his soul is wounded."

"His soul won't heal if he doesn't read his Bible or go to church, but I can't push him. I feel like God is asking me to be patient and gentle with him."

"God reveals Himself in many ways. It is for us to be right with the Lord so we can be light in the darkness."

"He won't talk at all about the war."

"I can imagine why not. A man who has witnessed the brutality of combat can bear wounds that only the Lord sees. Deep wounds don't heal rapidly."

"He came here to get away from those he loves. He told me he did it so he wouldn't hurt them. Perhaps this is a relapse of the pain that initially brought him to this place."

"We will pray. God is faithful. He will not let this warrior's wounds fester forever. There will come a time of healing."

"That is what is needed," Lorelei agreed. "A prayer for restoration."

※

The smell of sawdust filled the air. Russell moved down one more step and started to sand the next baluster. Mutt scooted down beside him. The dog shadowed his every move. Russell surveyed his work. He'd gotten almost all of this side of the stairs done; the other side had taken four days. Inch by inch, he'd been stripping varnish, sanding, pulling the wood in the house down to bare grain.

The wind off the ocean felt far stiffer today. He welcomed the refreshing change. Most of the month, record-breaking temperatures had scorched the coast. The marble floor of the entryway helped keep the center portion of the house cooler, so he'd purposefully planned to work in this area during the peak of the heat.

The sound of glasses clinking together made him pause.

"Russell!" Lorelei stood in the open front door with a huge smile on her face. "Look at how much work you have done!"

Mutt gave a happy yip of recognition and scuttled down the stairs to her side.

Russell stood and dusted off the front of his shirt and sleeves. "No, look at how much work you've done." He walked toward her and shook his head. "I told you, I don't need this."

"We agreed to sharecrop." She pressed the crate into his arms. "You will not take your portion of the money; the least we can do is see to it you have food put up in your pantry. Mama said you are to come to supper tonight."

"Your mother would have me eat supper with you every night. She must think I'm starving."

Lorelei laughed as she passed the crate full of jars to him. "Can you blame her? We saw the charcoal you tried to feed this dog. If that is your idea of a roast, it is a wonder both of you survive!"

The sound of horses made them both turn around. Pinkus Bayley rode right up to the veranda. "Folks," he greeted them curtly, " 'member how I insisted on the men making new storm shutters? Well, I brought the liveryman's boys to help you get 'em up and batten down the hatches. We've got us a big storm brewin', and the drop on my barometer makes me think it'll be a hurricane."

"Oh, my." The color drained from Lorelei's face. "I have heard they are fearsome things."

"Never been in one?" Pinkus shook his head. "Lock the covers on your wells to keep debris out, and board up the windows. You got a basement, just in case it gets bad?"

Russell set aside the jars. "I do. Lorelei, run down to get your mother. Grab kerosene, lamps, candles, and some blankets. Haul it back here in the wagon." He shook the old man's hand. "Thanks for rounding up help."

"Glad to do it." Pinkus nodded. "Those of us on the windward side of town are seeing boats make for storm anchor, but I reckoned those of you out here didn't know. Ships are reporting North Carolina's getting hit hard, and they've measured higher than thirty-four knot winds. Hurricane flags went up an hour ago. I'm going on to warn the Rimmons."

Four hours later, the boys had fastened the storm shutters built onto the upper windows and affixed the ones made for the lower ones. Russell helped them board up the windows down at the Goetzes' cottage. The boys had refused his offer to stay, delightedly accepted five-dollar bills apiece as payment, and ridden back home.

"I just filled the bathtub," Lorelei called from upstairs as he came inside. "It's cold in the basement. If you don't mind, I'll take the blankets from your beds and drop them down to you."

"There's only one bed. It's in the last room on the right." He turned as Mrs. Goetz emerged from the basement. "Is the fire in the stove out?"

"Ja. But first, I made a good stew and plenty of hot coffee. We will have a good meal as we endure this storm, but I have closed the flue so we will not have smoke come in."

The winds had been picking up steadily. Soon they shrieked, and rain pelted the house. As it sat atop a hill overlooking the ocean, the house groaned in the fury. He'd put it off for as long as he could, but Russell knew the time had come. He led the women to the basement door, sent them down along with the dog, then stared into the dank, dusty darkness. He broke out in a cold sweat. *It's like the trenches.*

Chapter 12

Wind howled louder. Lorelei pulled her sweater closed, more for comfort than for warmth, as Russell shut the door and descended the steps. She saw his steps falter. *His leg! The steps are steep, and it's dark.*

Lorelei grabbed a lamp and hastened to the base of the stairs to light his way. She forced a laugh. "Promise you won't be mad when you get down here and see where Mutt is."

Russell paused and scanned the dim basement.

"Look at the cot."

"We need more light in here." His harsh words echoed in the enclosed space.

"Ja, this I am seeing to." Mama laughed. "Seeing to—that was funny." She turned with two more lighted lamps, came toward the stairs, and handed one to Russell.

He breathes too fast. His face is sweaty. Lorelei shuffled back a bit. "You've worked hard for our safety, and we're trapping you on those stairs. Come. Sit and rest now."

He descended the last step and made a sharp turn to the left. Wordlessly, he prowled the basement, inspecting every last inch. The stairs marked the center of a narrow, fifteen-foot room. One end opened into a small, square room.

"This room, since it already has shelves, we thought was perfect for storing everything." Lorelei scanned what had probably served as an additional pantry in years gone by. "Do you think we have enough?"

Russell barely paid attention to the crate of canned food, the odd assortment of buckets and pitchers filled with water, and the folded stack of blankets. He grabbed a tin of kerosene and shook it. "Almost full."

"Yes. We also brought a box of candles." *Why is he so concerned about light?*

He exited the storage room and looked about as if he hadn't seen the main room before. He walked the full length and stopped by the clunky vacuum cleaner.

"Mama, she coughs when she gets around too much dust," Lorelei said. "I didn't have time enough to clean well, but the worst of the dust is gathered and gone."

He nodded. "There's not much of anything down here."

Mama sat down in one of the three chairs they'd brought down and patted the seat of another. "Come. Sit. Lorelei is right. You have worked hard. There is nothing to do now but wait."

Russell shook his head. "Things down here look fine for a fall-back position if the need is present. For now, we'll stay in the entryway."

"But is that safe?" Mama fretted.

He'd already started toward the stairs. "It's in the center of the house, away from the wind pattern."

Lorelei and her mother exchanged baffled glances.

"Hand me the coffeepot and the stew," Russell called from the top of the stairs. "I don't want you to spill and scorch yourselves."

They settled in the curved area of the entryway in the shelter of the staircase. Instead of sitting with them, Russell kept prowling around. He came back with something each time—an overstuffed chair from the parlor for Mama, a small table from the library for their food. After his fifth or sixth trip, Mama grabbed his arm.

"Come. Have coffee with us."

"Yes," Lorelei agreed. "You've done more than enough to make us safe and comfortable."

Russell sat on a wooden chair he'd brought from upstairs. He accepted a mug of coffee, curled his big capable hands around it, and took a big gulp. Mutt settled on the floor beside him. "Raining pretty good out there now."

"Does that mean it's started?" Lorelei listened as the wind whistled through the shutters.

"Perhaps." He shrugged. "Hurricanes can also have bands of rain clouds that come before the brunt of the storm. We'll sit tight."

"This is a good place to be." Mama craned her neck and studied the area. "It is like being in the cleft of the rock. I don't remember where that is in the Bible."

"Exodus thirty-three." Russell jerked his cup up to his mouth and took another drink.

"Let's read it." Lorelei strove to hide her surprise at how quickly he'd rapped out the citation. She took a small Bible from the pocket of her apron. "I tucked this in before we left the house. Exodus thirty-three. . ." She ran her finger down the page until she reached the passage.

"Starting at verse twenty-one. 'And the Lord said, Behold, there is a place by me, and thou shalt stand upon a rock: And it shall come to pass, while my glory passeth by, that I will put thee in a clift of the rock, and will cover thee with my hand while I pass by: And I will take away mine hand, and thou shalt see my back parts: but my face shall not be seen.'"

Russell didn't seem to be in the least bit interested in the scripture, but the fact that he'd known precisely where to find the verse hinted that he'd spent considerable time in the Word at some point.

Mama began to hum. She paused and smiled at Russell. "This is your house. You do not mind if we sing, do you?"

He shrugged.

Mama began to sing, and Lorelei joined in:

A wonderful Savior is Jesus my Lord,
   A wonderful Savior to me;
He hideth my soul in the cleft of the rock,
   Where rivers of pleasure I see.

He hideth my soul in the cleft of the rock
   That shadows a dry, thirsty land;
He hideth my life with the depths of His love,
   And covers me there with His hand,
And covers me there with His hand.

As they finished the last line, Russell leaned forward and reached for the coffeepot. Lorelei grabbed it and poured more for him. He'd tolerated the hymn, but clearly, he hadn't enjoyed the lyrics.

Instead of letting things fall into awkward silence, she said, "You've done much to the house. What will you do next?"

"I'm stripping the wood." He reached up and curled his fingers around one of the balusters. "Think I'll strip wallpaper out of the parlor, then do a lot of staining and painting."

"The wallpaper is ready to come down in there," Mama agreed. "If you mix vinegar and water, then put it on the paper with a sponge, it will make the glue let go."

"Vinegar?"

Mama nodded. "The day you do this, you will smell like the pickles or sauerkraut."

When he chuckled, relief poured through Lorelei. She settled back. "What color will you paint the parlor, and what will you do about curtains?"

Gusts of wind and rain pelted the house. They discussed his plans, gave suggestions, and finally ate stew. When Mama yawned, Russell took a second lamp, lit it, and ordered Mutt to stay before he walked off.

"I think he's getting the cot, Mama. I'll go get the blankets from that little room in the basement."

"Do you need the lamp?"

"No, Russell has one. It'll only take a minute."

Lorelei descended the stairs, took a few steps, and let out a gasp as something knocked her to the floor and hands closed around her throat.

Chapter 13

Rus-sell." His name came out in a breathless whisper. It took another second for him to realize his assailant wasn't fighting back. Long strands of hair filled his hands, too. *Lorelei!*

Russell let go and rolled to his knees. "Are you all right?"

Lorelei lay there, her eyes huge with fright, yet she nodded.

"Can you breathe?" He anxiously brushed her hair back as remorse clawed at him.

"Yes."

"Did I hurt you? Can you move?"

She rolled to the side and started to push herself into a sitting position. "You surprised me is all."

Gently as he could, Russell pushed her back down. He dragged the kerosene lantern he'd left on the floor closer. Even as he gently turned her head so he could examine her neck, she protested.

"Truly, Russell, I am fine."

Fear turned to anger. "Why did you sneak up on me?"

"The blankets—they're down here."

"If I'd had another second or my trench knife, you'd be dead."

She shook her head and rested her hand on his arm. "No, Russell. You would never hurt me."

"Buttercup, you have more faith than brains." He stood and loomed over her. "Go back upstairs."

She took his hand and got to her feet. He braced her, afraid she might suddenly collapse, sick at the thought she'd cower from him. Lorelei rested her hand in the center of his chest—more, it seemed to still the thundering beneath her palm than to steady herself. Standing there, she looked so fragile, so feminine. He'd scared the wits out of her, yet she smiled up at him and acted as if her heartbeat didn't match his. Being down here scared him; being around her scared him even more.

"I'll get the blankets, and you can get the cot," she decided.

He clamped his hands around her waist, lifted, and set her halfway up the stairs. "Get going."

She took hold of the stair rail, so he let go and turned his back on her.

"I'll wait here. If you go get the blankets, you can hand them to me."

"Stubborn woman."

Her laughter warmed the basement. "Yes, I am."

She's not leaving me down here alone. Russell didn't know whether to be relieved or mad. He strode to the small room, grabbed the blankets, and stomped back. "Here. Scat."

"Yessir!" Humor tinted her voice.

He grabbed the cot he'd been folding, snatched the lamp, and sped up the stairs. Though desperate to be out of there, he still wasn't ready to let matters alone. Russell set up the cot with a few practiced moves, then tugged Lorelei's hand. She lost balance and tumbled into his arms with a surprised cry. He laid her on the cot.

"What is this?" Mrs. Goetz hopped to her feet.

"Loosen your daughter's collar and check her out. I practically broke her neck." Russell paced away and kept his back turned.

As soon as the storm's gone, they'll be gone—and I'll make sure they don't come back. I could have killed her.

❦

"A week," Lorelei grumbled under her breath. "A whole week, and he still barely speaks to me." She scored the glass, tapped along the underside with her cutting tool, then snapped it neatly into two pieces. Ever since he'd set upon her in the basement, Russell had kept his distance.

"Now, Lori," her mother chided as she cleaned one of the windows, "don't be so impatient. Russell Diamond is a good man. He's been very busy clearing away all of those branches which fell—and didn't he cut them into logs for our very own fireplace and stove?"

"Yes, Mama. You don't have to convince me that he has many fine qualities."

"Well, you have been very busy, too. You were in town most every day, fixing windows that storm broke." Mama smiled. "I still thank God that it did not worsen and become all we feared."

"If that was a storm, I don't want to live through a hurricane!" Lorelei walked to the glass rack and selected a small scrap of green to use for a leaf. As she decided how to cut it to use the swirl pattern in the glass to its best advantage, she added, "God heard us when we were singing that He covered us with His hand."

"Ja, so this is true." Mama finished the window and set aside her rag. "And what about the gardens? I thought for sure the plants would all blow away."

"Having the gardens by the hedges helped. They served as a windbreak. If you take produce into town tomorrow, could you please tell Mr. Rawlin that this window is done? Maybe he can drive out to get it."

A shadow fell on the workroom. She glanced up. "Russell!"

"How big is the window?"

"Come see." She gestured to him.

He ordered Mutt to stay in the doorway, walked around the edge of the workroom as he had before, then came to her side to look at it. "Pretty, but not big at all."

"No, it's not." She nudged a piece into alignment. "Teddy broke one just like it when he was playing ball. It belongs to Miss Florina."

Russell winced. "I broke a neighbor's window once. Worked long and hard to pay for it." He stuffed his hands in his pockets and looked decidedly uncomfortable. "I. . .um. . .came to ask a favor."

"That is what neighbors are for."

"I don't know about that. I got a letter from home."

"Is everything okay?" Mama blurted out.

"Yes." He shot her a kind smile, and Lorelei liked him all the more for how nice he always was to Mama. "To put it in a nutshell, my mom and sister have decided they need to come see the house. It's nowhere near ready to have visitors, and I'm not even sure what I need to get."

"Curtains, towels, beds, and bedding for two rooms," Lorelei said at once.

"I like to sew." Mama smiled. "You get many yards of nice fabric, and I can make curtains and pillows and a cushion for a chair in each room."

Russell held his hand up in surrender. "Wait! I figured I'd have you come shopping with me tomorrow. We'll deliver the window while we're at it."

"Stay for supper. You need to eat better." Mama shook her finger at him and headed toward the door. "And come for breakfast. It will be a long day tomorrow."

୯ଡ଼

His head pounded unmercifully, his leg ached, and Russell knew they'd barely begun. He shot Lorelei a get-me-out-of-here glare.

"No, thank you, Mrs. Whorter. I am positive he won't want Chinese urns." She picked up a crystal vase and turned it toward the sun. It cast myriad rainbows about them. Unlike everything else in the store, it was American-made instead of imported. "This Heisey vase is the last thing. You will pack it with the rest so we can pick it up in an hour?"

"Yes. Of course." Mrs. Whorter set the vase on the counter next to an appreciable pile of towels and toiletries, then gave her a shrewd look.

"Good. We've got to get moving." Russell got out of Whorter's Imports and collapsed on a bench on the boardwalk.

"This is moving?" Lorelei plopped down beside him and giggled.

"I have to recover. I kept wanting to sneeze." He scrubbed his hand across his nose to try to stop the tingling from all of the perfumed soaps, powders, and whatnots. "What's wrong with getting all of that stuff at the mercantile?"

"Nothing." Lorelei tugged on the edge of her glove. "But Mrs. Whorter is a widow, and it is nice to give her business. We can go to the mercantile after we go to the china shop—unless you want to use those everyday plates we already bought for when we were feeding the workmen."

"I'm only doing this once. Since I have your help, we'll get the fancy china today."

Ten minutes later, Lorelei somehow managed to get Mrs. Sweeny to seat Russell in a dining chair at a table. "Now, then," Lorelei said, "it is easier to picture the place setting."

She coordinated so well things that made it all go together—the Garland pattern of the Fostoria crystal carried the same graceful motion as the swags between the historical cameos on the Virginia pattern of the Lenox china. The Mount Vernon pattern of Lunt silverware featured the same style of curve.

Even a year ago, this would have irritated him to no end. Now, having a young lady set pretty things on the table before him, worry about whether it harmonized with the other pieces, the soft rise and fall of her sweet voice, the graceful little gestures—it all rolled over him like a balm. War did that to a man, made him aware of the gentling effect women exerted in an otherwise savage world.

Lorelei shifted, bit her lip, and replaced the goblet with another. "There. What do you think?"

I think I'd like to stretch this moment for a long while. Russell lifted the plate to assure himself he'd not been woolgathering and misheard the pattern name. "Virginia." Russell raised a teasing brow. "The silver is Mount Vernon. Are you going for a theme here?"

"Of course." Lorelei set a pair of candlesticks nearby and crooked her head to examine the match. "You told me you were restoring the house. The patterns are old-fashioned looking and honor your heritage. Isn't that what you want?"

"I have the Hanover pattern," Mrs. Sweeny held out a plate with a touch of red amidst heavy gold embellishment around the edge. She cast a sideways glance at Lorelei, and her voice took on a decided bite. "It might suit your heritage, too."

Russell didn't like the undercurrent. He pushed to his feet and tucked Lorelei behind himself as if to protect her from any cruelty. One ugly comment, and the peace he'd craved died instantly. Once again, he was a warrior, and he'd defend Buttercup from anyone who dared pose any threat or unkindness toward her.

"The lady already showed her preference. We'll just go elsewhere—"

"No! Oh no, there's no need for that." Mrs. Sweeny blanched. "I misspoke."

"Yes, you did. Years ago, Americans didn't want my Irish ancestors to immigrate here. I went to war because our country believes all men are created equal."

As he spoke, Lorelei shifted to stand beside him. His arm went about her waist, and he tucked her close to shelter her. "It would be unspeakable if the freedoms we fight for were denied the citizens at home."

"Yes. Of course you're right."

Russell dared to look at Lorelei. Her eyes glistened with tears, but instead of looking pained, she glowed.

"Russell, your words are so wise. Papa would have been so glad to know such a good man as you. For those things, he went to fight, too."

"We don't have to do business here."

Lorelei traced the tip of her forefinger on one of the cameo pictures on the salad plate. "Mrs. Sweeny is sorry. Even before America entered the war, her son's ship was hit by a German U-boat."

Lorelei obviously didn't want to make a scene, and Russell knew it would be best to follow her lead. He bought the china and led her out of the china shop, silently vowing he'd never spend another cent there.

As they waited at the corner for a buggy to pass before they crossed the street, Lorelei turned her face toward the sunshine. The joy on her face sent pangs of envy through him.

"Is there some specific charitable cause I should know about at the next store?"

Lorelei spluttered, then laughed. "Russell, even when you are wry, your wit tickles me."

He smiled back at her. She made being grumpy seem so ridiculously selfish. Few were the people he knew who could laugh at themselves; Lorelei did so regularly. She also coaxed him out of being in a bad mood simply with her sunny disposition.

They'd dropped her mother off at the mercantile in the first place. While they were taking care of the other matters, Mrs. Goetz was supposed to arrange for several other items. Now Lorelei and her mother chattered like birds on a clothesline, and Lorelei kept insisting that Russell make a decision between two things. Finally he leaned back against the counter and folded his arms across his chest.

"This must be done today so the house is ready for your guests," Lorelei scolded playfully.

Russell turned to Mr. Sanders. "I've got dozens of rooms to furnish, and she's fussing like I wouldn't have someplace to stick another bedstead. Just take all of the stuff and dump it in my buckboard. If it won't fit, deliver it."

"But you didn't decide on the material!" Lorelei's mother glowered at him.

He gave Mr. Sanders a yet-another-tempest-in-a-teacup look. The storekeeper grinned as Russell said, "Just throw the whole bolt of whatever fabrics she liked on there, too. Now give me a bottle of Bayer aspirin. Domestic matters are a headache."

Lorelei waited until they reached the mansion and started to unload the wagon. Mama had taken an armful of goods into the house before she tapped Russell on the shoulder. He turned around, holding a gleaming teakettle.

"What?"

"Your headache—is it all you have? Is anything else bothering you? In Boston, the navy is having many cases of the grippe."

"I heard about that. They're calling it the Spanish Influenza. You don't need to fret. I'm fine. Besides, there haven't been any cases down here or out west, so you can stop worrying."

A heavily laden wagon trundled up, and a young man jumped down. "Mr. Sanders ordered me to help carry all of this in. Where do you want it all?"

For the next two days, Lorelei and her mother went up to Russell's house. Russell was more than generous each time they worked for him, and the sock with their savings finally bulged.

Lace curtains hung in the parlor, and Mama had sewn new cushions for the window seat. She'd salvaged the material on the underside of the cushions and made pillows that still matched the old settee they'd uncovered. Russell had already stripped the wallpaper and freshly stained the floor, so he painted the walls a creamy color and nodded appreciatively as Lorelei filled the Heisey crystal vase with a fistful of black-eyed Susans.

She'd concentrated on the bedrooms. He'd painted each of them a pale shade of green. An ornate, white, wrought iron bedstead in one room was covered with a deep green counterpane. It had taken very little time for Lorelei to stitch hems in the dark green material, and after she'd hung the draperies, she'd pulled them open with white, tasseled cords. The room had no bedside table, so she'd tossed a tablecloth over a barrel and set a flowery, globed lantern on it.

The other room boasted cabbage rose bedding and curtains, and fresh, fluffy towels graced the washroom bars.

"What do you think of this?" Russell knocked on the top of a small chest of drawers. "I'm finding stuff in the attic that looks salvageable. When I first got here, I didn't bother looking there, but since I'm going to need some furnishings, that place is full of stuff."

"That will be nice. Can you sand and stain it, or would it be easier to paint it white?"

"The grain's nice. I'll stain it. There are a few washstands and eight or nine chairs up there I'll bring down and either stain or paint."

"Your mother and sister—do they come from far away?"

He straightened suddenly. "Buttonhole. They live in Buttonhole."

"I am sure they will be very glad to see you." She gestured in a wide arc.

"When they see all you have done—"

"That's the idea," he said curtly.

Lorelei quietly studied him, then asked, "Do you believe they will be so busy looking at your house that they will not see the trouble in your eyes and heart?"

Chapter 14

Russell's face hardened, and he gave no reply other than to turn and carry the piece down the stairs and into the empty ballroom he used as his workshop.

Lorelei sat down at the top of the stairs. *Heavenly Father, Your voice holds together the universe. Please speak in a way that will soothe Russell's hurting soul. I dared to hope he'd been improving, but I was wrong. The changes were only on the outside, while inside he's so very broken. You, God—only You can heal the hurt he carries.*

≈

"You're Diamond?" A purser from the railroad scuttled up to Russell.

"Yes." Russell kept searching the trickle of folks disembarking.

"I was asked to give you this message. The phone and telegraph line to Buttonhole blew over in the gale, and the new one's not working."

Russell accepted the envelope and ripped it open. Just seeing his father's strong script brought back memories:

> *Dear Russell,*
>
> *Your mother and sister have both come down with a fever and are staying home. Mom says not to worry, that she'll come next week. She's missed you sorely, as have I. She complains your letters are too short. I would complain, too, but I'm no better, as you can see from this. We pray for you daily and trust the Lord to give you strength and peace.*
>
> *Love,*
> *Dad*
>
> *P.S. We've sent some furniture to you. It once belonged in your house, and we wanted you to have these pieces.*

Russell had dreaded seeing his mother, knowing full well Lorelei was right. Mom was far too perceptive to be deceived by a pretty bedroom and fragrant soap. She'd admire them, enjoy them, but she'd fuss over his leg and fret over how he'd changed.

What was a man to do? He'd gone to war with high ideals and heroic plans. He'd believed in God and country—well, country was still here, but where was

416

God? Where was He when men all around were dying? The first day out, Jonesy—Russell's childhood friend—had stood up and crumpled back into the trench, dead from a sniper's bullet. Men he considered brothers had died all around him.

The very first man Russell had killed had a rosary spill from his pocket. He'd undoubtedly thought God was with him, too. From that day on, Russell hadn't opened the Bible Dad had given him right before he'd left.

That had been the first of many lives Russell had taken. Kill or be killed—it was the most basic rule of warfare. The Bible said God created man in His image, and man was nothing but a bloodthirsty, cruel animal.

Mom and Dad lived such innocent lives. Their world was simple, their faith unshaken. Russell couldn't bear to look them in the eye and let them see what he'd become. Body, mind, and soul, he'd come home battered in ways no one would ever comprehend.

One more week of respite. . .but at what cost? *Is Mom really all right? And Sis? Is it the Spanish Flu?*

"Sir? Mr. Diamond." The purser scowled at him. "You need to claim your crates and sign for them."

"Sure. Fine."

He'd cleaned up an old buggy from the stable to come claim Sis and Mom. Clearly, he'd never manage the furniture. Russell arranged with the livery to deliver the large crates.

The house felt eerily empty when he got home. Once the oak secretary, rocking chair, and hall tree were in place, the feeling of loneliness intensified. Dad had often sat at the secretary, going over order forms. Mom had loved the rocking chair. The hall tree had no umbrellas, hats, or jackets on it to give it a homey air. As far as companionship, Mutt usually was all Russell wanted or needed, but tonight he felt alone.

Russell couldn't sleep. He worried about his mom and sister. Had Dad taken sick, too? Russell purposefully didn't read magazines or newspapers because the major features were all about the war. Even so, he'd overheard stories about the influenza up in Boston. It killed strapping, healthy soldiers.

Did I tell Mom I loved her before I left?

༈

"Hop in. I'm going to town to make a telephone call."

Lorelei took hold of Russell's hand and nimbly climbed into the buggy. "Telephones are amazing, aren't they? Hearing a voice over wires—it doesn't seem possible."

"My dad had one put in his emporium. I always thought it was a nuisance, because whenever anyone called, it fell to me to answer it and take messages."

Lorelei chuckled. "So now who will have to take the message?"

"I'm calling my dad. Mom didn't come yesterday. She and my sister are both sick."

Lorelei twisted on the seat to face him. "Oh, Russell, I am so sorry to hear this. I will have to pray for them."

"You do that, Buttercup." His voice sounded grim, and he said nothing more the rest of the way to town. As soon as they entered the mercantile, Russell bee-lined to the telephone on the rear wall.

Lorelei decided to buy ten-pound bags of flour and sugar instead of five pounds since she'd have a ride home and she and Mama hadn't bought any for themselves in a while. Then, too, she asked for a dozen brown eggs. Folks chatted and jabbered as usual. One of Mrs. Sweeny's sons had received a battlefield promotion.

After he finished his phone call, Russell prowled around the farthest aisles of the store. Noting his dark expression, Lorelei ventured over to him.

"How is your mother?"

"Dad said it's a nasty cold—nothing more." He didn't meet her eyes. "While I'm in town, I want to stock up. It'll take time. Is that a problem?"

"Not at all." She laughed. "With the unexpected ride, I'll still get home sooner."

By the time they left, Lorelei knew for certain they couldn't have wedged one more thing in the buggy. As it was, she held a crate on her lap that contained the oddest assortment of canned food she'd ever beheld. "Your larder will be full for at least a year with all of this."

"Don't blame me." He fished a can of chipped beef from the crate and held it up. "Mutt's the hungry one."

"She is by your side all of the time. How did you make her stay home?"

"It wasn't easy. Listen, Mom sent apples from our orchard back home. I'll eat a few, but they'll mostly spoil. Can you and your mom use them?"

"But of course. Oh. . .I should have bought more canning jars."

"I'll get you some if you promise to make cinnamon applesauce."

Lorelei laughed. "This applesauce—"

"Cinnamon applesauce."

"This cinnamon applesauce—I suppose it is also for your very hungry dog?"

Chapter 15

Russell carried Lorelei's measly ten-pound bags of sugar and flour into the cottage, barged into the kitchen, and started opening cabinets. "Where do these go?"

"In the canisters, silly." Lorelei put down the eggs and gave her mother a hug.

"You will stay for lunch." Mrs. Goetz made it more of an order than an invitation, but he'd been counting on that.

"I can't stay long, what with that stuff in the buggy. Let me help." He opened the pantry and scanned the shelves. *They hardly have anything on them.* He cleared his throat. "What do you want?"

"I want you to sit down," Mrs. Goetz said as she pulled out a chair.

"Yes." Lorelei's eyes sparkled with humor. "Having seen your roast, Mama is sure your cooking would give us stomachaches."

"I'm never going to hear the end of that roast, am I?"

Lorelei and her mother said in unison, "No."

At dusk, they stood side by side and said the same thing. "No, Russell."

He rotated his shoulders, but the action didn't relieve the stress. As soon as he'd finished lunch, he'd driven the buggy to his back door, unloaded the contents, then changed his socks to the ones Mrs. Molstead had knitted. He'd unhitched the horses from the buggy and changed them over to the buckboard.

It had taken considerable fortitude to drive north to the Molsteads' store. He'd done it for Lorelei, though.

Only Lorelei acted anything but pleased.

Russell folded his arms across his chest and glowered at the woman. "I didn't want to tell you this, but you're backing me into a corner. I have information that the flu is spreading."

"You don't read the newspaper, Russell." Lorelei made a dismissive gesture. "So far, they think it will stay up North. No one expects it to come down here, and experts say it will never go to San Francisco, either."

He'd hoped they'd simply accept what he told them. Clearly, Lorelei needed to be set straight. "You know I spoke with my dad on the telephone. He's got contacts all over because of the orders he places for his store. He said it's spreading—faster than folks realize. Dad's not one to panic, but he's not letting Mom or my sis come visit. That says plenty to me. After I spoke with him, I placed a few calls myself."

"You truly are worried." Lorelei gave him a compassionate smile.

"I am." He didn't mince words. "You're going to have to cooperate with me, because the less often we go to town, the lower the chances are that we'll contract it."

"But influenza strikes the feeble, the old, and the very young," Mrs. Goetz reasoned.

"Not this one. People fifteen through forty are getting hit the worst." He hated scaring them, but he had no choice. "It's killing them in a matter of a day or two."

Russell didn't give the women a chance to demure. He hefted twenty-five-pound bags of sugar and flour onto his shoulder and headed toward their kitchen door. Prices—especially of sugar—were high, so folks had been cutting back and buying smaller bags. He, on the other hand, was willing to pay top dollar, and the Molsteads gladly sold him as much as he wanted. Fatigue and the extra weight of the sacks made his limp worse. A sardonic smile twisted his mouth. His bum leg had provided a good excuse to buy several bottles of aspirin.

Glass clinked behind him. Funny, how he'd come to associate Lorelei with that sound. "Russell," she said in her singsongy voice, "I hope you bought some cinnamon for the applesauce I'll put in these."

He shouldered the door open and dumped his burden near their pantry, and more than just the weight on his back lifted. He smiled at her. "Are four big tins enough?"

"Four!"

The shock in her voice still rang in Russell's mind as he crawled into bed that night. Exhausted as could be, he lay there and experienced the oddest sensation—security. He'd not felt this way since he'd gone off to war. For the first time in ages, he'd been able to control matters and take action to make a difference.

The sickening knot in his stomach and the tension in his muscles eased as he closed his eyes and recalled his last glimpse of the Goetzes' kitchen. By the time he'd left, every last cabinet and shelf there had bulged with provender. Astonishment and gratitude had shone in Lorelei's eyes as she bid him sweet dreams when he walked past her toward the door. He rubbed his aching leg and let out a sigh. *She'll be safe now.*

ⳗ

"All set." The iceman shut the door to the icebox and pulled a newspaper from his pocket. "Here's the paper. News is bad all over. The missus said to thank you for the pumpkins."

Mama handed him a burlap sack containing more bounty from their garden. "She is welcome. They grew well this year."

Lorelei sat on the new porch and opened the newspaper. Mama came out

420

and settled on the chair. She started to shuck corn. "Read to me."

"Things look bad in the North," Lorelei said as she scanned the headlines. She didn't tell Mama about the article of another German store being vandalized.

"So Russell was right about the influenza?"

"Yes. Boston canceled its Liberty Bond parades and sporting events. In New York, they closed the theaters and symphony halls. The stock market is only open half day. The influenza is awful in Europe, too. They've canceled schools!"

"So terrible this is!"

Lorelei read aloud, and as she turned the page, Mama called out, "Good day, Russell!"

"How can you say it's good with what you're reading?" He waved his arm toward the newspaper.

Lorelei watched his gait as he approached. *He barely limps at all anymore. . .or is it just that I've grown accustomed to his walk? No. It is better, because on the days it pains him, I can tell by his bearing.*

"The day is beautiful, crisp, with the lovely autumn air and weak sunshine. The news is bad. Perhaps the church is doing something. We will see on Sunday."

"You can't be thinking of going to church!" Russell halted by the porch steps, leaned forward, and snatched the newspaper from Lorelei. "Public gatherings help spread the disease." He turned and appealed to Mrs. Goetz. "You've lost your husband; you can't possibly endanger your daughter!"

Lorelei folded her arms in her lap. *Dear Lord, let this be an opening.* "Will you make a deal with us, Russell? If we do not go to town for church, will you come to our house and worship with us?"

"Is that what it'll take?"

Lorelei glanced back at Mama, saw her nod, and turned back to him. "We would be pleased."

"Fine. Sunday." He stomped off.

"You know, it will be hard for him," Mama said softly. "He knows the Bible, but his faith is faltering."

"I know. He got angry when I was singing, 'Great Is Thy Faithfulness' out in the garden last week. He's still a soldier, but the battlefield is his soul."

"The Holy Ghost is wooing him. Maybe God will make something good happen out of all of this bad."

"With God, all things are possible." Lorelei scooted backward and reached up. Her fingers closed around her mother's corn-silk-tassel-covered hand. "Let's pray, Mama."

∽

"What was I thinking?" Russell angrily opened a can of chipped beef and dumped it in a bowl for Mutt. Russell plopped the bowl on the floor for the dog and didn't worry about the gravy that slopped over the edge. Mutt would make short work of it. He twisted and threw the empty can into the wastepaper basket with total disgust. "What under the sun was I thinking to agree to that ridiculous proposition?"

I care about them. The truth nearly knocked him off his feet. It was dangerous to care. How many friends had he made on the battlefield, only to lose them? How often had he shared a cold, miserable trench with someone, only to see him die? *This flu—it's killing people. It could claim any of us.*

The safest thing is not to grow attached. Even though she's freshly widowed, Mrs. Goetz has a pleasant outlook on life and a gentle warmth. As for Lorelei. . .

Russell didn't want to admit it to himself, but the truth glared at him. He yanked out a chair and dropped into it. *She has a way about her—a compassion and joy for living that lights the dark corners of my heart. It's too late for me to keep from caring. I'll be sure to keep as much distance as possible.*

Really, it wouldn't be all that hard. He'd been essentially solitary since he'd arrived. Other than interacting with the workmen as necessary, Russell made a point of not socializing. All he'd do was walk down to the cottage for an hour or so on Sunday mornings, then ignore his neighbors the rest of the week.

Satisfied with that decision, he stood and tugged open a cupboard door. Scanning the cans of food, Russell felt a twist of disgust. Overseas, he'd eaten out of tins for months and promised himself he'd never eat out of them once he got home. Now that he was home, it didn't matter. Nothing tasted good. For the most part, he ate only because hunger forced him to. The meals Lorelei and her mother made were the exception. Russell couldn't figure out why he suddenly developed a decent appetite and appreciated the flavor of their food. He grabbed a can of tuna and wrinkled his nose as he opened it. It occurred to him that anything he didn't have to fix or something fresh ought to rightfully be more appealing. *But when I've eaten at the diner, that might as well have been sawdust.*

He peeled off the lid and didn't bother to drain the can or mix it with anything. Hunched over the counter, he scooped out bites and shoveled them into his mouth.

Why did I agree to worship with them? I left the battlefield in France, but I'm still at war—only this is a personal war. I'm fighting with my soul, with God. Tradition and convention aren't good enough, and I'm not going to pretend.

Russell spent a sleepless night and a hectic day. He tried to find something to take his mind off the fact that he'd gotten roped into Sunday worship. Mucking out the stable and grooming both horses, raking and burning leaves—the heavy physical labor didn't distract him in the least.

The library beckoned—the one room he'd left entirely alone. Heavy draperies blocked out the sunlight, and sailcloth drooped in forlorn, dusty shrouds over the bookcases. Methodically, he removed and folded each piece of sailcloth from the outside to the middle, effectively capturing the worst of the dust. Whoever had closed up the house had taken great pains to try to preserve the books. Russell finally stretched his back and wiped his hands on the thighs of his jeans. He'd gotten a lot done—even if he'd been thinking of Lorelei all the while.

The next morning, he grudgingly put on a tie and walked to the cottage. Mutt trotted alongside him, and he figured it would be all right. *She'll probably behave better than I will.*

Lorelei opened the door, and a combination of aromas from the kitchen and her light, floral perfume greeted him. Her eyes sparkled. "We waited breakfast on you. There's even some applesauce—cinnamon applesauce."

He cracked a grim smile. They'd tried to do their part to make this comfortable. After breakfast, they moved from the kitchen table to the small parlor.

Lorelei smoothed her Sunday-best dress. "I thought to have us sing a bit, read a passage of scripture, and pray."

Russell shuffled his feet and cleared his throat. "Ladies, I'll not be a hypocrite. I won't sing the words to those hymns. I don't feel them, and a man ought not misrepresent himself to the Lord or to others."

Mrs. Goetz smoothly invited, "Then listen and hum. You can appreciate the music even if the lyrics don't quite match your thoughts."

Satisfied with that compromise, Russell sat down and hummed old, familiar hymns. Lorelei lovingly opened her Bible and paused a moment as she fingered the ribbon marking the passages she'd selected. She didn't start reading from the left page where the Psalms began. Instead, she shifted the Bible slightly and began reading. "Psalm four: 'Hear me when I call, O God of my righteousness: thou hast enlarged me when I was in distress; have mercy upon me, and hear my prayer. . . .' "

Three psalms she read, her expressive voice rising and falling, carrying a range of emotions that made the psalmist come alive. Before now, the Psalms had never been much more than pretty words to Russell. The depth and complexity in the verses struck several nerves.

After Lorelei finished reading, Mrs. Goetz prayed. Lorelei had once told him that her mother usually prayed in German, but at the meals they'd shared, she prayed in English. Even so, then, as today, she occasionally slipped and called God *Vater* instead of Father. Her prayer, so honest and intimate, made the ache in his heart double.

Seconds after saying, "Amen," Mrs. Goetz smiled at him. "Russell, you will stay for dinner?"

"I can't. I have to go." He stood and saw the surprise, shock, and chagrin on Lorelei's face. He couldn't help it. He had to get out of there, shift his thinking, and shut down the unexpected flood of emotions he felt from hearing David's words, the hymns, and prayer.

At home, the haunting passages played through his mind. He'd never appreciated how David was a warrior. He'd been besieged, seen comrades fall. *I will both lay me down in peace, and sleep: for thou, Lord, only makest me dwell in safety.* . . . The words from the psalm nagged him, taunted, and wouldn't let go. Even after enduring combat, killing and seeing his own men perish, David could lie down in peace—and he slept. *Oh, to have my head hit the pillow and not relive the horror of what I saw and did!*

David the soldier was also David the musician, the one who sang unto the Lord. *I can't sing. Nothing flows from me but anger and sadness. How did David manage?*

As the week went by, Russell found himself humming as the words of hymns Lorelei and her mother had sung seeped into his memory. "Abide with me! Fast falls the eventide. The darkness deepens. . ." Russell knew all about darkness—not just the pitch black of night, but the ugliness of the soul. In the silent moments when Russell paused from his work to rub his leg or catch his breath, he'd recall the lyrics again and again. "Lord, with me abide. . . ."

The next Sunday, he took a harmonica to worship, hoping to drown out the lyrics. He didn't want to remember how he'd once treasured those hymns and believed them, had held faith in a loving God. Russell hoped if he concentrated on playing, the lyrics wouldn't continually intrude upon his conscience, but nothing could drown out the sweet blend of Lorelei and her mother's voices as they worshiped the God they loved so dearly—the same one who turned His face away and allowed Russell to wallow in the aftermath of man's ultimate evil.

No matter how hard he worked, regardless of the physical difficulty or the mental acuity required for a task, Russell couldn't free himself from the persistent reminders and memories of what Lorelei and her mother sang, read, or said. Between the songs of reverence and praise and the scriptures, he left the Goetz cottage and lived with the echoes of worship all week long.

Daytime was hard enough; nights grew nearly impossible. Russell would lie in bed and fight to find a comfortable position. His leg troubled him after the exertions of the day, and that pain only compounded his inability to sleep well. He'd toss and turn, besieged by flashes of battlefield memories. Jolting awake, he'd struggle to reorient himself. In the moments after he established that he was safe in his bed, he'd try to substitute a different vision in his mind. Time and again, his thoughts would go to Lorelei as she held up a stained-glass window of Christ or as she read her Bible. Lorelei laughing. Sun shimmering on her golden hair as she bowed her head in prayer. She had the peace he craved. It didn't take a genius to figure out her peace ran soul deep—but the problem was, his trouble plumbed the depths of his soul.

Each Sunday, he kept his promise and went to their cottage. At first it was just to keep them safe, but in the following weeks it became a habit. Sunday morning became the only way he marked time. He'd left home and family behind in search of a refuge, to get away from others; yet he paid a weekly visit to his neighbors, sat in their parlor, and examined how others in the Bible had endured the separation from God he was experiencing.

Most of all, Russell identified with David. He'd lost his friend Jonathan. He'd gone to battle, been brave, then shook with fear. Psalm after psalm revealed the ups and downs he'd experienced—the joys, the sorrows, the fears, the depression. David was just as likely to cry in grief and sorrow as he was to sing in victory.

David—David had known the ugliness that lurked not only in other men's souls, but in his own, too. War had forced Russell to do things he'd never imagined himself doing. He'd slain—even rejoiced and taken pride in causing his enemies' deaths. That fact plagued him. . .but King David—the warrior, the psalmist—had done the same thing. And Lorelei had said David was a man after God's heart.

Right and wrong—they once were so clear. Now Russell struggled to reconcile a loving God with all He allowed to happen. As time passed, Russell's anger started to give way to unspeakable sorrow.

David had times of darkness when he couldn't see God's face. Why had he still called out to God? *And why can't I?* Russell shook his head. *I can't.*

Chapter 16

I t's cold in here."

Lorelei nodded absently and tapped a nail into the surface to keep the next piece of glass in place.

"Why didn't you light the fire?" Russell tromped across the workroom toward the potbelly stove.

"Please, don't light it." She looked over her shoulder at him. "The newspaper says it is best to leave the house cold. They think it kills the microorganisms for the influenza."

"The cold will kill you before it kills the germs. You don't dare catch a chill. It'll weaken your lungs and make you a prime target." He opened the grated front of the small stove, then slammed it shut.

"Come look at this window. I've been working on it for your parlor. Remember the pieces I couldn't match? I've removed the original edge, cut and used those pieces, and reformed the border with this opalescent gold. See how the amber makes the vertical lines shimmer?"

"What about that spot in the middle?"

"I couldn't quite make the glass stretch far enough, so I decided we'd put jewels here, here, and there." She touched the empty spots.

"Jewels?"

"Yes." She pulled a box from a shelf off to her right and opened the lid.

"Oh. Bauble things."

She laughed. "There are plain, smooth, round ones, or we can use faceted ones. What do you prefer?"

He reached over her shoulder and used his forefinger to push the jewels around in the box until he found one that appealed to him. "This kind." He picked it up and set it on her work board. "Yeah. I like that a lot."

"I agree. We need two more." Before he could respond, Lorelei hurriedly added, "In fact, there are many supplies I need to buy—more lead cames, more solder, and emery so I can smooth out the chips on some of your pieces in order to repair them best."

"Make a list. I'll go to town."

"I knew you'd offer, but it won't work. I need to look at the things and decide for myself." She could see the fire in his eyes, so she hastily added, "If I'm to stay out of town, at least I should have the things necessary to keep myself busy."

"Don't you understand?" Russell glowered at her. "My mother and sister just had a simple cold and fever. Even after they recovered, they stayed in Buttonhole, because by then, Dad wouldn't let them get on the train. It's utter foolishness to mix with people."

"I'm getting essentials, not going to a party."

"Lo-ri!" The frantic pitch of Mama's voice sounded from the house.

"Coming, Mama!" She started toward the house, and Russell rushed alongside her. "What is it?"

"We need to go check on Russell. Mutt is here. Perhaps something is wrong."

"Nothing's wrong, Mrs. Goetz." Russell brushed past Lorelei.

Her mother threw her arms around him and burst into tears. "I was so worried for you!"

"Shh," he murmured. Lorelei watched as he awkwardly embraced Mama. Seeing Mama's stark fear and how his tender nature surfaced touched her deeply. After a few minutes, Mama calmed down, and he announced, "Enough of this. I'm worried about the two of you, and you're worried about me. My cooking is so bad, I'm likely to kill myself with something I fix. I'm moving you into my house."

"You can't mean it." Lorelei stared at him in shock.

Crafty as a fox, he ignored her and spoke to Mama. "Lorelei can share my workroom downstairs to do the windows. It will make it easier than creating them here and moving them."

"This would be good."

Lorelei slipped an errant hairpin back into place. "I can't finish this window or start on more until I have my supplies."

※

I lost the battle but won the war. Russell shot Lorelei a surreptitious look as he drove the buckboard toward town. Her mother stayed home to pack up their necessary belongings. "This is a short trip."

"You've said that twice since we left home."

"I mean it." As they reached the edge of town, Russell felt her stiffen. "What is it?"

"The cemetery."

He leaned forward to look past her. Perfectly manicured grass normally graced the lot, but now it was pockmarked with multiple new graves.

"Mrs. Sweeny has black crepe on her door, but the stars on her flag are still white." Lorelei grabbed his arm. "Everyone is wearing masks."

Russell grimly hitched the horses outside the mercantile. "Stay put, and don't visit with anyone." He tied a bandana over the lower portion of his face and went inside. Moments later, he emerged with an entire bolt of cotton gauze. Hastily, he hacked at it with his pocketknife and folded the freed portion into a mask that he secured over her nose and mouth.

"Russell, look around us. There are posters in the windows, warning of contagion and how to battle it."

"It's bad, Buttercup." He squeezed her hand. "Give me the list. I'll leave it with Mr. Sanders. He'll fill the order while we take care of everything else. I want to get out of here as quickly as possible."

At the hardware store, they found everything they needed for her windows and the repairs Russell was making. The china shop was closed, and a black wreath hung from the door. Lorelei's eyes filled with tears. "I used to walk down the street and see the star flags in the window. Now there is black crepe everywhere."

Just then, a wagon started down the street. Two plain pine caskets rattled on it, and Mr. Sweeny sat in the back with them as the preacher drove the team.

"What time does the funeral start?" Lorelei asked in a subdued voice.

The pastor shook his head. "New orders are out. Family only. No church services—only fifteen-minute graveside commitments."

Russell reached around and tugged Lorelei into the lee of his body. He could feel her shaking. "We'll go home now."

"No, Russell. We must help."

He knew that look in her eye and the streak of stubbornness that ran straight through her. Instead of arguing, Russell let out a sigh. He searched for something that would satisfy her without putting her in danger.

"Tell you what, Buttercup. We'll go to the butcher and the mercantile. I'll load up and buy the biggest kettle they have and every last canning jar. You and your mother can bake bread and make soup. I'll bring it to town."

⌒⊘

"Here you go." Mrs. Goetz set one last paper-wrapped bundle in the bed of the buckboard. Flour streaked her apron, and she tried to brush it off. "You're starting out late today. The sun is setting earlier, too. If it gets too late, unhitch the wagon and ride home. The horses know the way."

"You go on in and rest. You're working too hard."

"Broth and bread are easy to make."

"You've made plenty of both for the past two weeks."

She pressed her hand to the bib of her apron. "In my heart, I make many more prayers than any loaves of bread. I pray God keeps you safe, Russell."

He reached town and took the list of homes from the light post. The pastor had arranged to hang a roster from a string he'd knotted around the post, telling Russell which families needed bread and soup. He'd drop off the food on their porches and pick up the jars from the previous day.

Each day the list grew longer. Russell worked his way across town from one street to the next. Folks didn't stop to visit—they scurried away, eyes big with fear above the ever-present gauze masks. At the last stop, Russell walked up to the door. To his surprise, little Arnie was sitting on the stoop. The five-year-old had been the first in his family to come down sick. He'd only gotten out of bed two days ago.

"Arnie, it's late for you to be up."

Arnie looked up, and Russell's heart skipped several beats. The little boy's face was ashen, and his eyes huge. Dried tear runnels etched his cheeks. "Mommy won't wake up."

Russell knocked, then invited himself inside. A quick check revealed the worst: Both of Arnie's parents and his baby sister were dead. It would be foolish to take anything out of the diseased home, so Russell took off his shirt, wrapped the little boy in it, and headed toward the parsonage.

The pastor took one look at Arnie and bowed his head in grief. He paused a moment, then motioned Russell inside.

"No one's left at his house." Russell chose his words carefully as he lowered the child onto the couch. Arnie wouldn't let go of him, though, so he sat on the horsehair-stuffed cushion and kept the boy in his lap. "What about the rest of his family?"

The pastor wearily rubbed his forehead and sat in a nearby chair. "They've already passed on. He doesn't have anyone. All the families who were able to help out are overburdened. I can't see any choice. Arnie will need to go to Tepfield."

"Tepfield?" Russell gave the parson an appalled look. An orphanage was never a good arrangement, but in the midst of the epidemic, it would amount to cruel neglect at the best and death at the worst. Over in France, Russell had hated seeing the ragged orphans wandering about hungry, frightened, and alone. He refused to resign an American child to that fate. He took a deep breath. "I'll take him."

"Do you know the way?"

Russell shook his head. "No, I meant I'll take him home with me."

"Praise be to God!"

Russell rose. "It's not temporary. I won't have him relocated later. He's been through enough."

"I agree." As the pastor led them back outside, he offered, "I'll handle the arrangements so you'll be assigned as his guardian."

Russell nodded. The commitment he'd just made ought to be staggering, but even amid the sorrow surrounding the situation, the decision felt right. He set off for home. Along the way, Arnie snuggled in his lap. "That house has a star. Daddy says they have a boy in the war."

"Yes, they do."

Arnie pointed out house after house, mentioning the star flags. "There's a lellow star at that house. That means they gave a son."

Russell wondered if Arnie understood what that meant. *So much death. So much heartache. Why, God? Why?*

The horses walked slowly since it had grown dark. They went past an open field. Arnie pointed up at the sky. "Look. Lots of stars. God has lots of boys like me."

"Yes, He does."

Arnie nudged Russell's chin. "Lookie. A big lellow star. God gave a Son, too."

It was all Russell could do to keep from roaring in his agony. Instead, he tightened his hold on Arnie. "What if I take you home and let you be my boy now?"

Chapter 17

lease, Lord, bring him home. It's grown so late. Keep Russell healthy and safe. He's been through so much, Father. Show him Your mercy and grace. The sound of the buckboard and horses jolted her. *Thank You, Almighty Father!* Lorelei raced out onto the veranda. "Russell!"

"I brought home a nice little fellow." Something about his tone and the sorrow in Russell's eyes made Lorelei's breath catch. "Arnie's going to be my boy now."

She reached up and accepted Arnie. Russell had sacrificed his shirt to bundle the small boy. "You look tired, Arnie. Let me carry you into the kitchen. I'll make you a nice, warm snack; then we can put you to bed."

Arnie clung to Russell while Lorelei spooned chicken noodle soup into him. Mama didn't bother filling the bathtub; the kitchen was warm, so she pumped water into the sink, added hot water from the stove's reservoir until it was just the right temperature, then sang quietly as she bathed the boy.

Lorelei went upstairs to set up the cot, and Russell called to her, "Put it in the little parlor off my bedroom so I can hear him during the night."

After she did as Russell requested, Lorelei came downstairs to catch Russell burning his shirt and Arnie's clothing. Neither of them said a word.

Mama came in with Arnie bundled in a towel. "Russell, our little boy needs to borrow one of your undershirts. Tomorrow I will sew some handsome clothes for him."

"I seem to recall trunks up in the attic with old clothes in them." Russell stood and gently took Arnie from Mrs. Goetz. "I'll tuck him in tonight and search for stuff for him first thing in the morning."

A short while later, Lorelei and her mother went up to bed. They peeked in on Arnie. Russell sat on the settee by the sleeping child's cot, looking as if the weight of the world had fallen on his shoulders. Mutt lay curled at his feet.

"You look so domestic," Lorelei whispered.

He raked his fingers through his hair in agitation. "He doesn't have anyone. Pastor said there isn't anyone left in his whole family. I promised I'd watch over him, but I can't do it alone. I can keep him warm and fed, but I don't have the love and solace he'll need."

Lorelei opened her mouth to refute his words, but Mama silenced her with a touch and said, "We will help you. Arnie needs a whole family, and together, with God's loving help, we will become what he needs."

"I'll fix up this little room for him. He was afraid to be by himself."

"We can do that tomorrow. For now, let's all get some rest." Lorelei gently ruffled Arnie's hair and smoothed his blankets. "No fair going to the attic alone, Russell. I want to see what's stored up there."

He leaned his head back on the settee and said, "There's something else."

Lorelei dreaded what else might have gone wrong. *Lord, please don't let him have lost someone dear to him. He can't take it.*

"Buttonhole is almost decimated by the epidemic. I got a telegram from my dad. So far, you and I have done well by staying isolated, and I'm thinking about having my mom load up some of my cousins who are the most vulnerable and having them come to stay here."

"This is something to pray about," Mama said sagely.

"We'll go back to our cottage. You'll have plenty of room." Lorelei smiled at him.

He bolted upright. "No! I thought you just promised to help me with Arnie. I just wanted to know if you'd mind having more people underfoot."

"God blessed you with a mansion, Russell. I think it would be a sin to leave rooms empty when they could harbor children who need a safe place."

"I'll think on it more tonight."

"And we'll pray," Mama said. She shook her finger at Russell. "I get to look in that attic tomorrow, too. If we are going to fix up more bedrooms, I might find things up there we can use."

❦

"Look at these!" Lorelei dusted off a pair of pineapple-topped bedsteads. "They'd be wonderful together in one of the larger bedrooms. It is odd, though, these pineapples."

"They're an old American symbol of welcome," Russell said absently as he lifted an old ceramic chamber pot.

Arnie, who clung to Russell's leg, announced, "I don't got one of those under my new bed."

"Then it must be yours." Russell chuckled.

Lorelei knelt and smoothed her hand over another piece of wood. "What is an altar doing up here?"

"Family lore is, the church burned down the night one of my ancestors proposed. He ran into the church and saved the altar for his bride's sake. He knew she'd want it for their wedding."

"Yes. Yes, I believe this. Part of it is burned."

Mama bent over a trunk that was pressed way beneath the eaves. "The top of this has had much rain, but inside it looks good. There are clothes here—old ones that belonged to a woman." She dug deeper. "Oh, bless the Lord! There are clothes here for a little boy!"

"Count your many blessings," Lorelei started to sing.

"Mommy sings that song to me. When is Mommy going to come get me?"

Russell sat on the floor of the attic and tugged Arnie around so the boy stood eye to eye with him. "Mommy was very sick. Daddy, too."

"And Baby 'Liz'beth."

"They died, Arnie. Do you know what that means?"

Lorelei knelt on the floor and said, "It means they sleep in heaven now with Jesus."

Arnie's eyes filled up with tears. "But what 'bout me?"

"You're going to sleep in your new room here," Russell said. "You're going to be my boy now."

The little boy's face puckered. "Am I 'posed to put lellow stars in the window?"

Mama came over and opened her hand. Three golden buttons in the shape of stars lay nestled in her palm. "Better than that, sweetheart. You'll wear the yellow stars."

❦

"I'm going." Lorelei set down her soldering iron so hard, the pieces of glass jumped. The room that had once been an enormous parlor and ballroom rang with her words.

"Don't be so stubborn. It's for your own good."

"You are my friend, not my father," she said hotly. "You cannot make me go to my room like a naughty child." *Even if you want to. . .*

"See reason."

"I am seeing reason. It will be necessary to get essentials."

"For crying in a bucket, Lorelei, I'm losing my patience. I have enough china and silver to feed an army."

"But you do not have towels enough, nor sheets. You don't even have mattresses for the beds! I know what to get; you do not. Of course I should go to town."

He stared at her. "I'll tell you what: My dad and mom own a mercantile. You make a list, and I'll have them fill a freight wagon. I'd rather have them ride here than come by train, anyway."

Jaw clenched to the point that the tiny muscles on the side of his cheek twitched, he bent over a little chest of drawers and resumed sanding it with long, heavy strokes. The grating *swish* against the sudden hush in the room sounded unnaturally loud.

The patter of little feet echoed on the marble entryway, giving warning that Arnie had awakened from his nap and would be with them in an instant. The little boy burst into the workroom and zoomed toward Russell. "There you are. I thought you were gone."

Russell let go of the sandpaper, knelt, and opened his arms wide. Arnie ran straight to him and hung on tight. His eyes and voice were filled with tears. "Don't leave me."

"Leave you?" Russell pulled away and gave the little boy a playful shake as he repeated in a voice full of patently mock outrage, "Leave you? Do you know what I've been doing this morning while you slept in?"

Arnie shook his head.

Russell thumped his palm on the top of the chest of drawers. "I was fixing this for your bedroom. You'll need it to hold the clothes Mrs. Goetz found for you."

Arnie stood on tiptoe and stared at the compact wooden piece. "What're you doing to it?"

"I didn't want you to get any splinters, so I'm sanding it."

"Can I help?"

Lorelei watched as Russell opened his arms and heart to Arnie. It came as such a surprise. He was normally so standoffish—but there he was, a tall, broad-shouldered, gruff man with a tattered-looking mutt on one side and an orphaned little boy on the other.

He'll make a good father.

The thought sent streaks of warmth through her. *Deep inside Russell, there is tenderness and goodness.* Surely, there must be hope for him. She pensively brushed flux on the joints she needed to solder. *Jesus, You are the lover of our souls. Please shower Your love on this man. Wash away the pain and doubts, and allow his spirit to flourish again.*

"Are you thinking about what to put on the list?" Russell's words made her look up. "I'll need to go place the telephone call this afternoon. While I'm there, I'll deliver the soup and bread and can pick up a few of the smaller things at the mercantile."

"You'll wear a mask the whole time?"

He nodded.

"Me, too." Arnie bobbed his head, a miniature replica of Russell.

Lorelei gave Russell a startled look. He wouldn't let her go to town; he couldn't possibly allow Arnie to. In those tense seconds, Arnie's eyes widened, and he grabbed a fistful of Russell's pant leg.

"Hey, now, buddy." Russell shifted and gave Lorelei a bail-me-out-of-this look.

"Russell doesn't want me to go to town, either." She came around the work-table and sighed. "I suppose we'll have to keep each other company and watch Mutt for him until he gets home tonight. In just a few days, some big, big boys and girls are coming to visit. We can surprise Russell with how much we get done on the bedrooms for them."

"It's about lunchtime." Russell ruffled Arnie's hair. "You can help us think of things our guests will need to bring."

"I didn't bring nothing."

"You most certainly did!" Lorelei laughed at Arnie. "You brought Russell back home in the dark!"

◦⧝

"Everybody's settled in for the night."

Russell didn't turn toward his mother's voice. Instead, he continued to stare out the bank of windows at the back of the house, out into the darkness where the sky and ocean met. *Moon flecks on the water and stars in the sky make it almost impossible to tell them apart.*

Lots of stars. God has lots of boys like me. Arnie's words kept echoing in his memory. *Lookie. A big lellow star. God gave a Son, too.*

"You have a beautiful view of the stars," Mom said as she stood beside him. She snuggled into his side. The top of her bun tickled his jaw, and she smelled like the peach soap he'd bought especially for her. "Thanks for inviting us to come, honey. I've missed you so much. Your father sends his love."

He pressed a kiss on her temple. "You're tired, Mom. Go to bed."

"My room is lovely. Did Lorelei help you with it?"

Lorelei had moved out of that very room and in with her mother. Still, Russell didn't want his mom playing matchmaker. "Lorelei and her mother did it together, just as they worked on the other bedrooms."

He'd managed to turn her around and walk her toward the entryway. She stopped and smiled. "The hall tree looks wonderful here."

"It does. Thanks for sending it. I want this mansion to look as much to period as I can make it."

"While we're here, the kids can help. Alan and Philip could help you paint and work outside—especially cut back some of the shrubs and pull out the dried weeds."

"I'll keep 'em busy."

"I brought bolts of fabric. I'll have the girls sew each day, and they can help in the kitchen."

"Mrs. Goetz will appreciate it. The town just started using the local dance hall as a makeshift hospital. Late each afternoon, I deliver soup and bread to it instead of going to individual homes as I used to."

"But is that safe?"

"It limits any exposure, and everyone has to help out." He took her arm and forced a chuckle as he escorted her up the stairs. "I can't believe you'd fret. I've spent my entire life watching you make baskets and deliver them to everyone in

Buttonhole who had so much as a bruise, bump, or boil."

"Those aren't catching, Russell."

"Nothing's killed me yet." Once he said the bitter words, he regretted them—they were truthful, but he'd promised himself he'd shield his mother and cousins from the ugliness inside. They'd just arrived early this evening, and he'd already stepped far over the line.

Chapter 18

Lorelei smiled as she watched Mrs. Diamond organize her nieces. She'd sent the dark-haired one to the kitchen to help Mama make bread. "Beatrice, Beatrice," Lorelei chanted under her breath to remember who was who.

Three girls, two boys, and Russell's mama made for quite an addition to the house. They ranged from thirteen to seventeen, and all had the look of children setting out on a holiday adventure instead of ones hiding from a terrible epidemic.

"Lacey, I know you girls brought your sewing boxes. Go fetch them and bring them to the parlor. Adele, wipe down the dining table so there's nothing sticky left from breakfast. We'll use that as a cutting table."

Lacey is blond, and Adele is the youngest.

While the girls all scattered to do as they were bid, Mrs. Diamond walked over to Lorelei's worktable. "Oh, this window is lovely, just lovely. Where is it going?"

"In the smaller parlor, just on the other side of that wall."

"I'm surprised at how few windows needed to be replaced. After the house sat vacant for so long, I expected it to be a hideous mess."

"Russell has done considerable work. He's put on a new roof, painted the outside, replaced more than fifty panes of glass, rebuilt the veranda. . ." She made a spiraling gesture. "So many more things, too. It used to look like a magnificent bridal gown that somehow ended up with torn lace, smudges of dirt and mud, and a sagging hem. Now when I look at the house, I see what the mansions in heaven must be like."

"Will you be doing any more stained glass for the house?"

Lorelei nodded. "Russell found an old photograph when he took the drawers out of one of the washstands. It showed that there used to be large, floral windows on either side of the front door. I'm to reproduce them, but first he must decide on the colors. Perhaps you could help him."

"Evidently my son hasn't told you my embarrassing secret."

"Russell is discreet. He would not speak badly of anyone."

Mrs. Diamond picked up a little scrap of glass and held it up to the light. Her voice lilted with merriment. "I love pretty things, but when it comes to putting them together, I'm hopeless. Why, when my husband courted me, he actually had to point out that my clothing was ragged and faded as a beggar's."

"You cannot mean this!"

Mrs. Diamond laughed and nodded. "It's the absolute truth. In fact, I was hoping you'd help me look at the bolts of cloth we brought along so I can start the girls sewing some quilts and pillows or cushions for the rooms. That bedroom I'm in is utterly charming, so I know you have an eye for these things."

"The bedroom where Adele and Lacey sleep needs curtains. Perhaps that would be a good project to do first. I have the measurements of the windows, so that will make it easy."

Mrs. Diamond set down the piece of glass and nodded. "Wonderful idea. I'm sure they'll enjoy decorating their room. I want to keep the children busy so they'll not get into trouble or be too homesick."

"Russell once mentioned he has a list of things he wishes to do. Perhaps you could read it to see what might make good projects."

"Aunt Rose, do you know where Russell is?"

They turned toward the door. A younger version of Russell stood there, still at the gangly stage where he was all knees and elbows. His voice cracked mid-sentence as he added, "I found a bunch of paint in one of the stalls, and I was thinking we could spruce up the stable. Russell has a pair of geldings out there."

"Out exploring, Philip?"

"Yes." He shrugged. "This is a nifty old place. Russell must be having a great time fixing it up."

Lorelei had seen Russell work. He wasn't having a great time at all—the work was demanding and pressed him to his limits. Nonetheless, he determinedly forged ahead. Sometimes she watched him as he toiled, and she'd arrived at the conclusion that he pressed himself until exhaustion would allow him to sleep. Still, he slept poorly. Every single night, he groaned or shouted out in his dreams. Refusing to reveal any of those facts, Lorelei looked about the room and said, "He's put much care into this place."

Philip wandered across the floor and gawked around. "It was too dark to see much yesterday. My dad said he'd been by a couple years ago, and the place was nothing but a dirty wreck. He ordered me to test the floors to be sure they hadn't rotted, but I can see that's not necessary."

"Russell replaced the veranda here and the porch down at the cottage." Lorelei noted the envious gleam in Philip's eyes and added, "Russell mentioned some of the rooms in the attic sustained rain damage. If you are as skilled as Russell, you might wish to ask him if he could use your help in repairing them."

"Wow. Yeah. I'd like that. I brought some tools along—in case he needed that kind of help."

"You said my son has a list of projects?" Mrs. Diamond shot Lorelei a conspiratorial glance.

"Perhaps we could ask him to show it to us at lunch. Mama always told me a man is easier to deal with when his stomach is full."

Philip sniffed and grinned. "Smells like the bread is out of the oven. The kitchen is like a big city bakery—loaves and loaves all laid out and more dough ready to bake."

Lorelei laughed. "Mama loves to cook. You should ask her about her cinnamon rolls. She would be happy to make you some."

"Really?"

Lacey, having entered the room with the sewing baskets, chimed in, "Cinnamon rolls?"

"Now I don't know. . . ." Russell's mother shook her head.

Lorelei laughed. "I'm sure. They're Mama's favorite, so it would give her a good excuse."

Russell called from the window, "What's going on in there, and why does someone need an excuse?"

~

Lorelei rolled over and blinked at the shaft of sunlight creeping though the chink between the halves of her curtains. *Lord, it's Your day today. Russell isn't going to let anyone go to town. Will You please grant him some comfort as we worship here with the children?*

She yawned and burrowed beneath the quilt for a few more minutes, mentally going through a list of hymns they might sing. "Stand up, stand up for Jesus, ye soldiers. . ." No, that wouldn't do. "Onward, Christian soldiers. . ." Lorelei grimaced. She'd never noticed how many songs used words like "soldier" or "battle."

Heavenly Father, help us to keep this day of worship holy and special. Let it unfold according to Your will, and make me sensitive to what You would have us say, do, sing, and read. Russell is hurting, and he needs Your healing touch. The children all miss their parents. Arnie clings to Russell, to Mama, and to me because he is so afraid of losing any of us. Tender Shepherd, we need Your touch and mercy. Guide and direct us, I pray. Amen.

"You're awake, Lori?" Mama whispered.

"Yes, Mama."

"I dreamed of your papa reading the Bible to us. Remember how he smoothed the ribbon back into the pages when he was done?"

"Every time." The memory made sorrow wash over her.

"I was thinking about how I wished the ribbon on that Silver Star medal the government brought us for your Papa was smooth, deep blue satin instead of striped grosgrain." Mama rolled over. Tears glossed her eyes. "I decided to put blue satin in the box the medal came in."

Tears spilled down Mama's cheeks as Lorelei reached over and pulled her into a tight hug. When she found her voice again, she whispered, "That's a nice idea, Mama."

A little while later, when they'd regained their composure, Mama sat on the bedside and combed her hair as she said, "Russell's mother tells me he got a medal, too—the same as your papa's."

"I'm not surprised. He's a man of honor and courage." Lorelei bent to tie her shoes and added quietly, "But I don't think we'd better ask him about his medal. He doesn't want to talk about the war."

"His eyes hold much hurt, Lori."

"So does his soul." She straightened. "Which makes me wonder, what shall we do for worship today?"

"I know just the right verses." Mama gave her a watery smile. "And Rose Diamond has a lovely voice. She can help us decide on some hymns."

They slipped downstairs, and Mama stirred up the fire she'd banked in the stove last night. Lorelei opened the kitchen door and pulled in the milk Mr. Rimmon had delivered. Before the epidemic, he'd delivered a single half-gallon bottle to each house twice a week. Now he left a half-full, ten-gallon tin milk can each dawn. He'd already strained it and left half a gallon of cream, too, so they could churn their own butter.

"Hi!" Arnie skipped through the kitchen, accompanied by Mutt. Only a step behind, Russell nodded and turned the knob to let them out. The three of them were nearly inseparable, and Mama and Mrs. Diamond both thought it slightly scandalous that Russell allowed the dog to sleep at the foot of Arnie's bed, but no one dared interfere since the three of them seemed to need each other.

Soon the kitchen smelled of yeast from the bread dough and cinnamon from the rolls. Beatrice sat in a chair over by the window, using the Daisy paddle-wheel churn. Mrs. Diamond had Adele setting the table as Lacey rearranged the parlor for "church." Alan and Philip went to muck out the stable. The routine in the household hadn't taken long to establish, and it carried with it a comfortable air. It didn't take much longer before everyone sat down to breakfast.

After the meal, Russell ordered the boys to carry their chairs to the parlor for worship. Everyone found a seat, and Mrs. Diamond led the singing. True to form, Russell didn't sing, but he played his harmonica.

⊷

Russell lifted Arnie onto his lap to stop him from squirming as Mrs. Goetz started reading from the second chapter of Nehemiah.

> *Wherefore the king said unto me, Why is thy countenance sad, seeing thou art not sick? this is nothing else but sorrow of heart. Then I was very sore afraid, and said unto the king, Let the king live for ever: why should not*

my countenance be sad, when the city, the place of my fathers' sepulchres, lieth waste, and the gates thereof are consumed with fire? Then the king said unto me, For what dost thou make request? So I prayed to the God of heaven. And I said unto the king, If it please the king, and if thy servant have found favour in thy sight, that thou wouldest send me unto Judah, unto the city of my fathers' sepulchres, that I may build it.

Russell stared at the worn Bible in her lap. He couldn't recall hearing that passage before now. *Sorrow of the heart. Yes, that said it well. And I'm also rebuilding what belonged to my ancestors. Nehemiah felt this way, too?*

"Russell is rebuilding." Adele smiled at him.

Arnie waved across the room at her, which seemed to serve better than the stingy smile Russell himself barely managed. *What am I doing with all of these tenderhearted children here?*

Alan cleared his throat. "I'm thinking of that verse about building a house. I don't recall where it is."

"The one about whether you build a house on rock or sand?"

"That's a nice one, but not the one that I had in mind. It's about laboring in vain if God isn't building the house."

Russell cleared his throat. "That's Psalm 127:1: 'Except the Lord build the house, they labour in vain that build it: except the Lord keep the city, the watchman waketh but in vain.'"

Mom patted Alan on the arm. "Russell's mind is like a camera. He need see something only once, and he remembers it forever."

And there are things I wish I'd never seen and wouldn't remember. . . . He stared at the floor. The autumn sun streamed through the stained-glass window Lorelei had restored, and the golden segments she'd cleverly borrowed from the border and stretched to fit by using the amber jewels he chose ended up casting a golden cross on the far wall.

Lorelei suggested, "Let's finish with sentence prayers. Anyone who would like can join in."

The prayers and the glass-cast golden cross don't bother me, he realized with shock. When he'd first come back from France, those things would have set him on edge. Now, after weeks of quiet worship and hearing Lorelei read the Word of God aloud, he'd let go of most of his anger. At times it still surged, but for the most part, a profound emptiness replaced the rage.

Their faith is touching, innocent. I was like that once. A sense of loss swamped him. He held Arnie and rested his chin on the little boy's soft hair. Wrapping his arms tighter, he realized how much he wanted Arnie to grow up believing that Jesus loved him. Lorelei's sweet, husky voice chimed in with a word of prayer.

Russell's leg ached, but his heart ached more. *Even if I can't patch together my own faith, I want this little guy to have the assurance and security Lorelei has.*

⌐ℑ

"Russell, I brought you your jacket." Lorelei knew she needed to speak before she approached him. He'd been lost in thought, and sudden sounds and movement always resulted in startling or angering him. The past week had been particularly bad. He'd been going to town and digging graves, coming home only to get the bread and soup, then returning again late in the evening. The bleakness in his eyes and the groans in his sleep bore testimony to the great cost of the work he'd done.

"The air, it is chilly much of the day now. It is good that we have so much wood piled up for the winter." Slowly, she walked across the veranda and out into the yard.

Russell pushed away from the tree and shrugged into his jacket. "Thanks."

"You are troubled."

"I'm not decent company, Lorelei. Go back inside."

An undertone of anguish in his voice made her stay. "I didn't ask if you were good company. If I wanted pleasant companions, there are plenty in the house."

"Are they getting under your skin?"

She laughed. "I just said they were pleasant companions, Russell. Your mother is a wonderful woman, and your cousins are delightful. My place is not with them right now; my place is to be with a friend who is hurting."

"Who's hurt?" He stiffened as he barked the question.

Lorelei paused a moment, then quietly answered, "You."

442

Chapter 19

*L*ord, I felt led to come out to Russell, but I feel so unsure of why You have me here. I have no understanding of the pain he feels or what to say to him.

"My leg's never going to get better." He snorted. "I'm going to limp for the rest of my life. The shrapnel left in there is too close to the nerves and arteries to mess with, so the ache's permanent. I'm a cripple. There. Did that clear the air?"

"The ache, this I am sorry for. The limp—it has gotten better over the months you have lived here. It does not keep you from doing the things you wish. Your body serves you well, Russell, and you use your strength and talents for others. I hold no pity for you, only gratitude. You have a battle raging inside you, yet you had the kindness and courage to think of others."

"Don't fool yourself. I came out here because I was thinking only of myself."

"You need time alone. What is wrong about that? There have been days when I sought solitude in my sorrow and confusion."

"Buttercup." His voice sounded ragged. She liked how he occasionally called her such a pretty name, even if he said it in a jaded tone. Somewhere deep inside, it meant that he still longed for good things, even if he denied himself.

"Yes?"

"I'm as splintered and jagged as the broken glass you sweep up. You don't know what you're dealing with."

"What I know is that even when glass is shattered, the pieces can be fit together in a new way to make something beautiful."

Russell shook his head. "Not me."

"You must be patient. Papa used to patiently fit the pieces of a window together. He refused to hurry. These things take time. He taught me that if something is to last, it must be tended with diligence now—whether it is a window or a soul."

"You still believe in fairy tales, Lorelei."

"I'm a grown woman, Russell. I didn't fight in a war, but I have lost my father, and I've worked hard to make a living and provide for my mother. I believe in God's love. I believe in family. I believe in friends. The pattern I envisioned for my life was shattered, but I chose to put the pieces back together. The picture is different, but the Source of my light never changed."

443

He smashed his fist into the trunk of the tree. "My friends died! Don't you get it? All around me, my friends bled and died. I used my rifle, my trench knife, even my bare hands, and killed Germans—men who had families and friends back in their hometowns. I've seen slaughter, I've slain, and I'm sick of death."

Lorelei quietly reached over and curled her hand around his wrist. He yanked free, but she persisted and took his wrist again. Gently, she brushed bark off his skinned knuckles. "You are hurting enough on the inside, Russell. Don't hurt yourself on the outside, too."

"There's blood on my hands and in my soul." He pulled free.

"Only the Living Water can wash that away." She folded her arms around her ribs. "Once, I told you the red glass was the most expensive. Right now, the only color you see in the window of your soul is red. Christ already paid the price to purify it. Regardless of the color, though, know that I care for you as a friend. Your pain doesn't frighten me away."

꙰

Russell sat at the head of the supper table long after the meal was over and everyone had left the dining room. Arnie didn't want to leave his side, but Adele promised to teach him how to play checkers. Laughter and chatter drifted across the marble entryway and into the dining room. The swinging door to the kitchen sat ajar, allowing a wedge of light and the musical conversation between Lorelei and their mothers.

At the first lunch they all shared, Mom, Mrs. Goetz, and Lorelei had created a schedule of chores. They'd all insisted on taking a turn at dishes, too. Mom and Mrs. Goetz spent a couple hours each day in the library, clearing off bookshelves and oiling the wood. In another day or so, that room would be an inviting haven of peace.

The girls rotated into the kitchen for a day, then sewed for two. They hadn't decided on any particular room—they'd stitched in the parlor, in a bedroom, on the veranda—so no matter where he turned, Russell seemed to run into someone. Simple, gathered cotton curtains hung from the windows in the kitchen, bedrooms, and washroom, and the duvets in the girls' rooms bore new, matching covers. A lacy, tatted doily lay in the center of the dining table beneath the mum-filled Heisey crystal vase.

The boys eagerly traipsed through the house and over the estate, then voiced which projects appealed to them the most. After the first day, Russell had decided he'd make assignments so he'd know where they were and what they were doing; finding Philip "fixing" the stairs to the attic reinforced the need for that decision.

So far, the washroom and four bedrooms sported fresh coats of paint, a wobbly chair's legs now measured even, and two doors that used to sag and stick had been planed and rehung. The stable sported a fresh coat of barn red paint, and most of the shrubs had been cut back to manageable level. Once set to work, the boys did fairly well. Their exuberance sometimes eclipsed their judgment, but overall, they hadn't been too much trouble.

How did I ever end up with this troop in my barracks? He stared at the hodge-podge of chairs about the table. Counting Lorelei, Mrs. Goetz, Arnie, his mother, and five cousins, he'd taken on responsibility for nine other people. *And to think I came here to get away from everyone.*

He let out a burdened sigh. His father hadn't asked him to take on these guests; he'd simply revealed how bad things were in Buttonhole and asked how Russell was doing since he lived so far on the outskirts of a town. Survival: the first rule of war—and they were fighting a deadly enemy in the form of an epidemic. Russell knew he'd made the right decision. It didn't make it any easier, though, when he craved solitude.

Suddenly rifle fire split the night air.

"Sniper!" He dove out of his chair and crawled to the doorway. "Down! Down! Everybody down!"

His pulse thundered in his ears as feet pounded on the floor.

"Russell? What's wrong?"

Someone burst through the front door. Russell grabbed Lorelei and yanked her to the floor. She tumbled over him, and he shoved her into the corner where she'd be safest.

"Alan bagged a buck! Come see!"

Sweat poured down Russell's temples, and tension made him jump as Lorelei gently rubbed his back. "A deer, Russell. Alan hunted a deer. In your yard in Virginia, Russell. You're home, not in the war."

A shudder rippled through him. It took another second or two to fully understand her. He bolted to his feet, yanked her upright, and strode as fast as his limp allowed him out to the front yard.

Alan stood over a buck on the far side of the hedges, chest thrust out and shoulders squared with pride. "How do you like this?"

Russell grabbed the rifle from him. "I don't."

"We'll have venison roast, and Mrs. Goetz can make stews for the folks in town."

"That's no excuse. None at all," Russell bit out. Memories of what a rifle shell could do to a human being burst through his memory, making his voice harsh. "In this light, you couldn't be sure what you were shooting. Do you understand me?"

"Hey, I was just trying—"

"No excuse," Russell repeated himself through gritted teeth. He stared at Philip. "If you have a weapon, you're to give it to me now. No one hunts without my permission."

Arnie started to sniffle. Lorelei stooped, pulled him into her arms, and rose. She patted his back and cooed, "It's okay, honey. It's okay. He's not mad at you. Russell worried that someone got hurt because he cares about us."

"You children go back inside." His mother gave the order firmly. Spreading her arms wide, she herded them toward the house and didn't leave any chance for objections.

Alan stood belligerently over his kill. Russell's hand curled tighter around the stock of the rifle he'd carefully kept aimed at the ground. He stared at Alan until the teen looked away, then commanded, "This is your kill—you dress it."

"I. . .um. . .don't know how."

"Then it's time you learn."

"I could help." Lorelei's soft, husky voice startled Russell. He shot her a strained look. She set Arnie on the ground and gave his little backside a pat to send him on his way.

The last thing I need is for her to weaken my stance with the kids—if that's possible.

Russell shook his head. "This is Alan's mess. He's not a child; he's a young man. A responsible young man handles his own affairs."

༭

The next evening, Mama and Mrs. Diamond declared it was a celebration night. All of the rooms on the second floor and the three maids' bedrooms in the attic were painted. The occupied rooms all had curtains; refurbished furniture; spreads, duvets, or quilts; and pictures. Beatrice had shown remarkable artistic flair, and her works hung here and there.

Mrs. Diamond fixed a big venison roast while Mama used bread crumbs to make dressing. Lorelei passed the okra over Arnie's head to Russell and teased, "Now aren't you glad you gave us that garden?"

"He's more likely to be thankful there are a bunch of us at the table to eat the okra." Mrs. Diamond laughed. "Russell doesn't care for it."

Lorelei gaped at him.

He cleared his throat. "I'd like some of your beans, though. Between the corn and beans you canned, I'm still glad you garden."

Mrs. Diamond took the bowl of green beans from Philip and passed them to her son. "Like father, like son. Did Russell ever tell you I have a fruit orchard?"

Lorelei nodded. "He shared the apples you sent."

"Mom makes peach everything—jam, tarts, pies," Russell began.

"Don't forget her cobbler!" Philip tacked on.

"Yes, well, Russell's father had me fooled about liking peaches for the longest time. It wasn't until he asked me to marry him that he confessed he can't stand the taste of peaches!"

While others laughed, Lorelei felt a twang of worry. "Did you give me the apples because you don't like them? Is that why you want cinnamon in your applesauce—to hide the flavor?"

"Love them." Russell tipped his head to the side and gave her an assessing look. "That apple I'm smelling—it's not the cider you're drinking?"

Arnie piped up, "Nope! Lorelei made apple doodle. It's a s'prise."

"Strudel," Lorelei corrected softly as she saw the deliciously greedy spark in Russell's eyes.

"You told!" Arnie glared up at her. "Now it's not a s'prise."

After dessert, everyone played musical chairs in the entryway with Russell controlling the tunes on the gramophone; then everyone bundled up and went outside.

A big pile of leaves and logs lay ready. Russell supervised Alan as he lit it. Sugar prices made candy cost an arm and a leg; marshmallows were a rarity. The bag of marshmallows Russell's mother brought out to toast counted as the highlight of the whole evening.

"Uh-oh. I burned mine!" Arnie's face puckered.

"Yum! Just the way I like it!" Russell swiped the charred, gooey mess and popped it into his mouth. "I suppose you like them all golden perfect like Lorelei's, don't you, Arnie?"

"Uhn-huh." The boy nodded.

"Shh. We have to be sneaky," Russell said in a stage whisper. He grabbed Lorelei's stick, and she obligingly let out a shriek.

"Lorelei, Russell has a marshmallow on his stick," Adele tattled. "He hasn't roasted it yet."

"What's sauce for the goose," Lorelei said as she tried to grab Russell's marshmallow.

Quickly, they were "fencing" with marshmallow-tipped sticks. Russell and Lorelei became the judges as they set up matches between the cousins. Arnie fought the boys, who gladly got on their knees to make for a fair fight.

After the final cry of "Touché!" they toasted the last few marshmallows and sat around the fire as it died down to mere embers. They sang "Shenandoah" and "Shoo Fly" and ended the evening with Arnie's request, "Twinkle, Twinkle, Little Star."

Russell poured water on the embers, and Alan raked the ground to guarantee they'd extinguished the fire entirely. Alan started coughing from the smoke.

Lacey giggled. "Don't pretend the smoke is bothering you. Lorelei is practically in a cloud of it, and she's not coughing."

"She's used to it." Russell stood with his arms akimbo and stared at her. The look in his eyes sent sparks through her. "Everyone knows smoke follows beauty."

Russell lay in his bed and closed his eyes. Instead of the hideous scenes of war that usually flashed across his mind, he pictured Lorelei with a speck of apple strudel on her lower lip. For the first time since he'd come home, he felt the knot in his chest loosen. He'd been able to horse around and laugh tonight—and it was because of Lorelei.

Arnie's cot squeaked as he tossed about in the little parlor. Accustomed to the little boy's restlessness, Mutt snuffled and settled back in. Lorelei had marked Arnie's height on the pantry door frame this morning—just another one of her little ways of making sure Arnie felt secure about this being his new home. She'd made this old house a home with her warmth, laughter, and hard work.

The house creaked as it always did—the settling sounds of old timbers easing after the burden of a day. *Like I do.* He smiled wryly.

Somewhere in the house, someone coughed. Russell rolled over, yawned, and drifted off to sleep.

"Russell. Russell! Wake up." Lorelei stood over him, her beautiful hair streaming like ribbons down past her waist. She shook his shoulder again. Desperation tainted her sweet voice. "I need your help. It's Alan."

Chapter 20

There. That's better." Lorelei eased Beatrice back onto the pillows she'd piled beneath her shoulders to ease the coughing. Unsure if it made any difference, Lorelei still kept pillows piled beneath the shoulders and heads of four of the kids and Mrs. Diamond. They'd all come down with the flu in the past day and a half.

At first, Russell moved Alan into the nursery in an attempt to isolate him. By daybreak, all of the teens except Adele were also sick. They'd been brought here, too. Russell argued hotly with Lorelei that she shouldn't help, that she'd get sick, too. She'd turned around, made a gauze mask, and returned. Since then, he'd not been able to send her away. With the girls sick, Russell needed a woman to help with their care.

They'd transformed the big nursery into a sick ward. Mama kept Adele and Arnie away from the doorway and delivered broth, tea, and fresh linen and towels.

"S—sorry." Mrs. Diamond rasped after being violently ill.

"Shh. It is nothing." Lorelei supported her head and held a glass to her lips. "Sip. Rinse your mouth. You will feel better for it."

"I want my mama," Lacey whimpered in her fever-cracked voice.

Lorelei watched as Russell tenderly sponged her blue-tinged face and made soothing sounds. They'd been going from bed to bed, doing their best to control the fever, ease the cough, and keep their patients hydrated. When Russell had first put up supplies, fearing the epidemic, he'd bought quinine and aspirin. The posters in town advised using both, so they'd diligently dosed each patient.

By afternoon, everyone except Alan seemed stable. Lorelei knew from the newspapers that many who died of the ravaging disease did so within the first day. As long as she and Russell kept them medicated and hydrated, they ought to pull through—all except for Alan.

Russell sat by Alan's bedside, hollow-eyed with grief. From Alan's rattled, irregular breathing, Lorelei knew he had little time left unless God intervened. She went over and sat on the opposite side of the bed. Taking up a damp cloth, she fought tears as she sponged his parched, hot skin.

"Eternal Father, we've done our best. You know how we love Alan. Please, Lord, if it be Your will, heal this young man."

Alan opened his eyes. They were glazed, yet he feebly reached for Lorelei's hand. "God is love."

"Yes. Yes, God is love."

Russell made an agonized sound. He stood, paced away, and came back. Standing over the bed, he muttered, "This is my fault."

"No, Russell. You did your best. You tried to protect these children."

"I made him take half of that buck to the Rimmons. Rimmon's son brought milk today—because his father is down with the flu. If I hadn't been so stubborn and—"

"Stop! You were right to want a young man to be responsible for his actions, and you were right to share the meat with a family who needed it. Life isn't lived on our power. We aren't in control, and we don't bear responsibility for tragedies like this."

"Then God is to blame." Russell buried his head in his hands. "God allows the war; God allows illness." He lifted his face. "How can you serve Him when He refuses to protect His own children? Look at Alan. Just look at him!"

"I see a young man in God's hands." Her mask didn't successfully muffle her sob. "I want him to recover and sit at your table again, but if he does not, I know his heart is right with the Lord and I will someday feast with him in heaven. This I cling to. It is the hope Jesus bought for us on the cross."

"That's where we're different—you still hope. Me? I've learned otherwise."

༜

"Leave him alone, Lori," Mama said softly.

"I can't." Lorelei slipped past her mother and headed toward the large oak tree. It was barren of leaves, and a fresh mound of dirt beneath it carried a lovingly made wooden cross that lay beside a small collection of old family headstones. The pastor had come out and performed the funeral. Russell refused to come inside after the burial. He'd been out there ever since, and sunset had given way to dusk; then the moon rose. Still, he stood alone beneath the barren branches, staring at the grave.

Lorelei said nothing at all. Leaves crunched beneath her shoes as she walked to his side and silently slipped her hand into his.

"It's too cold out here for you." Even as his words rejected her, his fingers curled about hers.

"My hand is warmer than yours."

"So is your heart. Go back inside, Lorelei. The chill inside me will freeze you. I've already caused enough heartache and damage."

"You've done no such thing."

He let out a gusty sigh and said nothing more.

"Come inside. Your mother needs to see you before she goes back to bed."

He cast a quick look at the second story of the house. "Her light's on. Your mom will take care of her. She'll sleep better in her own room tonight."

"I'll peek in on her during the night."

He looked down at her. "Just like you slip in to tug Arnie's covers up higher?"

"You knew I do that?"

"Buttercup, you're like a guardian angel around here. I don't think anyone does anything without you hovering over their shoulder." The gentle look on his face hardened. "But you can stop hovering over me. I'm a lost cause. God and I— we weren't on speaking terms before this happened." He gestured toward the fresh grave. "Now—well, now it's plain as can be that He's cursed me for what I've done."

"God isn't that way, Russell. God is faithful. His character is unchanging. Bad things happen in life—things we cannot understand. They hurt, but God is with us during the hurt to give us consolation. If there is distance between you and Him, He is not the one who pulled away."

"That's some snappy theology you've worked out."

His words cut her to the core. Lorelei gulped, then closed her eyes. *Please, God, give me wisdom so I speak only the words You would have me say.*

"Lost, Buttercup? It's not easy to try to make sense of it all when things go wrong. I've given up. There's no use pursuing God when all He does is turn His back on me."

"God does not turn His back!" She staggered back from his bitter words. "You once told me you gave your heart to Jesus when you were a boy. So now you think to snatch it back because life is hard? Is that all a vow means to you?"

He glared at her stonily.

"Think of what a vow is. It does not say you will be true to your words only if all pleases you. I think of my parents. When they wed, they promised for better and worse, for richer and poorer, in sickness and in health. When things were hard for them, they did not blame each other, pull apart, and curl in opposite corners. They clung together and gave their all."

"That's what marriage is."

"Yes. Two people make a promise to one another, and you expect them to keep their word. How can you think a vow made to God is less binding? You, Russell, made a vow to God. It was an eternal one—that no matter what life brought, you would follow Him. Instead of thinking of yourself, it is time for you to start serving Him."

"What more does He want?" Russell slashed the air with his hand in sheer frustration. "I've done everything I can. I deliver food. I dig graves. I've adopted an orphan."

"Your deeds are not what He wants. He wants your heart."

The air hissed out of his lungs. He flinched as if she'd struck him.

Lorelei watched the pain in his eyes. Even in the moonlight, the deep anguish he felt shone in them. She'd spoken the truth. The message wasn't a gentle one, and part of her wanted to soften the impact, but she couldn't water down the foundational truth. Until Russell chose to yield control to God, he'd fight a painful and losing battle.

After a prolonged silence, she murmured, "I left supper for you in the warming box." With a heavy heart, she walked back inside.

In the next two weeks, Russell worked from first light to well after dark. Arnie, shaken by another death, trailed after him like a second shadow. His cousins all leaned on him to be strong. "You're like the Rock of Gibraltar," Philip said as Russell helped him back upstairs after his first meal at the family table.

A rock? I can't let them see that I'm like a million grains of shifting, sinking sand. They depend on me.

Even with all his hard work, Lorelei's words rang in his ears. *Your deeds are not what He wants. He wants your heart.*

One evening, he came back from delivering food in town to find Philip in the large parlor, working on refinishing a piece of furniture. At first, Russell couldn't see what it was. By the time he reached a decent vantage point, Philip turned. "I saw this in the attic and decided it needed to be repaired."

Russell stared at the burned altar.

The teen reverently ran his palm across the surface. "When I saw it, I felt closer to Alan." His voice cracked, "I remember his last words."

" 'God is love,' " Russell remembered aloud.

Nodding his head, Philip started to sand the singed wood. Drawn to his side, Russell studied the damage. "We can fix it, can't we?" Philip asked.

"It won't be the same as new." Russell thumbed an edge. "I can plane it, and you could rout the edge. Then we can sand it to even out this other surface. A little putty and darker stain will cover any of the imperfections."

Late into the night, they worked on the altar. Every spare moment in the next three days went toward restoring it. Finally, late at night, all alone, Russell ran a polishing cloth over the surface. Though he'd put Arnie to bed upstairs, the little guy had crept back downstairs and fallen asleep beneath Russell's jacket on a small sofa. Arnie stirred and sat up. He rubbed his eyes.

"Russell?"

"Yeah, buddy?"

Arnie padded over and snuggled close. He wrapped his little arm around Russell's neck and curled his other hand around the edge of the altar. "Can we pray at this one, just like we do at the one in church?"

Chapter 21

Russell's breath caught. *I'm not equipped to do this. God, why are You putting me in this position?* One look at Arnie's innocent eyes forced Russell to tamp down his own doubts. "Would you like to?"

Arnie nodded. He slithered onto his knees, folded his hands, and frowned. "I'm too short."

"Here." Russell knelt on one knee and crooked the other up. He lifted Arnie to sit on it, and the little boy then folded his hands and rested them on the altar.

"That's right," Arnie said happily. He closed his eyes tightly and dove right in. "God, it's me, Arnie. You got my daddy and mommy and Baby 'Liz'beth with you. Please take good care of them. Russell takes good care of me. Night-night. Amen."

"Amen." Russell hugged him tightly. "Now go on up to bed."

"Yessir."

Russell sat on the floor by the altar as despair washed over him. *If only my soul could be restored like this house and altar. If only my faith were that simple and pure.*

❧

"The paper in town says the flu is still bad, but it's not claiming as many folks as it did in October," Russell said when he got home one evening.

"How much longer will it last?" His mother took a sip of tea.

Russell shrugged. "No one can say."

"I want to go home," Beatrice said quietly. "It's been good of you to have us stay, but in the end, it didn't make any difference. I'm homesick." She laughed. "I'd even be glad to have Mama scold me for slacking on my chores."

Lorelei cut Arnie's meat and didn't participate in the conversation. The Diamonds needed to make this decision on their own.

"Going home by wagon is going to be too taxing," Russell said.

His mother nodded. "We'll go by train."

"Tomorrow is Sunday," Mama said.

"We'll leave Monday," Mrs. Diamond decided.

After everyone left the table, Russell remained, as had become his custom. Lorelei started to clear the dishes. "Mama and I will return to the cottage, too."

His head shot up. "Why?"

"Because it is time."

"Arnie needs you!"

Silently, Lorelei left him and went to the kitchen. Alone and up to her elbows in suds, she scrubbed a plate and fought back her disappointment. *Why couldn't you need me, Russell?* Tears stung her eyes and nose.

Mama came in, picked up a dish towel, and started to dry dishes. "There was a time, I thought Russell was the answer to my prayers. You reminded me the pastor said we should pray specifically, and I did—just as you said—that God would put a husband for you on our cottage porch. Russell fixed that porch. I hoped with time, his heart would mend, too, Lori. It hasn't.

"You cannot be with a man who has hardened his heart against God. It is too hard for you to be under his roof and not set your affections on him. With his strength and kindness, he will woo you, but it is not what God would bless. On Monday, we will move back home, too."

Heartbroken, Lorelei whispered, "I know. I've already told him."

❦

"It's over!" Russell didn't bother to knock. He plowed straight into the cottage and repeated, "It's over!"

"What?"

He swept Lorelei up and swung her around. "The war! They declared Armistice! It's over!"

"Praise God!" Mama said from the kitchen doorway.

As Russell set Lorelei down, he still couldn't contain his relief. He held her shoulders and planted an exuberant kiss on her cheek. She gave him a shocked look, but he laughed and grabbed her mother in an enveloping hug. "It's done."

Arnie tugged on his slacks. "Do we get to cel'brate with marshmallows?"

"Better than that. We'll go to town. If you all promise to wear masks and stay away from others, we'll go in tomorrow. They're planning music in the park and a parade."

Arnie scratched his knee. "Daddy had mag'zines. They showed soldiers marching, marching, marching in parades. You gonna wear your soldier clothes, Russell?"

The question jolted him. Russell hadn't thought about his uniform since the night he'd happened across it before he left home. The very thought of ever putting it on again made him sick inside.

"The war is over, Arnie." Lorelei poked the little boy in the belly and made him laugh. "No more uniforms. What if we decorate the buggy? How would that be?"

"Terrific!"

❦

Indeed, the buggy did look terrific. Russell chuckled as he hitched the geldings to it the next afternoon. "You folks outdid yourselves. This is the fanciest buggy in all of Virginia!"

Even the black crepe on doors and fresh graves in the cemetery didn't dampen spirits. Folks from all around came to town to revel in the good news. The gauze masks couldn't muffle the shouts of victory. The War to End All Wars was over. Never again would man engage in such brutality.

For the first time in months, Russell felt a glimmer of hope for the future.

❧

Lorelei carefully cleaned each piece of glass, then wrapped the edges with copper foil. Once the foil cupped the edges, she used her crimper to burnish it in place. She'd decided to do this window as a gift for Russell—a thanks for his generosity. The copper foil allowed her to make this far more intricate, and she'd constructed it so he could place it in the library window since he often slipped into that room when he needed to ponder matters.

"What are you up to now?"

His voice startled her. She jumped and let out a gasp.

"Sorry. I didn't mean to scare you. Hey—you cut yourself!"

"It's nothing." She set down the small piece of ruby glass and grabbed a rag. "I'm used to cutting myself. It's just part of the job."

He encircled her wrist with his hand and turned the finger toward the light. "Poor finger. If this happened to Arnie, he'd want me to kiss it better."

"I'm not Arnie." She pulled away. A shiver ran through her, so she reached over and grabbed her sweater.

"No, you're not." Russell held the sweater for her. "I came over to talk with you about that."

"That I am not Arnie?" She glanced at her finger, decided it wasn't going to bother her and didn't need any bandaging, and set back to work on the window.

Russell chuckled. "No. Arnie's in with your mother. They get along famously."

"They do," Lorelei agreed. She tucked a finished piece in place and started to foil the edges of a deep green leaf.

"Will you please stop messing with that and look at me?"

Surprised at his request, she laid down the leaf and foil, then turned toward him.

"Arnie misses you up at the house. I miss you more."

His admission stunned her. Lorelei blinked at him in utter surprise.

Russell leaned forward. He traced her hairline with his forefinger and quietly said, "Buttercup, we've been through a lot together."

"We have." The tenderness in his touch and voice made her want to lean closer.

"I'm not very good with fancy words." He cupped her cheek. "But, Lorelei, I can be myself around you. There isn't anyone else I can say that about. You listen and are honest about what you think. I don't know another gal in the world with a heart as big as yours."

"Russell, those are fancy words. Kind ones. Your praise means much to me."

His eyes darkened as he rubbed his thumb across her lips. "And my love? Does that mean much to you? I want to marry you, Lorelei."

She sucked in a shocked breath. His words thundered in her ears, made her world tilt crazily.

"Don't you love me, too?" His voice dropped an octave as he asked those words in a velvety voice.

The chill she'd felt earlier doubled. Lorelei stepped back and wrapped her arms around herself. "Yes. No." She shook her head. "Russell, it does not matter how I feel. My love for you is strong, but my love for God makes such a marriage impossible."

His brow furrowed. "What is that supposed to mean?"

Hot tears scorched down her cheeks. Everything inside trembled as she searched for the right words. "Russell, the man I marry must love God. In marriage, two become one. My heart and body tell me such a union would be wonderful, but my soul tells me no. We would not be a good match because there is this difference between us. Faith matters. It matters much."

"It doesn't have to. I'll go to church if that's what bothers you. You can continue to say grace at meals and bring up our children with Bible reading." He got off the stool and came closer. Cupping her shoulders, he drew her close. "I wouldn't expect you to give up anything that is dear to you."

"But—"

"Your mother—she'd move in with us. She'll make a wonderful grandma for Arnie, don't you think?"

His words broke her heart. Lorelei pressed a hand to her mouth to hold back a sob.

He brushed away her tears. "Buttercup, this was supposed to be a happy moment. Things are looking up."

"My heart says yes, but my soul says no. Russell, you honor me with this proposal, but I cannot accept it. A woman should not marry a man in hopes of changing him. It is unwise. Though I love you, marriage would be wrong because the Lord is my Shepherd, but He is your enemy."

She could barely see him through her tears. Her legs felt rubbery, and she blindly reached behind herself for the table to keep herself from falling.

"If that's how you feel." Russell's voice sounded grim, muffled.

Instead of bracing her, the table slid. The sound of glass shattering filled her ears as the world tilted and everything went dark.

Chapter 22

M om!" Russell burst into the cottage with Lorelei draped limply across his arms. Ever since he'd come to the realization that he loved Lorelei, he'd begun to think of her mother as his, too. The horror on her face cut him to the core. "She fainted. She's running a fever."

"Put her in bed. Go get the quinine and aspirin." Mrs. Goetz hurried into the bedroom and yanked back the covers.

By the time Russell returned, Lorelei was dressed in a lawn nightgown and covered by a sheet. Her mother worriedly sponged her wrists and face. "She is so hot. Too hot. Please, Russell, hold her up so I can make her take your medicine."

Of the people he'd seen with the flu, no one had been as sick as Lorelei—no one except Alan. Russell sat at the bedside, nearly crazed with grief. He couldn't bear to lose Lorelei. He trickled broth into her, held her head when she was sick, sponged her to control the fever. Nothing helped.

She grew weaker by the hour. Her coloring changed to the telltale bluish white that indicated she didn't have long.

Russell stared at her and remembered when Alan was at this point. He'd whispered, "God is love."

Lorelei believes that, too. My beautiful Lorelei, whose world is so full of light and color. Her soul sparkles with the joy of the Lord.

What do I believe? He'd tried to make bargains with God in the trenches. *If You spare me and my buddy, I'll. . . Get me out of here and. . . Make this war end. . .* Now he sat at the bedside of the woman he'd grown to love. His hands and heart were empty.

I can't bargain. I never could. I have nothing to offer God. I have no power. You are God, and I am a man—one who cannot bear to lose this woman.

Lorelei had spoken of vows and promises and commitment. *When things got rough, I failed to rely on the Lord. I tried to live on my own terms, and I turned on God. What kind of fool have I been?*

He took the Bible Lorelei kept at her bedside and started to read where a blue ribbon that was purpled with age lay between the pages in the eighth chapter of Mark:

And when he had called the people unto him with his disciples also, he said unto them, Whosoever will come after me, let him deny himself, and take up his cross, and follow me. For whosoever will save his life shall lose it; but whosoever shall lose his life for my sake and the gospel's, the same shall save it. For what shall it profit a man, if he shall gain the whole world, and lose his own soul? Or what shall a man give in exchange for his soul?

Whosoever therefore shall be ashamed of me and of my words in this adulterous and sinful generation; of him also shall the Son of man be ashamed, when he cometh in the glory of his Father with the holy angels.

The words cut to the depths of his soul. He had nothing to exchange with God. . .nothing to give but a heart that was jaded and aching. The man in him wanted to bargain still—to beg God for this sweet woman's life—but that wasn't right. He couldn't make a deal with God. Sovereign, Almighty God owed him nothing. If in His grace He spared Lorelei, it would be a blessing beyond all hope, but if He didn't spare her. . .

Even then, I will serve You, Lord.

Russell slipped onto his knees. He closed both hands around Lorelei's and prayed. "Father, take my wayward heart and make it Yours. I beg Your forgiveness for letting anger and pride separate me from You. Lord, I love this woman. I promise to follow You no matter what her fate. She said there is always the hope of eternity—of being seated together at the banqueting table in heaven. Our only hope now is in Your promise of eternity and salvation. Merciful God, be with us, I pray."

※

Wrapped in her nightgown and two blankets and propped in the corner of the couch, Lorelei swallowed the apple cider and hummed appreciatively.

"Thirsty, Buttercup?"

"Yes." She sipped more as Russell held the glass to her lips.

He sat next to her and played with the tip of her frazzled braid. "You're looking miles better."

She managed a weak laugh. "That is a terrible thing to say. As you carried me out here, I saw my reflection in the mirror. I'm a fright!"

"You're beautiful." He scanned her face slowly. "I need to tell you something."

Please, no. Please, Russell, don't ask me to marry you again. It nearly tore my heart out, telling you no last time. I'm too weak right now for this.

"While you were sick, I did a lot of soul searching. I didn't like what I saw. Things have changed. I've recommitted myself to God."

"Oh, Russell!"

"It's not supposed to make you cry." A lopsided grin tilted his mouth.

"They are happy tears."

His woodsy, masculine scent enveloped her as he leaned closer and used the corner of the sheet to dab her cheeks. His voice deepened. "Before you got sick, I told you I love you. Do you remember?"

She nodded slowly.

He looked into her eyes. "You were right to refuse my proposal. We wouldn't have had the bond in our marriage that God gives to His children."

"I didn't want to hurt you, Russell. I never wanted to hurt you."

"Shh. I know. Because you stood firm in your faith, you challenged me. It wasn't in a spirit of cruelty—you held up a mirror to my soul and forced me to look at myself."

"Since I met you, I've held a burden for you. God gave me a special passage to lean upon."

"Tell me."

She felt weak as water. Without her saying a word, Russell tucked her into his side and pressed her head to his shoulder. She closed her eyes at the security and serenity she felt in that moment, then recited softly, "It's in the first chapter of Second Corinthians. 'Blessed be God, even the Father of our Lord Jesus Christ, the Father of mercies, and the God of all comfort; who comforteth us in all our tribulation, that we may be able to comfort them which are in any trouble, by the comfort wherewith we ourselves are comforted of God. For as the sufferings of Christ abound in us, so our consolation also aboundeth by Christ.' "

"We've had plenty of tribulation. I'm ready for that comfort and consolation." He pressed a kiss to her temple. "Lorelei, my heart overflows with love for you. Will you marry me?"

"I love you, too, Russell. Being your wife would be an honor."

Epilogue

T he altar is our something old," Lorelei told Russell's mother as she showed her the grand parlor where the wedding was to be held the next day. Once, it had been the workroom she and Russell shared. Now it would serve as a wedding chapel.

Though outbreaks of the flu had lessened, quarantine laws made it impossible to use the church. Family members and a few close friends would come to the mansion for the nuptials, and Lorelei loved the fact that she and Russell would still have an altar for their wedding.

"And you have a beautiful new gown." Mrs. Diamond smiled.

"The something borrowed is Mama's lace hanky, and something blue is from Papa's Bible. I'm using the ribbon marker from it for my g—" She stopped abruptly as Russell entered the room. Heat suffused her cheeks at the thought that he'd almost overheard her speaking of such a thing.

"Everything set to your satisfaction?" He looked about.

"Not exactly." Mrs. Diamond's words shocked Lorelei. Walking toward her son, she said, "Lorelei thinks that beautiful altar is her something old. To my way of thinking, the bride is supposed to wear something old."

Russell wore a smug smile. "I've got that covered." He gave his mother a peck on the cheek; then she left the room. Russell took Lorelei's hand and tugged her to the window. A veritable rainbow of color shimmered around them from the stained glass. He pulled a frayed scarlet cord out of his pocket.

Three tiny hearts dangled from it.

"This has been in the family for seventy-seven years. I'd like you to tie it in your bridal bouquet. Maybe it's not exactly wearing it, but I think carrying it qualifies for the tradition."

"Three hearts. . .for God, you, and me?"

He smiled. "I knew you'd understand." He kissed her, then cupped her face in his hands and shook his head. "In the myth of Lorelei, she was a siren who called men to their destruction. You, my sweet siren, were the voice God used to call me to restoration."

The next afternoon, sun showered through the window onto the altar where they sealed their marriage with a heartfelt kiss.

"Now?" Arnie asked as he wiggled off to the side.

Lorelei laughed as Russell motioned for him to come. "Yes, now."

Arnie pulled two roses from Lorelei's bouquet and turned to the small crowd. "I got a s'prise. I'm 'dopted, so Rus—I mean, Dad—said I get to give these to my new grandmas."

They had a lovely wedding supper, and as a special celebration that night, Russell arranged for fireworks to be shot off the main lawn for the guests' enjoyment. He and Lorelei stood by the window of their bedroom and held each other in the sparkling showers of light.

She walked her fingers up the buttons of his shirt. "It's Independence Day. I've heard men think marriage takes away their freedom."

"Not this man." He captured her hand and kissed the backs of her fingers. "I've found liberty from doubt and anger. It's not just the world that's at peace, Lorelei. I'm at peace."

"And I'm in love."

With a full heart and in a finished home that love had restored, he swept her into his arms and kissed her.

A Letter to Our Readers

Dear Readers:

In order that we might better contribute to your reading enjoyment, we would appreciate your taking a few minutes to respond to the following questions. When completed, please return to the following: Fiction Editor, Barbour Publishing, Inc., P.O. Box 719, Uhrichsville, OH 44683.

1. Did you enjoy reading *Virginia*?
   ❑ Very much—I would like to see more books like this.
   ❑ Moderately—I would have enjoyed it more if _____
   _____
   _____

2. What influenced your decision to purchase this book?
   (Check those that apply.)
   ❑ Cover   ❑ Back cover copy   ❑ Title   ❑ Price
   ❑ Friends   ❑ Publicity   ❑ Other

3. Which story was your favorite?
   ❑ *Precious Burdens*   ❑ *Ramshackle Rose*
   ❑ *Redeemed Hearts*   ❑ *Restoration*

4. Please check your age range:
   ❑ Under 18   ❑ 18–24   ❑ 25–34
   ❑ 35–45   ❑ 46–55   ❑ Over 55

5. How many hours per week do you read? _____

Name _____

Occupation _____

Address _____

City _____ State _____ Zip _____

E-mail _____

$\mathcal{H}$EARTSONG ♥ PRESENTS

Love Stories Are Rated G!

That's for godly, gratifying, and of course, great! If you love a thrilling love story but don't appreciate the sordidness of some popular paperback romances, **Heartsong Presents** is for you. In fact, **Heartsong Presents** is the premiere inspirational romance book club featuring love stories where Christian faith is the primary ingredient in a marriage relationship.

Sign up today to receive your first set of four, never-before-published Christian romances. Send no money now; you will receive a bill with the first shipment. You may cancel at any time without obligation, and if you aren't completely satisfied with any selection, you may return the books for an immediate refund!

Imagine. . .four new romances every four weeks—two historical, two contemporary—with men and women like you who long to meet the one God has chosen as the love of their lives. . .all for the low price of $10.99 postpaid.

To join, simply complete the coupon below and mail to the address provided. **Heartsong Presents** romances are rated G for another reason: They'll arrive Godspeed!

YES! Sign me up for Heart♥ng!

NEW MEMBERSHIPS WILL BE SHIPPED IMMEDIATELY!
Send no money now. We'll bill you only $10.99 postpaid with your first shipment of four books. Or for faster action, call toll free 1-800-847-8270.

NAME _____

ADDRESS_____

CITY_____ STATE_____ ZIP_____

MAIL TO: HEARTSONG PRESENTS, P.O. Box 721, Uhrichsville, Ohio 44683
or visit www.heartsongpresents.com